# THE VEILED PRINCE

IVY BRANNON

# Content Warning

*This book contains scenes of an adult nature including coarse language, strong sexual content, mention of sexual assault, and graphic violence including gore, torture, and an intense flashback sequence of severe child abuse (physical). A list of resources for survivors can be found after the acknowledgements section at the end of this book.*

*For Kari*

SAMHAIN
November 1
YULE
December 19-22
AUTUMN
EQUINOX
September 19-22
IMBOLC
February 1
LUGHNASADH
August 1
SPRING
EQUINOX
March 19-22
LITHA
June 19-22
BELTANE
May 1

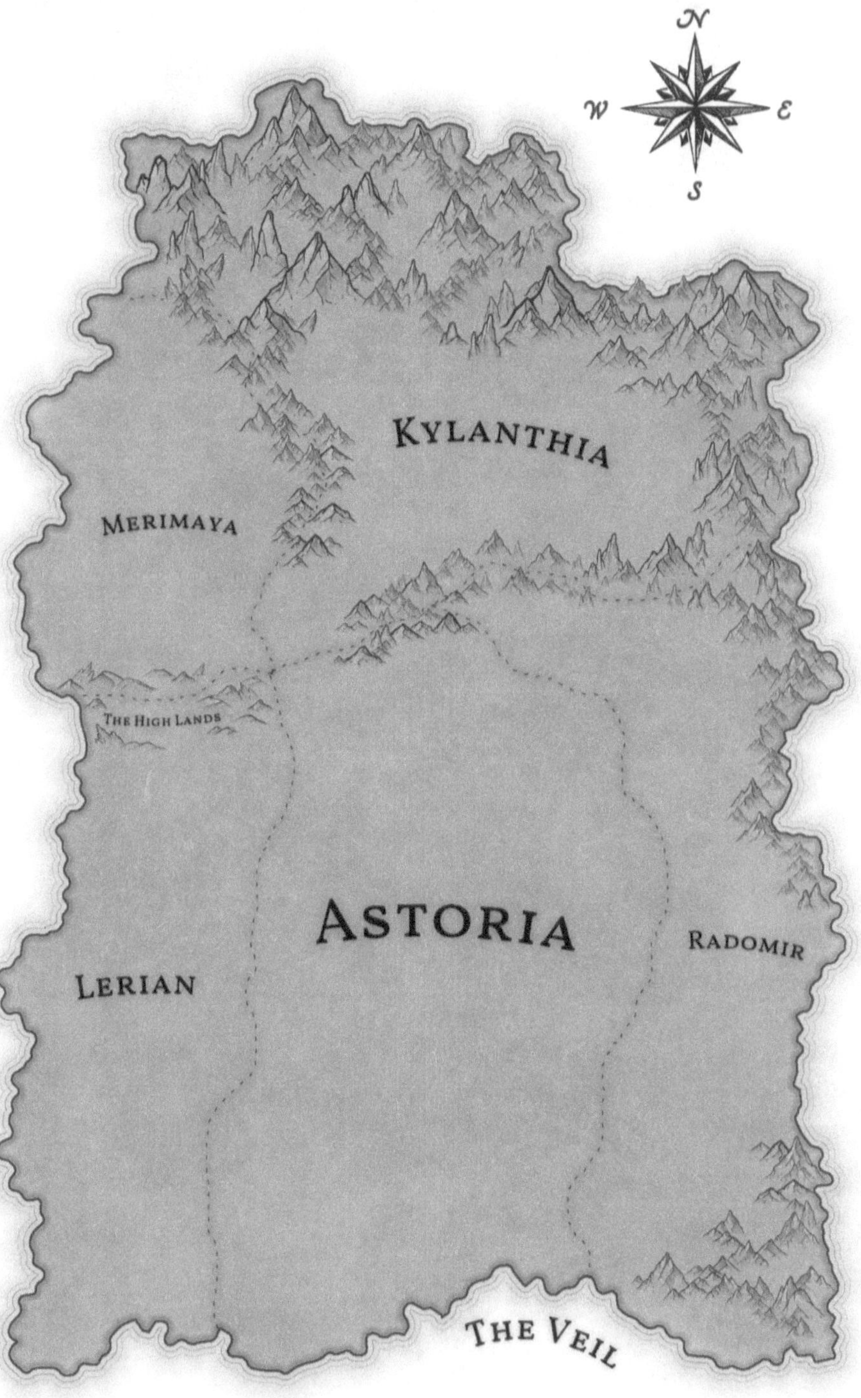

N
W
E
S
KYLANTHIA
MERIMAYA
THE HIGH LANDS
ASTORIA
LERIAN
RADOMIR
THE VEIL

# THE VEILED PRINCE

# CHAPTER 1



THE ONLY SOUND IN THE FOREST WAS THE STEADY DRIP OF melting snow.

A storm had blown through last night, and when I woke this morning the air was still thick with fluffy snowflakes that spiraled down and coated my nose and eyelashes. But lately the days had been getting warmer fast. Even now, not an hour after I'd set out, the sun was drenching the forest in warm gold light, which meant the fresh layer of pillowy snow underfoot was likely to be a muddy, slushy mess by the time I returned.

There was no doubt about it; spring was almost here.

I cautiously scanned my unfamiliar surroundings before stopping to readjust my cloak around my head and shoulders using my free hand. Partnered with the sun, the thick wool would have me profusely sweating come noon. For now, though, my chilled limbs were thankful for the extra warmth.

I glanced down at my left hand, tightening my grip around the fingers entwined in mine.

Wynn's hands were cold too. Not that he noticed. My little

brother didn't notice anything anymore. He stared straight ahead, his eyes milky and glazed over, his jaw slack, and his expression blank.

I frowned. It never got easier seeing him like this.

Spellbound.

Even after all this time, the sight of him comatose, just an inanimate shell of the sweet smiling boy he once was, still made my heart ache. I'd grown accustomed to it, but that didn't mean it hurt any less. It just meant I was no stranger to pain.

I brushed one of Wynn's frizzy blond ringlets out of his face. I didn't know why, though. It's wasn't like he needed to see where he was going. He couldn't see anything in his current state.

"It's alright, Wynn," I sighed. "Not much longer now. We're almost there."

To my left, a twig snapped.

I threw myself in front of my brother and ripped my dagger from its sheath at my hip. Usually the blade's home was strapped around my thigh, but today my dress was made up of multiple layers to keep out the cold, and hauling all those skirts up would take too much time. Time I wouldn't have if I was in a sticky situation.

Keeping Wynn pressed to my back, I spun in a circle, my eyes narrowing as I analyzed the snow-laden forest. My heart pounded in my chest, but my arm, extended straight out with my fingers curled tight around the hilt of the knife, remained steady.

When the source of the noise came into view, the muscles that had tightened in my body in preparation for a fight instantly loosened. I dropped my arm, letting the dagger fall to my side as I glared at two squirrels playing chase in the low-hanging branches of a nearby elm. I took a deep, calming breath in an attempt to slow my racing heartbeat.

*Inhale through your nose, exhale through your mouth,* I reminded myself, *just like when you have a nightmare.*

Which was still far too frequent for my liking.

More often than not, my nights were plagued by dreams of menacing monsters, dark omnipotent gods, and the pained expressions of my loved ones as the life seeped out of their blood-drenched bodies. Out of all those I'd lost, I saw two faces more than the rest. The first was a gentle, kind, and compassionate healer with alabaster skin and long white hair. The second was a man with a symbol that said "demon" branded into his neck, who had beautiful but tortured eyes so brown they were nearly black. I loved both of them in different ways, but the guilt of their deaths haunted me equally.

The thought of those dark eyes in particular threatened to overwhelm me and unleash a flood of tears, so I shoved my emotions down and took up my brother's hand again.

"Come on," I mumbled, wiping my nose with my sleeve as I sniffled, lying to myself that it was only from the cold.

I went to start off again, but motion to the right caught my attention. My head jerked up, and I stared wide-eyed into the forest.

What I saw was... No, it couldn't be. It was the glare from the sun dancing on the snow and messing with my eyesight. That had to be it, because there was no way in hell I'd actually seen what I thought I had.

I thought I'd seen Meer.

In my peripheral vision, it had looked like he was not ten paces from me, dressed in his silver overcoat and merrily waltzing through the fresh powder, with his hair billowing behind him in the breeze.

But it couldn't be him.

Not here.

And not when I'd seen him meet the end he had.

It had to be the snow playing tricks on my eyes.

... Or maybe it was some*one* playing tricks on me.

My blood chilled at the memory of a shapeshifter taking the form of my friend in a twisted way to toy with me.

I squeezed my eyes shut and furiously shook my head, forcing myself to remain calm.

*He couldn't be here,* I reminded myself. *The veil to the Netherworld was destroyed. And besides, he's dead. Aedan is dead. You killed him yourself. You stabbed him, you felt his blood in your hands. You, Lina the King Slayer, killed the king of the Netherworld. He can't hurt you or anyone you love ever again.*

The thought immediately eased the panic trying to claw its way up from my belly into my chest. I chose not to dwell on how strange it was that the nickname that had once infuriated and humiliated me now brought me comfort. I *did* still feel immense guilt about Valdir's death, and the blood gushing from the wound I'd sliced across his neck as his gray eyes went wide still made frequent appearances in my nightmares. But I'd become desensitized to the title, and oddly fond of it as well.

King Slayer.

Yes, it was an insult, but it also reminded me I wasn't helpless. I hadn't been led to the slaughter like a defenseless lamb the way Valdir had intended. I hadn't lain down and taken it; I'd fought back, and I'd won. I was not a victim. I was not prey. I was the godsdamned hunter.

I watched the woods a few seconds more, but when nothing moved, I reassured myself the image of Meer was just a figment of my imagination and continued on my way.

We trudged on through the snow until we crested a hill and a small frozen pond came into view, brown reeds sticking out of the ice across its surface like spines on a hedgehog. Air puffed from my mouth in white clouds as I panted from the hike.

"Finally," I breathed.

With a squeeze of Wynn's hand, I grinned down at him. For some reason, part of me still expected him to look up at me and smile back.

I shoved the foolish thought from my mind and moved my gaze from Wynn to the dilapidated shack nestled on the shoreline beside the pond. With its rotting shingles and the splintered gray wood planks of its walls, I wouldn't have assumed anyone inhabited the place, but a thin plume of black smoke spiraling up from the crooked chimney pipe told a different story.

"Why does this feel like a bad idea?" I mumbled, gingerly starting down the other side of the slope, slipping and sliding on the half-melted snow all the way down. Wynn trailed listlessly behind me.

When we arrived at the front door, I rearranged my brother's hair and smoothed the front of my dress, then raised my fist to knock. The hair on the back of my neck stood on end as the door creaked open before I could touch my knuckles to the wood.

"Yep," I muttered. "*Very* bad idea."

I peeked down at Wynn once more, my heart twisting at the sight of those once expressive turquoise eyes, now nothing but empty white orbs.

It was too late to go back now. We'd come too far, and this was Wynn's final hope.

With my hand gripping my brother's so tight it made my knuckles pale, I took a deep breath, lifted my chin, and stepped inside.

Dried herbs, charms, and animal carcasses dangled from the exposed beams, which meant upon entering, I came face-to-face with a dead rat hanging directly in front of the doorway.

It would have smacked me right in the face if I hadn't ducked out of the way in the nick of time.

"Good reflexes," a voice chuckled from the corner.

I blinked as my eyes adjusted to the dim light. Within seconds, my surroundings came into focus. A small cot was nestled against the wall in the corner, a crude table laden with stones, herbs, jars, and elixir-filled bottles stood at the center of the room, and finally, crouched on a three-legged stool in front of a soot-stained hearth, was an old woman.

She was wrapped in a tattered plaid shawl as she warmed her knotty fingers in front of the flames, her gray-streaked hair twisted and pinned at the back of her head. Shadows from the fire flickered and danced across her bony face, giving it life, but something about her eyes disturbed me. Maybe it was my imagination, but I could have sworn there was no reflection of the flames in her pupils. They seemed to swallow the light whole.

I fought the urge to shiver and squared my shoulders instead, taking care to avoid the dead rat and making note of my exit routes in case things got messy. There was the door I'd come through, then two small windows on the opposite side of the hut. Wynn could fit through them just fine, but my wide hips might have more trouble. Fighting my way out would be my only option if worse came to worst. The thought had my right hand instinctively moving closer to my dagger.

"Hello," I said stiffly. "I'm—"

"I know who you are." The woman waved her hand, shushing me, but kept her attention fixed on the hearth.

I raised an eyebrow. "You do?"

"Of course."

"Did someone tell you I was coming?"

The woman chuckled again. "No. I saw it."

She faced me then, her bottomless eyes meeting mine for

the first time. Again I fought the urge to shudder at the eerie way they gobbled up all the light in the room.

"What do you mean you saw it?"

The woman's lips pinched as she squinted at me. The look was reminiscent of the annoyed expression my mother had given me once when she'd told me to stop whining about going outside, sit down, and finish my sewing. *Your husband will expect you to know how to do this,* she'd insisted. I'd then tossed my needlework across the room and screamed, *Then I won't have a husband,* promptly earning myself a ruthless spanking.

Needless to say, I didn't especially like the look on the woman's face.

"I *saw* it," the woman repeated, her brows arching as she dropped her chin and looked pointedly up through her lashes. "Don't play dumb, girl, you know what I mean."

My free hand balled into a fist at my side.

*You have to behave, Lina,* I reminded myself.

I cleared my throat and attempted a somewhat pleasant tone. "So can all witches see the future?"

The woman stood and shuffled over to the table. There she grabbed a granite mortar and started tossing in ingredients, haphazardly sprinkling herbs here and drizzling liquids there.

"Only some can." She plucked a comatose lizard dangling from the rafters by its tail and promptly ripped off its head. The resulting crack made me flinch. "But even then, we only get snippets."

The woman dropped the reptile in her concoction and lifted the pestle from the tabletop. I tried not to fixate on the grinding of bones against stone.

"And did you learn my name in your vision?"

"No, but anyone who looks close enough can see who you are."

My spine went stiff, and I revisited my exit strategy as I

tightened my hold on Wynn. His fingers were turning purple from how hard I was gripping them.

"What do you mean?"

The witch rubbed her hands, brushing off any remnants of the mixture she'd been working with, before striding towards me. She unnerved me so much I wanted to bolt out the door and run all the way home, but I forced myself to remain. I did, however, subtly guide Wynn behind me.

The woman scanned my body from head to toe and pinched the sleeve of my dress between her thumb and index finger, rubbing the cornflower blue appreciatively.

"Decent clothing," the woman murmured, eyeing the white fur detailing at my wrists and neckline.

I yelped in alarm as she snatched up my right hand and traced her fingertips over the calluses along my palm.

"But the hands of a warrior," the witch added. "Or are they the hands of a commoner? Perhaps both."

I ripped my arm free and shoved Wynn further behind my back.

"And my guess is if I move this out of the way..." The woman reached for the hood of my cloak.

I instinctively slapped her hand aside.

The witch chuckled in amusement. "I assume I would find rounded ear tips." Her thin lips twisted into a grin. "You are clearly Lina Calder, the King Slayer."

I frowned and slid my hood off. So much for keeping a low profile.

The woman puttered back to her mortar and pestle and tossed in a few more items, one bearing a nauseating resemblance to a leech. "There were rumors you'd left the Fae realm."

I glanced down at where a long black scar lived on the inside of my right wrist, a lasting remnant of that first violent Samhain over a year ago. The night I watched two of my brothers die. The night I lost Wynn. The night I stumbled into this world and my life changed forever.

"I almost left," I whispered.

Actually, that was a lie.

I *had* left.

Soren had found me at the last second on the bank of the river and professed his undying love. He'd apologized for his past behavior and swore his life and love to me, and I'd wanted nothing more than to stay locked in his embrace for the rest of my days. I'd wanted what he offered. I'd wanted *him*. But I'd truly believed the solution for Wynn's healing wasn't here. I'd been absolutely certain if we went back home, back to the world we actually belonged to, then he'd finally be free of the Sluagh's spell.

So I'd tramped across the river, scooped my brother into my arms, and yelled across to Soren that I was returning to the human realm. He'd been heartbroken, but hadn't fought me on it. He'd swallowed hard and set his jaw, bowing his head in the gentlemanly way he does, and shouted back, "If that's what you want, then I support you." I'd turned to leave, and he'd hurriedly offered to accompany me to the boundary. I could take care of myself, and Soren knew it, but it had been his way of asking to spend just a little more time with me. I'd gladly accepted.

He'd waded over to me, and we'd walked in silence most of the way, content to simply listen to the soothing song of the other's breath. When we arrived at the burial grounds that marked the edge of the boundary, I'd nearly collapsed from the shock. The boundary of the veil was the same glade where my brothers had died. In the thick fog that night, and with the horrors happening around me, I hadn't noticed the graves; to the untrained eye, they were nothing but grass-covered mounds dotting the outskirts of the clearing.

I'd shared my revelation with Soren, and he'd held me while I cried pitifully in his arms. Then he'd proceeded to kiss my hair and rub my back while he recited a poem in the ancient Fae tongue. He'd said it had something to do with pain and love and honor. It was beautiful, and when he'd finished, I'd sung one of the lullabies my mother used to sing me and my brothers as children. I should have sung one of the hymns I'd heard at funerals before, one that begged the gods for safe passage to the Underworld, but in the moment it had felt right.

My brothers were being sung to sleep one last time.

After that, we'd left the glade and headed deeper into the forest. Once we were fully immersed in the human realm, we'd found a seat on a fallen log. There, with Soren beside me, I'd hauled Wynn onto my lap and waited.

And waited.

And waited some more.

I'd expected him to take one step over the boundary and snap back to normal. I'd thought he'd blink and look around and tell me he'd just had the longest, strangest dream. I'd stared down at him for what felt like an eternity, waiting for the light to come back into his eyes.

But it never did.

The Sluagh's spell was strong enough to extend into the human world. I had run from the Fae realm, but it still found a way to keep its claws in my brother.

A million panicked thoughts had rushed into my mind then. When the eastern horizon lightened with the promise of dawn, Soren had kissed me on the forehead and whispered it was time for him to go. He'd stood to leave, but I'd grabbed his hand to stop him. Then I'd sat in silence a few seconds more, warring with myself.

Could I go through life with a spellbound brother, searching for a cure while completely and utterly alone? Of course. I'd learned over the past year I could handle any hardship life threw at me, no matter how painful.

But I didn't *have* to.

People out there loved me and supported me. Leaning on them didn't make me weak. It just made the weight on my shoulders a little less heavy.

When I realized that, I'd stood, faced Soren, and stated I would take him up on his offer and stay with him while continuing to search the five territories for my brother's cure. But I'd also insisted that, despite our feelings for each other, I didn't want us to be together right away. Every fiber of my being protested the statement, the very blood in my veins screaming that not being with Soren meant living life missing a piece of my soul. But I'd wanted to focus all my attention on my brother, and get to know myself in the process.

After all, who was Lina Calder when she wasn't clinging to survival or weighed down by the world? I wasn't sure I'd ever found out. Growing up, I'd been told I should be something I had no desire to be, and when I'd paved my own way, I'd faced criticism and judgment because I didn't fit into the mold people thought I should. After my parents had passed away, I'd spread myself thin to provide for my family just so my brothers could go to bed with full bellies. Then my life had turned upside down when the veil lifted, and I'd spent a year grieving, falling apart, worrying about my brother, and fighting for my life. I'd grown, I'd healed, and while my brother wasn't the same, at least now he was safe. I was at a place where I could truly breathe for the first time, and I wanted to exist here for a while. I wanted to get to know the woman I'd become and fall in love with her too.

When I explained all that to Soren as best I could, he hadn't protested in the slightest. He'd nodded and told me he supported my decision, and he wouldn't pressure me. Wynn and I would live with him as his wards, unless I came to him and told him I wanted to be more. So here I was, nearly three months later, meeting the latest witch on the long journey towards healing my brother. She came highly recommended by Soren, who said she was well-known for her potions and elixirs and could personally attest to their power. I had nothing left to lose, so I'd set out the next day, following the directions Soren had given me, and ended up here.

So far, I was not impressed.

"What made you stay?" The witch sniffed her concoction, then dipped her pinky in and tasted it.

I winced and choked back a gag.

"Did a certain Fae king's cunning silver tongue convince you that there would be a future together?" She looked over at me and smirked.

It seemed the whole realm was aware the king of Astoria once had a special talent for spinning silken words that could bend women to his whim. Normally, I didn't mind Soren's past. In fact, his extensive experience meant nothing except that he expertly knew his way around a woman's body, which made for a deliciously toe-curling time in the bedroom for me. I *did*, however, mind when people tried to use his past to torment me.

*Behave.*

I'd been practicing polite smiles in the mirror lately, so I forced one onto my face. "*I decided* to stay. I thought there was a better chance of finding my brother help in a place with people who are familiar with these sorts of ailments." I ignored the disbelieving look on the witch's face and reached into one of the deep pockets of my dress. "That's where you come in. Unless you don't want *this*."

I pulled out a small drawstring purse and tossed it onto the table, the coins inside clinking as it landed beside the woman's mortar. Her eyes widened as she snatched up the bag and wriggled her fingers inside, eagerly counting the gold marks she found there.

"Well then," the witch snickered. "It certainly pays to be the king's pet, doesn't it?"

At that, a fire started inside me, and I forgot my manners.

"I am not his *pet*," I spat.

"Does he know that?"

"Of course he does!"

"His toy, then. Nothing but a shiny prize kept locked away on his shelf."

I frowned. I could see how it looked that way. No one besides the servants and a handful of nobles had seen me since Wynn and I had returned with Soren on Samhain. I never went into the nearby villages, hadn't attended any balls or dinner parties, and I typically hid in one corner of the garden and three or four rooms in the castle, only moving around freely under the cover of darkness. But that wasn't because of Soren.

It was because I didn't want to see anyone.

Every person I came in contact with made a split-second decision about me. Some agreed with my actions last year on Yule, but many didn't. Some hated me for being the stranger who'd brought violence to their realm, while others romanticized me for being the human their king had valiantly defended, offered sanctuary to, and fallen in love with against all odds. They scrutinized and gossiped and determined who I was before ever getting to know me, and it was exhausting. I'd made my peace with what I'd done, and sat with the guilt for countless nights, but I couldn't live in the past or it would eat me alive. Other things demanded my energy and attention. I had my brother. I had Soren. And I had people to mourn.

One more so than the rest. And he would have understood the feeling of being judged more than anyone.

I pushed the thought of Hale from my mind and

brought Wynn out from behind my back. "Not that it's any of your business, but Soren isn't keeping me from the public eye. That was my choice too. Now if you don't mind..." I gestured to my brother. "I have a little boy here who needs your help. Are you going to be useful, or should I take back my gold and leave you to your lizard maiming?"

The witch hurriedly tucked the sack of gold into the bodice of her dress. She then placed both hands on Wynn's shoulders and cocked her head as she examined him.

"What's wrong with the child?"

"He's spellbound."

The woman rolled her eyes. "Clearly." She cupped Wynn's chin with a surprisingly gentle touch, angling his head towards the fire as she inspected his glazed-over stare. "How long has he been like this?"

I anxiously rubbed my neck. "Since Samhain."

"Well, that's not so bad."

"Samhain last year."

The woman let out a low whistle, peeking at me out of the corner of her eye. "What took you so long to seek help?"

"He was in the Netherworld most of the time."

"The Netherworld." The witch threw her head back and cackled. "Right."

When I didn't join in, her laugh died off and her amused expression was replaced with one of alarm.

"You can't be serious."

My mouth pressed into a line.

The woman's eyes grew round and darted to Wynn. She took another look in his eyes. "What creature did this?"

"The Sluagh."

The witch staggered backwards, throwing out a hand to catch herself on the table behind her. When she'd composed herself, she rubbed her face and groaned into her palms. "Are you sure?"

"Positive."

"You've had no success with healers?"

"No. I've tried everything. Healers, potions, offerings to every god there is. The only thing that's worked remotely well is the touch of a witch."

The woman lowered her hands and raised a quizzical brow. "You've seen others?"

"Yes."

"And what happened when you did?"

I swallowed the lump that appeared in my throat and glanced down at my brother, silently begging the pinching behind my eyes to cease.

"He seems fine." My voice wavered, and I cleared my throat in an attempt to bring some strength back into it. "His eyes are clear, and he responds to our voices. He doesn't talk, but he'll nod yes or no. He'll stay like that for a few days, a week if we're lucky, but then one morning he wakes up and he's back to this." A rogue tear slipped out, but I quickly wiped it away, hoping the witch hadn't seen. "I don't understand why. I made the trek to the Netherworld and brought him back. That means they no longer have dominion over him and he's free, doesn't it?"

"It should." The woman stared at Wynn, tapping a finger against her lips. "And you're sure it's the Sluagh who have bound him? No one else?"

I shook my head. "No, it was the Sluagh. They claimed him as a Changeling on Samhain last year."

"Hmm..." The witch wandered over and smoothed the cowlick at the back of Wynn's head. Another surprisingly gentle gesture I hadn't expected from her.

"Strange," she mused. "Very strange."

"Can you help him? I've heard you're powerful."

The woman looked up at me and smiled, a sparkle finally coming into her vacant eyes. "We are all powerful in our own way, Lina Calder."

I groaned. "Oh, gods. Please don't. No strange wording. No riddles. I'm not in the mood."

My mind drifted to the memory of another witch I'd met almost a year ago, the one telling fortunes in the palace of Merimaya on Imbolc, who'd found me huddled on the floor after I threatened the prince of Lerian with a shard of glass to the throat. That woman had spoken in riddles too.

*A girl torn between two worlds,* the witch had said to me. *She searches for the Netherworld prince, but her path is one of darkness and pain. A great evil is growing, unable to be contained by one world alone. The Slayer of Kings will return before the end.*

Looking back, I knew now she'd been talking about me finding Wynn.

*Little princeling,* Aedan had fondly referred to him. And the Slayer of Kings had indeed returned when I stabbed that shapeshifter dead. All the seer's words had come true, and I personally wasn't in a hurry to hear any more ominous premonitions. I'd had enough excitement for one lifetime.

"Fine." The woman made her way back to her workspace and consulted a large dusty tome on the table before tossing a few more ingredients into her mixture. "I assume you have no interest in becoming a witch, then?"

"Why would I..." I trailed off and sighed, crossing my arms. I was starting to think this woman might not actually have any magical abilities at all and was just some crazy lady in the woods, conning desperate folk out of their money. "*No.* I don't have any interest in becoming a witch."

"Then I won't bother telling you what's in this." The woman jerked her chin towards her concoction. "I'll just tell you what it will do."

She dumped the fine powder she'd ground into a nearby bottle, corked it, and shook it firmly. The brew began to glow, the cyan light instantly reminding me of a place much darker, where monsters lurked and moonflowers grew out of cracks in cave walls. Panic tore through me, and I had to put a hand on Wynn's shoulder to remind myself where I was.

We weren't in the Netherworld anymore. We were safe. We'd gotten out. Others hadn't been so lucky.

I took a deep breath in through my nose and out through my mouth, forcing my body to calm.

The witch wiggled the bottle in her hand. "This will break the Sluagh's hold on him. He will be unbound and remain sentient for the rest of his days."

A flicker of hope cut through the tightly coiled tension in my chest, and I released a heavy sigh of relief.

"But..." The woman's gaze flicked to Wynn, her expression softening. In this moment, she seemed less like an old witch in the woods and more like a loving grandmother staring down at a grandchild. "I urge you to be patient with him. No one stays spellbound that long and comes back the same."

My heart sank again. Whatever hope I had of seeing my brother the way I remembered him was shattered. His innocence had been lost that night, which was exactly what my brothers and I had always worked so hard to keep from happening.

"But he is young," the witch added brightly, offering me the tiniest hint of an encouraging smile. "Children learn quickly. He is still your brother, and your love for each other has spanned worlds, proving no matter what happens, it above all else will remain."

At that, another tear toppled over my lashes and splashed down my cheek. I sniffled and rubbed my eyes, effectively stopping the others threatening to follow suit.

"Thank you," I croaked.

The woman bowed her head. "You're welcome. Now stop your blubbering and hold him steady."

I gulped and took hold of my brother's shoulders. The witch crouched in front of him, placing her hand on top of his head and muttering a few words in the ancient Fae tongue. She then brought a crooked hand to the cork of the bottle and yanked it free, allowing a puff of glowing blue smoke to snake out and waft towards Wynn. The movement reminded me of one night in a library in Lerian, when a ribbon of black mist sidled towards me in the same silky way and caressed my cheek while I cried.

I was pulled from my memory when the blue smoke slipped inside my brother's nostril and Wynn began to thrash wildly.

"What's going on?" I shrieked, gripping his shoulders tighter.

"It's normal," the witch replied. She placed her hand on Wynn's head again and shut her eyes, speaking the ancient tongue louder and more confidently. Within seconds, Wynn went limp, and his eyes fluttered shut.

"Wynn?" I knelt in front of my brother and took his face in my hands. "Wynn, come on! Look at me!"

I stared at him, unable to speak or think or breathe, until finally Wynn's chest rose and his lips parted as he sucked in a gasp. When his eyelids snapped open, my heart practically burst out of my chest and flew away, I was so happy.

Blinking back at me were a pair of clear turquoise eyes.

"Wynn, can you hear me?" I asked, trying to keep my excitement contained to avoid rattling him.

Slowly, Wynn nodded. He then looked around the shack, his brows inching together in confusion as he got his bearings.

"Do you know who I am?" I pressed.

My brother's eyes shifted back to me and narrowed as he studied my features. After a few seconds, recognition washed over his face and he nodded.

I pulled him into a ferocious hug.

"Thank the gods," I whispered.

When I broke away, I cupped my little brother's cheek in my palm and smiled. "Come on. Let's go home."

# Chapter 2

By the time Wynn and I had trudged back to the castle, the snow had melted almost entirely. Our boots were caked with mud, the hem of my dress was filthy, and both my brother and I were in desperate need of a bath.

I stopped Wynn on the front steps and helped him take off his shoes before we passed through the new doorway into the entry hall, one of the countless new sections of the castle.

After Soren, Xavier, and I fled the Yule attack last year, a handful of the Nethers had returned and set fire to the grounds to make a statement. When we returned from the Netherworld and went our separate ways, Soren's first order of business in Astoria had been overseeing repairs. Now everything looked relatively the same as it used to, but it felt different than before. Maybe because there weren't as many servants now as there once were. The castle employed only a handful of staff, just a fraction of what it had before the Nether attack. Understandably, many were uneasy about the idea of returning to work here. Despite Soren's assurances, they didn't feel safe. I understood all too well. I still slept with my dagger beneath my pillow, and he'd never tell anyone, but I knew Soren kept his sword at the ready beside his bed at night.

But I think the main reason the castle didn't feel the same was because it was missing a few very special people.

There was no replacing Meer as head of staff. No one could compare to him or the legacy he'd left. Soren had turned down everyone he'd interviewed for the position, for no other reason besides "they didn't feel right." My Sprite handmaidens were missed just as much. Before the attack, they had always been there to help me bathe and dress and do my hair, but now I purposefully chose to do those things alone. Unless Laurel, Cassia, or Acacia could be there to giggle and gossip and sneak me wine from the cellar or fresh bread from the kitchen, I didn't want help. It made doing up my corsets take significantly longer, but I used that time to reminisce about my friends and sit with the weight of their loss. Some days I didn't feel strong enough for that, though, so I'd started wearing shirts and trousers more and more.

"Look who's awake!"

Wynn immediately perked up at the chipper voice and whipped his head towards the dining room.

With her plum-red hair pinned in milkmaid's braids and her plump lips curved into a smile, Willow ambled over and extended a plate of warm brownies.

"Hungry?" she asked.

Wynn eagerly nodded and took two.

I frowned disapprovingly at the Wood Sprite. "It's morning, Willow."

She grinned back at me, mischief gleaming in her lavender eyes. "It's never too early for dessert."

She waggled the plate under my nose, cracking my stern expression. I pulled off a small chunk and popped it into my mouth.

"That's what I thought." Willow took the rest of the brownie for herself, moaning at the taste and nodding appreciatively.

Willow was nearly identical to her sister, Acacia. Not only did they share the same hair, rosy cheeks, and full figure, but both had joyful energy that was practically contagious.

I hadn't expected any family members of my slaughtered handmaidens to come work at the castle. I certainly wouldn't have if it were me. But Willow had heard Soren and I were looking for someone to help us with Wynn, and when she learned his story, her heart had gone out to him. They'd met the first time a witch managed to make him sentient, and all Willow had done was sit with him in the garden for two hours and finger-paint. When those two hours were up, she'd come to me, slipped my hands into her paint-splattered palms, and told me her sister had loved working here, and she'd loved *me*, and because of that, Willow would happily accept the position. I had, of course, burst into tears at her kind words, to which Willow had responded by giving me the warmest hug I'd ever felt and insisting we go find something strong to drink in celebration. It was at that moment I'd known we would be great friends.

Willow was a wonderful companion, both for me and for Wynn. Whenever he was sentient, Willow would work with my brother on basic reading, writing, and arithmetic, as well as some history lessons. I often chose to sit in on those. I figured if I was going to be staying here, and my focus was no longer solely on surviving long enough to find Wynn, then I needed to learn about this world I'd become a part of.

Something that was similar to the human realm, I'd discovered, was the Fae's caste system. In my world we had nobles, a middle class, and what my own family had been, peasants. The Fae had three main classes as well. First, there was the highest caste: the nobles, lords and ladies who owned estates and governed people of their own. They were often owners of impressive magic and a notable pedigree. Then there was the middle caste, generally made up of merchants, shopkeepers, and artisans. These Fae typically had less impressive magic, or sometimes none at all besides the standard heightened senses, accelerated healing, and long life. Finally, there was the lower caste. Low-borns, as the slur referred to them. They were no one of importance. It was extremely rare for them to have magic, and they did the jobs no one wanted, like working in the mines or scrubbing floors or tending the fields.

I would have been low-born if I were Fae.

Oddly enough, creatures like Willow were also lumped into the lowest caste. She was a Wood Sprite, a type of Fae with a close relationship to nature. Many Wood Sprites possessed a talent for growing things, and they often found success in agricultural professions. Willow's family had a particularly close relationship with plum trees, and had an extensive orchard in the northern part of Astoria, where they'd lived for generations. They shipped Willow a crate of their renowned plum brandy monthly, which I eagerly partook in. Gods, that stuff was strong. Absolutely delicious, but one glass too many and I'd be left with foggy memories and a pounding headache the following morning. Luckily for me, the Fae could heal themselves faster than I, so while I'd be suffering, Willow, utterly unaffected, would putter around making breakfast and herbal tonics to help me feel better.

There were Water Sprites too, which, I found out, was what Meer had been. These creatures were drawn to and energized by water, and some even had healing abilities. When I'd learned this, everything made sense. Meer had guzzled water before he healed Xavier, and his spirit was as refreshing as a cool drink on a hot summer's day.

I couldn't wrap my head around why Meer and Willow

were considered low-caste. Following the logic of the Fae, if Sprites had magic, then they should be regarded as nobles, or upper-middle caste at the very least.

*That's just the way it's always been,* Willow had said with a glum shrug, *and that's the way it always will be.*

That never did sit right with me.

"How was it out there?" Willow asked Wynn around the mouthful of brownie she was crunching.

My brother peeked down at the mud-stained legs of his trousers.

"Cold and wet?"

Wynn nodded glumly.

"Well then." Willow brushed a few stray crumbs from the neckline of her ruffled blouse and gestured to the freshly lacquered grand staircase behind her. "Let's get you washed and dry, how does that sound?"

Wynn beamed and reached up to her. She slipped her palm into his and led him in the direction of his room.

"We'll see your sister later, alright?" Willow glanced over her shoulder and tilted her chin towards the entry. "Lina, look. They're back."

I turned to the front door, and my stomach dropped.

Xavier, Soren, and Lord Magnus Tynan strode into the castle, their hair, skin, furs and leathers coated in the thick crimson of Nether blood. I gave each of them a quick scan, but when I saw no blood or wounds of their own, I relaxed.

"Hey," I greeted them. "How did it go?"

Soren's eyes lifted from the ground to meet mine, the rich blue of his irises instantly lighting up as his tense shoulders relaxed.

I'd already noticed how Soren's presence calmed me, but in this moment, anyone could see I had a similar effect on him.

"Good." Soren nodded and unstrapped the broadsword from his waist. "It was quick work."

I had no doubt. He'd been getting a lot of practice in.

Soren had taken it upon himself to pick off the Nethers who still prowled Astoria. Whenever there was an attack on a village or news came that some were seen close by, he, Xavier, and occasionally Lord Magnus would ride out and dispose of them. Soren told me he did it so none of his people would be subjected to any more danger. I knew how much guilt he felt for the bloodshed that had befallen them, but I also knew he did it to ease tension. Just like how people either loved or hated me, opinions on Soren were divided too. By getting his hands dirty like this, Soren was proving to his people that he cared enough about them to risk his life instead of theirs, and they respected him for it. Since he'd started his crusade two months ago, much of the discontented grumbling throughout the territory had quieted, and Astoria was headed back towards peace and harmony at last.

Xavier lifted a freckle-splattered nose in the air and inhaled deeply. "Do I smell brownies?"

I nodded and motioned to the staircase. "Talk to Willow."

Xavier eagerly rubbed his hands together, not even bothering to unbuckle the sword from his back or the two daggers from his hips before bounding upstairs.

"How that boy can eat after what we just did, I have no idea."

I peeked at Lord Magnus Tynan. Soren's new advisor was massive, towering above everyone, even the king himself, which was saying something. I'd remarked once that Magnus reminded me of a giant gold statue. He had shoulder-length golden hair with a matching well-manicured beard, his skin was sun-kissed, and his eyes were such a bright shade of amber they almost looked yellow. He stood regal and proud, and his expression was constantly stoic and stern. I'd never once seen the man smile.

I didn't like the lord, and the feeling was mutual.

He was always looking down his nose at me, both literally and figuratively, and even though Soren never said anything about it, I was almost positive Lord Magnus had advised him not to keep me around.

But luckily for me, the king was just as stubborn as I was.

I hadn't let Soren in right away. When my brother and I had come back to Astoria, Soren had kept his word and hadn't pressured me to be with him. Wynn and I were his wards, and the king had behaved just as he had when I first came to live at the castle. He'd been friendly in passing, but respectfully kept his distance.

I'd managed to keep things platonic for three weeks. I'd still felt a pull to Soren as I always had, and I could tell he did too. I'd catch him sneaking longing glances in my direction when he thought I wasn't watching, and looking like it physically pained him not to touch me. I was no better, but we both resisted temptation.

One night I'd decided to check in on Wynn before I went to sleep. He'd still been spellbound at that time, and when I peeked into his room, I'd found Soren sitting beside my brother's bed and reading him a bedtime story. I'd watched at the door, listening to Soren perform funny voices for all the characters and even act out a fight sequence, despite the fact my brother couldn't see or hear any of it. Soren had no idea I was there. When he finished, I'd intercepted him in the hall and dragged him into his bedroom, where I'd slept every night since.

Many of those nights we'd stayed up talking.

We'd spent hours discussing everything from our favorite childhood memories to the embarrassing habits we typically kept hidden away. We'd also had countless heavier conversations, including ones about the events of the past year and how things had transpired between us. Together, we'd agreed our night in Soren's tent hadn't bound us to each other, we'd both jumped to hasty conclusions about the other, and the two of us were absolute shit at communicating. Soren didn't hold it against me that I'd fallen for someone else while he'd been distant, but this time around, he'd made a point of asking me to be his, and *solely* his.

"I don't know," I'd teased him, "Xavier is looking pretty good lately."

Soren had responded by tackling me into the pillows and smothering me with kisses until I said the words out loud:

I was his, and he was mine. And we promised, from that point on, we would have no more lies and no more secrets.

"Nothing kills Xavier's appetite," Soren said, finding the buckle on one of his bracers more difficult than usual. "If Xavier says he's not hungry, it's time to start worrying about him."

Able to get a better angle, I unbuckled the strap for Soren. He offered me a smile, which caused a giddy flutter through my heart. I beamed back at him, keenly aware of Magnus's icy glare boring into the side of my head.

I helped Soren unfasten his other armguard, and when I finished, he caught my hands in his.

"How's Wynn?" he asked, his brows knitting with concern.

I smiled and used my thumb to smooth the lines etched in his forehead. "He's himself again."

Soren puffed a relieved sigh, and that blinding smile of his returned. "Thank the gods. I'll go say hello. Let me get rid of these clothes first."

"May I be of assistance, Your Majesty?"

If I were a dog, my hackles would have risen at that voice.

I turned as Lord Magnus's daughter, Mirielle, strode towards us. Like her father, she was tall and lean, and if Magnus was gold, Mirielle was copper. Her bronze tan was a shade deeper than her father's, and caramel brown curls cascaded down her back to her tailbone. She batted the long dark lashes surrounding her amber eyes as she stared up at Soren, a coquettish smile playing on her perfectly pouty lips.

"I was just about to drop some things off with the laundresses anyway."

No she wasn't. The woman wasn't carrying a single article of soiled fabric.

"That's alright, Mirielle," I cut in, plastering a fake smile on my face, "I can take care of him."

Mirielle shot me an even bigger smile back. "I'm sure you can. I was just trying to be helpful."

It took every ounce of strength in me not to roll my eyes.

I hated Lord Magnus, but I might hate his daughter more.

With Meer gone and the head of staff position still vacant, Magnus had advised Soren to bring Mirielle on to help around the castle. He'd been quick to point out I had no idea how to run a household, especially a noble Fae one, but Mirielle did. I'd hated it, but the lord had a good point. I would have no idea how to run things anywhere, *especially* a castle, and learning would require me actually being brave enough to leave my room and face people. Also with everyone so divided on their opinions of me, putting me in a position of authority would just fan the flames. So I'd begrudgingly gone along with the decision. Mirielle's frequent presence only added another reason for me to stay hidden away. If I was out and about, I'd have to see her throwing herself at Soren while constantly finding ways to belittle me and remind me of my place in society. Or rather, my lack of one. She was sweet as honey to all the important people she crossed paths with, but she was condescending and rude to anyone she deemed below her, including me and the staff. I actually thought she might make a good match with Kaspar of Lerian because the two were so alike in that regard. If she were nicer to me, I might have offered to set them up. I'd jokingly brought up the idea in one of my letters to Syrena, to which she'd written back, *Good gods, no. Either they'll burn the world down together or I'll murder them in their sleep. My money's on the latter.*

I looped my arm through Soren's as Xavier, who had stripped down to a sweat-drenched tunic, returned downstairs, happily munching on a brownie.

"I appreciate that, Mirielle," I purred, "but I'll be disrobing Soren myself, thank you."

One of Mirielle's eyes twitched, but she smiled so big it had to be hurting her cheeks. "Charming."

Xavier glanced at me and then to Mirielle before whipping off his tunic and tossing it to her.

"Here you go." He slapped her on the back. "You're so thoughtful, Mirielle."

He brushed past the lord's daughter, giving me a subtle wink before sauntering half-naked towards the kitchen. In search of more brownies, no doubt. How that man still had a defined six-pack was a mystery.

Mirielle balled up Xavier's shirt and pursed her lips. "Well, then. I'll leave you to it. Your Majesty." She gracefully dropped into a low curtsy. When she rose, she briefly looked me up and down before flashing the most pained smile I'd ever seen. "Good day, Lina."

My smile back resembled an animal baring its teeth.

"Remember," Soren muttered in my ear as I steered him towards the stairs, "we have to behave."

"Her first," I whispered back.

"Oh, and Lina?"

I glanced back over my shoulder. Mirielle blinked up at me with innocent doe eyes.

"I meant to tell you, I *really* like that dress on you. It makes you look so much less common than usual."

She then turned on her heel and pranced away, her father giving Soren one last disapproving frown before following after her.

I stomped up the rest of the stairs, dragging the king with me and well aware of my nails digging into the flesh of his arm.

"Wonderful," I grumbled. "Now I have to burn my favorite dress."

"Maybe she meant it as a compliment?"

I shot Soren a glare.

He sighed heavily. "I'll speak to her."

"You've been saying that for weeks now."

"It's complicated."

Now it was my turn to sigh. I *knew* it was complicated. Soren and I had discussed it countless times now.

Lord Magnus was highly regarded in the five territories. He'd served as an advisor to Soren's father, Stelios, and his opinion held sway over the majority of the noble families in Astoria. If he was in support of Soren, then multiple powerful families throughout the territory would be as well, and any rumors of insurrection would be tamed. Lord Magnus also happened to be incredibly protective of his only child, and if someone were to disrespect her or anger the spoiled brat in any way, then they would make an enemy of Magnus. And Soren couldn't afford to have any more enemies.

But sometimes no matter how much I *understood* something, it didn't help how terrible it made me feel.

When we arrived outside the king's bedroom, he pushed open the door for me. I entered, Soren following, but before I got too far, he caught my hand and drew me back towards him.

He pinned me against the wall by shoving his chest to mine and placing his hands flat on either side of me, pulling a gasp of surprise from my lips.

"You know," Soren murmured, brushing my nose with his, "if you're going to destroy this dress anyway, maybe I should just rip it off you."

My body hummed to life, acutely aware of his hips pressing into mine, while the muscles deep in my lower abdomen clenched at his seductive tone. Unable to help myself, I ground into him. "You do have a history of ruining dresses."

One side of Soren's mouth quirked upwards into a knee-weakening half grin, and his tongue swiped across the tip of one of his canines. I had no doubt he was thinking of that morning in Lerian when he'd returned from battle and we'd screamed the words we'd been holding back before taking out our frustration on each other in our favorite way.

*Then fuck me like you missed me,* I'd demanded.

And oh *gods*, did he.

Soren leaned in to catch me in a kiss, but I dodged him, ducked out from under his arms, and sauntered towards the bathing chamber at the other end of the room instead.

"I'm sure your little friend can think of some other clothes of mine she'd like you to destroy." I narrowed my eyes at Soren over my shoulder. "Ones that make me look *common*."

I pushed through the solid mahogany door into the washroom as Soren sighed in exasperation behind me.

The massive round tub carved into the center of the chamber's marble floor was already filled to the brim with steaming water and perfumed suds. Willow must have told one of the maids I needed to freshen up after my trek in the woods, and they'd prepared it ahead of time. They'd even drawn the room's navy-and-crimson curtains over the windows that overlooked the garden so I'd have privacy.

Soren entered the room just as I began unfastening the silver buttons down the front of my dress. Hovering near the floor-length mirror beside the arched doorway, he watched me undo each one, his gaze holding on the small sliver of skin revealed.

"You have nothing to be jealous of, you know," he said softly. He removed his fur and leathers, then grabbed the hem of his linen shirt and pulled it over his head. "I'm not interested in Mirielle. I only have eyes for you."

"I'm not *jealous*." I wriggled the dress off my body and let the thick velvet pool on the floor at my feet. "I just don't like her."

I peeked over at Soren. He'd raised one eyebrow like he didn't entirely believe me, but he'd also gotten distracted by my exposed breasts and stomach.

"Xavier doesn't like her either." I angled my torso away from him so all he could see was my shoulders and backside as I gingerly waded into the tub.

Soren's eyes followed me the entire way. "That's probably because she's never tried to sleep with him."

"That's probably because she's a fucking bitch," I snapped.

Soren threw his head back and laughed before untying the laces on his pants. The material slid down his hips and legs to give me a full view of his perfect body. My gaze wandered along his wide chest, then slipped lower, over the taut muscles of his abdomen and the carved lines along his hips that pointed to the object hanging between his legs. The sight caused another contraction deep and low inside me.

"I'm sorry," I mumbled. "It's just frustrating not being able to say or do anything back. I really am trying to behave."

Soren chuckled and stepped into the bath, sinking in deep enough that his long ash-brown locks spread out around him on the surface of the water. "I know you're trying." He swam closer and framed me with his muscular arms once again. "It's alright, I like it. You're not jealous, you're protecting what's yours. Like a bear defending its cubs."

I arched an eyebrow. "So you're my cub in this scenario?"

"Huh." Soren looked down at the soapy lather in the tub and chewed his bottom lip. "I didn't think this metaphor through entirely."

I giggled and slipped my right leg over the top of Soren's thigh. He immediately brought one hand to my skin and ran his fingers along the curvature of my hip. I'd always carried extra weight in my hips, but since I'd come back to Astoria, all the brandy and extra sweets with Willow had amplified their curve. But Soren didn't seem to mind. Quite the opposite, in fact. He couldn't seem to get enough, sometimes spending hours planting idle kisses over every inch of my lower half.

"I thought you were supposed to be good with words," I teased.

Soren responded to my taunt by sliding his other hand to my opposite leg and yanking it towards him so I straddled his hips. His long silky length rubbed against the tenderness between my thighs, eliciting an unintentional moan from my lips.

"I usually am." Soren wrapped his arms around my waist, and I moaned again as he nuzzled the side of my neck. His words came out breathy and muffled against my skin. "There's just something about you, Lina Calder. My mind scrambles when you're near."

My fingers found their way into Soren's hair and wove themselves through his tousled waves, latching firmly around the strands at the base of his skull.

"Come on, Your Majesty," I whispered in his ear, tightening my grip. I pulled lightly, forcing his chin to lift so he looked me in the eyes. "Tell me some pretty things with that silver tongue of yours."

Soren chuckled again, his yearning gaze breaking from mine to peer through the bubbles between us. "I think my tongue would rather be doing other things to you."

Without warning, Soren gripped my hips and pushed me up out of the bathwater onto the edge of the tub. I smacked my hands onto the marble behind me to brace myself as Soren swung my knees over his shoulders and settled between my legs. My body shuddered as he languidly traced his lips up the inside of my thighs while his fingers dug into the soft flesh at my hips, pinning me in place. I shut my eyes, relishing the sensation of his velvety mouth, the prickle of his scruff, and the way his appreciative groans reverberated against my skin. My hands wandered down his back, my fingernails lightly raking the skin between his shoulder blades.

"Imbolc is coming up," I murmured.

I hadn't meant to say the words out loud, but Soren's lips and the carnal twinges they were stirring made my mind go blank, and the statement had slipped out before I could stop it.

Soren lifted his head, the hunger in his eyes dimming. "It is." He sat up straight, unhooking my legs from his shoulders. "Have you decided if you'll be attending?"

I shifted uncomfortably and averted my gaze to a patch of bubbles frothing up from the tub. "I don't know. I'm not sure if I'm ready yet."

The idea of walking into a room full of critical eyes made my skin crawl. Aside from that, even if I had been facing the masses on the regular, I wasn't sure I was ready to celebrate another Imbolc. Last year, the holiday had been spent trying not to panic in a suffocating crowd, dodging advances from entitled princes, and processing news that Soren could be dead. My memories of that night weren't especially good ones, and if

I celebrated this year, there might be a chance I'd relive them. I relived enough of the past in my dreams. I had to pick my battles when I was awake.

Soren nodded. He wasn't annoyed or casting judgment; instead, his eyes were full of empathy and understanding.

"Well, if and when you feel ready, I'll be right there beside you."

I smiled and moved my hand to his face, where I delicately traced the raised white scar across his cheekbone. Scary things never seemed quite so nerve-racking whenever Soren was near. "Thank you."

"Of course." He gave my thigh one last peck. "I just have one request."

My brow furrowed. "What?"

That voracious grin of his made a reappearance, reminding me I was in for more than just a bath. "When you do decide you're ready to get back into society, please drink some of Willow's plum brandy beforehand. It makes you deliciously handsy."

I laughed and slid off the edge of the tub, back into the water, before draping one arm around Soren's neck. The other dipped between his legs. "You like when I get handsy, huh?"

Soren quivered and hardened beneath my fingertips.

"Do I even have to answer that?" he breathed, his hands clasping my backside like his life depended on it.

I touched my lips to Soren's neck in a loving kiss before nipping at the skin, giving him a taste of his own medicine. Soren sucked in sharply through his teeth.

"Alright, that's it," he growled. "Now you're just being rude. You need to be punished."

I burst into a fit of giggles as Soren wrapped his arms around me, hauled me out of the bath, and carried me into the bedroom.

# Chapter 3

I was back in the Netherworld.

Sobs racked my body as I hugged Wynn, dressed in black and gold robes, as tight as I possibly could.

Aedan, king of the Netherworld, wearing the face of my friend Meer, stood from his crystal throne. Hands in his pockets, he wandered over to where my brother and I embraced.

"It's a shame," he sighed. "I had high hopes for this one."

I pulled away from Wynn just enough to look up at Aedan as he smiled and stretched out an alabaster finger to caress my brother's cheek.

"Goodbye, little princeling. I'll miss you dearly." The king of the Netherworld's eyes shifted to me. "He is yours, Lina Calder. Go, and be at peace."

"Thank you," I whimpered. "*Thank you.*"

Aedan dipped his head and turned, starting back towards his seat. When he reached it, he stopped in his tracks, thought for a few seconds, and glanced over his shoulder.

"Actually... I think I might have phrased that wrong."

Dread washed over me. "What... what do you mean?"

A gurgle and a scream pulled my attention to my left. Erith was slicing her sword across King Ilris of Merimaya's throat while his wife wailed in horror.

"Oops," Aedan giggled, shrugging coyly. "It looks like you won't be leaving after all."

Then, he raised his right hand and snapped.

Wynn instantly shoved me away and walked towards Aedan, while I scrambled after him on my hands and knees.

"Wynn? Where are you going? *Wynn!*"

I latched on to my brother's robe, but he pried my fingers off and pushed me back with unnatural strength, then continued forward to take his place at Aedan's side.

A pained wheeze pulled my attention to my right. Hale was on his hands and knees with two arrows lodged in his back. He coughed and sputtered, blood staining his lips. He looked up at me, his expression twisted in agony.

"Why didn't you save me?" he gasped.

Someone snapped their fingers again, and when I faced forward, Aedan had disappeared and my brother had taken his place on the throne, jagged shards of an obsidian crown shooting up through his golden hair while his eyes glowed a haunting red.

I WOKE HALF SCREAMING, half sobbing.

Soren bolted upright, reaching for his sword beside the bed, but when he sensed no immediate threat, he scooped me into his arms.

"Shhh..." he hushed, repeatedly kissing the top of my head. "It's alright. You're alright. We're safe. Breathe."

My tears trickled down his bare chest as I buried my face in him. Soren tightened his grip, not letting go until my wails had quieted. When I was finally breathing normally again, Soren stroked my hair.

"Do you want to talk about it?" he murmured in my ear.

I hurriedly shook my head.

It was pointless to talk about the dreams anymore. They all played on a loop in my mind, so I'd only be repeating myself at this point. Besides, Soren had enough nightmares of his own. Sometimes he'd whimper in his sleep, sounding just like a terrified child, and when I'd wake him, he would huddle against me, lay his head on my stomach, and whisper, "I felt so helpless," over and over until he'd drifted back to sleep. He never told me what the dreams were about, and he'd seen too much violence in his life for me to know for sure, but I had a theory they involved one of three things: when he lost his powers in the Netherworld, the surprise Nether attack on Yule, or memories of his abusive father, Stelios, who used to beat him and his little brother Silvain half to death. That was another reason I despised Lord Magnus. He'd served under Stelios during that time, so he must have known what was going on behind closed doors. How anyone could stand by while someone did that to their children was something I couldn't fathom, and it made my blood boil every time I thought about it.

I sat up and squeezed Soren's hand. "I'm just going to check on Wynn."

"Do you want me to come with you?" Worry coated his voice.

"I'm fine." I forced a fake smile to reassure him. "Really. Go back to sleep. I'll be in soon."

I threw back the comforter and padded over to the velvet robe draped over the chaise at the foot of the bed, then slipped it on over my naked body before stepping out into the hall.

Guilt nudged me in the ribs as I tiptoed down the corridor.

I'd lied. I wasn't going to check on Wynn.

Instead, I went straight to Soren's study. My fingers found the cool metal knob, and with a twist, a slight lift, and a slow push, the door opened without a creak that would give me away. Inside, I moved gracefully through the dark. I couldn't see anything, but I'd lost track of how many times I'd made this same journey over the past three months, and I knew the steps by heart.

Once I hit Soren's desk, my hands ran along the smooth mahogany to the third drawer down. I lifted the crystal decanter of liquor from inside, then maneuvered my way back to the sofa in front of the hearth, where the embers had burned out hours ago. I sank to the floor, rested my back against the couch, and took a long pull from the bottle. The sweet, maple-tinged liquid burned as it slid down my throat, but I didn't mind. After enough of it, I wouldn't feel anything. Which was exactly what I wanted.

Soren could never know how much I did this. It would only make him worry about me more than he already did. He had real problems to focus on, like uprising and war and Nethers attacking the small villages along the border of Astoria and Kylanthia. Most of the time he acted completely fine, but anyone could see the truth. The stress of it all was slowly chipping away at him. I'd frequently catch him staring off into the distance with a concerned frown, lost in his own mind, or the littlest thing would set him off and he'd explode. He could barely sit still, and he insisted on working, training, or schmoozing with nobles at all hours of the day. The only time he ever seemed truly present was when we'd make love, or cuddle in bed before breakfast, or steal moments together between his meetings, where we'd just hold each other and breathe.

I refused to be another burden for him to carry, so I kept

these visits a secret. We'd agreed not to have any, but this was to help him. If it was done with good intentions, that made a secret alright.

... Didn't it?

Another gulp from the bottle silenced the guilt that disagreed.

I lifted my gaze to the lattice-paned windows in the corner of the room. There were no clouds tonight, giving me a perfect view of the veil of glittering stars blanketing the night sky. My mind wandered to a different night under the stars, when I'd watched a dark figure perched on a mountaintop as black mist rippled off his body into the valley below.

That was the last night I'd seen him alive.

My throat tightened, and this time I didn't fight the tears. Here in the dark, I didn't have to be strong. Here I could hurt.

Here I could still miss him.

I continued to drink for another hour, accompanied only by my hiccuping sobs and the shadows in the room.

Shadows I desperately wished that dark figure was still watching from.

"REMEMBER, *I* comes before *E*, except after the letter *C*."

It was such a beautiful day that Willow was holding Wynn's lessons outside in the garden. The snow had melted, leaving the lawn dry enough for us to lay out blankets and enjoy the sun. It was still relatively cool outside, but after twenty minutes, the bright rays warmed our skin, and we removed our jackets.

Xavier eagerly waved his hand above his head. "What about the word neighbor?"

Willow glared at him. He was lounging on a blue and green

quilt a few paces away, and to the surprise of no one, he was sunning himself without a shirt on.

"Neighbor is an exception." Willow tucked a loose strand of hair back into her bun and clasped her hands in front of her. "We'll go over that in another lesson."

She turned back to Wynn and opened her mouth to speak.

"What about the word weigh?" Xavier chirped.

Willow sighed and glared at him again. In response, he flashed her one of his signature lopsided grins. I had to bite into one of the hand pies we'd brought out with us to keep from laughing. Xavier had been tormenting poor Willow throughout the entirety of Wynn's lesson, and I suddenly felt sorry for all the schoolteachers and governesses in charge of him while he was growing up. As a child, he'd probably been even more of a menace than he was now. What a truly terrifying thought.

"That is *also* another lesson," Willow hissed through gritted teeth. "Now if you'll stop interrupting—"

"What about the word eight?"

Willow stomped her foot. "Damn it, Xavier!"

Xavier snickered, pushed himself up off his blanket, and sauntered over to her. "Such unwholesome language, Miss Willow!" He shook his head in mock disapproval and clicked his tongue. "You seem cranky. Are you tired? Maybe you should take a break."

"I *am* tired," Willow barked. "Tired of your bullshi—"

"How about some fight training instead?" Xavier crouched in front of my brother. "What do you say, Wynnie? Does that sound fun?"

Wynn nodded eagerly and shut his notebook, setting it on the blanket beside him before scrambling to his feet.

"Atta boy," Xavier chuckled, mussing Wynn's curls.

I smiled fondly at the memory of Dominic doing the same.

Willow frowned. "I don't condone violence."

Xavier cupped her chin in his hand, brushing his thumb over her plump bottom lip.

"Then look the other way, sweetheart," he purred.

Willow's cheeks flushed a bright shade of cranberry, and she quickly ducked her head before scurrying over to me.

"Can you believe him?" She huffed, settling in on the blanket beside me.

I snorted. "Yes."

We both watched Xavier lead my brother to an open patch of grass and motion for him to raise his fists in front of his face. It was the same stance he'd first taught me in our original lessons. The thought of Wynn gaining the strength and confidence I had over the past year brought another wistful smile to my face.

"I lied before."

Willow's voice was so quiet I almost didn't hear her. When I realized what she'd said and peeked over at her, I caught her staring at Wynn and Xavier, her fingers nervously toying with one of the ruffles on her skirt.

I scooted a little closer. "What about?"

Willow averted her gaze to her hands. She hesitated a few seconds before swallowing and taking a shaky breath. "I *do* support violence. I support it when it's in self-defense." Her eyes flicked to me, amethyst irises glistening with emotion. "I can't help but think that if my sister had actually known how to use a weapon, then maybe... maybe she might still be alive."

A weight settled in my chest. An image flashed into my mind of snow falling on my handmaidens' bodies as they lay in the courtyard, their blood a vicious red stain on the blanket of white beneath them. I shut my eyes and shook my head, banishing the memory.

"Anyway..." Willow sniffed and dabbed at her eyes before plastering a smile back onto her face, showcasing the dimples in her round cheeks. "What I'm trying to say is, I really am happy Wynn is training. Just don't tell Xavier."

I smiled and squeezed her knee. "Your secret is safe with me."

Willow dipped her head in thanks and refocused on the boys.

"Willow?" I asked.

She glanced back at me.

"Do *you* know how to use any weapons?"

Willow blushed. "Goodness, no! Wood Sprites are naturally gentle creatures. Not as docile as Water Sprites, but... no." She giggled and tucked another strand of hair behind her elongated ear. "Although, I used to chop fallen trees in the orchard back home. So I suppose you could say I'm rather handy with a hatchet."

"Do you want to learn?"

Willow's eyes grew round. "Oh no, I wouldn't want to impose." Her attention returned to Xavier and Wynn, who were now practicing bobbing and weaving. "Xavier should focus on Wynn."

"Xavier taught me everything I know. It's saved my life countless times. If you'd like, I could show you some things."

Willow's eyes glazed, and I knew she was thinking of her sister.

"Well..." Willow nibbled the inside of her cheek and smoothed her skirt. "If you're not busy... and only if you want to..."

As she trailed off, I grinned and stood. "Let me grab some dull blades."

Willow beamed, her eyes crinkling with joy. "Alright! I'll suppose I'll need to change into some trousers?" Her face fell, and she blushed beet red. "Oh gods, I never wear trousers! I don't even know if I own a pair."

"You can borrow a pair of mine. I'll be right back."

Off her relieved smile, I jogged into the castle.

When I hit the top of the grand staircase, I headed towards Soren's bedroom, passing his study on the way. Two voices reached my ears through the cracked door. My footsteps slowed, and I paused just outside the room, angling my head towards the thick mahogany.

"You're playing with fire, Soren."

Lord Magnus.

"People are still talking, and no one is happy about her being here."

I frowned. I had no doubt the *her* he was referring to was me.

"They had no problem with Lina when she first came to Astoria."

Soren. He sounded frustrated. How long had they been at this?

"That was before she murdered a king!"

The image of Valdir's eyes growing wide in surprise as I slit his neck flashed into my mind, and my stomach churned.

"How many times do I have to tell you, she did it out of self-defense! He allowed the Nethers entry and was going to make her a living sacrifice. If you'd been there, you would have seen—"

"Your people don't view it that way, and neither do the people of Radomir. The territory is in chaos without a ruler, and they blame—"

"I'm well aware of what's happening, Magnus."

"Then do something about it! You could easily appease both our people and Radomir's if you got rid of her! It's not unheard of for kings to keep secret mistresses. Just tell people she's been disposed of, and put her and the child in a cottage near the Kylanthian border. Visit whenever you feel the need to stick your cock in something, but get her *out of here!*"

My shoulder accidentally brushed the door, and it creaked open. I jumped and stood upright, meeting the stunned gazes of Soren and Magnus. The latter grunted and stormed out of the study, almost bowling me over.

"Sorry about him," Soren sighed, toying with the signet ring on his index finger. "He's in a mood."

I entered the room and cautiously made my way over to where the king frowned down at a stack of papers in front of him. I slipped my arms around his waist, pressing my chest to his back as I planted a tender kiss on his shoulder blade.

"Everything alright?" I asked.

Soren patted my hands. "Yes."

"I thought we agreed not to lie to each other."

He sighed again. When he faced me, he tucked a loose strand of hair behind my ear and traced his fingers along its rounded curve. "It's nothing. People are divided, as always. Magnus offered a ridiculous solution that I refuse to entertain."

I frowned. "Soren, if you don't want me here—"

"I do!"

"I know *you* do. But if it would make things easier for you, and if it would be better for the territory if I left—"

"You and Wynn are staying here," Soren stated firmly. He took one of my hands, drew it to his mouth, and pressed his pillowy lips to my skin. "Right where you belong."

I smiled, but something still ate away at me. Soren saw through me.

"What's wrong?"

"Nothing."

Soren caught my chin and angled my face up to look him in the eyes. "I thought we agreed not to lie to each other?"

I swallowed the guilt that rose at the thought of all those nights spent alone in the study.

"It's just..." I bit my lip, trying to put my emotions into words. "I'm... I'm not sure I *do* belong here."

Soren opened his mouth to argue, but I cut him off.

"I feel like I belong here when I'm with *you*. Or when I'm training with Xavier, or drinking with Willow, or when Meer was dressing me and holding my hand before I faced a crowd."

Soren wilted at Meer's name.

"But other times," I continued, "I... I wonder if I'm cut out for this. After Yule, crowds are hard. And I don't fit in with high society. Nobles are assholes, and I don't like them."

The king chuckled grimly and nodded in agreement.

Words were tumbling out now. A dam had been lifted, and my insecurities were releasing in torrents.

"And... and I'm *trying* to behave, Soren. I'm trying to be quiet and polite and take what people throw at me, but I've never been good at it. Even as a child, I always got in trouble for mouthing off to my parents or punching my brother Jaras. And having everyone watch you and judge you? I'm not Lina anymore. My sole identity is the King Slayer. Which is true, but I... I hate that people think they know me because of that title. I hate that all I am to them is a murderer."

Soren's arms tightened around me. "Lina, it was self—"

"I know," I interrupted him. "I *know* I was defending myself. But that doesn't change the fact I took someone's life. There's no escaping that. When people look at me, they just see a trail of blood." I shrugged weakly. "I don't know what I'm saying anymore. I guess... I guess I just feel a little lost. And it's draining having to pretend like everything's fine when it's not."

Soren nodded and offered a sad, tired smile. "Welcome to politics."

I huffed a bleak laugh. "It's definitely not what I expected."

"No?" Soren pulled me closer. "What did you expect?"

"Well, for one, I expected more thrones and royal scepters lying around."

Soren's hands dipped to cup my ass. "I don't have a throne, but I have something else you can sit on."

I threw my head back and laughed as I smacked his chest. "Oh *gods*, what a horrible line!"

Soren laughed too. "I know. But it made you smile." He raised an eyebrow, one corner of his mouth twisting up in a devilish grin. "And I wasn't lying. Any chance of making it a reality?"

I wrinkled my nose. "Not quite. You're going to have to try harder than that."

"Hmm..." Soren nuzzled into my neck and planted kisses up the side. "How about now?"

"Soren," I giggled. "Willow's waiting for me."

Soren's lips parted, his tongue exploring before he gently caught the tender skin between his front teeth. I gasped and shut my eyes, my hips instinctively rolling against his.

"How about now?" he whispered in my ear.

I groaned. "Not fair. You know what that does to me."

A chuckle rumbled in Soren's chest. "What were you saying about Willow?"

"I don't remember."

Soren lifted both hands to the sides of my face and dragged me into a kiss.

"Fine," I murmured against his mouth. "Make it quick."

Soren's tongue slipped between my lips as we both feverishly tore at the buttons on each other's clothes.

"*Ahem.*"

I jumped, and Soren hissed an angry expletive. Both of us turned to Mirielle standing in the doorway, a sour expression polluting her otherwise perfect face.

"Sorry to interrupt."

She most certainly wasn't.

"What is it, Mirielle?" Soren sighed, moving behind me so I blocked her view of the object straining against his trousers.

"I was just coming to let you know we're ready to go."

My head jerked up in alarm. "Where are you going?"

"He's coming with me to spend the night at my father's estate." She was smiling brightly, but her large amber eyes were cold as ice.

"Oh, right!" I forced a ditzy giggle to combat Mirielle's sickeningly sweet grin. "I forgot."

I hadn't known. Soren hadn't said anything about it, and I subtly kicked him in the shin to remind him of it. He squeezed my hand to signal his apology.

"Yes, for the dinner Magnus organized with a few of the lords and ladies of southern Astoria," Soren said, lowering his voice. "The one I didn't ask you to come to because I knew you wouldn't want to go."

I didn't, but it still would have been nice to be told about it. I ripped my hand from Soren's to communicate that. His heavy sigh proved he got the message.

"Are you packed, Your Majesty?" Mirielle asked, twirling a ringlet around her finger. "If not, I can do it for you."

I couldn't help myself and let out a loud scoff. "You are *not* going to go rooting around in our bedroom."

Mirielle's eyes flashed. "Last time I checked it wasn't *your* bedroom, it was the King's."

Sensing the rage bubbling inside of me, Soren reached forward and put his hand on my waist, giving it a squeeze in a silent plea for me to stay calm. He cleared his throat.

"Thank you, Mirielle. That's very thoughtful of you, but I can take care of it."

Mirielle shrugged. "Just trying to be helpful."

"Bullshit," I hissed.

Soren quickly stepped in front of me.

"Lina…" His voice was a low warning. "We have to behave. Please."

"But she—"

"*Please.*"

His eyes were wide in a desperate plea for me to rein in my emotions. I could practically hear the words he'd uttered countless times before whenever I'd complain about the Tynans. Either we bite our tongues, or we risk angering Magnus and have an insurrection on our hands.

So I grit my teeth, loosened the fists at my sides, and took a deep breath.

"Fine," I grumbled. I leaned closer and lowered my voice to a whisper. "But only if you promise to finally learn how to close that damn door."

"I promise." Soren popped a kiss on my cheek. "I love you. I'll be back late tomorrow night." He lowered his mouth to my ear and added, so quiet only I could hear it, "When I get back, I expect to find you naked and ready for my cock in *our* room."

The delicate area between my legs twinged at his words, but still annoyed with his lack of communication, I replied, sweet as sugar, "I think I'll be asleep by the time you get back. I need my beauty rest."

"Your beauty is already devastating." Soren pressed his lips to mine in a final passionate kiss before breaking away. "So prepare to be woken up."

And with that, he smacked my ass and exited the study, passing Mirielle, who respectfully curtsied to him. When she straightened, her innocent facade evaporated, and she glared at me with a look of pure contempt that would've had me cowering in the corner a year prior. It was reminiscent of the way a certain icy queen of Kylanthia had glared at me the first time we met at the harvest celebration.

But instead of recoiling, I stood tall and matched Mirielle's stare. "Is there something you would like to say to me?"

"Yes, actually." Mirielle looked me up and down, taking in my boots, leggings, and cable-knit sweater. She clicked her tongue disapprovingly. "This is what I was referring to when I said some things make you look common."

*Behave, Lina.*

I sniffed. "Good to know. I'll have Soren tear it off with his teeth when he gets back."

Mirielle's lips curled into a condescending smirk. "I don't care that you're sleeping with him, you know."

I actually cackled. "Right."

"I'm serious." Mirielle shrugged. "Everyone's slept with him."

"You haven't."

"Are you sure about that?"

"Yes."

I knew that for a damn *fact*. I'd pressed Soren about it the day I met Mirielle and got my first taste of her hatred for me. He'd told me every person in court he'd been with during the salacious days of his youth, at least all those whose names he'd actually known, and Mirielle wasn't on the extensive list. He'd sworn that even though she'd pursued him for years, he'd never given in.

When I didn't balk at her stare, Mirielle crossed her arms and narrowed her eyes. "Like I said, I don't care that you're sleeping with him. I care that you think you're important because you're sleeping with him. You're not." She started towards me, landing a step on every word. "All you are, Lina Calder, is a dirty low-born stray playing dress-up."

*Behave. Behave. Behave.*

Mirielle came to a stop directly in front of me, the tips of her toes nearly touching mine. "You're not special. You're the king's whore. A mistress at best, and that's all you'll ever amount to. Everyone knows it, even Soren. The sooner you realize that, the better for everyone."

She turned on her heel and started for the door.

*Behave, damn it!*

"Mirielle!" I blurted.

She glanced over her shoulder.

My entire body shook as I suppressed the words I really wanted to say. All the emotions churning inside headed towards their usual outlet, and my eyes pinched with tears.

*No. For once you will not fucking cry, Lina Calder.*

"Listen," I said as calmly as I could. "I know you don't like me. But I'm trying really hard to be kind—"

"Don't bother," Mirielle interrupted. "It doesn't matter. You won't be around much longer."

I squeezed my hands tight, pain shooting up my arms as my nails dug into my palms. "The king feels differently."

"Does he?" Mirielle raised an eyebrow. "Has he ever said anything about marrying you?"

I opened my mouth to speak, but promptly shut it.

Soren and I had never discussed marriage, but our relationship was still in the early stages. We were still learning about each other and enjoying the thrill of it all. We didn't need to have that talk yet. And if I was being honest, I wasn't sure marriage was something I wanted.

Not that Soren wouldn't make a good husband. I'm sure he would. But it was like I'd told Hale last year in Merimaya the night before Imbolc; growing up, I never imagined myself getting married. Marriage in my world meant becoming a mother too. I didn't want children, and never had. I didn't want my purpose to become producing my husband's heirs, and I didn't want to be confined to the house to mind the cooking and cleaning and sewing. I knew other women who *had* wanted that, and it made them happy, and that was wonderful! I was happy *for* them.

But that was their dream, not mine.

"What does the future look like in your eyes, Lina?" Mirielle cooly examined her fingernails. "Do you actually think you and Soren are going to live happily ever after?" She snickered like it was the most amusing thing she'd heard all day. "I can confidently tell you the five territories would burn before a human took the throne and started squeezing out mongrel children. Soren knows that." She looked me up and down once more. "You're Soren's pretty little pet until he finds a viable option for a wife. So by all means, have him tear your clothes off with his teeth as much as he wants. Sleep in his bed, fuck where people can see you, but never forget what you are. And never forget what you and the king are not."

When Mirielle turned and strode out of the room, I slammed and locked that stupid fucking door.

# Chapter 4



Soren hated all these people.

Well, all of them except Sorcha Umber. She and his little brother, Silvain, had gone to boarding school together in western Radomir. She'd been the quiet girl with thick spectacles and bushy hair, always following Silvain around like a puppy. Soren had said hello to her once when he paid Silvain a surprise visit, and she quite literally squeaked before fumbling her armful of books onto the cobblestones of the courtyard. Poor thing nearly cried when Silvain knelt to help her pick them up.

But here she was now, grown and graceful, sitting across from Soren at the dinner table with thinner spectacles and glossy curls, but still just as quiet. She'd said a grand total of three words all night. When Magnus introduced her at the start of the evening, she'd curtsied and said, *Hello, Your Majesty.* After that, the night was taken over by the more dominant personalities gathered around the table in the Tynans' dining room.

There was Cailin and Aimil Pollux, one of the more wealthy families in Astoria, but by far the most boring. How many ways were there to talk about your estate's overgrown hedges? Apparently, if you asked Aimil, countless. Poor Cailin. That explained the dull look in her eyes. She must have lost her mind as a result of all that talk, day in and day out, about her husband's stupid hedges.

Lord Judis and Lady Fennella Teague were slightly more animated, which was in part thanks to Lady Fennella's excessive drinking. If she had one more glass of port, Soren would be surprised if she could still stand. She and her husband were clearly trying to seduce Lord Tristan Rourke. Tristan, the handsome, hawk-eyed lord who only recently took his father's title, was a decade younger than Soren, so their respective social circles occasionally overlapped while they'd grown up. Soren knew enough about him to know Tristan would never take the Teagues up on their proposition, but it was entertaining to watch them try.

What wasn't fun was listening to Mildred Macrae drone on and on, her high-pitched voice grating on Soren's ears every time she opened her mouth, which had been, on average, every ten seconds for the past three hours. Her daughter, Vevilla, didn't speak as much as the lady, but she irritated Soren even more. Partly because she constantly tittered and whispered with Mirielle, but mainly because she hadn't quit staring at him for one single second.

Soren was used to having eyes on him. Even before he was king and every move became analyzed and criticized and picked apart, people paid attention to him. He'd noticed it as soon as he'd matured as a young man and realized the effect his appearance had on people. But Vevilla's gaze was so blatant and hungry, it was uncomfortable. The woman made no effort to hide the fact she was trying to seduce him. So was Mirielle, but that was nothing new. She'd been after him since they were young, but Soren was never tempted. Not when their fathers used to constantly pressure him about what a smart match it would be, and *especially* not now. Not after how she treated Lina.

Soren's fingers tightened around his goblet at the thought, the silver groaning as it strained under his strength. Soren had smiled and laughed and made perfect small talk all night, coddling and purring and charming the way he was known for, but inside a war was raging. Magnus sat on his right, Mirielle on his left, and it was taking everything in him not to flip the dinner table and crush them both under it.

When he took the throne, Soren had sworn he wouldn't keep the Tynans close the way his father had. And he wouldn't have if it hadn't been the one thing that promised to unite Astoria. It was a last resort, so he'd begrudgingly shoved down his emotions and brought the Tynans on. He was used to pushing aside his feelings for the good of the territory. He'd been doing it his whole life. But after seeing them torment the woman he loved... it took an unnatural amount of self-control to behave. Yes, Magnus had been hugely influential in calming discord in Astoria, and an uprising was no longer hovering over Soren's head. But somehow it didn't feel worth it if Lina was miserable. She'd never asked for this life. She'd left on Samhain to live a normal existence with her brother. But instead she was here, dealing with this. And that ate away at Soren every day.

Unfortunately, they'd gone down this road too far. It didn't feel like it, but this was best for everyone. If Soren was dethroned, he'd most likely lose his life in the process. No king in the history of the five territories had been usurped without violence, and if Soren was gone, then Lina would have no one. No money, no title, no one to defend her from the Fae dead set on seeing her blood spilled, and no one to hold her at night when the nightmares came calling. So whether they liked it or not, this was the way things had to be, and there was nothing either of them could do about it now.

Soren finished off his wine, the third goblet he'd downed within the hour. He couldn't help it. The company was repulsive, the conversation utterly mind-numbing, and the food mediocre at best. If Lina were here, she'd be drunk off her ass and probably getting handsy under the table. Soren caught himself smiling at the thought.

Fuck, he missed her.

He'd missed her presence at every event she'd avoided over the past few months. Xavier had been reclusive lately too, which meant Soren attended these functions alone, and it would always make him reminisce about that first harvest celebration with Lina, before either of them had confessed their newfound feelings, and when life had seemed so much more simple than it was now. They'd danced and flirted, and Lina'd had gold sparkles on her eyelids, and her smile had been so bright it lit up Soren's soul like the dawn. He wished things could be the same as they were then, but he knew that wasn't possible. Lina needed him not to rush her back into this life.

When he'd met her two Samhains ago, Soren hadn't understood her. He'd been impatient and judged her for hiding in her room and wallowing in her sadness during those first few days in Astoria. He hadn't known that was how she healed. She processed things on her own, in her own time. She'd go through phases of being social or blowing up in anger, something Soren understood far too well, but then Lina would find time alone to fall apart. Her healing wasn't linear, and even though he respected it, it killed Soren not being able to help. He wanted to take care of her, to distract her or hold her until he'd drawn all the pain out of her aching heart like sucking poison from a wound. But that only helped some of the time.

All Soren could do was wait, respect her space and her process, and let her have her secrets.

He knew about the study. He knew Lina would sit in the shadows and cry and drink until the guilt ebbed enough to let her sleep. A few weeks ago, he'd followed her. He'd been worried after she had a particularly disturbing dream and woke unable to catch her breath. She hadn't told him what it was about, but he'd known who it involved when he stood outside the study and heard her whimpering a name over and over in the dark.

Hale.

In that moment, Soren had known he couldn't give Lina what she really needed.

Soren couldn't be *him*.

Lina needed that secret, and gods knew Soren still had his own. So he let her keep it.

"More wine, Your Majesty?"

Knocked from his thoughts, Soren glanced over at Vevilla. She and Mirielle were both looking up at him with heavy-lidded come-hither stares.

Soren forced a smile that chipped away another piece of his sanity. "Yes, please."

Mirielle snapped her fingers at a lanky Wood Sprite in the corner. The woman jumped and rushed over.

"His Majesty's had a few glasses this evening," Mildred Macrae tutted. Her thin lips were pinched into a smile, but her eyes scanned him critically. She'd been a bitch to Soren ever since she'd cornered him at a Beltane celebration and attempted to seduce him. He'd been nineteen years old and had responded by laughing hysterically in her face. It was something she'd never forgive him for, it seemed.

Soren shrugged. "What can I say? I have a weakness for good wine, and the Tynans have exquisite taste."

A lie. The wine was shit.

"You're too kind, Your Majesty," Mirielle giggled.

Her voice was reminiscent of nails scraping across a chalkboard, and Soren had to physically fight the urge to wince.

Soren glanced back down at the table as the Sprite topped off his drink. Her hands shook uncontrollably.

"Thank you." Soren gave the woman a genuine smile, probably the first one he'd cracked all night. "What's your name?"

The Sprite's one green eye and one blue eye grew round, and she quickly peeked over at Magnus, her mouth fixed shut.

"We don't allow them to speak at the table," Magnus explained.

Soren's rage had been steady, crackling embers all night, but the lord's words stoked it into a blaze. The candles throughout the dining room burned a little brighter as a result.

Digging his fingers into his thighs to keep them from forming fists, Soren nodded. "Then what is her name, my lord?"

Magnus sawed off a slice of the venison on his plate and swirled it in gravy before lifting it to his mouth. "No idea. Mirielle?"

The lord's daughter shrugged. "I didn't know she had one."

Flames on the candelabra at the center of the table flickered wildly. Soren took a deep breath, in through his nose, out through his mouth, and the flickering calmed. He faced the Sprite.

"Miss. As your king, I hereby grant you permission to speak. What is your name?"

The woman gulped, her gaze bouncing warily between Magnus and Mirielle before her lips parted.

"Aspen, Your Majesty," she said, her voice a pained whisper.

Soren's heart ached at how fitting the name was. With

bright orange hair and constant trembling, she was exactly like a sad little leaf clinging to an aspen tree desperately holding on to the last leg of autumn.

"Thank you for serving us this evening, Aspen," Soren said earnestly. "You're working very hard. You deserve a raise."

Magnus scoffed and washed the venison down with a mouthful of brandy. Some spilled out, dripping down his lip and into his beard.

"She's paid well enough," Magnus grumbled, dabbing at his mouth with his napkin. "Besides, you can't pay the low-borns too much, or they'll start to expect it."

"Yes, gods forbid actually wanting to be treated like a person," Soren mumbled.

But his comment was heard by every keen Fae ear in the room, and awkward silence fell over the table. It was broken only when Lord Tristan snickered at the far end of the table.

"You always did have a soft spot for the less fortunate, Your Majesty," he said, tearing off a piece of bread and popping it into his mouth. His ice-blue eyes narrowed as a smirk lit up his face. "Good to see you haven't changed much over the years."

Soren couldn't tell if the lord meant that or not. Something about Tristan had always felt off. He'd been cunning and conniving their whole lives, and spent too much of his youth slinking around darkened hallways, eavesdropping on every-one's conversations, for Soren to ever feel comfortable around him.

"You're excused, Aspen," Mirielle declared.

Soren hadn't realized the Sprite was still standing beside him. He'd been too busy stewing and had forgotten to dismiss her.

Aspen dipped into a curtsy and darted back to her corner, trembling even more than she had before.

"How is all that going, by the way?" Lord Judis asked,

draping an arm around his wife, who had stopped making eyes at Tristan for the first time all night to focus on her king instead. They both tried to appear innocent, but they couldn't disguise the judgmental gleam in their eyes. Soren knew exactly what they were poking for information on.

Lina.

The flames on the candles swelled once again, this time larger than before, and Soren had to grit his teeth to keep from snarling like an animal. Lina was none of these people's gods-damned business, and he wanted her out of their venomous mouths.

He needed to get out of this situation. If he didn't leave soon, he feared he might actually burn the place to the ground.

Soren mustered one last painfully fake smile and shrugged nonchalantly. "When the gods have chosen to bless us, I firmly believe it is our duty to share those gifts with others, especially those less fortunate. I try to do so whenever the opportunity presents itself."

Lord Aimil opened his mouth to speak, most likely to prod Soren for more information, but his wife elbowed him in the ribs. Soren took that as his cue to mimic a yawn.

"Lords and Ladies," he began, extending his arms out wide in a languid stretch. "My apologies. I'm ashamed to admit I may have misjudged my tolerance and overindulged. Apparently I'm not as young as I once was. I must retire for the evening, before I have a little too much fun."

He shot the room a suggestive wink, earning a ripple of charmed laughter. Soren pushed away from the table and stood, the rest of the party following suit. He dipped his head, the others curtsying or bowing in response before Soren started for the door. He passed Aspen on the way, and lowered his voice so only she could hear him.

"I would love one last glass of wine as a nightcap. Could you make that happen for me?"

The woman refused to meet Soren's gaze but nodded obediently.

"Thank you." Soren turned back to the lords and ladies and raised his voice. "Good night."

They replied with their *"Good night, Your Majesties,"* unable to hear Soren grumble the word "fuckers" over their own miserable voices.

THE ROOM the Tynans put Soren up in was small, but just as luxurious as the one he and Lina shared back home. And despite what Mirielle had said earlier, his bedroom *did* belong to both of them now. The first night Lina had spent in his bed, it had felt right. Like a piece of the puzzle had always been missing, and Lina completed it. Soren didn't like to imagine how it would feel when he eventually lost that piece. Living without her would feel innately wrong. Even tonight, it was odd not having her here to burrow beside, or bury himself into.

Soren was standing in front of the hearth, staring into the flames and fantasizing about all the places he would take Lina in this room if she were with him, when there was a knock on the door.

"It's open," he called out.

A timid orange-haired Wood Sprite slipped in.

"The wine you requested, Your Majesty," Aspen muttered, keeping her eyes glued to the floor as she curtsied and extended a corked bottle to him.

"Thank you, Aspen." Soren walked over and took it from her hands, noting their vicious trembling.

The servant nodded, curtsied again, and started back for the door.

"Aspen?"

The Sprite jumped and spun, wringing her hands nervously. Gods, it was painful just watching her exist.

Soren set the wine down and leaned a hip against the back of a nearby armchair. "Are you happy?"

"I... I'm sorry?" Aspen squeaked.

"Are you happy working for the Tynans?"

The Sprite swallowed. "I'm very grateful to the Tynans for giving me employment."

"That's not what I asked." Soren softened his tone. "Are they good to you?"

If Aspen clenched and twisted her hands any harder, Soren was worried she might actually tear them off.

"The Tynans don't mistreat me, Your Majesty." She uncomfortably shuffled her feet. "My sister works for a powerful man in Lerian. He beats her, and worse. But the Tynans have never touched me like that, so I view myself as blessed."

Soren frowned. "Just because someone's never hurt you physically doesn't mean they're good to you."

The Sprite was quiet for a few seconds, her multicolored eyes shifting back and forth across the stone floor as she considered her next words.

"I'm invisible," she finally settled on. "And I'd rather have that than what my sister has."

Soren nodded thoughtfully before straightening. "Well, if you or your sister ever decide you want a change, you have a guaranteed spot on my staff."

Aspen's eyes jerked up from the ground in surprise, meeting Soren's gaze for the first time all night.

"You can send a letter explaining our conversation here

tonight and address it to someone named Xavier. I fear if you address it to me, it could be seen by eyes that are not my own."

Soren frowned again as he thought back to that stack of papers on his desk. Even though Magnus denied it, Soren knew he rifled through them.

"I trust Xavier with my life, and he was close with my last head of staff." A pang of sadness shot through Soren's chest at the mention of Meer. "Xavier will know what to do in preparation for your arrival."

Aspen tried to smile, but a heavy weight seemed to settle on her shoulders, making them slump as her eyes dimmed.

"I understand if you have reservations after the events on Yule," Soren added. "There's no pressure to accept if you don't feel comfortable with it. I want you to feel safe, and if you won't—"

"No, that's not it, Your Majesty." Color flushed Aspen's cheeks, her next words tainted with shame. "I... I can't read or write."

A sudden wave of guilt washed over Soren as Aspen fought the humiliated tears welling in her eyes and returned her gaze to the ground. Many low-caste Fae rarely had the time or resources to receive a proper education, and Soren had forgotten to consider that might be the case here.

Soren clasped his hands in front of him and shrugged. "Well, no matter. Even if you showed up unexpectedly, you'd still have a place."

"Really?"

Soren donned the warmest smile he could. "Yes. And I happen to have a very good teacher on staff. She's a Sprite, like you. She's always happy to have people sit in on her lessons. You'd be most welcome."

The tears finally overflowed from Aspen's eyes, but these weren't from shame. They were tears of gratitude.

"Oh, thank you," Aspen whimpered. "Thank you, Your Majesty."

She ducked her head and scurried for the door. When she got there she froze, and slowly turned to look back at Soren over her shoulder. "You're different than they say, you know."

Soren tilted his head. "What do they say about me?"

Aspen placed a hand on the door handle. "I hear things I wouldn't dare repeat, Your Majesty. But know that when *I* speak of you to others, it will only be of your kindness. This won't be forgotten. I swear."

And with that, she cracked the door and slipped into the hall.

Soren headed for the armchairs in front of the hearth, smiling to himself at the thought of Lina and Willow taking Aspen under their wing, plying her with food and drink and laughter until she felt comfortable in her own skin.

The door creaking open again made Soren turn. When he saw who had entered, his shoulders instantly tensed.

"How do you find your accommodations, Your Majesty?" Mirielle cooed, clicking the door shut behind her.

Soren tried to smile, but he had a hunch it came out more like a grimace. "The room is more than satisfactory. Thank you for checking."

"My pleasure." Mirielle locked the door.

Dread seeped into Soren's gut. He knew what was coming. He'd had countless moments like this in his youth, and back then he'd happily indulged. But things were different now.

*He* was different now.

"I'm about to retire, Mirielle," Soren said as politely as he could, willing his rage to stay under control. "You're excused."

"Your Majesty, you don't have to play coy with me."

Soren sighed wearily. "Coy isn't my style."

Don't try it, Mirielle.

The advisor's daughter lifted her fingers to the neckline of her dress and slipped it from her shoulders, the pink silk fluttering to the ground and pooling at her feet.

Fuck. She tried it.

Soren immediately averted his gaze before he caught a glimpse of Mirielle's naked body, now fully on display in front of him. If this was anyone else, he wouldn't need to tread as carefully as he did now. With anyone else, he would rage and threaten and say anything he wanted to get them out of his sight. But this was Mirielle Tynan, and her father...

Hell, her father owned him.

"I apologize," Soren cleared his throat, still keeping his attention directed elsewhere. "I don't know what I did to give you the idea this was something I'd be interested in."

Mirielle didn't reply. Instead, she stepped towards him. Soren responded by taking a step backwards.

"As I said before, Mirielle, I'll be retiring for the evening. Alone."

Another step from Mirielle, another step back from Soren. He collided with one of the armchairs and gripped the side, channeling his building fury into clawing the brown leather until he'd poked holes in its surface.

"With all due respect, you're a lovely woman, but I'm not interested in anything physical or romantic with you," Soren said, more firm this time. "I'm a happily taken man."

Mirielle continued to glide towards him. "Since when is Soren of Astoria ever content with just one woman?"

She sidled up and reached out, dragging her fingers seductively down Soren's chest. He couldn't contain himself anymore.

He grabbed Mirielle's wrist and wrenched her hand off him, making her wince in pain. "Since he met Lina Calder."

When he released his grip, Mirielle backed away and gingerly massaged her wrist. "Gods, I hope not. For *your* sake."

She spun on her heel and stalked back to her dress on the floor.

"What the hell does that mean?" Soren snapped, facing her but keeping his gaze fixed on the ground.

"Nothing," Mirielle grumbled back. She stepped into the gown and lifted it back onto her body. Only then did Soren dare look at her.

"Enjoy your new plaything while it lasts, Your Majesty," Mirielle huffed. "But all boys eventually grow out of their toys."

Soren kept calm, but when he spoke, the quiver in his voice exposed the storm raging inside. "Lina is not a toy."

Mirielle scoffed and smoothed the front of her gown. "You're right, she's not. She's a *weapon.* One I pray you don't die by."

The fire in the hearth roared to life at the same time as the fire in Soren's soul. Without thinking, he lunged across the room and shoved the door closed as Mirielle opened it.

"Is that a fucking threat?" he growled in her face.

"No, it's a warning," she spat back. "One that all those people out there are too afraid to give you themselves. They don't want to tell you what's really going on, but I will." She lifted her chin, eyes glinting with an edge Soren had never seen in her. "Rumors of insurrection are still circulating. Despite Lina's cowering, people know you've kept her around, even after everything she did."

"How many times do I have to say it? Lina did nothing wrong."

Mirielle squeezed her eyes shut and shook her head. "Gods, has this girl put you under some kind of spell? She *murdered* the king of Radomir! *Your* friend! Cut his throat like a pig at the slaughter!"

"I was the one who told her—"

"People are clamoring for her blood *and* yours! The entire

realm is on the verge of civil war, all because some pathetic low-born human—"

"Get out." Soren pushed away from the door and stormed back across the room.

"Soren—"

*"Get the fuck out!"*

The fire tore out of the hearth as Soren roared, its flames flaring and licking at the sheepskin rug on the ground in front. Mirielle recoiled in fear and hastily fumbled for the handle. When she finally managed to yank the door open, she looked back at Soren, her chest heaving as she attempted to catch her breath.

"You two don't have a future. Not one that ends happily. You have to know that."

The door slammed shut behind Mirielle, and Soren stomped across the singed rug to slump miserably into one of the chairs.

Yes. Unfortunately, he *did* know that.

# CHAPTER 5

"Mirielle's a bitch."

Xavier, Willow, Wynn and I were in our corner of the garden like the day prior, my little brother sitting cross-legged on a blanket under an apple tree, writing out the words Willow assigned him while the rest of us went over basic fighting maneuvers. Xavier was shirtless as usual, and he had lent Willow a pair of trousers and one of his tunics. I wore pants of my own and had rolled up the sleeves on Soren's shirt, which I'd slept in last night when I'd been missing him.

Xavier deftly tossed a dagger in the air and let it flip three times before catching it behind his back.

"She always has been," he continued. "Soren should've told her to piss off a long time ago. I don't know why he hasn't."

"Because the Tynans could turn half the noble families in Astoria against him if they wanted to." I absentmindedly scraped my thumbnail across the silver filigree vines decorating the hilt of my own dagger, the same one Soren had given me all those months ago when I first learned how to defend myself the same way Willow was now. I raised an eyebrow at Xavier. "Besides, I thought you liked bitches."

*Particularly royal ones with sea green eyes and dark hair,* I wanted to add, but kept it inside. It seemed I could tease Xavier about anyone and anything... *except* the queen of Lerian. Even if he was in the best of moods, any mention of Syrena instantly made him go sullen and moody.

"I like my women sassy, not bitchy. There's a difference."

"And that difference is?"

"Bitchy has ill-intent." Xavier's mouth curved into a grin, and his eyes sparked with mischief. "Sassy is just fun to play with."

Willow glanced at Wynn. "I'm sorry, but can we please watch the use of the B-word? There are innocent ears present."

"It's fine, he can't hear us." Xavier faced the apple tree and raised his voice. "How's it going over there, Wynnie?"

Wynn remained focused on his notebook.

Xavier turned back to us and shrugged. "See? Not even paying attention."

Willow pouted in protest.

"Stop worrying, Miss Willow," Xavier cooed. "He's being a good little schoolboy. But right now..." He pulled another dull blade from his waistband and slid it into Willow's palm, curling her fingers around the hilt. "Right now, I'm going to need you to be a very *naughty* schoolteacher."

He shot her a wink, and Willow's face turned cherry red as something that was half giggle and half squeak bubbled out of her.

I rolled my eyes. "Willow, this would be the part where you kick him between the legs and tell him to stop dicking around."

Xavier laughed and stepped backwards. "Point taken. Alright, from the top. What's the correct position?"

"Um..." Willow peeked at the ground and adjusted her feet

shoulder width apart, one slightly in front of the other. Then she raised one fist just below her chin, blocking her throat, while the other held the dagger ready to strike.

Xavier scanned her body. "Good girl. Nice form."

"Thank you," Willow mumbled, her face flushing again.

"And what do you *not* do with that front foot?" I chimed in.

"Don't put all my weight on it."

"Correct."

"Now I'll go slow, alright?" Xavier took a fighting stance of his own.

Willow set her jaw and tightened her grip on the hilt of her blade. "No, I can handle normal speed."

Xavier arched an eyebrow. "Miss Willow! Such an over-achiever."

This time, Willow was the one who rolled her eyes. "Stop dawdling. Let's see you work as hard as that mouth does."

Xavier's eyes glittered. "Oh, sweetheart, you haven't even seen half of what my mouth can do."

Willow's flush deepened as she gulped, but her expression remained determined.

Impressed with her tenacity, Xavier arched his eyebrows and stepped back. "Alright, Miss Willow. You want to dance? Let's dance."

I observed from the sideline as the two went through basic blocks and parries. Willow kept up well, but Xavier was clearly taking it easy on her. He was building up her confidence, and he'd work on honing her skills at a later date. It was the same thing he'd done with me when we first started training together.

I smiled at how far I'd come since that first day in the courtyard, when Soren had interrupted us and effortlessly knocked my pride down a few notches before gifting me my dagger. It was a crucial moment for me in my journey towards healing and strength, and not only did my dagger represent that, but it also reminded me of Soren and his heart for the hurting. Because of that, it had become my most prized possession. I never went anywhere without it.

I returned the dagger to its sheath at my thigh and wandered over to where my little brother sat scribbling intently in his notebook.

"How's it coming over here?" I asked, plopping beside him.

Wynn didn't look up at me. Instead, he kept his concentration on the page, his eyes narrowed and his tongue sticking out the side of his mouth. I'd never seen him so invested in his lessons before. Confused, I tilted my head to get a better glimpse of what he was working on.

My stomach dropped.

With his charcoal pencil, Wynn had drawn a large circle with spikes around the outside. It looked like the start of a symbol I knew very well, only that symbol had been a brand seared into the skin on a man's neck, left hand, and right hip.

"Willow?" I called, my voice cracking. I kept my gaze fixed on the paper, where Wynn was drawing a squiggly line and leaves along the outside of the jagged sphere. "Willow, can you come here for a second?"

The Sprite jogged over, Xavier trailing after her.

"What's wrong?" she panted, wiping at the small beads of sweat already condensing on her brow.

I extended a shaky finger to Wynn's drawing. Willow took one look at the paper and yelped, then snatched up the notebook and clutched it to her chest.

"Goodness!" Her cheeks on fire, Willow frantically shook her head. "I didn't teach him that, I swear! He must have looked ahead in one of my textbooks to the unit on the ancient Fae tongue."

"What did he write?" Xavier asked, angling his head in an attempt to see the drawing.

Willow jammed her shoulder in his way to block the view. "Don't worry about it!"

"Come on, Miss Willow," Xavier crooned in such a silky tone it finally made sense how he managed to seduce people so easily. Willow was utterly helpless against it.

She sighed and lowered her voice to a whisper. "It was the start of a slur."

Xavier laughed and ruffled Wynn's hair. "Attaboy, Wynnie!"

Willow smacked Xavier with the notebook and turned to me, her eyes earnest. "I'm so sorry, Lina. I promise, I'll watch him closer. I won't let it happen again."

I swallowed the lump in my throat, willing my pounding heart to settle. "It's fine, really. Let's just get back to training."

Xavier nodded and sauntered back to his spot in the grass, but I remained where I was, attempting deep, calming breaths while Wynn stared blankly off into the sunset.

THAT NIGHT, I dreamed about Hale.

Only it wasn't one of the usual dreams where crude arrows embedded in his back, and I held him in my arms as his lungs rattled and filled with blood while he cried like a babe.

For once, this dream wasn't a nightmare.

We were in Astoria, in a bedroom here in the castle. Hale and I were kneeling on the bed, completely shrouded in darkness, but I could see him clear as day. My arms were draped around his neck, and we stared at each other, those dark eyes of his piercing my soul in the most intimate way.

"I miss you," I whispered, tenderly nudging Hale's nose with mine.

"It's alright," he said. "I'm here now."

I reached up to run my fingers over his brow and brush back the strands of obsidian black hair falling in front of his eyes. My fingers drifted lower, running along his sharp cheekbones, then to the lips that were smiling instead of turned down in their usual frown. Finally my fingertips landed on his throat, where the skin was marred by a spike-covered circle and two crescent moons with lines through their centers to connect them.

"I never got a chance to tell you how beautiful I thought you were," I said, brushing my thumb over one of the moons. "Every inch of you."

Hale's hands tightened around my waist and pulled me closer. "I knew."

"Did you?" I touched my lips to his neck, grazing it tenderly before pressing a kiss to the scarred flesh.

His throat bobbed as I traced my lips along the outline of the scar. "Of course I did."

I worked my way lower, kissing down his throat, collarbones, and bare chest, inhaling the smoky scent of him like I was suffocating and he was the taste of fresh air.

"You saw me," Hale muttered, leaning his head back and shutting his eyes as he savored my mouth against him. "All of me. You saw me in a way no one else ever had. I couldn't hide from you, no matter how hard I tried."

Without warning, Hale threw me onto the bed and pinned me on my back, his fingers caging my throat and his dark gaze scanning my face.

"Are you scared?" he asked, his breathy words hot against my skin.

"No," I panted. "I've never been afraid of you."

"I know." Hale's lips hovered above mine, leaving me wanting. "That's why I loved you."

A heavy, all-consuming sadness settled in my chest. "You loved me?"

Hale moved his fingers from my neck to my face and dragged his thumb across my bottom lip. "You know I did. You felt it in your soul. We both did."

I swallowed, and even in sleep I was incapable of keeping the salty tears at bay. "I wish I could've heard you say that when you were alive."

"I wish I'd had the courage."

I couldn't fight the tears any longer, but Hale didn't flinch at the sight of them. Instead he bent his head to kiss them away.

"I'm saying it now, though," he murmured against my cheeks. "And I mean it. From the bottom of my heart... I loved you, Lina Calder."

I sniffled and nodded. "I loved you too."

His mouth spread into a bright smile, making my stomach dip.

"Well, now that we've got that out of the way..." His gaze licked over my body, achingly slow. "I need you to lie back and let me do what I do best."

Hale's hand returned to my throat, but his head dipped between my legs, making my back arch as I moaned with pleasure.

~

I JERKED awake gasping for air.

My body was slick with sweat, the blankets on the bed tangled around my neck, and there was a deliciously deep pulsing between my legs. I groaned and kicked the covers off before wiping my brow and flopping back to the mattress to catch my breath.

Gods, that dream had been vivid. Its realism rivaled even

my worst nightmares. I half expected Hale to materialize out of the shadows and tell me it wasn't a dream at all.

*He's not here,* I had to remind myself. *He can't be here.*

Still, I found myself scanning the room. Once I'd accepted the shadows were in fact empty, I took one last shaky inhale before rolling onto my side, shutting my eyes, and attempting to calm my racing mind. It took a few minutes, but I eventually settled, and sleep crept towards me again. When a door creaked open, however, I snapped back to awareness. I relaxed the second I recognized the heavy footsteps and clink of a broadsword as it was propped in the corner.

Hale wasn't here, but someone else was. Someone I loved desperately, and whose presence soothed my aching soul like a salve the second he entered the room, peeled off his shirt, and climbed into *our* bed.

Soren's muscular arms slipped around my waist and hauled me closer as he nestled his face in the crook of my neck. I let out a sleepy moan and snuggled my back into his chest.

"Hello."

"Hello," Soren replied, playfully nipping at my earlobe. "I thought I told you to be naked when I got home."

My core leapt at his hungry, demanding tone.

"Did you say that?" I leaned my head back so Soren had full access to my neck. He understood the silent request and pressed his lips to the sensitive skin before giving it a nip too.

"Mm-hmm." Soren's voice rippled from his body into mine. "I'll have to remedy this, I think."

He tightened one hand around my waist while the other explored my curves over my nightgown. I rolled into his touch, moaning softly as he ran his fingertips along my stomach, my breasts, and my hips.

"Come here, little rebel," Soren growled in my ear as he dragged me closer.

I ground my backside into him, gasping appreciatively when I discovered him already hard. Another carnal twinge shot through me, warming my blood in anticipation.

As if reading my mind, Soren let out a breathy chuckle and slowly dragged his fingers up the inside of my thighs. "It would already be inside you if you would've just obeyed me."

Those words caused another pang of lust, but they also stoked a fire in my soul. I pushed my hips against Soren even harder, eliciting a low groan of arousal from deep inside him.

"You can't *always* be the one in charge," I chided, swirling my ass against him.

Soren chuckled again and reached for the hem of my nightgown. "Oh, you want to be the one in control now?"

I grinned and flipped over, pushing Soren onto his back as I swung my leg over to straddle his hips. Grabbing hold of his wrists, I pinned them beside the pillow beneath his head. He raised his eyebrows in surprised amusement.

"Maybe I do." I pushed my face close to his and lowered my voice. "Is that alright with you, Your Majesty?"

Soren's eyes drifted lower. The way his gaze roved over my cleavage and hips was vaguely reminiscent of an animal assessing how it wanted to devour its prey. "Honestly, I think you could do anything to me right now and I'd be alright with it."

Keeping his wrists pinned, I leaned closer. Soren lifted his face to kiss me, but I made sure my lips stayed just out of reach, much like someone else had in my dream this evening.

"Anything?" I purred.

Soren's gaze softened for a moment. "If it makes you happy, then it makes me happy."

My heart swelled at the unexpected sincerity, and for a split second, I had the urge to stop my teasing and give Soren the biggest hug I possibly could. But then the lustful gleam reappeared in his eyes as quickly as it had left, and he angled his mouth as close to mine as he could manage, his puffs of breath tickling my lips.

"Tell me, Lina," he whispered. "What makes you happy?"

The game was back on.

"Hmm..." I bit my lip as I considered. "What makes me happy..."

Soren lay flat again, and I took the opportunity to nuzzle his exposed neck.

"Let's see," I mumbled against his skin. "I like watching sunsets."

Soren's throat bobbed as I planted a delicate kiss on it.

"And I like wine." I moved lower, pressing another kiss into the dip between his collarbones, following it with a quick lap of my tongue.

"Wine makes you horny. I like when you drink wine too."

I laughed a little and continued down his body, grazing my lips across his chest next.

"I like flowers..."

The faint smell of sweat on Soren's skin mixed with his own scent of wood and spice, making my mouth water. Other more intimate parts of me were having the same reaction.

Soren's chest rose and fell faster as my lips traveled towards his abdomen.

"What kinds of flowers?" he managed to gasp out.

A memory flashed across my mind of a yellow crocus tucked in the buckle of a black leather jacket.

I shoved the image away.

"All kinds." I sat upright and released my hold on Soren's wrists. He moved to grab me, but I smacked his hands.

"Ah!" I warned. "Not until I say. I'm in control tonight, remember?"

Soren grunted in frustration, but obediently returned his

hands to the mattress. I smiled proudly and tilted forward on my knees, lifting off him just enough to hoist my nightgown over my hips. I resettled on top of him, letting the sensitive area between my legs rest against the fabric of his trousers, which was now straining from the object swelling beneath it. Slowly I rocked my hips forward and back, forcing Soren to ball his fists in the sheets and clench his jaw. He twitched beneath me, growing harder still.

Oh, this was *fun*.

"What else do I like..." I mused, shifting my hands to Soren's bare chest and continuing to roll myself against him at an excruciatingly slow pace. "I like riding horses, feeling all that power between my thighs."

Unable to help himself, Soren reached for me once more. I glared in warning, to which he responded by exhaling sharply and begrudgingly returning his hands to the sheets to grip them tight.

"You're very good at riding," he forced through clenched teeth.

I ground my hips quicker. "I know."

Soren pressed his lips into a tight line, another deep groan resonating in his chest as I delicately raked my nails down his abdomen.

"I like that look you get." My fingers traveled over the curves and dips of the muscles on his stomach, headed towards the V-shape beneath his hips.

Soren impatiently wriggled underneath me. This time, it was my turn to groan as he pushed his hips upward, pressing himself against my clit, which now throbbed with desire.

"What look do I get?"

I dipped my hand behind the waistband of Soren's pants and traced my thumb along the line where his leg and hip connected. He pressed against me harder, but kept his fists bound to the sheets, gripping them so hard I thought for sure they would rip.

"*That* look." I tossed my chin in his direction. "Like you're dying of thirst and I'm a cool drink of water."

"I *am* dying," Soren panted. "Save me, Lina. Please."

I stopped rubbing against him and raised an eyebrow. "Huh. Apparently I like watching you beg, too."

Soren's body trembled with restraint while heat radiated up from where we connected, intensifying the ache in my core. I wanted him plunged inside me, filling me and stretching me and bringing me more pleasure than I knew what to do with.

But that would have to wait. Right now I was having too much fun.

I moved off Soren's hips and positioned myself further down on his legs. He grunted in protest, but was silenced as I pressed my lips to his abdomen, kissing each of the muscles individually, staring up at him as I did.

"Do it again," I demanded. "Beg for me."

The tone of my voice reminded me of words someone else had uttered once.

*Worship me.*

Again I pushed the thought of Hale away.

Soren slammed his head against the pillow and shut his eyes. "This is cruel and unusual punishment."

I giggled and nipped his hip bone, making him buck underneath me.

"Shit!" he hissed. He lifted his head off the pillow to look at me over his heaving chest. "Please, Lina. I have to touch you. I have to taste you."

My fingers wandered to the laces at the top of his trousers and unfastened the knot. The material instantly gave way to what was barely contained inside. "But what if *I* want to taste *you*?"

Soren twisted the bedsheets in his fists. "I think you'll fucking kill me."

*Well, I am the King Slayer,* I thought grimly.

I forced that thought from my mind too.

Instead I moved between Soren's legs and settled on my stomach, pulling his trousers all the way down to release what I was after. When it sprung free, the tension inside me screamed with need.

"So..." I wrapped my fingers around the base of Soren's cock and hovered my lips over the tip. "Does that mean you don't want me to do this?" I dropped my tongue to the skin and dragged it along the underside before slipping the head into my mouth and sucking lightly.

"Fuck!" Soren gasped, writhing beneath me and clawing frantically at the sheets. "You are a cruel, *cruel* mistress, Lina Calder."

*Mistress.*

Mirielle Tynan's words rang in my ears:

*You're the king's whore. His mistress at best. And that's all you'll ever amount to. Everyone knows it, even Soren.*

I pulled Soren from my mouth and sat upright, not even attempting to disguise the scowl on my face. "You know what? I'm not really in the mood anymore."

I crawled off Soren and flopped onto my side of the bed. He laughed and wrapped his arms around my waist, hauling me back towards him.

"Very funny."

I lightly smacked Soren's hands again, but this time it wasn't playful. "I'm serious! I'm not in the mood."

He released me, watching in confusion as I yanked the bedcovers over my body and tucked them under my chin as I angled away from him. A few moments of silence hung heavy in the air before Soren asked, "What the hell just happened?"

"Nothing," I grumbled.

"Did I do something wrong?"

"I don't know, did you?"

Soren sighed in exasperation. "I didn't think so, but apparently I'm mistaken."

I nestled further into the pillows. "Wonderful observation."

Soren hesitantly scooted closer. "Lina, what is it? What did I do? Please, I want to fix it."

I looked over my shoulder at him, anger camouflaging the hurt inside. "*Mistress?*"

Soren threw his head back and laughed. Usually I found his laughter contagious, but right now it felt like a slap in the face.

"It's just a figure of speech, Lina."

I threw the covers off and sat up again. "Alright. What would you call me, then?"

Soren's brows inched together. "You're... Lina."

"And what is Lina to you?" I crossed my arms. "If I'd been attending any of these events over the past few months, how would you have been introducing me to people?"

"I..." Soren looked around the room helplessly. "I'd say you were... my... uh..."

The hurt was amplifying now, carving a vicious hole in the center of my chest. "Your what? Your ward?"

Soren rolled his eyes. "You're clearly not my ward anymore."

"Then what would you call me?"

My prodding was making Soren's shoulders tense up, and when he spoke, his voice was gruffer.

"What do you want me to say, Lina? Do you want me to go around introducing you as my lover? Is that what you want?"

"Why not?"

Soren groaned and ran a hand through his hair. "Where is this even coming from?"

"Don't avoid the question!"

"I'm not avoiding the question, I'm just fucking confused!" Soren barked.

I recoiled at his outburst, and Soren groaned again, rubbing his eyes.

"I'm sorry," he said, his voice returning to its usual timbre. "I'm sorry, I didn't mean to yell."

He slipped my hand into his. I let him, but refused to meet his gaze.

"I'm not going to introduce you to people as my lover, Lina," Soren murmured.

I turned my face away so he wouldn't see my eyes welling with tears. "Are you ashamed of me?"

"No," Soren stated firmly. "That couldn't be farther from the truth."

He lifted his fingers to my chin and forced me to look at him. His eyes shone with sincerity as his grip tightened.

"I'm not going to do that because it would be an insult to *you*. You've been to the Netherworld and back again, you've slaughtered monsters with your bare hands, and you've brought a king to his knees. Saying you're *just* a lover would be a gross understatement. You're so much more than that. You're... *you*. And I can't think of a title that could encompass all that."

Soren's heartfelt words calmed me, but something still gnawed at the back of my mind. Now would be the time to bring up what Mirielle had said about Soren and me getting married. Was it even an option? Did either of us even *want* it to be an option? Did we feel that strongly for each other? If not right now, could we see our hearts there eventually?

But right now, my heart was tired.

Between the dream about Hale and now the argument with Soren, my spirit ached from the whirlwind of emotions churning inside. It needed a reprieve, and I needed a release.

"I brought you to your knees, huh?" I muttered, running my thumb back and forth along Soren's knuckles.

He sighed. "Lina, I will fucking crawl for you if you ask me to."

"Maybe another time. Right now I want you to do something else."

"Anything."

I rose to my knees, pulled my nightgown over my head, and chucked it to the floor.

"Worship me."

# CHAPTER 6



WILLOW AND I SAT ON A BLANKET IN THE GARDEN, OUR GOBLETS of water halted halfway to our lips and our jaws hanging slack as Soren and Xavier attacked each other with a vengeance.

Wynn had finished his lessons for the day and retreated to his usual spot under the apple tree to work on his sentences while Willow and I began her training. Then Xavier and Soren had returned from one of their Nether hunts and wandered into the garden to say hello, but when they saw Willow and me working, they'd both watched us with their arms crossed, critiquing our form and yelling out things like "You can do better than that" and "You forgot a step." I'd finally snapped, tossed my blade at their feet, and told them if they could do better, then they should do it themselves. Xavier had immediately stepped forward to take me up on the challenge, claiming he would be a much better teacher than Soren, to which Soren had laughed and reminded Xavier who exactly had taught *him*. Then Xavier had made a quip about Soren getting old and stiff, and Soren had told him he was all talk, and Willow had cooly suggested the two should duel to determine who the superior warrior was. Xavier had instantly whipped off his tunic, and when Soren didn't immediately do the same, Xavier asked if it was because the king was getting a potbelly.

Now both men were shirtless, sweaty, and panting as they furiously swung, sliced, jabbed, blocked fists, and landed kicks.

"Willow, you're a genius," I muttered as I fixated on a trickle of sweat between the dimples on Soren's lower back.

Willow grinned and bit her lip, her rosy cheeks a deeper hue than normal. "I know. I learned a thing or two from reading about Queen Evalarae of Kylanthia."

"Who?" I asked, not looking at her. I was too distracted by Soren spitting blood on the ground after Xavier landed a blow to his cheek.

"She was this ancient ruler who was as fearsome in battle as she was beautiful." The Sprite let out a small squeal of delight when Xavier made an especially guttural noise after Soren landed a punch to his side. "Supposedly she passed the time in Kylanthia by making her best soldiers fight one another for sport. Whoever won was awarded a night in her bed."

A shocked gasp of a laugh escaped me. "*What?* They teach that in the history books here?"

Willow winked back. "Only the good ones."

I laughed again and eagerly leaned closer. "Well, go on. What happened if there was a draw?"

"Legend says they *both* received their rewards." Willow's voice lowered to a scandalized whisper. "At the same time."

"You're joking!"

"No!"

I shook my head and refocused on the shirtless men in front of us. "Gods, why didn't I stumble into this world sooner?"

"Well, you're here now." Willow leaned back on the blanket, propping herself on her elbows to get a more comfortable view. "Might as well enjoy it."

I copied her reclining position. "Oh, believe me. I am."

We giggled and watched as Soren disarmed Xavier, knocked him to his knees, and proudly stood over him.

"That's right!" Soren rasped. "Bow before your king, boy!"

Xavier responded by tackling Soren to the ground, their grunts and shouts transforming into cackles of merriment. Willow and I joined in on the laughter, and for the first time in a long time, I felt at peace.

*Maybe,* I thought, a warm seed of hope sprouting inside my heart, *just maybe I might belong here after all.*

Once again Soren got the upper hand, forcing Xavier to frantically tap the king's shoulder as Soren's forearm dug into his neck. "Alright, I give! You win!"

Soren chuckled and straightened, hauling Xavier to his feet and brushing him off before swinging his arm around his shoulders and guiding him back towards our blanket.

"Not bad. You almost had me a few times there. All that practice has been paying off."

"Thank you." Xavier kept his expression cool, but by the way his eyes lit up and he fought the smile tugging at the corners of his mouth, it was clear what the compliment meant to him.

Xavier had done nothing but train since Wynn and I had arrived the morning after the most recent Samhain. When I'd asked Soren about it, remarking that Xavier seemed less social than he had before, he'd said Xavier had been this way ever since he recovered from his brush with death in the Netherworld. Once his wounds had healed, he'd woken every morning at the crack of dawn to exercise and train before fulfilling his duties for Soren. Apparently, Xavier had been fairly distant at parties too, only staying at this year's harvest celebration and Yule ball for an hour before retreating. It was highly out of character for him, and when I brought it up one night as we lay in bed, Soren had leaned over, kissed the top of my head, and explained, "He never wants to feel helpless again."

I understood that all too well.

The men wandered over, still breathing heavy from their tussle. I handed them their discarded shirts, trying not to focus on the long white scar running diagonally across Xavier's abdomen. I pushed aside the memory of him flayed open and hemorrhaging blood as Meer healed him, and I urged a smile onto my face. "Now that a winner's been established, should we have lunch?"

"Or should it be best two out of three?" Willow chimed in. She was teasing, but judging by the flush in her cheeks, she wouldn't be opposed to the idea of watching the show again.

Xavier sidled up beside her, raising an eyebrow and shooting her a mischievous grin. "I thought you didn't condone violence? Or was that before you saw me half-naked?"

The Sprite rolled her eyes. "You wish."

"Come on, Miss Willow." He playfully poked his finger in her side. "You can admit you appreciated the view."

Willow, who was exceedingly ticklish, squawked and batted Xavier's hand away as she attempted to button up her laughter. "Good gods, man! You are absolutely—"

"Shameless?" Xavier winked and slung his shirt over his shoulder as he strode away. "I'm going to take a bath before we eat. Let me know if you'd like to watch me do that too."

Willow huffed and whipped her head to Soren, glaring at him with a look that screamed, *Control your child.*

Trying and failing to hide his smile, Soren shrugged. "My apologies. The only magic Xavier has is the innate ability to get under people's skin. Who am I to deny someone the use of their gift?"

Willow snatched up the blanket we'd been lounging on and clicked her tongue. "Some gift."

I chuckled and melted into Soren as his hands slipped around my waist from behind.

"I'm going to wash up too," he purred, his breath against my ear sending a shiver down my spine. "Join me in the bath?"

I glanced innocently back at him, but pressed my backside into his hips and gave them a torturous swirl. "We'll be late to lunch if I join you."

Soren's upper lip curled into a lustful smirk. "I'm not that hungry. At least not for food."

I shook my head. "Gods, you're insatiable."

Soren's arms tightened as he brought his teeth to my neck and nipped it gently. "Is that a yes?"

I sighed, pretending my entire body wasn't desperately screaming the word. "Let me see if my brother needs a snack to hold off his hunger first."

Soren grinned and released me with a playful smack on the ass. I giggled and shoved him away.

*Love is strange. Look at me. Twenty-four years old and this man has me acting like a giddy school girl.*

I smiled to myself and faced the apple tree where my brother was writing out his sentences.

But Wynn was gone.

Suddenly, I was transported back to that foggy forest on Samhain, my brother's screams ringing in my ears and the life I'd known crumbling around me. Panic clutched my chest, and adrenaline fired through me, catapulting me into action. I darted towards the tree.

"Wynn?!" I shrieked.

I arrived at the empty blanket and frantically scanned my surroundings.

Wynn wasn't by the fountain.

There was no mop of golden curls bobbing through the hedges.

He wasn't dipping his toes in the pond.

He'd completely vanished.

"Wynnric!" I screeched again, my voice breaking.

Soren ran up beside me and rested a hand on my lower back to steady me. I hadn't realized I was teetering in place. I tried to speak, but my thoughts were scattered and my words came out in hysterical gasps.

"I... I don't... I don't know where..."

Soren grabbed my shoulders and shook me, forcing me to look him in the eyes. His gaze had hardened; the lover was gone and the warrior had taken his place, speaking not to his beloved but a soldier.

"He likes the reflecting pool in the courtyard, check there. Willow, check his room. I'll search outside the castle."

I nodded, thankful to have a task to channel my frantic energy into.

"We'll find him." Soren squeezed my shoulders reassuringly before sprinting towards the exterior wall. Willow was already halfway back to the castle. I inhaled a shaky breath and started for the courtyard.

"Look who I found!"

I spun at the voice.

Xavier strode towards me, hand in hand with my little brother, and a cry of relief leapt from my throat.

"Wynn!" I exclaimed.

I collapsed to my knees in front of them and hauled Wynn into a hug.

"Found him wandering west towards the stables," Xavier added.

I pulled away from my brother and cupped his face in my hands. "You scared the shit out of me! Don't you ever, *ever* do that again, you hear me? If you want to go somewhere, you take one of us with you, do you understand?"

Wynn's eyes went round with surprise and fear. I sighed and forced my voice back to something resembling calm.

"I'm sorry. I just..." I gulped in another breath and let out a wavering exhale. "I was worried about you. Please let us know where you're going next time, alright?"

Wynn stuck out his bottom lip and lifted a small hand to my forearm to give it a gentle squeeze. I took that to mean, *I'm sorry*.

I smiled and wrapped him in another hug. "I'm just glad you're alright."

Thundering footfalls prompted me to look up. Soren skidded to an abrupt halt in front of us.

"Where the hell was he?" the king snapped. He sounded furious, but relief shone in his eyes.

I opened my mouth to explain, but closed it when Wynn wriggled out of my hold and moved towards Soren. Still holding his lesson book, my brother stopped directly in front of the king, frowned, and raised the notebook high. Confused, Soren crouched and accepted the pad of paper, angling his head to see what Wynn had scribbled there.

All the color drained from his face.

"What's wrong?" I asked, scrambling to my feet and joining them. When I put a hand on Soren's shoulder and looked down at what had captured his attention, my heart skipped a beat.

Wynn had sketched the spiked circle, only this time he'd gotten around to drawing the two crescent moons facing away from each other, with two lines jutting through their centers to connect them. It was identical to the brand burned into Hale's flesh, except for one difference: vines wove in and out of the circle, entangling themselves in the barbs along the outside.

Soren stared at the drawing for a few tense beats, then

looked to Wynn. My brother stared back, his brows pinched in a somber expression. He then lifted one hand and pointed his index finger in my direction. Soren swallowed hard and slowly returned the paper.

My gaze bounced between the drawing and Wynn, then Soren. "What's wrong?"

Soren looked like he'd either seen a ghost or was about to be sick. He cleared his throat and stood, wiping his palms on the legs of his pants. "That's a slur in the ancient Fae tongue."

"I know, I've seen it before. It means demon, doesn't it?"

A muscle in Soren's jaw twitched. He refused to meet my eyes, choosing instead to keep his attention fixed on the ground as he shook his head. "Close. Hale's said demon. This says something else."

"What does it say?"

Soren didn't answer. Instead, he cleared his throat once more and straightened his shoulders. "Will you excuse me?"

Before I could respond, Soren spun and strode towards the castle.

A presence came up beside me. I glanced over at Xavier, whose mouth curved downward into a grim frown as he took up the notebook and examined Wynn's art.

"What does it mean?" I asked softly.

The usual merriment in Xavier's eyes was absent when his gaze flicked to mine.

"It means demon lover."

# Chapter 7

Soren stormed into his study, grabbed one of the armchairs in front of the fireplace, and hurled it across the room with all his might. The chair flipped in midair and crashed into a bookcase with a loud bang, sending papers flying.

Hand shaking violently, Soren balled them into fists and tried to rein in his emotions by taking deep breaths.

One more.

Two more.

Three.

Shit. This wasn't helping.

Soren whirled, crossed the study, and fumbled for the third drawer down in his desk. When he pulled out the crystal decanter, he mumbled another expletive. There was significantly less in it than the last time he'd seen it, which meant Lina had been drinking more than he'd thought when she hid here. The dreams must have been terrible lately.

Fuck. He should have been there for her.

He should've held her longer, insisted on talking about it

even though he was terrible at talking about emotions. He should have stroked her hair and kissed her forehead over and over until she fell back asleep. He'd thought giving her space was the answer, but the near-empty bottle proved him wrong. He'd failed her. *Again.*

Soren shook the miserable realization from his head and brought the bottle to his lips, finishing off what liquor remained in three gulps. He moved to smash the bottle against the wall, but froze when footsteps padded down the hall.

He lowered his hand as Lina peeked into the room and painted a cool smile onto his face. "Sorry for darting off. Everything's fine, I just forgot I had some work to do. I'm afraid it's urgent."

Lina tried to appear collected, but Soren could tell she was nervous. Her fingers inched towards her collarbone and rubbed it absentmindedly as she hovered near the bookcases to survey the destroyed armchair. The pounding of her heart reached all the way across the room.

"Anything I can do to help?"

"No. Thank you, though. I'll be back down in a little bit."

Lina nodded and moved towards the door. She set one foot in front of her before hesitating, as if deciding whether to stay or go. She finally turned and cautiously approached Soren. When she arrived in front of the desk, she kept her eyes downcast.

"He didn't mean anything by it," Lina murmured. "Willow said he looked ahead in one of her books and saw it—"

"No!" Soren's eyes widened, and he shook his head. "Oh gods, no! I'm not mad at Wynn!"

He should have told her that. Of course she thought his storming off had meant he was upset with the boy. Fuck. He was *still* failing her.

"I swear he doesn't know what it means," Lina continued.

"He probably saw the vines, and they reminded him of the ones on my dagger and your crown, so—"

"I know he didn't understand the meaning," Soren blurted, "but someone else does."

Lina just stared at him and blinked.

Soren sighed heavily and ran a hand through his hair.

"Words like that," he explained, "crude, cruel curses... those aren't found in textbooks."

Lina's brows scrunched in confusion, her hazel eyes searching Soren's gaze for answers. "What are you saying?"

"The only way Wynn could have seen something like that is if someone in the castle has been writing that of their own accord."

Lina's expression iced over. "Someone's saying that about me."

Soren sighed again and nodded.

Deep in thought, Lina stared out the window for a few seconds before quietly asking, "Who do you think it is?"

"It could be Willow. After what happened on Yule—"

"No." She cut him off. "Willow's my friend. Even after what happened with Acacia, she wouldn't talk badly about me."

"Mirielle, then."

Lina grunted and crossed her arms. "That's more likely."

A pang of guilt shot through Soren's heart, chipping away at his soul a little bit more. "I'm sorry. Even with the Tynans here, I thought this kind of talk wouldn't get to you."

Yet another way Soren hadn't kept the castle safe.

Yet another failure.

Soren grit his teeth and pushed down the guilt and fear that word, *failure*, conjured.

Lina wandered around the desk and leaned a hip against it. "Are you sure that's all that's bothering you?"

"Yes," he replied firmly, straightening his shoulders and offering up a smile.

A lie.

And Lina saw right through it.

She pushed Soren into the chair, slid onto his lap, and cupped his face in her hands.

"Talk to me. What is it?" She licked her lips as her heartbeat picked up in her chest, which meant she was nervous to say her next words. "Does it have something to do with Hale?"

"No."

Not a lie.

He could see why she thought that. There was no denying the two symbols shared similarities. The brand on the Night Sylph bastard's neck said *demon*; the symbol Wynn had drawn said *demon lover*. And the fact that symbol was being thrown around hinted someone knew about Lina and Hale's relationship. But despite its connotations, Soren wasn't ashamed of the woman he loved.

Or the man *she* had loved.

Last year, Soren had been too caught up in his quest for violence and vengeance, he'd pushed Lina to the back of his mind when she'd needed him most. He hadn't even thought twice about it, even though Xavier had urged Soren to write to her every day, a suggestion Soren simply shrugged off. Although they hadn't discussed their feelings for each other at that point, and she was in no way bound to him, Soren had arrogantly assumed Lina would be doing nothing but sitting around pining for him. It was what every other woman in his life had done up to that point. In his past, he could go months without so much as looking at a woman, then one furtive glance would have her melting at his feet. He'd never had to communicate, never had to work for someone's attention. Shamefully, it was all he'd ever known, and he hadn't comprehended the error of his ways until Lina quite literally smacked some sense into him.

It had been a bitter realization, but he understood why her heart had wandered. And eventually, he understood why it had landed on the man it had.

When he and Lina went their separate ways last year, Soren had spent days, *months* thinking about everything that had transpired. One night he got piss drunk, sat alone in his study, and did something that didn't come naturally or comfortably to him: he dug deep and searched his feelings.

Soren hadn't trusted Hale. He'd heard horror stories of Night Sylphs since he was a boy. Everyone had. He'd battled them and seen firsthand the atrocities they were capable of. Soren had thought Hale would be no different. He'd feared the man. But more than that, he'd been jealous of him. He'd been jealous that this creature, a monster in his mind, had gained Lina's affection just as quickly as Soren himself had. But in the Netherworld, Hale had proven he wasn't a monster at all. He'd chosen to give up the prestige and power offered to him by Aedan and sacrificed himself so those he cared about would be saved. He'd shown his true colors that day, and proven himself to be someone courageous, selfless, and horribly misjudged. He was the type of man Soren would want to ride into battle alongside. The type of man he'd want in his court. And he was exactly the type of man Soren would want looking after the woman he loved.

After that drunken, miserably eye-opening night, Soren had realized how wrong he'd been and come to the conclusion he didn't hate Hale at all.

He respected the hell out of him.

And if Soren could go back, he would let him know that. He'd take back the bargain they'd made, take back the inhumane way he'd treated him, and instead of passing through that veil back to the Fae realm, he would have stayed in the Netherworld and fought alongside him until the bitter end, like an equal.

No. More than that.

Like a friend.

"Are you sure it doesn't have anything to do with him?" Lina asked. She dropped her hand from Soren's face and threaded her fingers through his, squeezing them tight. "You're shaking."

Soren took a deep breath, Lina's observation making him embarrassingly aware of his pathetic trembling. "I just... I thought..."

He couldn't get the words out. He might break down if he did, and he had to be strong.

Kings had to be strong.

"Never mind, it's nothing." Soren flashed another bright smile and leaned in to distract Lina with a kiss like he always did. She immediately pulled away.

"Stop," she snapped, pushing him back into the chair. "No secrets, remember? Talk to me."

Another pang of guilt punched Soren in the gut at the mention of secrets.

They'd agreed not to keep anything from each other, but there was still one thing he hadn't told her. If he did, he would lose her, and Soren couldn't bear that. He knew he had to tell her eventually, but not yet.

He couldn't lose her yet.

Soren refocused on the conversation at hand and fidgeted in his seat. "It's stupid."

"It's obviously not stupid if it's got you upset."

"I'm fine."

"You're not."

"But I *should* be fine!"

There it was. The floodgates had opened, and there was no

stopping the rest of the words from spilling out, or the deluge of emotions he typically kept bottled.

"Nothing happened! Nothing happened to Wynn, but I thought something had. I thought they got in again. I thought they'd taken him and it was Yule all over again. I couldn't stop seeing it." Soren shook so badly his teeth chattered, and he shut his eyes as images from that night flashed across his mind.

Fae he'd known since he was a child running for their lives.

Screams of agony.

The never-ending rivers of blood.

*Gods*, there had been so much blood.

Soren's breath deteriorated into panicked gasps. "I failed everyone who lost their lives that night. *Everyone*. My people trusted me, and I failed them. I failed Meer. I failed the Sprites. I failed *you*, Lina. I swore I'd keep you safe, but I couldn't. I never have. Not in the castle, not in the Netherworld. No matter how hard I try, I just keep fucking failing—"

It was only when Lina wrapped her arms around Soren and pulled his head to her heart that he calmed slightly.

"I'm sorry," he panted, clutching her tight, "I'm sorry. I don't know why I'm acting like this."

"There's nothing to be sorry about," she replied, the gentleness of her voice soothing Soren's soul. "You don't always have to be strong."

Soren grit his teeth. "Yes, I do."

"You *don't*." Lina's arms tightened around him as she nuzzled her face against his ear and lowered her voice to a whisper. "You're my safe place. Let me be yours too."

Her intimate words made Soren's eyes sting. He dragged her closer, partially so she wouldn't see the watery gleam in his eyes, but mainly because her body pressed against his made the world fade away. It always had. Since the day they met, when Soren was with Lina, no problem seemed too large, no evil too terrifying, and no pain too great. Sure, the woman could push his buttons like no other, but her fire matched his, and she could douse it as easily as she could stoke it. Soren didn't understand it, but he knew without a shadow of a doubt that the two of them fit.

"You *are* my safe place, Lina," Soren mumbled against her skin. His heart rate slowed, his breathing calmed, and the tightness in his chest subsided when Lina's lips grazed his temple in a tender kiss.

He wanted it to always be like this. The two of them together, finding peace in each other's arms and helping the other face their demons. It was why Soren couldn't tell Lina that remaining secret. Because once he did, this would be over. And Soren selfishly wanted more time. He *needed* more time. He needed more moments like this.

"I'm ready."

Lina's voice brought Soren out of the thoughts he'd lost himself in. He lifted his head to meet her stare.

"Ready for what?"

Lina's eyes gleamed with fiery determination. "I'm coming to Imbolc."

# CHAPTER 8

"ARE YOU NERVOUS?"

Willow's voice in the bedroom was distant, like I was in the midst of a dream and she was morning birdsong sneaking through the cracks of consciousness. I almost didn't hear her as I stared at my reflection in the washroom mirror.

I had on the same white dress I'd worn last Imbolc in Merimaya. It was Lerian-crafted, made of the airy material most of its citizens dressed themselves in, and while it was a standard fashion there, in Astoria, a region that leaned more towards structured corsets and layer upon layer of fabric, this gown commanded attention. Sleeveless, with a hip-high slit, plunging neckline, and a crystal embellishment gathering the waist to draw attention to my curves, it would be verging on scandalous in contrast to the rest of the attire this evening.

Which was exactly why I chose to wear it.

A rebellious little voice inside me said people were already gossiping about me, so why not *really* give them something to talk about?

But mainly, I wanted Soren to see me in this dress. I wanted the man I loved to see how strong and powerful and beautiful I felt in it. This dress was for him and me, no one else.

I glanced down at the long black scar on my right wrist, a result of my first brush with the Nethers two Samhains ago. I'd considered sewing sleeves on my gown for the night, or wearing long white gloves to cover the marred skin, but decided against it. I wasn't ashamed of what I'd been through. I was a survivor, and I was fucking proud of that.

"No," I called to Willow, my lips curving into a smile as I traced my fingers along the scar. "Not in the slightest."

I looked back at the mirror and fluffed my hair, which I'd chosen to keep down for the celebration. It had been longer when Wynn and I had first come to Astoria, having grown out while we'd been staying in Lerian, but one of the first snide remarks Mirielle Tynan ever said to me was, "Long hair would suit you so much better. It would distract from your broad frame." To which I'd responded by immediately stomping down to the kitchen, stealing a steak knife, and sawing off my tresses at the shoulders. Luckily, the jagged cuts had grown out and now curled gracefully around my collarbones.

Giving my hair one last shake and pinching my cheeks to add some color, I turned and exited the washroom, passing through the door to the bedroom only to be met with a loud gasp from Willow, who was sitting on my bed with Wynn.

"Lina!" Willow clapped a hand to her heart in astonishment. "Gods, you look amazing!"

Shyly, I smoothed my skirt. "Really?"

"Are you kidding? *Yes!*" Willow exhaled sharply and fanned herself. "Good gods, I need to get some dresses from Lerian. What do you think, Wynn?" She turned to my brother and slid her arm around his shoulders, giving him a squeeze. "How do you think your sister looks?"

Wynn held up his index finger, signaling for me to wait, and immediately got to work scribbling something in his notebook. When he finished and held it up for me to see, my heart nearly melted. Written in shaky charcoal letters were the words *Lina looks good*.

"We've been working on double 'O' words recently." Willow beamed.

"Wynn!" I jogged over to the bed and lowered onto the velvet comforter beside him, hauling him into a hug. "That's amazing! I'm so proud of you. And thank you."

Wynn smiled brightly, patted my head, then got back to his doodling. Thankfully, he wasn't working on any more slurs.

"One more thing!" Willow bounced off the bed and bustled across the room to the fireplace. She jabbed her fingers into the ashes in the hearth before making her way over to me.

"Close your eyes," she demanded.

I hesitated but finally obeyed and flinched as Willow dragged her soot-covered thumb over my eyelids.

"This is a little trick my sister taught me," she mumbled. It sounded like her tongue was sticking out of her mouth as she concentrated on decorating the skin around my eyes with smudges of black.

At the mention of Acacia, a melancholy smile tugged at my lips. She'd acted the same way as her sister just before the harvest celebration, commanding me to shut my eyes before coloring my eyelids with glittering gold flecks.

"I miss her," I muttered to myself.

Willow's fingers stopped moving, and she let out a quivering sigh.

"Me too," she whispered.

I opened my eyes to meet Willow's dim gaze. "You're so much like her."

Willow ducked her head. "I know, we looked very similar—"

"No." I took Willow's hands in mine. "I mean *yes*, but it's more than that. Your sister brightened every room she walked into. She was always blushing and giggling and could make anyone feel welcome with nothing but a glance. She had a special gift for making you feel beautiful, not just by painting your face, but by the way she spoke to you. She made you see beauty in yourself, because she saw it in you."

Willow's eyes began to water, and her bottom lip wobbled. Her expression instantly brought tears to my own eyes.

"Don't start," I warned.

Willow giggled and wiped her eyes with the back of her hand. "Fine. We'll get together soon and drink two bottles of brandy and cry then."

I nodded eagerly. "Yes, please."

Willow laughed and stepped back. "Alright. I think you're ready."

"Wait, one last thing." I reached under my pillow and pulled out my dagger. I planted my foot on the bed, hauling my dress's flowing white skirt away from my leg so I could slide the blade into the sheath already strapped to my thigh. I glanced at Willow.

"If anything happens, I'll be ready."

The Sprite nodded solemnly. After a peek at Wynn to make sure he wasn't looking, she pulled back one side of her lilac cardigan to reveal a steak knife tucked into the waistband of her lacy skirt. She raised an eyebrow, a spunky grin finding its way onto her face.

"I'll be ready too."

Completely in awe of my friend and how far she'd come in just a few weeks, I smiled and gripped her shoulders. "One day I'll get you a dagger of your own, I promise."

The Sprite's violet eyes twinkled. "Can it be purple?"

I threw my head back and laughed. "Of course! It couldn't be any other color."

"Good."

She and I stared at each other for a few weighted moments, and I chalked it up to her Fae senses that she recognized I was losing my gall. Willow cupped my face in her palms and leaned in close.

"Hold your head high," she ordered, pressing her forehead to mine. "Keep your shoulders straight. Walk without hesitation and walk without fear. You've looked death in the eye. You're the human who passes beyond veils. You defeat Nethers and seduce Fae royalty."

I set my jaw. "I'm the King Slayer."

"You're Lina Calder," Willow declared. "And they should all be cowering before *you*, not the other way around."

I swallowed the lump in my throat and nodded.

Willow followed suit and released her hold on me. "Now go get 'em."

I obeyed and started for the door. "Are you sure you don't want to come with me?"

Willow waved me away and plopped back down on the bed beside Wynn. "If Astoria saw a Wood Sprite attending one of their balls instead of working it, I think it might burn itself to the ground."

Not taking no for an answer, I jerked my chin to the armoire in the corner of the room. "There's a gown in there Mirielle told me to wear. It's frilly and extravagant and so *not* me, but on you it would look incredible. If it just so happens Wynn goes to bed early and you feel like putting it on, I would love to see how you look in it."

Willow snorted. "First of all, there's no way a dress that fits you would also fit me." She motioned to her considerably fuller bust and rounder stomach.

"I'm taller," I countered. "Plus, I never had it altered so it's two sizes too big for me. And the back has laces, which means it's adjustable." I winked at her. "Do you have a second of all?"

Willow's mouth opened but promptly shut.

"That's what I thought." I rested my fingers on the handle of the bedroom door. "What was it you told me just before I got dressed?"

Willow toyed with one of the buttons on her sweater as she mumbled, "I said they can all take their opinions of you and shove them up their behinds."

"Exactly. If you want to go, don't let other people's opinions stop you. They can all take their opinions and shove them up their asses."

"Language, Lina!"

I grinned back at her. "See you soon."

And with that, I threw open the door and strode into the hallway, headed towards the daunting laughter and gossip at the base of the grand staircase ahead.

Time seemed to slow as I neared the stairs. I wasn't sure if the pounding in my ears was my feet hitting the wood planks of the floor or my heart about to thunder out of my chest. The last time I'd made this walk to a ball was on Yule, with my arm looped through Meer's. That night, I was fearless. I'd stood at the top of the stairs and met Soren's gaze, and when his jaw went slack at the sight of me, I couldn't help the smile that spread across my face. That smile had remained until all hell broke loose.

Tonight, everything was different.

Meer wasn't here to steady me, and I wasn't giddy and starry-eyed the way I was then. I was on edge, aware not just of the whispers and judgmental glares, but of everything around me. Every shadow made me tense, every tinkle of laughter or clink of sparkling wine flutes made my hand twitch towards the blade at my thigh. As I arrived at the top of the staircase, I tried to remind myself over and over that I was safe, but my body remembered what had happened here.

The only thing that calmed me was a pair of deep-set blue eyes looking up at me from the bottom of the stairs.

I breathed a sigh of relief at the sight of Soren. His hair was down and brushed smooth instead of his usual tousled, half-pulled-back style, while the slim vine-engraved silver crown of Astoria graced the top of his head. His clothing mirrored the headpiece, with silver vine embroidery detailing the long white jacket he was clad in. My heart sank a little at the sight of a ceremonial sword fastened at his hip. He never used to bring weapons to the balls Astoria held, and I suspected his change of heart had happened after the attack on Yule. This, along with his breakdown in the study a few days before, proved he was just as affected by the events of that night as I was.

Guilt washed over me. It had always been so easy to focus on my own problems, and Soren eagerly did the same. He preferred his feelings stashed away and buttoned up, while I was always breaking down. I was the one unable to handle the stress. I was the one constantly crying or hiding away or drowning my emotions in liquor. Taking care of me both physically and mentally was something Soren leapt at the opportunity to do, and he became antsy if he couldn't. I should have known that sometimes those quickest to help are the ones who need help the most.

I made a mental note to check in with Soren more regularly, and started my descent down the staircase.

A hush spread over the room at my presence. The sudden silence sent an eerie shiver down my spine, reminding me of the chilling quiet that precedes a Nether's presence. I faltered and slipped on the stairs at the thought, but I dug deep, reminded myself for the thousandth time that I was safe, and steadied myself. I lifted my chin high and focused on Soren, his soulful eyes a lighthouse guiding my ship through a storm.

The king reached out his hand as I arrived at the bottom of the stairs, and I gratefully took hold. The warmth of his touch instantly eased the panic creeping up inside me.

"Gods," Soren breathed, shaking his head and bringing my knuckles to his lips in a velvety kiss. "You are an exquisite work of art, Lina Calder."

He looked up at me with hooded eyes and smiled, and all of a sudden, my worries seemed significantly smaller.

"You don't look too bad yourself," I teased.

Soren chuckled and straightened, giving my hand a reassuring squeeze. "Come on. There's a procession in the garden to start off the festivities, but then I'm going to insist on stealing your first dance."

I smiled coyly. "Oh, I'm sorry. It appears you're under the impression you're back to being in charge."

One side of Soren's mouth quirked upwards in a wolfish grin, and he yanked my hand, dragging me closer to him. "When you have the audacity to come down looking that good, you're damn right I'll have you how I want you."

Heat swelled through me, forcing me to bite my lip to avoid letting out an appreciative moan. Judging by the sparkle in Soren's eyes, he knew exactly what his words did to me. And to stoke the fire further, he slipped his free hand around my waist and pulled me into him, pressing his hips against mine and angling his head down to kiss me.

"Your Majesty."

Soren froze just before his lips met mine. Lord Magnus appeared beside us, his face stern and his golden eyes cold.

"With all due respect, sire..." Magnus's voice was a low snarl. "I advise you to control yourself. People can see you."

Soren hesitated, furiously glaring at Magnus before his gaze shifted to the crowd. Everyone in the room was watching us. Some with curiosity, but many with disgust or contempt.

"You wouldn't want your behavior to upset your people any more than they already are, would you?" Magnus added.

A muscle in Soren's jaw ticked before he took a deep breath and curtly dipped his head to the lord. Then he released his hold on me and stepped away.

I understood why he did it, but that didn't make it any less humiliating.

For the first time since I'd known him, Lord Magnus smiled. And for some reason, it unsettled me more than any of his other expressions.

"Thank you. Now, the girl is permitted to walk behind you out to the garden, but she must keep her head low and her eyes downcast."

I rolled my eyes. "How very gracious, my lord."

Soren shot me a warning look. I averted my gaze and shuffled my feet, attempting to focus on anything other than the way my fingers were itching to find the hilt of my dagger so I could slice the smile right off Lord Magnus's face.

"Shall we?" The lord gestured to the entryway of the castle, then pushed through the crowd towards it.

Soren followed, glancing back over his shoulder at me as he mouthed the words *I'm sorry.* I pretended not to see it.

We exited the castle, the rest of the crowd filing out after us, and headed down the path lined with blazing torches to the garden. White rose petals were scattered along the smooth gray stones at our feet, the hem of my dress catching the blossoms and brushing them along with me as I trailed behind the men. The clutch of winter was still stubbornly hanging on before spring moved in entirely, but the full flames on the torches battled the bitter chill of the night and warmed the air around us.

As we passed through the flowering hedge archway that led to the southeast section of the garden, two Fae dressed in white hooded cloaks stood on either side of the pathway, handing out white candles. To Soren, though, they passed a torch, which he accepted with a courteous bow. He peeked at me and smiled, the shadows on his face from the dancing flames bringing me back to that moment in his study when I first arrived in the Fae realm, when he and I drank in front of the hearth and dared to let our guards down in front of the other for the very first time.

Neither of us could have ever guessed we'd end up here.

I winked back at Soren, widening his smile before he refocused on the path and pressed on. Magnus caught the exchange and glowered at me. I batted my eyelashes sweetly in return.

As the rest of the Fae accepted their candles from the hooded figures, a nearby flutist, dressed in similar hooded garb, took up a haunting melody that floated through the night like a gentle breeze. When Soren stopped at the far end of the garden beside another flowering archway, and the Fae nobles in attendance had all received their candles and gathered on either side of the path, a second musician took up a bowed lyre, its deep sensual strings perfectly complementing the flute.

Lord Magnus turned to Soren and dipped his head solemnly. A silent order to begin.

Soren brought the head of his torch to Magnus's candle and lit it. I was next in line to receive the flame, but the lord skipped me, and instead shared his candle with the Fae behind me. Another wave of humiliation hit me, but it was soon replaced with anger. I was busy imagining lighting Magnus's perfectly coiffed beard on fire when Soren subtly moved backwards so he stood shoulder to shoulder with me. There he angled his torch to the candle in my hand, igniting its wick.

"Thank you," I mumbled.

He nodded and shifted his attention to the back of Magnus's head, where he tried to bore a hole into it with a blood-chilling stare. I hoped he found a way to succeed.

The music swelled, and the candles in the crowd blinked awake like fireflies lighting up the night. Another white-cloaked figure passed through the archway beside Soren. They carried a bowl with an assortment of herbs, spices, and flowers. The figure, a woman, stopped in front of the king and lowered into a deep curtsy, extending the bowl to him. Soren bowed in response and pushed his torch into the bowl, the mixture inside instantly sparking and going up in crackling flames. A cloud of smoke wafted up from the bowl, filling the air with the scent of cinnamon, rosemary, lavender and...

Night-blooming jasmine.

My stomach knotted at the sickeningly sweet scent. Immediately it felt like I was back in the Netherworld, in that luminescent throne room inside a cave with Aedan's nauseating floral aroma stinging my nostrils, choking my throat, and burning my eyes. Once again my body remembered the fear and acted in response, and without thinking, I jerked my hand towards my dagger. Soren caught my arm before I could grip the hilt and rip it free. I peeked up at him. He was staring straight ahead, his eyes distant, his jaw clenched, and his shoulders tensed like he was preparing for a fight. It was clear the smell had brought him to the same place it had me, and was forcing him to fight the same instincts. For some reason that comforted me, knowing I wasn't alone with my fear. Someone else understood, which meant we could face it together. I looked forward again, and both Soren and I took deep breaths in through our noses, out through our mouths.

*You're safe,* I reminded myself. *The people you love are safe.*

I repeated that mantra over and over in my mind, and when

the words and breath had calmed my racing heart, I gave Soren's hand a grateful squeeze. He squeezed back even harder.

Drums joined in with the pipe and the strings, livening the melody. The woman with the incense continued down the path towards the castle while a procession of more caped figures made their way through the arch after her. Most held torches, but others spun or breathed the fire.

I inched closer to Soren and lowered my voice so only he could hear me. "Are you going to be doing any fire tricks of your own this evening?"

Soren chuckled, keeping his eyes on the activity in front of us. "No, not tonight."

"Why not?"

The crowd gasped and applauded as a man tossed three blazing torches in the air, alternating catching them.

"Not many people know I have that power," Soren whispered back.

"Really?"

The king shook his head. "I've kept it quiet over the years."

"How come?"

Soren sneaked a glance at me. "A few reasons. But mainly because it's tricky. It can get out of control fast. People would expect me to use it perfectly, and if I didn't... If I lost control or took it too far..." He trailed off. Even in the low light, the turmoil in his eyes was clear as day. He thought for a few long beats before murmuring, "I just wouldn't want to fail them."

I squeezed Soren's hand again and changed the subject to relieve his clearly tormented soul. "If you wanted to keep it a secret, how come you showed me that night in your study?"

I remembered that moment like it was yesterday. Shortly after I'd arrived in the Fae realm, after I'd woken from a nightmare, Soren had walked me into the room and waved his hand in front of the embers, bringing the fire roaring back to life so we had light to see while we drank together.

Soren's gaze landed on me fully, a charming smile spreading across his face. "I might've been showing off for you."

I had no control of the giddy laugh that bubbled out of me.

"Shhh!" Magnus snapped.

I wilted, but Soren's grip on my fingers tightened and adopted a slight tremor from the rage he suppressed. I nudged him, shrugging to communicate that the scolding hadn't bothered me. Begrudgingly, Soren eased.

The music grew faster and more complex, the masked figures with their flames increasing their speed to match it. I was admiring a woman gyrating a hoop of fire around her hips when an elbow prodded my shoulder. When I peeked over at Soren, he jerked his chin to my candle.

The small flame fluttered and elongated, growing taller and more slender before it bent into the shape of a heart. I bit my lip to keep from giggling again and looked up at the king. He was beaming down at me with a look so loving and tender my heart swelled and my breath caught in my throat.

The crowd clapped at something one of the fire-breathers did, the abrupt sound making the king flinch. The flame on my candle instantly snuffed out.

Soren frowned at the smoking wick. "See? It's tricky."

The music stopped, and the torchbearers extinguished their flames so they could begin stacking bundles of sticks and straw in a brush pile at the center of the crowd. A petite masked woman stepped forward, strands of curly hair sticking out beneath her hood. As she stopped in front of the growing brush pile, she raised her hands to the sky and opened her mouth. A silken soprano voice rang out, the lilting ancient Fae she sang in echoing through the garden and sending prickles across my skin at its haunting beauty.

"She sings to the Mother of Spring," Soren explained, leaning in close so his breath caressed the outer shell of my ear. "She asks for Her blessing this coming season, and welcomes new beginnings, light, and love."

I sank into Soren's side, savoring his warmth and the peace it washed over me. "It's beautiful."

Soren's hand slipped from mine and found its way to my waist instead, pulling me closer. "*You're* beautiful."

I glanced up at him and grinned. "What a horrible line."

"It's true."

The adoration in Soren's eyes as he stared back made my heart swell so much I wondered if my chest might actually explode.

Gods, how was it possible to love someone this much?

A looming figure brought the tender moment to an abrupt halt. Soren and I turned to Magnus scowling down at us.

"Your Majesty," he said tightly, "it's time."

Soren hurriedly removed his hand from my waist and stepped away from me, knocking me off-balance. I quickly composed myself, attempting to ignore the rush of embarrassment and annoyance I was left with.

After one last glare in my direction, Magnus led Soren out to the brush pile. When the king arrived in front, silence settled over the garden.

Soren raised his torch high, speaking in a clear, booming voice. "Blessed Imbolc to all!"

"Blessed Imbolc!" the crowd thundered back.

The king released his grip on the torch, letting it drop to the bonfire to ignite the brush in a roaring blaze. The Fae erupted in cheers, whoops, and hollers, and suddenly the world was a flurry of activity. People sang and danced and laughed and chattered, and before I knew what was happening, Soren had disappeared from view, his calming form replaced by a clamoring crowd. I stood on my tiptoes to look for him and caught a glimpse of Magnus and two male nobles dragging him in the direction of the castle, but I lost him just as quickly as I'd seen him.

I would be facing the frenzy alone.

I tried to shove down my discomfort as I circumvented the crowd, forcing myself to stand tall and proud even though the loud noises made panic claw at my chest. People constantly brushed against me, stepping on my toes or elbowing me in the back. Every muscle and tendon in my body went taut. I started to see things out of the corner of my eye. Flashes of what I thought were Nethers prowling in the shadows, but turned out to be a branch waving in the breeze or a couple wandering off into the garden to do gods know what. My heart beat faster and faster, while my breath grew more shallow and frantic each passing second. When someone screamed with laughter, the sound had my hand flying straight to the handle of my dagger, which I gripped tight enough to hurt.

I was wrong.

I couldn't do this.

I wasn't ready.

I squinted in the direction of the castle, plotting an escape route through the crowd, but there were too many people. To get through the archway we'd passed through, I'd need to navigate four couples dancing, two fire spinners, a bawdy group of drunken male nobles, and a cluster of ladies whose glares and whispers seemed the most daunting of them all. The idea of passing through that hell made me want to crumple to the ground, curl into a ball, and cry. The rational part of me knew pushing through this crowd wouldn't kill me. But I didn't feel rational. Every inch of my body screamed one thing.

*Run.*

So I did.

# CHAPTER 9



No nocturnal insects chirruped the night away.

Spring was still on the way, the beasts it brought with it still in hibernation, so the evening was eerily quiet. The only noise as I sprinted through the garden was the pounding of my feet against the ground and my own frantic breath. The calm resembled the ominous silence brought on by Nethers, only adding to my panic. Every shadow and shrub was a potential foe, and by the time I ended up at the apple tree Wynn did his lessons under, I was sweating, my body ached from being so tightly wound, and tears stung my eyes.

I skidded to a halt and stuck my hands on my knees, wheezing and gulping down air in a poor attempt at catching my breath.

"If you wanted to go for a run, you should've worn better shoes."

I bolted upright, threw my skirt aside, and tore my dagger from its sheath. Holding it at the ready, I searched the darkness for the source of the voice. Only when I looked up into the branches of the apple tree and caught a glimpse of a cocky, lopsided grin did I relax.

Xavier leapt out of the tree and landed rather ungracefully on the lawn with a grunt before brushing himself off. He wore a billowing white shirt, partially unbuttoned, with a matching satin double-breasted waistcoat. His cream breeches had a few scuffs and smudges from the bark of the tree, but it didn't take away from his appearance. Tonight, he looked every inch a handsome nobleman.

"What the hell were you doing up there?" I shouted. "You scared the shit out of me!"

"Maybe *you* scared the shit out of *me*," Xavier snapped, indignantly popping his fists onto his hips. "Didn't think about that, did you?"

His words were slightly slurred, and he woozily swayed in place.

I squinted at him. "Are you drunk?"

"Yes," Xavier replied matter-of-factly. He pulled a flask from his back pocket and shrugged. "Tree drunk is the best drunk."

A tiny confused giggle escaped me, and Xavier took that as his cue to toss the flask in my direction. I caught it and raised an eyebrow.

"Plum brandy," he said with a wink.

I sighed. "You're a bad influence."

"Obviously."

I cracked a grin and unscrewed the top of the flask. After a lengthy swig of its contents, I wiped my mouth and tossed it back to Xavier.

"So this is where you've been hiding during these things."

Xavier grunted and plopped onto the lawn. "Not just here. Any tree usually does the trick."

I snorted.

Xavier beamed up at me and patted the ground beside him.

I crossed my arms. "I'll get my dress dirty."

"You can sit on my lap, then." Xavier's eyes twinkled mischievously.

I clicked my tongue and stuck out my foot, firmly nudging his shoulder with the toe of my satin slippers. In his inebriated state, he lost his balance and toppled onto the grass, where he erupted in a fit of hysterical giggles.

"Shameless," I muttered, hauling up my skirt and settling beside him. I snatched the flask back out of his hand. "So why aren't you doing your usual thing?"

Xavier pushed himself upright, a dopey smile on his face. "What's my usual thing?"

I took another hearty gulp of brandy and licked my lips. "Flirting or fucking."

Xavier snickered and swiped the flask back. "You forgot eating."

"That too."

Xavier's face fell, and he mindlessly toyed with the flask's cap. After a long weighted pause, he huffed a sigh. "I think the game might be losing its allure."

"Oh gods!" I gasped in mock horror.

"I *know*." He stuck out his bottom lip in a pout.

"Will you even have a personality if you stop trying to sleep with everyone?"

"Exactly!" Xavier gestured wildly around him. "Who the hell knows?"

We both chuckled and fell silent. After a while, Xavier shrugged again. "It's probably just a phase. There's a new stable boy. I have no doubt he'll be looking extra good preparing my horse one of these days and I'll have a new target."

Xavier smiled, but it quickly dimmed. He looked away and focused on the ground between his legs.

"Also..." His brow furrowed, but he shook his head. "Never

mind."

I moved a little closer. "What?"

Xavier plucked a blade of new grass sprouting from the lawn and tore it apart between his fingertips. Deep pain colored his eyes when he said his next words, something I'd never seen in him before, even when he was balancing on the brink of death.

"Things just don't feel the same without Meer."

An ache seeped through my heart at the mention of our lost friend. Meer did have a unique talent of filling every event, small or large, with love and light and joy. He'd made such an impact on me in such a short time, I had no idea how hard his absence must be for Xavier.

I scooted closer, brushing the man's shoulder with my own. "You two had a beautiful bond."

Xavier stilled for a few moments, but soon gave up his cool facade. His shoulders sagged and he nodded. "Yes we did."

I considered my next words. A string of letters often seems so small and feeble compared to the monster of grief. No sentence or phrase could ever destroy it, but sometimes they held enough power to make the tiniest dent in its armor. So I thought back to when my heart was aching for my slain brothers, and said something that would have eased my own pain, if only for a few precious seconds.

"It's alright to miss him."

Xavier glanced over at me, eyes round, sad, and making him look decades younger than he really was.

"You're supposed to," I continued. "That means it was special. That it mattered. The pain has purpose. Every moment of missing them is just reminding you how incredible they were, and how lucky you are to have crossed paths with them. It's a gift, the pain. It's a reminder of them, a way they're kept alive inside us."

Xavier stared at me, his forest green eyes gleaming with emotion. He eventually blinked, cleared his throat, and angled away from me.

"You know, for someone who's a short-tempered baby, you're sort of wise sometimes."

I shoved him playfully, pulling another laugh out as he toppled onto the lawn once more. "Who are you calling a baby? You may have fifty years on me, but I'm much more mature."

Xavier hauled himself upright and brushed back the mess of curls from his face. "That's true."

"Could I get that written down?"

Xavier grinned and winked at me. "Never. And I'll deny saying it."

He gulped down the rest of the brandy in the flask and tossed the container into the rose bushes behind us before scrambling to his feet. He held out his hands for me to join him.

"Where are we going?" I asked.

"We, Miss Calder..." Xavier bopped his index finger on the tip of my nose. "Are going inside to brave the masses."

I frowned at the idea, much more content to stay here, where the world was quiet. "What about your tree drinking?"

Xavier discovered a twig in one of his curls and flicked it to the ground. "Listen. I don't know if you're aware of this, but *you*, Lina Calder, are my friend." His gaze hardened. "Now I've fought in wars, been eaten alive by Nethers, and flirted with death on its doorstep more than once. After all that, I can confidently say there is nothing in this world more terrifying than those entitled pricks in there." He pointed gruffly in the direction of the castle. "But there is no way I'm going to stand by while those wolves try and tear my friend apart. No way in hell."

Xavier smoothed my mussed hair, then ran his thumbs

under my eyes to fix the black powder Willow had smudged around them.

"You've come too far to be a slave to your fear, Lina. That's not you anymore. It ends tonight. No more running. No more hiding. They think they can bite?" Xavier's lips curled upward in a devilish grin. "Show them you bite back."

I frowned. "I'm supposed to behave, remember?"

Xavier threw back his head and cackled. "Asking Lina Calder to behave is like asking a fish to breathe air."

The comment earned him a playful smack to the back of the head.

"I *have* been behaving, though," I argued. "Soren needs me to—"

"Soren fell in love with a spitfire human who chucked a book at his head." Xavier crossed his arms. "Extinguishing your flame entirely isn't going to solve all your problems, or Soren's. So for goodness sake, stop making yourself small. Don't burn the place down, but burn bright. Blind some people."

He leaned forward, pressing his face in close before flicking my forehead with his middle finger. "And *that* you can get in writing."

With my arm looped through Xavier's, I entered the ballroom with my head held high. Everyone's eyes landed on me the moment we entered, but I refused to dwell on them. I focused on my breath instead of the overwhelming noise, methodically placing one foot in front of the other as we headed towards the refreshment table. I did my best to ignore a flicker of panic when I glimpsed a group of female Fae hovering near a tower of wine flutes, one of whom I recognized far too well.

No matter how much I hated Mirielle, there was no denying

the woman was beautiful. She commanded the attention of the room in a white ball gown with a skirt made up of layer upon layer of white feathers, while her gold-tinged locks were braided and piled on top of her head in an intricate pattern. The advisor's daughter clinked wineglasses with three women, all of them just as impeccably dressed as she was.

Mirielle's amber eyes locked on me from across the room and iced over as Xavier and I approached.

"Well," she cooed, tapping a sparkly white fingernail against her glass as she scanned my dress. "Look who decided to grace us with her presence."

Instead of saying all the things I really wanted to say to her, I forced a polite smile and turned to the other women in the group. "Who are your friends, Mirielle?"

The advisor's daughter glared at me but sighed and gestured to a woman beside her with strawberry blonde hair and blue eyes the size of saucers.

"This is Vevilla Macrae."

The woman shared an eerie resemblance to a porcelain doll as she pursed her mouth and eyed the slit in my dress. "Charmed."

She sounded like she most certainly was not.

"This is Lady Sorcha Umber." Mirielle pointed to a stoic woman with voluminous hair, tawny skin, and thin spectacles perched on a long straight nose. She looked just as uncomfortable on the outside as I was on the inside. Sorcha dipped her head to me, but kept her lips pressed shut.

"And *this...*" A genuine smile broke out across Mirielle's face as she wrapped her arm around the final woman and drew her closer. "This is Lady Rianne Craith. From Radomir."

When I met the woman's gaze, the floor went wobbly. Her gray-blue eyes, impressive bone structure, and rich brown skin looked exactly like someone else from Radomir I'd met before.

Someone I'd killed.

Rianne was nearly identical to Valdir. The two even shared the same long braids woven through an intricate headpiece. Looking at her immediately brought me back to that Yule Ball.

Valdir stood in front of me, his eyes wide with surprise.

His tendons and muscles snapped under my blade, skin peeling back as blood sprung from the wound.

The surprise stayed on his face, followed by horrified realization and sheer terror as death came to claim him.

I squeezed my eyes shut at the memory, my knees buckling beneath me, but Xavier gripped me tight and kept me on my feet.

"Hello, Lady Craith," I managed to croak, my heart a frantic drum in my chest. The crowd seemed too big again, and too loud, and *gods* why had I thought I could do this?

Mirielle arched an eyebrow and smiled sweetly. "Rianne, this is the King Slayer—Oops. *Sorry.* I meant Lina. Lina Calder."

Rianne examined me, the sheer intensity of her steely stare making it feel like I was standing before her stark naked. My dagger practically burned a hole in my thigh, and even though it was concealed, I worried Rianne could see it and recognize it as the weapon responsible for taking her king's life. Xavier's unfaltering hold was the only thing keeping me feigning a sliver of confidence.

When our eyes finally met, Rianne lifted her chin, stepped forward, and extended her hand.

"It's a pleasure to meet you, Lina," she said earnestly.

I glanced at Mirielle, trying to figure out if this was some cruel trick, but she was just as surprised as me. I looked back to Rianne and cautiously slid my palm to hers.

"I'm sorry about the pain my former king caused you," the lady of Radomir continued, firmly shaking my hand. Empathy flickered in her eyes. "He loved our territory fiercely, so much so that he became irrational in his fight to protect us. He abandoned compassion and mercy in exchange for fear. He wasn't a bad man, but he made a bad choice, and unfortunately those have consequences. But just so you know, not everyone agrees with his actions that night."

"Most do," Vevilla cut in.

Rianne shot her such a vicious glare it wiped the condescending smirk right off Vevilla's face.

"As I was saying." Rianne faced me again. "I'm sorry things happened the way they did, and I want you to know I admire how well you've been handling it all."

Mirielle scoffed incredulously, to which Rianne responded with the same icy glare she'd just silenced Vevilla with. Mirielle balked, but lifted her nose in the air to save face.

"Thank you, Rianne," I whispered. "That means a lot. And..." I licked my lips, thankful to have Xavier to rest my violently trembling hands on. "I know Valdir wasn't a bad man. I liked him a lot. Really, I did. But you're right, actions have consequences." I swallowed hard and hung my head. "And my actions that night still haunt me to this day. I wish things could have ended differently. I'm truly sorry for the pain I've caused, both to your people and your land."

Rianne dipped her head, accepting my apology, and offered me an encouraging smile. A voice inside me argued this was too good to be true, that it was all a cruel ploy and I shouldn't believe that this woman whose territory I'd thrust into disrepair was actually genuine. But I chose to ignore it and smiled gratefully back at her.

It was then Xavier leaned in front of me, intercepting the lady of Radomir's attention.

"Hello," he purred, extending his free hand. "I don't believe we've ever been introduced. I'm Xavier."

Rianne permitted him to take her fingers and pull them towards his mouth for a kiss, but yanked them free just before his lips brushed her knuckles. "Of course you are. You and your escapades are legendary."

Xavier's eyes sparked with devious delight. "Word of said escapades has traveled all the way to Radomir?"

Rianne tossed her braids over her shoulder and shrugged, suddenly very transfixed with her nails.

"Well then." Xavier battled the grin tugging at one corner of his mouth. "Maybe you should see for yourself if the man lives up to the legend."

I fought the urge to roll my eyes.

Rianne delicately sipped her wine. "Men rarely do, but if you play your cards right, I might do you a favor and investigate."

Now it was my turn to keep Xavier standing upright as an eager giggle bubbled out of him.

*Looks like the game* does *still have allure,* I thought wryly.

"Oh gods! What is *that*?" Vevilla's barking laughter snapped my attention back to her. She and Mirielle had locked onto something at the entrance of the ballroom. I turned to see what was so amusing.

Willow had found her courage and donned the dress I'd told her to wear. Despite her worries, the gown fit her just fine, with the wispy shards of tulle along the edge of its plunging bodice accentuating her ample bust in the most jaw-dropping way. The gown's layered skirt of varying shapes and sizes of airy fabric would have swallowed me, but it swept down Willow's curvaceous figure gracefully and elegantly. Instead of the dress wearing her, she wore *it,* and she did so beautifully. She'd chosen to scoop her plum locks into a bun on top of her head to let the dress speak for itself, and it looked like she'd applied a generous amount of blush to her cheekbones, but it was probably just her nerves making her natural flush extra rosy. My friend was undeniably breathtaking, which was why my blood boiled when snickers, whispers, and disgusted gasps began to swirl around the ballroom the moment she entered.

"This territory really *is* going downhill if the king's started bringing Sprites to his parties," Vevilla huffed. "Is her kind even allowed to be here? Who let her in?"

Mirielle's brows sank low over her spiteful glare as her head whipped towards me. "I'm assuming she was invited by—"

"Me." Xavier stepped forward. "I invited her."

I kept my face neutral but tightened my grip around Xavier's arm.

Mirielle scoffed. "*You* invited the nanny?"

"Yup." Xavier's eyes gleamed with defiance.

"Makes sense." Vevilla sniffed and twirled one of her long locks around her finger. "You really will fuck anything with a pulse, won't you, *low-born*?"

Rianne and Sorcha Umber gasped at Vevilla's slur.

The fire Xavier had mentioned in the garden suddenly roared to life inside me, obliterating any desire to behave. I instinctively took a menacing step forward, but Xavier dragged me back. His face wasn't twisted in fury the way mine was, but frozen in a cool smirk.

Xavier chuckled lightly and shook his head. "That didn't stop you from begging for a taste of this low-born cock at Litha last year, did it, Vevilla?"

This time, it was Mirielle and Vevilla's turn to gasp. Sorcha Umber was in the middle of sipping her wine but immediately spat it back into her glass. Meanwhile, Rianne fought a smile.

"You did *what*?" Mirielle shrieked, the curls trailing down from her updo whipping around her shoulders as she snapped her head in Vevilla's direction.

Vevilla's eyes grew even rounder.

"*Begged,*" Xavier repeated, snatching Sorcha's wine flute from her grasp. "On her hands and knees." He winked at Vevilla and downed the drink in one gulp.

Sorcha cleared her throat and dabbed her napkin to her mouth, and Rianne bit her lip to keep from laughing out loud. Vevilla refused to meet Mirielle's glare.

"Apparently she'd wanted it for ages." Xavier patted my hand, his signal to walk away. He called back over his shoulder, "At least that's what she said when I had her crawl to me. Have a good evening, ladies."

As soon as we were out of earshot of the women, Xavier and I burst into maniacal laughter.

"And *that...*" The Fae playfully poked me in the ribs. "...is when all the shameless flirting and fucking pays off."

"I promise, I'll never tease you about it again." I squeezed his arm. "Thank you for coming to my rescue."

Xavier waved away the comment with a flick of his wrist. "I like the way you think, Calder." He grinned and raised an eyebrow. "Wreaking havoc by putting a beautiful woman in a dress? Meer would be so proud."

My heart warmed. "He really would."

When we reached Willow, she looked two seconds from being sick all over the floor. Her knees nearly gave out from relief when she saw us.

"This was a mistake," she hissed out the corner of her mouth. Her violet gaze darted around the room, taking horrified stock of the countless eyes watching us. "I shouldn't be here. I shouldn't have come."

"You have every right to be here." I took her clammy hands in my own. "And you look incredible."

Willow gulped and shook her head. "I should have at least covered my ears."

I glanced at the ear tips on full display at the sides of her head. They were longer and more pointed than those of a traditional Fae, a dead giveaway as to Willow's Sprite ancestry.

"Your ears are beautiful," Xavier cut in.

Willow looked up at him, the candles catching her eyes in a way that highlighted the tears welling in them.

"And so are you." Xavier let go of my arm and slid his hand into Willow's, bringing her knuckles to his lips. He planted a tender kiss, then peeked up at her with hooded eyes. "I would be honored if you granted me your first dance at a Fae ball."

Willow shuffled her feet and glanced around the room again.

"Don't look at them, look at me," Xavier ordered. When Willow faced him again, he smiled brightly. "Do you like to dance, Willow?"

The Sprite sighed. "I *love* to dance."

"Good." Xavier's fingers tightened around hers. "Me too."

I inconspicuously slipped into the crowd as my friends drifted towards the dance floor. They would be safe together, too busy laughing and poking fun at each other to pay any mind to the cruel words and judgmental glances circulating around them. That was Xavier's magic; he always protected those he cared about, whether it be physically or emotionally, no matter the circumstance. Willow was better off with him than she would ever have been with me. Having the King Slayer close by would just attract more scrutiny.

The night had gotten colder, the torches placed along the terrace no longer strong enough to keep out the last of winter's chill. The moment I exited the ballroom I started to shiver, but outside fewer people milled and it was easier to breathe, so I stayed put. I gratefully accepted a glass of wine from a nearby servant and sipped it while taking in my surroundings.

A couple huddled in the shadows to my right, too preoccupied with whispering sweet nothings and exploring each other's bodies to pay much attention to me. To my left the rest of the terrace stretched, its railing decorated with white blossoms and boughs of evergreen dotted with cream pillar candles, their flames flickering wildly as a breeze whisked around the corner of the castle.

I glanced up at the trees swaying in the wind, their naked branches creaking and rustling with a thousand tiny whispers. Through the bare limbs of a mighty oak tree, I caught a glimpse of the moon rising on the horizon. The crisp silver light it cast over the shadowy land beneath it immediately brought me back to a cold, dark night in the Kylanthian mountains nearly a year prior. I'd sat on a boulder overlooking that ill-fated valley, a dark and beautiful creature perched beside me, silhouetted by a moon that shone exactly like this one. The familiar pang of longing and loss settled in my heart, and for the first time in a long time, I said a prayer to the gods.

I didn't pray much anymore. Hell, I didn't even know if I believed in the gods now. Too much had happened. There'd been too much pain and sadness for me to believe the gods, *if* they existed, ever showed us favor. But tonight, on a sacred holiday that ushered in new beginnings, I figured if the gods *were* real, they might hear a quiet prayer uttered by a human in a foreign land, cold and alone on the terrace.

"Let him be happy," I whispered to the sky. "Let him finally be at peace. He deserves that. If anyone deserves that, it's him. It's Hale."

The wind swelled and whistled through the trees, whipping my hair around my face and forcing the tear teetering at the edge of my lashes to slip out and trickle down my cheek. I sniffled and quickly wiped it away.

The breeze died down, and the world was silent once more, making it possible to overhear a hushed conversation near the ballroom doors. I angled my ear towards the voices.

"I just pray they won't be celebrating with any fertility rituals later." There was no mistaking the haughty tone of Mirielle Tynan. "Can you imagine a half-human bastard becoming next in line to the throne?"

The conversation was about me, a realization that had me frowning, but my curiosity got the better of me, and I inched closer.

"Who says the child would be a bastard?"

That clear, no-nonsense voice belonged to Rianne. I still wasn't exactly sure what to make of her, but I got the sneaking suspicion she didn't like Mirielle very much, and that solidified me liking her at least a little bit.

"If the king marries her," Rianne went on, "their child would be a legitimate heir to Astoria's throne."

At that, my stomach lurched.

I still hadn't told Soren about my desire to remain childless. The conversation hadn't come up yet, and I hadn't felt like it needed to. Our relationship was new, and there was still plenty of time to discuss those things at a later date. Of course, the thought had occasionally popped into my head... that Soren would require children in order to continue his line, but I'd always shoved the idea away and told myself I would deal with it some other time. It was something I didn't want to face, so I'd kept it stashed away at the back of my mind, where it waited and watched and lurked like a predator in the night. But deep down I knew the reality of our situation, and it slowly, quietly ate away at me...

Either Soren and I were not meant to last, or I would have to bear his children.

And both options filled me with dread.

A condescending cackle passed Mirielle's lips. "Marriage between the two is not something we have to worry about."

"What do you mean?"

I leaned closer, my thoughts mirroring Rianne's question.

"Soren marrying her isn't an option."

"You seem rather certain."

"I am. My father's spoken to the king about it a few times now. Apparently, he has no intention of marrying the girl."

I rolled my eyes. Mirielle was an arrogant brat who thought she knew everything. There was no reason to believe a single word that came out of that woman's mouth.

Still, her words stabbed me in the chest. It was one thing to ponder and doubt on your own, in the safety of your own mind. It was an entirely different thing hearing those doubts voiced between others.

"Are you sure?" This voice was soft and timid, and one I didn't recognize. I assumed that meant it belonged to the other woman I'd been introduced to but hadn't spoken with directly, Lady Sorcha Umber. "He seems rather taken with her. I think their story is quite romantic."

I sniffed.

*I like you, Sorcha. You can stick around.*

"His infatuation with her probably has to do with something else." That nasal tittering was undoubtedly Vevilla.

"What do you mean?" Sorcha asked.

"Tell them what you told me, Mirielle."

"Well..." Mirielle lowered her voice so much I had to take another step forward to hear her. "I have a theory that the King Slayer isn't all she seems. Think about it! She shows up out of nowhere, everybody is irrationally infatuated with her, even the Nethers. It's almost as if she's cast some sort of spell on everyone, don't you think?"

A scoff from Rianne. "You can't be serious."

"Wait," Sorcha pressed. "Let me get this straight... you're saying you think Lina is a—"

"Demon lover?"

Four heads whipped to face me as I stepped through the doors into the ballroom. Mirielle, Vevilla, Sorcha, and Rianne were gathered in a gossipy huddle in front of the dessert table, shock and shame coloring their features. I looked each of them in the eye, Mirielle and Vevilla the only ones who didn't shamefully avert their gazes.

"A witch," I clarified. "I suppose it makes sense, doesn't it?" I gave a matter-of-fact shrug. "I mean, how could Soren love someone like me, right?"

I wandered towards the group. Vevilla and Sorcha took cautious steps backwards, accidentally knocking into the table behind them and making the dishes rattle, but Mirielle and Rianne stood their ground. I locked eyes with Mirielle and came to a stop directly in front of her, our noses nearly touching. She was slightly taller than I was, and made sure to lift her nose higher in the air so she could look down it at me. Still, her chest rose and fell with shallow, nervous breaths.

"Because who am I? Just a human with average beauty and below average intelligence." I laughed lightly. "At least, that's how the god of the Netherworld described me. Right before I stabbed him."

In one swift move, I pushed back my skirt, pulled my dagger from my thigh, and embedded it in a bundt cake beside Mirielle. The girls gasped in alarm, but I smiled sweetly as I sawed myself off a piece.

"Anyway." I wiped a glob of frosting off the blade and popped it into my mouth, licking my lips before taking the slice to go. "Blessed Imbolc to you all."

# Chapter 10

I sat on the floor in Soren's darkened study, the piece of cake untouched beside me as I stared into the smoldering hearth and listened to the faint sounds of the celebration below. When the fire suddenly roared to life, I didn't flinch at the burst of flame. There was only one person I knew who had the power to manipulate fire like that.

I glanced over my shoulder at Soren. He stood in the doorway, lit from behind by the flickering golden light of the candelabra in the hall. He was smiling, but his eyes were sad.

"I've been looking everywhere for you," he said softly. He noted my melancholy expression as I hunched on the bearskin rug, clutching my knees to my chest. "Was it too much for you?"

I nodded sheepishly.

Soren wandered over, removing his ceremonial sword and laying it on the sofa before sinking to the floor beside me and wrapping an arm around my shoulders. I snuggled into him, inhaling my favorite scent of sensual cedar and spice from his chest. He angled his head to kiss the top of my hair.

"It's alright," Soren mumbled. "You tried. There will be other chances."

I nodded again and tightened my arms around his waist. We stayed there for a few precious, peaceful minutes, staring into the crackling flames and listening to the melody of the other's breath. But the longer we sat in silence, the more my heart ached. I tried to ignore it, tried to shove it back down like I had so many of my emotions lately, but tonight they seemed determined to fight back. Before I could bottle them, the words tumbled out.

"Is it going to be like this forever?"

Soren tensed at the word forever, and my heart sank even further. Maybe there *was* a grain of truth to what Mirielle had said. Maybe Soren really *didn't* see a future with me.

And somehow that hurt worse than my own doubts about us.

After a moment of hesitation, Soren cleared his throat. "What do you mean?"

"I mean your people hating me," I blurted. "And me cowering in the shadows because of it, then you going off to do your kingly duties and leaving me to face the wolves alone."

Soren recoiled slightly. "Are you mad at me? Lina, I just walked away for a second, and when I came back, you'd run off! I didn't know where you'd gone, and I—"

"Stop, I'm not..." I sighed and sat upright, removing my arms from around Soren's waist to rub my face. "I'm not mad at you. I'm hurting, and I lashed out. I'm sorry."

"What's the matter?" Soren took my chin in his hand, angling my face so I would look him in the eyes. Compassion glimmered in that deep blue gaze, the same way it had the night we'd met.

*Tell him,* the small voice inside me prodded. *Tell him every-thing. Your fears, your doubts, your desires. It's time to stop running.*

But I couldn't. I wasn't ready to lose him.

Soren was safe. He was stable. He loved me, and I loved him. He was *home*.

Where did I fit in this world if my home wasn't meant to last?

I squeezed my lips shut and looked away, fighting tears as I shook my head. Soren's hand slipped to the side of my neck and pulled me closer so he could rest his forehead against mine.

"Lina, talk to me," he whispered.

"I'm scared."

"Of what?"

I inhaled a quivering breath and finally managed to meet Soren's concerned gaze. "I'm scared it's not enough."

"What's not enough?"

"Love." Hot tears dripped down my face. "I'm scared it's not enough to keep two people together."

Soren stared at me, his eyes filling with a mix of fear, pain, sadness, and love.

*Gods*, there was so much love there.

I opened my mouth to say more, but couldn't get the words out. I wasn't ready to ask what we were or what our future held. I wasn't ready to ask him if I was just a placeholder for something, *someone* better. I wasn't ready to tell him I couldn't, *wouldn't* be a mother and continue his line. I wasn't ready to ask if we'd been fooling ourselves this entire time, if deep down we both knew we were never destined for our happy ending.

I wasn't ready for the truth to tear us apart.

We needed to face it eventually. All our secrets had to come to light. But right now I didn't feel strong enough to confront them. Maybe tomorrow, or the next day, but not tonight.

Tonight, I just needed him.

I slid my hands to either side of Soren's face and hauled him forward, pressing my lips into his. My flood of tears wet his cheeks and the collar of his jacket, but he didn't care. His arms encircled my waist, closing the distance between us. I freed myself from his claiming kiss just enough to murmur against his mouth.

"Make me forget. Make everything outside of us disappear. Just for a little while."

Soren nodded and crushed his lips back to mine, heaving me onto his lap so I straddled him. Usually in heated moments we were frenzied, practically feral with desperation, but tonight Soren took his time. He kissed me deeply, his hands exploring every inch of my body. His tongue lapped mine in slow, sensuous strokes while his fingers used the same tempo as they trailed through my hair, then over my back and breasts. When his hands cupped my backside, his grip tightened, and he pushed me down so the sensitive spot at my center pressed against his stiffening cock. I instinctively ground myself along it, moaning as deep-rooted pleasure swelled through me. I moved against him faster, eager for more, but Soren caught my hips and held them in place.

"No." His voice was commanding, but still breathy and seductive in my ear. "I'm taking my time with you."

Soren dragged my hips, painfully slow, up and down the raised outline of his cock, and a carnal twinge leapt through me. My breath picked up speed, my hips attempting to follow suit, but Soren kept me pinned how he wanted me. When he moved his mouth to my neck and began to suck and scrape his teeth over the skin, I had no control over the full-body shiver that came over me.

"Soren, please," I whispered, clutching at the buttons on his jacket, "I need you inside me."

"I told you," Soren mumbled against my neck, the vibration of his words only increasing the intensity of my trembling, "I'm taking my time with you."

I moaned in protest, which prompted Soren to snatch my hair in his fist and tug gently, forcing my head backwards so my neck was fully exposed. He shifted his tongue to the center of my throat while his hips drove against mine in steady, deliberate thrusts. With each lap and roll, the heat built, and soon I was aching with desire, unable to think of anything besides the frantic need to feel all of him.

"Please, Soren," I gasped. "Please just fuck me."

Without warning, Soren flipped over, planting my back in the fluffy fur rug and pressing his full weight on top of me. He continued his leisurely grinding as he stared me deep in the eyes, his intoxicating navy stare leaving me just as breathless as his movements.

"I'm not going to fuck you tonight, Lina." His lips grazed mine as he spoke, the words hot against the tender skin. "I'm going to make love to you."

I nodded eagerly and reached for his waistband, but Soren caught my wrists.

"No, no, no..." A hint of wolfish mischief tugged up one corner of his mouth. "I'm not done with you yet."

I started to object, but Soren ran one hand down the front of my body and lifted the skirt of my dress before dipping two fingers inside me. My words immediately morphed into a gasp of surprise and pleasure.

"I'm going to go slow." Soren's hand worked me with unhurried movements, providing just the right amount of pressure to coil blissful tension in my core as his fingers repeatedly curled inside me. "I want you to remember everything I do to you."

Soren slipped the strap of my dress off my shoulder with his free hand, exposing my chest. He then lowered his head to kiss and nip at my peaked breasts at the same moment his thumb started tracing persistent circles around my clit.

Formulating words no longer became an option. I tried to

say his name, tried to beg him to stop his delicious torment and give me what I really craved, but all I could manage was a string of stuttering groans. The sounds only motivated Soren, his eyes glittering with delight as he looked up at me to watch the pleasure manifest on my face. The sweet ache in my core intensified, growing more consuming with each stroke. My hips attempted to swivel in time with his fingers, but Soren planted his free hand on my lower abdomen, pinning me to the ground so I stayed still and steady. Just when the tension was about to snap and send a tidal wave of bliss crashing through me, Soren pulled his hand from between my legs and sat upright, grinning as I cried out in pitiful protest.

"Impatient *and* greedy," Soren teased. He slipped his fingers into his mouth and sucked the taste of me from their tips.

I bit my lip and groaned in frustration, angling my hips towards him. "Please, Soren. I need you. *Now.*"

Soren chuckled and unbuttoned his jacket, shrugging it off his broad shoulders and letting it drop to the rug behind him. "Now look who's begging."

"Yes," I panted, too damn turned on to be coy. Unable to hold off any longer, I sat up and tore at Soren's pants as he removed his undershirt, the ache inside me constricting sharply at the sight of his length springing free.

Soren pushed me to my back once more before settling on top of me and positioning himself between my legs. I glanced down at our hips and desperately wriggled closer. It was like my body had never needed anything but this, *him*, and it was so close yet so agonizingly far.

"Look at me," Soren demanded.

I dragged my gaze up to his. I was throbbing, the need for him maddening and overwhelming, and it only increased the longer I stayed connected with Soren's intense stare.

"I want to see everything," Soren continued, moving

forward so the head of his cock nudged my entrance. "Every breath. Every moan." He bent his elbows and leaned down, pushing his bare chest flat against my skin while he hovered his lips above mine. His voice lowered to a husky whisper. "I want to memorize the look on your face when you come for me."

At that, Soren drove himself inside.

I cried out, my hands latching on Soren's thick forearms and my eyes fluttering shut to savor the sensation.

"I said look at me," Soren growled.

My stomach dipped at his commanding tone, and I had no control over the eager smile that spread across my lips at the sound. I obeyed and opened my eyes.

Soren thrust into me again, deeper but slower this time. I matched his gaze, losing myself in the pleasure and the sea of deep blue staring down at me. Soren continued his languid pace, but the ragged breaths he sucked through gritted teeth proved he was having just as hard of a time holding back as I was.

We'd never been good at going slow. We'd been a whirlwind of fiery emotion since the moment we met, our passion taking off at a sprint after that first addictive dose of each other's lips. But tonight we were appreciating every second while we still could, something we should have done all along.

Our bodies rolled in tandem, moving in such perfect harmony even our gasps and moans synced. We both started to tremble at the same time, me from nearing my climax and Soren from restraint. I slid my arms around the king's back and dug my nails into the flexing muscles along his shoulder blades to pull him closer. I needed more of him, needed him deeper. Soren read my mind and thrust as far into me as he possibly could, keeping himself there until my bottom lip was quivering and my teeth were chattering from the decadent tightness.

Soren exhaled sharply at my response and smashed his mouth to mine.

"Fuck it," he hissed against my lips.

Without breaking the kiss, Soren rose to his knees and hauled me up to straddle him. His hands cupped my ass and guided me up and down his shaft, picking up speed and intensity. I laced my fingers around his neck, giving myself better support as I eagerly rocked my hips to the new pace Soren set. I pulled my lips free and returned my gaze to Soren's, our breath growing increasingly rapid and frantic.

This. *This* felt more like us. This wild, frenzied hunger. *This* was the fire I'd been drawn to since the moment I opened my eyes and saw the man who'd rescued me on Samhain. *This* was the flame I'd been drawn to like a moth, knowing it could burn me, *had* burned me, but still unable to resist its glow. *This*, for better or worse, was who and what I loved.

"Shit," Soren grunted, his fingers digging into the flesh of my backside with a grip so strong it was bound to leave bruises. "I fucking love you, Lina."

Maybe it was the raw emotion on his face and in his voice, or maybe it was my unfathomable pleasure as he slammed into me again and again, but tears squeezed out the corners of my eyes.

"I love you, Soren. Always. No matter what."

I could have sworn a sheen glazed Soren's eyes too, but before I could be certain, he shut them tight.

"Fuck!" He shuddered and finished, which sent me over the edge too. I buried my face in his shoulder and cried out against his bare skin as ecstasy exploded through me. Tears continued to stream down my face, an involuntary response to the overwhelming pleasure and the influx of emotions it stirred up. I clung to Soren, my scattered mind finally still as our ragged breaths became the only thing in the world for a few precious seconds. We stayed there, holding each other in iron clutches, until our breathing returned to its normal pace.

Wearily, I lifted my head from Soren's shoulder and brushed a sweaty lock of hair from his face. "Guess what?"

Soren pressed a kiss to my temple. "What?"

I jerked my chin to the door of the study, where a sliver of light from the hallway shone into the room. "You forgot to close the door again."

We both fell into a breathless fit of laughter.

"I really am bad at that, aren't I?" Soren's smile reached all the way to his eyes, crinkling the skin around them. Lately, seeing him thoroughly happy like this was rare. He'd have moments where he displayed charming grins or seductive smirks, but most of the time his mind was somewhere else, and he'd soon sink back into a state of worry or stoicism. But right now his smile beamed so bright it was a ray of sunshine pouring light into my stormy soul.

Soren carefully maneuvered himself out of me and laid me back down on the rug, settling in alongside me. "Oh well. Let people see. Maybe they'll learn a couple of things."

I grinned and nuzzled Soren's chest, the beat of his heart a soothing lullaby. He wrapped an arm around me, and my smile widened as his calloused fingertips traced mindless designs along my spine. Exhaustion set in, and I began to doze off, but I was still conscious enough to hear Soren's words, gentle and quiet.

"You look beautiful in white."

I opened my eyes to peek up at him. He was staring down at me with a thoughtful, almost pained expression.

"You think?" I murmured.

Soren nodded. He seemed sad about that for some reason. Why, I wasn't sure.

I opened my mouth to ask him what was bothering him,

but something in Soren's expression changed. His brows rose, his eyes widened, and his jaw clenched. The look immediately made my blood run cold.

That was surprise on his face.

Surprise, and fear.

Soren and I sat up at the same time.

"What's wrong?" I asked, tugging my dress back over my shoulders and grabbing my dagger from where it lay beside the cake. Soren had already laced his trousers and was shrugging his jacket on.

"I don't know." He didn't bother to fasten the buttons before snatching up his sword. Although it wasn't his typical broadsword, he could be deadly with it. I'd seen him terrifyingly lethal with far less.

I scrambled to my feet and followed him towards the door. "Nethers?"

He angled a pointed ear in the direction of the hall. The cheery sounds of the crowd celebrating still wafted up from the ballroom on the main floor.

"No." Soren frowned, his fist repeatedly clenching around the hilt of the sword. "Something else." His gaze shifted to the ground, eyes narrow as he searched his senses to determine what exactly they were telling him. Soren's back abruptly stiffened, and when he looked at me again, all the color had drained from his face.

"Lina, is Willow still watching your brother?"

A gasp leapt out of me like someone had reached in and ripped it out.

Soren threw open the door and sprinted in the direction of Wynn's bedroom. I followed as quickly as I could.

That run from one wing of the castle to the next took only seconds, but it felt like an eternity. Things moved in slow motion as a thousand scenarios flashed through my mind, each more gruesome than the last. The image that stayed with me the longest was of a creature with antlers and a black cloak raising my brother's brutally severed head high in bloody victory. The thought would have made me sick to my stomach if it weren't for the adrenaline pumping through my veins, giving my mind clarity and my feet wings.

By the time I arrived at Wynn's bedroom and stumbled through the door, Soren was already inside. I skidded to a halt beside him, my mouth falling slack as I took in the scene.

Scattered across the floor was page after page of a hurriedly scribbled Fae symbol:

Demon lover.

Over and over and over, everywhere we looked the word taunted us, written across notebooks, papers, novels and scrolls.

I couldn't focus on the sinking dread the scene invoked. There wasn't time.

Because when I looked at my brother's bed, it lay empty.

"Wynn!"

For a split second, I thought I was the one who'd spoken. The voice held the same panic and urgency I felt inside. But Soren was the one who had yelled my brother's name.

I turned to him, and when I saw where his stare was trained, a horrified scream tore from my throat.

Perilously perched on the ledge of an open west-facing window, its gauzy curtains billowing in the breeze, was my brother. He stood with his back to us, facing out into the night.

"Wynn," Soren said again, his voice calmer but still wavering. "Wynn, get down from the window."

My brother didn't move. He stayed as motionless as a statue, the pale moonlight shining down on him only adding to the effect.

"Wynn, get down from the window!" I demanded.

Still, he didn't move.

I stepped towards my brother, determined to snatch him down from the windowsill myself, but Soren threw his arm in front of me, barring the way.

"What are you doing?" I snapped, shoving him off. "My brother is—"

"Asleep." Soren returned his attention to Wynn, his brows nudging together with worry. "He's sleepwalking."

I followed his gaze and angled my head so I could see Wynn's face better. Sure enough, my brother's eyes were shut, lids and lashes fluttering wildly as he watched images moving back and forth beneath them.

"We have to be gentle with him," Soren continued, taking a tentative step closer. "If he wakes suddenly, he won't realize where he is, and he could fall."

My stomach sank at the thought, but I refocused on Wynn and anxiously waited as Soren inched forward, cautiously holding one hand out like he was taming a wild animal.

"Wynn?" Soren called softly, taking another step. "Wynn, can you hear me?"

A cold gust of air whipped around the exterior of the castle and burst through the window, causing Wynn to teeter on the ledge. Soren and I froze, both of us holding our breath. When my brother's feet stayed fixed in place, I huffed a sigh of relief.

Soren crept forward again, this time taking longer strides to reach Wynn faster. "Wynnric, you're dreaming. I need you to stay right where you are, alright?"

The bitter wind swept through the window again, knocking the shutters against the wall. I clapped a hand over my mouth to keep from screaming as my brother swayed in place.

"Wynn." Soren's voice was strained, like he too was fighting the urge to cry out. "Wynn, stay *exactly* where you are. Don't move. I'm coming to get you, alright?" He extended his arm even further, his fingers stretched in my brother's direction.

My heart hammered against its cage so hard my bones felt seconds from snapping.

Soren was almost to the window. Only a few more steps, and he'd reach Wynn.

Five paces away.

Four.

Three.

Wynn's head slowly swiveled to look at us over his shoulder. His eyelids were still closed, his lips parted.

"Wynn?" Soren asked gently. "Wynn, can you hear me?"

My brother's eyes snapped open, revealing an eerie milky-white haze that I'd grown to know too well.

He was spellbound.

Wynn's head whipped back around to face the night, and in the most terrifying moment of my life, more horrifying than any violent act I'd experienced up to this moment, my brother stepped off the ledge of the window into empty air.

I knew I screamed, but I didn't hear it.

I knew I shut my eyes and collapsed, but I didn't feel it.

My world went pitch black, full of nothing but pain and terror and guilt.

*I'd* brought my brother here. It was *my* fault we'd been in the woods two Samhains ago. I should have passed him off to one of the grannies in my village to keep hidden while Dominic, Jaras, and I fled to the mountains, but instead Wynn had whined that he was big and strong and could keep up with us, so I'd wrapped my arm around his shoulders and pleaded his case. Jaras and Dominic couldn't argue without upsetting him, so they'd begrudgingly agreed to bring him along.

I should have insisted on going with him when he wandered off to find firewood in that foggy forest.

I should have searched harder for him after he'd been abducted by the Sluagh.

I should have been stronger instead of selfishly asking Willow to come to the celebration tonight to keep me and my anxiety company.

All my brothers were now dead because of *me*.

Soren's voice cut through my hysterical spiral and brought me back to reality. He called my name, his words urgent and strained.

"Lina!"

I lifted my head, and through the watery fog of tears, I caught sight of Soren at the window, one hand gripping the jamb while something outside the window weighed down the other.

"Lina," Soren repeated, grunting with effort, "get over here and help me!"

I shakily pulled myself up off the ground and stumbled to the window. When I peeked over the windowsill, I screamed again, but this time in relief.

My brother dangled against the side of the castle, his wrist wrapped firmly in Soren's strong grasp.

"Help me pull him up," Soren demanded.

I scrambled forward and straddled the window ledge, grabbing the jamb with one hand the way Soren was while the other latched on to the back of my brother's nightshirt and heaved upwards. Together, Soren and I dragged Wynn back through the window. The three of us collapsed into a heap on the floor, the scattered drawings of the slur crinkling beneath us as we landed on top of them.

"Wynn?" I brushed my brother's unruly mane out of his face. "Wynn, look at me!"

In response, my brother's milky gaze stared back, emotionless and unflinching.

I smashed both hands to his cheeks and shook him, willing the haze over his eyes to diffuse.

"Wynn, come on! Wake up! Wake *up*!"

There was no response.

Helplessly, I looked to Soren. "I don't know what to do."

Soren swallowed hard. It looked like it killed him to admit, "I don't either."

# CHAPTER 11

*(250 years prior)*

PAIN SLAMMED INTO SOREN THE SECOND HE WAS CONSCIOUS.

It cut through his skin, his muscles, and his bones, instantly bringing him back to his last fuzzy memory:

He'd thought he'd avoided his father's wrath. But he was wrong, and the king had cornered him after the Lughnasadh ball let out.

Soren had accidentally been late for the evening's ceremonial bull sacrifice because he'd been trying to give that insufferable Mirielle Tynan the slip. He'd gotten caught up with some young servants in the stable, who had sneaked him a bottle of bilberry wine, and by the time the evening's first waltz rolled around, Soren, tipsy and bleary-eyed, had fumbled a few of the steps. He'd accidentally caused his pretty partner to trip, but he'd thought his mistakes might go unnoticed by the king. He hadn't even thought his father was paying attention.

But he had been.

Usually Soren's mother was there to stand up for him, but she'd been laid up with morning sickness for days and had missed the evening's festivities. Soren had no one to defend him when his father intercepted him outside his room after the party. The king had followed Soren into his bedroom and slammed the door behind them before shoving his son into the nearest wall. He'd screamed in his face, demanding to know why Soren was so hell-bent on making a fool of him and the rest of the royal family. Soren had sobbed miserably and tried to explain it wasn't his intention, but his words had only enraged his father.

One blow after the other had landed, each more agonizing than the last, until stars scattered across Soren's vision. The last thing he remembered was his father berating him with a list of his failures as he slammed his face into a mirror. The glass had cracked and shattered beneath him, a long jagged piece slicing deep into Soren's brow just above his right eye and slitting the flesh from eyebrow to opposite cheekbone. Despite his son's cries of pain and terror, the king had pushed even harder, grinding Soren's face into the glass until he'd passed out from the pain.

Now Soren had finally regained consciousness. His eyes snapped open as he woke, gasping and panting like he'd been thrust right back into the moment.

"Shhh, it's alright," a deep voice soothed.

Soren almost jumped. A stiff turn of his head revealed his father's advisor, Lord Magnus Tynan, sitting beside his bed. Soren moved to push himself upright but cried out when his arm gave out under him. He knew that feeling all too well. His wrist was broken. Bad.

"You're still healing," Magnus continued. "It would be best for you to lie still."

Soren obeyed, doing his best to relax into the pillows he was propped against. But being still only made him hyperaware of the way his bones ground as they fused back together.

"Does it hurt?" Magnus asked.

Soren watched the lord warily for a few seconds before replying. "I'm fine."

A lie.

Healing injuries hurt as bad as receiving them, and if Lord Magnus weren't here, Soren would be calling for one of the castle's healers to put him to sleep while they fixed him up.

The lord leaned forward and braced his elbows on his knees. "How old are you now, Your Highness? Fourteen? Fifteen?"

Soren fought the urge to cry out as one of his ribs popped back into place.

"Thirteen," he grunted.

"You look older. Do people tell you that?"

Soren nodded stiffly.

"You act older too. You hold yourself like a respectable young man. Your father taught you that, didn't he?"

Another nod.

"You know why he's doing that, don't you? You understand why he wants you to behave well?"

Soren lifted his chin, but winced as another rib started the healing process. "Because I'll be king one day."

"That's right." Magnus thoughtfully stroked his beard. "Your father is a very good king, you know. Our people love him, and they will expect the same from you when you take the crown. Your father wants to see you succeed. We all do."

After a brief pause, Magnus grasped Soren's chin in his hand, angling it to the left, then to the right to catch the light from the candle on the nightstand. He clicked his tongue as he examined the damage done by the mirror. Soren's face had healed enough that only two small cuts remained; one through his right eyebrow, and the other across his left cheekbone.

"Your father is strong, isn't he?" Magnus muttered. "More so than normal Fae. That's one of his powers, isn't it? Strength."

Soren nodded a third time.

"Maybe that will be one of yours too. Have you started seeing any magic of your own manifesting?"

Another rib slipped back into place.

"The other day at breakfast I thought I moved a fork without touching it," Soren said, forcing his voice as steady as possible. "But it could've just been my imagination."

"Maybe, maybe not." Lord Magnus released his hold and sat back in his chair. "Keep trying. It's still early for you. Most Fae don't come into their magic until their twentieth year. But you're not most Fae, are you?" He crossed his arms over his chest, staring at Soren like a hawk. "You're a prince from an extraordinary bloodline."

Soren swallowed, unsure exactly why the conversation was making the hair on the back of his neck stand up.

Magnus offered him a smile, but it was the farthest thing from comforting. "Do you know what my power is, Your Highness?"

Soren slowly shook his head.

"No, I suppose not. I like to keep it quiet. I find that it gives me an advantage. No one can use it against me or figure out a weakness, and like a viper laying wait in the grass, I'm able to strike when it's least expected." That eerie smile was still on the lord's lips as he leaned forward again. Soren would have scooted away if he'd had the strength. "Would you like to know what my power is, Your Highness?"

To be polite, Soren managed a tiny nod.

"Well, you're familiar with what healers do, of course. They fix things. I have the opposite power, though. I can keep things from fixing. And sometimes if I focus really hard..." Magnus latched a hand around Soren's wrist. "I can undo."

There was no holding back his screams as all the ribs in Soren's chest cracked at once.

The wounds that had been on the mend suddenly reversed progress. Bones separated. Gashes tore open. The cuts on Soren's face peeled apart, viciously shredding his skin and muscle the way the mirror had earlier. His tortured wails almost drowned out Lord Magnus's disturbingly relaxed words.

"Gods, that's a nasty cut on your face there. It could scar if it stays open much longer. You wouldn't want that, Your Highness. Appearances are so important. Especially for the royal family."

At that, Magnus tightened his grip, and the wound on Soren's face gouged deeper. A strangled sob wrenched from Soren's throat as he crumpled forward. Blood dripped from his face, soaking the stark white bedsheets tucked around him.

"I want you to listen to me very carefully, Your Highness," Lord Magnus hissed in his ear. "Your father is a wonderful king. Because of him, we have peace and prosperity and more wealth than all the other territories combined. If anything damaged his reputation, all that would be lost. You wouldn't want that, would you? You wouldn't want to be the cause of that."

"No," Soren choked out.

"Of course not. Because this is going to be your territory one day too. And you don't want to be the one to fail your people. You want what's best for them, right?"

It wasn't clear if the wetness trickling down his cheeks was Soren's blood or his tears. "Yes."

"And sometimes that's going to involve doing things we don't want to do. Like behaving as we should, and keeping up appearances. Do you understand what I'm saying to you, Your Highness?"

Soren inhaled a quivering breath, his rib cage screaming at the movement. "I'll behave. And I... I won't tell anyone what my father did."

"You swear?"

"Yes, I swear!" Soren whimpered. "I won't say anything. I never do."

Magnus's hand slid into Soren's. "Do we have a bargain?"

Soren stubbornly pressed his lips together.

The lord frowned. His nose scrunched in a silent snarl as he sent more magic tearing through Soren's body. Soren screamed again as his ribs broke further apart, their jagged edges piercing his skin and internal organs.

"I *said*," Lord Magnus repeated, "do... we have... a *bargain*?"

"Yes!" Soren wailed. "Yes, we have a bargain!"

"And you will never breathe a word of what happened here today?"

Soren collapsed, unable to breathe, unable to scream, unable to think of anything besides pain.

"I asked you a question, Your Highness," Magnus spat.

Somehow Soren managed to gasp out, "Yes."

"Yes, what?"

The dark of the room crept in, beckoning Soren back to unconsciousness or worse. He lifted his eyes to meet the lord's golden gaze, and with the final remnants of his breath he whispered, "Yes, my lord. We... we have a bargain."

Lord Magnus released Soren's arm, bringing an end to the unbearable pain. Soren frantically panted for air as his body filled with a different kind of pain, and his wounds started healing for the second time that evening.

Magnus tutted as he stood and gestured to Soren's mutilated face. "Pity. That's definitely going to scar. But I suppose that's alright. It will make you look tough. You are tough, aren't you? You're strong? Kings need to be strong."

Soren glared up at Lord Magnus blurred through the tears in his eyes, and through gritted teeth he replied, "Yes, my lord."

"That's what I thought." Ever the perfect courtier, Magnus smiled and politely dipped his head. "Feel better, Your Highness. And if you think *that* hurt, you should see what happens if you ever break that bargain."

As the lord walked away, Soren swore another oath, only this one was silent and to no one but himself:

One day, Soren of Astoria would kill Lord Magnus Tynan. Slowly. Painfully. And with a smile.

Splayed on his bed, Soren shivered and let the thought of revenge consume him. He welcomed it in, burying it deep so it simmered and stewed and warmed his soul with a fiery rage. It was a new sensation, but somehow it felt at home in Soren's body. Something deep inside clicked into place, like it had been waiting for Soren to find it and give it a home.

On the nightstand beside him, the flame on the candle suddenly flickered, swelled, and snuffed out.

*(250 years later)*

Soren absentmindedly ran his fingers along the raised white scar on his cheek. Magnus's voice eventually pulled him out of the dark memory he'd drifted to.

"Your Majesty."

Soren blinked and met the lord's gaze.

"Well?" Magnus asked.

"Well, what?"

Lord Magnus scowled and crossed his arms. "What do you plan on doing with her?"

Soren sighed and flipped through the stacks of paper on his desk. Notices, appeals, invitations. The pile was overwhelming and never-ending. And oddly enough, it was in a different order than he'd had it in the day prior. Magnus had been snooping again. No matter how many times Soren had told him the items in his study were private, the bastard wouldn't listen.

"I don't know why we keep having this conversation. I'm not sending Lina away."

"Don't you see how this looks for you?"

Soren's stomach twisted. Lord Magnus, always so concerned about godsdamned appearances...

"First that King Slayer in your court and now a Sprite—"

"Willow," Soren cut in. He glanced up, secretly enjoying the sight of Magnus bristling at the interruption. "Her name is Willow, and she's a lovely young lady and a wonderful addition to my staff, as was her sister, Acacia. Also that King Slayer you keep referring to has a name too. It's Lina Calder."

"I don't give a rat's ass what their names are!" Magnus snapped. He took a menacing step closer, and Soren's shoulders instinctively tensed. A tiny whisper of fear still remained inside, left over from that broken boy in his bed two and a half centuries before. But the truth soon rang out loud and clear in Soren's mind, drowning it out.

He wasn't that defenseless child anymore. He'd made sure of it.

The king stood and met the lord face-to-face, matching his defiant gaze. Magnus was slightly taken aback, but stood his ground.

"I want you to think very carefully about what you do next, my lord," Soren warned. "Remember, I am still your king."

Magnus's shoulders squared. "For how much longer?"

Soren's body hummed with restrained rage. The fire in his soul flared, begging to be let out through either magic or violence. He balled his hands into fists at his sides, partially to disguise their shaking, but mainly to keep from finally acting out all the bloody things he'd imagined doing to this man since he was thirteen.

"Your words are starting to sound an awful lot like treason, my lord."

The hardened gleam in Lord Magnus's eyes remained. "I'm telling you the truth, no matter how difficult it is for you to hear. People are talking."

"People are allowed to talk."

"They're saying you're unfit to lead."

"People have a right to their own opinions."

Magnus clenched his jaw and spoke through gritted teeth. "What is the point of bringing me on to advise you if you won't listen to a single word I say?"

For a brief moment, Soren considered telling the truth. *You, Lord Magnus, who cares so much about appearances, should understand you're only here to make me look good. You're nothing but a means to an end, and if it were up to me, I would see you flayed alive in the courtyard.*

But revealing that would defeat the lord's purpose. All the months of fake conversations and forced smiles would be in vain, and Lord Magnus would turn against Soren and spread dissent among the Astorian noble families. There would no doubt be an uprising, spearheaded by the lord himself, and Soren would likely lose the crown and his life, leaving Lina and Wynn alone in a world determined to end them too.

Soren wouldn't let that happen. He *had* to keep up this game, no matter how hard it was getting, and no matter how much it killed him to play it.

"I respect your opinion, Lord Magnus," Soren said, "but I'm

convinced there's a way to achieve peace without sending Lina away. As soon as people see her for what she really is, which is a victim in all this, I truly believe they'll come around."

Inwardly, Soren cringed at that word. Victim. He hated it, and hated the negative connotation attached to it. Lina was no more a victim of her past than Soren was. She'd fought tooth and nail to get where she was. Hell, what Mirielle said about Lina was more fitting than the term victim.

*She's a weapon.*

And if Soren had to die by a weapon, he'd gladly choose her.

"That's exactly the point," Magnus persisted. "People *aren't* coming around to her."

Soren sighed. His patience was fraying. "She's gone to *one* party, Magnus."

"Exactly! One party and she's already causing trouble!"

Soren threw his arms up in exasperation. "She put a low-caste woman in a dress! That's it! Gods forbid you rub elbows with a Sprite while she dances around in a fancy gown."

"The human also drew a weapon on my daughter and her peers, including a noblewoman from Radomir."

Soren blinked in surprise. Lina hadn't told him that part. But there hadn't been much time to. After they saved Wynn, Lina had looked after him while Soren saw to boarding up the boy's windows himself. He'd never returned to the Imbolc celebration, instead spending the rest of the night hammering planks in place so Wynn would never again have such a close brush with death. Now it was morning, and Lina was off readying her horse so she could take Wynn back to the woman in the woods. Only Soren knew where she was headed. With the term "demon lover" floating around, the last thing they needed was for word of her meeting with a witch to start circulating through the court. If anyone got hold of that information,

Soren would have more problems to worry about than a Sprite in a ball gown and knives pulled on gossipy girls.

Soren shrugged. "There are two sides to every story. I'm sure Lina meant no harm to Mirielle and her friends."

Magnus scoffed and paced the study. "Gods, I'm starting to think the rumors really are true. This girl must have you under some sort of enchantment."

"My mind has never been clearer."

Not a lie.

Lina had changed things when she stumbled into Soren's life. Changed *him*, though he'd felt a shift happening for years before then. After the falling out with Lerian, Soren had taken a long, hard look at the way he'd been living his life. His brother's passing a few years later solidified his feelings and made him realize he wanted to change. He wanted to be a better man. For his people, for all the lost and broken creatures he'd given a home to, but also for himself. Then Lina had come along, and she'd tested him. She'd forced him to think about things differently. She'd made him look at his behavior, his territory, his whole world from a different perspective. She'd violently shaken up his life, and it was one of the best things to ever happen to him. It was something others, especially Magnus, would think was madness, considering her presence was still making waves. But some people are worth a little choppy water.

Magnus shook his head grimly. "I swear, if your father were here—"

"I'm not my father!" Soren barked. Control slipping from his grasp, his rage tumbled out like an avalanche. "And I would never want to be!"

Magnus bristled and stepped closer. "Your father was the finest king Astoria has ever known—"

"Because no one knew the real him! Except *you*."

Magnus stared at Soren for a few weighted seconds before

sniffing and looking him up and down. He resembled a predator calculating if the animal in sight was something it could kill. "I'm beginning to worry you might be too far gone for me to help, Your Majesty."

"Helping me has never been a priority of yours."

Soren was visibly shaking now. He had to get out of this situation. A red haze had slowly started inching in on the outskirts of his vision, the same way it did before a battle. Soon all logic and sense would disappear, and he'd be left with nothing but an all-consuming lust for violence that turned his world the shade of blood. It was a rare power, one many of the famous warlords in history had carried too, but it was also a curse. If the Red Sight took hold, Soren would lose himself for a time, then wake in a pile of carnage with no memory of what had happened.

The thought of Lina pulled Soren back to his body. A voice in his head reminded him she'd be left with nothing if Soren was gone. Killing Magnus now would be Soren's death sentence too, and therefore Lina's. That thought pushed the haze back slightly, which gave Soren the strength to take a deep calming breath and turn away from the lord. Magnus, not one to be so cooly dismissed, gruffly grabbed Soren's arm, dragging him back.

"If you have something to say to me—"

Soren didn't hear the rest.

His rage flared, his vision flashed blinding crimson, and before he knew what he was doing, he'd slammed the lord into the nearest wall and wrapped both hands around his throat.

"Don't you ever, *ever* lay your hands on me again," Soren growled, baring his teeth like a rabid animal. "You don't get to do that. Not anymore."

Magnus gurgled and choked, his face flushing as he gasped for air.

The haze in Soren's eyes thickened, and a smile tugged at the corners of his mouth as he drank in the image of Magnus fighting for his life. The lord's hand landed on his wrist, same as it had all those years ago when Soren was a boy. He felt the lord's magic enter him, the power spreading through Soren's body and prodding around in his veins in search of a weakness, but it found nothing. Magnus was completely helpless, and that realization made Soren eagerly tighten his grip, that broken boy inside cheering him on.

A knock at the study door was the only thing that spared Lord Magnus's life.

Soren immediately released his hold on Magnus's throat and spun, blinking the remnants of crimson haze from his vision. Lord Tristan Rourke stood in the doorway, casually leaning against the frame. Soren hadn't seen him since that dinner at the Tynan estate, when the Teagues were attempting to lure Tristan into their bed. Now the lord was just as nonchalant as he watched the scene with a curious but calculating gleam in his eyes.

"Am I interrupting something?" Tristan's eyebrow arched as his gaze darted between the two men.

With Magnus bent over, coughing and sputtering beside him, Soren chose to ignore the question, and instead cleared his throat and plastered a smile on his face. "Lord Tristan. To what do I owe this pleasure?"

Seemingly unconcerned with what he'd stumbled upon, Tristan shrugged and ran his fingers through his slicked-back blond hair. "Lord Magnus invited me and a few of the other lords and ladies to breakfast. It was a tradition your father had, if I recall correctly. There was a feast with Astoria's most notable families the morning after every holiday when we were growing up, wasn't there?"

Soren forced his smile wider. "Yes, there was. Good memory."

"His Majesty and I were just speaking about how he wants to bring back more of his father's practices," Magnus said, his voice a ragged croak. He straightened, readjusting the collar of his overcoat and proudly lifting his chin as he wandered up alongside Soren. "King Stelios was an honorable man worth emulating, wasn't he, Your Majesty?"

Soren glanced at the lord. Cold and cruel, his stare was a silent challenge for Soren to speak up, to break the bargain he'd been manipulated into making all those years ago. For a moment Soren wanted to, even though he knew what breaking a bargain entailed. Once again the thought of Lina brought back his sanity. While setting fire to his father's reputation was tempting, it wouldn't be worth it if Lina was left alone in this cruel world.

So Soren turned back to Lord Tristan, faked another smile, and bowed his head. "Lead the way, Lord Tristan. It would be my pleasure to dine with you."

# CHAPTER 12

WITH THE SNOW GONE, THE TREK TO THE WITCH'S HUT WAS easier than it had been a few weeks prior.

Clutching Wynn in front of me, I urged my horse through the dense forest at a gallop. Before long, the freshly thawed pond and crooked chimney pipe came into view. I hauled on my horse's reins, and it dug its hooves into the ground, bringing us to a grinding halt at the top of the slope above the shack. I leapt from the saddle and tied the reins to a nearby birch tree before pulling my brother down to join me.

"Come on," I mumbled, snatching up his hand in my own and setting my sights on the hut below. I stomped down the hill with furious determination, towing my brother behind me while my mind raced through all the different ways I could handle this. Logic told me I should go in and explain Wynn's situation politely and respectfully. In Soren's words, I should *behave*.

But *gods*, was I tired of behaving.

For three months I'd been distant or demure, putting up

with all the rumors and cruel words and judgmental glances from Mirielle, Magnus, and everyone in between. And what had that gotten me? Nothing. I was still the King Slayer. I was still the demon lover. I was still the whore. Maybe there was no point in trying to be someone I wasn't.

I arrived in front of the door of the shack and raised my foot to kick the door in, stomp inside, and demand an explanation as to why my brother was once again spellbound. The snap of a twig behind me made me freeze. Every muscle in my body tensed, and my attention shot to my peripheral vision. When something white flashed by at the corner of my eye and another branch cracked, this time closer, I snapped into action.

In one swift move I spun, threw my brother behind my back, and ripped my dagger from its sheath. For a brief moment, I glimpsed a flash of white darting behind a tree. My heart skipped a beat as I foolishly thought it was a sweet and loving creature with pale skin, kind eyes, and long white hair. But he was dead, and no matter how much I wanted it to be him, it was impossible.

Meer couldn't be in this forest with me. Someone else was.

I watched the trees until my hand cramped from holding my dagger so hard, and eventually I swayed in place, the rigid muscles in my body losing strength from being so tightly wound for so long. Still, I continued to watch the forest, waiting for any signs of movement, but none came. Doubt that I had seen anything at all crept into my mind, and logic joined in to remind me I was jumpy from sleep deprivation. I finally came to the conclusion my mind was playing tricks on me, the same way it had when I made the journey here before.

I let myself relax and turned back to the door, but still warily kept an eye on my surroundings. Again I raised my foot to kick in the door, but this time it swung open before I could bring my heel to wood. I sighed and resettled on both legs before ducking through the doorway.

This time, I was prepared to dodge the carcasses dangling from the ceiling.

"There you are. I thought you would stand out there all day."

My eyes adjusted to the low light in the dingy space, and the witch came into focus. She was back on her stool by the fire, her sleeves rolled up to the elbow as she mixed a hearty stew over the flames.

This time, I didn't have the patience for quips and conversation. I pulled my brother out from behind me and thrust him in front of the woman.

"Explain."

The witch didn't even look at Wynn, choosing instead to keep her eyes locked on the thick wooden spoon stirring her cauldron. "Explain what?"

I took a menacing step forward, angling myself to make sure the woman could see the dagger in my hand. "You know exactly what I'm talking about." I jerked my chin to Wynn. Even in the shadows, the white film over his eyes was undeniable. "Your magic was bullshit!"

At that, the witch's head whipped towards me, her bottomless eyes narrowing in rage. "Don't insult me, girl! I was practicing magic thousands of years before you took your first breath. I don't make mistakes."

My self-control finally snapped.

I lunged across the room, caught the witch by the arm, and slammed the edge of my blade to her throat. Her breath hitched, but otherwise she remained calm and glared back at me with an unreadable stare.

"Then explain why my brother looks like that," I hissed.

The witch huffed an amused chuckle. "What are you going to do? Kill me?"

I pressed my dagger further into the woman's skin, forcing her to flinch. "I slay more than kings."

The witch pursed her lips. "You think I deceived you. I have not."

My hand shook as I fought the urge to push the blade deeper. "You said my brother would be healed."

"Wrong." The woman glanced at Wynn, who had mindlessly wandered over and was facing the wall on the west side of the hut, staring at nothing in particular like usual. "I said I would break the Sluagh's spell over him."

"You haven't!"

"Wrong again," the old woman countered. "I asked you if any other creature had bound the boy."

"I told you, *no!*" I shouted, giving her a rough shake. "It was the Sluagh who claimed him as a Changeling and stole him away to the Netherworld—"

"At *first*." The witch's hands found their way to the collar of my jacket to shake me back with surprising strength. "Think, girl! *Think!* When you slipped into the Netherworld, did you witness any other creature controlling your brother?"

"I already told you, *no*. I—"

Suddenly my mind raced back to that glowing throne room.

*Erith sliced her sword across King Ilris of Merimaya's throat while his wife wailed in horror.*

*"Oops," Aedan giggled, shrugging coyly. "It looks like you won't be leaving after all."*

*Then, he raised his right hand and snapped.*

*Wynn instantly shoved me away and walked towards Aedan, while I scrambled after him on my hands and knees.*

*"Wynn? Where are you going? Wynn!"*

*I latched on to my brother's robe, but he pried my fingers off and pushed me back with unnatural strength, then continued forward to take his place at Aedan's side.*

Stuck in a loop, the memory played over and over in my mind. I'd been seeing it in my nightmares for months, but the realization had never clicked.

It wasn't the Sluagh who'd had the power over my brother in the Netherworld.

It was Aedan.

"But..." I blinked, working to process the information. "I... I killed him."

More memories bubbled up.

Aedan's eyes widening as I plunged the antler blade into his stomach.

Hot, wet blood gushing from his body and coating my hand.

An ear-piercing, bone-rattling screech tearing out of his throat before he dropped me to the ground.

"I killed him," I repeated.

The witch frowned, her hands moving to mine and gently coaxing my dagger away from her neck. "When something dies, so does its magic. Any power they have over another dies with them, releasing the bond between the two. If they do not die, then the bond remains. I swear to you that what I did for your brother would have broken any hold the Sluagh still had on him. If he is not healed, then he is bound by another's magic. And it is a much stronger magic than I am capable of dealing with."

I swallowed the painful lump swelling in my throat. "So you're saying—"

"I'm sorry." The witch's eyes softened. "Whoever you thought you killed is still alive, and it is they who have dominion over your brother."

Those words hit like a kick over a cliff. My stomach

dropped, my knees threatening to give out with it, but somehow I stayed upright.

"But..." I croaked, keenly aware of my breath growing shallow and sharp in my chest. "If he's not dead, that means—"

"Yes," the witch interrupted. "No matter what my kind does for him, your brother will always return to this state for the rest of his days, as long as whoever holds sway over him still lives and continues to call to him."

"No, not that."

Another image floated to the surface of my mind.

*Aedan returned his attention to Hale. "So you see, my son? What you view as a curse is in fact the most glorious gift. Because of you, the Fae realm is ripe for the taking. It's led by inexperienced and arrogant rulers, constantly bickering and picking sides like children. Now's your chance to finally get what you deserve. Finally, my children can emerge from the depths and take back the land they've been chased out of for millennia. You'll be able to live normal, happy lives, all thanks to you."*

"The creature who controls my brother," I said slowly, the weight of the words squeezing the air from my lungs. "He wants to destroy the Fae. He's the one responsible for killing Soren's father and the kings and queens of Lerian and Merimaya. He used my... friend."

My heart sank at the memory of the guilt and shame in Hale's eyes when Aedan told him that whenever he used his power, Aedan could see through it too. "He used him to spy on the kings and queens so he could send Nethers to kill them, all so the Fae realm would be left vulnerable."

The witch stared at me with a furrowed brow and deep frown, but her expression wasn't one of doubt.

"Why?" the witch asked. "Why would he do that?"

A shiver ran through me as I saw Aedan in my head once again.

*Aedan beckoned to the Nethers prowling around us with their weapons still at the ready. "Please excuse my children, they're quite protective of their home. They're not welcome anywhere else, you see. In your world, they're treated like pestilence, hunted down and slaughtered like animals."*

"He wants to take this realm for his own so the Nethers can roam free." I shut my eyes and shook my head to try and rid my mind of the horrific image of Nethers slaughtering innocents. "He thinks they're owed it, that they've been unfairly persecuted for all these years."

The woman nodded again, her gaze drifting to the floor of the hut.

"I suppose you mistreat a people for long enough, they're bound to rise up," she mused.

I grabbed her arm, desperate for her to feel the same urgency I did. "If Aedan's alive, that means he'll be coming after what he feels he's owed. It means he's coming for us. All of us."

The witch's thin lips pressed together in a determined line, the crow's feet around her eyes crinkling as she glared at me. "So what are you going to do about it?"

I almost scoffed. "*Me?*"

"You."

When I realized she wasn't joking, I let go of the woman and stepped back, suddenly feeling very small in an overwhelmingly large world. "What can *I* do?"

The woman moved her shoulders in an easy shrug and gently intercepted Wynn as he tottered towards the door. "A powerful ruler needs to be killed. Sounds like a job for a King Slayer, wouldn't you say?"

This time, I actually did scoff. "I already tried to kill him and failed."

The witch grunted and handed my brother off to me before heading back to her cauldron. She sniffed it appreciatively and took up her wooden spoon, leaving me standing in uncomfortable silence.

"Besides," I added, "the way in was destroyed. I couldn't get to the Netherworld even if I wanted to."

The witch peeked at me from one corner of her eye. "So wouldn't that mean the Nethers can't escape to enact their vengeance?"

I frowned. "I guess so."

"Then we're safe."

At her words, I breathed a sigh of relief. "Right."

The witch dipped her head in a curt nod and refocused on the pot.

I continued to watch her casually stir the soup, asking myself why I didn't feel as calm and relaxed as she did. The thought sneaked up on me like a thief in the night, and before I could stop myself, I spoke it out loud.

"Unless there's another entrance to the Netherworld."

The witch stopped her stirring.

"Do you know what makes a witch?" she asked suddenly, as bright and cheery as a summer day.

I blinked at the abrupt subject change. "What?"

"A witch." The woman clasped her wooden spoon in front of her. "Do you know what makes one?"

"Uh... no, not really." I shook my head and rubbed my eyes. "Sorry, can we stay focused here—"

"We have magic," the witch interrupted.

I dropped my hands to my sides and exhaled impatiently, glancing at my brother, who had again wandered across the shack to stare at the wall.

"But many creatures in this realm have magic," the woman continued, gesturing to the world outside the window with her spoon. "So what gives someone the title 'witch?'"

"I don't know."

I *did* know I was fighting the urge to smack her.

"We are not born with the magic." The woman smiled again. "We're unnatural because we are painfully ordinary, but find extraordinary power by alternative means."

"I don't see how this is relevant."

The witch ignored my comment, choosing instead to brush past me and putter over to her worktable. "To achieve power, we've had to gain extensive knowledge and dabble in both the light..." Her gaze flicked back to me. "And the dark."

Her words made my fingers tighten around my dagger.

"It can be frightening for some." The witch grabbed her mortar and pestle and poured the powder it contained into a jar, capped it, then came to stand in front of me. "But you love the dark. Don't you, King Slayer?"

I opened my mouth to voice my distaste for witches' riddles, but before I could, the woman gave the jar a solid shake, the contents taking on a glowing cyan hue. It was the same concoction she'd made for Wynn when we'd visited before, and the realization had me blinking in surprise.

"I had a vision of rounded ear tips and a dagger with silver vines at my throat," the witch explained with a shrug. "I thought it might have something to do with you needing this, so I prepared it ahead of time. Again..." She peeked at Wynn sadly, that flicker of grandmotherly warmth returning. "I'm afraid it will only help him for a short time."

"Right." I frowned. "Unless I find another way to the Netherworld and kill its king?"

"Precisely."

I sighed and rubbed my eyes again. The stress had ignited a dull pain there. Outside, a breeze rustled the trees and howled as it whipped around the branches. It was only when the wind died down and the howling remained that I realized it wasn't wind at all.

It was wailing.

I angled my ear towards the window. "Do you hear that?"

When I looked to the witch, her face had gone pale.

"It sounds like someone crying," I added.

The woman gulped and nodded. "We need to hurry."

I obediently followed her over to Wynn and gripped his shoulders tight in anticipation of what was to come.

The witch rested her hand on Wynn's head like before, muttering the same rhythmic phrase of ancient Fae before uncorking the bottle and letting the luminescent blue smoke slither out. It swirled into my brother's nostrils, and this time I was ready for the way he went rigid and thrashed. The witch set the jar down and placed both hands on top of Wynn's head, closing her eyes and raising her face to the heavens as she spoke the ancient chant.

When my brother went limp, I swept him into my arms.

"Wynn?" I asked, cradling him the same way I had seven years ago when my mother returned from the midwife's cottage, handed me his tiny swaddled body, and told me to say hello to my new brother.

Wynn's lashes fluttered, and his eyes opened.

They were clear and bright once more.

I smiled and opened my mouth to say hello, but then I heard it again.

Miserable, pitiful wails.

And this time, they were louder. And much, *much* closer.

"There's that sound again," I mused.

"Yes." The woman reached for the door with a trembling hand. "You need to go. *Now*."

I straightened and helped Wynn settle on wobbly legs. "Shouldn't we see if they need help?"

"No," the witch said firmly. She beckoned us to the doorway, then grabbed her wooden stirring spoon from where she'd set it on the table. "Come. Quickly."

I took up Wynn's hand and followed. The second we exited the shack, a deep pit opened in my stomach.

The forest was unnaturally silent.

# CHAPTER 13

———————

No wind. No birds. No insects. Nothing.

Nothing except the wailing.

The witch froze, Wynn and I following suit when we glimpsed what she was staring at.

A woman stood a few paces in front of us, wearing a simple white dress, a tangle of white hair cascading down her back all the way to the ground. Her slender hands were covering her pale face, her body shuddering and shaking as she sobbed miserably into them.

"Miss?" I asked. "Are you alright?"

I started to approach her, but the witch's hand flew out and latched on to my arm, holding me back.

"Don't!" she hissed.

Confused, I turned back to the woman in white.

"Enough with the act," the witch shouted at her. "I know what you are, *Ben Síde*."

My blood chilled at those words.

We'd all heard the tales as children, the name used in

haunting ghost stories murmured around campfires for as long as I could remember.

The Ben Síde. Heralds of death.

The woman in white's shoulders immediately stopped shaking. She straightened and removed her hands from her face, and I swallowed a gasp.

Her eyes were completely white, illuminated with an otherworldly glow.

"Hand over the princeling, demon lover," the Ben Síde said.

I'd expected a chilling voice to come out of her like the other Nethers I'd met before, but she sounded... sweet. Normal even. Which was somehow far worse.

The witch raised her chin defiantly. "Let the boy be. He's innocent in this war—"

"I wasn't talking to *you*," the Ben Síde interrupted her. She angled away from the witch, her eyes settling on me instead.

I gulped.

The Ben Síde took a step forward, prompting me to protectively shove Wynn behind my back.

"My master called, but did not receive an answer," the woman in white went on. "He wants what is rightfully his."

I readjusted my grip on my dagger. "Over my dead body."

The Ben Síde's petal pink lips curled upwards, producing a blindingly white smile. "I was hoping you'd say that."

A nauseating crack cut through the silence as the woman's mouth opened and her jaw unhinged, her teeth elongating to points. Her nails followed suit, the black hue they adopted a stark contrast to her pure white exterior.

"Get back inside," the witch whispered urgently beside me.

The Ben Síde took up her keening again, only this time her wails were a higher pitch, like an eagle screeching before the kill.

"Get inside!" the witch yelled.

I grabbed Wynn and dragged him back into the shack just as the Ben Síde lunged, her fingers outstretched like razor-sharp talons.

The witch flew inside the hut after us and slammed the door closed, whirling her wooden spoon above her head in a wide circle as she did. Before, I hadn't seen the runes carved into the shack's rafters, but with one flick of the spoon, they lit up like rays of sunlight.

The Ben Síde collided with the door, letting out a shrill shriek as she bounced off.

"My wards will only hold her off for so long," the witch said, nodding to the glowing symbols in the rafters.

The Ben Síde attacked the door again, and this time the hut shuddered and the runes flickered like a flame on a torch.

"What do we do?" I asked. I peeked down at my brother. Wynn's arms were wrapped around my waist, clutching me for dear life, his eyes wide with terror and confusion. I held him tighter, praying he couldn't see I felt the exact same.

"I'll distract her." The witch tucked her spoon in the waist-band of her skirt and grabbed two elixirs from the table before starting for the window. "You take the child and run for your horse, then get back to the castle as fast as you can."

The hut shook as the Ben Síde continued her assault. The runes in the rafters dimmed.

My gaze darted from the Nether at the door to the witch at the window, who now seemed so small and frail by comparison. "Are you going to be alright?"

At that, the woman stilled.

The planks in the wall creaked as the Ben Síde attacked again. The runes nearly extinguished.

The witch glanced over her shoulder at me, her eyes melancholy but a smile on her wrinkled lips. "I've lived a good long life, Lina Calder. Your story is just beginning. Take the boy, and don't look back."

As she turned back to the window and began to haul herself out, my throat constricted at the weight of her sacrifice.

"Why?" I asked, my voice breaking. "Why help us?"

The witch looked over her shoulder again, her eyes shuttering. "Because my pain will have purpose. You have a job to do, King Slayer, and you can't do it if you're dead."

Without another word, the witch crawled through the window and faced the monster outside.

I swallowed my emotions and faced the door, rubbing Wynn's shoulder to comfort him.

"Get ready to run," I ordered.

My brother nodded obediently, but his bottom lip quivered. I bent and kissed the mop of hair on his head.

"We'll be fine."

The Ben Síde's screech sounded, followed by a scream of pain from the witch. I squeezed my eyes shut, my stomach lurching, but forced a calming breath.

"Alright, on three. One... two... *three!*"

I shoved the door open, and together Wynn and I sprinted outside, headed towards the horse perched on the hill, and trying our best to ignore the violent struggle behind us. I winced as the witch screamed again, and I squeezed Wynn's hand tighter to propel him forward.

My horse was whinnying and pulling at the reins tied to the birch branch when we arrived, the Ben Síde's keens riling it into a frenzy. I ran my palm down the horse's nose in an attempt to calm it.

"Shhh..." I whispered. "Easy!"

The horse shook its head, tossing its mane left and right. There was no way Wynn and I could ride it in its current state.

I nervously glanced over my shoulder to see if the Ben Síde had spotted us yet, and my breath hitched.

The witch, bloodied and battered, was crawling on her hands and knees towards the last bottled elixir she'd brought with her. She uncorked it with her teeth, then chucked it in the Ben Síde's direction. A bright puff of red smoke exploded in front of the Nether, the impact sending her stumbling backwards, but it only slowed her down. The witch started to run, but the Ben Síde scrambled after her, tackled her to the ground, and sank her claws into the woman's back, ripping an agonized scream out of her.

I sucked in a breath and refocused on my horse, the bite of guilt bitter on my tongue.

"Easy!" I urged, stroking the beast's muzzle. "Easy…"

The horse repeatedly stomped its hooves, but it relaxed just enough for me to grab Wynn and shove him into the saddle. He latched onto the horse's mane, his chest heaving in shallow pants. I moved to pull myself up behind him, but looked back over my shoulder one last time.

The witch had found the strength to grab the wooden spoon from her waistband. She swung it in a circular motion again, chanting a line of verse, and a small whirlwind of dust, rock, and leaves billowed up from the forest floor and knocked the Ben Síde back a few paces. The witch collapsed onto her stomach from the exertion.

I glanced at my brother, back to the witch, then shut my eyes tight.

I'd left someone to battle Nethers alone before, and it ate away at me every day since. I couldn't abandon her.

I couldn't leave her like I'd left Hale.

I opened my eyes and set my jaw, then took my brother's hands in mine. "Wynn, go back to the castle. The horse knows the way home. All you have to do is hold on."

Wynn furiously shook his head.

"Wynnric," I said, more firm this time. "I'm not asking you, I'm telling you. Go back to the castle. If anything happens to me, Soren, Xavier, and Willow will take care of you, alright? You listen to them like you would me."

Wynn's eyes glistened, and his lower lip trembled. I kissed his hand.

"I love you. I love you so much."

Tears slipped down Wynn's round cheeks, and his mouth opened, but no words came out. I gave him a tender smile, my vision blurring with tears of my own.

"It's alright," I whispered. "You don't have to say it. I know. I know you love me too."

Wynn nodded, his shoulders shaking as more and more tears slid down his cheeks. I gave his hand one last kiss before loosening the reins from the tree.

"Hold on," I ordered.

Then I slapped the horse's flank as hard as I could and watched it carry my brother to safety.

When the mess of blond curls had disappeared into the tree line, I turned back to the shack below. The Ben Síde had hurled herself at the witch and embedded her needle-sharp nails into the woman's back. The witch cried out, her scream weakening.

My muscles tensed and my blood pounded in my ears as I took a final calming breath.

Then I launched myself down the hill.

By the time the Ben Síde heard me coming, I'd picked up too much momentum for her to react fast enough. My body collided with hers, sending us both hurtling to the forest floor, rolling across stone, branch, and leaf to land in one solid heap. We came to a stop on the muddy bank of the pond, both of us wriggling out of each other's grip and scrambling upright to face the other. Miraculously, I'd kept a hold of my dagger.

The Ben Síde bared her teeth like a wolf, the high-pitched wail tearing out of her mouth so loud it shook the reeds around us. I flinched at the noise, my ears ringing, which the Ben Síde used as her moment to strike. She lunged at me quick as lightning, but I managed to block her first swipe by slicing my blade along her wrist. The sudden movement made me lose my footing, and the slippery slope gave way beneath me. I attempted to duck out of the way, but the Ben Síde's hand caught my right shoulder as I passed, her elongated nails ripping my jacket and raking across the flesh.

I cried out and fell face-first into the mud, gritting my teeth against the stinging pain. Behind me, the Ben Síde screeched from the wound my dagger had inflicted on her arm.

Groaning, I rolled onto my back and mentally prepared for another attack. I tightened my grip around my dagger—

But my hand was empty.

I sat up, my eyes darting around me for a glimpse of the blade. It must have landed in the mud of the bank when I fell. It had to be here somewhere.

On hands and knees, I felt through the mud, but found nothing. I frantically peeked over my shoulder at the Ben Síde. She was raising herself up tall, blood flowing from her right wrist, her white eyes narrowed into furious slits. She bared her teeth again, her jaw cracking as it stretched further apart before she rushed towards me. I could do nothing but grab the only weapon at my disposal.

I whipped a handful of mud in her direction, hitting her square in the face. The move halted her for a split second as she shook the muck from her eyes, buying me a little more time. I searched the bank again, elbow deep in stinking pond sludge.

"Come on, where are you?" I muttered.

The mud squelched as I crawled forward, my breath

growing increasingly panicked as the weapon remained hidden. I blinked back tears, then glanced over my shoulder to see how much time I still had.

The answer was none.

The Ben Síde loomed over me, her good arm raised to strike. My luck had finally run out. I was completely and utterly defenseless, and there was nothing I could do but close my eyes, curl into a ball, and brace for the pain.

The Ben Síde's claws soared towards me, but just before they made contact with my skin, a whirling coil of leaves, branches, and pebbles blasted her off her feet and into the depths of the pond. Cautiously, I peeked out between the arms I'd thrown over my face. The witch stood on the shore with her spoon in hand, rallying what little strength and magic she had left. She collapsed to her knees, gasping for breath, and jabbed a gnarled finger at the Nether in the water.

"Finish it," she rasped.

Filled with renewed strength, I sent her a determined nod, pushed myself to standing, and turned to the creature in white sloshing back into the shallows. Her gown and hair had soaked up the water, weighing her down and slowing her movements.

Seeing my chance, I mustered my strength, bolted towards her, and tackled her around her midsection, pushing her deeper into the pond. Her nails clawed at my back, tearing more of my jacket and drawing blood, but I didn't care. As the Ben Síde thrashed, I held her facedown in the water, thinking of Soren, Wynn, Xavier, Willow, and Syrena, all of them people this creature and her master would see dead if they had their way. The thought of them consumed me, giving me strength and steady hands as I grit my teeth against the pain. I kept the Ben Síde submerged until she stopped moving and I was certain she never would again.

I released my hold on the woman in white, paddled back

into the shallows, and collapsed on the bank to watch her body float to the surface and bob lifelessly towards the center of the pond. Only then did something shining in a clump of nearby reeds catch my eye, its silver filigree hilt glittering as it reflected one of the sun's morning rays.

With a heavy sigh, I crawled through the mud to retrieve my dagger from its hiding place.

"Thanks for nothing," I mumbled to the blade as I shoved it into its sheath.

Feeble coughing reached my ears. I searched my surroundings until I found the witch lying in a heap on the ground. I sloshed back onto the shore and fell to my knees beside her.

"Hey, it's alright," I said, gently scooping her head into my lap.

The woman drooled blood from cracked lips, her lungs wheezing with every shallow breath.

"You stupid, reckless girl," she croaked before bursting into another miserable coughing fit. More blood flew from her lips.

I gently dabbed away the trickle of red with my sleeve. "You're welcome."

To my surprise, the witch smiled.

"I'll find you a healer," I said as brightly as I could. But one glance at the bloody pool around the woman revealed it was too late for her. Still, I faked a comforting smile. "You're going to be fine."

The witch shook her head and tried to laugh, but she choked and dribbled more blood onto my lap. Something unspoken passed between the two of us.

She also knew it was too late for her.

"Listen." She gestured with a trembling hand for me to lean closer. "Kill the Netherworld king, and the prince will be free." The witch choked again, her body jerking as she fought for air. She clasped my hand, and I stroked her hair as I shushed her, the same way I used to do for Wynn whenever he had a bad dream.

"It's alright," I said. "You're alright. You're not alone. I'm right here."

The witch continued to twitch and seize, but gratitude filled the depths of her eyes.

"You think the boy blind," the woman managed to gasp out, "but he sees. You think him mute, but he speaks. Listen... and follow."

The witch's body stilled, and with her final exhale, she breathed, "Follow him, Lina. Follow, and embrace the dark."

Her fingers feebly squeezed mine before going limp, and the forest swelled with birdsong once again.

# Chapter 14

Fuck.

Fuck. Fuck. *Fuck.*

Soren had barely touched his food. He'd been too busy mentally kicking himself for losing his head with Magnus. The lord hadn't looked at him the entire meal, and despite both his and Soren's fake smiles and cool, casual demeanors, he could tell the others in the room felt the tension too.

Soren glanced at Tristan Rourke to his left, who quickly averted his eyes to the teacup in front of him. His piercing gaze had been palpable all morning, weighing on Soren constantly. Would Tristan be the first to say something? Soren wasn't close with him, so he had no idea where his loyalties were. Would he paint Soren as a villain in front of the most powerful people in Astoria, or would Magnus be the one to land the fatal blow?

Fuck.

Soren readjusted in his seat and tried a bite of ham, but it tasted like ash in his mouth, and he subtly spat it into a napkin. He couldn't eat right now. His stomach roiled with anxiety and his mind raced through every possible worst-case scenario.

Magnus could tell everyone what Soren had done. He could say he'd lost his mind and was unfit to lead the territory and should be forcibly removed, or he could spread more rumors that Lina was a witch and needed to be killed so her enchantment over Soren would be broken. Gods help him if he did that, though. If Magnus tried *anything* with Lina, he'd be dead within the hour.

Mirielle said something that had the whole room laughing, but Soren didn't hear it. He was nervously toying with the signet ring on his index finger, scrambling to think of a way to salvage things.

He could go to Magnus and grovel. He'd say he was stressed and hadn't been thinking clearly, maybe offer him more money or land or titles as an apology. Would that be enough, though? Doubtful. Mercy wasn't a word in Lord Magnus's vocabulary.

Fuck, this was bad.

A loud bang echoed from the entrance of the castle, causing Soren and the rest of the Astorian nobles to look up in surprise. When Lina came tearing into the dining room, Soren shot to his feet. She was sopping wet and covered in mud, her clothes torn and stained red with blood.

"Lina!" Soren rushed over and took her face in his hands, scanning her from head to toe. "What happened? Are you hurt?"

Shit, she *was* hurt. There were claw marks down her back and right shoulder.

"I'll call for a healer." Soren slipped his hand into hers and moved to lead her out, but Lina's feet stayed put.

"My brother," she panted. "Where's my brother? Is he alright?"

"I heard Willow taking him upstairs. Why—"

"Aedan is alive."

Soren froze at the name, a chill stiffening his spine. The

anxiety in his stomach morphed into a thick vat of panic and dread.

"I thought you killed him."

Lina swallowed hard, her hazel eyes shimmering with the tears she was fighting. "I thought so too."

A memory rose in Soren's mind. An image of a dark place that had seeped all the magic out of his veins, its god lurking in the shadows and toying with them like puppets. A place that had made Soren more helpless than he'd been since he was a child. A place that had left him so shaken and lost he'd pushed away the woman he loved in the hopes of finding himself again. The only way he'd bounced back to normal the months following was because he'd told himself he would never, *could* never experience that dark place again because Aedan was gone.

But if he was alive...

The whispers of the nobles pulled Soren back to reality before he could finish the thought, and he glanced over his shoulder at the lords and ladies leaning in close. Their critical eyes were glued to Lina. Soren faced her again and gestured to the door.

"We should discuss this in private."

"She's not joining us?" Mirielle chirped. "But she's perfectly dressed for the occasion."

Laughter rippled through the room.

Soren glanced down at Lina. Her pulse raced, her body shook, and she stared at the nobles with wild eyes.

"Lina," Soren warned, "we have to behave."

But as soon as her gaze snapped to Soren's, something behind her eyes changed. In an instant, he knew she would do no such thing ever again.

... Oh, *fuck*.

Lina brushed past Soren. "You all have no idea what's coming! We'll see who's laughing when Nethers are running rampant and eating *you* lot for breakfast."

A few of the nobles gasped at her outburst, but Magnus was glaring at Lina with bloodthirsty eyes.

"Lina, *please*." Soren grabbed her nonbloodied arm and attempted to draw her back towards the doorway. "This isn't a good time."

Down the table, Mirielle sighed and raised her teacup to her lips. "See, this is exactly why pets are kept on leashes."

Lina wrenched her arm free from Soren's grasp, stomped forward, drew her dagger, and thrust it menacingly in Mirielle's direction. "For the last time, I am not his fucking pet!"

Oh fuck, oh fuck, oh fuck.

Mirielle set her cup down and raised a taunting brow. "What are you going to do with that? Cut some more cake?"

"No, I'm going to cut out your fucking tongue, you poisonous bitch!"

Lina lunged across the tabletop at Magnus's daughter, knocking over platters and glassware along the way. The nobles screamed in shock and horror, and Mirielle had to scramble backwards out of her chair to keep out of Lina's reach. Soren swooped in and wrapped his arms around Lina's waist to haul her off the table.

"Lina, stop it! You're hysterical!"

"I... am... not!" she grunted, still flailing to get at Mirielle.

Magnus threw himself in front of his daughter and snarled. "Your Majesty, subdue this woman!"

Lina kicked in the lord's direction. "Go fuck yourself, Tynan."

Magnus's eyes blazed. "How dare you speak to me like that!"

Lina spat at him.

Like a feral fucking animal.

Magnus rushed towards her, his hand outstretched and murder in his gaze, but Soren dragged Lina towards the door in the nick of time.

# CHAPTER 15



Only when we were out of earshot did Soren release me.

He planted me on my feet and spun me to face him. "Have you lost your fucking mind? What the hell is wrong with you?"

My chest heaved as I threw a shaky finger in the direction of the dining room.

"I just fought a Ben Síde that Aedan sent for my brother while you all were sitting around having fucking tea!"

"Lina, breathe. You're hysterical."

"I am *not* hysterical!" I screeched, wildly waving my dagger above my head to prove my point.

Dodging the blade, Soren caught my wrists and pinned them at my sides.

"Stop it!" he hissed. "You've already made enough of a scene."

At that, I went completely still.

Quiet, simmering rage seeped through my bones, and when I spoke next, my voice was as calm as the eye of a storm.

"A *scene*? That's what you're worried about? I tell you Aedan is alive, and you're worried about how I'm making you *look*?"

"How I look is important!" Soren glanced over his shoulder at the dining room and guided us further away. "I've explained this a thousand times, how many more do I have to say it? You have no idea what thin ice I'm on. Appeasing Magnus—"

"Keeps that precious crown on your head, I *know*," I spat.

Soren's eyes flashed. "May I remind you that precious crown also keeps a roof over *your* head."

"For how long?"

The bitter statement tumbled out as my soul finally cracked, and all the emotions I'd stuffed down the past three months flooded out at once. I wasn't thinking. I was a pot boiling over, rapidly overflowing with anger, fear, and hurt, unconcerned about who or what would burn in the process.

I rammed my dagger back in its sheath and frantically paced the hall. "How long do we pretend I fit here? How long do we act like we're not affected by what people think? How long do I be the well-mannered pet until you grow tired of me and throw me out like a used whore?"

Stunned, Soren stepped backwards. "Where the hell is this coming from? I never once said—"

"Exactly! You've never once said anything about what you plan to do with me!"

"Plan to *do* with you?" Soren shut his eyes and shook his head in confusion. "Lina, I have no idea what you're—"

"Who am I, Soren?"

I shouted the question even though I was terrified of the answer.

I wanted to keep living in a whimsical land of denial and make-believe. A land where we were happy and carefree and didn't have to worry about our love causing an uprising. A land where a king didn't require heirs to continue his royal bloodline, and it could just be me and him living a blissful existence together. A land where I didn't have to settle for the title of mistress to be with the man I loved. A land where we low-borns could be viewed as equals, and dance and love and celebrate alongside all castes without judgment.

But it was blissful ignorance, and part of me had always known that. As much as I wanted to keep pretending, the time had come. I'd started down this road after weeks of avoiding it, and there was no turning back now.

"Who am I, Soren?" I repeated. "Am I your future wife?"

Soren froze like an animal caught in a trap.

"Well?" I prodded.

The longer Soren stayed silent, the more my throat tightened, the more tears welled in my eyes, and the more my heart broke.

Soren finally averted his gaze.

"We'll talk about this later. You're hurt, and you're emotional. This is not a good time." His voice had adopted that gruff, no-nonsense tone. My Soren had disappeared, and the king stood in his place, calmly ordering one of his subjects into subservience.

"No, we're going to talk about this right now." My voice shook, but I forced myself to stand tall and strong. "Do you see yourself marrying me?"

Soren sighed and rubbed his face. "This conversation has gotten so off course—"

"It's a simple question, just answer yes or no."

"How did we go from talking about Aedan—"

"Do you see yourself marrying me?"

"Stop interrupting me!"

"Then answer the question!"

"See, this is exactly why I didn't want to talk about this—"

"Just answer the fucking question!"

"You're too fucking emotional right now—"

"*Do you see yourself marrying me?*"

"*No!*"

A word had never felt so much like a slap to the face.

Soren wouldn't look at me, so I stared at him until he had no choice. When his eyes finally lifted from the floor, I willed my voice steady in spite of the tears streaming down my face.

"Why?"

Soren took a quivering inhale and shook his head, guilt shadowing his features.

"Lina," he said softly, his voice cracking. He reached for me, but I recoiled.

"No, don't touch me. *Talk* to me. No more secrets. Tell me why you don't want to marry me."

Soren exhaled sharply and swiped a hand through his hair. "It's... it's not that I don't want to."

"Is it because of how it would look?" The words were acid on my tongue.

"*No,*" Soren said earnestly. "That's not it."

"Are you sure?" I chuckled bitterly. "I mean, a human queen? Gods, what would Lord Magnus think?"

"Fuck what Magnus thinks," Soren mumbled.

"Alright then." I crossed my arms and stepped in front of him so he couldn't avoid my gaze even if he tried. "Say he wasn't in the picture. Say you didn't have an image to save. Would you marry me then?"

Soren searched my eyes, his brows knitting. "Would *you* want to marry *me*?"

My stomach lurched.

It was the same question I'd asked myself countless times and never quite knew the answer.

Until now.

I loved Soren. I loved him so much it hurt. I didn't want to know a life *without* him.

But... no.

I *wouldn't* want to marry him.

I desperately wanted a lifetime with him, a thousand lifetimes with him, but not if they involved bearing heirs, biting my tongue, keeping my eyes downcast, and making myself small. I couldn't be that woman. I *wouldn't* be that woman. Not even for the man I loved.

As the realization dawned on me, I racked my brain for how exactly to express it. It barely made sense in my own mind. How could I voice it so it made sense in someone else's?

I opened my mouth to speak, and like a damn coward I did what I'd been doing for the past three months and avoided the problem.

"I asked you first," I countered.

Soren blew out a shaky breath, his eyes darting around the hall like he was looking for an escape. "I would *want* to..."

"But you wouldn't," I finished for him.

The guilt in Soren's silence was so tangible I could taste it. "Why?"

Soren blinked back his tears, so I cried them for the both of us.

"Please, Soren," I pressed. "Just tell me why. You owe me that much."

He reached for me again, trying to slip his arms around my waist and pull me close like he had so many times before, but I pushed him away.

"I said don't touch me! Talk to me!"

I wanted him to say something, *anything*, offer me any kind of explanation, but he kept his jaw stubbornly clenched. After the agonizing silence became too much and my heart couldn't crack any further without killing me, I straightened my shoulders, wiped my nose on the back of my sleeve, and cleared my throat.

"Well, since communicating with me is so hard, I'll be the

one to do this for us." Weakly, I raised my hands in defeat. "I'm done."

Soren's gaze jerked up from the floor, something like terror coloring his eyes. "Lina, please—"

"I'm *done*, Soren." My words were barely audible. If I spoke any louder, I'd start crying again, and if that happened, I wouldn't be able to resist falling into Soren's arms for comfort. "I can't do this anymore. *We* can't do this anymore. We can't keep pretending we get our happy ending."

Soren released a puff of air like some unseen foe had just landed a punch to his stomach.

I swallowed the sob threatening to choke out of me, pinched my lips together, and turned towards the grand staircase.

"Lina?" Behind me, Soren's voice trembled, but I refused to look back at him. I kept my eyes fixed on the dark wood planks of the floor and focused on placing one foot in front of the other.

When I arrived at the bottom of the staircase, Soren's footsteps pounded up behind me.

"Lina," he repeated, more firm this time.

Still I refused to look at him. I stomped up the stairs, Soren matching my stride as he followed alongside me.

"Lina, look at me." He slid his hand to my waist once more, but I shrugged him off.

My breathing was rapid. Soon it would be impossible to breathe and the tears would be uncontrollable, so I hurried up the rest of the stairs, determined to put space between me and Soren so he wouldn't see. He sprinted after me as I turned down the hallway to our bedroom.

"Damn it, Lina, just look at me!"

But I couldn't do that.

I'd lose my nerve if he glanced up at me with that charming

look that always got him exactly what he wanted, or if he pulled me close and whispered sweet words in my ear, or if I looked at him a little too long and convinced myself we should pretend just a little longer.

We'd come to the bedroom door, and Soren darted in front of it before I could reach for the handle, intercepting my attention at last.

"Please," he choked out. "I don't want to lose you yet."

I had to bite my cheek to keep the words from escaping: *You already have.*

I ducked beneath Soren's arm, opened the door, and slammed it shut behind me. When the lock clicked, he immediately slammed his knuckles to the wood.

"No, don't do this. Don't shut me out this time."

I settled my back against the door and covered my mouth with my hand so Soren wouldn't hear me as I finally let go. Hot, salty tears flooded out as sobs racked my body, making me quake and shudder until my teeth chattered.

"Lina, open the door." Soren continued to pound his fist against the thick mahogany. "*Please.*"

He tried the handle.

"I love you. I love you with all my heart. Please, I want more time with you. I *need* more time."

My hand dropped from my mouth. I didn't care if Soren heard me anymore. I let out a wail and sank to the ground.

The handle shook again, this time so hard it rattled the door. "Lina, open the door."

He tried it a third time, the wood vibrating so much that the back of my head knocked against it.

"Lina, this is childish! Open the door," Soren barked, his panic transforming into anger.

Another jolt, another strangled sob.

"Dammit, Lina, just open this fucking door!"

At his furious demand, the slumbering embers in the hearth roared to life. I screamed in surprise and instinctively threw my arms up to protect my head. Out in the hall, Soren gasped, and the fire died as quickly as it had surged.

"Shit! Lina, I'm so sorry! Are you alright?"

I didn't get up. I slumped over onto my side, my tears soaking the rug beneath me, and miserably watched Soren's feet dart back and forth through the crack under the door. When I didn't respond, he dropped to his knees.

"I'm sorry," he repeated, his voice trembling. "I didn't mean to do that. Please just open the door, let me see you're alright."

I sniffled and drew my legs to my chest, taking care not to jostle my mangled arm. The wounds the Ben Síde had inflicted on my back and shoulder throbbed, but it was nothing compared to the pain in my heart.

"I love you, Lina. I'd do anything for you, anything at all. *Please.*"

My eyes fluttered shut.

"Then let me go, Soren," I whispered. "Just let me go."

# Chapter 16

I CRIED UNTIL I HAD NO TEARS LEFT.

Soren had eventually retreated to his study. Even from the bedroom, I could hear him tearing it apart and yelling curses until his voice was hoarse. Only when the castle fell silent did I push myself upright.

I glanced at the window. The sun was still high in the sky, but it dipped towards the western horizon.

My body was stiff, and everything ached, but I ignored the pain, hauled myself to my feet, and headed to the washroom, where I stripped off my soiled clothes and dabbed a wet rag to the wounds on my shoulder and back. Miraculously, they weren't so deep I needed stitches or a healer, but I wouldn't be surprised if they left scars.

I discovered strips of cloth in a cupboard and fashioned makeshift bandages, then returned to the bedroom to change into clean trousers, a lace-up shirt, and a jacket. Then I went to Soren's armoire, dug around until I found the pack he used for hunting, tossed it onto the bed, and loaded it up. I packed only the essentials, plus a few shirts of Soren's I'd fallen in love with and two of my favorite dresses. I had no doubt when I got to where I was going, I would be showered with countless more.

With the pack slung over my good shoulder, I cautiously unlocked the bedroom door and peeked out, looking both ways before slipping into the hall. I stealthily padded down the dark wood walkway, avoiding the creaky planks, and held my breath as I passed Soren's closed study.

*Look at that,* I thought bitterly, *he finally learned how to shut a door.*

I sneaked away, picking up my pace as soon as I was out of heightened Fae earshot. When I got to Wynn's room, I gave a quick a knock and darted inside.

"Lina!" Willow leapt from her armchair by the window and rushed over to me, Wynn trailing behind her. Her face was flushed and her eyes red-rimmed.

"What happened?" the Sprite demanded, taking my hands in hers. "Are you alright? Wynn rushed in crying, but all he could do was write a few words and make some drawings. I couldn't piece it together. I was so scared!"

Wynn ran over, papers in hand, and flung himself into my side to latch his arms around me in a ferocious hug. I caught a glimpse of the words *Lina woods* and *bad lady* on the pages, as well as a crude sketch of a woman with sharp teeth.

"I'm fine." I gave my brother a squeeze and kiss. "I'll explain later."

Willow noticed the pack on my shoulder for the first time, and her brow creased in confusion. "Where are you going?"

The tears were threatening to start all over again, so I distracted myself by smoothing Wynn's curls. "We're going to Lerian."

"Oh." Willow's head tilted. "I hadn't heard anything about Soren traveling to Lerian."

I swallowed hard. "He's not. It's just me and Wynn."

Willow glanced between the two of us. "I don't understand."

Wynn tightened his embrace. I smiled at his silent encouragement and sniffled, blinking rapidly to clear my watery vision.

"Soren and I are through. It's been brewing for a while now, but neither of us have wanted to face it. So Wynn and I will go live in Lerian with Syrena. I have a long-standing invitation there, and she says I'm welcome anytime."

I could only peek up at Willow for a second before needing to look away. Heartbroken tears welled in her own eyes, and her plump bottom lip trembled.

"Maybe it'll be a good thing," I continued, trying to sound cheery. "Maybe the salty breeze is exactly what Wynn needs. He's never seen the ocean before." I playfully ruffled my brother's curls. "You'd like that, wouldn't you, Wynn? You'd like to see the ocean?"

Wynn shrugged, then wistfully scanned his room. My heart sank at his expression. I'd forgotten this place was his home too, and me uprooting him was taking him away from the one bit of normalcy he had to cling to.

"What about me?"

I turned back to Willow. She wrung her hands, not even attempting to wipe away the tears that streamed down her cheeks and soaked the lacy bodice of her dress.

"You were just going to leave without me?" Despite the tears, Willow's voice was clear, strong, and utterly indignant.

"I couldn't ask you to leave Astoria, Willow. Your family's here."

"Well, you're my family now too, Lina Calder!" Willow snapped. "You *and* Wynn. And I think... I think..." She popped her fists onto her hips and stuck her nose in the air. "Well, I think it is just *damn* rude you would leave me behind."

We blinked at each other.

Slowly, my lips cracked a smile. "Willow, you just swore."

The Sprite turned cherry red. "I did. That's how strongly I feel about it."

I sighed and glanced down at Wynn again. He nodded eagerly.

"Willow... would you want to come with us?"

The Sprite airily tossed her tresses over her shoulder. "I'll think about it."

I managed a chuckle, and Willow grinned and yanked me into a warm hug.

"Of course I'll come with you. Family doesn't abandon each other when they're needed most."

Willow's palm rubbed comforting circles along my back, and I buried my face in the frilly shoulder of her dress to hide my emotion.

"You don't have to face everything alone," she whispered in my ear. "I'm here for you."

I gave my friend a grateful squeeze. "Thank you."

We pulled away, and Willow wiped my tears with her thumbs, offering me a bright smile that poured sunshine into my soul. "I'm going to pack the cutest outfit for the beach."

WHILE WILLOW GATHERED her things from her bedroom, I bustled around Wynn's, stuffing a bag with his belongings. He didn't need much, just a few clothes, some textbooks to continue his studies, and a couple of notepads to draw in. When I was finished, I took my brother's hand and headed towards the door, but he dug in his heels and tugged on my arm. I turned around.

"What is it? What's wrong?"

Wynn pointed to the bed.

Nestled between the pillows was a plush toy wolf that Soren had given him as a present the first time my brother turned sentient. I knew Willow put him to bed with it every night, but I had no idea it meant so much to him.

That *Soren* meant so much to him.

The ache in my heart intensified, but I forced a cheery smile on my face and nodded. "Alright, you can bring that too."

Wynn bounded over to the bed and grabbed the wolf, clutching it tight to his chest as he returned and followed me into the hall.

We met Willow at the bottom of the staircase and followed her out the servants' passages towards the stables. Once there, I pulled my horse from its stall and saddled it up.

"Will we all fit?" Willow asked, anxiously analyzing the three of our bodies and the packs.

"Huh. Good point." I chewed the inside of my cheek, scanning my horse's silhouette. It was a powerful gelding, but if the three of us climbed on with our bags, we'd probably break the poor thing's back.

The rebellious fire that lived inside me flickered to life, inspiring me to set my jaw, stride over to the first stall, and lead Soren's massive steed out to the hitching post.

Willow gasped. "What are you doing? That's the king's horse!"

"We'll call it a going away present," I muttered, tossing a saddle pad over the beast's broad shoulders. "You can use mine and Wynn and I will ride this one."

"Going somewhere?"

Willow and I spun at the voice.

Xavier came trotting into the stables on his chestnut mare, his usual smile bent into a frown and his brows knitting together as he surveyed us.

"What's going on?" he asked, swinging one leg over the

saddle and gracefully dropping to the ground. He stalked over, his gaze trained on our full packs. It was strange to see him so serious, and it made me instinctively step backwards.

"We... uh..." Willow gulped and glanced at me, then back to Xavier.

"Soren and I are done." I wrapped my arm around Wynn and held him close. "My brother and I are going to Lerian to live with Syrena."

Xavier blinked and shook his head, the two rings through the top of his ear tinkling as he did. "Wait, what? What happened?"

I sighed and raised my gaze to the ceiling of the stable, mostly so that Xavier wouldn't see the tears that were beginning to form in my eyes again. "It's too long of a story to get into."

"But..." Xavier looked around helplessly, his face no longer solemn but worried and slightly frantic. "You two can fix things, can't you? You always fix things!"

My tears were on the cusp of falling again, but thankfully Willow came to my aid.

"Xavier." She reached out and gently touched his arm. "It's done."

With eyes that resembled those of a wounded puppy, Xavier slumped against a nearby stall and let out a heavy exhale as he ran a hand through his tousled curls. "Well, shit."

I nodded sadly, and we all stood in somber silence until Xavier broke it.

"Wait a minute." He popped upright again and narrowed his eyes at me. "You were just going to leave without saying goodbye?"

"That's what I said!" Willow huffed.

I opened my mouth to protest, but Xavier cut me off.

"You're a bad friend, Lina Calder!" His voice was sharp, but it dripped with hurt.

Willow smacked his shoulder. "Don't say that! She's going through a hard time!"

"So?"

"So you try ending things with the love of your life, then stick around to—"

"He's right, Willow."

The two of them peeked at me, and I shrugged. "I'm sorry, Xavier. I should have said goodbye. I just... I felt like I needed to get out of here as fast as I could. If I see him, I know he'll convince me to stay. And I can't let that happen. Not this time. He and I can't keep fooling ourselves."

Xavier stared at me, his eyes roving back and forth across my face, studying my pained expression. Finally he sighed, and his head bowed. "I understand. I don't like it, but I understand." His attention drifted to our bags. "So Lerian, huh?"

"Yes. I think it'll be good for us. Wynn's never seen the ocean before."

Xavier sniffed and ruffled Wynn's hair. "That'll be fun, Wynnie. You'll love it, I promise."

Wynn's response was giving Xavier's leg a solid hug, gouging the wound in my heart even deeper.

"Maybe you can come visit," Willow offered, blinking up at Xavier with glossy eyes.

"Not sure the queen would approve of my presence there," Xavier mumbled, absentmindedly toying with one of Wynn's ringlets.

"All the more reason to come," I teased, nudging him with my elbow.

That notorious grin finally made an appearance, and a chuckle rumbled from Xavier's chest. "You know me well, Calder."

His gaze drifted to the packs on the floor of the stable a third time. "You ladies have everything you need?"

"Yep." Willow began to count on her fingers. "Clothes, books for Wynn, Lina has her dagger—"

"Food?" Xavier asked, raising an eyebrow. "It's over a day's ride to Lerian."

"Oh." Willow nibbled her bottom lip. "Uh..."

"And the sun will be setting soon. Do you have flint to start a fire?"

Willow and I exchanged glances.

"How about bedrolls to sleep on? Or a map in case you get lost?"

Willow grimaced while I sheepishly kicked at a mound of hay on the cobblestones at our feet.

Xavier sighed and rolled his eyes. "Gods. Alright, sit tight. I'll be right back."

He jogged off towards the castle, leaving us to finish saddling Soren's steed and loading the horses with what we did remember to pack.

When Xavier returned a half hour later, he looked like a pack mule himself. He had a rucksack strapped to his back, a sack of food from the pantry in one arm, a bundle of bedrolls in the other, and a map clamped in his teeth. Grunting with exertion, he shuffled over and dumped the load beside our horses.

"This seems like a lot for the three of us," I mused, counting the bedrolls. There was one, two, three, and—

"Four of us." Xavier spat out the map and shimmied off his knapsack, throwing it over his mare's back and strapping it to the saddle. "I'm coming with you. Soren would kill me if he found out I let you travel alone. There are still Nethers prowling around out there, you know."

I shivered at the thought of the Ben Síde I'd faced a few hours prior. I hadn't even considered there might be more. I hadn't been thinking about anything except leaving as fast as I possibly could.

Maybe what Soren had said earlier held a grain of truth. Maybe I was a *little* bit hysterical.

Maybe.

"Soren was still holed up in his study brooding, so I left a note on the door telling him where we were going." Xavier finished fixing the bedrolls to the horses and turned to me, shaking his hair out of his face. At my disapproving frown, he added, "I know you wanted to make a statement and leave in a big dramatic huff, but I have responsibilities here. I needed to explain so he doesn't think I just up and defected."

I hesitated a few seconds, but eventually gave him a curt nod. Xavier offered me a melancholy half-smile back and jerked his chin to the horses.

"Come on, then. Lerian awaits."

# Chapter 17



Lerian was exactly how I remembered it.

Sunny and warm with a refreshing ocean breeze, its quaint villages along the rocky coastline a constant hub of activity.

Vendors and merchants at the outdoor bazaars shouted out the day's deals and offered fresh samples to passersby while artists displayed their work in town squares. Performers danced or played stringed instruments on street corners for spare coins while fishermen hauled their catches through the sandstone streets, the scent of fish mixing with the exotic perfume of spices and flowers wafting up from the marketplace. No matter where we walked, the air was filled with the shouts of men down on the docks as they loaded cargo in and out of the trade ships harbored there. Everything was colorful and loud and welcoming, but even though Xavier, Willow, and Wynn happily tried every sample, watched each musician, and admired all the art they laid their eyes on, I couldn't share the same cheer.

I still remembered how this place had treated Hale.

I still remembered the way they'd spat at him in the street, the way they'd cursed him, hid their children from sight, and boarded up their doors and windows after one glance at the brand on his neck. Everything seemed happy and carefree now, but I could still see the hatred spewed towards him then.

Maybe I was just grumpy from not sleeping the night before.

We'd ridden away from Astoria until darkness fell, then camped in a small meadow for the evening. Willow and Wynn had fallen asleep right away, and after I'd told him I'd take first watch, Xavier wasn't far behind. I was thankful for the time alone. No one had been awake to hear me crying into the night.

As we neared the grand palace perched on the cliffs overlooking the sea, the hustle and bustle of the city died down, making way for increasing elegance. Aromatic flowering vines decorated the lavish sandstone villas that lined the way to the castle, their bright blossoms and intoxicating scents creating the illusion of passing into a luscious garden of the gods. Wynn's mouth was agape the entire way.

When we finally arrived at the entrance of the palace, we were stopped in the teal and gold mosaic archway in the outer wall by a palace guard and told to dismount our horses and state our business. I gave him my name and said I was friends with the queen, and we were ordered to wait while he checked with his superiors. Twenty minutes later the guard returned, and he brought with him a man I recognized as the new captain of the guard.

When I stayed in Lerian after we returned from the Netherworld, Syrena and Kaspar had begun the process of finding a replacement for Hale. When I left on Samhain Eve, a head of security hadn't been decided on yet, but recently I'd received a letter from Syrena where she stated they'd finally secured someone for the position: Commander Roric Pax, who had served the royal family as captain of the guard before Hale and had been in charge of one of Lerian's battalions that

Syrena had brought to Merimaya in response to Erith's siege last year.

Seeing Roric now, I vaguely recognized him from that day. I'd only seen him in passing, but a man like him was hard to forget. With skin bronzed from countless hours under the sun and a hulking body whittled by centuries of training, Roric commanded attention. His silky black waves were tied back in a bun at the nape of his neck, and the gold hoops through his eyebrow and nose glittered as they caught the light of the afternoon sun. With two long, curved swords strapped across his back and tattoos covering one arm from knuckle to neck, he was as handsome as he was intimidating. Even the finest soldiers would think twice before picking a fight with the Fae warrior.

"Commander Roric," I said when he came to a stop in front of us. "I'm Lina Calder. We crossed paths last year when Syrena brought your battalion to Merimaya."

Roric nodded, his olive green eyes roving over our horses and packs. "Of course. You're Soren of Astoria's... human."

*Well, at least he didn't say his whore.*

"Yes." I gestured to Willow and Xavier. "These are my friends, Xavier and Willow."

Roric dipped his head to Xavier. "Sir."

Xavier curtly returned the greeting.

The commander then faced Willow and gave her a small smile before bowing politely. "My lady."

Willow wheezed a laugh, her face and neck flushing. "Oh! No, not a lady. Just normal. Normal lady. Sprite lady, actually. Wood Sprite. My family likes plum trees."

I nudged Willow with my foot. She cleared her throat to compose herself. "People call me Willow."

Roric's mouth twitched in an attempt to keep his face stern. "Noted."

"And this is my brother Wynnric." I rubbed my brother's back as he leaned into my side, tightly clasping his plush wolf to his chest as he stared up at Roric's towering form with round eyes. "We stayed here last summer."

Roric tucked a loose strand of hair behind his pointed ear and knelt down so the two were face-to-face. "Welcome back, Mister Calder. I like your wolf. Does he have a name?"

Wynn looked Roric up and down with a scrutinizing gaze, then peeked at me.

"He doesn't talk," I explained.

"That's alright." Roric offered Wynn a warm smile. "Most people talk too much, and about nothing important."

Wynn nodded, prompting Roric to chuckle dryly and return to standing.

"What brings you to Lerian, Miss Calder?" he asked cooly, clasping his massive hands in front of him.

"I have a long-standing invitation from the queen."

"Right." Roric nodded thoughtfully, then glanced over his shoulder as if someone was watching him. He then jerked his head to the side, motioning for us to follow.

Roric led us a few paces from the archway and sighed, scratching at his short beard as he chose his words carefully. "I'm afraid I can't allow you entry."

My brow furrowed. "Why not? The queen—"

"Isn't the only one I take orders from."

It took me a few seconds, but the realization finally dawned on me, and my hands subconsciously balled into fists at my side. "Kaspar told you not to let me in."

Roric scrunched his nose. A silent *yes*.

"May I ask why?"

"He gave the impression you were a danger to him."

"A *danger* to him? That's ridiculous!" I flung my hand

towards the palace. "I lived here peacefully for months this past summer!"

"But you did threaten his life once before, did you not? Last year on Imbolc?"

I promptly shut my mouth.

"Exactly." The commander shrugged helplessly. "I'm sorry. You're welcome to submit a formal request for the order to be lifted, but until then—"

"Lina!"

Relief flooded through me at that voice. It was beautiful and powerful, much like the woman it belonged to.

It was hard to look at Syrena straight on as she rushed out of the archway. Her radiance was blinding, in part due to her gorgeous features, but mainly because the sun caught the thousands of sparkling jewels sewn into her high-neck gown and matching cape. The outfit probably weighed more than Wynn, which made Syrena's fluidity and grace all the more impressive.

Syrena blew past her captain of the guard and tackled me in a hug.

"What the hell are you doing here?" she squealed, bouncing up and down excitedly. The diamonds in her cape clacked together with the movement. "Oh, what a wonderful surprise!"

The queen pulled away and looked down at Wynn, gasping and clapping her hands to her mouth. "Wynn! Look at you! I've never seen you awake before!"

Wynn blushed and buried his face in his wolf's fur.

"Syrena, this is Willow." I brought my friend forward, and the Sprite immediately dropped into a low curtsy.

"Your Majesty, it's an absolute honor."

Syrena laughed and hauled Willow upright, hugging her just as ferociously as she had me. "There's no need for formalities. Lina's told me all about you in her letters. Welcome to Lerian."

When Syrena pulled away, her bright green gaze flicked to another's.

Xavier winked. "Miss me, Princess?"

"Ugh," was all Syrena said, rolling her eyes. When she looked back at me, she took my hands in hers.

"Please, come inside. I'll have your rooms made up right away, and I'll tell the kitchen to whip you up something to eat. You must be starving after that journey."

The queen turned to lead us back towards the archway, but Roric stepped in front of her.

"I'm sorry, Your Majesty, but I have strict orders not to allow Miss Calder on the premises."

"What? Who told you to..." The light of realization illuminated Syrena's eyes, and her face fell into a scowl. "My brother?"

Roric dipped his head in confirmation.

Syrena sighed and glanced at me, anger rippling from her like heat radiating off the sand. "I give my brother one responsibility, *one*, and he still manages to fuck it up."

She turned back to Roric and pursed her lips. "I'm overruling the king's order. Kaspar gets a say on everything else that comes in and out of the palace, *except* Lina Calder. Are we clear?"

That tiny smile toyed at Roric's lips once more. "Crystal clear, Your Majesty." He warily glanced over his shoulder again, like Kaspar was a ghost haunting his every step. "But if anyone asks, I put up a much larger fight."

A courteous bow, and the commander retreated behind the palace walls.

Xavier watched him go, then turned back to us and let out a long whistle. "What a delicious hunk of Fae, huh?"

Syrena made a noise of disgust and crossed her arms, sending her stack of gold-and-emerald bracelets crashing together. "Please tell me you'll be leaving as soon as your horse is watered and rested."

Xavier's eyes sparked with mischief. "Actually, I think I might stick around for a while. I've had this nasty cold, you see. I think the salty sea breeze might be good for it." He brought a fist to his mouth, gave a pathetic and very fake cough, then grinned wickedly. "Good to see you, Your Highness."

"It's Majesty!" Syrena cried, stomping her foot.

But already sauntering towards the stables with our horses in tow, Xavier didn't hear her.

"You *had* to bring him," Syrena grumbled, glaring at Xavier's back as he disappeared from view.

"Sorry. It wasn't really planned."

"How long will you be staying, by the way?" Syrena's face lit up, and she clapped her hands. "Oo! Will we have enough time to throw a party in your honor?"

The smile disappeared from my face, my shoulders slumping as my gaze slipped to the ground. "Yes... there'll definitely be enough time."

Sensing the looming conversation, Willow slipped her hand into my brother's. "Wynn, how about we head down to the beach? I'll teach you how to make a sand castle."

I managed to muster a grateful smile, and the Sprite nodded knowingly before guiding my brother towards the tiled steps leading down the cliffs to the crashing waves below. When they'd gone, Syrena's head whipped back to me, her thick, defined brows drawing together with concern.

"What's wrong?" she demanded.

Familiar stinging started behind my eyes, and my throat tightened, making it hard to speak. "I ended things with Soren."

Syrena blinked.

Then blinked again.

Finally, she whispered, "Are you alright?"

The tears welling in my eyes spoke for me, but I still forced myself to admit the truth. "Not really, no."

Syrena clicked her tongue and opened her arms to wrap me in a comforting embrace, but I flung a hand up, halting her. Her head tilted in confusion.

"This will be the last time I cry over him," I stated firmly.

Syrena studied me, taking in my trembling lip and hardened gaze. Understanding washed over her face, and she nodded solemnly. I nodded back, then dropped my hand to my side as Syrena closed the distance between us, giving me strength as I melted into a hysterical wreck on her jewel-encrusted shoulder.

BY THE TIME I'd finished crying, it was nearly dark.

I'd told Syrena about everything, from the fight with Soren and doubt sowed by Mirielle, to my desire to remain childless. I even told her about the witch's revelation that Aedan wasn't dead, information that caused all the blood to drain from her face, but she never interrupted me. She let me vent, nodding and listening until I asked for her input, to which she usually responded with something belittling about Soren followed by fierce encouragement or validation of my feelings. And just as I'd thought she would, she'd insisted Wynn and I were welcome in her home for as long as we wanted.

When Willow and Wynn, sun-kissed and sandy from the beach, found us, Syrena invited us to dine with her. I was too emotionally drained to be around other people for one second longer, so I left Willow in charge of my brother and retreated to my old room, which Syrena had asked a servant to prepare while we'd been talking. I was told my belongings were already there along with an array of the finest Lerian fashions, all my size and ready to be worn. Gods bless Syrena. Nothing sounded better than changing into pajamas made from Lerian silk and curling up in bed to sleep off the events of the past few days.

I made my way down the familiar hallway and shuffled up to my bedroom door. I reached for the handle, but stopped abruptly. My eyes drifted to the crack between the ground and the door, barely even noticeable, too small for even a mouse to squeeze through.

Only big enough for a wisp of black mist.

A pang of loss cut through my already aching heart. I glanced at the door further down the hall, halfway between mine and Syrena's. The door to that room had remained shut since the day Hale closed it, never to return. When I stayed in Lerian before, I'd frequently found myself standing in front of that door, imagining he was on the other side, and I would foolishly tell myself if I just had the courage to open it, I'd see him again. I'd never turned the handle, though. I hadn't felt strong enough to face what was inside. Now, though...

I hesitated for a moment, then shook my head and entered my own room.

Not tonight.

I could only handle the grief of one loss tonight, not two.

# CHAPTER 18



THE DAYS TURNED INTO A WEEK.

A week of resting on the beach, reading to the symphony of gulls and waves, and playing in the sand with my brother. Wynn smiled more in seven days than he had the entirety of our time in Astoria, which helped ease the ache in my heart ever so slightly. But despite that, and despite Syrena and Willow's constant attempts to cheer me up, I couldn't stop thoughts of Soren from weighing on me. When it wasn't Soren, something in the palace would remind me of Hale. My heart felt a little like a battlefield; battered, bloodied, and haunted by the emptiness left behind by those it had lost.

"Ilora's coming."

I blinked and turned away from where I'd been staring off into the distance for gods know how long.

"Huh?"

"Ilora's coming," Syrena repeated. "She's coming down from Merimaya to attend your party."

Lounging on the sand beside me, the queen angled her face towards the sun and moaned softly at its warmth. With all our time spent outside at the beach over the past few days, her olive skin had deepened to a gorgeous bronze, making her sea green eyes pop even more than they already had. My fair skin, on the other hand, had just burned and freckled even more.

"Oh, fun." I smiled and returned my attention to the orb of liquid gold dipping towards the horizon. "It'll be good to see her."

Apparently, Syrena hadn't been joking about throwing a party in my honor. A few days ago she'd informed me of her plans, insisting a Welcome Back to Lerian party with all the territory's most eligible bachelors was all I needed to get my mind off Soren. She'd hired the best musicians, ordered new outfits for the both of us, and made sure there would be plenty of booze to go around. I was truly dreading it, but then I'd remembered what Meer had told me once.

*The Fae can and will find any excuse to hold a ball.*

So I let Syrena have her fun.

"Maybe all three of us can find a special someone." Syrena waggled her eyebrows suggestively.

I chuckled grimly. "I'll leave the search to you and Ilora. My heart is taking some much needed time off."

"Suit yourself," Syrena said with a shrug.

Neither of us mentioned the other reason the queen of Merimaya was coming.

We needed to tell her about Aedan and discuss the possibility of his threat to the realm.

"Are you alright?" Syrena asked.

Not realizing I'd stared off into space again, I plastered a smile on my face before nodding brightly.

Syrena tossed sand in my direction. "Liar."

I sighed and toyed with one of the gold tassels on the hem of my top. "It's just... do you think I made the right decision?"

"With that outfit?" Syrena raised an eyebrow. "I'll be honest, I've seen you look better."

I playfully shoved a pile of sand back at her. "You know that's not what I'm talking about. Do you think..." I averted my gaze and swallowed the lump that immediately appeared in my throat as I prepared to say the name that had been haunting every waking thought for the past week. "Do you think I did the right thing leaving Soren?"

Syrena's lighthearted expression waned, and she rolled over onto her side, propping a fist under her head. "Do *you* think you did the right thing?"

I frowned and faced the ocean again. "I don't know." The familiar ache in my heart grew heavier as I replayed my last moments with Soren. "I love him. I *do*. I didn't even think it was possible to love someone so much. I didn't want to leave him, and..." I fidgeted uncomfortably. "I'll admit, I was a *tad* hysterical and could have handled things better. But I also know I couldn't be his wife. Not with what it would require of me." I sighed and hugged my knees to my chest. "Maybe it's selfish, but I keep expecting him to show up. I still want him to fight for me. I want him to run after me and tell me he'd do anything for me, that he *is* willing to marry me and he'd go to the edge of the world for us if he had to. Even though it wouldn't change anything, I still want it."

I peeked at Syrena, who was nodding thoughtfully as she processed my words.

"Maybe I acted too rashly," I muttered. "I didn't even give him a chance to speak at the end. I just ran off."

At that, Syrena sat upright and threw a finger in my face. "Don't make excuses for him. Might I remind you Xavier left a note telling him you were coming here. He knows exactly where you are, and *could* fight for you if he really wanted to." The queen crossed her arms and haughtily lifted her nose in the air. "He could come here and make some grand gesture or beg for your forgiveness on his proud little knees. At the very least he could send a fucking letter, but no! He's not speaking to you. *Again*. So on top of him refusing to admit why he doesn't see a future with you, he's pulling the same shit he did last year. You deserve better."

I looked away and nodded sadly. "Maybe you're right."

"I *am* right." Syrena scooted closer and looped her arm through mine. "I know it's hard right now, but it'll get better. I promise you're better off without him. You're a Lerian girl now! We have cuter clothes, better tans, and absolutely no time for drama."

Her words pulled a small chuckle out of me at the same time Xavier passed by on his way to the ocean. He jerked his head in our direction.

"Evening, ladies."

"Go sit on a cactus," Syrena spat.

"Pull it out of your ass and hand it over," Xavier quipped right back.

Syrena tried to think of a comeback, but settled on sticking out her tongue at him instead. Xavier scoffed and breezed past us.

"Very mature, Your Highness."

Syrena yowled like a wildcat and chucked a seashell at Xavier's head. He narrowly dodged it.

"Stop calling me that!" Syrena snarled. "I'm a queen now, dammit! You're supposed to call me Your Majesty!"

"And I *will* when you stop acting like a bratty little princess." Xavier went to continue on his way, but stopped and looked back in Syrena's direction. "Oh, and in case you were confused. Stuff like this?" He mimicked the way she'd stuck out her tongue. "Is *exactly* what I'm talking about."

Syrena settled back on the blanket, simmering like a tea kettle about to scream.

"Now if you'll excuse me, I'm going for a swim." Xavier yanked off his tunic and tossed it at Syrena's bare feet. "Enjoy staring at me while I walk away."

"I would enjoy staring at you more if you were sitting on a cactus!" she shouted at his retreating back.

"So you admit you enjoy staring at me?"

Syrena stood up to chuck her next seashell, and Xavier giggled like a giddy schoolboy as he ducked out of the projectile's path and trotted off towards the sea.

"That man is the most infuriating creature I've ever had the misfortune of knowing," Syrena grumbled as she sat again, but her eyes stayed glued on Xavier's form as he waded into the waves. "Why is he even here? I thought Soren would have called his loyal dog home by now."

Her lips were pinched in an annoyed pout, but her gaze was fixed on Xavier's toned arms as he slicked water through his hair. I smirked.

"You know, a lot of people find Xavier quite charming."

"Those people must be mentally unwell."

I raised an eyebrow. Syrena quickly looked away and tossed her ponytail, pretending she wasn't still keeping one eye on the lithe figure in the shallows.

"You have to admit," I mused, casually tracing designs in the sand beside me, "if you had a special someone like Xavier by your side, there would never be a dull moment."

"I like dull," Syrena replied with the speed of a striking viper.

I barked a laugh and pointedly stared at Syrena's emerald-adorned, midriff-baring top. It was the epitome of flashy Lerian fashion.

She rolled her eyes. "Fine, let me rephrase. I *need* dull." Her shoulders slumped, and her fire dissipated. "I'm basically running this place on my own. I have an army to worry about, an armada, trade and commerce, an entire territory of people to rule... The last thing I need is a man constantly joking around and teasing me and making me forget all the stressful things that control my life."

I nibbled my bottom lip as I considered her words, then shrugged. "It actually sounds like that could be exactly what you need."

Syrena shut her mouth, her brow crinkling as she weighed my words, but she finally shook her head and flipped onto her stomach to sun her back. It was an unspoken signal that the conversation was over.

I moved onto my front as well and changed the subject. "Kaspar isn't helping you much?"

Syrena huffed a laugh, puffing a cloud of sand off the blanket. "If by helping you mean stumbling through his days in a drunken stupor and busying his nights with sticking his cock in anything he can, then yes, he's a huge help."

I rested my chin on the back of my hands as I watched my friend. She expertly kept her cool and unaffected mask intact, but I knew better. I knew the toll that watching a sibling self-destruct took on a person all too well. Jaras had been helpful and happy once, but after our parents died, his path had looked disturbingly similar to that of Kaspar's.

I moved closer to Syrena.

"What happened?" I asked gently. "When you two were crowned last summer, he was still pulling his weight."

Syrena was quiet for a few seconds, staring intently down at the sand as if it would speak for her. Finally, her lips parted, and while her mask stayed put, the emotion was evident in her choked voice. "Aside from everyone we ever loved dying around us... you know very well how people like to talk. It's nothing new. Our line has been highly scrutinized and talked about since I can remember. 'Do they have magic?' 'Don't they?' 'If they don't, then they aren't fit to lead'... that sort of thing." She sniffed bitterly and gestured to her copious amount of jewels. "So we overcompensated over the years, tried to distract people from learning the truth: that we have no magic. We're not exceptional or extraordinary. We're normal. Nobodies. Nothing but average Fae, just with significantly more money."

She chuckled, but a glimmer of pain and insecurity appeared in Syrena's eyes as her throat bobbed. "The scrutiny's given Kaspar a chip on his shoulder. After our coronation this summer, people began to talk again... only this time, it was directed solely at him." Her gaze flicked to Xavier's silhouette in the distance. "It seems after the siege on Merimaya, many of our people shared the same sentiment *he* did."

The memory of Xavier punching Kaspar in the face when the prince chose to stay behind while Syrena put herself in harm's way flashed across my mind.

*Your sister has more balls than you ever will,* Xavier had stated in the heat of the moment.

I assumed that to be the sentiment Syrena was referring to.

"So," Syrena continued, rolling over onto her back. "I think he's just... given up. Our whole lives, we've tried to keep up appearances and prove people wrong. And now... it's almost as if he's showing people he's exactly what they think he is. I don't understand it."

Syrena shut her eyes tight, and I wasn't sure if it was to block out the glare of the sun or to hide the tears forming there. "He's kept minor duties like approving visitors and monitoring the items coming in and out of the palace so it seems like he still has sway, but ultimately I'm the one in charge of everything important. He doesn't offer to help. He doesn't want to."

When Syrena opened her eyes and angled her head to look

at me again, she spoke in a voice more soft and vulnerable than I'd ever heard from her. "I love my brother, Lina. But I don't like him. I don't like the person he's become. And I have no idea what to do about it."

I sighed and nestled closer to my friend, gently leaning my head against hers. She snuggled into me, thankful for the silent act of love and support. Together we watched Xavier wade out of the shallows and plop on the shore beside Wynn, who was busy burying Willow in sand from the waist down with one hand, while the other was clamped firmly around the paw of his plush wolf. He seemed like a normal, happy child now, but it was only a matter of time before the darkness came calling and he was nothing but a shell once more.

"I don't know what to do about my brother either," I whispered.

# Chapter 19



Nearly three weeks had passed since we'd arrived in Lerian, my body bearing proof of the long hours spent under the ever-present sun. A constant rosy flush colored my cheeks, my freckles had become so dark they looked like someone had splattered paint across my face and arms, and the auburn streaks in my hair had grown so bright they resembled streaks of fire running through the brunette locks.

Seeing myself in the mirror now, I couldn't help but notice I looked the way I had when I first came to the Fae realm after working at Lord Olin's estate all summer. Except now my hips had rounded out from having more than enough to eat, and the dark bags under my eyes had lessened now that my days weren't spent breaking my back in the fields. My clothing was another significant change as well. My outfit tonight would have been considered vulgar in the human realm, too revealing even for those who worked in the brothel at the outskirts of my village, but here among the Fae in Lerian, my clothes were all the rage.

I ran my hands over the red silk top Syrena had picked out

for me, which was nothing but a glorified strip of fabric trimmed in beads and jingling gold coins that wrapped around my neck, crossed over my chest, and tied behind my back. The matching high-waisted pants had high slits along the sides of the legs, but Syrena knew about my compulsive need to have my dagger on me at all times, so she'd had this pair specially tailored so the fabric overlapped, camouflaging the sheath fastened to my thigh. With one quick movement the material could be pulled aside to access the blade.

I brushed my fingers along the outline of my dagger, my heart stinging as I thought of the one who'd given it to me, but I lifted my chin and pushed the thought of him out of my mind. The sole purpose of the party tonight was to forget about Soren. I was going to have fun, damn it. Even if it killed me.

After one last glance in the mirror, I nodded at my reflection and opened my bedroom door. The hallway already echoed with laughter and chatter wafting up from the ballroom below.

I exhaled long and slow, then squared my shoulders as I stepped out into the hall.

"Fun," I reminded myself. "You're going to have *fun*."

Despite my urging, my feet stayed fixed in place. Something weighed on me, holding me back from continuing towards the party. It wasn't my normal anxiety or fear pulling at me, although that was still here. It was something else, some invisible tether connected to my heart and tugging gently. My throat pinched, and I warily peeked over my shoulder like whatever beckoned might pounce.

But it didn't.

Hale's bedroom door stood just as still and silent and lonely as he used to be.

Again I willed myself to move down the hall, down to the

lavish party where I could laugh and drink and dance with my friends, but my feet remained planted.

Tonight was about letting go and moving on.

Of *everyone*.

It was finally time to say goodbye.

The realization hit me like a tidal wave, knocking the air from my lungs as we collided. My feet moved before my mind had caught up, carrying me down the hallway to finally face the truth. In a daze, I rested my hand on the knob and turned it, the gears inside the latch creaking as they woke from their long slumber, and with a trembling hand I gave it a firm push. The door groaned open, and before I could talk myself out of it for the thousandth time, I stepped inside.

I don't know why a small part of my heart still clung to the hope that Hale would be there. I knew he couldn't be. And the simple space covered in dust, its only inhabitants the spiders and mice that had taken up residence in its musty corners, only confirmed it.

That tiny piece of remaining hope broke apart, and I couldn't help but think how strange it was that something so small could inflict so much pain.

My tears forged rivers through the makeup I'd powdered on my cheeks, the same way my fingertips cut through the dust as I traced my hand over the surfaces I passed. To my right was a dresser, so old it was practically crumbling, with a row of half-melted candles in brass candelabra along the top. Beside the dresser, a few hooks were nailed into the wall, and from them hung various belts, a threadbare towel, and a black shirt. My breath hitched as I took the shirt in my hand and rubbed the rough linen between my thumb and forefinger.

Did it still smell like him? I could barely remember his scent of smoke and musk, or the way it captured the sultry essence of sweat-dusted skin beside a crackling campfire.

I quickly released the shirt and moved on to the nightstand, but froze when I noticed its only decoration.

Buried beneath a film of dust, its petals now wrinkled and brown, lay the pathetic remnants of a yellow crocus.

My heart wrenched, and I had to grip the nearby bedpost to steady myself. I knew without a doubt it was the same flower I'd tucked into the buckle on Hale's jacket the night of the spring equinox. I remembered seeing it there even after the Nethers attacked. It had been crumpled and wilted, but still fixed in place, a testament to how smooth and efficient Hale moved when he fought. After we'd all parted ways to decompress after the battle, I'd assumed he'd thrown it away. Apparently, I'd been wrong, and it had meant so much to him that he chose to keep it.

I pressed my lips together to keep a whimper from escaping as I delicately scooped the flower into my hands. I was too scared to even breathe, worried that so much as an exhale would destroy the fragile thing, so I spoke in the softest, most tender whisper I could.

"I'm sorry," I said, turning my face to the ceiling so my tears wouldn't soak the flower's paper-thin petals. "I'm sorry I couldn't save you. I'm sorry I did exactly what everyone else did your entire life and abandoned you when you needed me most. I'm sorry I failed you."

My voice cracked on the last sentence, unleashing the sobs I'd been holding back. My shoulders shook violently, and I tried desperately to keep my trembling hands from smashing the blossom in my palms.

"If I could go back, if I could do it all again, I wouldn't leave you. I wouldn't let you be alone at the end. I would have died alongside you before I let you be alone again."

*Crash!*

I screamed and spun towards the opposite corner of the

room. An unnervingly large rat skittered away from the jumble of books it had just knocked off their shelf onto a table. Heart nearly hammering out of my chest, I heaved a sigh of relief and grunted my frustration at the rodent's tail as it disappeared through a hole in the wall. When I looked down at my hand again, I wilted. I'd been so surprised by the noise I'd accidentally crushed the crocus, leaving it nothing but dust in my palm.

Now there was nothing left of me and Hale except memories.

I sighed miserably and brushed the flower's crumbs from my skin before wiping my eyes with the back of my hand and wandering over to inspect the rat's damage. The grime-coated books had smashed directly onto the table's cluttered contents, which included knives, short swords, and... figurines?

My brow crinkled in confusion as I wrapped my fingers around a small wooden fawn and lifted it to a beam of light peeking through the shuttered window. It was the size of my palm with impressively whittled details; large innocent eyes, speckles along its back, and little nubs on its head where antlers were readying to sprout. I glanced back at the table, noting the wood shavings and blocks of pine for the first time, as well as the woodworking knives mixed in with an extra stash of Hale's black-bladed daggers. I sniffed and shook my head.

"Carving," I muttered, a smile sneaking onto my lips. "You liked to carve."

I didn't know why I hadn't thought of it before.

Hale had fashioned a blade from the antler of the Nether I'd killed on the spring equinox. He'd gifted it to me just before we left for Merimaya, and it had saved my life in the Netherworld when I used it to stab Aedan. I hadn't considered it wasn't the first time he'd made something like that.

I chuckled softly and set the pinewood fawn back beside

the assortment of woodland creatures scattered across the tabletop.

"It kept his mind busy."

I whipped around at the voice, yanked my dagger from its hiding place, and held it at the ready.

Commander Roric Pax stood in the doorway, his hands defensively rising as I whirled on him. His thick brows arched in amusement, and he jerked his chin towards my blade.

"You're fast at that."

"I've had a lot of practice, unfortunately."

"That is unfortunate." Roric lowered his arms and clasped his hands behind his back. He seemed far less intimidating now that he was dressed in his formal guard attire and his swords were absent from their usual posts at his back. But the warrior still lay underneath, wired and ready to spring into deadly action in the blink of an eye, so I kept a firm hold on my dagger just in case.

"May I enter?" Roric asked.

I blinked at the polite request. *I* was the one snooping, after all. He could easily pull rank, tell me to stop trespassing in private spaces or forcibly remove me. But the commander did no such thing. He stood just outside the door, waiting for my permission, like he understood and respected the intimate moment he'd interrupted.

I warily lowered my blade and nodded before tucking it back into its sheath. Roric dipped his head in thanks and stepped inside the room, looking around curiously.

"You see it in the military a lot," he stated, batting at a cobweb that threatened to drift down from the ceiling and tangle in his hair.

"See what?"

Roric beckoned to the carvings on the table. "Activities to keep the mind and body occupied."

He wandered over, the light in his eyes dimming as they scanned the wooden figures. "Sometimes people who have experienced violence need them, or else their thoughts start to wander and their hands get antsy, and eventually the darkness calls to them."

Roric frowned, picked up the rendering of a rabbit, and turned it over and over in his wide palm. Something told me he understood the truth of his words firsthand.

"What does it say when it calls?" I asked softly. "The darkness."

Roric set the rabbit back down. "When all you know is violence, violence becomes instinct. You either inflict it on yourself, or others." He offered me a sad smile, then nodded to the figurines. "But finding little activities that bring you joy helps immensely, which I believe is what this was for Hale. It looks like he used this, or target practice."

The commander gestured to a beam running up the wall opposite the bed. I stepped forward and squinted as I examined it closer. The texture on its surface came from hundreds, maybe even thousands, of tiny nicks from a blade. My mind filled with the image of Hale reclining on the bed, one arm propped behind his head while the other threw knives into the beam the same way he'd flung one into the face of a Nether to save my life. I smiled at the thought and slowly traced my fingertips over the divots in the wood.

After a few moments, I became aware of Roric's stare. I peeked at him, and his eyes narrowed ever so slightly.

"You're the first person to open the door to his bedroom since he left."

*Here comes the scolding.*

"So?" I defensively crossed my arms.

Roric shrugged. "So nothing. I was just making an observation. No one else dared to enter this room."

His gaze left my face and returned to the table. He picked up another figurine, a horse this time.

"It seems the fear and dread of the Night Sylph remains, even after death," Roric mused, rubbing the dust from the beast's face with a tattooed knuckle.

"He wasn't someone to fear," I said, probably a little too quickly.

"You two were close." Not a question. A statement.

"We didn't know each other that long. We were no closer than he and Syrena were."

"Well, that's a lie," Roric chuckled.

I froze. My lips parted to speak, but no words came out. Roric nodded, like my stunned silence was his native tongue and he heard the words I was incapable of forming clear as day.

*How did you know?* I wanted to ask.

And the commander answered.

"In all my long years, Miss Calder, I've been fortunate enough to have never experienced the death of a lover," he said, his voice taking on a surprisingly gentle tone, "but I imagine if I did, the look in my eyes would resemble the one in yours now."

I swallowed hard, and Roric offered me a small smile as encouragement.

"You should take something of his," he suggested. "He would have wanted you to own something that makes you think of him. He would have wanted to be remembered fondly."

I wrapped my arms around myself. "You're right. He would have."

He would have wanted to be remembered as anything other than a monster.

I scanned the clutter on the table once more, searching for something to remind me not of the monster, not of the demon, but of the lover.

"What about this?" Roric picked up a squirrel figurine and beamed as he extended it to me. "This is cute."

I smiled politely, but reached past him and grabbed one of Hale's black-bladed daggers from the stack of weapons on the tabletop. Pulling aside the fabric of my pant leg, I slid the knife into the leather band strapped around my thigh, right into the sheath behind another lost lover's blade. When the material was smoothed back in place, I met Roric's stare.

The commander snickered and shook his head. "I should have known."

"Probably." I cracked a hint of a smile. "Now I believe there's a party we're both expected at."

"There is." Roric motioned to the door. "May I accompany you down to the ballroom?"

Again, I was taken aback by the rugged male's politeness. I shook off my surprise and raised a mocking eyebrow as I brushed past him. "What's the matter? Worried the King Slayer will find her next victim along the way?"

Roric fell into step beside me. "Well, she *is* doubly armed now. I have to be doubly careful."

"Well, who the hell let her arm herself a second time?"

A chuckle rumbled in Roric's chest. "A godsdamned fool who had the audacity to assume a beautiful woman would prefer something cute and worthless to something deadly and powerful."

"Hmm..." I clicked my tongue. "He does sound like a fool."

"He is. And he'll freely admit he doesn't know the first thing about women."

"Then maybe he's not a complete fool after all. Close, but not entirely."

We fell silent as we began our descent down the winding staircase that led to the palace's main floor. After a few seconds, Roric cleared his throat.

"What you said before, about Hale not being someone to fear..." His olive green gaze met mine, the dark brows over them drawing together in earnest. "I know he wasn't. If I thought differently, I wouldn't have trained him."

I stopped in place. "*You* trained Hale?"

He bowed his head. "Recommended him for the captain of the guard position when I stepped down, too."

Words were evading me again, but luckily Roric continued with an explanation without my urging.

"The king, Syrena and Kaspar's father, was wary about having a Night Sylph bastard under his roof. Which is completely understandable, of course."

My face dropped into a scowl, and every muscle in my body went taut with protective fury. Roric's gaze shot to me so fast it was as if he'd heard the blood start to roil in my veins.

"You've never seen the Night Sylph in action, Miss Calder. You've never had to witness the aftermath, or listen to the screams, or watch the violence through barricaded windows. You've never had mothers or sisters or friends or children stolen from you in the most horrific way possible. The Night Sylph's presence has haunted our kind since the beginning of time, so you can imagine the generations of fear passed down along the way." Roric's cold expression melted. "I am not, by any means, saying my people's mistreatment of Hale was correct. It wasn't. But I do understand where their fear came from."

I stared at Roric for a tense beat before begrudgingly dousing my defensive instincts.

When he seemed sure I wasn't going to tear his head off, Roric continued with his tale. "To ease the king's worries, I told him to let the boy start working with me and my men. I said he would thrive with structure and might find the physicality beneficial."

"You wanted to make sure the weapon could be used *for* you, not against you," I muttered, unable to hide the contempt in my voice.

Roric went quiet again. He dropped his gaze to the floor and sighed as he chose his next words.

"You don't know me very well, Miss Calder. I hope eventually you come to realize I'm not that kind of person." He glanced up at me again, his expression sincere. "While that was indeed the king's thinking, it wasn't mine. I wanted to give Hale an outlet. A purpose."

"Why?"

"I recognized something in him." A distant expression washed over Roric's face, like he was watching a far-off memory in the empty space between us. "I knew that look in his eyes... all that pain and sadness and anger. And I knew if he didn't find a release, it would eventually kill him."

I sniffed bitterly. "I would have thought most people would encourage that."

"Many would, yes. But not all." Roric straightened his shoulders. "Hale wasn't the only half-Nether I've ever come in contact with, you know."

I blinked, certain I hadn't heard him correctly. "What?"

Roric nodded, then followed it up with a sly smile as he leaned forward and lowered his voice. "Can you keep a secret?"

"Too well."

Roric glanced warily over both shoulders before speaking again. "I come from a long line of fishermen. My father would spend his days out on the boats while my mother stayed on shore and sorted their catch in the harbor. Many of the workers down on the docks are Water Sprites, so when my mother brought me to work with her as a boy, I would run around playing on all the crates of cargo with their children. And what most people don't know is that Water Sprites sometimes grow close to others who share their affinity for water... Merrows."

Merrows. The creatures Aedan had sent to drown Soren's father. Or, as I'd heard Syrena once refer to them, *fish bitches.*

I winced at the thought of some strange fish woman pulling me into the water and holding me there until I stopped breathing, like they had the previous king of Astoria.

The look on my face made Roric laugh. "Despite what you may have heard, they're actually quite beautiful and alluring creatures. Terrifying and deadly if you piss them off, but what woman isn't?"

He looked pointedly at where I had two daggers disguised on my person. I smirked and leaned against the bannister, planting my hands along the railing on either side.

"So you knew someone who was half-Merrow?"

Roric looked around once more to make sure we were the only two within earshot. "Like I said. Growing up, many of my friends were Water Sprites, and I was a rough kid with anger issues. So when someone would shout slurs at my friends or treat them poorly, I'd take it upon myself to go and teach the bullies a lesson. When I got back, my friends would stitch me up with whatever blossoming healing powers they had. I did it enough times that I earned their respect and trust, and after a while, a few of them shared with me the truth behind their heritage." He leaned in close again, his voice so low it was nearing a whisper. "And here's another secret: if you ever see a Water Sprite with a faint blue sheen to their skin, it's a dead giveaway there's Merrow in their blood too."

"Huh." I nodded thoughtfully. "I think I have seen that before."

"There you go." Roric shrugged and clasped his hands in front of him. "You've met other half-Nethers too."

I ruminated on the thought, then finally let my walls come

down fully and gave him a genuine smile as a peace offering. "Your friends' secrets are safe with me."

A matching smile spread over Roric's face, and he inclined his head in thanks.

Laughter burst from the ballroom, startling both of us, but I caught myself before my hand shot towards the knives at my side.

"Sounds like things are getting lively." Roric turned to me, his pierced eyebrow arching as he teased, "Last chance to bail."

In response, I channeled the queen of Lerian herself.

I tossed my hair, lifted my nose high in the air, and sauntered towards the party like I owned the place.

# CHAPTER 20

My confidence was overinflated and short-lived.

I stood in the ballroom's gilded archway, attempting to rub at my collarbone, but the high neck of my silk top was blocking it. Despite wearing so little, it somehow felt like significantly too much, and the fabric around my throat was strangling me. The more I thought about it, the more suffocating it became, and before I knew it I was tugging frantically at the neckline and gulping air like an out-of-water fish.

"It's a lot."

Roric's words pulled me from my silk-induced panic.

"Yes, it is," I croaked, swallowing hard as I surveyed the packed room for the fifteenth time and tugged at the material around my neck for the twentieth.

"What helped me when I first started coming to these sorts of things was thinking of it like a battlefield."

I peeked at the man out of the corner of my eye. "A what?"

Roric chuckled. "Here, I'll show you." He crouched so our faces were on the same plane. "It takes the same amount of strategy. In war, you find your allies..."

I followed Roric's gaze across the room to where Syrena stood, looking majestic in an outfit similar to mine, only instead of pants she wore a long flowing skirt, with a floor-length glittering shawl draped over her gold and ruby crown.

Roric's calloused hands alighted on my shoulders, and he gently angled my body to the left. "Then you take note of where you can retrieve nourishment."

He stopped me when we were facing the dessert table, and I stifled a giggle.

"Then you search for a weakness in your opponent." Roric removed his hands from my shoulders and motioned to our right. "Take that woman by the punch bowl, for example."

He was pointing at a Fae noble dressed in a frilly blue ball gown that looked more like an extravagant cupcake. Fixed haphazardly to the side of her head was a matching hat that resembled a feather-stuffed pincushion.

"That has got to be the most ridiculous hat I've ever seen," Roric mused.

I bit my lip to keep in another laugh.

"*But.* She clearly wants to show it off, so if you walk up and compliment her, she'll go on and on about it for ages. If you act even remotely interested, you'll be her new favorite person in no time." Roric straightened and brushed his hands together like he was wiping imaginary bread-crumbs from his palms. "There you have it. First opponent slain."

I grinned and surveyed the room again. This time, it didn't seem nearly as daunting, and my shirt was starting to feel a little less tight.

"A battlefield," I repeated to myself.

"Oh! And most importantly," Roric added, "you should *always* have an exit strategy. Fainting is a popular option with the ladies."

I glared at him, but a smile teased my lips. "Do you really take me for a fainter?"

Roric shrugged. "There's a first time for everything."

I scoffed and crossed my arms. "I may run, freeze, or fight, but I'll never faint."

Roric chuckled and ruefully rubbed the back of his neck. "I can respect that."

He caught my eye again, and his eyes softened with that earnest sincerity I'd seen in them before.

"Miss Calder." He stepped forward to give us some privacy as a group of chatty female Fae passed us on their way into the party. "In all seriousness, I hope you know that despite our rocky introduction a few weeks ago, you are very much welcome here. This place can be a home to you if you let it, and I will be your friend if you'll have me."

I offered a grateful smile, then hesitantly reached out to give his arm a squeeze. "Thank you, Roric. I need friends right now."

The commander's gaze broke from mine, a smile spreading over his face as he looked past me. "I don't know about that. I think you've got some pretty great ones already."

He tilted his chin in the direction he was looking, and I turned.

Willow walked hand in hand with my brother, whose smile stretched ear to ear as he eagerly dragged her across the ball-room. Xavier trailed behind laughing.

I knelt to meet Wynn and smoothed a curl that had popped off the side of his head. "Look at you! Don't you look handsome!"

My little brother was dressed in a hilarious jumble of Lerian fashions. A gold-trimmed turquoise shirt was paired with an embroidered burgundy vest, while patterned green-

and-orange trousers were fastened with a silver sash at his waist.

"He wanted everyone to know he picked out his clothes himself." Willow sighed, shaking her head at the garish ensemble.

It took every ounce of strength in me not to laugh, but somehow I managed to keep my expression serious. "I never would have guessed."

A large presence loomed behind me.

"Mister Calder." Roric bowed grandly to my brother. "You look every inch a Lerian gentleman."

Wynn beamed and admired his outfit, his proud expression lighting up every shadowy part of my soul with joy. It was moments like this where my brother seemed like any other normal seven-year-old child, and the false hope that he actually could be came sneaking in again.

"But your friend's not dressed," Roric continued, motioning to the plush wolf in Wynn's arms.

The toy was filthy now, its fur plastered with sand and grime since my brother never let it out of his sight. Willow informed me he refused to allow the palace laundresses to wash it, going so far as kicking them if they tried to pry it out of his arms.

"Here." Roric pulled the gold pocket square emblazoned with the Lerian crest from his jacket and gestured to the wolf. "May I?"

Wynn considered for a moment, then nodded and extended his toy to the commander.

Roric dipped his head to thank him, then let my brother keep his hold on the wolf while he fastened the handkerchief around its neck like a scarf.

"There," he said, fluffing the fabric. "Now you're both equally dashing."

Wynn lowered the toy and stared at it like it was the finest piece of art he'd ever seen.

I looked up at Roric with a grateful smile, but he didn't see it. His gaze was fixed on Willow.

"And you look radiant, as always," he told her.

The pink hue that flushed over the entirety of the Sprite's body complemented her lilac gown and its matching waistcoat. Her plum-red braid whipped around her shoulders as she averted her gaze and glanced nervously at her ample bosom on display.

"I like purple," was all she could sputter in response.

"It's a good color," Roric replied. "Especially on you. It brings out your beautiful eyes."

Willow gulped, spun on her heel, and declared to no one in particular, "I need wine."

Roric's eyes followed her as she scurried away, his mouth curving downward in a concerned frown as he turned to me. "Did I say something to offend her?"

I exchanged a glance with my brother, who just shook his head and buried his face in the wolf's fur.

"You said it yourself, Commander." I chuckled. "You don't know the first thing about women."

"Don't worry, Pax." Xavier, who had been leaning against a nearby pillar and observing the interaction with wry amusement, stepped forward and clapped Roric on the back. "I can teach you a few things."

Roric threw his head back and laughed heartily. "Oh, is that so?"

That cocky grin made its first appearance of the night, and Xavier paired it with a playful wink in the captain of the guard's direction. "Play your cards right, and I'll let you pick my brain."

Roric laughed again. "I like your confidence, boy."

A tug on my pant leg drew my attention away from the men.

My brother looked up at me with hopeful eyes and pointed at the dessert table.

"Hungry?" I asked, smoothing another one of his curls.

He nodded passionately and squeezed his toy to his chest in anticipation.

I gestured for him to lead the way. "Alright, let's go. But not too much chocolate, or you'll hurt your stomach."

My brother rolled his eyes and scampered off, headed straight for the chocolate fountain at the center of the table. I followed, leaving Roric and Xavier to continue their banter.

When I arrived at the table, I grabbed a plate and scanned the sweets. As I loaded up, I couldn't help overhearing a conversation between two young Fae women hovering next to a platter of truffles.

"Who is that gorgeous creature speaking with Commander Roric?" one whispered to her friend.

I smirked but kept my attention glued to a tray of candy-coated strawberries.

"I think that's the low-caste boy the king of Astoria adopted," the other woman replied.

"Is it?"

"I believe so."

"Gods, he's not a boy anymore, is he?"

"Imogen! You can't honestly be considering what I think you are."

"What? Who cares about caste when they look like that?"

"Well, I would never lower myself—oh gods, he's coming over here. How's my hair?"

Unable to mind my own business any longer, I peeked up in time to catch Xavier sauntering up to the table, his swagger oozing confidence and charisma.

"Excuse me," he said, his voice taking on a deep, velvety timbre. "I saw something over here I just had to have a taste of."

Without breaking eye contact with the second woman, Xavier reached past her and picked a truffle off the platter, then swept it into his mouth with a flick of his tongue. After an appreciative groan, he sucked the remnants from his finger and glanced at the other female.

"Divine," he drawled.

The woman's knees must have buckled because she threw out a hand to grip the side of the table like her life depended on it. Xavier scanned her body appreciatively, one side of his mouth quirking upwards before his gaze returned to the first woman. He cordially dipped his head.

"Have a good evening, ladies."

I discreetly mouthed the word *shameless* to him as he passed, to which he winked. When I looked back at the women, they were still staring at Xavier's retreating form with slack jaws.

"His name is Xavier," I offered.

Snapping out of their dazes, the women faced me. I wrangled my brother, whose mouth was now smeared with chocolate, and steered him away from the table.

"Try asking him about his scars," I added over my shoulder. "It works every time."

One of the women nodded dumbly while the other just muttered, "Xavier, you say..."

I laughed to myself as I led my brother through the crowd, headed for a regal queen across the ballroom, who was scowling at the ladies I'd just left.

"Everything alright?" I asked Syrena.

Her eyes never left the Fae noblewomen. "What did he just say to them?"

"He described chocolate."

Syrena's frown deepened, and she let out an unimpressed grunt. I sighed and glanced back at the table. The women had found Xavier again, and he was currently unbuttoning his green and gold vest to show them the long, diagonal scar across his chest and abdomen. One of the women pressed her fingers to his bare skin and traced the jagged outline, a move that made Syrena roll her eyes and snatch up two goblets of wine.

"Pathetic," she hissed, passing me one.

I sipped at the drink while Syrena took a hefty swig of hers.

"Anyway." She finally peeled her attention from the trio and painted a smile on her face. "How are you doing? How do you like your party?"

I nodded and looked around the room. "It's nice. It's..." I trailed off.

Syrena read my mind like a book. "I know. It's strange for me too, not having Hale here."

I swallowed and peeked down at where the black blade was hidden on my thigh, its presence somehow making me feel slightly closer to its previous owner.

"I've found myself looking around, half expecting to see him grimacing in a corner somewhere," Syrena continued, causing us both to chuckle at the image. "He hated these sorts of things."

I tapped a finger against my glass thoughtfully, my mind again drifting to the spring equinox the year before. I'd slipped the crocus into Hale's jacket, then danced with his darkness in the shadows while he lit them up with a smile as radiant as the sun.

"I think he would have liked them if people let him," I muttered. "He would have liked to dance."

Syrena scoffed. "Hale? Dancing? Never in a million years."

I fell silent, knowing with every fiber of my being she was wrong.

Syrena suddenly stiffened, her grip tightening around her

drink and her chin lifting proudly. By her body language I knew who was approaching before I saw him.

"Nice party, Your Highness," Xavier stated. "Great music, good food, and your guests are delightfully handsy."

The queen examined her fingernails. "Glad you like it. Maybe you can learn a thing or two about class and bring it back to Astoria with you. Which will be when exactly?"

Xavier breathed in deep, then let out a leisurely exhale. "You know, I'm not sure. I quite like it here. I'm thinking about petitioning for citizenship."

"It will be denied," Syrena snapped.

"What's the matter, Your Highness?" Xavier raised an eyebrow. "Want me to get on my knees for you and beg?"

"I'd prefer if you stop trying to spite me and just leave already." Syrena went to take another sip of her wine, but Xavier plucked the goblet from her fingers and took a gulp before she could.

"And you say *I'm* the immature one," she huffed.

Xavier lowered the drink and wiped his mouth with the back of his hand. "Arrogant of you to assume it's you I'm staying for, Your Highness. Maybe I'm sticking around to seduce your delectable captain of the guard."

Syrena laughed so hard she snorted. "Oh, please! Roric would never."

Xavier's brows dropped low over his eyes. "You shouldn't tell me that. I love a challenge."

"Well, *he* loves *women*."

"So do I." Xavier's gaze never left Syrena's face as he took another swig and licked his lips. "Are you a gambler, Your Highness?"

Syrena looked him up and down curiously before folding her arms. "Why?"

"Because I'd like to propose a game." He sidled closer, but

Syrena didn't flinch. "I wager I could sleep with that man before you do."

The manner in which Syrena laughed in his face would make most men cower, but not Xavier. "You can't be serious."

"What's the matter? Scared you couldn't do it?"

Syrena's lashes shuttered, and in a sultry voice that nearly had *my* toes curling in my shoes, she purred, "Oh, I *know* I could do it."

Somehow unaffected by her vixen eyes and silken voice, Xavier raised another eyebrow. "Worried about your performance in the bedroom, then?"

Syrena smiled. A sweet, calm, utterly deadly smile. "For your information, I perform majestically."

"Oh, really?"

"Really."

The tip of Xavier's canine came into view as he flashed a primal grin. "Prove it."

I caught myself holding my breath as my gaze darted between the two, worried even the smallest movement would snap the tension between them. Unleashing what exactly, I wasn't entirely sure.

Finally, Syrena leaned in closer, her gaze dropping to Xavier's lips. His tightly wound body stayed frozen, but his eyes moved to her mouth too.

"I'm a queen," Syrena said, her words as sharp as shards of glass. "I don't take orders."

For a moment it looked like she was going to lean in even further, dangerously close to making contact with Xavier's lips, but she moved past him, roughly knocking his shoulder as she did. A muscle in Xavier's jaw twitched as he ground his teeth, and he exhaled sharply through his nose before turning to watch Syrena strut across the room. When she came across her captain of the guard, however, she struck up cheerful conversation, laughing at something he said and touching his bicep a few seconds too long. She then looked over her shoulder and shot Xavier a devilish smile.

Xavier huffed a low laugh and shook his head. "You little snake."

He downed the rest of his drink, tossed the empty goblet to me, and moved through the crowd towards Roric with the intensity of a wolf locked onto the scent of its prey.

"What the hell did I just watch?"

I spun on my heel. "Ilora!"

The queen of Merimaya beamed back at me, looking like a goddess in a deep violet and emerald green trouser and jacket set with a plunging neckline and floor-length train. The simple gold circlet that marked her status sat on top of her hair, which had been twisted into slender cords and adorned with an array of gold cuffs and charms. The flames of the torches in the room were practically reflected in her glossy umber skin, highlighting her golden undertones and sculpted features.

Ilora stepped forward and wrapped her lean arms around me in a warm embrace.

"How are you doing?" she asked softly. Her voice was as calm and soothing as the water lapping against the shore of the lake beside her palace.

"I'm alright. There are good days and bad days."

"I know." Ilora nodded and rubbed my back in encouragement. "I feel the same."

We pulled away and shared a melancholy smile, both silently acknowledging the bond of loss that connected us.

Ilora had changed since I met her. Before, she'd been a bubbly, carefree princess bickering with her twin brother and sunning herself on the decks of ships at breakfast. But then her brother was murdered in front of her eyes, her parents were slaughtered in front of mine, and her entire world flipped upside down as she rose to a position of power overnight. She had to piece together her territory and herself at the same time, and she'd done it so swiftly and with such grace and strength that I was completely in awe of her. Everyone was. Even in Astoria, when people spoke of the new queen of Merimaya, they did it with respect and reverence. She was without a doubt the strongest person I'd ever met, and I was honored to call her a friend.

"Anyway," Ilora said brightly, clapping her hands and looking around the room in search of a servant. "What are we drinking?"

I giggled.

*Good to see some of the old Ilora is still in there.*

"Oh!" The queen turned back to me and eagerly bounced on her toes. "And I want to finally meet your brother now that he's awake!"

I nodded. "Of course! He's right here—"

I reached for the hand at my side, only to find it missing. I frowned and turned to my other side, then spun in a circle. My brother wasn't there.

"Lina?"

"Um..." I stood tall and surveyed the crowd near the dessert table. No signs of Wynn sneaking back into the chocolate fountain for seconds. "Sorry, hold on. He was right here a second ago. I just have to find him."

I craned my neck and found Syrena, Roric, and Xavier across the room. Maybe my brother had wandered over to eavesdrop on their conversation.

But he wasn't there either.

My heart beat faster, its thumps growing louder in my ears along with the chatter of the crowd.

"You can't miss him." I squeezed out a nervous laugh. "He's wearing every color of the rainbow."

Wynn wasn't by the punch bowl.

Not on the outskirts of the dance floor either.

He wasn't listening to the musicians or playing in the drapes or hiding under any of the tables.

My breath was shallow now, and the talk and laughter of the party guests had turned into a dull roar. Ilora called my name again, but her voice was muffled. I barely heard her as I pushed through the crowd, treading on feet and elbowing guests in the back.

When I discovered Willow in a dimly lit corner by the refreshment table, sipping from the two glasses of wine in her hands, I caught her by the elbow.

"Willow," I rasped, my mouth drying up from panic. "Have you seen Wynn?"

The Sprite's eyebrows knit. "No, I thought he was with you."

Ilora shouldered her way through the crowd after me. "Lina, what's wrong?"

I couldn't breathe. Frantically tearing at the silk around my neck, I replied in gasps. "I can't... I can't find him."

"I'm sure he's around here somewhere," Ilora stated calmly. "Where did you last see him?"

"When I was with Syrena and Xavier." I crouched low, trying to peer through the ocean of legs and skirts in the hopes of catching a glimpse of blond curls. "I told him not to go anywhere without telling us. He's supposed to tell us..."

Willow put a hand on my shoulder.

"We'll find him," she insisted, but her voice was a high squeak, proving she was just as worried as I was.

"He can't have gone far. We'll spread out, ask around," Ilora declared. "Maybe someone saw him."

I started off before she'd finished speaking, grabbing the first nobleman I passed.

"Excuse me, have you seen a little boy?" I asked. "Blond hair, blue eyes, and freckles?"

"No, dear. I'm sorry."

I bolted to the next.

"Excuse me, have you seen my brother?" I motioned with my hand. "He's about this tall, curly blond hair."

"No, sorry." The woman offered a pout of remorse. "I hope you find him."

In the distance, Ilora could be heard having similar conversations.

I spun in a circle, helplessly searching the room. The roaring in my ears was deafening, my shirt was suffocating, and dread was seeping through me like a fast-acting toxin.

"Lina!"

I jumped at Willow's urgent tone. It took me a moment to find her among the throngs of people, but I caught sight of her rapidly waving her arms overhead to get my attention. She stood at the mouth of a hallway that led into the depths of the palace. I shoved my way over to her.

"I found this," she said, lifting something off the floor.

It was a piece of gold fabric, emblazoned with the Lerian crest.

My stomach dropped at the sight of the pocket square Roric had tied around my brother's toy. I snatched the cloth from her hand and immediately sprinted down the hallway, only slowing to search the alcoves and darkened doorways I passed.

"Wynn!" I called.

The only response was Willow's footsteps pounding behind me.

"Wynnric, where are you?" she shrieked. Terror and guilt choked her voice. I knew her well enough that if anything happened to my brother on her watch, she would never forgive herself.

I understood the feeling well.

"Wynn!" I shouted again.

We were nearing the end of a long stretch of hall, where the passage continued after a sharp curve right. It led to a part of the palace I'd only been a few times, but it had the most magnificent view I'd ever seen. Massive floor-to-ceiling windows looked out over a long balcony that stretched across the coastal cliffs. When I first discovered it, I'd thought it would be the perfect place to watch the sunset over the sea with a special someone. But romance was the farthest thing from my mind as we neared it, especially when Willow and I tore around the corner and glimpsed the door that led to the balcony hanging wide open.

"No, no, no..." I muttered, unable to block out the image of my brother standing on that windowsill in Astoria. Sleepwalking, spellbound, and a split second away from ending his life. What if it was happening again? Oh *gods*, what if this time I was too late?

I shoved the horrific thought down and grit my teeth, focusing all my attention on putting one foot in front of the other until I'd darted through the doorway to the balcony outside. I couldn't think the worst yet. Who knows, maybe we'd gone in the wrong direction and my brother was—

"There!" Willow panted, pointing at the bench placed at the end of the balcony.

A colorful character with blond curls ruffled by the wind was climbing onto the west-facing seat, dangerously close to the balcony's railing and the precarious drop it guarded.

"Wynn!" I screamed at the top of my lungs.

My brother's head whipped around, his eyes wide.

Wide, but clear.

He was still himself.

"What the hell are you doing?!" I demanded, storming over

to my brother, grabbing his wrist, and yanking him and his toy wolf off the bench. "I told you not to wander off! I told you, Wynn! You can't do that, you hear me? You can't! I had no idea where you went! I was so scared!"

I hadn't realized my words had transformed into panicked sobs until I was kneeling in front of my brother and shaking his shoulders.

"I was *so* scared," I repeated, my voice cracking. "You can't keep doing this. Please. *Please.*"

Wynn frowned, his bright puppy dog eyes full of remorse. He then raised a hand and pointed to his ear.

I sniffled and wiped my nose on the back of my hand. "What?"

Again, my brother put his index finger to his ear.

Confused, I looked up at Willow.

"You..." The Sprite's brow furrowed as she attempted to piece together the puzzle. Eventually, her eyes lit up. "You heard something?"

Wynn nodded eagerly.

"What did you hear?" Willow asked, kneeling beside him.

My brother swallowed nervously and pointed to his chest.

"Your heart?"

Wynn shook his head and tapped himself once more.

"You heard..." Willow scratched her temple. "Your voice?"

After a frustrated stomp of his foot, my brother shook his head and touched his chest a third time.

"I'm sorry." Willow sank back onto her heels, her shoulders slumping in defeat. "I don't understand."

Wynn's gaze slid over to me. He looked me pointedly in the eyes and patted his hand against his heart. Suddenly, it hit me.

"His name," I mumbled. "He heard his name."

My brother triumphantly bounced on his tiptoes and nodded.

Willow scanned the balcony. It was entirely empty, populated by nothing but two humans, a Wood Sprite, and the symphony of crashing waves below.

"Who was calling your name, Wynn?" Willow asked.

My brother frowned and faced the sea, his expression going blank as he stared into the darkness. He didn't need to reply. I knew exactly who he'd heard as the Ben Síde's words echoed in my ears.

*My master called, but did not receive an answer. He wants what is rightfully his.*

# CHAPTER 21



"I THOUGHT AEDAN WAS DEAD."

We'd gathered in a private sitting room off the main hall. The party was still in full swing, its faint laughter and music echoing in the distance.

Bent forward with my elbows resting on my knees, I looked up at Ilora, who was curled on the low couch across from mine, her long legs tucked to her chin. She sat as motionless as a statue as she processed what Syrena and I had just told her, her expression unreadable.

"We all thought he was dead," Syrena muttered as she paced the room. "Lina stabbed him. I heard him scream. The whole damn mountain collapsed. We had every reason to believe he was gone."

Air hissed through Ilora's teeth as she exhaled and rubbed her face. "This whole time, I've been resting easy because I thought that monster was gone."

A knock at the door made the three of us tense. We relaxed when Xavier slipped in, carrying a blue and green quilt in one hand.

"Wynn's in bed," he said with a half-hearted attempt at a smile. "Willow's with him. Roric's assigning a guard to keep watch too."

"Windows?" I asked.

"All locked." Xavier draped the blanket over me. "Checked them myself."

He squeezed my shoulders, then busied himself with a nearby tea set, lifting a silver pot off its serving tray and pouring a fragrant liquid into individual cups before passing them to me, Ilora, and finally Syrena, who accepted hers as warily as if it were filled with poison.

"So Aedan is alive," Ilora mused, staring into her tea like it held all the answers. "Which means he and Erith will be continuing their crusade to take the five territories so the Nethers can run free."

"But they can't," Syrena cut in. "The entrance to the Netherworld is sealed. That mountain crumbled, and the whole valley flooded. *If* the veil is still there and they tried to come through it, they'd have to dig out from the rubble and swim through all that water."

Ilora raised her shoulders in a weary shrug. "Stranger things have happened."

Syrena sighed and tapped a fingernail against her cup. "I guess you're right. I'll have Roric send scouts to Kylanthia, then. See if there's anything suspicious happening in that valley we should know about."

"Merimaya is closer, I'll send mine. I've done it before. I sent some men to Kylanthia a couple of months ago to see what was happening now that its civilians are without a queen."

"What *is* happening there?" I asked.

Ilora shrugged again. "Same thing that's happening in Radomir. Utter chaos. Especially with the amount of Nethers there. Kylanthia's always had the highest concentration of them since it's so rural. There they can hide in the forests and mountains undisturbed. But without Erith or her army, half of which didn't even return home after the siege, the Kylanthian people are at the Nethers' mercy."

I sat upright. "They didn't return? Were they wiped out?"

Ilora shook her head. "From the amount of bodies that were recovered, it doesn't add up."

"Maybe she took them to the Netherworld with her?"

"Either way, the territory is in bad shape. Merimaya has taken in as many refugees as we can, but again, the land is so rural it's hard to get to them."

"Evil Kylanthian bitch," Syrena mumbled. "Who abandons their people like that?"

"I'm going to kill her," Ilora stated.

And when she looked up at me, her expression revealing no emotion, no pain, nothing except serene, terrifying promise, I believed her.

Syrena plopped beside me, ripped off her crown, and tossed it onto the couch beside us so she could place her head in her hands. "Should we be preparing our troops in case your scouts come back with news that Aedan's somehow gotten out?"

Ilora sighed and rubbed at her neck and shoulders. "I don't know."

"We should find a witch," I chimed in. "I've met a few lately who can see visions of the future. Maybe they'll be able to see if Aedan and Erith have found a way out of the Netherworld."

Ilora nodded thoughtfully. "The Hag."

Xavier sat down opposite me. "I forgot about the Hag! I haven't heard stories of her since I was a child."

I raised an eyebrow. "Who's the Hag?"

Ilora leaned forward. "There are tales of a powerful all-knowing woman in the High Lands between Merimaya and Lerian. They call her the Hag. She's a hermit, practically myth. No one knows where to find her, or even what she looks like."

I readjusted the quilt around my shoulders. "How are you supposed to find her, then?"

"Word of mouth," Syrena replied, settling deeper in the couch and clutching a pillow to her chest. "Witches talk."

"And you think this Hag will help us?"

"If anyone can, it would be her."

I exhaled slowly and sat a little taller. "Alright, let's do it."

Syrena nodded in agreement, toying absentmindedly with one of the tassels on the pillow. "There's a witch who still lives on the outskirts of my mother's old village. She was the first person who told my mother about the Hag, so maybe she knows how to get a message to her. I'll send her a summons to the palace."

"Then what?"

Syrena shrugged helplessly. "Then we wait."

The door to the sitting room banged open, making all of us jump in alarm. The person who stumbled in did nothing to ease the tension.

"Oh," Kaspar slurred, his arm tightening around the shoulders of a tittering woman clinging to his side. "Didn't know this room was taken."

I winced as the scent of alcohol hit my nose, the fumes so strong my eyes stung. It was coupled with a bitter burnt smell, and from the glazed look in Kaspar's eyes, I had a hunch it meant he'd also smoked one of the outlawed substances that still circulated down on Lerian's docks. I raised a hand to my nose to try and block out some of the stench.

The movement caught Kaspar's attention, and when his eyes landed on me, they narrowed into hostile slits.

"Well, look who it is," he sneered, letting go of the woman

and tottering towards me. "I heard the king-slaying whore was back. On the hunt for another royal cock to stuff yourself with?"

My fingers twitched, practically screaming to feel the calming steel of my dagger, but before I could move, Xavier stood and blocked the king's path.

"I think it's best you return your attention to the beautiful companion you already have and finish your night somewhere else."

Xavier's voice was as cool and controlled as an experienced diplomat, but there was ice in his eyes, and the muscles between his shoulder blades had gone taut, primed for violence.

Kaspar had to blink a few times to see Xavier clearly. When he did, his face twisted into an enraged snarl.

"You! You're that low-born who can't seem to remember his place."

He roughly pushed Xavier in the chest, sending him stumbling backwards a few steps. Xavier responded by lowering his gaze to the ground and sighing.

"Listen, I don't want any trouble. I'm just here to support my friends."

"No one's in the mood for your shit tonight, Kas," Ilora called from her spot on the couch.

But the king ignored her and neared Xavier again. "Without your master here to protect you, I could do whatever I want. I could have you arrested for what you pulled last time. Or better yet, I think I'll string you up, have you flayed alive in the town square so everyone can point and laugh at Soren's dog as the rats and vultures pick it apart."

A smile crept onto Xavier's face in a silent challenge.

"Enough!" Syrena chucked her pillow aside and scrambled off the couch. She wedged herself between the men and pushed her brother backwards. "He's my guest, Kas."

"He's low-born scum who needs to be taught a lesson," Kaspar barked.

"Well, *I* say he's welcome here, which means *you* have to play nice." She gave him another shove to make her point. "Got it?"

Kaspar stared at his sister, the tension so palpable it could be cut with a knife. Finally the king sniffed, spun on his heel, and shuffled back towards the woman he'd entered with.

"You know, this whole shared crown thing is getting old."

Syrena sighed and popped one hand onto her hip while the other rubbed at her eyes. "What would you suggest we do about that, Kas?"

Kaspar glanced over his shoulder, his lip curling with contempt. "If you keep pissing me off, I'd suggest you watch your back. Lerian royals have a funny habit of disappearing, and you've always been so good at following in Mommy and Daddy's footsteps."

All the color drained from Syrena's face, while every hair on the back of my neck bristled at the blatant threat. Across the room, Ilora bolted upright, her lips parting to protest, but before any of us could respond, there was a flash of movement and suddenly Xavier was beside the king, the silver serving tray from the tea set in his hands. Without a second of hesitation, Xavier bashed Kaspar upside the head, eliciting a scream from the woman next to him and a surprised yelp from Syrena. Kaspar crumpled but managed to stay on his feet, something Xavier quickly remedied with a solid kick to his back that knocked him to his knees.

Syrena finally formed words.

"What are you doing?" she shrieked, eyes wide as saucers.

Xavier didn't reply.

Instead, he tossed the tray aside and took the king's neck in the crook of his elbow, squeezing tight.

"Xavier, no!" Ilora shouted, but it was a half-hearted command, and she made no move to stop him. None of us did.

Kaspar gasped and sputtered and kicked, frantically clawing at Xavier's bicep and face, but the younger man's grip didn't budge.

"You're going to kill him!" Syrena cried.

"No I'm not," Xavier grunted, dodging one of Kaspar's flailing hands.

The king's movements slowed, and his eyelids fluttered shut. As soon as his body was limp, Xavier released his hold, letting Kaspar flop to the floor. The second he rose to his feet, the door to the sitting room flung open again, and this time, Roric burst in.

"What is it? What's wrong?" he demanded. "I heard yelling."

Xavier shook a lock of hair out of his eyes and motioned to Kaspar's unconscious body. "The king's had a little too much to drink and took a nasty fall. He'll probably have a pretty big lump on his head from it. I trust you can put him to bed?"

Roric crouched and examined Kaspar, placing two fingers against his neck to check his pulse.

"Afraid so," Roric mumbled. "I've done it countless times now."

He flashed a tired half smile, then scooped Kaspar in his arms like a babe and started for the door.

"Wait a minute," Xavier called after him. He jogged over and dipped his hand into Kaspar's pocket, fishing around until he pulled out an overstuffed coin purse. He nodded to Roric, dismissing him. When the captain of the guard was out of sight, Xavier wandered over to Kaspar's female companion, who was still huddling in the corner, scared half to death. He placed the purse in the woman's trembling hands, curled her fingers around it, and rested his own over top.

"Looks like you have the night off." With a charming smile that seemed to calm the woman's nerves, he added, "This is for your trouble, as well as your silence."

The woman nodded earnestly.

"Good girl." Xavier winked at her before jerking his chin towards the door.

Understanding the cue, the woman scurried away.

As if nothing out of the ordinary had happened, Xavier picked up a nearby teacup and resettled on the couch beside me to sip at its contents.

"What happened to playing nice?" I asked.

Xavier shrugged. "I did."

After sending a message home to Merimaya that commanded her best scouts into Kylanthia, Ilora decided to stay in Lerian until we met with the Hag. She claimed it was so we'd all be informed at the same time, but I suspected it also had something to do with her not wanting to be alone. In Merimaya, she was surrounded by memories of a family she'd lost. Here in Lerian, *we* were her family.

One balmy morning just over a week after the party, I stood in the palace courtyard, Soren's dagger in my right hand while I tested the balance of Hale's in my left. I hadn't picked up fighting with two blades quite as easily as I had one, but with Xavier and Syrena's consistent help, I was slowly but surely getting a grasp on things. Having Hale's dagger helped too. It was slimmer and more lightweight than Soren's, so it was significantly more comfortable for my weaker hand, and made my movements considerably more fluid.

I glanced at Ilora. Her weapon of choice today was a long, slender staff, which wouldn't have been all that frightening except for the fact she could spin and whip it around her body with effortless precision.

"I thought Merimaya was a peaceful territory," I hollered across the yard at her.

"It is." Ilora used her teeth to tighten the strips of fabric she'd wrapped around her palms. "Peace is always the goal, but sometimes others don't believe in peace, so you have to speak to them in a language they understand."

I was starting to regret challenging her to a duel when we were tipsy on fizzy drink the other day.

"What language is that?" I asked hesitantly.

Ilora looked over and grinned, eyes glinting eagerly. "Pain."

I gulped.

"My parents didn't condone violence, but my brother and I argued we should be able to wield a weapon for ceremonial purposes, so they eventually caved and let us attend some basic training sessions with our guards. The beautiful thing about Merimayan guards, though, is they'll do virtually anything for a little extra coin, including secretly continuing the training of a sneaky prince and princess." She smiled fondly at the memory and deftly tossed the staff between her hands as she wandered over. "Our guards are all armed with weapons similar to this, only they have blades at both ends to stab with. You can even decapitate someone if you swipe hard enough."

I grimaced. "Lovely."

"It's my favorite weapon," Ilora added, beaming.

I suddenly became painfully aware that I had some very scary friends.

"Teach her a lesson, Your Majesty!" Xavier shouted across the courtyard. He and Roric had just returned from a run on the beach when they'd come across us. Ilora had proceeded to explain the situation, and now the men sat on the palace steps shirtless, dripping sweat, and munching on a post-workout snack of oranges while they awaited the show.

I shot Xavier a dirty look. "Traitor."

He shrugged and popped a piece of fruit into his mouth. "You've been getting cocky lately. You need to be knocked down a few pegs."

"*I'm* getting cocky?" I scoffed. "That's rich, coming from you."

"*I* have every reason to be cocky. You not so much."

"Your ego's gotten so big that the other day you claimed you could, and I quote, 'take Roric any day.'"

Taking him in a fight wasn't what Xavier had been referring to, but that was beside the point.

Roric dropped the orange wedge from his lips and turned in Xavier's direction, brows lifting towards his hairline. "Is that so?"

Playing it cool, Xavier sighed. "Well, what can I say? You've been looking a little stiff lately, old man."

Roric barked a laugh. "You must like pain, boy."

Xavier's lips curled into a seductive smirk. "If the mood is right."

"Up," Roric demanded, standing and kicking Xavier's boot. "*Now.*"

"No, don't," I wailed, but eagerly darted out of their way.

Ilora joined me on the sidelines, her eyes narrowing. "What are you doing?"

"Taking a cue from Queen Evalarae of Kylanthia," I murmured, watching Xavier and Roric square off in front of us.

"This isn't over."

I put my index finger to my lips to shush her, then patted her shoulder. "Just sit back and enjoy the pretty, sweaty show."

Ilora rolled her eyes but didn't protest, propping her staff against a nearby wall and leaning beside it as she took in the view.

"Any last words?" Roric asked, bouncing on his toes and craning his neck from side to side.

"Yes." Xavier pointed at Roric's abdomen. "How many extra sticky buns did you eat to get that little belly pooch?"

Unable to help myself, I checked if Xavier's claims were grounded in truth. They weren't, and there was nothing on Roric's stomach except rock-hard, sweat-licked muscle. I hurriedly averted my gaze and told myself the warm flush in my cheeks was from the sun.

Roric chuckled and shook his head. "I won't be making this quick for you."

Xavier cocked a suggestive eyebrow. "Promise?"

"Your Majesty, will you count us down?" Roric called, his head lowering like an adder readying to strike.

Ilora stepped forward. "One..."

Xavier cracked his knuckles.

"Two..."

Roric clenched his jaw.

"Thr—"

"What's going on out here?"

At Willow's voice, the men dropped their fists and bolted to attention like two boys who'd been caught with their hands in a cookie jar.

The Sprite ambled down the palace steps with my brother in tow, one of his arms clamped firmly around his wolf like usual.

"Nothing." Roric casually smoothed his dark hair. "Just basic training."

"Yup." Xavier bobbed his head in agreement. "Hey, Wynnie! It's been a while since we've worked on your skills. Feel like giving it a go today?"

My brother considered for a few moments before nodding.

Xavier eagerly rubbed his hands together. "Great! Come on down."

As Wynn shuffled over, Roric caught Xavier by the back of the neck and hissed in his ear, "That child just saved your life."

"Keep telling yourself that," Xavier whispered back with a wink.

When my brother arrived at the men's feet, he lifted his free hand to the buttons on his shirt and began unfastening them. Xavier burst out laughing and ruffled his hair.

"It's alright, Wynn, you don't have to take your shirt off too. It's optional."

I shut my eyes and groaned. "I knew you were a bad influence."

Xavier snickered and led my brother a few paces away. Somehow, Wynn managed to keep his toy clenched between his arm and side even as he raised his fists into position. Willow fell in beside me, absentmindedly smoothing the pleats on her pink and purple trousers as she watched them.

"So when are we going to continue *your* training?" I asked, nudging her.

Roric perked up at my words and wandered over. "You're learning to fight too?" His eyes sparked with surprise, a tinge of admiration in his voice.

Willow blushed and ducked her head, fixing her gaze on the tile at our feet. "Sort of."

I threw an arm around her shoulders. "She *is*. And she's picking it up faster than anyone I've ever seen."

"Maybe sometime you could show me what you've learned so far." Roric smiled at her, but Willow didn't see. Her round eyes were still glued to her toes.

"She'd love to," I replied for her, giving her a squeeze. She responded by subtly elbowing me in the ribs. "How about right now?"

At that, I got a firm heel to the foot.

"I'm free now." Roric smiled again, and this time Willow peeked up and caught a glimpse, her face flushing a bright strawberry hue at the sight.

"Don't worry," he soothed. "I'll be gentle."

Willow swallowed and stood a little taller. "I'm not some delicate flower. I can handle more than people think."

Roric's brows arched, but he nodded solemnly. "Noted."

"And..." Willow gulped again, eyes briefly flicking to Roric's glistening chest. "I would like to keep my shirt on."

Roric's lips twitched as he fought another smile. "Understandable. Would you be more comfortable if I put mine back on?"

"No, keep it off!" Willow blurted.

Roric blinked.

"I mean..." Willow nervously wrung her hands. "Whatever you feel comfortable with is good. If you want that, then it's good. If you feel good, I feel good. Do you feel good?"

"I do feel good." Roric rubbed the back of his neck. "Are you sure you feel good?"

"Yup." Willow smoothed her palms down her thighs, leaving sweaty streaks in their wake. "Good. Very good. Shirt off... good. We're good."

"Good."

"Great," I chirped, clasping my hands in front of me. "Have fun, you two."

Roric headed off to join Xavier and Wynn, and Willow shot me the dirtiest look I've ever seen as she followed him. I grinned and waggled my fingers at her as she passed.

Ilora sidled up beside me and crossed her arms as she gazed

out over the courtyard. "Look at that. Just a few months in Fae court and you're already a master manipulator."

"I have no idea what you're talking about," I purred, innocently batting my eyelashes.

She laughed and readjusted one of the gold cuffs in a lock of her hair before tucking it back into the bun she'd fashioned on top of her head. "I'm going to petition for a new nickname for you. Lina Calder, the Puppeteer."

"Better than King Slayer," I said with a shrug.

Ilora sniffed wryly and fell silent, a small smile spreading across her lips as she watched Wynn throw jabs at Xavier's open palms.

I glanced at the queen out of the corner of my eye. Words tugged at my tongue, but I hesitated speaking them for fear of the answer. Eventually, my curiosity got the better of me.

"It doesn't bother you?" I asked softly. "Being friends with someone of my... reputation?"

"No," Ilora stated, the word so firm it made me jump a little. Her eyes darted to me, the light in them honest, resolute, and unwavering.

"People think they know me too, but they don't," she continued. "It doesn't matter. The only thing that matters is who you are when no one is watching."

Ilora took my hands in hers and gave them a solid squeeze. Though she remained composed on the outside, her voice strained as it held back emotion.

"You put your life on the line for my family even though you barely knew them. Innocent lives were in danger, and you dropped everything to go after them. You fought for them, nearly died for them. That proves who Lina Calder is more than some nickname."

I swallowed the tightness in my throat and looked down at our clasped hands. "But what I did to Valdir—"

"Valdir played dirty," Ilora interrupted, tugging my hands to snap me out of the dark place she knew I was drifting to.

I still dreamed of that Yule. Just last night, I'd felt the tendons on the king of Radomir's neck separating beneath my blade, saw his blood spurting from the wound and splattering across my face. The guilt still ate away at me, and more often than I'd like, a little voice at the back of my mind told me I was evil for doing what I had.

"While I understand Valdir's point of view," Ilora continued, "he went about things the wrong way. He should have called all the rulers of the realm to Merimaya for a peaceful summit to discuss options."

"Was that a possibility?" I'd never heard of anything like that happening before. During my time with the Fae, I'd seen the territories mainly keeping to themselves, only dealing with the others if there was trade to do or a party to attend.

"It's not unheard of," Ilora replied. "It used to happen more, but over the years everyone retreated into their own little worlds. But it *should* have happened the second rumors of war started circulating. Instead, Valdir took matters into his own hands."

Ilora cupped my cheeks in her palms, forcing my gaze up from the ground to look her in the eyes.

"Remember what I said before," she urged. "Peace is always the goal, but sometimes others don't believe in peace, and you have to speak to them in a language they understand. You spoke to Valdir in a language he started speaking *first*."

Ease washed over me at her words. Even though it seemed the whole of Astoria hated me, it was nice knowing I had allies in Lerian and Merimaya. Wise, strong, beautiful allies I had the immense honor of calling my friends.

Even if they were *very* scary at times.

"I have your back, Lina," Ilora insisted. "Always. And that's a promise."

I smiled and placed my hands over hers. "Thank you. And likewise."

"I know." She matched my smile and pushed her face closer to mine, lowering her voice. "But keep in mind, this changes nothing. I'll still be beating your ass the next chance I get."

We burst into a fit of giggles, and Ilora slung her arm around my shoulders as we returned our attention to the four figures training in the courtyard. We were so focused on watching them that we didn't notice Syrena exiting the palace and making her way over until she was directly beside us.

"Fate has spared me from Ilora's wrath, Syrena," I joked, playfully bumping Ilora with my hip. "Looks like I'll live to see another day."

"Good, because I just received word." Syrena's lips pressed into a tight line. "Tomorrow, the witch is coming."

<h1 style="text-align:center">Chapter 22</h1>

<hr>

"Where the hell is she?"

Syrena's words rang through the sitting room like a clap of thunder, mirroring the storm raging outside. For the past thirty minutes the only noise had been the constant patter of rain on the roof and the diamond beads on Syrena's fringe gown swishing and clacking together while she paced. Ilora and I sat on the low couch, both lost in thought while the former gnawed her nails raw and I rubbed at my neck absentmindedly.

"I'm sure she'll be here soon." Ilora patted the couch cushion beside her. "Will you please sit down? You're stressing me out."

Syrena obeyed, but the beads on her dress continued to rattle as her leg bounced. Ilora threw a hand to Syrena's knee, stilling her.

"Focus on *anything* else," she hissed.

Syrena glared at her friend. "Like what?"

"Tell us what we can expect."

The Lerian queen sighed and fiddled with the stack of gold-and-emerald bangles on her wrist. "I don't remember much about her. I was a child when my mother brought me to her. I just remember her being odd."

I leaned forward. "Odd how?"

"I don't know. She barely made any sense. It was almost like she—"

"Spoke in riddles?"

"Yes!"

I nodded. "They do that."

"Well, I just remember my mother being very unimpressed when we left her."

Ilora leaned back in the couch and draped her arms across the back. "Why did your mother take you to see her?"

"She wanted to see if I had any special gifts."

"The witch could tell if you had magic?"

"I guess so." Syrena's gaze floated to the ground, and even though she forced a playful smile on her face, her slumping shoulders proved how disheartened she was by what she said next. "Despite how difficult she was to understand, her answer was a very clear *no*. It's been over a hundred years since, and nothing's shown up, so it seems she was right."

"Maybe she'll be able to see what happens with Aedan, so we won't need to find the Hag," Ilora mused, mainly to herself.

Syrena huffed a frustrated sigh. "Maybe. If she ever decides to show up."

"My apologies, Your Majesty."

All three of us shot to our feet at the voice. I, however, was the only one who drew a weapon.

The witch standing in the doorway lowered the hood of her cloak, offering a kind smile to ease the tension. I blinked, taken aback by how young she was. Most of the witches I'd met over the past several months had been silver-haired and etched with wrinkles, but this one looked barely older than Soren. My stomach knotted at the thought of him, so I quickly refocused on the woman in front of me before the ache in my heart became too distracting.

"I had trouble gaining entry at the gate," the witch said, removing her suede gloves and draping them on a nearby tea table. "It seems someone doesn't want you receiving any visitors."

I exchanged a look with Syrena, the name silent but heavy between us. It was no doubt the same person who'd tried to keep *me* from entering the palace when I first arrived.

Kaspar.

"Sorry about that." Syrena frowned. "Thank you for making the journey here, Rosheen."

The witch, Rosheen, nodded and tucked a stray lock of sandy blonde hair behind her ear, an ear slightly more elongated and slender than the Fae. She was a Water Sprite, and it was barely noticeable in the torchlight, but her skin carried a slight bluish tint.

As Ilora and I returned to our seats, Rosheen wandered over to Syrena and gave her a quick curtsy before taking her hands. "Your Majesty, you are the spitting image of your mother. Down to the details." Her gaze held on the stack of bracelets at Syrena's wrist.

Syrena smiled politely but slipped her fingers out of the witch's grasp and tucked them behind her back. "Would you like some tea?"

"No thank you," Rosheen replied, shifting her attention away from Syrena to study the rest of the room.

"Wine, then?"

"No."

"Water?"

"Where is the dark one?" the witch asked abruptly.

Syrena's thick brows knit. "Who?"

Rosheen didn't look at her. Her eyes continued to bounce

around the room, soaking up every detail like a sponge. "Your shadow."

"My brother?"

Rosheen shook her head, entwining her fingers in one of the silk curtains dividing the room. "The child your mother's handmaid bore."

"Hale."

"Yes." The witch's eyes locked on my face. "The one the night spills from."

Her gaze was unwavering and intense, almost uncomfortably so, but I refused to be intimidated and matched her stare. I barely heard Syrena in the background.

"Hale passed away last year. Commander Roric Pax is our captain of the guard again."

"You," Rosheen muttered, still staring at me. She wandered over and lowered herself onto the cushion beside me.

"You were not afraid of the dark?" Rosheen asked, head tilting with curiosity.

Something told me she already knew the answer. Still, I replied with the truth.

"No, I wasn't."

A smile played at one corner of Rosheen's mouth. "What is your name?"

I swallowed, mentally preparing myself for the snide remark or crude jab sure to follow like it always did. "Lina Calder."

But the witch didn't scoff and call me the King Slayer, or Soren's pet, or a human whore. She simply closed her eyes and nodded slowly, like my name was the answer to a puzzle she'd been trying to solve. When she opened her eyes again, she brushed my hair behind my shoulder, then gently traced her fingertips over the rounded shell of my ear. I had to force myself not to shiver at her feather-light touch.

"Lina Calder," Rosheen repeated softly, studying my features like a map. "The lover of fire and shadow."

Something in my chest twisted at her words. An image leapt into my mind of that night on Imbolc when I stood beside Soren, the flame on my candle forming the shape of a heart at his command. My own heart had ached then too, only that night it was because it had filled to the brim with unfathomable love, a stark contrast to the pain now. A result of all that love being ripped away. In its wake was a gaping wound that, despite everything that had happened, still desperately yearned for him.

The witch nodded again and patted my hand, as if she understood everything I was thinking and feeling. She then returned her attention to Syrena.

"May I ask what I have been summoned here for, Your Majesty?"

"Yes." Syrena stepped forward. "You see things. Things other people can't."

Rosheen shrugged one shoulder. "We would all see more if only we had the courage to be still and look."

I peeked at Ilora and rolled my eyes, mouthing the word *riddles*. She disguised her giggle by taking a sip of tea.

"We were wondering if you can look for something for us," Syrena continued.

"What do you seek?"

"Any information on something brewing up north. In Kylanthia, specifically."

"There is much turmoil in Kylanthia."

"Yes, but is there anything..." Syrena looked up at the gilded ceiling, searching for the words. "Is there anything *big* coming? Something evil, emerging from the rubble."

Rosheen chuckled and stood, slipping her hands into the wide bell sleeves of her rain-drenched cloak. "You say I speak in riddles, but your tongue is dancing around the truth more than mine."

Ilora set aside her tea and leaned forward in her seat. "Is the king of the Netherworld releasing his army of Nethers to rain terror down on the Fae?"

The witch's brows arched with amusement. "This one refuses to dance."

She moved forward, her unflinching stare once again taking on that inquisitive intensity she'd bored into me with, this time directed at Ilora.

"You've had to become both king and queen," she mumbled. "You've adopted your mother's kindness and wisdom and combined it with your father's poise and authority."

Ilora balked slightly, her brow furrowing as she considered Rosheen's words. Finally she mumbled, "I... I never really thought about it like that."

Rosheen nodded knowingly, a warm smile spreading over her face. "They would be immensely proud of the ruler you've become."

Ilora sat a little taller, and gave the witch a small smile back. "I know."

Rosheen dipped her head in respect to the queen, then returned her attention to Syrena and shrugged helplessly. "I cannot see what you want me to. The sight I have only permits me to see what is inside, not what looms on the horizon."

Both Syrena and Ilora wilted.

"I'm sorry," Rosheen added. "I know it's not what you wanted to hear."

I scooted forward so I was sitting on the edge of the sofa. "Then will you get a message to someone who *can* see what we need?"

Rosheen arched an eyebrow. "Who do you have in mind?"

"The Hag."

The witch blinked in alarm. After a few weighted seconds of silence, she tossed her head back and cackled.

Ilora, Syrena, and I exchanged glances, all three of us entirely unsure of what was so funny or how we should respond.

"The Hag is a myth," Rosheen said, finally composing herself and wiping the tears of merriment from her eyes. "Just a tall tale told to children."

I crossed my arms. "Everything in this realm was a myth to my people, yet here you are."

The witch's attention settled on me, and she smirked. "I am but a lowly cottage witch. What makes you think *if* the Hag exists, *I* would be able to reach her?"

I shrugged and repeated the simple phrase Syrena had uttered the other day. "Witches talk."

"Everyone talks," Rosheen countered. "In their own way, of course."

She lowered herself onto the cushion beside me and slipped her hands into mine.

"And when I say everyone, Lina," Rosheen whispered, leaning in close, "I do mean *everyone*."

I looked the witch up and down, unnerved by the sudden hushed urgency in her voice and pointed stare.

"What is that supposed to—"

The door to the sitting room flew open. Our heads whipped to Willow stumbling inside, panting for air.

"Please tell me Wynn is here with you," she gasped, tears streaming down her flushed cheeks.

A wave of dread flooded through me when I caught sight of a well-loved plush wolf clutched in her trembling hands.

I bolted to standing and stomped across the room towards her. I couldn't see my expression, but whatever it was, it instantly had Willow cowering in fear. "You weren't supposed to let him out of your sight!"

"I didn't!" Willow wailed, crumpling against the doorjamb. "He was asleep and started shivering, so all I did was go to the other room to grab him a blanket! The windows were barred, and the guard was supposed to be at the door!" She choked back a sob. "I was just gone for a minute. It was just one minute..."

Ignoring her cries, I moved to brush past her, but froze when I saw Wynn's notepad in her arms beside the wolf. I ripped it from her grasp and held it up to the torchlight. At the center of the page was a hurriedly scribbled symbol.

A spiked circle entwined in vines, with two crescent moons at the center and lines connecting them.

Demon lover.

My heart a deafening drum in my ears, I looked over my shoulder at Syrena, Ilora, and Rosheen. The seer stared back at me, her expression unnervingly peaceful.

"Everyone talks in their own way," she repeated.

Setting my jaw, I shoved the notebook back in Willow's arms and blew past her.

I didn't have to think about where I was going. Something deep in the recesses of my mind knew exactly where I'd find my brother.

After all, I'd seen this before.

I'd seen it the other day.

I'd seen it on Imbolc.

I'd even seen it before then, too.

For months my brother had been drawing symbols and wandering to the west in search of a voice only he could hear. He'd been speaking this whole time, I just hadn't heard him.

My thundering footfalls echoed through the empty corridor as I rounded the corner, headed for the balcony on the cliffs. In the distance, I glimpsed a head of curly blond hair nearing the balcony's bench overlooking the sea.

"Wynn!" I shouted, my voice so sharp and firm as it cut through the silence that I half expected the windows to shatter as I tore through the doorway.

"Wynn!" I called again, throwing myself out into the night and nearly losing my footing on the balcony's slick stones. Water fell from the sky in torrents, gusts of wind whipping it around the palace's exterior so fast it stung my bare arms and cheeks.

I squinted and raised my hand to shield my eyes against the biting rain. Through the heavy downpour, I could barely make out my brother's form. He was only revealed fully when a flash of lightning lit up the sky.

"Wynn!" I screamed.

But my brother didn't respond, and continued hauling himself onto the railing of the balcony.

I lunged towards him, but my silk slippers lost traction on the flooded stones, and I toppled forward. Too numb from adrenaline, I barely processed the pain as my knees cracked against the rock. My brother was swinging one leg over the rail, followed by the other. I screamed his name again, but received only a loud clap of thunder from the heavens in response.

I scrambled upright just as my brother settled on the balcony's edge, both legs dangling precariously over the side. Even all the way up here, surrounded by the wind and the rain, the tumultuous roar of the ocean filled my ears. His back to me, my brother leaned forward, staring down at the roiling waves far below.

"Wynn!" I shrieked, my voice breaking.

Another vein of lightning cut across the sky, followed by a crack of thunder so loud it shook the ground. I ducked, then watched in horror as my brother teetered on the ledge. I jerked forward, reaching out for him, a name instinctively passing my lips.

"Aedan!"

My brother froze.

Chest heaving, I inched forward and craned my neck to see Wynn's face.

"Aedan," I repeated more confidently.

Slowly, my brother's head swiveled to look at me over his shoulder.

Water streamed down his face.

His curls were sodden and plastered to his forehead.

And his eyes were glazed in spellbound white.

I tried to rein in my frantic breaths. "You can hear me, can't you? When he's like this, you can hear and see through him. Just like you could see through Hale when he used his magic."

As expected, Wynn said nothing. He just stared.

I started towards him again, moving at an agonizingly slow pace.

"Aedan, please," I said, trying to force my voice strong and steady. "Have mercy on him."

Tears slid down my cheeks, but they were indistinguishable from the raindrops battering my face. My brother seemed unaffected by the cold and damp. He was nothing but a crust of a child riddled with the gaze of an evil creature in a realm far away. I knew that creature was cruel and conniving, but part of me hoped he still had a sliver of a conscience, a tiny moral compass that still pointed north. If he did, then maybe, by some divine miracle ordained by the gods, he would find it in himself to have some compassion.

"Aedan." I clasped my hands in front of me the same way I used to as a young girl when I'd kneel at the foot of my bed and pray to the gods. "Please. He's all I have left. Don't take him from me. I'm begging you... just let him go."

My brother smiled.

Then he faced the ocean, released his grip on the rail, and jumped.

Wynn's name tore from my throat, but it was drowned out by another deafening peal of thunder. I raced to the edge of the balcony, a bright flash of lightning making it possible to catch a glimpse of a tiny figure hitting the choppy water below before disappearing into its depths.

I hesitated for a half second, considering the route to the beach through the palace's maze of hallways and staircases. Even if I ran as fast as possible, it would take too long. Minutes.

But Wynn didn't have minutes.

Before I could talk myself out of it, I threw both legs over the railing, took a deep breath, and leapt into open space, plummeting down the side of the craggy cliff towards the churning waves.

I hit the water so hard the wind was knocked from my lungs.

Cold jolted through me, shocking my body and scrambling my mind. For a few seconds, nothing existed except icy dark and the burning sensation in my chest from lack of air. A flash of lightning lit up the ocean around me, bringing submerged rocks and tall tendrils of kelp into view, snapping me back to reality. Without thinking, I opened my mouth to heave in a lungful of air, accidentally letting a flood of saltwater in. I choked, sending a cloud of bubbles into the space around me.

The survival instincts that had been lying dormant until now suddenly woke up and screamed.

*Air! Get air!*

I flailed my arms and kicked, propelling myself towards the surface. Just as my lungs nearly gave out, I burst up through the waves, coughing and sputtering to gasp in glorious life-saving air. When I'd composed myself, I searched the choppy waves around me, peering into every dip and crest as the ocean tossed me along with it.

"Wynn!" I shouted.

The night lit up with another flash of white, revealing the world around me for a few brief seconds. There was no sign of my brother. Not in the swells, not on the rocks, nowhere on the surface. Which could only mean one thing.

I took a deep breath and dove back into the watery abyss.

The pitch black was bone-chillingly cold, but it was nothing compared to the terror that gripped my chest as I faced the unknown. Was it just fingers of kelp reaching out and brushing my arms and legs, or was it a sharp-toothed predator hungry for a taste of helpless human flesh? Was I actually swimming towards the ocean floor, or was the current dragging me towards the razor-sharp rocks?

For any other reason, the murky depths would be frightening enough that I'd give up and swim back to the safety of the surface. But one word played over and over in my head, spurring me onward.

*Wynn.*

Far away thunder boomed, its bang muffled by the water in my ears, while lightning flashed and illuminated the ocean around me once more. Something moved to my left. I waited for another burst of light, praying it wasn't a shark or a Merrow or something with long tentacles and serrated teeth on a mission to tear me apart. But when the world lit up again, I'd have breathed a sigh of relief if I could have spared the air.

Alive, unharmed, and swimming towards a jagged reef was my brother.

Everything went dark again, and I furiously kicked towards Wynn and the rock, trying not to focus on the desperate ache my lungs had started to take on. Something solid and slimy nudged my shoulder, and I winced. Whatever it was, it hadn't been kelp. Praying it was only a fish just as jostled by the turbulent water as I was, I swam on.

My chest stung, begging for the fresh air at the surface, but I couldn't risk going back up for another breath. Wynn had already been under longer than I had. Who knew how much longer he could last?

I continued to paddle through the dark, gulping down a desperate hiccup that tried to bubble out of me. I had to be getting close. Wynn had been moving slow, and I was tearing through the water like I was being chased by another Ben Síde. Unless the current had turned me around and I hadn't noticed, I had to be right above him.

As if in answer, my hands collided with a wall of rough coral. Relief flooded over me, and I dragged myself along the reef with one hand while the other searched the surrounding water. My fingers brushed something firm and slimy, and I gasped in surprise, sending a glob of air burbling upwards. My lungs screamed again, pulsing as they desperately fought to expand. I twisted my head left and right, searching for any sign of my brother, but I was blind in the darkness. I needed light.

I lifted my face towards the surface, silently pleading for the gods to send another flash of lightning. As if on cue, the water around me illuminated.

Only the light didn't come from the sky above.

Confused, I whipped my head towards the ocean floor. There, at the base of the reef, a narrow crack led to an underwater cave.

A cave that glowed with an otherworldly cyan hue.

A cave whose entrance a small human child was wriggling through.

Another burst of air bubbled from my lips as I pushed off the reef and dove towards my brother, scaring away a shoal of fish gathered nearby. Wynn slipped through the crack, but I caught his hand just before he disappeared through entirely. Bracing my feet on either side of the crevice, I yanked him backwards as hard as I could, cringing as his clothing snagged and his arms scraped along the rocks, but it was better than the alternative.

I shot a wary glance at the eerie blue radiating from the cave and managed one final solid tug. Wynn tore free of the reef at the same time my lungs gave out, releasing all the air I'd been holding. I latched a hand on to the back of Wynn's shirt and kicked for the surface. My chest tightened, my head felt like it was going to burst, and stars scattered across my vision. My body couldn't fight its natural urges any longer. My mouth opened, and I heaved in a lungful of water. I choked and coughed it out, but inhaled another mouthful immediately after. I became too preoccupied with the water rushing in and out of my lungs to put much effort into swimming, my movements growing weaker and more erratic. The surface of the ocean still seemed painfully far away.

I shut my eyes, choking on the water spilling into my mouth, but tightened my grip on my brother.

He'd made it so far, he couldn't die now.

*We'd* made it so far.

Since that fateful night in the woods on Samhain, both my brother and I had gone through hell and back. He'd been kidnapped and spellbound. I'd been hunted, tortured, and had battled unimaginable monsters. We'd beaten worse odds than this. This couldn't be how the last of the Calders went out. They couldn't die alone in a cold watery grave. They would go out in either a blaze of glory or surrounded by the ones who loved them—or both at the same time.

Choosing that as our fate and refusing to accept anything else, I dug deep, mustered what strength I still had, and kicked as hard and fast as I possibly could. After a few seconds that seemed more like an eternity, we burst out of the sea and gasped in precious air.

The wild waves tossed us against a nearby rock, which I feebly clung to as I hacked up the remaining saltwater from my lungs. I then shoved my brother on top of the algae-slick stone so he was out of harm's way before crawling up after him. I leaned Wynn on his side and slammed a hand to his back to knock loose any water from his lungs. He was cut and bloodied from the reef, but miraculously still breathing.

I collapsed back on the rock beside my brother, shutting my eyes against the rain as I attempted to catch my breath. As we lay there, I replayed everything that had just happened. There was no denying the similarities the underwater cave shared with another cavern I'd stumbled into in Kylanthia. *That* was the entrance to the Netherworld, though. It couldn't be here too.

… Could it?

I opened my eyes and angled my head to look at my brother. All at once, the words uttered by the witch in Astoria played in my ears.

*You think the boy blind, but he sees. You think him mute, but he speaks. Listen… and follow.*

The witch had said something else after that, a final command spoken with her dying breath. I ruminated on those words, let them sink into my bones and relight the fire in my veins, and for the first time in a very long time, I was sure of what I needed to do.

I SLOSHED back into the palace sitting room with my brother's wrist locked in an iron grip. Syrena, Ilora, and Willow were nowhere to be seen, probably still searching the palace for

Wynn, but Rosheen hadn't left. She was perched in the middle of the couch, waiting patiently with her hands clasped on her lap.

I came to a stop directly in front of her, water dripping from my body to pool at our feet and soak the hem of her dress. She blinked up at me, eyes as wide and innocent as a fawn's.

"Give the Hag a message." My words were both command and threat. "Tell her Lina Calder is ready to embrace the dark."

# Chapter 23

"I don't know how much more of this I can take."

I glanced at Ilora on the horse next to me. She stared straight ahead, her mouth taut and her shoulders tense.

"I swear," she said in a strained whisper. "If this goes on for one second longer, I *will* kill them."

I peeked over my shoulder at Xavier and Syrena. Xavier was currently singing a song at the top of his lungs that Syrena had mentioned she hated, and she was retaliating by trying to force her horse to run his off the narrow dirt path.

"This little *thing*, whatever it is, was funny a week ago. It was funny a few days ago. Hell, it was funny an hour ago. But now?" Ilora shook her head. "Now I'm losing my damn mind."

I snickered and leaned down to give my horse a pat on its silky neck. Since Xavier hadn't returned to Astoria yet, I still had possession of Soren's massive steed. I'd never planned to hold on to it for so long, but after all this time, I'd grown fond of the beast and hated the idea of returning it. Also, in a way, it made me feel closer to Soren. As much as I wanted to deny it, it felt like part of me was missing without him. Almost as if I'd left a piece of my soul in Astoria the day I left, and no matter what I did, I couldn't capture it again. There was nothing but a hole in its place and a gnawing, ever-present sensation of being incomplete. Syrena told me the feeling would pass in time and insisted getting rid of anything Soren had ever given me would help, starting with both the horse and my dagger, but I couldn't bear to part with either. Not yet, at least.

I glanced down at Soren's blade on my thigh, a twinge of sadness twisting my heart at the sight of the silver and steel, but I quickly pushed it away and refocused on the rugged rock and green that made up the barren High Lands between Lerian and Merimaya. Mist drifted down from the craggy hills, not so thick it was impeding our journey, but heavy enough it set a damp chill in our bones.

I pulled my cloak tighter around my shoulders. "Don't worry, we're almost there."

"Thank the gods." Ilora nudged her horse into a trot, putting more distance between her and the bickering duo behind us. I stifled another laugh and followed her lead.

"I'm still surprised the Hag told you where she lived," Ilora mused. "I thought she'd want to keep her location a secret and she'd come to us instead."

I squinted at the rocky outcrops flanking either side of the path. "Maybe she assumed coming all the way out here would deter us."

"Maybe." Lost in thought, Ilora chewed the inside of her cheek. "Did she say anything else to you?"

"No," I lied.

I hated keeping secrets from my friends, but they couldn't know the truth.

If anyone knew what was discussed in my letters to and from the Hag that Rosheen had been ushering back and forth over the last few weeks, they would've never let me come. But as terrifying as it was, I had to do this. For Wynn, for my friends, for all those I'd lost, and most importantly, for myself.

The path we'd been following veered to the left, leading us around the rocky outcrops and into the open. Without the hills to shield us, the wind picked up considerably, clearing the fog so jagged coastal cliffs and choppy ocean waves came into view. Tucked slightly inland from the bluffs was a cozy cabin, complete with a stone chimney puffing gray smoke and a small barn for the herd of fluffy sheep grazing nearby.

"There it is!" I shouted over the deafening gusts.

Syrena rode up beside me, her curls whipping wildly around her face despite the silk scarf she'd wrapped around her head to contain them.

"Then what are we waiting for?" she hollered back. "I'm fucking freezing!"

"Should've worn a more practical outfit, Your Highness," Xavier called over his shoulder as he trotted past her, "but no, you just *had* to dress to impress."

Syrena shot daggers at the back of his head, but judging by the way her teeth chattered, Xavier was right. She was dressed like a queen, but there was a reason queens didn't live out here.

I led the rest of the way, guiding my horse through the front gate of the dwelling and dismounting before tying its reins to the nearest fence post. The rest of the party followed suit. Xavier blew into his hands and vigorously rubbed them together to ward off the cold.

"So who wants to be the one to knock on the mythical magic lady's door?"

None of us had to decide, though, because the door swung open on its own.

Ilora instinctively jumped backwards, and Xavier's eyes went round, while Syrena gasped and moved closer to him.

"Don't worry, that's normal," I explained.

My friends exchanged wary glances.

I faced forward again, checking in with myself a final time to make sure I really wanted to do this. But I already knew the answer. I'd made up my mind while I lay out on that rock in the storm.

No matter the cost, I would do everything in my power to stop Aedan.

So I straightened my shoulders, clenched my fists at my side, and stepped over the threshold to meet the Hag.

I expected something similar to the witch's shack in Astoria: jars of lizard guts, strange runes, and an eerie wrinkled woman mixing elixirs in the dark.

But this house was the opposite.

It was warm and inviting, homey even, with the scent of fresh-baked bread wafting around the room, a kettle simmering on a roaring fire, and a shaggy old sheepdog snoozing on the rug in front of the hearth. Curled up in the overstuffed armchair beside him was the last thing I expected to see in a dwelling belonging to the most powerful witch in the realm.

Peering up at us with round eyes and a friendly smile... was a teenage girl.

A wool throw was draped over her lap, and she had a book in one hand and a steaming cup of peppermint tea in the other.

"Hello," she chirped, her voice as bright and sweet as the tinkle of a bell.

Caught off guard, I did another scan of the space. There was no one else here besides the dog.

I turned back to the young girl. "Hello. I... I think we might have the wrong house."

"You're looking for the Hag," the girl said as nonchalantly as discussing the weather. She closed her book and set it aside, blinking up at us with a face as fresh as morning dew.

I peeked at my friends, who shrugged back.

When I returned my attention to the girl, she was reaching down to scratch the sheepdog behind the ears. "Yes, we are. Is she... out?"

"No," the girl said simply. "She's here."

"Oh." I nodded casually and stuffed my hands into my pockets, glancing around the room once more. "Um... where exactly?"

The dog huffed and stretched, rolling onto his back for belly rubs. The girl grinned and obliged. "Right here."

Xavier arched one eyebrow. "The Hag is a dog?"

The girl laughed and shook her head, one of her braids slipping out from behind her shoulder, its tail narrowly escaping a dip in her tea. "Xavier, you're a breath of fresh air, you know that?"

Xavier tensed. "How do you know my name?"

The girl finished off the contents of her mug, then set it beside her book. "You hear whispers over the years."

Syrena scoffed. "What years? You can't be a day over sixteen."

The girl beamed proudly. "It does look that way, doesn't it?"

The dog's tongue lolled from his mouth as he panted happily, relishing the girl's fingers in his long fur.

"It's amazing the things that can be accomplished when there's magic coursing through your veins, especially in regard to one's appearance."

Ilora hesitantly stepped forward, her eyes narrowing as she slowly looked the girl up and down. "*You're* the Hag?"

The dog woofed happily, and the girl giggled. "Indeed I am."

Syrena rolled her eyes and crossed her arms over her chest. "This is ridiculous. We clearly have the wrong house and the child's teasing us."

The girl sighed and shifted her focus to the ribbon at the

end of one of her braids, where she began readjusting its dainty bow. "You have the tendency to lash out when you're afraid, Syrena. You might want to work on that. It's a good way to lose the ones you truly care about."

"I don't lash out when I'm afraid!" Syrena snapped.

The girl smirked and tilted her chin to Xavier. "How come you're so nasty to him, then?"

Syrena's cheeks drained of their color, and her mouth clamped firmly shut. Xavier's gaze darted between her and the Hag, his brow furrowing in confusion.

"I don't mind changing if you'd prefer someone else." The girl nestled back in her chair, calmly folding her hands in her lap. "Perhaps something more expected? Like how I looked when I first met Lina?"

Everyone's eyes turned to me. I stiffened. "I've only spoken to you in letters."

The sly smile that spread across the girl's lips looked out of place on her innocent face. "Oh?"

When she opened her mouth again, the voice that escaped it was no longer the melodic warble of a young girl. Instead it had the weathered timbre of an old woman.

"A girl torn between two worlds," the voice stated. "She searches for the Netherworld prince, but her path is one of darkness and pain. A great evil is growing, unable to be contained by one world alone. The Slayer of Kings will return before the end."

I stumbled backwards, bumping into Ilora, who put a hand on my shoulder to steady me.

"The seer last year on Imbolc," I murmured, the realization making my head spin. "That was *you*?"

I still saw that woman in my mind as clear as the day it happened. I'd been slumped against a door, shaken after threatening to slice Kaspar's throat, when the witch found me and took my face in her wrinkled old hands to whisper that ominous premonition while I stared deep into her unseeing eyes.

The girl shrugged cooly, her voice returning to normal. "Merimaya knows how to throw a good party. I couldn't resist attending."

I glanced behind me at Ilora, who appeared just as shocked as I was.

"But..." I refocused on the girl and shook my head. "But the woman then was—"

"An old hag?" The girl grinned, her gaze darting between the four of us. "With extraordinary magic running through your veins, the opportunities are endless. You can create something out of nothing, alter your appearance, even see incredible things if you dare peek behind the curtain into the dark."

When the woman's eyes landed on me, her mischievous smile widened.

"Are you afraid of the dark, Lina Calder?" she asked. Her question was genuine, her stare glimmering with curiosity. In answer, I stood a little taller and clung firmly to the decision I'd made on that rock out at sea.

"No," I replied. "I'm not."

The girl nodded, then returned her attention to my friends, who were still uncomfortably fidgeting in response to the information they'd just been given.

"I don't know why it has your feathers so ruffled." The girl tutted, carelessly waving away their discomfort as she stood and carried her empty cup to a nearby washbasin. "I'm not the first creature you've come across who can change their shape, am I?"

She looked over her shoulder at us and smiled again, her eyes sparkling like the entire universe danced inside them.

"After all, that's why you've come, isn't it? You wish to know about the king of the Netherworld and his frigid Fae queen."

Xavier leaned his mouth to Syrena's ear. "Still think we have the wrong house?"

She responded with a swift elbow to his stomach.

"I understand you're not fond of riddles, so I'll speak plainly now." The girl dried her hands on her skirt and intertwined her fingers in front of her. Her playful demeanor abruptly changed, her face falling into an expression no longer childish and kind, but cold and foreboding.

"Death is coming," she stated. "For you and your loved ones, young and old, the guilty as well as the innocent."

A chill of fear raked its claws down my back at her words. Of course, I'd considered the idea before. I'd lain with it in the dead of night when worry and anxiety kept me awake and tied my stomach in knots until morning. But hearing it declared as fact was far worse. Now it wasn't just a made-up scenario only alive in my overactive imagination. It was real.

"The entire realm will end in destruction," the girl continued. "Unless you return to the Netherworld and inflict it first."

Ilora exhaled through her teeth and rubbed the back of her neck. "You mean we have to kill Aedan."

The girl dipped her head in acknowledgement.

"We tried that already," Syrena argued. "It didn't work."

The girl shrugged and returned to the dog in front of the hearth so she could gently stroke his head. "So this time you'll need some help."

Syrena stepped forward, her long nails digging into the biceps of her folded arms as she attempted to keep her composure. The queen, it seemed, hated witches' riddles just as much as I did.

"Who would you suggest?" Syrena ground out. "Even the most powerful Fae magic is useless in the Netherworld. Not even the king of Astoria could do anything. We could have an army of Sorens and it would be pointless."

My heart ached as I relived the shock and terror on Soren's face in the Netherworld when he realized he was utterly defenseless against Aedan. In that moment, all I wanted was to wrap him in my arms and kiss away every ounce of fear that tormented him.

Hell, I *still* wanted that.

I shoved the thought away, telling myself this was *not* the time to act like a lovesick fool, but the pain in my heart stayed put.

The girl's playful demeanor returned, and she winked at the queen of Lerian. "That is exactly why you all are here."

Ilora's brows nudged closer. "We're here to find out how and when Aedan and Erith will attack the Fae realm."

"Not entirely." A smile toyed at the girl's lips. "Would you like to tell your friends, King Slayer, or should I?"

I shrank at the room of questioning stares. Even the dog was blinking my way and whining softly with his chin propped on top of his paws.

"Lina?" Ilora asked, touching my forearm. "What's going on?"

I took a deep breath and willed my voice steady. "Our weapons are useless against Aedan, and I doubt we'll get another shot with a Nether-made blade. If we're going to take him down once and for all, we'll need something else. Something—"

"Extraordinary," the Hag finished for me. She was smiling proudly, eagerly even, and although I had no real reason to trust her, I did. What I was doing was reckless, but I was doing this. Good or bad, right or wrong, I *was* doing this.

"Did you bring what I requested?" the girl prodded.

I wilted at her words. I'd known this time was coming, but

now that it was finally here, I didn't want to face it. I wanted a little more time.

But time had finally run out.

I sighed and lowered my fingers to the weapon at my thigh, wrapped them around the glittering vines on the silver-filigree hilt of Soren's dagger, and slowly pulled the blade from its sheath. Its metallic hiss sliced through the silence that had descended on the room, and I paused for a moment, admiring the beauty of the blade and reminiscing on all I'd survived because of it. But mainly, I thought about the man who'd given it to me. The man who'd saved a girl he found dying in the forest, who'd taken her in even though she hated him for it, who'd fought for her even though his people hated *him* for it, and loved her even though it left them both broken in the end.

I curled my hand around the blade and shut my eyes.

*Thank you, Soren. Thank you, and goodbye.*

Then I took a deep breath and offered the dagger to the witch.

"My most prized possession," I stated, nodding to the blade. "Just like you asked."

The girl carefully took the dagger and lifted it to a beam of sun cutting through the paned windows, her eyes narrowing into slits as she analyzed it. After a few seconds, she grunted and dropped the knife to her side.

"No."

I blinked. "No?"

"No," the girl repeated.

"I don't understand." I glanced at Xavier and Syrena like they could somehow give me an explanation.

"I asked for your most prized possession."

"And I gave it to you," I snapped.

*Witches and their stupid fucking riddles—*

"You gave me *one* of them." The girl stepped forward, her gaze shifting back to my thigh. "*You* have *two*."

It took me a few moments to realize what she was referring to. Only when I glanced down at my leg and glimpsed a sliver of black glinting inside the sheath did I remember the knife I'd taken from Hale's room as a memento and wedged behind Soren's dagger.

"Two blades from two men who mean the world to you." The girl extended her free hand, waggling her fingers.

I hesitated, tugging at the buckles down the front of my jacket in an attempt to somehow relieve the ache in my chest, but I eventually conceded and slid the onyx-hued blade from its resting place. I surrendered it in an outstretched palm.

The girl plucked the knife from my grasp and examined it beside the other, a pleased smile lighting up her face.

"Sorry, I'm a little confused." Syrena's words cut through the air, tight and high-pitched. "What the hell are you doing, Lina?"

I turned to meet the savage darts shooting from my friend's gaze, her hardened exterior only there to disguise the distress inside.

"This time we need to bring something into the Netherworld that will help us."

"And what exactly would that be?"

I lifted my chin. "Me."

# Chapter 24



My statement was met with blank stares.

Xavier finally broke the silence. He sighed, then brought thumb and forefinger to his closed eyelids and rubbed them in circles. "You're going to need to expand because I'm having a hard time following."

The Hag slipped over to Xavier and slid her hand into his palm, smiling up at him as he looked down at her in surprise.

"You must fight like with like," she explained. "Hence why only something made of a Nether had an effect on Aedan. You need darkness to fight in the dark. And luckily for you..." She squeezed his hand tenderly. "A witch has knowledge of both the light and the dark."

Xavier blinked at the girl for a few seconds before his eyes narrowed. "No offense, but that isn't the slightest bit helpful."

For the sake of time and my friends' sanity, I decided to finish the riddle for them and repeated the words the Hag had uttered earlier. "With extraordinary magic running through your veins, the opportunities are endless."

Ilora and Syrena continued to stare, but Xavier's eyes widened.

"You're putting magic in her?" he blurted, ripping his hand from the girl's grasp.

The Hag chuckled and bopped him on the nose with the tip of her finger. "Very good. Not just a pretty face, are you?"

Syrena finally snapped, and she latched a hand around Xavier's arm to tug him away from the girl. The witch just smiled.

"There is a way to surpass the blocks of the Netherworld," she said cooly. "I can make it so that a Fae's magic will extend across the veil to the dark realm. Their power may be weakened, but it will still be intact. I accomplish this by combining the magic of one, or..." She waved Soren and Hale's daggers in the air. "... in this case two, with the magic inside another to create something else entirely. Something extraordinary. Something not bound by the barriers between worlds like the magic of the Fae."

Xavier shook his head and scraped his fingers through his shaggy curls. "Wait a minute... what do you mean, you're combining the magic of one with the magic inside another? Lina's not Fae, she doesn't have magic."

"Right. So this could be a waste of time."

Xavier relaxed slightly.

"Or it might kill her," the Hag added with a careless shrug. "Can't be entirely sure."

"*What?*" Syrena shrieked.

The witch rolled her eyes. "With Fae, it works perfectly. But I've never done it to a human. I don't know if it will have the same effect."

Syrena's hands balled into fists at her side. "I thought you were supposed to be all-knowing."

"Only the gods are all-knowing, child," the girl spat. "While I'm honored you think so highly of me, keep in mind I am nothing but an old hag."

"You knew about this and didn't tell us?" Ilora asked, cutting the tension between the two as she took hold of my elbow and maneuvered me to face her. "Why?"

"You would've told me it's a bad idea."

"It *is* a bad idea!" Syrena screeched. "It's a *very* bad idea! Why can't we just try a bigger knife next time? Or, I don't know, aim better?"

I shot her a dirty look. "And what if that doesn't work?"

"What if *this* doesn't work?" she countered.

My confidence faltered. That thought had been quietly sneaking around the shadowy outskirts of my mind for some time now, and Syrena had just shone a light on it. Maybe the Hag was lying. Maybe unnatural magic was just as useless against Aedan as the Fae's. Or maybe this process would get the better of me and take my weak mortal life before I even got the chance to find the Netherworld and challenge him again. Before doubt could sink in any further, I spoke.

"It's worth the risk."

Syrena stomped her foot and opened her mouth to argue, but I interrupted her before she could.

"I'm doing this, Syrena," I declared. "I'm finding a way back to the Netherworld, and when I do, I won't be helpless again."

Syrena grunted in exasperation and looked to Ilora for help. But the queen of Merimaya's eyes had softened. Several weighted seconds passed before she peeked at the Hag.

"All you need is our most prized possession?" she asked.

Syrena gasped. "What are you doing?"

Her words fell on deaf ears.

"Yes," the girl confirmed. "An object you love more than anything else, given as a sacrifice."

Ilora nodded thoughtfully. She then reached beneath the high neck of her blouse and pulled out two rings strung on a gold chain.

"These were my parents' wedding bands," she said, gently brushing her thumb across the smaller of the two. "My father never planned to wed. He'd ruled for a thousand years and never even considered it. But one day he was visiting Lerian, and he went for a walk down on the docks where a ship had just arrived from the lands across the sea. When he looked up, he saw my mother silhouetted by the sun as she stood at the bow. He said at that moment, he knew she was the one he would spend the rest of his life with. He went out and bought these rings the next day."

A faint smile spread over Ilora's lips at the memory of her parents. She quickly blinked away the moisture forming in her eyes before lifting the chain off her neck and holding it out to the Hag.

"It's all I have left of them. Everything else burned in the siege. It's without a doubt my most prized possession."

The girl nodded, took the rings, and pressed them to her heart. "Thank you for your sacrifice."

"Has everyone lost their minds?" Syrena squawked, flailing her arms overhead. "Am I the only sane one here?"

Ilora glared at her, the tenderness in her eyes making way for a vengeful gleam. "My parents were helpless in the Netherworld, Syrena. Their daughter won't be when she avenges them."

Syrena's bristles waned, but she still shook her head, her normally plump lips only a sliver of pink as they squeezed together in a disapproving pout. "This is reckless. Completely and utterly idiotic, ignorant, and irrational. You should both be ashamed of yourselves."

But while she was speaking, she'd started yanking off the gold-and-emerald bangles on her right arm one by one.

"So stupid," she grumbled, tossing the jewelry on top of the book the Hag had set aside earlier. She gruffly motioned to the offering. "There. I haven't taken those off since my mother gave them to me when I was ten. Hope you're happy."

The girl lifted one of the bracelets to the light, nodding as she scrutinized it. "Ecstatic."

I'd seen the bracelets countless times, but I'd never noticed they were made to look like coiled snakes, the small emeralds embedded in them acting as the creatures' eyes.

As if reading my mind, Syrena explained. "My mother used to tell me that to be a good queen, one must be like the serpent. Graceful, yet cunning." She shrugged. "I didn't really care what they stood for, I just liked that she cared enough to pass them down to me."

I gently nudged Syrena's bare wrist with my own. "You don't have to do this, you know."

"Yes, I do." She sighed, glaring at me with a look as frustrated as it was full of love. "You're my friends. And friends don't let friends do crazy shit alone."

An unexpected giggle burst out of me, Ilora following suit, and even Syrena eventually managed to crack a smile.

*Bang!*

We jumped as the door to the Hag's house slammed shut behind Xavier. We hadn't even noticed him leaving, but his absence now hung heavy in the air.

"Huh." Syrena blinked at the door. "Maybe *he's* the only sane one."

"He's probably just worried about us," I said. "I'll go talk to him."

I started towards the exit, but I'd only made it three steps before the door creaked open again and Xavier slipped back inside. Slung over his shoulder was the bedroll he'd had strapped to his horse's saddle.

Xavier cleared his throat and set the roll on the ground, then knelt beside it. He looked pained as he fiddled with the straps fastening the bedding, and his mouth opened and closed as he fought to find words. Sensing his discomfort, the dog rose from his cozy spot by the fire and came to investigate, giving Xavier's hand an encouraging lick. Xavier stroked the hound's head in thanks.

"It was cold," Xavier muttered. "The day my father died. It was the harshest winter Astoria had seen in centuries. I was shivering when Soren came into the house, so he took off his jacket and put it around my shoulders. Then he told me my father died a hero, and that he'd lost someone he loved in the battle too." Xavier's eyes went glossy as he drifted to the distant memory. "Soren said it was alright to be sad and scared, that he was too. Then he asked if I had anywhere to go, but I didn't. So he said we could help each other be strong. Together. When we finally left the house, it had started snowing. I was barefoot, and Soren's jacket was so big on me I kept tripping on the hem. Eventually, he lifted me into his arms and carried me the rest of the way."

Xavier blinked and returned to the present, focusing again on the bedroll in his hands.

"He never asked for that jacket back. I grew into it, and wore it every day until it fell apart. Meer had the remaining scraps sewn into a quilt so I wouldn't have to part with it."

Xavier unfurled the bundle, lifted a blue and green quilt from the top of the bedding, and presented it to the Hag. He cleared his throat a final time. "This means everything to me."

The girl clicked her tongue and gently took the blanket in one hand while the other cupped his cheek.

"Thank you for your sacrifice," she whispered tenderly.

Xavier swallowed and forced a cool shrug. "Couldn't let the girls have all the fun."

The Hag chuckled and draped Xavier's quilt over the armchair beside the fire before clasping her hands in front of her. "Now then. Who wants to go first?"

I summoned my rapidly waning courage and stepped forward. "It was my idea. I'll go."

"Very well." The girl cheerfully patted the chair. "Take a seat."

I wanted to, but my feet had different plans and stayed fixed firmly in place. I anxiously ran my fingers along the dip of my collarbone.

"Is it going to hurt?"

"Yes," the girl replied simply.

I loosed a puff of air and nodded.

*You're no stranger to pain, Lina Calder, physical or emotional. Whatever the Hag has in store, you can survive it.*

The thought propelled me forward, and I took my place in the chair. I rested my hands on the plush armrests, unable to help the grim smirk that crept onto my face at the realization my life was about to change forever, and it was going to happen surrounded by fluffy pillows and lace doilies.

"When the magic floods through you," the girl said, grabbing Hale and Soren's daggers and wandering over to the fire, "it will leave a mark on you."

I jerked my head to the side to look at her. "What? You didn't tell me that in our letters!"

The girl waved the comment away. "You didn't ask."

"What kind of mark?" Ilora asked, frowning. "Like a scar?"

"There's no way of knowing. The magic decides in the moment how and where it wants to be represented on your skin."

Xavier raised a skeptical brow. "Why can't you just look into the future and see what we get?"

The Hag reached out and playfully twirled one of his ringlets around her finger. "In the visions I've had, you have the marks hidden. Which is wise. Just like when playing cards, you don't want to reveal your hand to your enemies too early."

I glanced at Syrena. Her glare was as sharp and deadly as a double-edged blade is it carved into the side of the Hag's head.

The girl let Xavier's curl spring free, then grabbed a nearby rag to protect her hands as she reached into the fire and guided out a cast-iron kettle.

"Ilora, be a dear and pass me a mug, please," the Hag said, maneuvering the lid off the kettle and plopping my two daggers inside, one after the other.

Her face was etched in confusion, but Ilora obeyed, pulling a pewter cup off a nearby shelf and handing it to the girl.

"Now..." The Hag poured the contents of the kettle into the mug. "Lina is going to drink this, and the process will begin. She'll need the support of her friends, because as I said before, this *will* hurt, and I assume because she's human and this is Fae magic, the pain will be significantly worse."

I set my jaw and settled back in the chair. "I'm ready."

The Hag dipped her head and extended the mug. Wisps of steam wafted up from the liquid inside, sending the earthy perfume of herbs and a faint metallic note swirling through the air around me. I slid the cup into my hands and gingerly sniffed the contents. When I caught my friends' worried stares, I mustered a smile.

"Here goes nothing," I said, raising the mug in salute before bringing it to my lips. The liquid burned, but I decided to act fast before I could talk myself out of it and gulped the contents as fast as I could. When I was finished, I wiped my mouth and let out a hacking cough at the acrid aftertaste.

"How do you feel?" Ilora asked, kneeling beside me. Her brown eyes were round with worry as they scanned my face.

I glanced down at my hands, wiggling my fingers warily. "I... I feel alright, actually."

Syrena turned to the Hag, who had nestled beside the dog on the floor and was feeding him scraps from the kitchen table. "How long does it usually take?"

"Can't know for sure," the girl chirped. "Everyone's body reacts to it differently."

"Maybe it won't do anything at all," Xavier mused, thoughtfully rubbing his chin as he circled the armchair. "You said that was an option."

"True." The girl nodded and tossed a bit of bacon to the hound, who deftly caught it in midair. She patted him on the head as he proudly chomped on his prize.

I readjusted in my seat, squaring my shoulders and bending my head to one side, then the other. "Huh. I really don't feel anything at all. I'm completely fi—"

My body was thrown back against the armchair as what felt like a thousand invisible blades slammed through my skin and plunged into my flesh.

Every limb went rigid, and I thought I heard Syrena or Ilora screaming, but when I saw their mouths were shut, I realized the sound was coming from mine. Time slowed, and the world around me went quiet as the pain consumed me. Something hot sliced through me, fraying every muscle, bone, and vein in its wake.

There was no space for terror. No space for wondering how long this torment would last. There was only excruciating pain.

I barely clocked the figures darting around me, couldn't hear my friends' voices or read their lips as they shouted and gathered close. A high-pitched ringing started in my ears, shattering my hearing as the pain shattered my body. When I began to shudder and shake, I was suddenly looking down at myself from above, watching my friends yell and cry and hold me down as I violently seized in the chair. Froth dribbled from my lips, and my eyes rolled back in their sockets so only their whites remained visible. It mirrored the look of Wynn's spellbound gaze, except my brother was still alive when his eyes looked that way.

I, on the other hand, was dying.

The foam at my mouth turned pink as it mixed with blood, the sight of which sent my friends into a frenzy. Xavier positioned himself behind the chair, gripping my shoulders to pin me in place as best he could. Ilora stayed on her knees at my feet, her body curled around my thrashing legs and her eyes squeezed shut as her lips muttered something over and over, igniting a flickering pale blue light in her palms. Syrena had my wrists locked in an iron grip and was leaning forward to scream in my face. At one point, she may have even slapped me, but I was pulled back down into my body before I could see for sure.

The agony was too much.

It hurt worse than the Nethers who'd taken bites out of my flesh and sent paralyzing pain shooting through my body with a single claw.

It hurt worse than all the lost brothers, broken hearts, and fallen lovers combined.

It hurt worse than anything I'd ever experienced or imagined, and my body withered and faded under the torment.

My strength shriveled, causing my limbs to grow heavy and weak. My heartbeat slowed to a near undetectable rate. My breath halted, the ringing in my ears stopping with it, and for a beautiful brief moment, everything was peaceful.

I could have stayed in that place forever, where no pain or heartbreak or fear existed. I wanted to bask in that safe, sweet nothingness for all eternity, but it ended as quickly as it had come on. Before I had time to process what was happening, my body collapsed, the pain evaporated, and I gasped frantically for air.

"Lina!" Syrena wailed, wiping her eyes on the back of her sleeve. "Fuck you! You scared the shit out of us!"

Ilora hauled herself to standing. "Are you alright?"

I couldn't say yes. Not when every bone in my body was still throbbing.

"I'm alive," I groaned.

Xavier ran to get me a cup of water while Ilora and Syrena helped me sit upright in the chair. Through the sweaty strands of hair plastered to my face, I caught a glimpse of the Hag, still sitting on the floor with the dog and watching me with a smile on her eerily angelic face.

"Welcome back, King Slayer," she said. "That was a close one, huh?"

The dog woofed in agreement.

I wanted to think of something biting and witty to say back, but I was too exhausted.

Xavier returned with the water and helped me sip at it, then gave my arm a light squeeze. "Glad we didn't lose you, Calder."

I winced at his touch and sucked sharply through my teeth.

Xavier yanked his hand back. "What's wrong? What did I do?"

"I don't know." I brought my fingers to the place on my forearm he'd just touched and hesitantly squeezed, yelping as another jolt of pain shot through me. It was a different type of pain than before. This wasn't as extreme. It was skin deep, like a burn.

"Here, let's see." Ilora knelt beside me again, her healer's hands delicate but efficient as they rolled up my sleeve. The vertical black scar on my wrist from that first fateful Samhain came into view, followed by the impression of a flesh-eating Nether's bite that was barely noticeable. All normal marks that told my tale. A map of the past.

It was only when Ilora pulled the material up to my elbow that everyone gasped.

Something new lived on the widest part of my forearm, just above my scars. Embedded in my skin like a wax seal was a glittering silver spiked circle, with vines twining around the outside. Inside the sphere, two crescent moons faced away from each other, connected by two lines running through them.

In awe, I raised my arm towards the window to catch the sun, the ancient Fae symbol shimmering in its rays.

"Demon lover," Xavier muttered.

The Hag twirled one of her braids around her finger, beaming proudly at the mark. "Or in other words..."

"Witch," I finished.

The girl looked up at me, her grin widening. "I see no lie, do you? You're a creature born without magic, who has acquired it by unnatural means. You are fond of both the light and the dark. You fit the description perfectly."

I nodded, carefully running my fingers across the symbol now that the pain had lessened. The vines were identical to the ones that had encircled the hilt of Soren's dagger, and the symbol was practically a twin to the brand in Hale's skin.

Both men forever written on my skin, both loves a part of me and my story.

Unsure if the ache in my heart was from that thought or left over from the agony I'd just experienced, I rolled my sleeve down and faced the Hag. "So I have magic now. What can I do?"

The girl shrugged. "I don't know."

I blinked in surprise and opened my mouth to speak, but Syrena beat me to it.

"You don't know?" she barked. "You put her through all that and you don't know?"

The Hag's eyes flashed. "Your magic is yours to discover on your own, in your own time. That is, *if* it decides you should be blessed with any." She crossed her arms and challenged Syrena with a sneer. "So what do you say, little serpent? Do you think it will deem you worthy of such gifts? Do you want to risk it? Or will you back down and finally come to terms with how ordinary you really are?"

Syrena's back went straight as a board, every muscle in her body tensing. She looked seconds away from bursting, prompting me to instinctively reach towards the sheath at my thigh for my weapon, only to find it empty.

It was Xavier who finally moved, taking a hesitant step between the Hag and Syrena to intercept the queen's attention. Like she was waking from a spell, Syrena blinked rapidly and inhaled through her nose. She then lifted her hand to the scarf on her head and tore it off.

"Despite what I was raised to believe..." She huffed, tossing the silk to the ground before doing the same with her shawl. "There is absolutely *nothing* wrong with being normal. But to answer your question." She glared at the Hag. "*No.* I will *not* be backing down. Not because of your promise of power, but because of the promise I made to my friends."

Syrena flipped her hair and descended into the armchair, daintily crossing one leg over the other.

"So what do *you* say, Hag?" she pressed, her voice dripping with venom. "Are we doing this, or are you just going to stand there and continue being a condescending bitch?"

The Hag stared at Syrena for a few beats before throwing her head back and laughing. "I like you."

"The feeling isn't mutual," Syrena snapped back.

The girl continued to snicker under her breath as she returned to the kettle by the fire, grabbing Syrena's bracelets along the way. Just like she'd done to my knives, she tossed the bracelets into the tea one at a time, each resounding *plop* cutting through the tense silence that had settled over the house. When the tea was poured into a fresh mug, the Hag had barely extended it before Syrena snatched it out of her hand and downed the drink in two large gulps. She slammed the cup down and wiped her mouth, beads of liquid spilling from her lips down into her cleavage.

"Delicious," Syrena gagged.

We waited with bated breath.

And waited.

*And* waited.

Seconds turned into a minute.

Then five.

Ten.

The dog in the corner eventually rolled onto his back with his hind legs in the air and started snoring softly.

When Syrena broke the silence, the Hag had retreated to the kitchen to clean, Ilora was chewing her nails to nubs, Xavier was sitting hunched on the floor, toying with a loose string on his jacket, and I was perched on the chair's armrest, the skin around my neck nearly rubbed raw.

"I don't think it's happening for me," Syrena said, her words so abrupt they made us all jump.

Ilora wandered over and rested a hand on her friend's shoulder. "You don't know that."

Syrena shook her head, adopting her perfect practiced smile. "It's fine. I don't mind. Like I said, there's nothing wrong with being normal."

Xavier sniffed and shook his head. "You're the farthest thing from normal, Your Highness."

He peeked up at her, and when Syrena caught his gaze she rolled her eyes, but a genuine smile dared to lift the corners of her mouth. "It's Your Majest—"

She made a noise like the wind had been punched from her lungs.

Xavier bolted upright. "Are you alright?"

Syrena cleared her throat and nodded, smiling again. "Sorry, I don't know what that was. For a second I couldn't breathe."

Xavier crouched in front of her so he was directly in her eyeline. "Are you sure you're alright?"

"Yes, I'm fine." Syrena wiped her brow, where a few beads of sweat had accumulated. "Is it hot in here?"

I glanced over my shoulder at the dwindling fire. "Not especially."

"Huh." Syrena licked her lips, which had dried up so much in the last ten seconds they'd started cracking. "Strange. It feels warm all of a sudden."

She tugged at the deep V-cut neckline of her dress.

Ilora knelt beside Xavier. "What's wrong?"

"Nothing. It's... it's just this dress," Syrena muttered, her movements growing more frantic. "It's too hot. And tight. And I can't... I can't breathe in it. I can't breathe. I can't—"

She cut off again as air whooshed from her lungs. Syrena leaned forward, grasping wildly at nothing. Ilora caught one of her hands while Xavier intercepted the other.

"I can't... I can't breathe..." Syrena wheezed, her eyes wide with terror.

"It's alright," Ilora soothed. "It's just the magic. It'll be over soon. Just hold on, alright? Hold on."

Syrena nodded, but her legs kicked and her lips parted and closed over and over as she desperately gulped for air that wouldn't come.

Then we watched helplessly as our friend's skin ripped apart.

# CHAPTER 25

———

It started along the breastbone.

Her deep tan split down the middle, her skin disintegrating like paper under a flame. Blood gushed from the wound and soaked the neckline of her dress. Syrena's gaze shot to the carnage, but Xavier jerked her arm, forcing her attention forward again.

"Squeeze my hand," he demanded, tightening his grip around her fingers.

Tears slipped out the corners of Syrena's eyes as a trail of crimson snaked down the bodice of her dress. An agonized wail wrenched itself from what little air she had left in her lungs.

"Squeeze my hand," Xavier commanded again. "Try to break it."

Syrena's eyes grew wide.

"Do it," Xavier pushed. "I bet you can't."

Ilora and I exchanged confused glances.

"You're not strong enough," Xavier continued, pushing his face mere inches from Syrena's. "There's no way you could break my hand."

Although Syrena struggled for breath, her eyes narrowed. Her hand clamped firmly around Xavier's. He laughed in her face.

"Is that all you've got?" he asked. "That's pathetic."

The blood trail coiled around Syrena's stomach now.

She grunted and tightened her hold, her hand shaking.

"Gods, you're weak." Xavier chuckled. "I barely feel anything. I knew you couldn't do it."

Syrena leaned forward, now so close to Xavier her nose pressed against his. She squeezed even harder, turning his fingers purple.

"That doesn't even hurt," Xavier replied. "You're squeezing like a weak little princess."

Syrena snarled through gritted teeth and yanked Xavier's arm closer, maneuvering it so she got a better grip. Something appeared in the wound between her breasts; something with a metallic sheen that rose from inside her and breached the rivers of blood.

"Come on, Your Highness," Xavier barked, "is that all you have in you? Squeeze harder!"

Breath finally rushed into Syrena's lungs, her chest rapidly rising and falling as she greedily sucked in air, but she didn't let go of Xavier's hand. Both sets of eyes stayed fixed on each other, both hands locked in a violent embrace.

"I said *harder*," Xavier growled. "Go on, break it. Do it. Come on, just break it. Fucking break it! *Break it!*"

Syrena screamed in fury and squeezed as hard as she could, and a sharp *crack* cut through the room. She immediately gasped and released Xavier's hand, clapping a palm to her mouth in shock. A pained yet proud smile stretched across his lips as he stood. Syrena's eyes tracked him all the way to the kitchen where he stiffly retrieved a cup of water. After a few seconds, Syrena blinked, then looked around the room.

"Is it over?"

"It's been over for a while," Ilora said softly, gesturing to Syrena's chest.

Syrena glanced down, witnessing for the first time the golden viper embedded in her skin, its beady emerald eyes at the center of her chest reflecting the low flames burning in the hearth. We didn't have to remove her dress to see the rest; the blood trailing beneath her breast, coiling around her abdomen, and ending on the side of one thigh revealed the extent of the mark.

In a daze, Syrena lifted a hand to the gilded symbol, nearly identical to her mother's bracelets. "I didn't notice."

I peeked at Xavier as he placed the cup of water beside Syrena with his uninjured hand. The one Syrena had been gripping hung limp at his side.

"It looks nice," he mumbled. "It suits you."

"Thank you," she murmured, carefully tracing her fingers along the serpentine head ingrained in her flesh.

Ilora pulled off her jacket and draped it around Syrena's shoulders before helping her out of the chair. "Since you and Lina made it look so fun, can I go next?"

An unintentional laugh bubbled up at her dry remark, and I smacked my hands over my mouth in horror. But my outburst pulled an amused snort out of Syrena, which Ilora found hilarious, and eventually Xavier was chuckling to himself as he watched the three of us fall into a fit of giggles. Together we laughed and laughed and laughed until our cheeks hurt, there were tears of merriment in our eyes, and the weight on our shoulders felt a little less overwhelming.

Bracing her hands on her knees, Ilora caught her breath. "In all seriousness, I'd really like to get this over with. It looks terrible."

"It is," I said, still laughing.

"It's torture," Syrena confirmed, before accidentally letting slip another snort, which set us off all over again.

A sudden *plop, plop* quieted us down, drawing our attention to the teenage girl with a cast-iron kettle, which two wedding bands had just been dropped into the depths of.

"Shall we, then?" the Hag asked, merrily shaking the kettle like it was a box of sweets.

Ilora's face fell, but she bravely straightened her shoulders and lifted her chin.

"Just remember who it's for," Syrena whispered, squeezing her hand.

Ilora nodded as her eyes iced over. She took her potion from the witch's hand, blew the steam from its surface, and lowered herself into the chair. She calmly sipped at the tea, wrinkling her nose at the taste, but saying nothing as we all looked on. She'd only finished half the liquid when sweat dotted her forehead and the skin on her neck prickled like it was kissed by a cool breeze.

"Hot?" Syrena asked nervously.

Ilora's shoulders shuddered as she shook her head. "No. Cold."

The dog in the corner whined.

"Are you in pain?" I asked.

Ilora shifted in her seat. "No... yes... sort of?" She struggled to speak through her chattering teeth. "It feels like... a river. An ice-cold flood in my veins."

Sweat slid down her temples as her entire body quaked. Syrena removed Ilora's jacket from her own shoulders and went to tuck it around her friend, but leapt backwards when Ilora groaned suddenly and bent forward, miserably wrapping her arms around herself. It was then that two matching gold bands materialized in the skin around one of Ilora's upper arms, far quicker and significantly less bloody than the process had been for Syrena. Within seconds Ilora stopped shivering, sat up straight, and wiped her brow.

"Phew!" She laughed in relief. "That wasn't so bad."

Syrena frowned and huffily tossed Ilora's jacket back to her. "I hate you."

Ilora smirked and stood up, teetering uneasily for a moment but quickly righting herself and sauntering away like nothing had happened. My aching bones envied her.

"Like I said," the Hag stated, "everyone's body reacts differently. And if I'm counting correctly, it seems we have one last body to do."

She blinked expectantly at Xavier.

His throat bobbed as he gulped, but he still threw on one of his signature slanted grins and drawled, "I thought you'd never ask, sweetheart."

When he passed me on his way to the chair, I hooked my fingers around his elbow, halting him.

"Don't die," I pleaded.

He playfully knocked my chin with his knuckles. "You know I never do." He then continued on to the chair and made himself comfortable in his padded prison, peeking over at the girl as she took up the quilt. "So how are you going to fit all that—"

A rip of cloth silenced him as the Hag tore off the bottom hem of the blanket, then dropped the strip into the kettle before handing the remainder of the quilt back to him.

"Congratulations," she said brightly. "Just a piece is needed from your sacrifice. Consider yourself lucky."

Xavier beamed down at the fabric in his hands and absent-mindedly ran his fingers over one of the scraps of navy blue. "I do."

The Hag presented the final potion. "Then let's see if the magic agrees."

Xavier's face grew solemn as he dutifully took the cup and downed the contents like a shot of liquor. When he finished, he smacked his lips and shrugged.

"I've had worse things in my mouth."

I snickered and started to make a playful jab, but Syrena sent me an icy glare that had me swallowing my words.

Xavier nestled back in the chair and shut his eyes, taking deep, calming breaths. After a few moments of silence, he inhaled sharply through his nose. His eyes squeezed together tighter as a vein protruded from his neck.

"Fuck," he muttered.

The word was followed by a low, guttural groan. Disregarding the injury in his hand, Xavier gripped the armrests to ground himself. Another vein appeared in his forehead, his face flushing an unnatural shade of red.

I glanced nervously at Syrena, but her attention was glued to Xavier, her brow furrowed and her lips pinched in a taut line.

An animalistic noise ground through Xavier's clenched teeth. He threw his head back in the chair, his chest heaving. Movement flashed at the corner of my eye—Syrena.

She rushed over, skidded to her knees beside him, and took his uninjured hand in her own, prompting Xavier to open his eyes in surprise.

"Go on." Syrena jerked her chin to their interlocked fingers. "Try to break it."

Xavier let out a tortured laugh. Syrena smiled and scooted closer.

"Just breathe," she ordered.

Xavier nodded and slowed his shaky breath. When blood soaked through his shirt, he stomped his foot so hard the dishes in the kitchen rattled.

"*Fuck!*" he shouted.

Syrena tightened her grip.

Xavier's back arched, his legs kicking wildly. The sight was eerily similar to an animal in its death throes. Nausea churned in the base of my stomach at the realization.

"He never dies," I whispered to myself, letting Xavier's words calm my nerves.

But I wasn't even sure Xavier believed those words anymore as the magic ate away at him, and fear manifested in the wide whites of his eyes.

Ilora moved beside me and slipped her palm into mine.

"Come on... come on..." She kept her focus glued on Xavier as he jerked and seized. "You can do this."

I squeezed her hand tight, and the two of us held our breath as Xavier let out a final tormented wail and went limp.

Ilora and I raced over to join Syrena, the former anxiously checking his pulse and pressing her ear to Xavier's chest to listen for a heartbeat. "Shit. He's not breathing."

"What?" Syrena squeaked in terror, still gripping Xavier's hand.

"No, no, no..." I scrambled over to Xavier and took his face in my hands. His skin was cold and clammy, his mouth slightly agape, and his eyes empty, staring off into a great expanse of nothing.

"No," I repeated, my voice cracking. "This isn't happening. He never dies."

I patted Xavier's cheek once.

Twice.

Then I shook him.

"Xavier!" I snapped. "Wake up!"

He didn't, and Syrena still hadn't let go of his hand.

"Xavier!" I shouted this time, my voice breaking again. "Wake. *Up!*"

Ilora shouldered me out of the way. "Move."

I sniffled as I made room for her, but refused to let myself cry. If I cried, that made it real. And it couldn't be real. It *couldn't.*

Ilora hovered her hands over Xavier's blood-drenched chest and closed her eyes, muttering something in ancient Fae. In a flash, a blinding blue light appeared in her palms. The light spread and pulsed in time with Ilora's racing heart, soon covering Xavier's body entirely.

"It's not working," Syrena mumbled. She hadn't moved from her spot on the floor, hadn't pulled her fingers from Xavier's limp grasp.

I turned to the Hag, who was busy prodding the smoldering embers in the hearth.

"Do something!" I screamed at her.

She didn't even look at me as she shrugged. "It is done. The magic made its choice."

I swallowed a sob, turning back to Xavier, and brushed his sweaty curls out of his eyes. Their deep green usually sparkled and danced, but now the color was dull and faded.

"Ilora, please," I begged.

"I'm *trying,*" Ilora replied. Her hands were starting to shake, the light in them blinking before flickering out.

"Try *harder!*" Syrena demanded.

I stared at my friends, the scene seeming less and less like reality and more like some hazy dream.

It was wrong. So, *so* wrong. Xavier didn't die. He always found some miraculous way to survive. He beat the odds, *always.* And if he ever had to die, he wouldn't go out like this. Not without...

"Soren," I mumbled. "Soren should be here."

Ilora's light fluttered, then fizzled out completely.

"Shit!" she panted. With a grunt and wince, she conjured it again. It was weaker this time, barely glowing.

"Ilora, *please!*" Syrena wailed.

"He should be here," I repeated.

"I'm *trying*, Syrena!"

The Hag continued to poke at the fire.

"Why isn't he here?" I whispered, my tears finally coming to terms with the truth and slipping out.

Ilora managed to summon her healing light a third time, but within seconds she collapsed from the toll.

"No!" Syrena finally yanked her hand from Xavier's and shoved Ilora out of the way.

"We didn't let Lina go," Syrena growled, furious determination written across her face. "He didn't let me go, and I will *not* let him go."

Syrena pulled back her fist and sent it hurtling into Xavier's chest with a sickening *thud*.

Ilora tried to pull her friend away. "Syrena, don't—"

But Syrena shrugged Ilora off and punched Xavier again.

Then again.

Again.

"No!" she shouted.

Another punch.

"*No!*" Her voice broke.

I looked away to sob pitifully into my shoulder.

"No one else—"

Punch.

"Gets to go—"

Punch.

"Without saying—"

Punch.

"*Goodbye!*"

Punch.

Then a *crack* as one of Xavier's ribs broke under Syrena's fist.

... Followed by a desperate gasp for air.

Xavier's eyes brightened with beautiful life as he clutched a hand to his chest.

"Ow!" he cried indignantly. "What the hell?"

Relief washed over me, forcing me to collapse into a blubbering heap on the floor.

But Syrena had a different reaction.

She slapped Xavier as hard as she could.

"*Ow!*" he shrieked, smacking his palm to his cheek. "What the *hell*?"

Syrena jabbed a finger in his face. "Fuck you!"

Xavier irritably batted her hand away. "I told you I never die!"

"Well, you did for a bit there," Ilora laughed, breathlessly clapping him on the back. "So maybe you should stop saying that."

Xavier grunted and turned his attention to the bloodstain on his shirt, pulling his collar down to inspect the damage. On the left side of his chest, over his heart, was an intricate knotted pattern. It appeared to be stitched in thick blue and green threads.

He chuckled at the sight. "An ancient Fae symbol. Just like Lina's."

Composing myself, I craned my neck to see it more clearly. "What does it say?"

Xavier's grin reached all the way to his eyes. "Family."

"See?" The Hag padded over with the kettle in hand. "Wasn't that easy?"

Ilora, Syrena, Xavier and I all glared at her.

The girl hatched a sly smile. "You simply needed to have a little faith."

In one swift move, she pulled off the kettle's lid and dumped the container upside down.

Two daggers, two rings, a set of gold-and-emerald bangles,

and a strip of quilt slipped out and slopped onto the floor. The items were more slender than before, like they'd been whittled down, but each of our individual treasures were still wholly intact.

"Now with all due respect..." The Hag motioned to the door. "Please take your belongings and get out of my house. My book was just starting to get good."

~

WHEN WE LEFT the Hag's home, Syrena and Xavier took up their bickering again.

I clicked my tongue, urging my horse forward to catch up with Ilora, who was ignoring them as best she could as she led the way back to Lerian. She was more quiet than normal, and after what we'd just gone through, I wanted to check up on her.

"Hey," I called out, riding up alongside her dappled gray stallion as it crossed a shallow brook trickling through the rocky terrain. "Everything alright?"

She nodded and smiled feebly back at me.

"Liar," I chided.

Ilora sighed and adjusted her cloak to better protect her neck from the bitter breeze. "It's nothing. Just something that happened when I tried to help Xavier."

"What happened?"

Ilora shrugged. "It... felt different. Summoning my power, I mean. It didn't hurt."

I frowned. "Healing hurts you?"

"Always." Ilora absentmindedly rubbed the spot on her arm where two gold rings now lived. "It's exhausting and miserable, but healers do it anyway because we're helping someone, and that makes the pain worth it."

I thought back to the times Meer used his calming white

light to heal both me and Xavier. I'd seen it take a toll on him too.

"This time, though..." Ilora continued. "It was strange. It didn't hurt in the slightest. But I'm used to the pain. When it wasn't there, I didn't know what to do without it. I had trouble pulling the power out of me. I still feel it in there, of course, I just don't know how to get it all out. I feel like I'm a child coming into her magic all over again."

"Wait, you *feel* your magic?"

Ilora glanced at me, her brow furrowing. "Of course. Don't you feel yours now?"

I stared at her blankly.

"It's almost like a hum," she explained. "The energy, that power, just vibrating inside you like it can't wait to get out. Almost like it's an entirely different entity, but somehow still you. You don't feel that?"

I chewed my bottom lip and brought my awareness to different parts of my body, checking in with various limbs, organs, my skin...

Nothing.

"I don't feel any different," I admitted.

Ilora's face grew solemn as she looked away. "Oh."

I wilted. Maybe the Hag's magic hadn't worked on me after all. Maybe I'd gone through hell for nothing but a shiny tattoo.

"Maybe you should stay behind with your new friend. You two make quite the couple."

Ilora sighed and dragged her attention from the trail to the squabbling duo behind us.

Xavier made a retching noise. "Don't even joke about that! She's a child!"

"No, she's a witch as old as time itself."

"Well, she *looked* like a child. And for the last time, she wasn't flirting with me."

"Then how do you explain all that 'thank you for your sacrifice' nonsense?"

"She said that to Ilora too."

"She said it *differently* to Ilora."

Xavier cackled maniacally. "You're jealous!"

Syrena scoffed. "Don't be ridiculous. I just want you to be honest for once."

"When have I not been honest?"

"I'm going to kill them, Lina," Ilora muttered out the side of her mouth. "I am *not* in the mood for this right now."

I shouldn't find it funny, but for some reason Xavier and Syrena grating on Ilora's nerves like naughty children tormenting their mother was the most amusing thing I'd seen all day. It took everything in me not to crack a smile.

"For one, you're lying about Roric."

"I swear to every god there is that Roric wants me. He practically told me so."

"Bullshit. There is no way that man is going to fuck you."

"Who said *he'd* be fucking *me*?"

"Gods have mercy," Ilora grumbled, pinching the bridge of her nose.

"You can't honestly expect me to believe *you* would be the one in control in that scenario."

Xavier's eyes narrowed. "Your Highness, you have no idea the delicious things I'm capable of in the bedroom."

"For the last time, I'm a queen, and you will call me Your Majesty—"

Ilora's frayed nerves finally snapped.

She hauled on her horse's reins, spinning the stallion around so she could hurl a finger at Xavier and Syrena.

"Good gods, will you two just *shut the fuck up*?"

What happened next was so surreal it made me wonder if

I'd drifted off to sleep and was now in the midst of some absurd dream.

Ilora's words boomed, their echo bouncing around the rocky outcrops surrounding us. At the same time, a stream of water shot up from the nearby creek and hurtled towards Syrena. Xavier dragged his horse in front of her to shield her from the downpour, but the water bounced off a wall of nothing, leaving them both untouched.

My jaw dropped and my horse's reins slipped from my grasp.

Ilora repeatedly blinked in shock, then peeked over her shoulder like some strange water-hurling monster might be behind her. "What... what just happened?"

Xavier gulped. "You tell me."

Syrena pointed a shaky hand at Ilora. "Did you just...?" Her eyes darted to Xavier. "And did you just...?"

Xavier defensively raised his hands. "I didn't do anything."

Ilora nudged her horse forward, trotting up beside Xavier. "What did you feel?" she pressed. "Did you feel anything?"

Xavier raked his fingers through his curls, exhaling sharply. "I... I don't know. A... jolt, maybe?"

"Go on," Ilora urged.

"A jolt of... excitement I guess? Like when you land a blow on an opponent or eat too much sugar or kiss someone new for the first time, only it was a thousand times stronger."

"Yes." Ilora grinned. "And then?"

"And then..." Xavier squinted, analyzing the moment prior. "There was... a release."

Ilora laughed triumphantly. "Xavier, I think you just figured out the power the Hag gave you."

Xavier's eyebrows arched. "The water?"

Ilora jumped off her horse and trudged towards the creek. "No, I think that was me. Both of my parents could manipulate water. Why do you think they chose to put our palace on a lake?"

"The nice view?" I offered.

Ignoring me, Ilora knelt beside the crystalline stream and scooped a handful into her palms. "The Hag said when she put magic inside us, she was combining another's power with our own. So what I'm thinking is, whoever gave us the item we sacrificed, we take on similar power to the one they have in addition to our own. For example..."

Ilora stood and focused intently on the liquid in her cupped hands. After a few seconds, the water rose, rolling and wobbling like jelly, until it was hovering just above Ilora's hands, nothing but a weightless sphere.

Without warning, Ilora's eyes darted to Xavier, and the orb followed, hurtling through the air and splashing him in the face.

"I can manipulate water now." Ilora laughed. She touched her upper arm fondly, as if giving a silent thanks to the ones whose power now coursed through her veins.

Wearing a sour expression, Xavier brought his sleeve to his face and dabbed at the moisture dripping from it.

"Funny," he griped. "But I'm still not clear on what it is you think I can do?"

Ilora's eyes lit up, and she knelt beside the stream once more. "Soren can put up walls of force, right?" She looked to me for confirmation, and I nodded.

"He can push things like they weigh nothing, without ever laying a hand on them."

"Exactly!" Ilora dipped her hands into the water. "Xavier, you put up walls too. Only your walls aren't force."

Xavier scratched his temple. "What are they?"

Ilora flung the water again, this time aiming for Syrena.

Again, Xavier threw himself in front of her, blocking the spray. The droplets bounced off as they hit an invisible barrier.

"Protection," Ilora stated. "They're walls of protection."

Xavier looked around him, taking a few seconds to clock the fact that, despite the splash, he and Syrena remained untouched. A laugh bubbled out of him.

"Magic," he muttered in disbelief. "I have magic?"

Ilora chuckled and sat back on her heels. "Seems that way."

Xavier glanced at me. His joy was palpable and his smile contagious.

"You have magic," I confirmed, beaming back at him.

Xavier laughed again, then did it a little louder. Then he tossed his head back, howled like a wolf, and punched his fists high into the air as he screamed so loud they probably heard him all the way in Kylanthia, "This low-born scum has magic!"

# Chapter 26

ON THE WAY BACK TO LERIAN FROM THE HAG'S HOME IN THE High Lands, both Syrena and I tried everything we could think of to see if we too had newly appointed gifts like Xavier and Ilora, but we were unsuccessful. Syrena had laughed it off and said she didn't care, but I knew better. For centuries her family had desperately desired magic, and I had no doubt Syrena had gotten her hopes up, thinking that acquiring it might become a reality. I, on the other hand, just wanted to feel like I would be going into the Netherworld with some sort of advantage.

But despite the marks on our bodies and the torture we'd endured, any semblance of power evaded us, and by the time we all said good night for the evening, both Syrena and I had come to terms with the fact that adding magic to our veins had been nothing but a miserable waste of time.

But that didn't change my mind.

While I lay awake in bed that night, waiting for the palace to quiet, I replayed the plan I'd hatched weeks ago over and over in my mind. When the scullery maids had finally stopped gossiping and the guards had grown groggy at their posts, it was time.

I slipped out of bed, silent as a mouse, already dressed in clean trousers, a tunic, and a lace-up vest, with my two daggers strapped to my thighs. All I needed was to slip on my boots and grab the rucksack I'd quietly packed instead of washing up for bed like I'd told my friends I was doing. They couldn't know what I had planned. If they did, they'd insist on coming with me. They would protect me, and put their own lives in danger doing it, and I couldn't let them do that.

I'd put my loved ones in danger too many times. No one else would suffer the consequences of my actions. Not anymore. This was my journey. My battle. My dragon to slay. And if I couldn't, at least I'd be the only one who got burned. I'd thought the Hag would make me better equipped for the fight, but I'd been mistaken. Nevertheless the war was still on, and I had no choice but to suit up and head to the front lines whether I had a weapon or not.

I carefully maneuvered the bedroom door open to avoid it creaking, then dipped out the narrow crack into the hall and crept towards the opposite wing of the palace. When I arrived at my brother's bedroom, I pulled a sealed letter addressed to Willow from my pack. Since Wynn fell spellbound again, Willow slept in a cot beside his bed while the door stayed locked tight, the only key located on a cord around her neck. She would find my note the next morning, and when she did, it would read,

*Dear Willow,*

*I hate saying goodbye this way, but if I spoke to you in person, you'd tell me not to do this, or you might tie me to my bed to keep me from leaving. But I'm doing this for you. You, Wynn, our friends, and every other innocent creature in this world.*

*Aedan is coming. When, I can't be sure, but he won't stop until he*

*destroys every last one of us. He's been toying with Wynn like a cat with a mouse, and the other night when my brother fell under his spell again, I glimpsed my fate.*

*I believe there is another entrance to the Netherworld here in Lerian, deep in the sea beneath the palace. I plan to go through it, find Aedan, and end his threat once and for all.*

*I haven't wanted to pray to the gods much anymore, but lately I find myself praying a lot. I pray I'm right and this veil to the Netherworld isn't just a figment of my imagination. I pray I'll find Aedan and finish what I started last year. But mostly, I pray I'll see you again. If I don't, please take care of my brother. He loves you as much as he loves me, probably more, and despite everything that's happened, there's no one I trust with his life more than you.*

*You are my best friend, the sister I never had but desperately wished for, and I love you with all my heart.*

*-Lina*

*P.S.*

*I believe Roric Pax is a good man. He is respectful and kind, and I think you should be brave and ask him to dinner. Ask him about his childhood friends on the docks, and Sprites with blue skin, and give him some of your family's plum brandy. Don't let Syrena and Xavier make a game of him. He deserves better. And you, my friend, deserve the world.*

Before my fragile heart could shatter like it was threatening to, I knelt in front of the door, pressed a kiss to the paper in my hands, and begged whatever god was listening that this wouldn't be the last time my loved ones heard from me.

But I wasn't delusional. I knew it very well could be. My destination was a world full of monsters, and I had no idea where I was going or what to do when, or *if*, I got there. Still, despite my recent doubts about their existence, I prayed the gods would show mercy to an unexceptional human and spare her long enough to see her little brother smile again.

I slipped the paper under Wynn's door, whispering a soft goodbye as I did, and stood.

"What are you doing skulking around in the dark?" a male voice slurred behind me.

I yelped in surprise and spun, reaching for my dagger, but someone caught my wrist before I could and slammed me against the polished sandstone wall. I grunted as my body collided with the rock, and pain jolted through my head as my skull met stone. I wriggled against my attacker, trying to free one of my legs so I could land a strike to his groin, but he dug his knee into my thigh, pinning me. The scent of alcohol stung my nose as he leaned in, his breath damp on my face. The smell gave away my attacker's identity.

"I could ask you the same question, Kaspar," I grunted.

The drunken king let out a condescending laugh. "I live here. I can do whatever I want."

"Well, I live here too."

I struggled, but Kaspar's grip didn't budge.

"Right." The amusement drained from his voice. Instead, it turned darker. Resentful. Dangerous. "You made sure of that, didn't you? You just seeped right into another court like poison."

He leaned in, and I turned my head to keep his mouth from touching mine.

"How'd you do it this time, huh?" he pressed. "Did you do it the same way you did in Astoria?"

"I don't know what you're talking about."

"Yes, you do." Kaspar jerked my wrist, twisting it enough to pull a cry from my lips. "You're sleeping with my sister, aren't you?"

"*What?* No!" I jerked against him, but he kept me trapped. My anger and disgust dissipated, replaced by building panic.

Kaspar was bigger than me, significantly stronger, and if he tried something, I wouldn't be able to stop it.

"You're drunk, Kaspar," I said as calmly as I could. "Go to bed before you do something you'll regret in the morning."

"If I'm going to bed, you'll come with me." Kaspar's knee ground deeper into my leg, spreading my thighs farther apart. "Since fucking royalty is all you're good for."

I swallowed my fear. Fear was what he wanted, and I'd die before I gave it to him.

Kaspar's lips grazed the side of my neck, a sensation that usually made me weak in the knees, but now, coming from *him*, it had acid rising in my throat. "I always wondered what Soren found so special about you. Think I should see for myself?"

"Kaspar, please." Desperation crept into my hushed whisper. "My brother is asleep inside."

The king's laugh held no compassion or mercy. Just cruel, sadistic enjoyment. "Not so brave without a broken bottle, are you?"

"I'm sorry," I hissed. "Is that what you want to hear? You want me to say I'm sorry for what I did last year?"

"No, I want you to disappear, you king-slaying whore!" Kaspar spat. "You've ruined my realm, just like the Nether scum you prefer fucking."

Rage tore through me at the spite directed at Hale's memory. On instinct, I jerked forward, smashing the top of my head into Kaspar's nose. Something cracked, and he shouted in surprise and pain, but his firm hold remained. Instead of responding the way I'd hoped, Kaspar yanked my arm again, dragging another cry from my lips as he twisted me around so my back was flush against him. I struggled, but he slammed my face into the cold stone wall, scattering stars across my vision. Fear sank its claws deeper into my chest.

"*Please*, Kaspar," I begged. "You don't have to be this person."

The king's grip eased slightly at my words. Finding hope in his hesitation, I shut my eyes against their stinging and took a deep breath.

"We all have a choice. There are people who love you, Kas. They're on your side, and they want to see you succeed. The path you're going down will only lead to your own destruction, but it doesn't have to be that way. It starts with a choice. One choice, right now, to do the right thing."

His silence hung heavier than the dense rain clouds in the night sky, only visible from the window thanks to the light of the waxing moon illuminating their edges. The sight should have been beautiful, but what Kaspar said next made it the backdrop of a nightmare.

"Where's the fun in that?"

Dread chilled my blood.

I jerked to the side, attempting one last escape, but Kaspar caught me in violent fists and dragged me back. I opened my mouth to scream, but again he caught my head and bashed it against the wall, silencing me with another explosion of stars. I crumpled at the pain, my head swimming and leaving me defenseless against Kaspar's ruthless touch.

"Sometimes, Lina..." he said, his voice eerily sweet as he drew a small knife from the inner pocket of his coat. "Sometimes people are too far gone for you to save."

I mustered my strength as the stars faded, kicking at Kaspar's shins and stomping on his toes, but the liquor had numbed him and made him impervious to my struggle. He smacked my head into the wall a third time, drawing out a weak groan as I collapsed against him.

"Goodbye, King Slayer," he purred in my ear as the blade

rose to my throat. "When you see Hale in the Underworld, make sure to say hello for me."

*Thwack!*

The king suddenly went limp and slid to the floor.

I scrambled around, panting from fear and adrenaline, but relief washed over me when I peered through the shadows and caught a glimpse of my saviors.

Syrena and Ilora stood in front of me, while Kaspar lay in an unconscious mound at their feet. Syrena lowered the dagger in her hand, its blunt pommel glinting red in the moonlight with her brother's blood, while Ilora stared down at the king's body, her expression one of repulsion and betrayal.

"What are you..." I trailed off as my gaze landed on their hooded cloaks, the packs slung over their shoulders, and the weapons at their sides.

They were coming with me.

How they'd found out what I'd planned, I had no idea. But if Syrena had picked an outfit for the occasion, there would be no dissuading her now.

"Are you alright?" Ilora asked, dropping her bladed staff to the ground so she could search my body for anything in need of healing.

"I'm fine."

The queen of Lerian hadn't looked up from her brother's body. Her face was cold, her normally expressive eyes hollow. Ilora and I glanced at each other, unsure of what to say to her.

Syrena slid her blade back into its sheath on her hip, the blood on its handle staining her blouse, and her lips pursed as she dropped to the floor to straddle her brother's body. Then she pulled back her fist and threw it forward, connecting her knuckles with her brother's face.

"Syrena," Ilora said gently. "He's out. He's not going to wake up for a while."

But Syrena punched him again.

Then again.

Ilora peeked over at me, worry marring her features.

Again Syrena punched her brother. Her eyes were still empty, but a tear slipped from one corner.

Warily, I knelt beside her.

She kept her eyes glued to her brother's face as she hit him again, bloodying her knuckles, but another tear trailed down her cheek. She got two more punches in before I caught her raised fist and pulled it to my chest.

"Syrena, it's alright," I whispered.

"It's not," the queen spat back, struggling against my hold.

I gripped her hand even tighter. "You're right, it's not. But *I'm* alright. I promise."

Syrena's gaze lifted to mine. Doing so sent another tear trickling down her face. They were the only cracks in her otherwise perfectly crafted mask.

She swallowed and nodded firmly. "I'll talk to him." Confusion, guilt, and shame riddled her voice.

My heart broke for her. I knew the distress of hating someone and loving them at the same time far too well. I'd experienced it with my own brother. It was the most conflicting type of pain, and nothing seemed to help except time to accept that sometimes you love the idea of a person more than who they actually are.

I did the only thing I could think of, which was to squeeze Syrena's hand and give her an encouraging smile. "I know you will."

Syrena nodded again, trying her best to remain collected, but her bottom lip quivered. Her eyes moved to her brother's body once more, then darted back to me like she was afraid to look at it for too long. "I... I'm so sorry I let him become this."

I tightened my grip on her shaking fist. "He made the choice to be this person. Not you."

Syrena sat with my words for a few seconds. Then, as if someone had snapped their fingers and unbound her from an enchantment, she wiped her face and looked up at me, all traces of heartache disappearing. Fire ignited behind her eyes again, and as if fully embracing the golden viper in her flesh, she hissed, "Where the *fuck* were you going without us?"

I sighed in defeat. "I'm going to the Netherworld."

Ilora scoffed. "I knew it!"

"You did?"

"Of course." Ilora crossed her arms. "What you pulled with the Hag today was reckless, and I had a hunch that once Lina Calder starts doing reckless things, she doesn't stop."

Well, that wasn't *un*true...

"Why didn't you tell us?"

"Why?" Now it was my turn to scoff. "Because I knew you'd do *this*."

"So?"

"So you can't put your life on the line, you have territories to rule!"

Ilora shrugged, then stated as casually as discussing what she'd eaten at breakfast, "I don't plan on dying."

"Neither do I," Syrena added. "And if I do, there's somebody else who can take my place." Her gaze drifted to the brother she was still kneeling on. "Maybe it would be good for him. He'd have to step up and become something other than a giant heap of shit."

She threw one final punch into Kaspar's battered face before allowing Ilora to help her up.

I, however, stayed on the floor. "I can't ask you to do this."

"You aren't asking." Ilora gripped me by the shoulders and

hauled me upright with surprising strength. "But we *are* doing it."

I opened my mouth to protest more, but Syrena interrupted by sighing and examining the curling end of her side-braid. "Lina, let's be honest. You have some skill with a blade, yes, but all your success in battle so far has mainly been due to the element of surprise or sheer dumb luck."

"You're scrappy too, we'll give you that," Ilora added.

"But against a legion of monsters, you're doomed. You need us. And we need to do this too, because if we didn't go with you, we'd never forgive ourselves. It's like I told you before, friends don't let friends do crazy shit alone. And this is by far the craziest thing I've ever heard. So the question is..." Syrena threw the braid over her shoulder and readjusted her pack. "What the hell are we waiting for?"

Without waiting for my response, Syrena spun on her heel and blazed ahead, aiming for the staircase down the hall.

I begrudgingly shouldered my own bag and moved to follow her.

"Wait." Ilora stopped me, her warm eyes round with concern. "Are you sure you're alright?"

I squeezed her arm and smiled gratefully. "Yes. Thank you."

"If you need to talk about it—"

"Really," I cut her off. "I'm fine. It's not the worst thing a man has tried to do to me."

Ilora's eyes widened. After a few moments of processing the information, she leaned in and kissed my forehead, then cupped my face in her hands.

"You're the bravest person I know, Lina Calder."

When she turned to follow Syrena, I glanced back at Kaspar and stuffed my trembling hands in my pockets.

*I wish I felt like it.*

# CHAPTER 27

———

We tiptoed through the palace so stealthily even Hale would have been impressed had he been alive to see it.

On the way, I explained to my friends what I'd seen in the water the night Wynn jumped from the balcony. They agreed the crack in the rock, the glowing blue light, and Wynn's behavior were too odd to be a coincidence.

"You should've just told us," Syrena muttered under her breath for the tenth time. She peeked around the corner of the servants' entrance, cautiously looking both ways before signaling the coast was clear.

I didn't respond. She'd been talking at me like an angry jabbering parrot for the past ten minutes, but it was making her feel better, so Ilora and I let her get it out of her system.

We padded into the darkened corridor, the air around us cooling as we made our way towards the faint roar of the sea in the distance.

"So we don't know where this veil will lead exactly?" Ilora asked in a hushed whisper.

"No," I replied. "The one in Kylanthia came out in a cave

that led straight to Aedan. For all we know, this one could do the same."

Ilora nodded and readjusted the bladed staff she'd strapped to her pack. "We'll be ready."

"Quiet!" Syrena shushed, throwing up her hand to stop us in our tracks.

We listened intently for a few seconds. I heard nothing, but the two Fae went rigid, tilting their heads so their pointed ears were angled down the hall.

"Shit!" Ilora looked around in a panic. "Someone's coming! We need to hide."

Syrena ran to a nearby door and tried the handle. "Fuck! It's locked!"

I tried another. "This one too."

"Shit!" Ilora hissed again. "We have to turn back. Maybe if we run, we can—"

"Your Majesty?"

We froze at the deep voice.

"Or should I say..." Roric Pax materialized out of the shadows, his head cocking to the side in curiosity. "Majes*ties*?"

I held my breath and remained as still as a statue, but the captain of the guard's keen gaze landed on me a second later.

"Lina." He blinked in surprise, his brow furrowing. "What are you...?"

Roric trailed off when he noticed our packs. All amusement drained from his face, and his expression grew stern.

"Where are you going?" he demanded.

"Hunting," I blurted without thinking. "We're going on a hunting trip."

It wasn't *technically* a lie.

"Yes," Syrena affirmed, clasping her hands in front of her and adopting a radiant smile. "We'll be back tomorrow night."

Roric's gaze darted between our various weapons. "And what is it you're hunting, exactly?"

"Boars," Ilora said at the same time I blurted, "Pheasants!"

"Uh-huh." Roric's eyes narrowed. "So let me get this straight. You're going hunting for boars *and* pheasants in the middle of the night without telling anyone?"

"We were going to tell you," Syrena insisted. "That's what we were doing down here. We were looking for you."

"Thank the gods we finally found you," Ilora stated, slapping a hand to her heart.

"We've been looking everywhere," I added with batted eyelashes.

Roric sighed and barred his arms over his burly chest. "Alright, ladies. What's really going on?"

The three of us exchanged nervous glances. There was no way the commander would go along with our plan, and we were clearly not the best at spinning lies without previous preparation.

Before we could decide what to do, a familiar *thwack* rang out, and Roric grunted as he crumpled to the ground, unconscious. He revealed Xavier behind him, spinning his dagger in his hand before wiping its hilt on the leg of his trousers.

"Took you three long enough." He tutted, popping the knife back into its sheath. "I was starting to think you got scared and backed out."

"You knew about this too?" I shot a dirty look at the girls.

Ilora threw her hands up. "Don't look at us, we didn't tell him."

"I guessed." Xavier checked Roric's pulse, then grabbed his tattooed arm, bent it at the elbow, and propped it under the captain's head like a pillow. "After what happened earlier, I thought Lina might have some more tricks up her sleeve. And where one goes..." He pointed at me, then jerked his thumb to

Ilora and Syrena. "Two usually follow. So *then* I figured, wherever you ladies are going, you could use some extra protection. Thanks to my new friend the Hag, I can provide myself as a solution."

Syrena grunted in exasperation and stomped her foot. "Gods, why is it so hard to get rid of you?"

Xavier glared at her. "A simple thank you would suffice, Your Highness."

"A thank you for what?"

"For distracting your captain of the guard. If it wasn't for me, he would've been patrolling the palace and caught you sneaking around long before you got this far. Instead, he and I were here."

Syrena surveyed the corridor. "What were you doing in the servants' tunnels?"

A slow, utterly diabolical smile spread over Xavier's lips as he leaned in close and lowered his voice to a whisper.

"I win."

I groaned and smacked a palm to my forehead.

Syrena gasped and frantically shook her head. "No! There's no way!"

Xavier gestured to his ruffled hair and partially unbuttoned shirt, pointedly arching a brow in Syrena's direction. "Oh, no?"

Syrena's gaze raced over him. Once. Twice. Three times. Then her mouth dropped open.

"Don't play a game you can't win, Your Highness." Xavier winked as he strutted towards a nearby broom closet. When he opened the door, he pulled out a stuffed rucksack, a navy cloak, and a crossbody sling that contained his sword and daggers.

"I packed enough food for a week," he added. "Wasn't exactly sure how long saving the world takes."

"Xavier," I muttered, shaking my head. "Please rethink this. If anything happened to you, Soren would—"

"Soren's not here." Xavier straightened and buckled his weapons around his chest. "If he were, he'd do the same thing. He taught me that you do everything in your power to protect the ones you love."

My heart sank at the truth of his words. Soren *would* do the same. He fought tirelessly, fearlessly, often recklessly for the people he loved.

Gods, I missed that stupid reckless love.

"We should go before anyone else sees us," Ilora urged. "Or before our trail of bodies starts waking up."

I nodded and gingerly stepped over Roric before hurrying after Xavier and Ilora as they headed towards the beach. Syrena followed, still stewing in stunned silence.

Xavier whistled as he stared out over the waves bashing against the jagged rocks on the beach beneath the palace. "I can't believe you and Wynn survived that fall, Lina."

"It's the tide," Ilora explained, motioning farther out to sea. "This is the only time it's this high. Any other time of day you'd be smashed to pieces if you swam out there, but right now the swell is deep and calm." She eyed a wave tearing through two peaks of coral jutting up from the depths. "Calm*er*, that is."

"You're sure about this?" Syrena asked, finally finding her voice.

I sighed and tightened the straps on my pack to ensure it wouldn't get knocked off in the surf. "Not really, no."

Syrena turned back to the ocean and frowned. "Wonderful."

Xavier eagerly rubbed his hands in front of him. "Everyone can swim, right?"

"No, I grew up on the beach and never learned how to

swim," Syrena sneered.

Ilora massaged her temples. "Good gods, not everything needs to be an argument with him."

"Thank you, Ilora." Xavier huffed.

"Traitor," Syrena grumbled.

Ilora rolled her eyes and waded into the shallows, sharply sucking air through her teeth at the cold. "Lina, lead the way. We'll follow you."

I squinted at the horizon, searching the darkness for a familiar shape.

"There!" I pointed at a flat rock directly off the center of the cliff. "Wynn and I washed up there."

I trudged into the icy waters, flinching at the sting as they soaked through my clothing. As soon as I'd dipped in past my shoulders the chill became more bearable, but my teeth still chattered uncontrollably as I paddled towards the rocky point.

Our waterlogged packs weighed us down, making the going slow, but eventually we arrived at the rock and clung to its rough edges to catch our breath. The water was choppy, but not nearly as bad as it had been during the storm.

"It should be around here," I shouted at my friends' bobbing heads. "I'm going to duck under and look around."

"Be careful," Syrena pleaded.

I nodded, took in a lungful of air, and dipped beneath the surface.

This time, there were no flashes of lightning to help me see. The brewing storm remained stuck in the distance, leaving me no choice but to search the dark unaided. The world beneath the waves was foreign; I'd been too frantic and jostled by the chaos before to mark my surroundings carefully. I had to come up for air three times before I finally discovered a large mound of coral rising from the sandy sea floor with an unassuming crack at its base.

I breached the surface, gulping hungry breaths as I waved my arms over my head to capture my friends' attention.

"Over here!" I shouted at them. "I found it!"

Ilora, Xavier, and Syrena paddled towards me, and one by one they took turns diving to examine the crevice.

"Are you sure the veil's there?" Syrena panted when she popped up from the deep. "What if it's not? What if there's a shark instead, or a sea serpent?"

"Then you should go in first," Xavier offered. "Maybe they'll accept you as one of their own."

Syrena irritably splashed water in his face. "I'm being serious."

"So am I, little serpent." Xavier's eyes twinkled at the nickname the Hag had given her.

"We just have to trust Lina's instincts," Ilora cut in before the two could take up their bickering again. "Now let's go before the tide changes and we're skewered on these rocks. Who's going first?"

"Me." I swam over so I was directly above the rift, but Xavier shouldered me out of the way.

"You went first last time. Let someone else be reckless for once."

"Xavier—" I started, but he interrupted me.

"It's too small for us to go in with these packs on, so everyone swim through first and pull them in after you."

"Alright." I gulped, trying not to focus on my furiously pounding heart. "Don't die."

Xavier winked back. "Never do."

His gaze drifted to Syrena, and even though the darkness made it impossible to see her perfectly, I was fairly certain she smiled at him.

"See you on the other side." Xavier saluted us, took a deep breath, and sank beneath the waves.

We waited.

For what, exactly, we weren't sure, but none of us breathed. We hugged the rock, staring intently at the swirling depths below. No sharks emerged, but more importantly, no Xavier. After a while, I couldn't take it anymore.

I loosened the straps of my pack and dove into the dark.

Keeping one hand on the coral to guide me towards the ocean floor, I kicked my legs to propel me forward. My fingers met the top of the crevice, and I looked around for any sign of Xavier. He was nowhere to be seen in the water around me, so he must have gone inside.

Pushing away the sea serpent idea Syrena had planted in my mind, I shimmied off my pack, shut my eyes, and wriggled through the crack, wincing as its jagged edges sliced at my hips. When I popped through, I turned and yanked my rucksack in after me, tearing one of its edges on the same piece of rock that had grabbed at me. When we were both free, I flipped back around, treading water as I tried to see my surroundings, but the world was pitch black. My lungs were starting to burn, reminding me I needed air, while my panic spiked, reminding me there was none. Unsure what to do next, I kicked my feet and flailed my free hand forward, hoping to make contact with Xavier.

What I found instead was a veil.

A sensation shot through me, one I'd last experienced under a mountain in Kylanthia. Icy cold bit through my body even more than the ocean already had, reaching down to the roots of my teeth and the very marrow in my bones. My mind scrambled like I'd been flipped upside down and dropped on my head, and I lost all sense of self and time and space. The water around me grew heavy and thick, making me feel like a fly in a vat of molasses.

I had no idea how long I fumbled through the dense and dizzying dark. Seconds? Days? Months?

It was an eternity and the blink of an eye all at once, but then the world around me turned to water again, only now it was bright and clear.

I found myself in an underwater cavern inside a reef, a ray of light beaming down from a hole in the coral above to light my surroundings. I became acutely aware of my aching lungs, so I kicked towards the light as fast as my body would permit.

When my head broke the surface of the water, I gasped in a lungful of air at the same time a familiar laugh hit my ears.

"You made it!" Xavier paddled over to me, the freckles on his face popping against the rosy flush on his cheeks. "That wasn't so bad, was it?"

Not three seconds later, Ilora bobbed up beside me, spitting a stream of briny liquid from her lips.

"That was horrible!" She shuddered, her teeth still clacking from the cold.

"That was the veil," I corrected, slipping an arm through one of the straps of my pack while the other continued to tread water. I squinted upwards. "At least I think it was."

High in a gray-hued sky, a silvery orb lit up the world around us. Fog hung low over the sea as it lapped against rocky black sand beaches, and in the distance, craggy terrain covered in thick mist stretched as far as the eye could see.

We had left the Fae realm at night, but here it was daytime in a murky world of gray and black.

"Wait a minute." Ilora's voice dragged my attention from the shore.

I twisted to face her. "What?"

Ilora frantically searched the water around us. "Where's Syrena?"

My stomach dropped. Xavier and I both looked around, but

there was no one else bobbing in the choppy waves. Our eyes dropped to the cavern below at the same time. Realization hit, but it was Xavier who moved the fastest.

Tossing his pack aside to float on the surface, he didn't even stop to take a breath before diving towards the reef. Ilora and I followed shortly after, but by the time she and I swam into the hole, Xavier had already disappeared through the veil. I imagined that thick, visceral cold he must be experiencing, my body instinctively shuddering at the thought of going back through it, but I didn't have to.

Within seconds Xavier reappeared, towing a limp body behind him. Air bubbled from his lips as he motioned for us to help him haul Syrena to the surface. We obeyed, both latching on to our friend and speeding towards the light.

When we broke the surface, Xavier immediately barked orders.

"Get her to the shore! Hurry! She got caught on the coral and couldn't swim through. Ilora, help me carry her. Lina, grab our packs."

I snatched up the bags floating in the swells and followed as they splashed towards the dark sand in the distance.

When the water was waist deep, Xavier swept Syrena into his arms and clambered out of the sea onto dry land. He laid her in the sand, then put an ear to her chest to listen for a heartbeat. Ilora and I sloshed over and knelt beside him.

"Come on, Syrena," Xavier muttered to himself before tilting her head backwards, pinching her nose, and pressing his mouth to her lips to puff air into her lungs.

He pulled away after one long exhale, waited a few seconds, then did it again. On his third puff Syrena's chest jerked, and on his fourth, she retched, her eyes flew open, and water shot out of her mouth. Xavier heaved a relieved sigh and sat back on his heels as Syrena flipped onto her side and vomited salty fluid into the sand. When she finally lifted her head, her eyes narrowed.

"Fuck you," she sputtered.

Xavier's eyes widened in shock, but her words also had him bristling.

"What?" he spat.

Syrena hacked another mouthful of water onto the beach.

"That was not," she gasped, "how you were supposed to kiss me again."

"He wasn't kissing you," Ilora snapped, "he was saving your life! The least you could do is say thank you."

I shook my head. "I'm sorry, did you say *again*?"

Syrena breezed past my question and hoisted herself onto all fours. "You're a healer, Ilora. You could have saved my life just fine."

Xavier's face was devoid of all its usual playfulness as he stood, brushed black grit from his knees, and stormed further up the shore.

"You're a real bitch sometimes, you know that, Syrena?" he shouted, not even bothering to look back at her over his shoulder.

The queen of Lerian frowned, but stubbornly kept her mouth sealed as she straightened onto uneasy legs.

Ilora sighed and stooped to pick up her soggy rucksack, following Xavier as she mumbled, "I'm starting to understand why my father chose to be alone for so long."

I glanced at Syrena. She was hugging herself and shivering, but despite the wounded look in her eyes, they bored holes in the back of Xavier's head. I had no idea what was going on between the two of them, but whatever it was, they would have to work through it. We had far bigger problems to worry about.

We were back in the clutches of the Netherworld, and only the gods knew what horrors it had in store for us this time.

# CHAPTER 28

The next hour was spent in silence.

We foraged on the shore for driftwood dry enough to start a fire, and once Xavier had a blaze crackling behind a cluster of boulders, we picked our packs apart and laid our belongings out to dry. Xavier eventually broke the silence with a disappointed click of his tongue as he lifted a box of soggy pastries from the depths of his bag.

"Damn. My sticky buns are ruined."

Syrena scoffed. "You brought sticky buns?"

Xavier didn't respond. He simply tossed the box over his shoulder and continued rummaging around in the rucksack's contents. Syrena wilted at his purposeful silence.

Ilora laid out a pair of damp wool socks on the rock next to the fire. "A more important question would be, what happens next? Do we just aimlessly wander in the hopes we stumble on Aedan?"

I squeezed seawater out of one of the oversized lace-up shirts I'd stolen from Soren. "I hadn't really thought that far ahead." When I chucked the top to the ground, the loud *slop* rang through the air around us. "A scouting mission wouldn't be a bad idea. The last time we were here, Aedan was in a palace, in some sort of cavern carved out of moonstone that glowed from a strange algae. Maybe we search for anything that looks big enough to contain caves that size? Mountains, cliffs, things like that."

Ilora crouched and poked at the fire with a stick. "Decent idea."

"We have no clue how big this place is, though," Syrena cut in. "We could be searching for days, weeks, months even."

"Do you have any better ideas?" Ilora countered.

Syrena sighed and found a boulder to perch on. "I just want us to keep things in perspective. I don't think we should stray too far from the veil. We can always go back through and assign watchmen on the point day and night, so we'll know first thing if Aedan, Erith, or any Nethers manage to come through."

I sank to the sand, digging my hands into the coarse grit behind me to prop myself up. For one, that didn't help my brother. Leaving Aedan to his own devices meant Wynn would remain a slave to the voice in his mind. The second reason I spoke aloud.

"We thought there was one entrance to the Netherworld, the one in Kylanthia, but now we've discovered a second. How many others are there that we don't know about? And what are the odds that Aedan, Erith, and their army of Nethers already know about them and will use them to their advantage?"

"But we also don't know how long we can last in this place." Syrena skeptically surveyed the barren terrain. "How are we supposed to find anything to eat? Now that sticky buns are off the table."

She smirked at Xavier, but he wouldn't look at her, and her face fell once more.

"We'll hunt," Ilora offered with a casual shrug. "We'll kill some Sluagh, or cook up a nice Ben Síde."

"Fry up a Night Sylph wing," I offered.

Ilora licked her lips. "Mmmm... crispy *and* nutritious."

Syrena scowled and tightened her cloak around her shoulders. "You two are starting to get delusional."

Ilora and I giggled uncontrollably, proving her right.

Without warning, both Syrena and Xavier shot to their feet at the same time, peering into the incoming fog like guard dogs on watch.

"What's wrong?" I asked, scrambling upright too.

"Don't know," Xavier replied.

"Heard something," Syrena added.

Xavier's gaze met hers for the first time since their heated exchange on the beach. "Dangerous?"

Syrena considered her senses. "Don't know. It keeps changing."

"Exactly." Xavier's eyes flicked back to the fog. "What the hell is out there?"

Ilora slowly backed towards her bladed staff propped against one of the rocks. "Should we run or fight?"

A massive shadow appeared in the fog.

Xavier gulped and drew the broadsword from his back. "I don't think we can outrun this."

The shadow moved closer, expanding until it was taller and alarmingly longer.

"I don't think we can fight it either," Syrena whispered, her eyes growing wide.

I backed away. "Oh gods... what is that?"

"It's a—"

But Xavier didn't get a chance to finish before a massive serpentine head lashed out from the mist, jaws of glistening fangs snapping in his direction. Before it could make contact, though, Syrena darted forward and tackled Xavier around his midsection. They fell into a heap in the black sand, and when he realized Syrena was now in the snake's path too, Xavier's magic surged, throwing a protective barrier in front of them. The viper's black scales glinted in the sun as it coiled, reared up to its full height, and struck again, but this time its mouth bounced backwards like it hit an invisible wall. The serpent hissed, the force blasting my hair around my face as I remained frozen in place.

The creature struck once more, careening off Xavier's shield a second time. The snake's nostrils flared with fury. It then tried a different tactic and circled Xavier and Syrena, its forked tongue darting and lapping at the barrier in search of a weakness. When it found none, it hissed again, snatched the discarded box of pastries from where Xavier had tossed it in the dirt, and slithered off to the beach, where it slipped into the waves and disappeared from view beneath their crests.

I let out the breath I'd been holding and sprinted over to my friends, Ilora on my heels.

"Are you alright?" I asked, kneeling beside Syrena.

She continued to look past me, blinking at the ocean in shock. "I told you there were sea serpents."

I settled beside her and slipped my arm around her for comfort. She rested her head on my shoulder as Xavier murmured wistfully beside us, "My sticky buns..."

WE DECIDED it wise to move locations.

Exhaustion should have been taking its hold, but all of us were too tightly wound to notice the weariness in our limbs and the weight behind our eyelids.

Xavier and Syrena led the way, walking in silence ahead of

me and Ilora, but every once in a while their shoulders brushed and the two would glance at each other before quickly looking away and stepping apart.

Eventually the silvery sun dipped towards the horizon and darkness crept over the bleak landscape.

"We should make camp," Ilora called ahead. "But maybe no fires in the open this time?"

Syrena and Xavier muttered their agreement, and together we found a slanted rock formation jutting from the ground that provided us the smallest bit of protection against the elements. The wind worsened as night fell, forcing us to huddle together beneath the slabs of granite. We sat around a tiny fire and nibbled at apples and dried meat unspoiled by our dip in the sea earlier, but none of us had much of an appetite. Our eyes played tricks on us in the growing dark, and after a time, our attention was drawn upwards as the sky changed from slate gray to a dark purple that glittered with diamond stars and interstellar clouds.

"It's beautiful," I mused, leaning my head back on the stone to get a better view of the heavens above. "Strange, but beautiful."

I waited for someone else to comment on the sight, even if it was Syrena adamantly disagreeing, but no one spoke.

When I glanced at my friends, they were all staring straight ahead into the night.

"What's the matter?" I asked.

"Something's still out there," Xavier replied around a mouthful of apple.

I gasped and sat upright, but Ilora clapped a hand on my shoulder.

"Relax. If it wanted to attack us, it would have done it back at the beach."

"It's been following us since the *beach*?" I scanned our

surroundings, straining my eyes trying to see what my friends' heightened senses were picking up on.

"It explains why we were getting such conflicting feelings at first," Syrena said, twirling one of the thin bangles around her wrist. "If it had just been the serpent, it would have been more straightforward."

I swallowed. "So it's a Nether, but it won't hurt us?"

"Not necessarily." Ilora tore off another piece of meat. "It's currently not *trying* to hurt us."

"Will it?"

"That's what we're waiting to see."

I slowly returned my back to the stone, shifting uncomfortably in my seat. "How the hell am I supposed to relax now?"

"Exactly," Syrena sighed. "But yes, the sky is pretty."

Silence settled again, only this time, knowing we were being watched, I didn't find it as peaceful.

By the time an hour had ticked past, my body was so weary from being on edge that my exhaustion morphed into anger.

I sat up again and huffily crossed my arms, my stiff limbs crying out at the movement.

"Why isn't it doing anything?" I snapped.

"Maybe it's waiting for us to fall asleep to make its move," Syrena said, her voice now raspy from fatigue.

I huffed a frustrated sigh. "Coward."

My statement carried further than I intended it to, the word echoing off the rocks around us and dissipating into the dark, which prompted Ilora to clap a hand over my mouth. We waited with bated breath, but nothing happened.

"Do *not* antagonize it," Ilora hissed.

But exhaustion and anxiety were making all rational thought slip from my grasp. I refused to wait around for my demise, helpless and unaware. If I was to face death, I was going to meet it head on.

I peeled Ilora's fingers from my lips, snatched the apple from Xavier's hand, and jumped to my feet. "I'm just saying, if it's hungry, then it should stop waiting around and come *eat!*"

On the last word, I chucked the apple as hard as I could, sending it flying into the darkness.

"You want dinner?" I shouted after it. "Come and get it!"

"Lina!" Syrena grabbed my sleeve and attempted to yank me back down to my seat. "You fucking hothead, have you lost your mind?"

Ilora buried her head in her hands like I'd just signed our death warrants. "What the hell is wrong with you?"

"I was eating that!" Xavier whined.

A crunching noise pulled our attention back to the darkness.

The noise was quick at first, hesitant almost, but then another small crunch followed, then one a little bigger. Before long, the sound of constant munching filled the night.

"Maybe it's a vegetarian?" Syrena suggested.

When the sound stopped, the world around us fell silent again, leaving us more confused than before. After a few seconds, there came a rustling, followed by the grind of gravel, then a glossy pebble hurtled through the darkness and landed at my feet.

I stepped backwards in alarm, but composed myself and stooped to pick up the rock. I ran my thumb over the smooth, flat surface before smiling into the night.

"Thank you," I called.

Only silence responded.

"Xavier, give me another apple," I demanded, stretching out my hand.

He clutched his pack to his chest, but Syrena smacked his arm, and he begrudgingly dug inside for another piece of fruit.

"It won't last a week at this rate," he grumbled.

I plucked the apple from his fingers and rolled it forward into the darkness.

The crunching started again, this time without pause. When it was finished, there came more rustling and scuffling, and within a matter of seconds, another rock bounced to my feet. This time it was square and blue.

I grinned and picked it up, rolling it over in my palm with the first.

"Thank you," I said again.

Ilora stood and joined me.

"What are you doing?" she asked warily.

"I don't think it wants to hurt us. I think it's just hungry, and it's repaying us for what it takes." I shook the stones in my hand.

Ilora nodded, chewing her thumbnail as she considered my words. She then bent and picked up the piece of meat she'd been nibbling and tossed it forward into the dark. There was a moment of silence, then some sniffing, then faint chewing. The rustling started again along with a frenzy of scuffling, then something gleamed as it shot through the air and landed with a thud at Ilora's boots. A large abalone shell, its iridescent interior glimmering in the light of the fire, rested in the dirt.

I chuckled. "I think it's some kind of scavenger."

Ilora crouched and took up the shell, admiring it before tucking it into her back pocket.

"Can you come out?" she called to the darkness. "We'd like to see you."

Again, we were met with silence.

"We won't hurt you," Ilora added.

Nothing.

I licked my lips and stepped forward. "We know you're scared. We're scared too. But I think it would make us feel better if we saw what you looked like, since you can see us. It would establish some trust, and we would feel safer."

Still nothing.

"I have one more idea." Ilora pulled one of her cords of hair forward, wriggled off the cuff at its base, and tossed the gold into the dark. After gesturing to the other gold pieces adorning her twists, she added, "You can have some more if you just let us see you."

We waited, but nothing happened.

I looked to Ilora and shrugged. "It was a decent idea."

We both moved to sit back down, but a rustling in the dark made us freeze. When we faced forward again, our breath caught at what emerged from the shadows.

She was tall but didn't seem it because of how low to the ground she crouched as she crept towards us. She was so thin her bones were practically jutting out, and her round eyes were sunken and desperate. Despite her starved appearance, the woman was stunning. Her hair was the same inky blue-black as the feathered wings that sprouted from her back, and her hooked nose only added to her unique beauty. Despite our fears, she wasn't frightening at all. The only thing that had me slightly concerned was the curved black nails on her fingers and toes, more talons than anything else.

"I don't believe it," Ilora breathed. "I thought they'd all died off or migrated somewhere else."

"What are *they* exactly?" I asked, my eyes never leaving the Nether in front of us.

Syrena stood, her sudden movement causing the winged woman to scuttle backwards a few paces. "Feathered beasts found in the Kylanthian mountains. There are stories of them snatching civilians in broad daylight and flying them to their nests in the cliffs to feed their young."

"There are also stories of them being terribly misunderstood," Ilora countered. "Nothing but scavengers who steal fruit from your orchard or rummage through your trash. They've also been known to swipe pies off window ledges or shiny things you accidentally leave unattended, like a key or jewelry."

Syrena subtly lowered her sleeve over her bracelets.

I stole another look at the woman. Scraps of fabric clung to her hips, and her long hair was matted with twigs, shells, and black feathers that camouflaged her bare breasts. She also had a worn burlap sack draped over one shoulder.

"I heard travelers talking at the market in my village once," I muttered. "They told legends from their country about a creature that was half woman, half bird. They called it a Harpy."

Xavier stood, flashing his signature grin in the woman's direction. "Why don't we just ask her what she wants to be called?"

The woman tilted her head and sniffed in Xavier's direction, her wings rustling behind her.

"Here." Ilora bent so she was on the winged woman's level and pulled another cuff from her hair, then gently rolled it towards the woman's feet.

The woman instantly snatched the gold up and popped it into her sack. After scanning us with wary brown eyes, she straightened to standing, her wings folding behind her as she wrung her taloned hands with worry.

"Veshti," she mumbled.

"You're called a Veshti?" Ilora asked.

The woman shook her head furiously, tapping a long nail to her chest.

"Veshti," she repeated, then blinked at us expectantly.

"Oh!" Xavier's eyes widened, as did his smile. "Your *name* is Veshti."

The woman's feet shuffled happily, the curved nails on them clicking against the rocks.

"Veshti..." Xavier beckoned to the woman, then put a hand on his own chest. "Xavier." He motioned to the rest of us. "Syrena, Lina, Ilora."

Veshti's head tilted to the side, and after a few moments she licked her lips, cleared her throat, and recited in a voice that mimicked Xavier's so perfectly it was almost eerie, "Ilora, Lina, Syrena, Xavier."

We all laughed a little and exchanged stunned looks.

"Yes, exactly." Xavier beamed at the Nether before performing a graceful bow. "It's nice to meet you, Veshti."

Her wings rustled, and her feet tapped again.

"Why were you following us?" Syrena demanded.

Veshti looked Syrena up and down. "Snake."

"There's no need to be rude—"

Veshti shook her head, then inched a little closer and jerked her chin to Syrena's chest. "Snake."

Syrena glanced down. The top buttons of her blouse had come undone, revealing the gold viper with emerald eyes between her breasts. She quickly fastened them.

"Oh. Yes, that's a snake. It's a snake... uh... tattoo."

Veshti's eyes narrowed. "Tat... too?"

"A marking on the skin," Ilora explained. She pulled the collar of her tunic down over her shoulder, shrugging her arm out of its sleeve to reveal the twin gold bands. "See? I have one too."

"Me too." I pulled up my sleeve to show my scars and the silver symbol above them.

Veshti nodded in understanding. "Tattoo."

"Yes!" Ilora grinned. "Tattoo."

Veshti thought for a bit, then spun so her back was to us. Her wings were scraggly and missing feathers in places, revealing bumpy pink skin underneath. When she raised the wings, however, stretching them out wide to reveal her bare back, I had to press my lips together to keep from gasping in shock.

Veshti's back was covered in scars, the flesh marred in savage white slashes that created a tangle of deep fissures through her skin. She peeked at us over her shoulder.

"Tattoo?" she asked innocently.

I inhaled a quivering breath and shook my head. "Not quite."

Veshti tucked her wings back to her body and faced us. Her head angled to the side, and she uncurled a finger to point a nail at my arm.

"Tattoo?"

I looked down at my wrist and ran my fingers over the vertical black line running up it. "No, this is a scar, but this..." I patted the silver impression above it. "*This* is the tattoo."

Veshti nodded slowly. "No pain?"

I glanced at my friends. "No, the tattoos caused us pain too. But we... *chose* them, I guess. Did you? Choose yours, I mean?"

Veshti seemed to melt, the tips of her wings sinking to the ground as her shoulders slumped. She shook her head.

"Well, you're still very beautiful," Xavier admitted, unable to resist the urge to wink at her.

Veshti sniffed in his direction once more, then narrowed her eyes into a chilling glare. "Man."

Syrena snorted. "My sentiments exactly."

"Xavier is a man, yes, but he's good," I assured her. "He's safe."

The woman's wings rustled as she considered. "Protect?"

"Yes, Xavier protects."

Syrena sneaked a peek at the man in question, who was already looking at her.

"Veshti?" Ilora stepped forward, offering another piece of the gold in her hair. "Do you have anyone who protects you?"

Veshti grabbed the cuff and started to tuck it into her bag, but thought better of it. After analyzing Ilora's hair, she fastened it in one of her own locks.

"Beautiful," she murmured, nudging the piece with her knuckle.

Xavier chuckled.

The Nether looked back up at us, shaking her head as she tapped a talon to her chest. "Just Veshti."

"For how long?" Ilora pressed.

"For..." Veshti's brow furrowed, and her eyes grew distant. "Long."

I glanced at the tattered rags on her body.

*Years, by the looks of it.*

"Veshti?" Ilora pulled another piece from her hair, this one a dangling charm, and held it out in her palm. "Do you think you could help us find something?"

Veshti pinched the charm between two fingers and held it up to the light of the flames, poking it with her nail to make it sway back and forth.

"We're looking for a person."

Veshti shook the charm, her feet shuffling merrily at the way it tinkled.

"His name is Aedan."

Veshti immediately dropped the charm to the sand.

Her wings flared, and she furiously shook her head. "Bad."

"Yes, we know he's bad—"

"*Bad.*" Veshti backed up, her wings flapping in a frenzy as her head continued to shake. "Bad, bad, bad, bad—"

"We're going to kill him," I interrupted.

Veshti went still.

"We're going to kill Aedan," I repeated. "Do you know what kill means?"

Veshti nodded, her wings twitching. "Pain."

"Yes." My mouth set in a determined line. "We want Aedan to feel pain, but we don't know where he is. Will you show us where to find him?"

Veshti nervously clacked her nails together.

"*Please,*" Syrena insisted, stepping forward and slipping off one of her mother's bangles. She hesitated for a split second and stared at it in her palm, then straightened her shoulders and held it out to the woman as an offering.

Veshti gasped in awe, then hooked the hoop with her finger and lifted it to admire in the light.

"Snake," she breathed.

I grinned proudly at Syrena, who caught me watching and rolled her eyes. "What? The girl's clearly got good taste."

Veshti lowered the bracelet and wriggled her hand inside, her feet tippy-tapping as she jangled it around her wrist.

Another glance at Syrena found her almost smiling.

Veshti finally looked away from the bracelet, her gaze icing over as she rose to her full height and flared her wings.

"Come," she stated firmly. "*Kill.*"

# CHAPTER 29

WE WALKED THROUGH THE NIGHT UNTIL OUR EYES COULDN'T STAY open a second longer.

After we made camp, we took turns keeping watch while the others slept, with Veshti huddling just far enough away for her to feel comfortable. She was still wary and would jump if we moved too quickly or made a loud noise, but she seemed to be warming to us. The fact she trusted us enough to fall asleep with her wings wrapped around her like a shell to block out the cold was a vast improvement from a few hours prior.

In the morning when the sky transitioned from purple to gray, and the silver sun rose over the horizon, Veshti led us back to the coast. Shortly after, she flew out over the ocean and returned with two fish skewered on her talons, which she timidly presented to us before clacking her talons together expectantly. Ilora handed over another gold cuff in thanks, which Veshti proudly displayed in her hair next to the other.

After breakfast, we continued to follow the Nether woman up the coastline. At first, she would either fly above us or shuffle ahead, keeping a good distance between us and cautiously checking over her shoulder every few seconds. By the end of the day, though, her nerves had calmed, her trust blossomed, and she allowed herself to walk alongside us.

Veshti was an incredibly fast learner. She was constantly listening and watching and studying, picking up words we said as well as our mannerisms. Even conversations we had while she was flying above us weren't safe, and when she'd alight back on firm ground, she'd mimic our voices or repeat terms she wanted an explanation of. By the time night fell at the end of the second day, her broken speech had significantly improved.

"Veshti," Syrena asked as she watched Xavier get to work starting a fire. "What happened to your family?"

Ilora elbowed her in the ribs. "Syrena!"

"What?" Syrena cried, ruefully rubbing her side. "I'm curious!"

Veshti watched the two bicker, her head tilting quizzically. "Fam... illy?"

"Family," I repeated. I beckoned to Ilora, Syrena, and Xavier. "See? This is *my* family."

My words made Ilora and Syrena quiet down, and they sheepishly smiled at me and then each other.

"Your flock," Xavier explained. He balanced a few pieces of driftwood over the smoldering grass he'd ignited and sat back to watch them catch flame.

"Oh." Veshti's wings sank sadly, brushing the ground. "Flock killed."

"By..." I hesitated saying Aedan's name. "By the bad man?"

Veshti shuddered at the thought of him, then pulled her wings around her in a feathery embrace.

"Some, yes. Bad man killed mother. Veshti small then. Father..." Her wings tightened around her. "Father killed by... by..."

Veshti's brow wrinkled as she tried to find the word. She eventually gave up and instead tilted her head back, perfectly mimicking a wolf's howl.

"Wolves," Ilora finished.

Veshti nodded solemnly. "Veshti's kind food for many."

"Well, don't worry," Xavier assured her with a smile. "You're not food for us."

She studied his face and attempted a smile of her own, curling her lips and baring her teeth. It wasn't nearly as pleasant as she'd intended. "Xavier, Syrena, Lina, Ilora not food for Veshti."

"Good." Syrena settled against a rock and looked up at the deep purple sky, twisting her bracelets absentmindedly as she lost herself to her thoughts. After a few moments of quiet, she muttered, "Syrena's mother and father were killed too. Like Veshti's."

The Nether studied her, then leaned back in the cradle of her wings and toyed with the bangle on her own arm. "How?"

"The bad man sent creatures who ate them."

"What creatures?"

"Not sure. We live near the ocean, so maybe Merrows." Syrena glanced at her. "Do you know what Merrows are?"

Veshti blinked.

"Bluish." Syrena gestured to her skin. "Looks sort of like us, but with gills and dorsal fins? You know, a fish bitch."

Veshti squinted. "Fish... bitch?"

Ilora smacked Syrena's arm but stifled a snicker. "Don't teach her that!"

The girls couldn't hold back their laughter. Veshti watched them for a few seconds, then mimicked their sounds of joy.

"Veshti?" I scooted closer to her. "How long until we find the bad man?"

The Nether woman shuddered again. "If fly, by morning."

"We can't fly like you," I reminded her.

Veshti nodded. "Then by night."

I took a deep breath and leaned my head into the stump I was propped against, my heart thumping in anticipation of what the next day would bring.

After another period of weighted silence, Veshti cleared her throat to get our attention.

"Veshti not go all the way," she said softly. "Veshti too... too..."

Ilora gave her an encouraging smile, empathy written on her face. "Too afraid?"

Veshti's wings wilted. "Yes."

"That's alright," I reassured her. "Just take us as far as you can."

Veshti nodded, then shot me a sidelong glance.

"Yes?" I asked.

Veshti blinked, then shimmied a little closer. "What... what is Lina?"

I sat up, confused. "Huh?"

She extended a hand, poking the rounded top of my ear with a curved nail. "Different than flock."

"Oh." I noted my friends' pointed ears and gestured to my own. "Yes, I'm different than my flock. They're Fae, I'm human. I'm from a different place than them."

"Fae..." Veshti tapped her talons together as she considered the word. "Veshti Fae too?"

I glanced at Syrena and Ilora, all of us unsure exactly how to respond.

"In a way," Xavier replied for us. "Yes, you are."

Veshti nodded, her wings rustling happily. She was pleased with that.

She thought for a few seconds, then looked out at the

barren landscape surrounding us. "Different place... There is different place than here?"

"Yes," Ilora said. "Much different."

"Maybe you can come visit us sometime," Syrena offered. When Veshti perked up, she added, "Maybe I could take you shopping."

The Nether woman blinked. "Shop... ping?"

"Yes. We'll get you some more jewelry." Syrena gestured to her bangle on Veshti's wrist.

Veshti's eyes grew round with the realization. "*More* snakes?"

"Yes," Syrena giggled. "More snakes for Veshti."

Veshti nestled further into her wings, her toes tapping with excitement. "Veshti like that."

Syrena beamed. "Believe it or not, Syrena would too."

THE MOUNTAINS WERE TERRIFYING.

Not because they were precarious or desolate.

Not because they looked identical to the ones in Kylanthia.

They were terrifying because they were upside down.

At first we didn't know what we were looking at. In the distance, something was protruding out of the sky, only instead of rising from the ground, it poked down from the clouds above. We thought nothing of it, thinking it was just the mist playing tricks on our eyes. But when the sun had risen and burned off the layer of morning haze that coated the land, the jagged crags became clearer.

Jutting down like massive stalactites in a giant cave of gray sky, the mountains made us dizzy just looking at them, a sensation only worsened when we craned our necks back to try and see where they ended, but their bases were impossible to glimpse through the thick clouds. The sight was so peculiar and foreign that it was almost unfathomable, and that put us even more on edge. A condition only aggravated when the clouds darkened and blanketed the world in a heavy drizzle.

"Veshti?" Xavier called ahead, uncertainty tingeing his voice as he squinted up at the looming peaks with his hand shielding his face against the elements. "Quick question. How are we supposed to get up there?"

Covering her head with her wings and shaking them every so often to scatter the droplets pooling on her feathers, the only thing Veshti said in response was, "Follow."

The closer we got to the mountains in the sky, the more things around us started to change. The bleak landscape transitioned into something more lush. Small coastal shrubs sprouted from the sand, the grass thickened and swayed wildly in the wind, and crystal clear streams trickled down from the rocky inland to meet with the sea.

We pressed on, and the farther we went, the more the mountains stretched towards the earth. They reached down at us like rocky fingers threatening to pluck our feet off the ground and steal us into the heavens. As we passed under the range, the jagged peaks loomed overhead, the threat of them making us instinctively hunch, like we were afraid we'd accidentally knock our heads against their razor-sharp tips if we weren't careful. I couldn't look up without getting disoriented and falling over, so I chose to focus on Veshti's ragged wings as she plodded through the mist in front of us.

As night slowly sneaked in, we weren't just ducking our heads because it felt like the mountains would hit us if we didn't. It was a genuine concern. The tips of the peaks had stretched down so far from the sky that we had to maneuver around them, weaving in and out of the rock as it reached towards the black sand beach and formed a natural maze of spikes for us to navigate.

"What is this place?" Ilora mused, crouching so as not to hit her head against a row of craggy rocks.

Gusts of wind whistled and whipped through the spikes, stinging our faces with the rain and making it so we could hardly hear Veshti when she said, "Bad man where sky meets land."

"Sky meets land," I repeated, carefully running my fingers over a nearby stone's serrated edge.

"There!" Xavier pointed ahead.

Veshti had stopped moving. Frozen in place, she stared at something in front of her. A gust of wind cleared the fog around us, bringing the object into view.

The tip of what would be the highest mountain peak had finally connected with the black sand on the beach, forming a solid wall of rock in front of us.

And carved into that wall was a tunnel.

There was no way to see where it led. The inside was pitch black, disappearing into the depths of the mountain where the dwindling sun couldn't reach.

The Nether woman turned to look at us, her talons clicking and her wings twitching nervously.

"Veshti stop here." She shook her head fervently. "No more, no more, no more—"

"It's alright," Syrena soothed, hurrying over and placing a comforting hand on her arm. To our surprise, Veshti let her.

"You don't need to do more," Syrena went on. "This is good. Veshti is good."

Her wings rustling, Veshti calmed slightly but continued to clack her talons with worry.

I wandered up beside them, my mouth gaping as my gaze

followed the wall up. It seemed to go on forever, disappearing into the swirling fog in the darkening sky.

"Aedan is inside?" I asked, trying not to dwell on how small and frail my voice sounded, or how small and frail I felt.

"Yes," Veshti replied. She'd started trembling, and her eyes repeatedly darted to the tunnel like she was waiting for something to jump out.

Noticing her discomfort, Syrena quickly slipped off a bangle and held it out to her. "You've done enough now, Veshti. Thank you."

Immediately transfixed by the gold, Veshti gasped and snatched up the bracelet. "More snake!"

"Yes." A faint smile played on Syrena's lips as Veshti twirled the piece around her finger. "My mother gave me those, you know."

Veshti stopped playing with the bangle, immediately clutching it to her chest as her eyes widened. "Killed mother?"

"Yes." Syrena folded her hands in front of her. "They mean a lot to me, but... but you being brave even though you didn't fully trust us, even though we're different than you... Well, that means a lot to me too." She forced a chuckle. "I think I could probably learn a thing or two from you."

Veshti blinked.

"Anyway." Syrena sighed and casually waved away the intimate moment. "What I'm trying to say is thank you. And... take care of yourself."

Veshti nodded, then slipped the bracelet onto her opposite wrist. She held both of her arms out for Syrena to see, jangling the bracelets on them proudly.

"Beautiful?" she asked with hope.

Syrena swallowed hard, then nodded. In earnest, she replied, "Yes. Veshti is beautiful."

Veshti attempted another smile. This time, it was more successful than her first.

"We hope to see you again, Veshti," Ilora said, bending her head in respect. "And we look forward to taking you shopping."

Veshti shuffled excitedly. "Yes. Shopping."

Xavier chuckled and stepped forward, bowing grandly. "Until we meet again."

Veshti hesitated for a moment, skeptically looking Xavier up and down, but she soon outstretched one of her wings and caressed Xavier's cheek with the tip.

"Protect," she said. Her voice was gentle, but it was a clear command. Xavier understood and dipped his head in acknowlededgement.

When Veshti turned to me, she reached out her wing again, the feather at its tip grazing the curve of my ear. "Lina has good flock."

I grinned and peeked over at my friends, who beamed back at me. "I know."

When I looked back to Veshti, her face had fallen, and she leaned forward, lowering her voice to a desperate whisper. "Kill bad man, Lina. *Please.*"

The fear and pain in her eyes relit the fire in my veins, fueling my purpose and giving me renewed strength.

"I will," I declared. "I promise."

Veshti nodded. Then, stepping away, she tickled her feather across my cheek in a final farewell.

"Veshti not forget faces," she stated.

She then threw her wings out wide and exploded into the sky.

# Chapter 30

We could only muster up enough material to fashion two torches, so we had to pair up.

Ilora and I led the way into the tunnel, the flame lifted high in front of us, while Xavier and Syrena brought up the rear. All of us kept our weapons drawn as we walked, and everyone, even the typically chatty Xavier, stayed as silent as the grave. Every noise echoed around us; our hushed shallow breaths, a pebble being kicked and bouncing off a nearby rock, even the pad of our feet through the sand was deafening in our ears.

We had no idea how long we walked. It could have been hours or only minutes. The darkness was disorienting, and time seemed to stop down here. Or was it *up* here? Sometimes it seemed like the tunnel was elevated, gradually leading us up into the depths of the mountain, while other times it dipped low as it curled around what felt like the thousandth shadowy corner.

Over time, the tunnel widened. It happened so slowly that at first we didn't notice it, but eventually the craggy ceiling was high above us, and the rough gray walls had stretched far enough apart they no longer suffocated us. The passage finally opened entirely, and we arrived in a massive domed cavern, dripping spikes of rock and shallow pools of murky water everywhere we looked.

"I don't like this." Syrena's whisper might as well have been a roar as it reverberated off the cave walls. "I don't like there being only one way out."

"Agreed." Ilora wiped her sweaty palms down the front of her cloak. Her hands had to be aching from how tightly she'd been gripping her staff. She'd thrust it into a defensive position every time she'd heard a strange noise or seen a rogue shadow, which meant she'd been doing it every few seconds since we entered the tunnel.

"Then let's hurry and find this guy so we can kill him and get the hell out of here." Xavier lifted his torch and shone it along the walls, the shadows cast by its flames confusing our eyes even more. "I think the cave system goes on that way."

He pointed to the far end of the cavern with the tip of his sword, where a darkened corner disguised a crevice cut between two pillars of rock.

"I never would've noticed that," Syrena murmured. Maybe I imagined it, but she sounded impressed.

Either Xavier didn't notice or he just didn't care, because he motioned for us to follow and pressed on without calling attention to it.

The black sand of the path transitioned to slate and limestone as we pushed deeper into the cave, and we had to take hold of the boulders and stone spikes rising from the ground to keep from slipping on the slick surface.

"Lina?"

I looked over my shoulder at Xavier and Syrena. "Yes?"

Xavier blinked and peeked at Syrena. She shrugged and shook her head. "We didn't say anything."

"Oh." I turned to look at Ilora. "Sorry, did you say something?"

"No."

My gaze darted between my friends. "None of you just said my name?"

Ilora glanced back at Xavier and Syrena warily. They looked just as confused as she did. "No."

My brow furrowed. "Strange, I could've sworn someone said my name."

"Lina?"

My head jerked up as the faint voice called out again. "There! Did anyone hear that?"

"That one I heard." Ilora spun her staff into position. "It sounded like—"

"Lina!"

Syrena's head tilted. "Like a child."

"Lina, I'm here!"

"Oh gods." I snatched the torch from Ilora's hand. "That's Wynn!"

"Lina, no! Wait!" Xavier shouted.

But I'd already sprinted across the cave and wriggled through the crack into the passageway on the other side.

Maybe it was the exhaustion from days of walking and restless nights, or delirium induced by the cave and its ever-shifting shadows. Whatever the cause, I wasn't thinking clearly. I'd forgotten where I was and what monsters lived here, and where I'd heard creatures mimicking my brother's voice before.

I soon remembered, though, when I fumbled blindly through the cave system, accidentally tripped over a rock jutting up in the middle of the path, and tumbled to the ground. The torch flew from my grasp, extinguishing in a puddle and leaving me defenseless in a pitch-black world.

"Lina?" Wynn's voice called again. It was louder now. Closer. "Lina, is that you?"

I pushed myself up and rapidly blinked my eyes in an attempt to see something, *anything*, but I remained blind in the dark.

"Lina! You found me!" His voice was even closer now, to my left, and the overwhelming stench of rotting flesh wafted around me.

In the distance, Xavier, Ilora, and Syrena called my name.

"I'm here!" I shouted back.

"Lina," Wynn's voice whimpered from my right. My skin prickled, sensing someone near. "Lina, I'm so scared."

"You're not Wynn," I whispered, palming the hilt of my blade.

"Of course I am!" my brother's voice wailed. It sniffled pitifully, and when it spoke again, it was choked with tears. "They stole me away again, Lina. Please save me."

The rancid stench increased, and something brushed my left cheek. I spun and slashed at the air with my dagger, but hit nothing. In the distance, my friends' voices called for me again. They were getting closer.

"I'm over here!" I called to them. "Hurry!"

"They're going to kill me, Lina," Wynn's voice cried from behind me. "They're going to kill me like they killed Hale!"

At that, my fear was replaced by rage.

"Don't you dare speak his name," I snarled to the dark.

This time, Wynn laughed. "Oh, Lina. You stupid, *stupid* girl..."

On its last words, the voice changed. It was no longer my brother, but a sinister mix of a whisper and the hiss of a snake, and it spoke directly into my ear.

I tore my dagger through the air again, this time lower, and this time the blade hit flesh. When it found its mark, a pair of glowing yellow eyes snapped open in front of me, and the creature's mouth gaped as it let out an ear-piercing screech, revealing a row of rotten teeth, the same teeth that were forever scarred into my skin after my brush with these Nethers in the woods last year.

I leapt back from the monster, yanking my dagger from where I'd lodged it deep in the withered charcoal skin of the creature's abdomen.

But to my horror, we weren't alone.

My back collided with something, and I yelped in alarm and spun to face it. The monster was faster. Its claws sank into my skin, and I shut my eyes tight as I braced for the pain. Agony tore through me like lightning. My jaw became an immovable vice as every muscle went taut. Uncontrollable tears squeezed out the sides of my eyes as my body seized.

But I'd felt this pain before.

I'd *beat* this pain before.

Just like the last time I was in the Netherworld, I dug deep and willed strength to my limbs, forcing my body to move. I lifted my rigid, trembling arms, and aimed for the Nether's glowing eyes. Last time I'd seen eyes like those, I'd gouged them out with my bare hands in order to survive, so I readied to do it again.

But another Nether materialized out of the dark and pierced its claws into my side, sending another bolt surging through me. My arms dropped as the pain ravaged my body.

A third Nether appeared and plunged another talon through my skin. My jaw clenched so tight I was certain my teeth would crack under the pressure, and my heart pounded harder and faster than it ever had before. It ached under the strain, the pain there more urgent than anywhere else in my body. It was frenzied, frantic, desperately screaming for relief.

But none came.

Even though darkness already engulfed me, it moved in further. It became more visceral, seeping into my mind and coaxing me to surrender with a seductive caress. My eyes fluttered closed, unconsciousness descending fast, and the world drifted away, leaving me weightless in a deep expanse of black. My heart grew too tired of fighting, and it beat one final, weary time before snuffing out like a light.

NOTHING.

Nothing at all.

No pain. No fear. No panic. No grief.

No love. No joy. No compassion. No hope.

Just all-consuming black.

But then... a glimmer in the dark.

A fleck of silver sparkled in the distance. It grew larger, revealing itself as a vine. A tiny, hopeful, twinkling thing bravely sprouting in the vast expanse of black.

I reached towards it, hesitantly at first. When my fingers grazed its leaves, it burned.

But I liked the pain.

It sent out a shockwave that shivered through me long after it had gone, leaving behind a constant hum of energy I could feel inside, outside, everywhere.

It was the heavy silence after a lightning strike while the world waits for thunder.

It was the tight pause before a kiss.

It was the breath before a climax.

It was addicting, and I wanted *more*.

I reached towards the vine again, and this time I ripped it up by the root. It erupted, its light blasting through me like vicious, magnificent wildfire.

And it was all mine.

Pure, uncontainable power.

THE WORLD WAS BRIGHT, and I was screaming.

I screamed until my throat was raw and all the air in my lungs had been used up. Then I collapsed, and the brightness in the room faded as my back found stone. I laid on my back, panting until my racing heart had slowed to a manageable rate.

"Lina?"

I turned my head to the side.

Xavier, Syrena, and Ilora were huddled together on the floor of the cave, their eyes wide and their expressions a strange mix of shock, horror, and confusion.

Suddenly remembering where I was, I scrambled to a sitting position.

"Be careful!" I shrieked. "There are Nethers in here! They're... they're..."

Frantically, I searched the space. There was no sign of the corpse-like creatures with their yellow eyes and claws of pain. Suddenly, it dawned on me that I could vaguely see my surroundings. Things weren't as dark as they'd been before. How could that be? My friends' torch lay doused beside them, and everything had been pitch black when the Nethers attacked.

"They're right there," Xavier croaked, pointing a shaky finger to the space beside me.

I followed his gaze to the ground.

Piles of smoldering embers surrounded me, their glow brightening the room.

*When did someone light a fire?*

"No, they... they were..." I trailed off and rubbed my face, trying to piece together what had happened. Any image I managed to pull up was covered in a dark haze and rapidly retreated back into my mind, like a dream dissipating with the first glimpse of morning.

Syrena continued to stare at me, her mouth agape, but Ilora scooted a little closer.

"What happened?"

"I was attacked." I rubbed at my forearm. The silver symbol there ached, like a scab trying to heal. "They were the same type of Nethers who attacked me and Xavier in Astoria last year. There was pain and darkness and then..." I lifted my head, my brow furrowing in confusion as a word unintentionally slipped through my lips. "Wildfire."

My friends exchanged glances.

"Whatever that means." I shrugged and clutched my knees to my chest. "That's all I remember. Pain and dark. Why? What did you see?"

Ilora gulped and looked to Xavier. He exhaled sharply and raked his fingers through his hair, eyes still glued to the coals beside me.

Syrena was the one to finally answer.

"A flash," she muttered, still in a daze. "Like lightning. We ran in and saw you, but... your eyes were black. The blackest black I've ever seen."

"And you screamed," Ilora added.

Syrena nodded dumbly. "And the light exploded, but when it left you, it turned into this horrible black wave that..."

"Did *that*." Xavier motioned to the circle of embers and ash around me.

When I looked down again, realization hit me like a blow to the face.

These were bodies.

Bodies reduced to nothing but cinders.

"It would have happened to us too if it hadn't been for Xavier." Ilora finally managed to compose herself and shuffle over to me. "He threw his magic in front of us just in time."

She arrived at the smoldering remains of the Nethers and gingerly stepped over them, hesitating briefly before reaching out to me. "Can you stand?"

I nodded and accepted her hand. She hauled me to my feet.

"You're shaking," she observed, brushing the dirt from my back. "Are you alright?"

I took stock of my body. No broken bones, no life-threatening injuries, only a few scuffs and scrapes, but... something else was here too. Slumbering, smoldering like the embers around me. It was still me, just... *more*.

"I'm good," I said, an accidental laugh bubbling out of me. "I feel good. I feel... I feel..."

"Powerful?" Xavier stood too, offering a hand to Syrena. Too stunned to throw him her usual attitude, she accepted it.

"Yes." I laughed again and ran my thumb over the glittering symbol in my forearm. The ache was gone, but now it seemed to buzz in my skin. "Is this what magic feels like?"

"Sometimes." Ilora chewed her bottom lip. "Although, I'll be honest... I've never seen magic quite like that. I've never seen it that..."

"Intense?" Xavier finished for her.

"Yes," Ilora repeated, her frown deepening. "I can't imagine what you must be feeling right now. What that kind of power feels like inside you."

"Is it scary?" Syrena asked, finally starting to look and sound more like herself.

I glanced down at my trembling hands, searching my feelings a second time.

"Yes," I admitted. "And no. It's strange. I like knowing it's there, and using it feels good. *Gods*, it felt good, but it also feels... dangerous. And big. And confusing. And I'm feeling everything all at once, and I love it but I also hate it and I can't... I can't..."

Without warning, I turned and vomited violently against a rock.

Ilora patted my back. "It's alright. I threw up my first time too."

I stood and swiped my sleeve across my mouth, groaning as the sudden burst of nausea returned to the depths of my stomach. But emptying its contents made it feel significantly better, and the humming in my veins quieted, the embers of power inside reducing to nothing but smoking coals. The magic was still there, but harmless.

For the time being, at least.

~

WE DECIDED to keep moving in case the disturbance in the cave had alerted any other Nethers to our presence. This time we kept our wits about us as we traveled through the belly of the mountain.

The caverns grew increasingly larger, so large we could no longer see the ceilings or walls, and soon a familiar cyan luminescent algae dotted the rocks and illuminated the pools we passed. The air smelled less stuffy and more crisp, and that, along with the space, made it seem like we were no longer in the bowels of a giant rock, but in an entirely different world.

Gradually the pools expanded, meeting to form one massive underground lake stretching as far as the eye could see. A path of stepping stones was the only way across its surface. We had no choice but to trek single file along the rocks and pray we didn't slip and fall into the bottomless blue on either side. It was impossible to see how deep the watery chasm went. To the naked eye, it seemed to go down forever.

Ilora led the way, followed by Syrena and then Xavier, who occasionally talked among themselves, but I hung back, their words a dull drone in my ears. Over and over I traced my fingertips along the symbol on my arm, still struggling to process the power hibernating under its surface.

The magic felt normal to me now. Not normal in the sense it wasn't an extraordinary, terrifying thing. Far from it. But it felt normal inside my body, like it had made a home inside me, entwined itself in my very blood and bones to become one with them.

"You alright there, Calder?"

Xavier's voice dragged me from my thoughts. I glanced up to see him peering at me over his shoulder. The glowing water around us made his eyes the color of moss after the rain.

"You aren't going to explode again and burn us all to a crisp, are you?"

Ahead, Syrena gasped and spun to give Xavier a rough shove, nearly sending him toppling off the rocks into the water.

"That's not funny!"

Xavier's echoing laughter proved differently. "You have to laugh at the pain sometimes, Your Highness. How else are you supposed to get through life?"

"I get through life just fine," Syrena grumbled, facing forward again and leaping to the next rock.

"The stick up your ass would disagree," Ilora quipped from the front of the line.

Syrena gasped again, prompting Xavier to laugh harder. Even I couldn't help cracking a grin as I rolled my sleeve back down.

Ilora peeked back at Syrena pouting like a child. "I'm sorry, I couldn't resist."

Syrena huffed and irritably tossed her braid. "Lina, apparently you're my only friend. You can burn the others up."

Ilora cackled, and Syrena looked back over her shoulder, her eyes twinkling with amusement.

"Well, look at that." Xavier shot her a wink. "Someone found a sense of humor."

"What can I say?" Syrena cooed, batting her eyelashes. "You're a bad influence."

Xavier chuckled low, his teeth catching his bottom lip as he shook his head. "Oh, I assure you, Your Highness, I am *very* good."

Despite the darkness, there was no hiding the flush of color that appeared in Syrena's cheeks. She arched a brow. "Oh?"

Xavier's gaze licked over her once more. "Just ask Roric."

Syrena's face fell into a scowl, and she returned her attention to the stones ahead and picked up her pace to catch up with Ilora.

"Come on, Your Highness," Xavier called after her. "Don't be a sore loser!"

His echo chased after her, but did nothing to persuade her to return.

Xavier puffed a sigh.

"Really, though." He refocused on me as I reached him. "Be honest. Are you alright?"

"Yes. I'm just trying to make sense of it all."

Xavier nodded knowingly. "Fae born with magic will never understand what we're feeling. Their power has always been there. They've felt it for as long as they can remember. They grow up together, them and the magic. It spills out gradually, sometimes over the span of a few years. But us? We just... have it. All of it, all at once, in the blink of an eye." He exhaled slowly, then peeked at me, eyes gleaming eagerly. "It's intoxicating, isn't it? You want to take it out and play with it."

I frowned. "Maybe *you* do. But apparently if I take mine out, people die."

"Just because it's wrong for you doesn't stop you from wanting it. Does it?"

I froze at his words, unsettled both by how he saw through me, and the fact he was right.

Letting his question go unanswered, I shook my head and toyed with one of the straps on my rucksack. "It doesn't matter. It's stuck. I don't know how I got it out the first time, and I don't really feel like almost dying again to try and figure it out."

"It'll take practice. Even I don't know what the hell I'm doing."

My head swiveled towards him. "But you've been using yours constantly."

"I know." Xavier winced. "But I don't always mean to."

"Then how do you get it to come out?"

He shrugged and kicked a pebble into the water. "I just get scared."

I sniffed and playfully nudged his ribs with my elbow. "A big tough warrior like you? Scared?"

Xavier grinned and ruffled my hair. "Don't tell anyone."

*Splash!*

A yelp of alarm followed, then Syrena was screaming.

Xavier and I turned just in time to catch the water splattering in all directions as Ilora disappeared into the lake, bubbles trailing upwards from her cries as something dragged her into the depths. Syrena fell to her knees and peered over the edge of the stone, frantically searching the pool for any sign of our friend.

Xavier and I bolted towards her.

"What happened?" he shouted, leaping the stepping stones two at a time to get to her faster.

Syrena looked up from the pool, terror written across her

face.

"Merrows!"

The word had barely left her lips when something long and slender flew from the lake and tackled her off the rock into the water on the other side. Syrena disappeared from view with a gurgle.

"Syrena!" Xavier roared, lunging after her.

Another splash, then a flash of blue, then Xavier was knocked off his rock as something hurtled through the air past him. He caught the stone's edge before he fell all the way in, his hand gripping it for dear life and his legs furiously kicking as he attempted to haul himself back up again.

Crouching low, I ran towards him, holding out my hand.

But another hand rose from the lake before I reached him, this one powder blue with fingers webbed like a frog's. It latched on to Xavier's curls, pulled, and dragged his head backwards. I slid to my knees on the rock and fumbled for his grip, but I was one second too late, and he slipped into the water before our hands could latch. Xavier disappeared from sight and sank into the abyss.

I barely had time to process what had happened before there was another splash, and something solid and wet hit my back so hard it knocked the air from my lungs and sent me toppling face-first into the pool.

The water was the kind of cold found in alpine lakes, but the adrenaline pumping through my body helped keep its bite at bay. Once submerged, I peeled my eyes open and swam for the surface, kicking and paddling as fast as I could. I'd just burst from the water and gulped in a desperate breath when something grabbed my ankle and yanked me back down again. I squirmed and thrashed, but my struggle was in vain, and I watched in horror as the cavern faded farther and farther from sight, eventually disappearing altogether.

The deeper I went, the darker things got, the world around me transitioning from cyan to azure, then cobalt and navy. My lungs ached and stung, desperate for air. They gave out as soon as navy faded to black, and for the second time today, I wandered into unconsciousness to flirt with death on its doorstep.

And for the second time today, death slammed the door in my face.

Before I'd slipped away completely, I landed with a *slop* on something cold, hard, and smooth. Coughing and sputtering reached my ears, and when my eyelids fluttered open, I woke on my side in a puddle, facing Xavier, who was propped on all fours, spewing excess liquid from his lungs. Beyond him, Syrena and Ilora were doing the same.

Water dribbled from my own lips as I rolled over to push myself upright. I froze when I noticed the cool surface under my palms.

Moonstone.

My heart skipped a beat, and when I lifted my nose to the air and sniffed, dread washed over me.

There was no mistaking the nauseating scent of night-blooming jasmine.

"Well, this is a surprise."

The voice sent a shudder through me. It was as sickeningly sweet as the floral aroma polluting the air, and it had done nothing but haunt my dreams since the last time I'd heard it.

Long white hair flowed gracefully from a canvas of alabaster skin, and gray eyes so similar to the original's stared back at me. Only these eyes didn't share a single drop of the empathy Meer's had.

Now they were empty, cruel, and fixed on me.

"What's the matter?" Aedan purred. "Did you miss me?"

# CHAPTER 31



To my surprise, I wasn't afraid.

I'd thought I would be. I'd always jolt awake drenched in a cold sweat from my nightmares of Aedan, and his voice would haunt me long after I glimpsed the dawn.

But seeing him face-to-face, wearing Meer's form like he owned it, it wasn't fear that consumed me.

It was rage.

Maybe it was the power inside me giving me courage. It had been rattled awake as I was dragged through the lake, and now hummed in my blood like a blade sings after it's pulled from the scabbard. Even though I didn't know how to use the dark thing inside me, it reminded me I wasn't powerless.

I was not helpless.

I was not a victim.

I was a weapon, and they should all be afraid.

With a grunt, I pushed myself to standing. "Well, we left in such a hurry last time. We didn't get a chance to say a proper goodbye."

Aedan's brows arched at my calm tone, his calculating eyes scanning me for any sign of fear. I refused to give it to him and smirked instead.

*Still underestimating me, I see.*

Aedan crossed his arms, the wide sleeves of his black-and-gold robes rippling with the movement. "So you came all the way here to bid me your final farewell? You're making this too easy." His eyes flicked to Syrena and Ilora still soggy and panting on the moonstone floor. A sinister grin spread over his lips. "Two Fae queens delivered right to my door? I owe you my thanks, Lina Calder. Killing them is going to take so much less effort now."

Xavier leapt to his feet and drew both daggers. "Try it. See what happens."

A chorus of hisses rose behind us.

Warily, I peeked over my shoulder. A row of Nethers lined the edge of the underground lake where water met stone. They were slender creatures with female bodies, except their skin and hair were varying shades of iridescent blue, and there was webbing between their fingers and toes. All of them were naked to give full mobility to the spiny dorsal fins on their backs, and every last one bared her teeth as she snarled in Xavier's direction.

"It's alright, ladies." Aedan chuckled and motioned for them to stand down. "The guard dog here is all bark and no bite."

Xavier spun one of the knives in his palm, nose scrunching at the scent of a challenge. "Trust me. I like a little biting."

Ilora stood and bowed with the dignity and grace of a practiced politician. "My lord Aedan. It's an honor to meet you. We've come to negotiate peace."

Aedan blinked.

Then blinked again.

Then he burst out laughing.

I glanced at Ilora. She still held her head high, her face unreadable, but her eyes darted to me for a split second. The expression was pointed, a silent way of saying, *Just go with it.* When she looked back at Aedan, she straightened her shoulders.

"Is something funny, my lord?"

Aedan wiped away tears of merriment with his thumb. "My apologies, Your Majesty. It's been a while since I've heard a joke that good."

"It wasn't a joke." Ilora casually folded her hands in front of her. "The queens of Merimaya and Lerian have journeyed here to meet with you, as well as two ambassadors for the king of Astoria."

"Oh yes, how is the silver-tongue, Lina? And how are you enjoying being his little pet?"

*He doesn't know Soren and I aren't together.*

The revelation hit me so hard I had to dig my nails into my palms to keep my shock from surfacing. If Aedan did come to realize the truth, the ruse Ilora had crafted would be exposed. Even though I wasn't sure where exactly she was headed with it, I trusted my friend.

Forcing my face neutral, I gestured to my clothing, made of the finest Astorian suede. "I'm certainly reaping the benefits, aren't I?"

"Indeed." Aedan appeared in front of me and slipped a finger under my chin. He jerked my face upright, lifting it to look him in the eye. The move had me fighting the overwhelming urge to bite his hand.

"Ambassador, hmm?" he asked, scanning my expression.

"That's right."

"See, I'm having a hard time believing that. *That* one..." He nodded to Xavier. "That one I understand. He's been a loyal dog for years, but the king's whore? And one always so quick to use a blade?" Aedan clicked his tongue and shook his head in mock sadness. "Poor King Valdir. I'm sure *he* would have liked to negotiate. If only you'd given him the chance, *Ambassador*. So why would Soren send *you*? His King Slayer?"

I racked the depths of my mind for an answer, but came up empty. Panic crept in, ruining any chance I had of thinking clearly, so instead I desperately reached out to my magic. I begged it to blast out like it had before and destroy this creature in front of us so we could go home, but it stayed stubbornly rooted inside.

Aedan's head tilted abruptly. His nostrils flared, and his gray eyes narrowed as they scanned my face.

"You smell different."

"What?"

"You *smell* different," Aedan repeated, roughly snatching my jaw in his hand and dragging me towards a nearby patch of algae to examine my features in its glow. "Before you were fresh. Untouched. Unspoiled. But now there's something else." He pressed his nose to my cheek, inhaling deeply.

I clenched my hands into fists at my side, practically gagging at his touch and his scent and how much it hurt not to wrap my fingers around one of my daggers and jab it into his heart the way I had before. But an *ambassador* wouldn't do that, so I kept my homicidal instincts in check.

"There's something inside you," Aedan mumbled, his face buried in my hair. "There's something... Fae."

After several tense beats, he released me and stepped back, his eyes wide. "You're carrying his child, aren't you?"

I almost laughed and opened my mouth to inform him of my personal stance on bearing children, but Syrena cut me off before I could.

"Yes, she is."

My head whipped to face her, and panic nearly punched a hole in my gut at her words. But then I remembered just last week Ilora and I had been commiserating about the painful cramps we'd both been experiencing thanks to our monthly bleeds. It was impossible I was pregnant. Still, Syrena stood from the floor and haughtily angled her nose to the ceiling.

"Just imagine the wrath a warlord of Astoria will rain down if anything happens to his sole heir."

Her gaze briefly flicked to me, subtle but poignant; a silent order to continue with the lie.

Returning my attention to Aedan, I swallowed and lifted my chin. "It's true. I'm... insurance."

Aedan rubbed his chin as he analyzed each of us individually. "A risky move by His Majesty."

"Everyone knows my king has the military strength and prowess to avenge his loved ones," Xavier said, studying his cuticles.

"But peace is important to us," Ilora stated. "And it's worth a little risk."

"Now the question is..." Syrena haughtily tossed her hair. "Are you going to keep standing there gawking like a spoiled child who's been denied dessert, or are you going to be a good host and show us to our accommodations?"

Aedan stared for what felt like minutes before a slow smile stretched his lips wide. Without breaking eye contact with Syrena, he motioned to the Merrows.

"Ladies? Show our guests to a room. I'll set some extra plates at the table."

~

THE SHORE the Merrows had dropped us on was where the limestone cave met the start of Aedan's crystalline empire.

We walked through a maze of moonstone hallways, each of us flanked by two Merrows who studied our every move like wildcats waiting for the opportunity to pounce. If I didn't know where we were, who ruled here, or what its inhabitants would do to us given the chance, I might have found the space beautiful. With its alcoves of illuminated opal and quartz, and vines of moonflowers encircling the pillar-lined passageways, it looked straight out of a fairy tale.

The tension only increased as we navigated the crystal world. None of us spoke or looked at each other too long, and it was only when we were wholly scrambled by the twists and turns of the halls that Xavier had to shatter the silence before he lost his mind. He casually cleared his throat and turned to the Merrow next to him.

"So." He stuffed his hands into his pockets. "Do you live around here?"

The Merrow, a muscular female with cobalt skin and navy hair, peeked at him out of the corner of her eye, like she was unsure he was actually speaking to her. Xavier blinked at her expectantly.

After a few seconds of confused silence, the Merrow hesitantly replied. "Sometimes our master permits us to live in the sea or the system of pools running through the mountains, but mainly he likes to keep us here so we may serve him."

Xavier nodded as if having conversations with bloodthirsty Nethers was something he did every day. "So there are places here for you to swim, then?"

The Merrow averted her gaze to focus on the tunnel ahead. "Besides the lake you just took a dip in, there are only small bathing pools."

"Wouldn't you be happier if you had bigger bodies of water?"

"Obviously."

"So why stay?"

"Our master wants us here. There's no other option."

"I can think of one." Xavier looked back and forth between both Merrows on either side of him. "How about you just leave?"

"Many have," the Merrow next to Syrena piped up. She was shorter, with cornflower blue skin and a long wavy mane made up of teal and turquoise streaks. "We're tracked down if we leave."

"Tracked down?" Ilora asked.

"You know very well the types of creatures our master has made," the first Merrow snapped, a glimmer of fear in her eyes.

"So you're hunted down by other Nethers? By your own kind?"

The Merrow didn't respond, but her grim frown said enough.

"There's only one place that's safe to run to," the second Merrow continued. "That's your realm."

Xavier arched his brows. "You consider our realm *safe* for you?"

"Compared to here," she mumbled.

Merrows were hunted in the Fae realm too. I'd seen their hides strung up in Lerian's outdoor bazaars, and heard Willow mention a luxurious bed-and-breakfast in the mountains of Radomir that served Merrow steaks for a hefty fee. They were rare creatures because the Fae had made sure of it. If that was a better alternative than here... Gods, what kinds of horrors must they experience in this place?

When I turned to the Merrow at my left, a female with ice-blue skin, my heart tugged at her pained expression. "If it's so horrible for you here, why haven't you just risen up against Aedan? You all just proved how fast and strong you are. If you worked together, maybe you could—"

"He can't die," the Merrow replied, anticipating where the conversation was headed. "You tried it yourself. Even the King Slayer can't take a god's life."

"This is strange talk for ambassadors," the first Merrow interrupted, shooting us a suspicious glare.

Syrena slipped effortlessly back into her role of the peace-seeking queen and adopted a regal tone. "It's important to understand the people of a territory before determining the best way to go about helping them."

The Merrow scoffed. "*You're* going to help us?"

"Since when have the Fae wanted to help Merrows?" the second grumbled.

"I hear you sell our skins in your markets," one declared.

"And our feet are eaten as a delicacy," another added.

"Well, maybe it's time for change," I cut in. "For a revolution."

The first Merrow sniffed and shook her head. "I'll believe that when I see it."

We fell silent again, all of us lost in our own thoughts. I didn't know what the others were thinking, but I found myself wondering if it was just Merrows, Night Sylph bastards, and creatures like Veshti who were misunderstood and demonized, or if it was all Nethers too.

I hadn't noticed it while it was happening, but by the time we arrived at our room, the Merrows' appearance had changed. As they'd dried off, their webbing disappeared, their dorsal fins receded into their backs, and their coloring became more muted. Now they just looked like nude Fae women in various shades of shimmering blue.

The first Merrow opened a round wood door and gestured inside. "You'll stay here for now."

We filtered in and surveyed the space. The door opened to a common room made entirely of raw emerald, with couches and tables carved out of the stone and arched doorways in the wall that led to bedrooms and washrooms. At least the black silk throws and suede cushions draped over the seating provided a hint of comfort. Otherwise, the room would have felt like a green prison cell.

"You'll be summoned when our master is ready for you," the tallest Merrow stated.

Without another word, the door groaned shut, and we were alone.

"So." Xavier tossed his pack to the ground and plopped on one end of the crystal sofa. "What do we do now?"

"Brush up on our negotiating skills?" Syrena offered. A grunt escaped her as she lowered herself into one of the carved-out seats and propped up her feet.

"How about we get our stories straight?" I asked, glaring to say, *Pregnant?! Really?*

She winced and mouthed *sorry*.

"Whatever we decide that story is," Ilora interrupted, "we stick to it. No matter what Aedan or anyone else says. We're the only ones we trust down here. Got it?"

Xavier nodded. "And we stay calm. I'm looking at you, Lina."

I opened my mouth to protest, but promptly shut it. There was no point. Everyone knew there was fire in my blood long before magic burned there.

"We all need to be reminded." Ilora absentmindedly rubbed her upper arm. "We all have our own reasons to want Aedan dead, and he's going to try everything he can to get a reaction out of us. We can't give it to him. We're playing this game, ready or not, and we need to win. So we lay low, search for Aedan's weakness, and when the time is right, we strike."

The gravity of our situation weighed on us as we sat with her words. After a few minutes, I scanned the faces around me. They were weary and held traces of fear, but there was determination too, combined with an admirable mix of courage and strength. My heart tugged with pride at the fact I could call these brave souls my friends.

I cleared my throat, and when everyone's eyes landed on me, I spoke. "I wish I hadn't dragged you all here and gotten you into this mess."

Ilora opened her mouth to argue, but I held up my hand.

"*But*," I continued, looking out over my friends again as I mustered a grateful smile, "I'm glad you're here. I can't imagine facing this alone, and there's no one else I'd rather be facing it with."

Syrena's eyes glistened with emotion, but she quickly blinked it away and nestled in beside me.

"We're your flock, Lina," she said, slipping an arm around me and squeezing tight. "You're stuck with us."

I chuckled and rested my head on her shoulder, shutting my eyes and letting myself relax into the warmth of her embrace.

A knock on the door made us all jump. Several tense seconds followed before the knock sounded again.

Xavier huffed an exhale and stood. "I'll get it. I'm the protector, after all."

"Knew that would go to his head," Syrena mumbled.

We held our breath as Xavier strode across the room and placed a hand on the knob. He paused, and quietly mumbled a count of three. Then he threw aside the deadbolt and yanked open the door to reveal a single female in the hallway on the other side.

Something about her seemed familiar, although I was sure I'd never seen her before. She had straight black hair, pale gray skin, and dark upturned eyes wide with terror as they stared back at us. Her irises were larger than average, taking up more of the whites of her eyes than normal, and even though she was draped in a baggy gray dress and hooded cowl, it did nothing to disguise her violent trembling.

"Hello," the woman squeaked, wringing her hands. "My master will see you now."

# Chapter 32

The painfully nervous creature led us down hallway after hallway, refusing to look at us.

She kept her head hung and her shoulders slumped, and even Xavier's charms were useless on her. He could barely get her to speak more than four words to him, and even those were hesitantly whispered, like making too much noise might actually kill her. The only words she said loud and clear took place when we arrived at a pair of towering double doors forged from thick black tourmaline.

"Please, be careful," the woman pleaded, blinking up at us with anguish in her eyes.

My chest tightened at her obvious pain. What monstrosities had this poor thing experienced here? And at whose hands?

Deep down, I knew the answer.

The door groaned on its hinges as it opened, and speak of the devil, Aedan greeted us with arms stretched wide.

"You made it," he sang, disturbingly chipper. "Please, come in."

One by one we filed inside, taking in the domed room

carved from smoky quartz, the long dining table laden with platters of obscure fruits, and finally, the Fae woman at the head of the table, reclining in her chair as she sipped from a golden goblet. Her white-blonde hair was coiled around a circlet that dangled a raw diamond onto her forehead, her dark burgundy lips were pinched in a scowl, and sharp blue eyes that could make any man cower shot icy daggers in our direction.

"You remember Erith," Aedan said, walking over and taking the Kylanthian queen's hand so he could brush a tender kiss across her knuckles.

Erith didn't look at him. Her eyes stayed fixed on Ilora, one side of her mouth turning up in a smirk.

Though it must have killed her inside, Ilora smiled politely and dipped her head. "Hello, Erith. It's been a long time."

"Indeed, it has." Erith arched an eyebrow. "How's the family?"

Ilora looked away, but a muscle in her jaw spasmed as she clenched her teeth.

"You've already met my slave, Tallys," Aedan continued, clapping his hands at the woman in gray. She jumped and hurried over. The scent of fear practically wafted off her.

Aedan pushed back the hood of Tallys's cowl and stroked her hair like a pet. She pinched her trembling lips to keep from crying out.

"We just adore our little Tallys. Don't we, my love?"

Erith didn't respond. Her unnerving stare continued to bore into Ilora.

"She's a cute little combination of two of my creations," Aedan went on, pinching Tallys's cheek hard enough that she winced. "She's half Merrow, which explains these good looks. But don't worry, the fins and webbing don't show up unless she's in water. Then, of course, there's the other part of her. My favorite part. Tell them what your father was, Tallys."

The woman kept her eyes fixed on the ground, shame heavy in her voice. "A Night Sylph."

*That* was why she seemed familiar. Her features shared similarities with another half Night Sylph I'd known. Straight black hair and angular dark eyes hiding a world of pain, with pale skin providing a stark contrast. But out of the two of them, only Tallys's skin had taken on the gray hue of the Night Sylph.

"Isn't that funny?" Aedan's gaze landed on me. "Turns out Night Sylphs have an appetite for more than just Fae, and if a Merrow falls asleep sunbathing on the rocks... well, some would say she should know better and had it coming."

Xavier's hands clenched into fists at his sides. "I'd like to have some choice words with whoever says that."

Tension was growing, and we needed to shift courses before one of us snapped. Me being the most likely culprit.

"Shall we eat?" I asked to change the subject. "The baby's hungry." I slid a hand to my lower stomach to make the fib more convincing.

Erith pulled her cold stare from Ilora and drove it into me instead.

"Of course," she sneered. "Wouldn't want the half-breed to starve."

"You're too kind, Erith," I said sweetly, lowering myself into the seat at the end of the table opposite her. "When Soren and I are deciding on baby names, we'll keep yours in mind."

Erith blinked in surprise, which had me fighting a laugh. Apparently, Mirielle had actually served a purpose and prepared me for moments of fake civility such as this. If I survived this, I should send her a thank you card.

Syrena slid into the seat at my right. "This is quite the spread. You're very generous, Aedan."

The king of the Netherworld draped himself in the chair beside Erith and rested a hand on her knee. "I'm a generous man, Syrena, in many ways. You should come see for yourself." He gave her a lascivious once-over and turned to his queen. "What do you say, my love? Should we include her sometime?"

Erith grunted and took a sip of wine. "I bet she just lies there like a dead fish."

"Hmm..." Aedan turned to Xavier, snapping his fingers to get his attention. "You. Dog. Do you know? Or have all your attempts to woo the lady been in vain?"

Without missing a beat, Xavier adopted a smug grin and winked. "A gentleman never tells."

Aedan watched him for a few seconds before snorting a laugh and grabbing his wine to raise high in a salute. "I think I might grow to like you, boy."

Xavier raised a glass back. "Everyone likes me."

"Well, not everyone," Aedan chuckled, pointedly angling his chin at Syrena.

Xavier settled back in his chair, the confident smile still on his lips. "I don't think you know as much as you think you do."

"Ah, but I know everything."

"A new friend told me recently that only the gods are all-knowing."

"Exactly."

"But you're not a god." The words slipped out of my mouth before I could stop them.

Everyone went still. I flinched, inwardly kicking myself for letting Aedan get under my skin. But my slip was justified. Aedan could insult *me* as much as he wanted. Hell, I was used to it. I'd grown accustomed to names like King Slayer and human whore and Soren's pet. But my friends were being attacked now, and that made the rage simmering in my blood ignite to a full-fledged boil. I would fight tooth and nail for my friends, and *no one* spoke badly of them.

I lifted my gaze from the table to meet the stare weighing down on me.

"What do you think I am, then?" Aedan asked curiously.

In that moment, I made a split-second decision.

I could still behave. I could still play the politician. But I didn't have to play nice. Truth could be the deadliest weapon.

I sat back in my seat, folded my arms, and spoke life to the theory I'd been forming over the past few days.

"You're a witch."

My friends looked at each other in shock, realization washing over their expressions. Aedan, however, continued to stare at me, but he failed to hide the way one of his eyelids twitched before he adopted his cool smirk. "Don't insult me, girl."

Beneath the table, Syrena nudged me with her foot. It was her subtle way of asking, *What the hell are you doing?*

But I'd started down this path, and there was no turning back now.

"What's wrong with being a witch?" I asked.

Aedan sniffed and took another sip from his goblet. "Witches are weak."

The dark fire crackling in my veins adamantly disagreed.

"Really? I've met some pretty powerful witches recently. Some could even see the future."

Aedan shrugged. "Party tricks."

Under the table, Syrena nudged me again, this time harder. *Stop.*

I kicked her back. *I'm not finished.*

"Some could make something extraordinary out of the ordinary," I went on.

"We call that arts and crafts, my dear," Aedan chuckled, examining a ring on his middle finger.

"I've even met one who can change shape."

Aedan's gaze snapped to mine.

*Got him.*

"Is that so?" Aedan smiled, but I could have sworn panic flickered behind his eyes.

I reclined in my seat, interlocking my fingers over my stomach. "With extraordinary magic running through your veins, the possibilities are endless. So who knows? Maybe you could create a twisted sanctuary for yourself and all the creatures you made so you can play out a delusional fantasy that you're some omnipotent god."

Beneath the table, Syrena kicked me hard enough to bruise, then giggled and dabbed at the corners of her mouth with a napkin. "I apologize for the ambassador's behavior, my lord. She's been an absolute nightmare since the morning sickness started. Isn't that right, Lina?"

The daggers in her eyes were sharp enough to cut glass.

I took a deep breath, pried my attention from Aedan's furious stare, and cleared my throat. "Yes. Sorry. The baby makes me moody."

Ilora set aside her utensils and pushed her chair back as she stood. "We've had a long journey, and we're exhausted. Let's pick this back up tomorrow when everyone is rested and thinking clearly."

"I think that's a good plan." Syrena stood too, latching a hand around my collar to haul me to standing. "Good night. And thank you again for your hospitality."

After a shake from the fist gripping my shirt, I begrudgingly mumbled, "Yes. Sleep well."

Aedan sniffed. "Gods don't sleep, girl."

"Gods don't bleed, either," I bit back.

And with that, Syrena shoved me out the door as fast as she could.

We'd barely exited the room when Xavier froze in his tracks, thought for a split second, then darted back inside without saying another word.

"Where are you going?" Syrena hissed, but he didn't hear her. He was already speaking to Aedan.

"My lord, in my realm it is customary to present guests of your court with a gift. If you need ideas... your slave is pleasing to the eye."

A moment of silence followed before Aedan's laugh echoed out into the hall.

"I knew I liked you for a reason, boy. You're a man after my own heart. Tallys, go with Soren's loyal dog. Throw him a bone, and let him chew on it as long as he wants."

Her, "Yes, Master," was barely audible, but seconds later Xavier hurried out of the room with Tallys's hand clasped in his.

"What are you doing?" Syrena demanded, her voice hushed.

"Improvising," Xavier whispered back.

WHEN WE GOT BACK to our room, Syrena tossed me inside and planted her hands on her hips.

"What the hell happened to staying calm?"

"I *did* stay calm," I snapped, jerking my collar back into place. "I calmly told the truth."

"Did you mean it?"

We turned to Tallys, who was huddling in a nearby corner and wringing her hands as her gaze darted between each of us.

"Did you mean what you said? That..." She gulped. "That you don't think my master is a god, but a witch?"

Ilora and Syrena glanced at each other, the former shaking her head to urge us not to say anything, but Xavier stubbornly set his jaw and stepped forward.

"It would make sense," he said.

Tallys instinctively recoiled from him.

"It's alright." Xavier threw his hands up in defense. "I'm not going to touch you, I promise. I just said all that before so you could get away from Aedan. You looked like you could use a break."

Tallys's brow furrowed.

Xavier frowned and rubbed the back of his neck. "With all due respect... he doesn't seem like the kindest master."

Tallys gasped.

"You shouldn't say such things," she whispered. "He punishes anyone for speaking poorly of him."

"Then we have to make sure he doesn't find out," Syrena stated, her gaze hardening. "Right?"

Understanding the threat behind the words, Tallys shook her head earnestly. "I won't say a word. I swear."

"Good." Syrena dipped her head curtly. She analyzed Tallys carefully before choosing her next words. "He hasn't been kind to us either, you know."

Tallys looked up at her, eyes big enough for us to see the broken spirit underneath.

"He's killed people we loved," Syrena continued. "Like my parents."

Ilora hugged herself. "And mine."

"And he wears the face of one of my dearest friends," Xavier added, fury and pain distorting his normally cheerful expression. "A friend who one of his creations slaughtered in cold blood."

"And he took the life of a man I loved," I finished, my fingers grazing the black blade at my thigh. "One fathered by a Night Sylph just like you."

At that, Tallys's eyes widened. "You loved a Night Sylph?"

My heart squeezed. "I loved a man who was resilient and selfless and brave. Who his parents were made no difference."

Awestruck, Tallys stared at me until Xavier spoke again.

"You can sleep in my room tonight."

When she flinched, he quickly shook his head. "Sorry, I mean you can sleep there *alone*. I'll sleep here." He gestured to the sofa carved into the wall.

Tallys slowly looked around the room, blinking over and over like it was all too much to comprehend. After a while she mumbled, almost to herself, "My master makes me sleep on the floor."

Xavier and I exchanged glances. From the pained look on his face, he felt for her just as much as I did. When we turned back to Tallys, his voice was playful, but gentle. Like he was speaking to a child.

"Well, what your master doesn't know won't hurt him."

Tallys opened her mouth to speak, thought better of it, then darted into the other room. Ilora watched her go, her brows low over her eyes and her full lips pinched thin. A strange emotion flashed across her face, one that looked foreign on her features. She had always been the queen of comfort and warmth, or a firm and opinionated ruler. She never seemed to mix the two, and it was even more rare for her to be torn about which side of herself to lean into. But as she watched Tallys go, there it was, shimmering in her eyes clear as day. An internal battle that filled her with uncertainty.

Her best friend must have seen what I did too, because Syrena lowered her voice. "Remember what we said before. We don't trust anyone but ourselves."

The statement pulled Ilora from her thoughts, and she blinked before nodding firmly. "Agreed."

We stood with the weight of everything for a few minutes more until we all decided to follow Tallys's lead. We retreated to our separate rooms, unsure how sleep was supposed to find us after a day like today.

~

Miraculously, sleep did eventually find me, and I dreamed of a battlefield.

It was a bloody, violent space filled with both Fae and Nether, their bodies so crammed together and covered in crimson it was impossible to distinguish who was who. I was on my knees in the middle of the field, screaming in agony, my eyes the darkest shade of black I'd ever seen.

~

I was startled awake from the dream by a hand clapping over my mouth.

"Shhh!" a timid voice hushed. It took me a few seconds to blink the sleep from my eyes so I could see who it belonged to.

"You need to come with me," Tallys whispered. "Quickly!"

The urgency in her voice made me bolt upright and swing my legs over the edge of the bed. "What's the matter?"

Tallys frantically twisted her hands, eyes darting to the doorway. "There's no time. Just come. *Please.*"

I nodded and reached for my boots, but she grabbed my hand.

"No time," she repeated, dragging me towards the door.

We dipped out to the common room and shuffled past Xavier, who was sprawled on the couch, snoring softly with an arm bent over his face to block out the light. My bare feet slapped against the cold moonstone as we slipped out to the hall, Tallys towing me behind her as she raced down the maze of passageways at a surprisingly fast pace for such a feeble being.

"What's wrong?" I panted. "Where are we going?"

Tallys stopped running as quickly as she'd started, and I bumped into her as we skidded to a halt. We'd stopped in front of another black tourmaline door, similar to the one we'd passed through to visit Aedan.

"You're in danger." Tallys glanced warily over both shoulders. "I meant it when I said my master would kill you. Even now, I worry it may be too late for you."

Fear pricked the hair at the back of my neck, but I stubbornly lifted my chin. "We're not defenseless, Tallys. If Aedan tries anything—"

"No!" Tallys snatched my hands in hers, gripping tight as she looked up at me with haunted eyes. "He can do terrible, *terrible* things. You need help, and if anyone can help you, it's him."

Confused, I shook my head. "Who?"

Tallys gulped and turned back to the door, twisting the handle so it creaked open.

"No one can know I did this," she said, beckoning for me to enter.

I shot Tallys a sidelong glance before tiptoeing inside against my better judgment.

"Don't scream," she warned, then firmly shut the door behind me.

Silence never sounded so loud.

Heart pounding, I faced the dimly lit space I'd walked into. Its floor, walls, and ceiling were made entirely of glossy black obsidian, with a roaring fire in the large hearth on one side, a massive bed draped in black silks at the center, and a small emerald green bathing pool to the left.

"Hello?" I called, my voice wavering.

Something rose from the depths of the bathing pool.

I leapt back in alarm, throwing my back against the door in the hopes my presence in the shadows would go unnoticed. But when I saw what it was, the air rushed from my lungs.

Knee-deep in the pool, water dripping down his naked body, stood a man with chin-length jet-black hair, a brand on his neck, and brown eyes so dark they were nearly black.

"*Hale?*"

# Chapter 33



We stared at each other.

Not moving.

Not blinking.

Not breathing.

I couldn't think. My mind was frozen, same as my body, not a thought going in or out except his name.

*Hale.*

It couldn't be him.

I'd seen the arrows lodged in his back.

I'd heard his lungs rattling as they filled with blood.

I'd seen it splatter on his lips, lips that had kissed me so passionately in those final moments that it left me as stunned as I was now.

And I'd seen him bring down a mountain that crushed him beneath it.

... Right?

Of course. This couldn't be Hale. Whoever was in that bath—

My mind finally registered that the man in front of me was

completely naked. I tried to look away, but my eyes betrayed me and stayed fixed on his body, taking in the countless scars, the lean torso, and the crude symbols seared into his neck, hip, and left hand. The pool's green glow radiated upwards, highlighting his whittled muscles so he looked like some exquisitely carved marble statue. My eyes drifted lower still, sneaking a glance at what hung between the man's legs, something I remembered far too well and still craved the taste of.

I hurriedly shook the thoughts from my head and tore my eyes away, forcing them back to his. He hadn't broken his stare for a second. His eyes were exactly as I remembered them. Dark, analytical, and somehow able to see into the very depths of my soul. They could make you feel simultaneously exposed and understood, and I'd forgotten how erotic that was.

I swallowed hard.

*It's not Hale. Hale is dead. This is a trick. It's Aedan taking Hale's form to toy with you.*

I opened my mouth to tell him off, but the man in front of me spoke first.

"Aedan, if this is some kind of sick joke, it's not funny."

Words fell flat on my tongue. My stunned response made the dark eyes across the room widen slightly as they raked over my face.

"Lina?"

Hearing his voice utter my name instantly set my body trembling. I'd heard it so often in my dreams, hearing it out loud didn't feel real. All I could do was nod and slap a hand to the wall to keep myself from crumpling to the floor.

Hale's throat bobbed as he swallowed. He slowly stepped out of the pool, keeping his eyes glued to mine. "You're not real."

My whisper was barely audible over my frantic heartbeat. "I am."

Hale's eyelids flickered as he sucked in a breath. He continued to stalk towards me. "You can't be real."

The man moved with the fluidity of a natural predator. Maybe that was why I pressed my back further into the wall. Or maybe it was because the space between us felt like the crackling air before a lightning strike. My breaths came in shallow pants as he neared, and by the time he was standing directly in front of me, the heat from the bath radiating off his skin, my mouth had completely dried up.

"You can't be real," he murmured. His voice was low and raspy, like the words he was trying to convince himself of physically pained him.

When he stepped closer, halting his body just a hairsbreadth from mine, I stopped breathing entirely. His gaze flicked to my chest, where my heart feverishly pounded against its cage of flesh and bone. His brows knit, and when he looked up again, realization sparked in his eyes.

"It's actually you." He huffed an incredulous laugh and reached his branded hand towards my face, but it stopped just before its fingertips brushed the skin. My cheek prickled as he hovered there, and the longer he waited the more I trembled.

A flicker of worry colored Hale's eyes as he hesitated, but he soon set his jaw and pushed his hand forward. When we connected, I nearly melted into his touch. Hale must have felt the same because his shoulders slumped and he released a heavy sigh.

"You're really here," he whispered, shaking his head in disbelief and closing what little space remained between us.

I gasped at the movement, shaking for an entirely different reason now as his bare hips pressed into mine.

Hale brushed a strand of hair from my eyes, looking over my face with wonder, and slowly leaned in. My lips parted, tingling with desire at his teasing breath.

"What the *fuck* are you doing here?" Hale snapped.

I blinked. Then blinked again. "What?"

Hale pushed off the wall and stomped across the room, snatching a pair of loose black pants from the bed and turning his back to me as he slipped them on.

"I said what the fuck are you doing here?" he barked over his shoulder, yanking the drawstring to fix the pants low on his hips.

His sharp words woke me from my daze, and I stormed across the room after him. "What am *I* doing here? What are *you* doing here? You're supposed to be... I thought you were..."

I trailed off as the gravity of the moment hit me. All my tears, all those nights of drinking to numb the pain, all that agonizing grief... it had all been pointless, and it was stirring up the strangest mix of gratitude, confusion, anger, and about a hundred other emotions I didn't know how to process all at once.

"You thought I was dead?" Hale finished for me, spinning around. His expression had softened, but only just. He lowered onto the edge of the bed, then leaned forward and braced his elbows on his knees. "I almost was."

I had so many questions, but the most foolish and unimportant one threatened to bubble up first.

*Did you miss me?*

I shook the thought from my head, and instead asked a question that was actually important. "How?"

Hale sighed and ran his fingers through his hair, the front pieces immediately falling back in front of his eyes. "The tunnel came down, but a few of the Nethers dragged me out just in time. They risked their lives to save mine."

"You mean *after* they tried to kill you?"

Hale frowned. "Right. To make a long story short, I was on

death's door, but they healed me, and I've been living among them ever since."

"Nethers can heal?"

"A few of them can." Hale shrugged, a fond smile tugging at one corner of his mouth. "They're amazing creatures."

"Amazing creatures who tried to kill you."

Hale's gaze hardened. He stood abruptly, making me step back in surprise. "Like many things, they're incredibly misunderstood."

His tone had me bristling, and on instinct, I snapped back, "How about your father? Are Night Sylphs misunderstood when they attack defenseless women?"

Hale wilted. "They're the exception."

"What about all the Nethers at the spring equinox last year in Lerian who were slaughtering children?"

Shame shadowed Hale's face. "Another exception."

"And how about the ones who attacked me in Astoria?" I pressed. "Then again in the caves yesterday?"

At that, Hale's eyes darkened with primal fury.

"Who attacked you?" he asked, the calmness of his voice a chilling contrast to the vengeful gleam in his night-dark gaze. It was so unnerving that I took another step backwards.

"I don't know what they're called. They mimic voices and paralyze with pain before eating you alive." I subconsciously rubbed at my sleeve and the teeth marks beneath, left over from my brush with death in Astoria.

Hale nodded as he processed my words, his expression colder than the stone beneath our bare feet. "I'll take care of it."

The power inside me hummed proudly. "I already did."

Hale didn't seem to hear me. Instead he shook his head, huffing another exhale as he returned to the edge of the bed and rubbed his face. "See, this is *exactly* why you shouldn't have come here. Everyone is going to want you dead."

"But they're misunderstood?"

A world of conflicting emotion swirled in his stare as he peered up at me. "It's complicated."

On instinct, I moved to pull him into an embrace, but caught myself. We'd never truly grown accustomed to being close. Our moments together had been fleeting, and after last year's spring equinox, when we'd busied our troubled minds by giving in to our desire, we hadn't so much as brushed hands before he'd given me that final parting kiss just before he'd brought the mountain down. I'd wanted to touch him before then, *ached* to touch him, and after I'd lost him, I'd dreamed of it more times than I could count. Being close with him had become second nature in my mind, but now in real life, I wasn't sure it was something Hale would welcome. So instead, I wandered over and sat on the bed beside him. His attention remained on the symbol burned into the back of his left hand as he traced his thumb over its edges and curves.

"You're right," he muttered. "The Nethers have done terrible things."

It was nearly impossible to resist the urge to slip that scarred hand into mine and hold it until all the pain had disappeared from Hale's expression, but I did.

"Yes, they have." I paused as I considered, then sheepishly added, "But the same thing could be said about the Fae too. And humans. And... you're right too. I've met a fews Nethers lately who are pretty amazing."

An image of Veshti's happy tippy-tappies flashed into my mind.

Hale nodded, still staring at his hand. His fingers had migrated to a gold ring set with a glossy black stone, which he twisted in circles around his middle finger.

"I've been trying to help them as best I can," he murmured. "They respect me here. They listen. They say I have an outsider's point of view and can see both sides to their plight. I've been trying to convince them to seek peace instead of violence. Aedan's been very receptive to it."

I blinked in surprise. "Really?"

"Yes." Hale finally met my gaze, his face aglow with hope. "He says he'd be open to considering other options."

My frown returned. "You mean other options besides murdering every man, woman, and child in the Fae realm so he can reign there?"

Hale's eyes shuttered, controlled anger disguising his pain as he relived a distant memory. "You don't know what it's like to be viewed as a monster, Lina. It will kill you if you let it. Rage and violence gives you strength. It takes time to overcome those instincts."

"I understand that. It's just..." I winced as I repeated the words Kaspar had hissed in my ear the night I left Lerian. "Don't you worry that some people are too far gone for you to save?"

Hale weighed the question, then shrugged. "He spared my life and gave me a home here."

"He views you as one of his children."

"But your presence here means he spared you too. He wouldn't do that if there was no good left in him. And that means there's still hope for him."

I opened my mouth to protest, but quickly shut it. Hale was talking about Aedan like he was his oldest and dearest friend. Now was not the time to debate the Netherworld king's morality, or to reveal our plot to eradicate him once and for all. But a king wasn't the only threat needing to be eliminated.

There was also a queen.

"What about Erith?" I asked, trying not to spit the name. The woman had abandoned her territory, betrayed her people, and murdered innocents in cold blood. Speaking about her casually seemed wrong, and it took more effort than I'd anticipated. "Is she understanding too?"

Hale sighed and hung his head. "So far, she's been the hardest to reason with. But I'm trying. And I'm sure with time she'll come around."

I forced a smile, but inwardly I rolled my eyes. I'd seen the steel in that woman's gaze, felt the hatred spewing from her as she enacted her vengeance on the king and queen of Merimaya. It was clear her heart had iced over with no hope of thawing. I hated to admit it, but unfortunately what Kaspar had said was true. Sometimes, people *were* too far gone to be saved, and I was certain Erith was the perfect example.

The hope shimmering in Hale's eyes had me biting my tongue, and words escaped me entirely when his gaze flicked to my mouth. His expression grew softer, almost shy. Silence fell heavy around us, but it wasn't uncomfortable. It was peaceful and safe, like it had always been with him. Before long I was smiling for no apparent reason, which made Hale chuckle.

"Are you sure I'm not dreaming you?" he asked. "You're actually real?"

A flush crept into the apples of my cheeks. "Pretty sure."

"How? The way out was destroyed."

"There was another way in. Another veil. I found it in the ocean beneath the palace of Lerian when Aedan called to Wynn and—"

"What?"

At Hale's confused look, I explained. "Wynn is still spellbound, but it's not the Sluagh binding him anymore. The magic holding him belongs to Aedan."

Hale's brow wrinkled. "No, that... that impossible. There has to be some kind of mistake."

"There isn't."

"Why would he do that?"

"Because he's evil!" I barked, then flinched at my slipup.

*So much for holding off debating Aedan's morality.*

Hale sighed wearily and shook his head again, clearly not sharing my stance. "I'll talk to him about it."

I scoffed, prompting Hale to slide my hand into his. My breath caught at his touch, his skin still warm from the bathing pool. The calloused pad of his thumb swept back and forth across my knuckles.

"I'll talk to him, Lina," he insisted. "I promise."

I forced myself to exhale, and when I looked up, a wistful smile had found its way onto Hale's lips.

Gods, I'd forgotten how beautiful he was when he smiled.

"I never thought I'd see you again," he whispered, almost as if he was talking to himself.

A sudden lump appeared in my throat. "I thought the same."

Again, Hale's eyes drifted to my lips, holding there a second too long before he cleared his throat and pulled his hand away. "How's Soren?"

A twinge shot through my chest, but I wasn't sure if it was from Hale no longer touching me or the miserable heartache Soren's name dredged up.

"I don't really know," I admitted. "I'd been staying in Lerian when we went through the veil, and—"

"Wait," Hale cut me off. "What do you mean, *we*?"

"Me, Syrena, Xavier, and Ilora."

Hale's eyes widened. "*All* of you are here?"

I winced. "I tried to come alone, but they insisted."

Hale groaned and rubbed his face before standing. "Where are they? Are you all together or separated?"

"Together. We have a room not far from here—"

"Go back and bar the door," he ordered. "Don't go anywhere until morning, do you understand?"

His urgency relit the panic in my blood. "Where are you going?"

*I just got you back, I don't want to lose you again*, I wanted to say. *Can we please just sit here and catch up? Can I just hear your voice and push that hair out of your eyes and see you smile one more time?*

But I didn't say any of that. Instead, I followed Hale to the door, where he grabbed an oversized black sweater from a hook on the wall and yanked it over his head.

"Change doesn't happen overnight," he stated, wriggling his arms into place. "If peace is the goal, I need more time. Most of the creatures here aren't ready for it yet, and you won't be safe until they are."

When Hale turned back to me, my expression must have been as pathetic as an abandoned puppy's, because his eyes softened and he reached out to cup my cheek.

"I won't let anything happen to you, Lina. I promise."

His thumb skated across my skin, leaving a trail of tingles in its wake. We stayed that way for a few breathless seconds before Hale dropped his arm and started towards the exit.

"Hale?" I blurted.

He glanced over his shoulder at me, brows arched expectantly.

There were a million things I wanted to say, and a million more I wanted to do.

"It's good to see you," was what I finally settled on.

One corner of Hale's mouth twitched upwards, and he dipped his head. "It's good to see you too."

Then the tourmaline door shut behind him, leaving me on my own in a lonely black room.

~

I'D FOLLOWED Hale's instruction and gone back to the common room, where sleep eventually found me.

The following morning, laughter woke me from a restless slumber.

I sat upright in my bed, blinking the fog from my eyes before fumbling off the bed slab and shuffling out to the common room. There I found Xavier and Ilora practicing their newfound powers while Syrena looked on with a sour expression, her hair and blouse damp. I barely paid attention to their antics; I was too busy replaying last night in my head, reminding myself over and over it wasn't just another dream.

Hale was alive. I'd seen him. I'd talked to him. I'd touched him.

With a groan, I rubbed my eyes and quickly pushed away the image of Hale's naked body pressing me against the wall. When I got back from his room last night, everyone had been asleep, and I hadn't had the heart to wake them to share the news. Not when I still needed time alone to process it.

"Alright, try stepping a little closer to Syrena," Ilora ordered. She held a large basin in her hands.

Xavier obeyed, shuffling over to the Lerian queen, who was huffily wiping water droplets from her face.

"I don't see why this is necessary," Syrena grumbled.

"He needs to practice stretching it as far as he can," Ilora explained. "He can't be directly beside us all the time."

Syrena sighed and tossed her soggy curls over her shoulder. "Fine. Try again."

Ilora nodded and focused on the bowl. She squinted, her brow furrowing, and soon a large orb of water lifted from the bowl.

"Ready?"

Syrena nodded and flinched as she shut her eyes, readying for contact.

Ilora focused on the sphere, nostrils flaring. After a flex of her muscles and a furious grunt, it shot across the room towards Syrena. Just before it hit her, Xavier threw his hands in front of him, and the water smashed against an invisible barrier. Syrena breathed a sigh of relief.

"Well done." I applauded as I wandered over to them. "You three have had a productive morning, I see."

"Unlike some people." Xavier playfully ruffled my pillow-mussed hair. "You slept forever. Did you stay up late?"

Again I forced away the memory of Hale stepping out of the emerald pool. "I did."

After beckoning for the rest of our friends to join us, they congregated in a circle around me. Ilora's warm chestnut eyes urgently searched my expression.

"What's wrong?"

"There's something I need to tell you. Something happened last night—"

A deafening noise cut me off, forcing us to clap our hands over our ears. The sound resembled the blow of a conch shell horn, only so deep and thundering it shook the ground beneath our feet.

"What is that?" Syrena shrieked.

"I don't know," Xavier replied, grabbing his knives from the nearby table and stuffing them into their sheaths at his hips. When the door to the room flung open, he immediately ripped them out and held them at the ready, but it was only Tallys who raced in, out of breath and her large eyes brimming with tears.

"My master calls," she choked out. "Everyone must come. You, and every Nether close-by."

Syrena laughed bitterly and planted her hands on her hips. "Absolutely not. They'll all take one look at us and tear us to pieces."

"Please," Tallys begged, her words morphing into

hiccuping sobs. "I was sent to fetch you, and I'll be punished if you don't come. My master said *everyone*. Everyone must come. *Please.*"

"We're here for peace," Ilora cut in, shooting a deliberate look at Syrena to remind her of our cover. "Peace requires a level of trust."

Syrena swallowed and nodded, but her normally tan cheeks drained of their color.

Xavier subtly moved beside her and nudged her elbow. "Don't worry. I won't let anything happen to you, Your Highness."

To everyone's surprise, she didn't roll her eyes at the title. Instead, she gave him the smallest hint of a smile, lifted her head, squared her shoulders, and exited the room with the confident swagger of royalty. Xavier trailed close behind. Ilora filed out after them, but when I made to follow, Tallys yanked me back into the room, checking over my shoulder to make sure the others weren't listening.

"Did you tell him?" she asked, her voice hushed.

I clasped her shaking hands tight to offer her some kind of stability. "Tell who what?"

"My master! Did you tell him what I showed you last night?"

"No, of course not." I squeezed her fingers and lowered my voice too. "I only spoke to Hale, and I never mentioned it was you who showed me to his room. I haven't even gotten the chance to tell the others he's alive."

She nodded, but the way her bottom lip quivered proved my words had done nothing to ease her panic.

"He must have found out some other way," she whispered to herself. Her whole body trembled, and her teeth knocked so hard the sound echoed off the emerald walls. "He's going to kill me, I just know it!"

"You're fine, Tallys. He's probably calling everyone together for another reason—"

"You don't understand," Tallys wailed, bursting into another bout of hysterical sobs. "He only calls us like this when there's going to be an execution."

Dread swept through me like a poison, spreading into my limbs and paralyzing me in place. Had Aedan found out about Tallys's act of rebellion? Or was it my friends' executions scheduled instead of hers?

"It'll be alright," I said to soothe Tallys's nerves as well as my own.

The words gave Tallys enough strength to shuffle out to the corridor. With her head bent towards the ground, she hurriedly led us through the twists and turns, and with each step, the sinking sensation inside me worsened. By the time I recognized my surroundings, I was sick to my stomach and it was hard to breathe.

I glanced to my right and caught Syrena's eye. "Did you notice—"

"That we've been here before?" She frowned, working hard to keep the blank, unamused expression on her face. "Yes, I noticed."

She'd taken the words right out of my mouth. The tunnel's low ceiling had lifted into a vaulted, cathedral-like moonstone roof. Either it was the same space we'd arrived in the first time we'd stumbled into the Netherworld, or it was eerily identical. It was even complete with hoards of snarling Nethers forming a sea of nightmares, which parted as we passed through.

I smelled Aedan before I saw him.

His nauseating sweetness seeped through the room like a toxin, so strong that an ache was already forming at one corner of my forehead. When the crowd parted entirely, they revealed the Netherworld king front and center on a raised platform at the far end of the room. As he always seemed to when we were around, he wore Meer's appearance, dressed in black-and-gold robes as gaudy and extravagant as the spiked crystal throne he sat on.

Aedan stood and spread his arms wide when he glimpsed us.

"Peacemakers," he boomed. "My children and I would like to officially welcome you back to our home."

Ilora moved first, curtsying grandly to Aedan and then to the Nethers on either side of her. "We're honored to be here as ambassadors of our realm."

Syrena hesitantly followed suit, then Xavier. But I remained still, my eyes locked on Aedan.

He could have mentioned Hale yesterday, but he hadn't. He could have told Hale about us, told him to come see us, but he hadn't. Hale had said Aedan was a changed man, but his actions proved differently. Every fiber of my being screamed this man had no good intentions, and he most definitely didn't deserve a single ounce of my respect. At this moment, my hatred was stronger than logic, and despite our cover story, I found it physically impossible to fake civility.

Aedan's grin stayed put, but his eyes narrowed at my defiance. "Haven't they taught you any manners during your time in Astoria, King Slayer?"

"Pets don't need manners," I replied. "They just sit on a pillow and look pretty."

Aedan chuckled. "Well, at least you finally understand your place."

I smiled sweetly, but inwardly I reached down and grasped at my power, begging it to come to the light. But the magic stayed stubbornly entwined around my bones like the flowering vines on the pillars beside Aedan's jagged throne.

"Children?" Aedan turned to the Nethers around us. "Our guests have come to discuss peace."

A mix of snide laughter and furious growls erupted throughout the room. When Aedan extended his hand to silence them, an obedient hush swept over the crowd.

"They want to talk to us," Aedan went on, his voice as smooth and sweet as caramel, but his mouth curling upwards in a bitter sneer. "They want to dine with us. They want to understand our ways. After countless centuries they've decided it's finally time to *think* about treating you like you matter. Isn't that gracious of them?"

Syrena stepped forward, briefly forgetting her airs and graces as she snapped, "Leave the cattiness to the best of us and get to the point, Aedan."

The lord of the Netherworld threw his head back and cackled, then licked his lips as his gaze slid down her body. "You're even more beautiful when you're angry, Your Majesty. I swear, if every Fae looked as delicious as you, I'd have been so much easier on them over the years."

Beside me, Xavier tensed, his fingers inching towards one of his blades.

"I said get to the point," Syrena repeated through gritted teeth.

Aedan tucked his hands into his wide sleeves. "My point is, I'd like you to understand how things work around here, and thus take it into consideration when plotting your so-called peaceful delegation. To do that, though, I'm going to need some help. First, I'll need my queen."

Like an actress awaiting her cue to enter the stage, Erith appeared from the tunnel at Aedan's right. She was dressed in identical black-and-gold robes, only hers had a neckline plunging all the way to her navel. Her hair was curled and piled on top of her head, still adorned with the Kylanthian circlet that dangled the diamond between her eyes, and her painted crimson lips were turned down in their usual disapproving frown.

"*And*," Aedan continued, his stare settling on me, "I am going to need my prince."

When I followed his extended arm back to the tunnel, time stood still.

Dressed in matching gold and black, a circlet made entirely of obsidian shards resting on his head, Hale stepped out from the shadows and stalked across the platform with the same predatory confidence he'd exuded the night before. When he took his place at Aedan's left, the only thing that kept my knees from buckling was Syrena gripping my arm to support herself as she fought the same instinct. I placed my hand over hers, willing us both strength.

"I believe you know my second-in-command." Aedan clapped a hand on Hale's shoulder, giving it a fond squeeze.

The statement swallowed up all the air in the room, making it impossible to breathe. The words conjured an image of Hale from the night prior.

He'd been toying with a signet ring on his middle finger, the same way Soren would fiddle with his. Only Hale's was identical to the black and gold band now resting on his shoulder as the king of the Netherworld clutched him like a father would a son.

Bile churned in my stomach, forcing me to hold on to Syrena tighter.

"The truth is, though, you don't know him at all." Aedan turned back to us, eyes gleaming with delighted mischief. "Not really. You had no idea what kind of power was at your fingertips. In fact, you barely scratched the surface of what Hale is capable of. So we've decided to give you a demonstration."

Aedan snapped his fingers, and a group of Nethers pushed

through the crowd, hauling one of the corpse-like men from the cave behind them. They flung the creature to the foot of the throne, its withered charcoal skin already flayed and streaked with blood.

"Please, masters!" the Nether wailed, throwing itself prostrate and raising its claws like a beggar reaching for scraps. "Please, have mercy!"

Aedan thoughtfully clicked his tongue and angled his face to Hale. "What do you think, Your Highness? Do we show mercy?"

Without a second of hesitation, a tendril of black mist shot from Hale's palm and curled around the Nether in front of him like a whip, its tail snaking up into the creature's mouth and nostrils. The Nether began to writhe and vibrate, the light in its glowing yellow eyes flickering in and out.

Despite their intimidating appearance, the crowd grew increasingly uneasy by the display of violence. The longer the Nether suffered, the more they shifted and winced, and when it let out a string of agonized screeches, nearly all of them looked away or shut their eyes to block out the sight. I wish I could have done the same, but something kept my gaze glued on the creature on the dais, as well as the dark figure standing above it with an expression devoid of emotion.

I didn't recognize that person.

I knew his features. I knew that black mist flowing from his palm. But the man who smiled when the Nether cried out for compassion and sent in another vicious dark ribbon to join the first... I'd never met that man before.

He wasn't a Night Sylph bastard dancing in the shadows with a flower pinned on his chest.

He was a cold, cruel ruler carrying out an execution.

The Nether uttered a final tormented scream before a sickening *crack* silenced him. The creature's skull split in two like an overripe fruit, scattering blood and brains across the crowd as it burst from the inside out. The body had barely hit the floor when Hale spoke loud and clear.

"No one lays a hand on the newcomers," he stated calmly. "If you do, you suffer the same fate."

The Nethers stayed silent, their heads bowed in subservience and their eyes downcast in both respect and fear.

"Do I make myself clear?" Hale asked the crowd.

Every creature in the room nodded in unison.

Hale cooly stepped over the mutilated body at his feet and approached us, coming to a stop directly in front of me.

"I told you I'd take care of it." He used his thumb to wipe a splatter of blood from the side of his mouth. Then he glanced at my friends, clocking their expressions of shock and horror.

"What's wrong?" he chuckled. "You look like you've seen a ghost."

# Chapter 34

Syrena's fingers dug into my arm so deep I worried she might cut off blood flow. When she spoke, her words came out a hoarse whisper.

"Because you *are* a ghost."

Hale's brows knit. "Lina didn't tell you I was alive?"

Syrena released her hold on me so fast I almost toppled over. Her vicious glare made it seem like I'd just buried a knife in her back. "No, she most certainly did not."

I shrugged helplessly. "You were asleep."

"This is something worth waking us up for!" Syrena bit back, her voice growing increasingly high-pitched.

Before her panic could boil over, Xavier stepped forward, catching Hale's eye. The two regarded each other for several tense beats, Hale's fingers feeling at his sides. He carried no knives there anymore, but instinct still held sway over his limbs.

"You're alive," Xavier declared.

"So are you," Hale replied.

"And I have you to thank for that." Xavier lifted his chin and extended his hand. "If you hadn't done what you did, no one would have made it out. I'm in your debt."

Hale blinked at Xavier's palm, his fingers twitching again as he hesitated. After a weighted pause, he warily extended his own hand to meet Xavier's. The men shook curtly.

"There is no debt. Everything worked out in the end."

"For you," Ilora muttered under her breath.

Hale's gaze snapped to her. "Is there something you'd like to say?"

The queen confidently matched his stare. "A prince, huh?"

Hale shrugged. "It's just a title."

"One that comes with power." Ilora jerked her chin to the body pooled in scarlet at the foot of the throne.

Hale observed Ilora for a few seconds before sniffing bitterly. "Still don't trust me, I see. Some things never change."

"Trust?" Ilora scoffed. "You just executed one of your subjects to make a statement, *Your Highness*."

"The Fae execute my subjects all the time," Hale countered. "Wasn't it your father who hosted a Merrow hunt in Merimaya once a year?"

Ilora immediately shut her mouth.

"Unfortunately, violence is a language these creatures have grown to understand all too well, and sometimes it's the only thing that gets through to them." Hale jerked his chin to the body. "There are beings here who would listen if all I did was ask nicely, but the Fear Gorta are not one of them. What happened here today was a necessary evil to keep you all safe."

Syrena blinked up at Hale, opening her mouth to say something but thinking better of it. He noticed the movement and tilted his head in her direction.

"What?"

"Nothing, it's just..." Syrena shifted from one foot to the other. "You seem... different."

Hale frowned. "I'm still me, Syrena."

"You are. You're just..." She nibbled her bottom lip. "Just... more."

"More?"

"More confident. More talkative." Her bright green gaze analyzed every inch of him the same way he'd done to her countless times before. "And you hold yourself different now. You hold yourself like—"

"A prince?"

Aedan and Erith strode towards us. Invisible hackles rose on the back of my neck at the sight of them; the embodiment of evil and his traitorous bride.

"He fits right in, don't you think?" Aedan beamed at Hale, who produced a small smile in return.

Rage boiled my blood at the exchange. Hale's smiles were precious, a gift he rarely bestowed on anyone. They were an honor, more beautiful and breathtaking than anything else in this world. Someone like Aedan couldn't appreciate them.

"Sorry I kept him a secret before." Aedan chuckled and shrugged one shoulder. "I simply wanted to surprise you is all."

"We're definitely surprised," Xavier mumbled, scraping the toe of his boot against the ground to rid it of a stray chunk of Fear Gorta.

"Your Highness, why don't you take our guests on a tour?" Aedan squeezed Hale's shoulder again. "Show them the Netherworld's finest. Give them a glimpse of your new kingdom."

"That's alright," Ilora cut in, faking a gracious dip of her head before spinning on her heel. "We're a little tired. We'll just have Tallys show us back to our room, thank you."

Xavier followed her, but Syrena and I hesitated. Ilora glanced at us over her shoulder and raised an eyebrow.

"Aren't you coming?"

Syrena considered before turning to me and lowering her voice so only I could hear her.

"I'll go back with Ilora, you go with Hale. Have some time alone with him. I know how much you've missed him."

I took her hand in mine. She was still trembling from the shock of everything. "You've missed him too."

Syrena chuckled and shook her head. "Not like you, Lina. No one missed him like you."

She gave my hand a knowing squeeze, then turned to Hale and threw her arms around his waist, hugging him tight as he blinked in surprise.

"It's really nice to see you again," she murmured into his chest.

He fondly patted her back, and she pulled away, sent me one last encouraging smile, and jogged after Ilora and Xavier as they met up with Tallys and followed her down a nearby passageway. When I faced Hale again, he stretched out his arm. Stomach dipping, I slid my hand into his. He offered one of those rare smiles of his, then pulled me into the depths of his new empire.

WE WALKED IN SILENCE, both of us stealing glances when we thought the other wasn't looking and averting our eyes when we caught the other already staring. It resembled the summer I turned eleven, when I'd walk through the village market with a cute neighbor boy and we'd play the same game. My stomach was even in the same state, fluttering relentlessly whenever I peeked at Hale and found him already looking my way.

Together we aimlessly wandered the moonstone corridors, headed nowhere in particular. I racked my brain to find something to talk about, but there was simultaneously too much and not enough to say. Commenting on a cavern of luminescent bathing pools or a glittering crystal alcove seemed pointless in the grand scheme of things, and so much had passed that picking just one thing to discuss was overwhelming. I considered bringing up the lie I was wrapped up in, the fabricated pregnancy and fake negotiations, but the scene earlier only strengthened my theory from last night. Something told me Hale wouldn't react well to the idea of us only sticking around to murder his savior. Especially not when that savior had made him a prince, one who Nethers out of my worst nightmares cowered at the sight of whenever we passed them in the tunnels.

"So am I supposed to refer to you as Your Highness now?" I finally asked, jerking my chin to the circle of black stone resting on top of Hale's hair.

He let out a low chuckle and pulled the crown off, turning it over in his hands as he examined it. "To be honest, this thing is a hassle. All it does is give me a headache." He set the circlet down on a nearby ledge, then toyed with his signet ring. "It's all just for show. Nothing but a costume." He slid the gold and obsidian band off his finger and stuffed it into the depths of his pocket, then lifted his hands and waggled his fingers. "See? Still me."

A laugh found the courage to escape my lips, prompting Hale to grin back at me. His expression sent my stomach into another fit of somersaults.

"I know Syrena doesn't think it, but I really am the same person I was. I'm just..." He trailed off and raised his eyes to the ceiling in search of the right words.

"Happy," I finished for him. "You're truly happy for the first time."

Hale's smile disappeared. Several weighted seconds passed

before he averted his gaze and chuckled. "You always could see me better than anyone else, couldn't you?"

My stomach dipped once more.

When he looked at me next, we stared until the air between us went as warm and dense as a humid Lerian night. The longer Hale stared, the more a flush crept into my neck and the apples of my cheeks. His eyes tracked the color as it moved, his gaze so palpable it could have been mistaken for his fingertips brushing over my skin. One side of Hale's lips sneaked upwards, making it clear he knew the effect he was having.

"What's your favorite color?"

I nearly gasped in surprise as his voice shattered the silence.

"My what?" I laughed.

"Your favorite color."

"Why?"

"Just answer the question."

Even when I narrowed my eyes at him in suspicion, his face betrayed nothing. The Hale I once knew was back, standing as still as a statue with an equally stony expression.

"Red," I admitted. "My favorite color is red."

"Red," Hale repeated, lifting his eyes to the ceiling again as he pondered the word. Then that hint of a smile returned, and he brought one finger up, curling it at me as he backed away down the hall.

"Follow," he ordered.

Too intrigued to rebel, I jogged after him.

After leading the way down more twisting hallways, Hale arrived in front of a slender stone door—gray, bumpy, and unremarkable in every way. It blended into the wall so much I wouldn't have even noticed it if Hale hadn't slid his hand into a hidden latch and pushed it open. He gestured inside.

"After you."

I hesitated, but grimly reminded myself that Hale had just

proven he'd slaughter someone before they could hurt me, so with that in mind, I pushed down my trepidation, took a deep breath, and slipped into the passage.

Keeping my hand on the rough stone wall as a guide, I fumbled through darkness for about ten paces before I rounded a turn. When I did, my mouth dropped open.

The passage had opened into a cavern made entirely of rubies, complete with a small waterfall trickling into a large pool at the center. The only source of light was the glowing algae in the water, but it brightened the entire space by bouncing light off the glittering red walls.

"You like it?" Hale's voice came from over my shoulder, but it echoed off the walls around us.

I looked behind me. Hale was bathed in crimson light, but his dark eyes shone blue from the reflected light of the pool.

"Trying to impress a woman by giving her jewels?" I clicked my tongue in mock disapproval. "Typical male behavior."

Hale let out that low chuckle again, its deep rumble pushing the flutter in my stomach lower in my abdomen. "You're right. What was I thinking? If Lina Calder wants something shiny, she'd prefer it be deadly too."

His gaze dipped to the sheaths at my thighs. Soren's dagger was strapped on my right, and Hale's obsidian knife was fixed to my left.

"You added to your collection, I see," he murmured, stepping closer. He moved so quick I barely had time to blink, and before I knew it, the black blade was in his hand.

I was suddenly transfixed by the way Hale's fingers traced the dagger's razor-sharp edge. He moved so tenderly, so familiar, it was like he was saying hello to an old lover whose face he'd memorized the lines of long ago.

"It reminded me of someone I've missed very much," I whispered.

Hale froze. Slowly, his eyes rose to mine, the crude scar on his throat bobbing as he swallowed. His next words were quiet, almost fearful, like speaking them too loud might cause the ruby world around us to come crumbling down.

"He felt the same."

My breath hitched as Hale took another step closer. The last time we'd been this close he'd been bare and dripping and pressed against me, sharing the same breath as he insisted I was nothing but a figment of his imagination.

But this was real. *We* were real. I didn't know much in this life, and often struggled to sort through the influx of emotion flowing through me at all times, but I knew without a shadow of a doubt that this heat, this connection, this tangible pull between our souls was real.

Hale carefully slid the dagger back into place, his thumb brushing my thigh and leaving behind a tingle on my skin.

"Besides myself, you're the only other person who's ever gone into that room," Hale said, clearing his throat and backing away.

With his absence, I managed to breathe again. "What about the maids?"

"They were too scared. Had to make my own bed, I'm afraid."

"And..." I licked my lips. "What about women?"

Hale searched my gaze to confirm I was actually talking about what he thought I was.

"I went to them," he admitted. "In brothels, or the forest. Occasionally a meadow." At my confused look, he explained, "Wood Sprites. Their affinity for nature extends to all circumstances. But it was never..." Hale hesitated, and judging by the single wrinkle between his brows, he was fighting with himself on whether he should say it at all.

"You can tell me anything," I offered gently.

He nodded, his features relaxing. "When I was with others... it was never how it was with you."

The air was suddenly humid again.

"With everyone else, I had to be careful. I had to prove to them I wasn't the horrible thing they thought I was. But you... you knew I wasn't. You trusted me. You wanted me, *all* of me. The light, and the dark. So for once, I felt free to truly... be *me*."

Memories from last year's spring equinox flooded through my mind.

*Get on your knees.*

*Worship me.*

Him pushing me onto the bed.

Pinning me in place.

His ravenous kisses and unyielding tongue.

Confident and demanding, focused on my pleasure but controlling it... all because he felt safe enough to entertain his true desires, and knew I felt safe enough with him to desire the same.

Gods, the air was *really* humid.

Hale licked his lips, and tried to sound nonchalant as he asked, "And you? Was it just Soren who taught you... what you did that night?"

The memory of his muttered curses as I pleasured him with my mouth played in my mind, instantly shooting a carnal twinge between my legs before settling deep and low. This time, it was my turn to clear my throat.

"No. I was with men before in my world, even though I wasn't supposed to be. Where I'm from, women are expected to give themselves to their husbands only. But I've never really responded well to being told what to do."

Hale fought a smile. "Sounds about right."

"Although..." I cocked an eyebrow. "Presumptuous of you to

assume those men taught *me*." I shrugged and adopted a coy smile. "Maybe it was the other way around."

Hale sniffed with amusement, but became distracted by my lips. His gaze stayed there until the pressure between my legs grew heavier, and only when he'd returned his eyes to mine did I decipher how to speak again.

"My turn."

"To be the student?"

"To pick where we go next." Ignoring the voice in my head that was wailing, *Cover story be damned, just kiss the man,* I stepped away from him and planted my hands on my hips. "I want you to take me to the first place that took your breath away."

Hale finally revealed that rarest smile of his, the one that was wide and bright and lit up his eyes like the moon does the night.

"Follow me."

# Chapter 35

"No. Absolutely not."

Hale stood knee deep in the underground lake, gesturing to the flimsy driftwood raft he'd pulled from the shore and dragged into the water. "It's not going to sink, I swear."

My feet stayed stubbornly planted on dry ground. "That's not what I'm worried about."

Hale sighed. "The Merrows won't knock you overboard either."

I chewed the inside of my cheek and glanced at the serene water in both directions, rubbing my neck anxiously as I considered.

Hale sloshed out of the shadows and extended his hand. "Lina, I *promise*. You're safe with me."

The earnest look in his eyes finally swayed me, and against my better judgment, I slipped my hand into his, still grumbling under my breath. When we reached the water's edge, Hale gripped my waist with both hands and lifted me into the air like I weighed nothing, eliciting a yelp of surprise before setting me on the raft. He climbed on board after me and grabbed the long paddle he'd stashed there, dipping it into the water and pushing us from the shore.

"Now stay low and keep your head down so the Merrows don't get you."

My eyes went wide with panic, but when the corners of Hale's mouth twitched with a contained smile, I reached over the raft's edge and splashed him. "That wasn't funny!"

"Maybe not to you."

Comfortable silence settled over us as Hale rowed, the lap of the water against the raft and the gentle splash of the oar creating a calming symphony to accompany us on our journey. I even relaxed enough to lay on my stomach and trail my fingers through the ripples flowing behind the raft. I kept my gaze on the water, but I could always sense when Hale's eyes came to rest on me. They would stay so long that not looking up at him became agony, and fighting the urge to meet his potent stare became a strange form of torture.

"Thank you for coming even though the others didn't," Hale eventually said, the echo of his voice carrying across the lake like the ripples in our wake. "Your fearlessness still knows no bounds, Lina Calder."

The way his tongue formed my name, fond and tender, had my cheeks flushing worse than Willow's. I flipped onto my side and propped my fist under my head so I could look up at him. "I'm not fearless."

"I've seen you leap into battle without hesitation. What do you call that?"

"Poor impulse control."

Hale stifled a laugh. "It looks like bravery."

"Well, I've been scared shitless every time."

The quiet started rolling in again, but a hesitant statement passed Hale's lips before silence could take over completely.

"You befriended me."

When I looked over at him, he shrugged one shoulder, but it couldn't disguise the whisper of pain that flickered over his features. "That was fearless of you."

I pushed myself upright. "You weren't scary."

Hale sniffed wryly and focused on digging the paddle through the waves. "And *that* is how I know you're fearless. Lina Calder heard there was a monster born of a monster, and she tried to dance with it."

The memory washed some of the torment from his face, which brought a smile to my own. I nudged him with the toe of my boot.

"I still want that dance, by the way."

Hale froze, but his eyes darted to mine, and I caught another glimpse of the man I used to know as he scrutinized my expression, sifting through every detail on my face in search of the truth.

"You do?"

"Yes."

"Even after what you saw earlier?"

I couldn't help flinching at the memory of the Nether's skull bursting and scattering its contents across the crowd of onlookers. Hale hadn't so much as batted an eye at the violence, and if this was anyone else, maybe I would have let that sway me. But this wasn't just anybody. This was someone whose selflessness, strength, and resilience had saved my life and left a mark on my soul long after we'd parted ways. And maybe he did have darkness inside, but there was also so much light.

I slid forward so I was curled at his feet. An image floated up from the depths of my mind, one from this very angle, with Hale's head thrown back in ecstasy as his sweat-slick chest heaved. The flush returned to my cheeks, and judging by the way Hale had stopped breathing, he was thinking of the same moment.

"We're all capable of terrible things, Hale. I've done my fair share." I reached towards his hand, his eyes tracking me the whole way. I expected him to jerk away when I slid my fingers into his palm, but he didn't. He gripped my hand and released the breath trapped in his throat.

"I trust you," I continued. "And I'm not afraid of you. Not then. Not now. Not ever."

Another smile twitched at Hale's lips, but it was soon taken over by a pensive frown. His thumb swiped back and forth across my knuckles, setting my skin on fire.

"If only the Fae thought like you, Lina. There might be more hope for the Nethers if they did."

Hale pulled his hand from mine and returned to paddling. "If they only had the courage to look outside themselves, they might realize the Nethers aren't monsters. Most of them aren't, at least." His frown carved deeper, his mind likely drifting to the Night Sylph or some other grisly form of nightmare fuel. "But like you said last night, not every Fae is good either. And the Nethers were pushed into the position they are now. Outside these caves, the world is barren. There's no food and barely any shelter."

My mind drifted to Veshti's protruding ribs and tattered rags. "I saw."

"Many had to migrate in order to survive. Then they were persecuted by the Fae, and their fear turned to anger, and anger turned to violence. You know the rest. If they didn't have to fight tooth and nail to survive, I wonder how different things could be."

"Why can't their king provide for them?" I asked bitterly.

"He tries. He gives them homes in the caves where he can."

"Homes they don't always want," I countered. "The Merrows who took us to our room said they'd rather live somewhere with open water."

"They have this." Hale gestured to the lake around us. "And the pool system."

"Why can't they have the ocean outside the caves?"

"Aedan keeps them here because it's safer. It's dangerous out there."

I rolled my eyes. "It's just as dangerous here. I see how Tallys acts. She's terrified just walking around."

Hale grunted and rubbed his eyes. "I know. I'm... I'm trying to talk to Aedan about her. It's hard because he... he does so much good—"

"And so much bad."

Anger flashed across Hale's face. "You just said everyone is capable of terrible things. You have to give them a chance to show you they're capable of more."

"How many chances can you give?"

"As many as it takes," Hale barked. His shoulders immediately sagged with shame at the outburst. "I'm sorry. I just... I know what it's like to be considered a monster. I know how that weighs on you. And I wish someone had given me the option to take that pain away."

A pang of heartache cut through my chest. I empathized with Hale, and creatures like Veshti who were clearly misunderstood. Hell, I'd even started considering the idea that the Merrows might be friend instead of foe. But something I couldn't comprehend was Aedan having a scrap of morality left in him.

I licked my lips and chose my words carefully. "So... ultimately, what do you hope to accomplish by growing close to the Nethers the way you have?"

"Peace between Nether and Fae. Same as you."

Guilt sank my heart into my stomach. I sure as hell couldn't reveal our deception now. Not when the truth would unravel everything Hale had been working towards. If he knew we'd come here to assassinate Aedan, he'd try to change our minds.

Or worse.

I immediately shoved the thought from my mind. Hale wouldn't betray us by telling Aedan. The Netherworld clearly had its claws in him, but Hale wouldn't let any harm come to us. He'd just proved that with his disturbing demonstration earlier.

"It's hard to believe Syrena and Ilora are willing to discuss it," Hale went on. "After everything that happened, I figured peace would be the farthest thing from their minds."

Nervously, I fiddled with my sleeve. If someone looked close enough at the material, they'd catch a hint of silver glimmering up from the symbol on my arm. "Yes, it's certainly hard to fathom."

"I'll do what I can to make sure negotiations go well for you."

I peeked up at him. "And what if they don't? What happens then?"

Hale sighed wearily. "Then... I guess things go back to the way they were. Fae versus Nether, until one has wiped the other out completely."

"And what happens to you?"

"Would you have me go back to a people and place that hate me?"

I wilted at his words. I'd been so consumed by the fact he was actually alive and standing next to me, breathing the same air and staring at me with those intoxicating eyes, that I hadn't stopped to consider he wouldn't be returning with us. But of course he wouldn't. Here he was a prince, the right hand to a god. But that also meant he would be our enemy. Something he might welcome once he found out we'd come to kill his king.

Attempting to ignore the ache in my chest at the thought of

losing Hale a second time, I pulled my knees close and hugged them tight.

"A lot of people in the Fae realm hate me too," I mumbled.

Those dark eyes landed on me again, prodding me for more information.

"To them I'm just a king-slaying, troublemaking whore." I glanced up at Hale and mustered a small smile. "Some even say I'm a witch."

The magic in my veins thrummed proudly at the word.

Hale shook his head and turned his gaze forward so I wouldn't see the murderous gleam it had taken on, but he was unsuccessful. "To the ignorant, there's nothing more terrifying than a powerful woman."

"And if you're not ignorant?"

"There's nothing more seductive."

Hale lifted the paddle from the water and set it down, then sat beside me.

"We're here," he whispered in my ear before settling.

I followed Hale's eyeline, then gasped at what had captured his attention.

We were drifting towards a forest, only the massive evergreens were growing down from the ceiling, their pointed tops dangling just above the water. At first I thought all the trees were coated in the Netherworld's usual glowing algae, but then the substance moved. It wasn't algae, but a shimmering dust weaving in and out of the tree boughs and dancing on the surface of the lake. Once we floated closer, the powder revealed living things. It was trailing behind tiny creatures barely the size of my thumb. Drifting closer still, their forms became clearer. They were Fae in appearance, only with iridescent wings resembling those of a dragonfly.

"Piksis," Hale explained. His face was already alight with joy, but with the gold powder highlighting his features, he was positively radiant. "Don't worry, they're completely harmless. Although, they can be a little mischievous."

One of the creatures darted over the raft, creating an arc of luminescent dust overhead. Hale leaned in, lowering his voice like he was telling me a ghost story as the flurries of powder drifted around us like snow.

"They're notorious for hiding keys and stealing one sock from every pair in the drawer."

I gasped in mock horror. "True evil!"

Hale laughed. A genuine laugh where he threw back his head and shut his eyes, their corners crinkling with joy. At that moment, he was so beautiful it hurt, but I couldn't look away.

One of the Piksis alighted on the corner of the raft. Hale grinned and reached his finger towards it. It hopped on, its wings splayed out on either side to help it keep its balance as Hale brought the creature between us. The powder on its skin illuminated our faces in a golden glow as we moved closer together to peer down at it. The Piksi was female, and I could have sworn a tiny voice warbled hello as she performed an elegant curtsy.

"They live here?" I asked.

"In nests near the trunks of the trees, yes." Hale offered the creature his whole palm, and she happily skipped to the center. "Over time, some have migrated to the Fae realm. In fact, you may have seen a few. They come out of their nests at dusk, and they're often mistaken for fireflies. They prefer to live here in the Netherworld, though."

The Piksi began a beautiful dance in Hale's palm, bounding and twirling and whirling her limbs in graceful sweeps. Shades of pink, blue, and gold sparkled in her paper-thin wings.

"Why?"

"I've been told they're quite the delicacy for owls."

At the mention of owls, the Piksi stopped her performance and frantically shook her head.

"She's beautiful," I breathed.

"Yes, she is."

But Hale wasn't looking at the Piksi when he said the words.

He was looking at me.

I blushed and quickly averted my gaze to the winged woman in his hand. She curtsied one last time before darting into the air in a spiral of shimmer, and I caught myself waving goodbye to her.

"See?" Hale leaned back, bracing his hands behind him on the raft. "I think if everyone witnessed this, they'd realize not every Nether is a monster that needs to be slain. It's what finally convinced me. I saw this and thought it was the most breathtaking thing I'd ever seen. Well..." He sneaked another glance my way. "Second most breathtaking."

My heart skipped a beat at his words, but I forced myself to break his heavy-lidded stare.

"Syrena's right," I mumbled. "You are different."

"In a bad way?"

I exhaled a quivering breath and pulled my knees back to my chest. "Not at all. Happy looks good on you."

*Too* good.

Almost enough to make someone lose sight of what they'd come here for.

WHEN I GOT BACK to the common room, I ignored Xavier, Ilora, and Syrena when they tried to interrogate me about my time with Hale. Instead, I retreated to my bed, where I curled up in a pile of silk and lost myself to a barrage of miserable thoughts. Both Soren and Hale were at the forefront of my mind, and they each caused an ache in my chest so hollow it was hard to breathe.

I desperately wished Soren were here. I'd crawl into his arms and have him hold me until the task at hand seemed less daunting. And Hale *was* here, but I couldn't touch him either, not without ruining my cover and risking foiling the plan to kill Aedan before it had ever really begun.

Stressed, anxious, and sexually frustrated, I drifted into a fitful slumber.

I dreamed of the Piksi forest burning, flaming branches breaking off the trees and dropping into the water below.

I dreamed of the pool in the ruby cavern running red with blood.

Finally, I dreamed of the battlefield again, with my black eyes looking up at the sky as I screamed, followed by a flash of bright light and a heavy veil of dark shadow.

Rapping at the door eventually woke me.

Draping a blanket around myself, I scooted off the bed and shuffled out to the common room just in time to witness Ilora opening the door, revealing Tallys on the other side. She was trembling worse than usual, and walked with a slight limp.

"My master requests you dine with him," she sniffled, wiping her face with her wide gray sleeve.

Ilora frowned and caught her arm, making Tallys flinch. When Ilora pushed back the fabric on the dress, it revealed a patch of pale gray skin tarnished with a slew of dark bruises.

"Aedan did this?" Ilora asked, anger choking her voice.

Tallys lowered her gaze to the ground to hide the tears pooling in her eyes. "It's not so bad. I've had worse."

Ilora's expression twisted into one I'd never seen on her. A mixture of intense rage and sadness colored her features, but when she led Tallys over to the sofa and sat her down, Xavier and Syrena making way for them, her voice was gentle.

"Why don't you leave this place?"

Tallys shook her head. "He'd find me. There's nowhere I can run where he won't find me."

"What about..." Ilora froze and blinked repeatedly, like she was surprised by the next words out of her mouth. "What about the Fae realm? What if you came there?"

Syrena and Xavier exchanged glances.

Tallys laughed miserably. "That's the same death sentence as here."

Ilora scooted a little closer. "You're half Merrow, right?"

"Yes."

"So you like to swim?"

Tallys shot her a wary look but nodded. "It's my favorite thing. Underwater, things are quiet. You feel weightless. Free."

Ilora smiled at her, instinctively lifting a hand to wipe her tears away. Both women hesitated before Ilora made contact, studying each other with curiosity and confusion, wariness and wonder. Then the queen's fingertips brushed her cheek, and Tallys melted into the kindness of her touch.

"Where I'm from, there's a huge lake," Ilora said. "The water is as blue as sapphires and sparkles like diamonds, and there are hills as far as the eye can see, dense with flowers and trees and vines the shade of emeralds. What if... what if you came there?"

Tallys looked up at her, her eyes round with surprise.

"You could be a guest of the palace," Ilora continued, "and stay in one of the villas right on the water, with a terrace that meets the shore. You could go swimming anytime you like."

Syrena glanced at me. She frowned, but reluctant compassion glittered in her eyes.

Tallys twisted her fingers in her lap as she searched Ilora's face. "I've heard of your home. You hunt my kind."

Ilora shook her head, then took Tallys's hand in her own.

"That was my father. And we are not our fathers. You know that better than anyone."

Tallys's bottom lip quivered, and she nodded, returning her attention to her hands so she could glare bitterly at their shade of Night Sylph gray.

"Your home sounds like paradise," she whispered.

"It is." Ilora gave her another radiant smile, easing Tallys's pained expression.

To my surprise, Syrena plopped beside them. "You could sunbathe on the decks of boats and eat breakfast on the terrace, and there's this delicious fizzy drink they have there that tastes like honey and peaches."

"What are peaches?"

"You'll see." Syrena helped Tallys to her feet and cupped her cheeks in her hands. "Now go and wash your face, because we never, *ever* let them see how much they've hurt us."

Tallys dipped her head obediently and scurried into the other room. When she'd gone, Ilora stood too. Her eyes were cold, her jaw set, and her hands balled into fists at her sides.

"I want to amend our original plan," she stated, her voice steadfast and confident. It was the voice of a born ruler making a declaration to her troops. "We came for Aedan, but after the past few days, I think it's become clear to all of us there are some innocents who've gotten caught in the crossfire."

She looked to Syrena, who nodded and toyed with her remaining gold bracelets, then to Xavier, who was chewing the inside of his cheek and craning his neck to check if Tallys was alright. Ilora shut her eyes and took a deep breath.

"I'm still scared. I still don't trust this place, or the majority of its inhabitants. I'm still going to cut that Kylanthian bitch's throat for what she did to my family." Her eyes snapped open. "But my mother and father raised me to seek peace and kindness first, and always offer a hand to those in need. They didn't extend those principles to the Nethers, but their daughter will."

"What are you saying?" Xavier asked.

"She's saying we kill Aedan and Erith, then save the Nethers who want to be saved." Syrena turned to her friend. "Right?"

Ilora dipped her head.

Syrena lifted her nose in the air and planted her hands on her hips. "I second the amendment."

I pulled the blanket from my shoulders, and tossed it onto the couch. "Third."

"An assassination *and* a Nether rescue mission?" Xavier scoffed, his arms crossing as he leaned against the wall and shook his head. "This is the craziest shit I've ever heard."

His eyes lit up like the dawn. "I'm in."

<h1 style="text-align:center">CHAPTER 36</h1>

<hr>

Here in Aedan's empire, it was impossible to tell time. There was no sun to compare to the horizon, no moonrise to brighten the night, nothing but never-ending darkness. The only reason we knew it was time for dinner was because Tallys told us so. She led us back to the tall tourmaline doors of Aedan's dining room, only this time, Hale was the one who greeted us.

He'd changed out of the black-and-gold robes he'd worn when he'd shown me the ruby cave and Piksi forest, and opted instead for trousers and a simple black linen shirt. Now he looked more like the Hale I used to know, especially with his hair pulled back tight and the front pieces falling forward to tickle the sharp line of his jaw. The only thing missing was the stash of black knives on his thighs.

"Hello," Hale said in the doorway, a knee-weakening smile sneaking onto his lips at the sight of me.

"Hello," I couldn't help but giggle back.

His smile stretched wider as he stepped aside, beckoning for us to enter. "Come in. Food's on the table."

We filed inside, Aedan's sickening scent and singsong voice welcoming us as we did.

"You made it! Let's try this again, shall we? No negotiations, just pleasant dinner conversation. Can you do that?"

"Can *you*?" I grumbled.

Aedan tossed his head back and laughed. "Oh, Lina. You're so fiery now, I love it!"

*You have no idea,* the magic inside me crackled in reply.

Tallys limped to a corner behind Aedan and stood in silent submission, while the rest of us gathered around the table at our designated places. Hale clocked Tallys's slow, pained movements, his lips curving down in a frown, but he said nothing. Instead, he slipped into the chair beside me.

Aedan leaned forward and sniffed appreciatively at the fragrant steam wafting up from the massive slab of meat on the platter at the center of the table. To his right, Erith poured herself a large goblet of wine.

"Smells great," Xavier chirped. "What is it?"

"A type of winged Nether we have here," Aedan replied, grabbing a nearby knife and jamming its serrated edge into the rare flesh. "They look a bit like Fae, but taste just like chicken. Would you like some?"

I scanned the fare. Because of its wings and the size, I thought the meat was some form of wild turkey, but looking at it closely, it was far too big. It was roughly the size and shape of a woman's torso.

A Veshti-sized torso.

Air whooshed from my lungs so fast I had to grab the side of the table to steady myself.

"Everything alright, Lina?" Erith cooed.

A glance in her direction found her smirking at me, one elegant hand wrapped around her goblet, while the other twirled one of her earrings. The jewelry was made of a dainty gold chain and glittering diamonds... with raven black feathers dangling at the ends.

Xavier noticed them at the same time I did, his eyes darting between Erith and the carcass in front of us, before he slowly lowered his fork to the table. "Gods, that certainly looks delicious, but I'm afraid I've recently stopped eating meat."

"Oh?" Aedan's head tilted in curiosity before he gestured to a platter of crispy bite-sized morsels. "So you wouldn't be interested in trying any Piksi, then?"

I peeked at Hale. His frown had deepened, but he still said nothing. He did, however, stick to eating nothing but fruit.

"I'm alright." Xavier dipped his head politely, but the color was rapidly draining from his cheeks. "Thank you, though."

"Suit yourself." Aedan shrugged and tore into a piece of the meat, its resounding squish a deafening roar in our ears.

Apparently the others had experienced the same epiphany as Xavier and me, because across the table, Ilora disguised a dry heave by burying her face in her cup and pretending to drink her wine. Syrena cleared her throat and tucked a stray curl back into place. She appeared composed, but at just the right angle, someone could see the nails on her opposite hand digging into her thigh.

Keeping her eyes off the meat at the center of the table, she adopted her winning smile and purred, "So how did you two lovebirds meet, Erith?"

Aedan's gray eyes lit up as he leaned forward, gesturing between the two of them with his fork. "It's a funny story, actually. It was just over a hundred years ago when—"

"I can speak for myself," Erith declared.

Aedan stopped chewing and stared at her for a few tense beats before cracking a smile and easing back in his chair. "Of course you can, my love."

Erith's icy turquoise stare flicked back to Syrena. She set her wine down and slowly tapped her long red nails on the tabletop next to it, sending a pointed *click, click, click* echoing throughout the room.

"You're alone for long enough, you turn to whoever you can for company." Her voice was deadpan, devoid of any emotion, but her eyes were full of cold, calculated rage. "No one travels to Kylanthia for parties or festivals like they do in the other territories. No one comes with aid when its people are dying of plague. No one comes to protect its civilians when raiders from the lands across the sea invade and burn its villages to the ground. No one comes when monsters from the Netherworld make a home in its mountains, hunting down every man, woman, and child like wild game. No one ever comes, not because the road in is too dangerous or the land is too harsh like they all claim, but because we have nothing to offer. No agriculture, no export, just the occasional mine or quarry, which the other territories use up and leave ravaged before disappearing without a trace. After centuries of being treated like an outsider, you start to wonder if you're a monster too. So you befriend the other demons, and show them your own, and soon you realize you're not the villains at all. The true monsters are the ones who watched your suffering and did nothing."

Erith turned to Aedan, and for the first time since I met her, she smiled. "When someone comes to you in the night and sees you, *really* sees you, and they offer you a way out, you take it."

Aedan intercepted her hand, brought it to his mouth, and planted a tender kiss against the skin.

"People are still suffering, though," Ilora blurted. "Merimaya has been taking in Kylanthian refugees, but it's not enough. They're dying at the hands of the Nethers."

Erith shrugged, then lifted her wine to her lips once more. "They had their chance to show the Nethers mercy, but they refused. What's happening now is fair, and they brought it on themselves."

Ilora looked ready to argue, but Aedan wiped his mouth with a napkin and waved the conversation away with a flick of his wrist. "Enough talk about suffering. It's boring and bad for digestion. Let's talk about something else. Lina, how are you feeling? How's the morning sickness?"

Hale's fork clattered to the table.

"Oh, that's right! Hale, I forgot to tell you!" Aedan beamed at me like a proud father. "The King Slayer is bearing the silver-tongue's child!"

The very air around Hale seemed to cave in on him. His expression went blank, his eyes lost their gleam, and his voice was monotone as he muttered, "Congratulations."

His expression made me sick. I wanted to scream it wasn't true. I wanted to swipe that smug grin off Aedan's face. But mostly, I wanted to carve out that shapeshifter's heart and serve it up next to the innocent Nethers on his godsdamned dinner table.

Instead I could do nothing but keep my eyes glued to my plate. If I moved, they'd without a doubt fill with frustrated, helpless tears, and I was doing my best to take Syrena's words to heart.

*We never let them see how much they've hurt us.*

With a patronizing click of his tongue, Aedan swiveled in his seat to face Hale. "I'm sorry, son. I know how excited you were when she showed up again. Your mind was racing with all the possibilities of a future with her."

My foolish heart fluttered at that.

"But don't worry." Aedan patted Hale's hand. "There will be other women. You can have your pick of the ones here." He chuckled and winked at Xavier. "And let me tell you, our prince has certainly been sampling what the Netherworld has to offer.

The Merrows rave about his skills in the bedroom. He won't touch Tallys, though. I think he's afraid she might be his sister. Speaking of Tallys, how was her night with you in the kennel, dog?"

Without missing a beat, Xavier raised a glass and winked back. "A howling good time."

I had no idea how Xavier was keeping his composure, but I'd never admired my friend more.

Aedan cackled and slapped his knee. "You're too much, boy. I really do think we could be friends." He popped a Piksi between his teeth, crumbles from its wings puffing out as he spoke. "Going back to what I was saying, Hale's favorite thing is still to watch. Lina, you'll love this bit. Every so often, Hale asks me to take *your* shape so he can look on while Erith and I—"

"Aedan, please," Hale interrupted.

I sneaked a glance in his direction. His face betrayed nothing, but the scar on the back of his hand did. The symbol moved up and down, the tendons beneath it flexing as he repeatedly clenched his fist. What Hale's black mist had done to that creature this morning was gruesome, and in the moment I never wanted to see it used in that way again, but now I wished he'd do the exact same to Aedan. To my dismay, Hale's dark power stayed dormant.

Aedan sighed and shrugged, then took another savage bite of meat. Beside me, Syrena's nails dug deeper into her skin, and her leg started to bounce. Under the table, I slid my foot to hers to offer some support.

Across the table, Erith popped a Piksi into her red-rimmed mouth, its crunch making the acid in my stomach rise further.

"Oh! I just remembered!" Aedan sat back and clapped his hands eagerly. "We wanted to formally invite you all to the celebration tomorrow night!"

"What celebration?" Ilora asked. Her words were pinched,

like her throat was constricting to hold back the contents of her stomach.

"For the spring equinox, of course! It's my favorite holiday." Aedan grinned at Syrena. "It's yours too, isn't it? Although, Lerian's celebration last year didn't quite go as planned, did it?" He snickered like a naughty child. "Sorry about that. At least it all worked out. Lina and Hale ended up having quite a bit of fun that night."

The screech of wood against rock echoed throughout the room as Hale shoved back his chair and stood.

"Will you please excuse me?" he said tightly.

He turned before anyone could stop him, and I was running after him before I realized what my feet were doing.

"Hale!" I called once we'd exited into the hall.

He continued with determined strides, making it difficult to catch up with him. When I managed to get within arm's reach, I caught his hand and jerked him around to look at me. I was immediately met with a solid wall of anger.

"Why the fuck didn't you say anything?" Hale snapped.

I flinched at his tone and the fury in his eyes, suddenly hit with the realization I'd never actually seen his anger manifest in another way besides the occasional outburst or his typical silent brooding. My own emotions flared at the verbal attack, and despite my eyes stinging with tears, I matched his anger with my own.

"Why the fuck didn't *you* say anything?" I barked back. "I saw what you did to that Nether this morning. You could silence Aedan in a heartbeat, but instead you just sit there and take it."

Hale stepped menacingly closer, the steel in his eyes raking fear down my spine.

"I sit there and take it," he ground out, "because it's the smart thing to do."

"You sit there and take it," I spat, "because he's paying you with power, and that makes you just as much of a whore as me."

Hale shot forward, trapping me with my back against the wall as his hand smacked the stone above my head. A scream tore from my throat, mixing with the slap of Hale's palm, and I shut my eyes tight to brace for pain. I stood there cowering, but the blow never came. When I peeled one eye open, Hale's face was inches from mine.

"Tell me you want it," he panted.

My stomach dropped. "What?"

Hale moved closer, sliding his other hand to the wall beside the first so I was caged between his arms. When his chest pressed against mine and his breath puffed warm and damp against my lips, fear made space for arousal.

"Tell me you wanted his child," Hale breathed.

The lie weighed heavier on my shoulders, followed by guilt viciously gnawing through my chest. I tried to look away, but the intensity in Hale's eyes held me captive.

"Because when we were in Merimaya last year, you told me you didn't want this life for yourself," he continued. "You said that in your world, people thought you were strange because you didn't want children. So did you change your mind, or did Soren pressure you into having his heir?"

I hesitated, battling every fiber of my being that screamed at me to tell him the truth. I waited too long, and Hale hit the wall again.

"*Did he pressure you into having his baby?*" he shouted.

"No!" I wailed, tears pricking my lashes and blurring my vision.

"Promise me," Hale demanded. He slipped one hand from the wall down to my neck, forcefully cupping my jaw to make me look him in the eye. "Promise me he didn't make you change for him. Because I'll kill him, Lina. I swear, if he manipulated you into this—"

"He didn't, Hale! It's not what you think. It's..." I trailed off, miserably settling on, "It's complicated."

Hale's stare felt like it was digging through my soul, slicing it into pieces and dragging them into the light. I thought for sure he'd find the truth lurking there, cowering in some shameful, dusty corner, but Hale eventually sighed and shook his head.

"What are you not telling me?"

A lump lodged in my throat, making it impossible to speak the truth even if I wanted to.

I wanted to be honest. Hale had seen me at my best and at my worst. He'd seen me lose myself to my anger, seen me in the midst of my most intimate moments. He'd seen *all* of me, mind, body, and soul, and that made not being honest with him now seem so innately wrong it physically hurt, but I forced myself to remember *why*.

The well-being of my brother, my friends, and all the people I loved was at stake.

Aedan had to die. No matter what, and no matter whose heart got caught in the crossfire.

Hale's words pulled me back to reality.

"I don't like being lied to, Lina."

I swallowed the tightness in my throat, somehow managing to whimper, "And I don't like lying."

A rogue tear toppled over the rim of my lower lashes. At the sight of it trickling down my cheek, Hale's expression softened. Carefully, almost timidly, he caught the droplet with his index finger, wiping it away before bitterly flicking it to the ground like that particular drop of saltwater was the source of all my pain. Then he leaned in so close his mouth was a hairsbreadth from mine, and it took everything in me not to angle my head up just enough to make our lips meet after all this time.

"Get some rest," Hale whispered. "I'll see you tomorrow."

Then he turned and disappeared down the hall, leaving me free to fall apart.

## CHAPTER 37

—————

THE NEXT DAY WE DIDN'T LEAVE OUR ROOM, AND INSTEAD SPENT every second practicing our power.

At least, Xavier and Ilora practiced their power. I spent all day screaming at mine.

I desperately tried to bring out the burning dark festering in my veins, but it felt like it was laughing in my face when it gave me nothing more than a pathetic black spark at my fingertips. By nightfall, however, Xavier could extend his shield of protection in front of something ten paces away, while Ilora could manipulate an entire pool of water from across the room without even looking at it.

By the time a knock rapped at the door that evening, we were exhausted from our day's practice, making us dread the spring equinox celebration tonight even more.

Defeated by my pathetic attempts at handling magic, I shuffled over to the door and hauled it open, expecting Tallys on the other side, but instead I was met by the sunken eyes of an alarmingly thin woman who was simultaneously young and old.

I gasped in surprise and went to slam the door, but I'd forgotten how eerily fast the Sluagh were, and she darted inside just before it shut.

"That was not kind," the woman huffed. Her voice still resembled the mix of old and young, scream and whisper, but with a box in her hands and tired defeat in her eyes, it wasn't nearly as frightening as I'd once thought. Nevertheless, I reached for my blade just to be safe. Unfazed, the Sluagh continued into the center of the room.

"Calm yourself. We come in peace."

"Sure you do," I sneered.

The Sluagh sighed, her frail arms shaking as they lowered the box onto the emerald coffee table.

"Our master sent your wardrobe for this evening," she explained. "He requests you be ready within the hour. The one at the top is for the human."

The Sluagh started back towards the door, but stopped in her tracks and thought for a few seconds before peeking over her shoulder.

"We should tell you... we meant no harm to the child." Her hollow face fell, and what little light she had behind her eyes dimmed. "You see, it is difficult for us to bear children. When we finally manage, they often die. They come out thin and sickly, just like their mothers."

The Sluagh sniffed grimly and wiped her palms on the tattered skirt of her dress. "Most do not survive the first days of life. The human child in the forest on Samhain was strong and energetic and shone bright as the sun. He smelled like summer and looked like joy, and for the first time in a long time, he made us feel something akin to hope. That night, we saved him for the correct reasons, but we kept him for selfish ones. And for that, we owe you our apology."

My grip loosened around my dagger's hilt.

"But..." The Sluagh lifted her chin, all the vulnerability on her face washing away. "We have not forgotten your debt."

I swallowed. "My debt?"

"A life in exchange for that of our sister, the one whose skull you crushed in cold blood."

I winced at the memory of that first fateful Samhain I spent in the Fae realm.

"A life for a life," the Sluagh repeated. The same words they'd uttered that night. "Until then, we will be civil as long as it serves us."

"And when it doesn't serve you?" I asked warily.

The Sluagh said nothing. She only smiled, snapped her fingers, and disappeared, leaving me anxious and unsettled on top of everything else.

THE CLOTHES we were given were simple, but made from the same luxurious satin Erith typically dressed in. Xavier's black ensemble consisted of loose trousers and a wide-sleeved tunic. It also came with a collar attached to a gold chain, the note pinned to it reading, *This is for the loyal dog.*

"Fucking prick," Xavier grumbled, ripping off the gold chain. But never one to pass up an opportunity for good fashion, he draped it around his throat like a gilded scarf.

The dresses for me, Ilora, and Syrena were free of rude messages. The formfitting long-sleeved gowns had plunging necklines and high slits at the leg. The only difference between them was that my friends were dressed in black, while I was clothed in ruby red, and my skirt was complete with not one but two slits to show off both blades strapped to my thighs. I knew exactly who was responsible for the design. Clearly it was someone who knew my favorite color and believed there was nothing more seductive than a powerful woman.

When Tallys met us in the hall, she respectfully dipped her cowled head, her normal baggy, draping dress exchanged for a similar one in black.

"The ceremony will start shortly," she said, beckoning for us to follow her. She was still limping, and grimaced every time she put pressure on the leg. "The prince has commanded tonight be without violence, but if I were you, I'd still be wary. The upper beasts may interpret it as suggestion instead of law."

"Is there usually violence?" Syrena sounded angry, which meant she was terrified.

Tallys shuddered. "You're encouraged to do whatever the drumming inspires in you. We lesser beasts are often at the whims of the upper ones."

"What drumming?" Xavier asked.

Almost in answer, a resonant gong sounded in the distance, followed by the slow, steady rap of rawhide drums. Tallys immediately began to quake, as if the reverberations of the instruments controlled her body. Ilora instinctively wrapped an arm around her shoulders, taking care to avoid the fresh bruises.

"We won't let anything happen to you," she said gently, but hardened determination gleamed in her eyes. "Just stick with us, alright?"

"If my master calls and I don't come—"

"He can take it up with me."

Tallys peeked up at Ilora, her oversized pupils dilating with wonder. "You are a very brave woman, Your Majesty."

"You're just as brave, Tallys, if not more." Ilora glanced down and smiled shyly. "And you don't have to be so formal. You can call me by my name."

Tallys mustered a smile back, then ducked her head and

nestled a little further into the safety and comfort of a kind embrace, something I wasn't sure she'd ever known, but Ilora was more than happy to give.

The farther we walked, the louder the drumming became, and when torches appeared, lining the dark tunnel we were passing through, the sound had amplified so much it vibrated the soles of our feet. The persistent beat mirrored the pace of my heart punching against my chest. The passageway widened, revealing a cavern beyond with light spilling out the same hue as a red sand desert.

"If I could give you any advice," Tallys peeped from beside Ilora, "it would be to keep quiet, keep to yourself, and keep to the outskirts. The shadows are your friends. If you stick to them, you're more likely to go unnoticed."

This was clearly something she'd done too many times. My heart ached for her, and I could tell Ilora's did too because her grip around the Nether's shoulders tightened.

When the mouth of the tunnel opened entirely and we passed into the glow of the adjoining cave, we stepped into something out of my worst nightmares.

The circular cavern was as tall as it was wide, its domed ceiling reaching up so far I nearly fell over trying to see the top. The roof and walls were dotted with torches and riddled with precarious stone spikes, ones all manner of horrifying beasts were perched on. Creatures with bat wings and serpentine faces clung to the walls just above our eyeline, their forked tongues flicking towards us as we passed, and monsters that looked like a boar-sized combination of both scorpion and crab skittered across the ceiling, quick as cockroaches. The rest of the space was packed with other Nethers, ones I'd never seen and hoped I never would again, as well as others I'd encountered before, like the Sluagh and Fear Gorta and one of the horned beasts that had slaughtered Meer.

We'd wandered into a vicious sea of talon and tooth, and every evil eye watched us like they were preparing to rush in for the kill.

"Quick," Tallys urged, gesturing as she hurried into a darkened corner and inched her way along the wall to avoid prying eyes.

We followed in her footsteps until she'd led us to a group of Merrows we took shelter behind. They glanced over their shoulders at us, no longer wearing the cold expressions they'd welcomed us with when we first arrived. Instead, they looked just as terrified as Tallys, and nodded to us in grim acknowledgement when we fell in beside them. The drums still thundered, now so loud and deep the beat rattled in my chest, and when I lifted onto my toes to look out over the crowd, I saw why.

Not twenty paces away was a large circle of Nether percussionists striking animal-skin drums in perfect rhythm. Others stood beside them, armed with different types of natural instruments: bowls full of coarse black sand that made a distinct *shwick* when tossed, sticks of rattling seashells, and bones that clacked together on beat with the drums.

Inside the garish orchestra was another circle of Nethers currently piling bundles of brush around a larger stack at the center. Dead animals on spits waited nearby, ready for roasting, but no one moved to light a flame. The air was tight. Expectant. Like everyone was waiting for something.

I glanced at Tallys, clocking the way her dark eyes darted past the activity in front of us towards the other end of the cave. The other Merrows were doing the same, and when I peeked at a group of Sluagh, their attention was directed there as well. My curiosity getting the better of me, I sneaked out from behind a teal-haired Merrow and stepped into the torchlight to get a better view.

I felt his eyes on me long before I saw him.

It was the same sensation I'd experienced when I first visited Lerian. Back then, I would wander down the corridors with my skin prickling and the hair at the back of my neck standing on end thanks to the constant nagging sensation of someone watching me. I didn't know it at the time, but the feeling was Hale using his power to keep an eye on my movements around the palace. And since he'd been gone, I'd wished every lonely, empty shadow would feel like that again.

Now the feeling was finally back. The hair on my arms pricked, my skin pimpled, and my neck and collarbones heated. I couldn't see him, but the weight of Hale's stare was practically tangible. I rose to my toes again, searching the crowd for a glimpse of him.

My attention was intercepted by a mob of rowdy men and women at the far end of the drum circle. They had an array of different skin tones and hair colors, but each shared one similarity: bright golden eyes that reflected light at certain angles like those of a carnivore in the night. They could have easily been mistaken for Fae, except for the fact that when they smiled, their curled lips revealed two sets of elongated canine teeth, top and bottom.

"Aedan's hunters," Tallys explained, gliding up beside me so quietly I jumped when she spoke. "Traditionally he favors his more gruesome creations." Her eyes drifted to one of the chittering beasts stalking across the ceiling. "We call them upper beasts. They're creatures like the Night Sylph, or the Fear Gorta. Ones who inspire terror just by the sight of them. But the Weir..." She gestured to the pack across the cave. "Those can turn into a feral animal in the blink of an eye, and they can track anything. They're who Aedan sends if anyone tries to escape, and they rarely come back empty-handed."

Tallys shivered, prompting Ilora to slide over and rub her back in encouragement.

Across from me, one of the Weir men lifted his nose to the air and sniffed, following a scent on the wind until he'd turned in my direction. When his eyes landed on me, I stiffened. I could have maybe found him attractive, with his chiseled bone structure and long hair streaked in gray, but the way he was looking at me...

His gaze was that of a predator who had dinner in sight.

"Don't let them sense your fear," Tallys whispered. "It's their favorite flavor."

"I'm not afraid," I murmured. As a silent warning, I spread the slits on my dress further apart so the man and his hungry eyes would see the weapons I'd stashed there. Undeterred, he cracked a wolfish grin and licked his lips.

But I didn't balk, because someone else was still watching.

I looked past the Weir man, finally finding the gaze I'd been sensing.

Powerful, confident, and locked on my face, Hale's eyes blazed like a beacon, demanding the attention and respect of every creature who dared meet them as he sat on the sleek obsidian throne beside Aedan's. My breath hitched at the sight of him, my heart joining in with the thump of the drums as they beat faster.

He was captain of the guard no longer. Now he was every inch the dark prince.

The obsidian crown atop Hale's raven hair was the most extravagant thing he wore, the rest of his ensemble consisting of nothing but silky fitted trousers and a sheer black wide-sleeved robe he wore open to expose his carved muscles and the scars scattered across them. Scars he once hid, but now showed off proudly. His own personal battle scars.

Hale lounged in his seat, unafraid to take up space with his legs sprawled out wide, while one hand rested on the arm of the chair and the other lifted a goblet to his lips, the black and gold signet ring back on his finger to confirm his status. He watched me over the rim of the cup as he drank, the charcoal smudged around his eyes making his stare more piercing than usual.

Like him, Erith was dressed in black and drinking wine as she perched in an identical chair at Aedan's right. Skintight satin clung to her body, her usual red nails exchanged for a shimmering black, and her white-blonde hair swept over her shoulder in a graceful waterfall cascading all the way to her hips. The sight of a spiny, high-neck collar fixed around Erith's shoulders made my blood run cold. It was made up entirely of long inky feathers, and I couldn't help but wonder if they belonged to who she and Aedan had served up for dinner last night. A wave of nausea roiled in my stomach at the thought.

The self-proclaimed god of the Netherworld sat higher than his queen and prince, the shards of glittering crystals at the base of his throne shooting up around him like rays of light. Dressed entirely in pearly white save for his own signet ring and jagged obsidian crown, he looked like the blinding sun nestled between two storm clouds, and judging from the smug expression on his face and the Nethers gathering at his feet, he was going to be worshipped like it.

# CHAPTER 38

Aedan stood, and the drums stopped. The room fell eerily silent.

"My children," Aedan boomed. "My finest creations and my greatest joy. It was on this day at the dawn of time that the Netherworld was born, and your ancestors along with it. In honor of this, I urge you to celebrate in whatever way you see fit. Shut your eyes and listen to the beat of life inside you, feel it moving you, swaying you, and when you embrace the base instincts it churns up inside you, I want you to indulge them, then give thanks to the one who gave them to you."

Aedan raised his arms high and threw back his head.

Then his eyes went pitch black.

A blinding flash of light was followed by a wave of furious darkness that shot from his hands and tore into the brush pile at the center of the cavern as fast as vengeful wildfire.

I gasped and stepped back as the pile instantly disintegrated into crackling embers, the sight jerking awake a memory buried in the recesses of my mind.

Black.

A distant vine of silver.

Pure unadulterated power exploding, overflowing in a veil of shadow that swept over the Fear Gorta surrounding me and turned them all to embers.

As the Nethers in front of the dais brought torches to the coals, igniting them and passing the flame on to light the other bonfires, I peered over at Syrena, Xavier, and Ilora in disbelief. Judging by their shocked expressions, we'd all had the same realization about Aedan's newly revealed power.

It was the same as mine.

We barely had time to process the discovery, because soon as the fires were lit, the drums took up their pounding again. This time they were faster, which riled the Nethers into a frenzy. Some tore into the food, others began playfully brawling or flailing to the frantic beat, but the group of Merrows in front of us pushed further into the shadows, warily keeping an eye on the commotion as they huddled together for support. What would have befallen them if Hale *hadn't* requested a ceasefire on violence? Considering the haunted look in their eyes, it was far from good.

"So what now?" Xavier asked.

One of the Merrows regarded him over her shoulder. "Now you do whatever you're inspired to."

"Whatever the music drums up in you," another added, her sky blue eyes holding on the large white scar jutting diagonally over Xavier's chest.

Xavier chuckled. "Nice pun."

"Thank you," she giggled back. After a moment of hesitation, she moved closer, gingerly reaching out to touch the scar and delicately trace her pale blue fingertips over the marred flesh. The first Merrow watched them curiously.

"What happened here?" the second woman asked.

"Fear Gorta," Xavier replied with a lighthearted shrug. "Apparently I look good enough to eat."

"Well, that *is* true," the first Merrow cut in, twirling a wavy strand of indigo hair around her finger as she sidled up beside the other, whose fingers still hadn't lifted from Xavier's chest.

Xavier tilted his head to the side at the Merrow's remark, one corner of his mouth curling upwards. "Miss, I'm not sure if you're flirting with me or sizing me up for dinner."

"I only eat fish," she replied.

"And only on special occasions," Sky Blue Eyes offered with a coy tilt of her head.

Xavier laughed again and sheepishly rubbed the back of his neck. "Ladies, forgive me, but don't you drown men for fun?"

The Merrows laughed like it was the funniest thing they'd ever heard.

"We do other things with men for fun too," Indigo Hair purred.

Xavier bit his bottom lip. "We have that in common, then."

The women tittered again.

In the background, the drums increased their intensity, now accompanied by the clacking of bones on the downbeat.

A glance at Syrena caught her pretending she wasn't watching Xavier out of the corner of her eye.

Another Merrow joined the first two, this one batting a pair of long periwinkle eyelashes in his direction. "Do you find us attractive?"

Xavier respectfully kept his eyes from drifting down to her bare breasts. "Miss, if a man doesn't find you ladies attractive, it's because he leans entirely in the other direction."

"So what's the problem?" Indigo toyed with the gold chain draped around Xavier's neck.

Xavier's gaze darted to Syrena. "The problem is I don't want you to feel like you have to do something you don't want to."

"Who says we don't want to?" Sky Blue asked, her bright eyes deceivingly innocent.

"Don't you find the drums inspiring?" Periwinkle prodded.

Syrena huffed a sigh and crossed her arms.

"The what?" Xavier fought to keep his eyes up as all three Merrows pressed their naked bodies closer.

"Shhh," Indigo hushed, placing a finger to his lips. "Just listen."

"Shut your eyes," Sky Blue encouraged. "Feel it in your heart."

"In your soul," Periwinkle added.

"In your whole body," Indigo whispered, just as Sky Blue's hand floated lower on Xavier's abdomen. "Can you feel it?"

Syrena was no longer trying to disguise the fact she was watching them.

Xavier's laugh was tight as he pretended he wasn't as flustered as his flush suggested. "Believe me, I feel it."

Hell, *I* could feel it.

The beat of the drums was deep, pulsing, pounding through all of us. It rattled our bones and warmed our blood, and even *I* would have been weak in the knees if those three Merrows pressed their bare skin against mine.

I wiped the back of my sleeve against my forehead, blaming the blazing circle of fire in front of us for the temperature increase in the room.

"Don't you feel alive?" Periwinkle Lashes pressed, toying with one of Xavier's curls.

"Don't you feel inspired?" Indigo twirled her finger around Xavier's chain.

"I do," Syrena blurted, whirling on her heel to face the four.

Three pairs of blue eyes and one green shifted to her.

Syrena's expression was so abnormally tranquil that no one

bought it for a second. "Personally, I feel inspired to leave. Everyone have fun tonight."

She turned to go, but Xavier caught her elbow. "Syrena, wait—"

"I *said*," Syrena snapped, ripping her arm from his grasp, "have *fun*. I want you to."

Her glare was so intense Xavier shuffled backwards in alarm.

"Really?" he asked, squinting at her.

"Yes." Syrena took a deep breath and smoothed her hair before gesturing to the Merrows looking on. "They seem like lovely girls. Go. Enjoy yourself."

"But—"

"*Go,*" Syrena spat, the fire in her eyes flaring. "I don't care. Good night."

Without another word, she stomped through the crowd, pushing a nearby Nether out of her way so gruffly it tumbled to the ground.

Ilora mumbled something to Tallys, and both of them hurried after Syrena, leaving me and Xavier alone with the Merrows.

"What do you say now that you have your lover's approval?" Indigo asked, tugging Xavier's gold chain, causing it to tighten slightly around his throat.

He licked his lips, finally allowing his gaze to move lower. "She's not my lover."

"No?" Sky Blue asked innocently. "Not even once?"

"No." Xavier gulped as Periwinkle threaded more fingers through his hair. "Well... She kissed me once."

I acted distracted with a thread on the bust of my dress but angled my head so I could hear better.

"When?"

"Last year." Xavier groaned in appreciation as Periwinkle tightened her grip. "Right after we came here the first time."

"Nothing ever came of it?"

"No," Xavier panted, whether from Indigo yanking the chain on his neck taut or Sky Blue teasing the button on his trousers, it wasn't clear. "And we never mentioned it again."

Rattling shells joined in with the pounding of the drums, and the temperature in the room swelled.

"Then you're free to embrace your..." Periwinkle glanced between Xavier's legs, her eyebrows rising appreciatively. "Inspiration."

Xavier's gaze darted to me, but all I could do was shrug helplessly.

"I suppose I can't argue with that logic." Xavier adopted his signature grin. "Promise not to drown me?"

"Promise," Sky Blue cooed, dragging him by his waistband as she backed into the crowd. "But I can't promise we won't get close."

"I'll risk it," Xavier conceded, disappearing from sight just as the three women feverishly descended on him.

I exhaled slowly.

*Godsdamned drums.*

I looked around the room, my heart continuing to race as I was hit with the sinking realization I was alone. One of the winged beasts on the wall swooped off a nearby spike and lunged for a boar on a spit, the force of its wings pushing a gust of air into my face and forcing me a step back. My back collided with something warm and solid.

"What's the matter?" a sinister voice rumbled. "Not scared, are you?"

I spun, coming face-to-face with a pair of golden eyes.

The gray-haired Weir I'd seen earlier stood in front of me, irises reflecting the torchlight while his hands gripped my shoulders to steady me. His touch felt anything but supportive.

I wriggled free and moved further away from him. "I'm fine. Just startled."

The Weir sidled forward, his gaze lingering uncomfortably long on my chest. "Have to keep your wits about you here. You never know what's lurking around the corner."

I swallowed, my fingers inching towards both my knives. "Thanks for the advice."

The Weir stepped closer, prompting me to move backwards.

"Why'd your friends leave a pretty thing like you all alone?" He cocked his head as he examined the high slits in my dress. "Don't they know it's dangerous?"

I lifted my chin to hide the way his gaze made my skin crawl. "Your prince said there wouldn't be any violence tonight."

The man laughed, flashing razor-sharp canines that could easily tear my flesh to pieces. "That's like asking a Weir not to breathe."

The man stepped forward once more, but when I tried to move away, my back hit the wall, the stone spines along its surface nudging into my skin. My eyes darted to my right and to my left, but large spikes jutted out, blocking my way. I was trapped.

Both upper and lower fangs appeared as the Weir caught wind of my plight and licked his lips. "I like a little fight in my prey. I hope you don't disappoint."

He hungrily reached forward, but there was a flash of black behind him, and something whipped through the air to catch his wrist.

"I wouldn't do that if I were you," a deep voice warned. "Not if you'd like to keep that limb."

Hale strode out from behind The Weir, one hand casually

tucked in his pocket while the other remained locked on the man's arm. The Nether wrenched free from Hale's grasp, his top lip curling into a contemptuous sneer that showcased his fangs. "What are you going to do, *Your Highness*? Cut it off?"

"No." Hale's gaze flicked to me. "*She* will, while I watch. Then I'll take the other one for fun."

A grating rumble started in the Weir's throat, resembling a dog's growl, but Hale just stared back with an amused expression, like the idea of someone challenging him was a joke. Knowing what the power coursing through his veins could do in the blink of an eye, it practically was.

The Weir must have had the same realization, because he huffed in frustration and turned to retreat.

Quick as lightning, a tendril of black bloomed from Hale's back and shot forward, coiling around the Weir's neck like a noose. The man froze, his body going rigid as the dark mist extended to caress his cheek in a silky, taunting threat.

"Apologize to the lady," Hale commanded, casually examining his nail beds.

Another growl rolled in the Weir's throat, but he begrudgingly peeked back at me and mumbled under his breath, "My apologies."

Again he turned to go, but Hale's darkness swept upwards, swirling around the Weir's nose and prodding menacingly at his lips.

Hale shook his head, chuckling softly. "I don't think you understand." Taking his time, he stalked up to the Weir and folded his arms as he pressed his face close to the man's ear.

"You," he hissed, enunciating each word clearly, "are going to get on your knees and beg for her forgiveness."

My heart raced as the Weir hesitated. Or maybe it was pounding because of the music, keeping pace with the shells as they rattled faster in tandem with the drums.

After a few tense, hair-raising seconds, the Weir slowly lowered to the ground, glaring up at Hale the whole way.

"Good boy," Hale crooned, a smug smile twitching at his lips. "Now *beg*."

The Weir shook with rage and humiliation, but nevertheless his eyes shot to me and narrowed, the gold in them glinting as the firelight flickered in his pupils. "I sincerely apologize for my inappropriate behavior, miss. Please forgive me."

Without waiting for my response, the Weir went to stand, but in another flash Hale was by his side, kicking him back to the ground and pinning the man's neck with his foot. I clapped a hand over my mouth to keep from crying out in surprise.

"Maybe you didn't hear me." Hale's voice was steady, his movements unhurried, and his eyes devoid of emotion despite the way he was furiously grinding his heel into the Weir's skin. The man choked and sputtered, turning an unnatural shade of red from the lack of air.

Hale propped one elbow on his knee as he bent to look into the whites of the Weir's wild eyes. "I *said*... beg for your fucking life."

He lifted his foot just enough for the Weir to raise his head and pant, "I'm sorry! I'm so sorry! I made a mistake, it won't happen again! Please!"

Hale clicked his tongue. "I'm not sure I believe you."

Then he stomped his foot back down, trapping the Weir on the ground once more. The man coughed and flailed frantically, his face changing from red to purple.

I stepped forward, glancing nervously between the two of them. "Hale, I think he gets the point."

But Hale didn't look at me. His eyes stayed fixed on the Weir beneath him.

"Hale," I said again, this time louder, "that's enough."

Still he ignored me.

His darkness swirled around the Weir like sharks circling a capsizing vessel, waiting for the right moment to dart in for the kill.

"Hale!" I shouted. "Stop!"

Hale blinked, his gaze finally breaking from the Weir. He looked up at me with a bewildered expression. When the Weir let out a desperate wheeze, Hale glanced down as if seeing him for the first time and hurriedly removed his weight, allowing the man to scramble to his feet and lope into the crowd.

When he'd gone, Hale shook his head and gingerly rubbed his eyes.

"I'm sorry," he mumbled. "That was... that was fucked up. I don't know what came over me."

I hesitated for a moment, unsure which part of my heart I wanted to listen to. One part of it told me I knew this man, that I'd danced with him in the shadows and given him flowers from my hair and held his hand a little too long while he talked about his pain. But the other part was telling me this man had become something else entirely while he'd been here, and now he was nothing but a wild animal that had finally been let out of its cage, one that would bite me if I wasn't careful.

I took a tentative step closer. "It was probably just these damn drums inspiring you."

The steady beat was pounding in my legs, abdomen, and chest, bringing warmth with every pulse. My breaths were already shallow as they kept time with the beat, but when Hale's gaze met mine again, I almost stopped breathing entirely.

The world faded away as we stared at each other until there was nothing left except him and the drums.

"I'm sorry about last night." Hale's words were barely audible over the thundering melody. His eyes stayed fixed on me, guilt heavy in his gaze. "I shouldn't have acted the way I did."

I licked my lips and ran my slick palms over the thin fabric shielding my thighs. "I'm sorry too."

Sweat was beading at the back of my neck and between my breasts, and one glance at the dark prince's bare chest confirmed his skin was doing the same.

The bones and shells clacked faster.

Slowly, Hale extended his hand. "Dance with me."

My breath caught again.

Hale closed the distance between us. "Finally have that dance with me, Lina Calder."

An uneasy laugh bubbled out of me. "I don't know how to dance to music like this."

"I'll show you."

My skin tingled at Hale's touch as he slid his fingers into mine. Keeping his eyes glued to my face, he backed towards the fire, the crowd parting behind him to let us through. Nethers turned to watch us as we passed. I should've been riddled with anxiety at their attention, and any other time I would have been, but Hale's grip was an anchor for my emotions.

We strode through the outer circle of musicians, the cave floor rumbling beneath our feet as they played with passionate vigor. As we neared the fire, the air around us quivered from the heat rising off the flames. It only increased the closer we came, causing loose strands of hair to stick to the sharp lines of Hale's cheekbones and jaw. Despite the noise and the heat, his eyes never left mine.

When we arrived in front of the smoldering remnants of Aedan's demonstration of power, *our* power, the Nethers already dancing there made space for us. They paid us no mind as they yipped and chittered and whirled with erratic movements. There was no pattern or flow to their dance, but somehow every leap and bend and twist fit perfectly with the melody.

Hale stopped and ran his fingers up the back of my arm, urging it to lift and drape around his shoulders. His other hand found my hip and guided it closer, bringing our bodies flush. I wasn't sure if the pulsing between my legs was from the drums or my own carnal desire, which was becoming more and more evident the longer I stared into those deep dark eyes.

"Don't listen to the music," Hale directed me, delicately tracing his fingertips down my side until they joined his other hand at my hips. "Just focus on how it makes you feel. Then let your body follow."

Slowly, he moved us side to side. His hips brushed mine at every pass, and soon it became the only thing I could think about, the clamor of the instruments nothing but a dull roar in my ears. Somehow I could still hear Hale breathing, the air wavering in and out through his nose as he fought to keep his breaths steady. When I slipped my other arm around his neck with the first, he exhaled sharply, then slid his hands around my waist and pulled me in tighter.

I had to bite my lip to keep from moaning at the movement, and my heart beat as frenzied as the drums. I wove my fingers into the damp hair at the nape of Hale's neck, causing him to groan and lower his face to graze his nose along my ear and the side of my neck. The move sent a shiver across my molten skin.

The drums swelled, our swaying increasing speed to follow. One of Hale's hands trailed up and down my spine while the other dared to sink a little lower, inching towards my tailbone and the curve of my backside. A reluctant voice in my head told me to stop, that I had to remember who I was pretending to be and what I was here for.

*You're an ambassador. A pregnant lover bearing her king's heir.*

But my body and soul were screaming for more contact, more heat, more *Hale*, and they drowned the words out.

As another layer of clacking bones added to the symphony around us, I changed direction, rolling my hips forward instead of side to side. Hale instantly matched it, angling his body so his knee was wedged between my legs. Moisture was gathering there, but I was unsure if it was from the external heat or what was happening inside. I didn't care. Hale pressed against me perfectly, creating a delicious ache that was all-consuming, and it was impossible to stop.

Hale glanced down at where I straddled his leg, the high slit in my dress leaving one thigh completely bare save for the black blade strapped there. The sight of his blade on my body had Hale hissing an expletive.

"You're so fucking beautiful," he whispered, grinding harder against me.

A moan accidentally leapt from my mouth, to which Hale responded by pulling us apart and spinning me around so my back was pressed against him. His hands caught my hips again, and his face nuzzled the crook of my neck as we continued our rolls forward and back. My core throbbing in time with the drums, I shut my eyes and leaned my head back against Hale to savor the beat, the heat, and the way his rapidly hardening cock was grinding against my ass. Every inch of me was on fire with desire, quaking at Hale's touch as his hands lazily explored my abdomen and upper thighs. One of his thumbs grazed the underside of my breast while his other hand skated dangerously close to the vertex of my legs, the pressure from the hard outline of his signet ring eliciting another moan from deep inside me. I was panting now, and so was he, our bodies perfectly in time with the feverish rhythm. When Hale couldn't help himself any longer and pressed a slick kiss to the side of my neck, my hands developed a mind of their own and grappled behind me for the front of his trousers. I opened my eyes for a split second, only to catch a glimpse of Aedan on the dais, staring at us with a triumphant smirk.

A tidal wave of realization crashed over me, jerking me from my haze of lust and reminding me where I was.

I dropped my hands from Hale's waistband. "We need to stop."

Hale's mouth continued to graze my skin, his tongue undeterred by the layer of sweat blanketing it. Forcing myself to ignore how weak in the knees that tongue made me, I caught his hand just before it dipped between my legs and ripped it away.

"Hale, stop!"

I spun out of his hold, putting space between us because I didn't trust myself to be close. Hale stared at me for a few beats, then furiously blinked and buried his head in his hands.

"I'm sorry," he muttered. "I don't know what I was... I didn't mean..." He sighed and rubbed his eyes. "Will you excuse me?"

Without another word, he pushed into the crowd.

"Hale, wait!" I called after him.

I shouldered my way through the Nethers, struggling to keep up in the sea of writhing black the room had turned into. I glimpsed Hale's form heading towards the entrance of a nearby tunnel, furiously ripping the crown from his head and dropping it to the sand before storming inside. Ducking my head to avoid being decapitated by an intoxicated Nether's flailing claw, I darted after him.

When I passed into the cave, my eyes took a few seconds to adjust to the dimmer light. When they did, I caught sight of Hale's form disappearing into the dark at the other end.

"Hale!" I shouted again, the echo of my voice chasing him. "Talk to me, please!"

"There's nothing to talk about," he called back. "I'm going to bed. I have a headache."

I broke into a run to catch up with him. "I know that's not true!"

"Yes, it is."

I was on his heels now, and by lunging forward and reaching out, I caught his shoulder and pulled him to a stop.

"Just talk to me!"

"What the fuck do you want me to say, Lina?" Hale snapped, whirling and taking a threatening step forward so he loomed over me. "Do you want me to say it feels so fucking wrong not being able to touch you? Because it does."

My racing heart skipped a beat.

His mouth tight with tension, Hale breathed sharply through his nose, working hard to control his emotions. "I dreamed of you every single night I've been here. Horrible dreams. Every single night I saw you and heard you, but I couldn't fucking touch you, and it made me crazy. Then one day you *were* here, standing in my bedroom like a dream come true, so beautiful I didn't even think you were real, but I still can't fucking touch you?"

Tears stung my eyes at the pain bursting through the cracks in his facade.

Hale sighed and raked his fingers through his hair, slicking the sweat-drenched strands away from his eyes only to have one flop back again. "I'm happy you're happy, Lina. Truly, I am. But..." He hesitated at the vulnerability rushing to the surface, but finally swallowed hard and admitted, maybe for the first time, "I'd be lying if I said being around you didn't hurt. I'm no stranger to pain, so I thought I could handle it, but I don't think I can. And I... I just think I need to stay away from you until it stops hurting so much."

I ducked my head, thinking that might keep him from

seeing the tears, but I should have remembered there was no escaping Hale's ever watchful eye. Gently, he lifted my chin so I was looking up at him, and with one quick swipe of his thumb he wiped them away.

"I never wanted to hurt you," I said miserably.

Hale gave me a sad smile. "I never thought you could. I didn't even think I was capable of someone having this power over me. For my sake, for my *sanity*, I'm begging you, Lina." He caressed my cheek, agony coating his voice. "Please, just let me go."

"I can't."

"You can. Just focus on the negotiations with Aedan, then you can go back to Soren and—"

"I left Soren."

Hale froze.

In the distance the beat still thrummed, but it was drowned out by the pounding of my own heart.

"Over a month ago," I added in a hoarse whisper.

A tense silence followed.

Finally, Hale's face darkened.

"Did he hurt you?" he asked, deadly calm. Like the stillness before the violence of a hurricane.

I thought back to the way Soren had refused to be honest with me, and the way I'd covered up my own hurt and doubt by unleashing everything I'd kept bottled for months.

"We hurt each other," I said softly, a vicious pang of loss shooting through my heart at the realization. "But that wasn't the reason. It broke our hearts, but we were doomed from the start, and I think deep down we both knew it."

Hale's gaze dipped to my belly. "The baby?"

"A lie we made up to ensure Aedan didn't harm us. Threat of Soren's wrath kept him at bay."

Hale stepped backwards, a slow exhale puffing from his lips.

"I'm sorry," I croaked, tears blurring my view of him. "I wanted to tell you, but we all agreed to only trust each other, and I wasn't sure how you—"

"You're telling me," Hale rasped, "that I could have kissed you this entire time?"

It was my turn to freeze.

Hale's stare bored into me, his breath stuck in his throat the way mine was.

Somehow, I managed to gasp out a single word.

"Yes."

The silence stretched on, growing heavier each second. Hale's expression betrayed nothing, but his chest heaved faster, and his hands clenched into fists over and over at his sides. I fidgeted under his stare, nervously tearing at a hangnail while I waited.

"Hale, say something!" I finally blurted.

He didn't.

Instead, he closed the distance between us, grabbed my face, and hauled my lips to his.

# Chapter 39



IN THAT MOMENT, NOTHING EXISTED EXCEPT HALE'S KISS.

I melted into him, my knees threatening to buckle, but Hale kept me upright, holding me in place as his tongue swept into my mouth and explored with luxurious strokes that set my core on fire. On instinct, my hips responded by feverishly grinding into him. Hale retaliated by flattening my back against a nearby moonstone pillar and pressing his body to mine, rolling it forward and back in rhythm with his lapping tongue. I moaned against his mouth and slid my fingers under the sheer material covering his shoulders to dig my nails into the clammy skin of his back. One of Hale's hands slipped lower, grasping at my breasts and hips and cupping my ass before dragging one of my legs up and hooking it around his waist. He broke the kiss and found the sensitive skin at my neck instead, licking and sucking until I was a quivering, gasping mess in his arms. I buried my fingers in his hair, holding him close and reveling in his heat against my own.

Hale pulled his lips away from my skin and pressed his

forehead to mine, his pupils aglow with the light of the algae clinging to the pillar at my back.

"I need you," he panted. "Right now."

At my eager nod, Hale grabbed my hand and pulled me from the shadows, headed in the direction of his bedroom.

"There you are."

The voice surprised both of us, and we spun, Hale instinctively hurling himself in front of me while my hand surged towards Soren's dagger.

Erith emerged from the darkness, one eyebrow quirked in amusement as she twirled Hale's discarded crown around her finger.

"You know," she purred, nodding to the crystal circlet, "I'm starting to think you don't appreciate this. You keep leaving it lying around."

Hale snatched the crown from her hand. "Do you need something?"

"No." Erith casually polished the nail of her index finger against her dress, then scratched at it with her thumb. "Aedan does, though. He's looking for you."

Hale sighed, his shoulders slumping. "Can't it wait?"

"Urgent, I'm afraid." Erith wrinkled her nose in mock sympathy. "Sorry. Better hurry. I can accompany Lina to wherever it was you were going." Her eyebrow arched again, her smug smirk hinting she knew *exactly* where we were going.

Hale grunted in frustration, then turned to me and lowered his voice so Erith wouldn't hear. "Take two rights and then a left, three doors down. I'll find you as soon as I can."

His fingers subtly brushed my waist as he backed away, and he shot me one last apologetic grimace before placing the crown back on his head and jogging towards the sounds of celebration in the distance.

Erith's eyes stayed fixed on me after he left, her arms crossed and her nails tapping against her skin.

"Where *were* you two headed?" she finally asked, sweet as sugar. "Off to work on some peaceful negotiations, Ambassador?"

Ignoring the way my blood boiled at her tone, I forced a smile. "Just catching up with an old friend."

Erith chuckled, but her lips didn't lift from their frown. "That's my favorite way to catch up too."

I shifted my weight, looking casually around the darkened hallway. "Is there something you need from me, or can I be on my way?"

A few beats passed before Erith stepped closer, her heels clacking against the stone beneath our feet while her gaze slid down my body like she was analyzing a mare at market. "Let me offer you a little piece of advice."

When she stood toe to toe with me, her cold eyes lifted to mine and for a split second, the anger behind them fizzled.

"Be your own person," she stated, her voice uncharacteristically gentle. "Find yourself outside the shadow of a man. You may actually surprise yourself and discover who you really are."

"That's good advice. When are you going to take it to heart?"

Erith scoffed, her expression almost offended. "You think I *need* Aedan? He's a means to an end, one that never ceases to keep me entertained. But in the grand scheme, he's merely a pawn on a board where I'm the queen."

I tensed as she reached forward, but her finger simply hooked a strand of hair behind my ear, lingering on its rounded shell a few seconds too long.

"You should take notes. Maybe you could learn a thing or

two." Her long black nail tenderly grazed my cheek. "You'd look good as a princess dressed in black, you know."

No longer trying to hide my disdain, I lifted my chin. "I look better in red."

Erith sniffed and scanned me one more time. "Red. Of course. Like a sweet little rose."

"No. Red like blood."

A suggestion of a smile tugged at the queen's mouth as she searched my hardened gaze. "You know something? In another life, I think we could have been friends." Her head tilted. "By the way, I've been meaning to ask you... how's Wynn?"

Her smile made a full appearance then, those painted lips curling in delight as her tongue dirtied my brother's name.

My hands began to shake with the maddening desire to wrap around her throat, so I interlaced them behind my back and squeezed as hard as I could to combat the urge. "Thank you for your original offer, Erith, but I can find my own way back. Have a good night."

"Think about what I said, Lina," she called as I started down the hall. "You have the capacity to be so much more than what you are."

I stopped and glanced at her over my shoulder. "You have no idea what I am. But one day, I'd love to show you."

Then I stomped away, just as a seed of my power sprouted and manifested as two tiny black sparks in my palm.

I paced Hale's room for what seemed like hours.

The heat of the moment gone, I passed the time by nervously gnawing my nails to nubs, dipping my toes in the emerald pool, and panicking that Erith knew the details of our deception. I reminded myself over and over that just because I'd been caught sneaking off with a past flame didn't mean I couldn't *also* be a pregnant ambassador for peace. It just meant I was a cheating lover.

As I splashed my feet through the warm water of the bathing pool, I finally allowed my mind to drift to Soren, something I'd forced myself to avoid since the day I left him.

*If he were here, what would he do?*

No doubt *he'd* keep up appearances. He'd be so perfect and effortlessly charming that everyone would buy the story, and if he did eventually snap, he'd have no problem unleashing his vengeance with a terrifying demonstration of power. When I'd inevitably break down, he'd hold me tight in those sturdy arms of his, kiss the top of my head, and whisper over and over that I was safe and loved. Then, knowing us, he'd probably bend me over the side of the bathing pool and reset my cluttered mind by distracting it with knee-weakening pleasure, something he'd done countless times in our own washroom back in Astoria.

My eyes stung at the thought of him, and at the hollow space his loss had left in my heart and soul. But remembering the promise I'd made to Syrena the day I arrived in Lerian, I refused to let myself cry over him. No matter how badly I wanted to.

He was still on mind when the door creaked open and Hale slipped in. I pulled my legs from the water and scrambled to standing.

"Is everything alright?"

Hale nodded, crossing the room, and slid his arms around my waist to pull me into a kiss. My stomach fluttered at the taste of him, but my anxiety had me pushing away.

"What did Aedan want?" I asked.

Hale ignored me and moved in for another kiss, but this one I dodged.

"Really, I want to know. What was it?"

He sighed in frustration and shifted his mouth to my neck. "It was nothing."

I shut my eyes and tried to enjoy his lips and tongue and—

A sudden sharp nip on my skin made me recoil and clap a hand to my neck. "Ow!"

Hale laughed. "What? I thought you liked it rough."

My brow wrinkled.

Hale had never bitten me before. Kissed and licked and devoured me like he was starving and I was the only thing that would satiate him? Yes. But he never bit. That was something Soren did, and even he'd never done it that hard. His nips were primal and claiming, but this just felt plain mean.

I squinted at Hale's face. The way he was staring at me... his eyes didn't have their usual intensity. There was no trace of a haunted past, or a heart that felt everything so deeply but had been forced to put up a wall over the years to protect itself. Now his eyes were just... empty.

Warily, I stepped back.

Hale reached out for me, laughing again. "What are you doing? Come here."

I ducked out of the way of his hand. "You're not him."

"What?" he asked with another laugh.

Hale never laughed this much about nothing.

I yanked Soren's dagger from its home on my right thigh and thrust it forward, pressing the blade flush against the skin on Hale's neck.

"I *said*... You're. Not. Him."

Hale stared back at me, wounded betrayal plastered across his face, but after a few seconds it morphed into an amused smirk.

"Oops," he chuckled, his voice as sickly sweet as night-blooming jasmine. "You caught me."

I stumbled backwards as Hale disappeared in a swirl of

black. When the smoke cleared, Aedan, wearing Meer's form, stood in his place, grinning like he'd come out victorious in some twisted game of hide-and-seek.

"Forgive me," he purred, smoothing a hand over his hair. "I couldn't help myself. I've been too curious, I just had to sample what has everyone in an uproar."

Suddenly I was back in another time, practically another life, fighting off violent men who'd tried to take a piece of me just like this.

Squaring my shoulders to disguise the remnants of fear the memories pulled up, I shoved my dagger back in its sheath.

"You're sick," I hissed, gruffly knocking Aedan's shoulder as I stormed towards the door.

"Oh, don't be like that," he called after me. "If you can be a little naughty, so can I. Your secret's safe with me, by the way. I won't tell your beloved silver-tongue all the dirty things you've gotten up to with my prince."

His laugh followed me into the hall. It haunted me after I'd slammed the door shut, after I'd miraculously found my way back to the common room, and even after I shuffled inside and found Ilora on the couch, stroking Syrena's hair as she sobbed pitifully in her lap.

Ilora looked up, noting my shaking hands and the tears in my own eyes, and with a bittersweet smile, she offered me her free arm. I sniffled and crossed to my friends, snuggling into the crook of Ilora's shoulder just as the first salty drop fell.

"You want to talk about it?" Ilora asked gently.

I miserably shook my head.

"Men," Syrena answered for me, the word uttered with too much contempt and pain for it to be solely about my situation.

I sighed and shut my eyes. "Yes. Men."

# Chapter 40



Hale had returned to his room only to find it empty.

His heart had sunk to his stomach at the sight, and hundreds of worst-case scenarios about what had happened to Lina filled his mind, but when he'd rushed out into the hall, ready to burn the whole godsdamned world down in search of whoever had harmed her, he came across Tallys. She'd been huddled in a darkened doorway, waiting for him, so one with the shadows she was practically invisible to the untrained eye. It seemed both she and Hale shared the skill of stealth, a trait no doubt inherited from their fathers.

Tallys informed Hale that Lina was safe with the other women in their room, but that she'd seemed frazzled and upset when she left. Hale thanked her for the information, then offered her the safety of his bedroom while he was gone so she could wait out the night's adrenaline-fueled festivities. The poor woman was so thankful she had tears in her eyes. As Hale left her, he shuddered at the thought of what had befallen her in the past. He'd only heard stories, but they were enough to turn his stomach.

Hale's heart pounded as he raised a fist to knock at the door. Faint voices talked among themselves on the other side. Hale could make out Syrena's clipped tone and Ilora's motherly one, but Lina's was absent. He knew she was there, though. Somehow, he just knew.

Three loud raps, then Hale stepped back. The voices inside fell silent. There was the scuffle of movement, but no one answered.

Hale sighed, his heart still pounding. And his head. Gods, his head hurt.

He groaned and readjusted the obsidian circlet, hoping it would provide some relief, but the pain remained, pulsing behind his eyes and shooting down the tight muscles of his neck.

"Lina, I know you're in there," Hale barked, then flinched at his tone. He hadn't meant for it to come out so gruff. He wasn't thinking, and the events of the night had left his mind scrambled. Plus the pulsing behind his eyes was getting sharper. Gods, this stupid fucking crown.

Hale grunted and ripped off the crystal halo, easing the ache only slightly. He sighed and pulled off the sheer black robe and signet ring too, then rubbed at the charcoal around his eyes. The whole getup made him feel like a fraud anyway, but with the night in shambles, it had never looked more like a bad costume. He tried speaking to the door again, this time softer.

"Lina, what's wrong?"

Still no answer, but Hale thought he could make out Ilora's voice whispering, "What should we do?"

Hale pushed his face closer to the door and flattened his palm against it. "I'm sorry I left you alone, Lina. I should have told Erith that Aedan could wait, but..." He trailed off. But what?

But he feared Aedan? He felt indebted to him? He'd become attached to this place and these people and this new role he'd been given?

All pieces of the murky, convoluted truth.

Hale sighed again and leaned his forehead against the door. "Lina, I'm sorry. Please, just let me in so we can talk."

There was a tense moment of silence, and in it, Hale allowed himself the freedom to hope. But then the deadbolt locked, followed by a rustling at his feet, and when Hale glanced down, a blanket wedged between the crack at the base of the door and the ground.

It was to keep his darkness from slipping in and watching them the way it had in Lerian all those months ago.

Hale's shoulders sagged as he shifted his back to the door and slid to the ground. He leaned his head against the wood and shut his eyes, trying to figure out exactly how he continued to fuck up so badly. His head still ached some, and it made thinking too hard about anything feel daunting. So instead he gingerly massaged the tender muscles on his neck and shoulders to release some of the tension. Not long after, the wet slap of feet and sloshing of water-logged silk caused him to open his eyes.

Xavier trudged up from the depths of the hallway, his skin marred with hickeys and his hair dripping. He stopped in his tracks when he saw Hale, eyes darting between him and the door before he nodded knowingly.

"Women, am I right?"

Hale grunted in response.

Xavier waddled over, splattering Hale as he went, and firmly banged a fist on the door.

"It's Xavier!" he called. "Let me in."

An indignant scoff sounded from behind the wood,

followed by the distant slam of one of the bedroom doors. Syrena's, Hale assumed.

"That's what I thought." Xavier sighed and retreated to the ground beside Hale, who watched him wring water from his trousers out of the corner of his eye.

"Merrows?" Hale asked.

"Uh-huh."

"They try to drown you?"

"Uh-huh." A shrug, and then, "They said it was an accident."

"It wasn't."

"I know."

"Was it worth it?"

A moment of hesitation as Xavier's eyes darted to the door again. "Yes."

"You sure about that?"

Another moment of hesitation before Xavier sighed and slumped against the wall.

Hale angled so he could look him straight on. "What's going on between you and Syrena anyway?"

"Nothing," the younger man replied far too quickly.

"I don't care," Hale assured him. "All the feelings I ever had for her—"

"Seemed to melt away when you met Lina?"

Hale blinked. He opened his mouth, then shut it, then opened it again before promptly closing it. All the while Xavier just stared at him, a suggestion of a smile at the right corner of his mouth.

"I'm not stupid," he said softly. "A lot of people assume I am because I'm young and I like to joke around. But I see things." He turned his attention to a loose gold chain dangling around his neck and toyed with the ends absentmindedly. "I see the way you look at her, how you've always looked at her. From that very first moment I brought her through the war camp. It's the same way Soren does. Like you've been raised in the dark and she's your first sunrise."

Hale swallowed and averted his eyes, fighting the panic rising in his chest at how on display he was. His whole life he'd found protection and solace in the shadows, but here he was, out in the open with a stranger shining light on his heart, revealing things not even Hale had realized until now.

He anxiously rubbed at the scar on the back of his hand. It hadn't been obscured by gloves since the day he came to the Netherworld, but sometimes he still thought about wearing them. That way, he wouldn't have to see the damned thing. Wouldn't have to see that fucking word, *demon*, over and over. Wouldn't have to remember the torment it had caused him or all those years of loneliness even though he'd been surrounded by people.

"He really loves her?" Hale croaked, his throat tight for a reason he couldn't quite put his finger on.

Xavier nodded. "They love each other. More than anyone I've ever seen."

A pang of jealousy cut through Hale's chest. "How come she left him, then?"

Xavier jerked, clearly thrown by Hale's knowledge of the truth, but he soon composed himself and looked to the ceiling for inspiration. "Because... because they love each other so much it makes them feel *too* much, and they don't know how to handle it. They're too similar. Two flames with no water to quell them, and when it's good it's great, but when it's bad..." He smirked and shrugged. "Well, when it's bad, Lina runs away and tries to sneak into the Netherworld all by herself."

Hale let out a low chuckle and shook his head. "Of course she did."

"Of course she did," Xavier snickered.

When their laughter died down, Hale was content to sit in the silence, but the longer they were quiet, the more agitated Xavier became. Eventually, he burst.

"I owe you an apology."

Hale peeked over at him. "For what?"

"I was unkind to you the day we met."

"Everyone was unkind to me."

"That doesn't make it acceptable." Xavier swallowed and set his jaw, squaring his shoulders and lifting his head high. In this moment, he looked less like a boy and much more like a man. "I was afraid, and I judged you before I knew you. I of all people should know better. People judge me all the time." He frowned. "Low-caste scum, Soren's loyal dog... I got used to the taunts over the years, so I forgot how much words can hurt. I'm ashamed of the way I treated you, and I understand if you never forgive me for it, but I sincerely hope you will. You're a good man. An honorable man. I'm sorry I wasn't one back."

Again, there was that tightness in Hale's throat, and he had to look away from Xavier's earnest green eyes to make it return to normal. "I think you're the first person who's ever said anything like that to me."

"Soren would say the same."

Assuming that statement was some kind of sick joke, Hale forced a laugh.

"I'm serious," Xavier insisted. "He and I talked about it."

A wary, jaded voice in Hale's mind scoffed at the idea, but despite himself, he met Xavier's gaze again.

"Lina grieved for you a long time. She holed herself away so she could work through everything. She does that sometimes." He motioned pointedly to the door. "When she was working through losing you, she did it by herself, in her own time, and sometimes there was nothing more Soren could do for her than let her be. But he had things he needed to work through too.

And that's where best friends come in." Xavier smiled and shrugged. "He admitted to me he'd been wrong about you, and he thought you were a good man. He regretted how things ended, and he especially regretted the bargain he forced you to make."

Hale sighed, his heart sinking at the mention of that fateful oath he'd stupidly agreed to. He turned his hands over and examined the pads of his fingertips, ones that could never touch Lina in the Fae realm unless her life was in danger.

"He told you about that?"

"Yes." Xavier scooted closer. "Have you told her?"

Hale sheepishly shook his head, then raised an eyebrow in Xavier's direction. "Soren didn't tell her either?"

"No. Everyone thought you were dead. It seemed pointless to bring up the past."

Hale nodded, balling his hands into fists. "I probably would have done the same. Maybe the king and I aren't so different after all."

Xavier grinned, playfully nudging Hale with his elbow. "Now you're starting to see what I do."

They chuckled again, and the world around them went silent, not even the drums audible in the distance. After a while, Xavier hung his head and cleared his throat, his voice taking on a serious timbre that was very much out of character for him.

"She kissed me once."

Hale caught his eye.

"Syrena," Xavier clarified. He went back to toying with the gold chain, nervously tying its ends into a knot. "When you brought down the mountain last year, it flooded the surrounding valley. We had to climb into these trees to get out of the way, and the one Syrena and I were in started falling down. I'd lost so much blood, I barely remember it. I was woozy, and everything was foggy, but I think... I think I remember telling her that dying by her side would be an honor, and my only regret in life was not kissing her when I had the chance. When the tree cracked, she grabbed me by the collar, shook me, and made me swear the next time I kissed her, it would be special. The last thing I remember is her lips on mine before everything went black, and when I woke up it was days later. I was in a healer's tent, and she'd already returned home. The day I saw her at Ilora's coronation in Merimaya, she acted like nothing had happened. Part of me wondered if I'd imagined the whole thing and it was nothing but a hallucination from the blood loss. But then I started noticing the way she'd watch me out of the corner of her eye, and how she'd get angry if I didn't look back at her, or gods forbid I looked at a different woman. But she never said anything, and was never willing to let me get a word in either, so... I guess that's it. It was just something that happened in the heat of the moment, nothing more."

He sighed heavily and ran a set of fingers through the tangles of his damp curls. Then, almost to himself, he added, "No matter how many times you replay it in your head, sometimes it just doesn't mean anything at all."

Hale watched the young man a few seconds more, tracking the way his fingers fiddled with the golden chain, the muscles in his jaw twitching as he clenched his teeth, and the bump on his throat bobbing as he swallowed. Hale knew these symptoms very well, had displayed them himself for too many years.

This poor man was under the spell of Syrena of Lerian, a painful, maddening, intoxicating magic that was near impossible to break. Impossible, that is, unless he miraculously found a Lina Calder of his own to shake him awake.

Hale thought for a moment before inching closer and cautiously nudging Xavier with his elbow. "Hey."

Xavier peeked up at him, trying not to look vulnerable but not quite succeeding.

"I've known Syrena for a long time," Hale stated. "She's at war with herself. Who she was raised to be and who she wants to be are two different women. She chooses the first woman more often than not because it's instinct, and it's easy, and it's what people expect from her. But that's not who she really is. Deep down, she knows that. And I think it kills her to deny her true self. But that just proves how strong she is. She kills herself,over and over, day after day, and she does it with a cutting smile to pretend it doesn't hurt her. But I'm not so sure that's the case."

Xavier's brow furrowed. "What's your point?"

"My point is... you're *not* stupid. And if you feel something there, then... trust that. Don't lose hope."

Xavier considered Hale's words, then leaned his head back against the wall and shut his eyes to ruminate on them.

Maybe it was poor advice and Hale had just condemned the boy to more heartbreak, but he hoped all the sidelong glances he'd caught Syrena giving Xavier over the past few days actually *did* mean something.

Because she'd never acted like that with him, or with anyone for that matter. Not even a charming, silver-tongued prince a hundred years prior.

———————

The door had to open eventually.

I would have been content to keep it closed forever, but we had to let Xavier in at some point even though Syrena vehemently argued against it. Ilora, however, finally persuaded us to unlock the deadbolt the following morning, and when we did, Xavier sheepishly slipped inside while Hale, who had stayed in the hall with him all night, stood on the threshold.

"Can we please talk?" he asked earnestly, his gaze so intense it burned like fire.

I went to shut the door again, but Syrena caught the handle to keep it from closing.

"Lina," she chided, her voice shockingly similar to my mother's when I'd get in trouble as a child. "The silent treatment solves nothing."

"Tell that to yourself," I hissed back, angling my chin towards Xavier's room.

Syrena smiled sweetly and opened the door wider. "Do as I say, not as I do."

I was wrong. She sounded *identical* to my mother.

At Ilora's firm nod of agreement, I sighed, straightened my shoulders, and stepped out into the hall.

"What?" I asked, rubbing my arms as a shiver rattled my body. I'd changed into something more comfortable to sleep in, and now my thigh-high knit stockings and Soren's oversized shirt were doing nothing to fight the chill of the drafty corridor. I wanted to be back inside, huddled under a cozy blanket and hiding from the world's problems as soon as possible.

"Can we please talk?" Hale repeated calmly. He hadn't changed yet, but he'd discarded most of his ensemble in a pile on the floor and stood in front of me in nothing but his trousers. There were dark circles under his eyes, and his hair was ruffled from a night of obvious unrest.

"How can I be sure it's really you?" I barked, my voice betraying me and wavering with emotion. I thought with all the tears I'd spilled last night, I'd worked through everything, but apparently I was wrong.

Hale's brows nudged together in confusion. "What are you talking about?"

I sniffled and wiped my nose with the back of my hand, forcing my words steady. "Tell me something only you would know."

Hale squinted quizzically. "What?"

"Tell me," I repeated through gritted teeth, "something only you, *Hale*, would know and someone else, like *Aedan*, wouldn't."

"Why?"

"Just do it."

Hale huffed an exhale and yanked a hand through his hair. "Alright.... you put a yellow crocus in my jacket on the spring equinox last year."

"You used your power that night. Aedan could have been looking through it and seen that."

Hale sighed and raised his eyes to the roof of the moonstone tunnel above us, searching it like a map. "You... you were wearing men's clothing the first time we met, a shirt that was too big for you and baggy pants. Except your shoes. Your shoes were gray satin, and had little pearls on them."

I hesitated for a moment, my heart fluttering that he'd noticed something as minuscule as my shoes. But Hale had been trained to observe everything. He was a guard with a keen eye, one who picked up on anything and everything, even someone's footwear.

"Syrena and Kaspar were meeting with Soren that day," I countered. "We were in his war camp. No doubt you were using your power to keep an eye on things in case there was any trouble. And there was. You alerted us to the Nethers in the distance. So you *were* using it, weren't you?"

Hale winced and rubbed the back of his neck. "Yes, I was."

"So Aedan could've been peering through you then too."

"Lina, what's this about?"

"Just answer me." I tucked my shaking hands in the crooks of my arms. "Tell me something only the two of us would know. Something that happened when you weren't using your power."

Hale watched me for a few seconds, his stare so searing that my heart picked up speed. That alone should have proved to me he was who he said, but then he spoke.

"When we rode back from Merimaya after Imbolc, you thought Soren was dead," he said softly. "You were so overcome with grief that you'd start falling off your horse. I had to keep catching you and setting you upright again. I wanted to ride with you to hold you in place, but I felt you needed space."

My breath hitched.

Hale licked his lips before continuing. "When we returned, you stayed locked in your room for six days, and for six days I would pass by your door every hour and listen for your breath on the other side to make sure you were still alive. Not because Syrena or Kaspar ordered it, but because I wanted to. And I... I missed you."

My knees started to tremble.

"And..." Hale's eyes lifted to mine, the crude symbol burned across his throat dipping as he swallowed. "After the attack on the spring equinox, when we shared a bottle of wine and you called my darkness beautiful, you later got on your knees, looking up at me with the most eager, lust-filled look I'd ever seen, and I told you to worship me. And when you did, you did it fucking flawlessly."

I exhaled sharply, my insides now quivering in time with my legs.

"Alright," I breathed. "You're you."

"Why wouldn't I be?"

I opened my mouth to speak, but paranoia took over and I eyed the shadowy passageways on either side of us. When it came to Aedan, there was no such thing as too careful.

"We need somewhere private," I declared.

At the urgency in my face, Hale nodded without hesitation and beckoned for me to follow.

I kept close on his heels through the winding hallways until we arrived at the black tourmaline doors of his bedroom. Hale hauled them open and gestured inside, and after one last cautious look over my shoulder, I entered.

"Alright," Hale said, shoving the doors closed behind us, "what's going on?"

I wrung my hands, taking a moment to admire his calm expression before I destroyed it. I was about to set fire to everything he'd come to know and love about his new king, but I had no choice. This wasn't the same game anymore. Aedan was playing dirty, and it was time to let Hale in.

It was finally time for the truth.

I shut my eyes and took a deep breath. "Last night, when you went to find Aedan, he found me first. He came to your room pretending to be you."

Hale let out a single stunned laugh. "Why would he do that?"

"Because he was trying to trick me into sleeping with him."

Hale stepped back like an invisible foe had just socked him in the mouth.

"He's not a good man, Hale. And no matter how much you try to talk to him or reason with him or negotiate, he will *never* be a good man. He's sadistic and power-hungry and he needs to die, which is exactly why I'm here." I stood taller. "I'm going to kill him."

Hale was looking at me like I was a stranger, and it made me want to crawl into a corner and hide.

"I thought you were here for peace," he said, betrayal thickening his voice.

"Fuck peace," I bit back.

Hale's chest rose and fell faster, his eyes narrowing into sharp slits as his shoulders shook. He looked practically feral, like a wild creature who'd been trapped in a cage, frothing at the mouth to get out. His calm voice was a delicate caress in contrast, making it all the more terrifying.

"Why the fuck didn't you tell me?"

"Because I needed to be sure you wouldn't tell Aedan."

"You think so little of me?"

"I think the world of you, Hale." I took a hesitant step forward, wanting to wrap the wild animal in front of me in my arms but wary of the way it was poised to strike. "I always have. But I also know Aedan is deceitful and manipulative and he's given you more than you could have ever dreamed of, and that kind of power is intoxicating and maddening and makes you think you can take on the world without anyone else at your side to help."

Those last words were to myself as well as him, the magic in my blood thrumming in shameful agreement.

Hale's eyes dipped to the ground, his hands clenching repeatedly into fists at his side as his body shook with restraint.

My previous bravado waned, and no matter how hard I fought it, my vision grew hazy as tears began to well.

"I'm sorry," I whispered. "I'm so sorry. I wanted to tell you. Please... please don't be mad at me—"

"I'm not," Hale barked, the punch of his voice knocking me back a step. "For fuck's sake, I'm not mad at *you*, Lina."

Before his words could entirely process, Hale turned and slammed his fist into the solid stone of the door, letting out a furious roar so loud it sent ripples over the surface of the bathing pool in the corner. I flinched, not just at the raw torment in Hale's voice but the heart-wrenching anguish written across his face. I wanted nothing more than to take away that pain, to hold him in my arms and soak it all up until there was barely a drop left.

I closed the distance between us and threw my arms around him, pressing my chest to his back as Hale rested his forehead against the door with his hands braced on either side. I held him the way Soren used to hold me when I woke screaming and sobbing from my nightmares, channeling all my strength into a loving embrace that was a fortress where, just for a moment, nothing and no one could hurt us.

Eventually Hale stopped shaking, and his breath returned to a normal rate.

"I'm so stupid," he murmured, his words muffled by the rough black stone of the door.

"You're not." I tightened my grip around his waist and

nestled my face into the scarred skin on his back. I breathed deep, relaxing into the scent of smoke and musk wafting up from it.

"I should have seen it," Hale pressed. "I should have seen *him*. Or maybe I did, and just chose not to believe it."

"But you do now, don't you?"

A heavy sigh followed. "Yes."

I released my hold on Hale as he faced me.

"I don't know if I can kill him, Lina," he muttered, shaking his head.

"You don't have to." I slid a hand to his face, cupping his cheek in my palm and gently forcing him to look me in the eyes. "I can."

I pulled up the right sleeve of my shirt, revealing the mark of glittering silver embedded above my scars. Hale's mouth parted at the symbol, quietly mumbling the word to himself before he lifted a hand to the flesh. He gently swiped his thumb over the spikes and vines and crescent moons at the center, which now made the ones seared into his own body seem a little less lonely.

"What is this?" he asked.

His fingers traced the mark, my skin prickling beneath the delicate touch of his calloused hands.

"I went to a witch, and she gave me a way to fight fire with fire." At Hale's confused expression, I continued. "It's a combination of two of the most powerful men I know, and in me, it created something to match Aedan's power."

Hale's fingertips froze on one of the silver vines. "You can change your appearance?"

"No. At least, I don't think so. I'm not entirely sure what I'm capable of yet. But what he did last night, to the fire. I've done that before. I'm still figuring out how exactly, but it's inside me. It's possible."

Hale stared in awe at the symbol a few seconds more before shaking his head. "When you go back, no one can ever see this."

"Why?"

"Because they'll say you're a witch. They'll call you—"

"Demon lover?" I chuckled. "King-slayer. Whore. Pet. What's another name? And besides..." A timid flush rushed to my cheeks. "It's true."

Hale sucked in a breath but otherwise didn't move. He only stared, a still marble statue with eyes of onyx that had embedded themselves in my soul.

"People will be cruel," he said, his voice barely a whisper.

"Yes they will. But I'm not afraid." I raised my chin. "I'm not ashamed of who I love."

Again, Hale inhaled sharply, his eyes a whirlwind of emotions. Confusion, disbelief, denial, desire, and maybe, just maybe, the smallest suggestion of love himself.

"You say that now," Hale said, his face trying and failing to keep its unfeeling mask, "but when you have hordes of people wishing you dead, you'll feel differently."

"I won't."

When he looked like he didn't believe me, I slipped my arm out of Hale's grip and lifted a hand to his face again. This time he let out a shaky exhale and nestled his cheek into my palm.

"Hale," I began, skating my thumb across his skin, "your entire life, you've had to be strong all by yourself. But you don't have to be alone anymore. Not if you don't want to."

Hale's breaths were coming in short bursts now, and he shut his eyes as he listened to my words, his brow wrinkling as he fought some vicious internal battle.

I lifted my other hand to scrape the stray hairs out of his face, letting my fingers entwine in their silky ends as I drew his forehead to mine and lowered my voice.

"I'm here now, Hale." Moisture stung my eyes, and I trembled when his arms slid around my waist to pull me close.

"I'm not going anywhere," I whispered. "Not again. Through good or bad, thick or thin, in this realm or any, I'm never letting you go. That is… if you want me."

At that, Hale's eyes fluttered open. "Lina, I've wanted you since the moment I saw you."

A tiny laugh squeezed out of me at the same time the first tear made its escape. Hale quickly wiped it away, brushing it into the hair at my crown as he took my head in his hands to make me look him in the eye.

It didn't need to be stated because we both knew, but I wanted to say it anyway.

"Then I'm yours, Hale."

"And I yours, Lina Calder. Until the dark calls me home."

More tears continued to fall, but these Hale kissed away. I'd never enjoyed crying until this moment, when each salty drop was replaced by the warmth of Hale's lips and the nuzzle of his nose. His fingers tightened as he held me close, like he was afraid I was a dream that would dissipate with the morning. I angled my lips to his, channeling all the nights spent missing him into that one kiss so he could know what it meant to me. What *he* meant to me.

Hale understood, and in answer, caught the nape of my neck in one hand, holding my mouth flush to his, while the other hand dipped behind me to grip my backside and scoop me off the ground.

I wrapped my legs around his torso as he carried me to the bed, his tongue never leaving its fervent dance with mine. When his knees hit the mattress, Hale fell forward, never breaking the kiss as he threw my back to the cool silk sheets and landed on top with effortless grace. He settled his hips between my thighs, his body and tongue moving in identical sweeps, sending heat rushing through me from the top of my head down to the tips of my toes.

Losing myself in my lust, I eagerly pressed hungry kisses across his neck and toned shoulders. He responded by hauling me to a seated position and yanking Soren's shirt over my head. The sight of my naked body had him sucking sharply through his teeth.

"Fuck," he groaned.

I leaned forward to kiss him again, but he raised a hand to the center of my chest and firmly pushed me down to the bed so I was back on display for him.

"*Fuck,*" he repeated to himself as his free hand slid up and down the curves of my body, caressing the rounded domes of my breasts and the slight line between the muscles of my abdomen. Then he slipped lower, down to the dip of my hips and the soft flesh of my upper thighs, which hours of rigorous training never seemed to have much effect on. But Hale touched me like I was the most exquisite thing he'd ever seen, clutching my form with reverence and desire, holding off to either savor the moment or drive me into delirium.

My hips instinctively lifted towards him, but Hale brought them back to the bed with a solid shove. He stared at me, chest heaving as he attempted to catch his breath, and one corner of his mouth lifted to form one of the most knee-weakening smirks I'd ever been on the receiving end of. He shook his head in a playful taunt.

I pouted at Hale's pause, impatiently reaching forward to fumble at his waistband, but he only caught my right wrist and pinned it above my head. Then he hovered his lips above mine, his whispered words hot against my skin.

"Tell me how you want me."

My insides clenched, and an involuntary whimper rose from my throat.

Hale turned his face to drag his lips across the vertical black scar along my wrist, and I couldn't help but utter a soft moan when he pressed a tender kiss to the faded impression of teeth just above it.

"I want you now," I breathed.

Hale's low chuckle vibrated against my skin, causing another pang of desire between my legs.

"That's *when* you want me, not *how* you want me." Hale moved higher, tracing his tongue along the silver symbol at the center of my forearm before firmly sucking the skin between his lips. Even though the movement was nowhere near them, my hips bucked in response. Again, Hale pushed them flat with his free hand.

I was panting with need, but Hale still took his time. He continued to work his way up my body, grazing his mouth along my upper arm, then pressing a kiss to the shoulder marred with scars from the Ben Síde. Then his lips were trailing along my collarbone and down the center of my breasts. When his tongue lapped into my navel, I jerked with pleasure, but his hand on my wrist held steady.

"Just like this," I gasped. "I want you just like this."

Hale's mouth dipped even lower, torturously teasing the skin near my clit.

"Are you sure?" he muttered into the ache.

My hips greedily wriggled towards him, every ounce of carnal flesh begging for anything he was willing to give. "Gods, yes. *Please*."

At my desperate plea, Hale released his tongue, drawing it up my center, slow and appreciative. I cried out at the sensation, throwing my head into the pillow and arching my back as pleasure shot through me. Then he did it again. And again.

Then he lapped in quick, firm circles at my most sensitive spot until my breath caught and I could do nothing but string together a chorus of deliciously tortured moans.

Just before I toppled over the edge, Hale sat upright, still keeping his grip on my right wrist with one hand while he undid the buttons on his trousers with the other. When the fabric slid off his hips he sprung free, as large and firm and mouthwatering as I remembered him. I could only stare in appreciation as he positioned himself between my thighs, so overcome with pleasure and need that words were an afterthought.

"Are you ready?"

I barely registered his question, too busy licking my lips at the sight of a slick bead pilling at the tip of his shaft.

"Lina, look at me."

I met his equally lustful gaze. With an eager nod, I took it upon myself to guide him to my opening, where he pressed in just enough to make my insides constrict with the want for more.

Hale froze, halting the welcome intrusion and forcing me to cry out in frustration.

"Please," I begged, my need for him nearly unbearable. "Please fuck me, Hale."

"Slow at first," he replied, his grip around my wrist tightening as he quivered with restraint. "I've thought about this for too long."

My skin flushed at his husky voice, and the way his eyes flicked down to our hips to watch as he inched inside me ever so slightly.

"I'm going to enjoy every..."

A little further.

"Glorious..."

Further.

"Second."

By the time he was halfway inside, I was breathing in haggard gasps. By the time he'd slid in all the way, I let out a noise that was half moan and half expletive, my center pulsing as it adjusted to his size.

"*Fuck*, you feel perfect," Hale groaned, the front pieces of his hair falling forward to tickle my cheeks. "Are you alright?"

In answer, I hooked my ankles behind him and pulled him deeper.

Hale laughed breathlessly, his dark eyes lighting up. Then he tackled my lips in a ravenous kiss before breaking away, raising up on his knees, sliding himself out almost entirely, only to crash back in.

I cried out in pleasure, then again when Hale pumped a third time, and a fourth, his deep grunts on each thrust harmonizing with my moans to create our own symphony of lust. We stayed there, stares locked, panting together as we basked in every deep, purposeful stroke, until a film of sweat had broken out across our flushed skin and filled the room with its heady scent.

Suddenly inspired, Hale pulled out of me and flipped me onto my hands and knees in one fluid motion. Then he lowered his face between my thighs and used his tongue on me the way he had before. I moaned into the pillow, my hands clutching the sheets beneath us and twisting them as I ground my hips to the rhythm Hale set. He took hold of my ass, a cheek in each hand, and squeezed to offer silent encouragement as I journeyed towards a climax. His appreciative groans vibrating against my clit only increased the tension coiling there, building just under the surface until my legs were quivering and Hale's fingers were digging into my backside to hold me in place as his tongue finished the job it had set out to do. Tension snapped and shot through my core, unraveling me from the inside out.

I was still riding the waves of the orgasm when Hale sat up on his knees and pressed himself inside me again, adding another ripple of pleasure to the shockwave. I shakily moved to prop myself up on my elbows as he fucked me from behind, but Hale's hand slid to the back of my neck and pushed me back to the pillows, holding me there to rest while he pumped into me. He was slow and sensual at first, using languid strokes so I experienced every inch, and only when I was moaning his name did he graduate in speed. He drove into me, strong and deliberate, unashamed of how or what he wanted.

His breath shifted into ragged grunts as he neared his own release, but still Hale continued his momentum, hauling me upright on my knees and holding me flush to his chest to get a better angle. His hand on the back of my neck slid forward and cupped my jaw, pulling my face to look over my shoulder so my lips could meet his, while his other hand dropped between my legs to rub circles against the still-sensitive skin. I let out a stuttering breath at his touch, one Hale shared as his tongue parted my lips and swept into my mouth.

There we stayed in a passionate embrace, tasting each other, breathing the same air, until the sensation became overwhelming and I rushed towards another fit of pleasure. My insides frantically constricted around Hale's cock, prompting him to curse through his teeth while his thrusts sped up to match the urgent circles he stroked. I lifted my arm to grasp a handful of hair at the base of his skull, holding him close as our individual pleasure swelled and toppled both of us over the edge in unison.

We collapsed forward onto the bed, our bodies still melded together, and lay there until our breathing had slowed. Then Hale pressed a kiss to my back and carefully slid out of me, falling onto his side next to me with a satisfied huff. Exhaustion quickly setting in, I peered through half-lidded eyes and swiped the hair from Hale's face so I could see it in its entirety. His stare on my skin and his branded hand resting on top of my own were the final pieces of the puzzle I needed to give in to weariness and plummet towards a well-earned slumber.

# CHAPTER 42

Hale watched Lina sleep until his own eyes couldn't stay open any longer.

When he woke again, he continued to stare, partly because she was so damn beautiful, but also because he needed to reassure himself she was real. He'd seen her too many times like this in his dreams. She'd seemed real then too, so much so he'd been certain she was actually there with him in his bed until morning came and he had to endure the torture of watching her image dissipate into nothing.

But she was here. She was actually here.

And she loved him.

Hale rolled onto his back and stared up at his reflection in the glossy obsidian ceiling, dragging his hands through his hair and shaking his head in disbelief.

This woman next to him. This beautiful, strong, brave woman loved *him*. A demon. She was willing to endure the harsh words and dirty looks and senseless, targeted violence. For *him*. Hale still couldn't fathom it, but it was making his chest hurt and his throat tight whenever he thought about it.

Fucking her had felt so good, so *right*, that despite the trials that lay ahead, Aedan and Erith and a whole realm of Nethers who would seek vengeance if their master was slaughtered, there was no place Hale would rather be than with this woman, listening to her snore softly and mumble in her sleep.

Hale leaned over and pressed a small kiss to the tip of Lina's freckle-dotted nose, smiling to himself when it twitched beneath his lips.

Once upon a time, he didn't think he was capable of love. But now, looking at her, he decided that *if* it was possible for a creature like him to fall in love, Lina Calder was the woman it would be with.

Too bad the only place they could be together was here.

Guilt weighed in the base of Hale's stomach. He should tell her about the bargain. He should have mentioned it to her when it first happened, or when she'd first arrived. But he was selfish. He'd wanted to make up for lost time by enjoying every moment with her as much as possible. And something told him a conversation starting with, *I swore a magical oath to your lover that I wouldn't touch you*, might not go over well.

Beside him, Lina stirred, and Hale quickly rolled away from her in the hopes she'd stay ignorant to the amount of time he'd spent watching her. He'd only just gotten her into his bed, he didn't want to scare her off already.

Lina's breathing changed, and movement in the bed informed Hale she was waking up and stretching her legs, the soft grunt that followed her quiet confirmation. Hale stayed still, eyes closed, and waited with bated breath to see what she would do next. Would she fall back asleep? Slip out and tiptoe back to her room? He'd never experienced sleeping in a bed beside a woman before. In his past, Hale had always done the women a favor and run off before their haze of lust cleared and regret set in as they came to terms with who, and *what*, they'd just been intimate with. So in this moment, Hale had no idea what to expect.

He especially didn't expect Lina's fingers to meet the skin on his back and gently trace the outlines of the scars she found there.

Hale swallowed. He knew exactly which ones she was touching. Her fingers ran along the divots left by two arrows that had plunged into his back as they attempted to make their escape from the Netherworld last year. Those two arrows had nearly sealed his fate, and had kept the two of them apart longer than Hale ever wanted them to be again.

When Lina's hand pulled back, he thought that was the end of it. But then warmth puffed against his skin, and a pair of lips pressed against the marks. Hale's heart and throat ached again, the sensation only increasing when Lina continued to kiss the rest of the scars scattered across his back. Ones from countless scuffles and battles, and the oldest ones, the ones that had long since grown white and faded, from the torture he'd endured as a child.

Hale rolled over to face the woman in his bed, putting an end to her gentle torture. He was worried if she continued much longer, his throat would close up entirely and he'd suffocate from her love. But if he had to go, Hale figured that was a near perfect way to do it.

Those big eyes of hers stared back at him, blue, green, gold, and amber all glittering together like jewels in a chest of treasure as Lina blinked away the final remnants of sleep from her vision.

"I've never gotten a chance to tell you how beautiful I think you are," she murmured, her morning voice raspy and by far the most seductive sound Hale had ever heard.

Lina leaned forward, nestling close to the symbol burned

into Hale's neck and pressing a delicate kiss to the moons at its center.

"Every piece of you," she mumbled against them.

Hale froze, not wanting to swallow the agonizing tightness in his throat because it might move the lips on his skin, and he wanted them to stay there for all eternity.

Lina migrated down to his chest, kissing every nick and scar she came across, and Hale hurriedly shut his eyes so she wouldn't see the moisture accumulating at their corners.

He should tell her about the bargain.

But her lips were soft and warm, and no one had ever done this. No one had ever made him feel like this.

Like he was something worth loving.

Lina's lips met the brand on Hale's lower right hip, and he had to bite his cheek and clutch the sheets to keep from jerking beneath her. It felt good, verging on divine, but he still viscerally remembered how much it had hurt to receive those burns, his screams of fear and agony doing nothing to deter the villagers as they held him down and brought the hot iron closer. They'd chosen the spots for the symbols purposefully. Hale could still hear their voices discussing it as he begged for mercy.

*Put it on his neck, so everyone will see it.*

*Put it on his hand, so anyone he touches will know what he is.*

*What if he covers them up?*

*Then put it somewhere he can't hide from anyone he tries to fuck.*

Hale squeezed his eyelids closed tighter, willing away the tears behind them. They weren't from the past. He'd stopped feeling pain for that a long time ago. These tears were for the present, for the beautiful woman who saw the villagers' marks, knew exactly what he was, and wanted him anyway.

He should tell her about the bargain.

But he couldn't. Not yet. Just a few more seconds with Lina's lips, and her hands running over his skin, and the vanilla scent wafting up from her hair.

Lina's mouth dipped lower, nearing his cock, and Hale's eyes fluttered open.

"You don't have to," he gasped out.

A radiant smile broke out across Lina's face. "You have no idea how bad I *want* to."

And with that she slipped him into her mouth and moaned at the taste of him.

Hale shut his eyes again, a deep groan accidentally rising from his chest. It felt better than he remembered, her mouth and tongue doing things he'd only ever fantasized about. Somehow she was more eager than the first time, more precise, and had him close to a climax in record time. But he wasn't finished with her yet.

Hale opened his eyes and dragged Lina off him, flipped her onto her back, and maneuvered himself between her legs. She still wore those navy blue socks that reached halfway up her thighs, just those and nothing else, but Hale made no move to take them off her. She looked like a painted masterpiece splayed open before him. Her freckled skin flushed with arousal, her breasts heaving, and her desire slick and glistening.

Gods, he could come just looking at her.

Hale grabbed both of Lina's stockings and used them to haul her legs over his shoulders as he settled onto the bed and placed wet kisses along the soft flesh of her inner thighs. She eagerly angled her clit towards him, and Hale smiled to himself before putting a hand on top of her lower belly and gently applying pressure to hold her down. The girl was so damn impatient. That would be fun to toy with one day, but today Hale was just as impatient.

The musky scent of her arousal was so fucking delicious his

mouth was watering, and when Hale's lips connected with flesh, he instantly hardened at the taste of her. She was a rich port wine; luxurious, sweet, and something Hale would happily consume every night no matter the consequences in the morning.

Lina moaned and squirmed beneath him, prompting Hale's hands to fly to the socks on her thighs and grip them tight in his fists to hold her steady. He was getting drunk on her and refused to be moved until he'd had his thirst quenched.

"Hale, I need you inside me."

Hale looked up Lina's torso at her but kept his face buried as he shook his head and lapped quicker.

Lina cried out with pleasure, her knees instinctively jerking together, but Hale yanked the stockings in his fists, dragging her legs wide again. He smiled to himself as her breath stuttered and her eyes shut as she savored his tongue.

There it was. *That* was the rhythm and pressure she liked.

Hale's cock pressed against the bed, swollen and pulsing with the need to feel her walls around it, but he made no move to get up. He'd set his sights on something, and he was going to have it.

Lina's hips moved faster, and she kept herself positioned so Hale's tongue was working her clit and nothing else. He let her control the pace, watching in admiration as she ground into his face and her breaths grew more sporadic. Her hips started to lift off the bed and little urgent moans escaped her parted lips. She was close.

Even though his own ache was maddening, Hale stayed focused. He kept his mouth working at the same pressure, but increased speed slightly. He released one of Lina's stockings to prop one hand under her lower back, keeping her hips angled so she was perfectly open to him.

Her moans increased in volume, the frantic pulsing in Hale's cock increasing along with them, but he mumbled his encouragement and kept steady. When a slow shudder made its way through Lina's body, starting in her legs, then her hips, then her stomach and chest, it was time to push her over the edge.

Releasing the last sock, he slipped a hand between her legs and pushed two fingers inside her, curling them upwards until she constricted around him. When she cried out his name, her body quaking uncontrollably, Hale changed tactics with his mouth and sucked at the sensitive skin, drawing her orgasm out even more.

Lina collapsed back on the bed, breathless and twitching from aftershocks of bliss. Only then did Hale finally remove his fingers and lick them clean of the decadent taste of paradise itself.

To his surprise, Lina still had energy. Fire in her eyes, she popped off the mattress and pushed him to his back.

"Your turn," she panted, throwing one leg over his hips so she straddled him.

Before Hale could get a word in edgewise, she'd grabbed hold of his cock and eased herself down on it. At her tightness, Hale grasped at the fabric dressing Lina's thighs, his eyes nearly rolling back in his head at the sensation.

"Fuck," he groaned. "You feel too good."

Lina leaned forward to move herself up and down his shaft, but Hale gripped the stockings again to hold her in place. He then lifted a hand to her chest and pushed slightly, angling her so her hands were braced on his legs behind her.

"Let me watch," he demanded.

Lina's smile widened at the command. Keeping her body on display for him, she slowly rolled her hips forward and back, grinding him into her on every pass.

Hale hissed another expletive, his hand drifting over the soft skin of her torso in awe. "Gods, how are you real?"

At his words, she began to grind faster.

Hale settled back into the pillows, still keeping an eye on her exquisite performance but relaxing into it.

Warm and tight and fucking perfect—*gods*, how could he have ever lived without this? Without *her*? And how was he supposed to do it again?

Fuck the bargain.

They never had to go back to a place he couldn't touch her. He couldn't handle it. They could stay here. Somehow, they could find a way to stay here, and they could slip in and out of paradise anytime they wanted.

That word, *paradise*, was playing over and over in Hale's mind when Lina tossed her head back to look at the ceiling. Curiously, he followed her gaze to see what had caught her attention.

In the reflective gloss of the obsidian ceiling shone the mirror image of the two of them, their naked bodies moving in perfect harmony. Lina met his eye in the reflection and beamed brighter than the sun, the sight of which immediately shot Hale over the edge. His cock went rigid and pulsed, bliss sweeping through the entirety of his body, mind, and soul, as he released inside her.

Lina collapsed forward onto his chest. There the two of them rested until their sweat had dried and Hale had finally stopped panting like he was dying of thirst. When he'd recovered enough to move, he raised his hands to Lina's bare back and traced the knots of her spine with his fingertips. She moaned her approval and snuggled her face further into his neck. Her sleepy voice brought Hale back to reality.

"You can't stay here, Hale."

Could the woman read minds too?

Hale swallowed the lump in his throat, but his words still came out hoarse. "I know."

"It's alright." Her lips pressed to his skin once more. "We'll find a place somewhere. Together."

*Together.*

Hale pulled Lina closer and shut his eyes tight.

He should tell her about the bargain.

Tomorrow. He'd do it tomorrow.

Or the next day.

Or maybe the day after that.

# CHAPTER 43

I COULD HAVE STAYED IN HALE'S BED FOREVER, BUT WE HAD WORK to do.

When I got back to the common room, Syrena and Ilora pounced on me and dragged me into one of the bedrooms for an interrogation. I told them what had happened, and Ilora scolded me for revealing the lie to Hale, but Syrena eagerly cut in to ask how he was in bed. Surprisingly, the question made Ilora back off her tirade and admit she was curious too. At their incessant prodding, I broke down and told them the answer to everything they asked in great detail, except for Syrena's impertinent, "So who do you prefer more, Soren or Hale?"

I didn't answer because I didn't know.

Both men brought equal amounts of pleasure in their own ways, so I simply shrugged and said, "Should we discuss my sex life or make a plan to get rid of Aedan once and for all?"

Thankfully my friends had their priorities straight and chose the latter, so later that day, Hale met us in the common room to begin plotting.

While Syrena filled him in on our decision to rescue Tallys

in addition to assassinating Aedan, Xavier informed him of his and Ilora's new powers, complete with a demonstration. Hale nodded thoughtfully as he watched, his eyes narrowing as he worked through potential strategies. When he finally spoke, he stated that we needed to make Tallys aware of our motives as soon as possible. She spent most of her time with Aedan and could offer insight into his comings and goings, and with her stealth, she could potentially be our eyes and ears during moments Aedan and Erith thought no one was around to witness them. While usually the responsibility of spying would fall to Hale, he reminded us that Aedan could see through his darkness if he wanted to, so it was best to keep it contained.

I suggested Ilora be the one to talk with Tallys. How Ilora had comforted and supported her during the spring equinox proved she was someone Tallys trusted and gravitated towards, and the queen agreed to the task without hesitation.

When Tallys came to our door to offer us dinner, Ilora took her into one of the bedrooms to discuss everything privately. The rest of us milled around the common room and waited anxiously, trying not to dwell on the nagging worry that maybe Tallys was too far under Aedan's thumb to be saved. What if she instantly turned around and informed him of our mutiny? We heard her crying a few times, then Ilora soothing her, and finally, almost an hour later, the two emerged, Tallys tear-streaked and shaking in Ilora's arms, but her jaw set firmly and her large eyes glimmering with the tiniest flicker of courage.

"Alright," she said, her voice steady for once. "Let's come up with a plan."

Hale dipped his head to her, the smile on his face so full of pride you would have assumed the two of them actually were brother and sister.

"Great." Xavier, leaning casually in a doorway, clapped his

hands in front of him. "So who all do we take with us when we bust out of here?"

"The Piksis," I stated firmly.

Hale peeked at me out of the corner of his eye and smiled.

"And the Merrows," Ilora said, tightening a reaffirming embrace around Tallys's shoulders. "All of them should be on board. They're treated as nothing but toys to be played with at the whims of men, and they've had enough."

Tallys nodded adamantly, the words Ilora had spoken clearly hers.

"And the Sluagh healed me when I was near death," Hale added. "I think a few of them would be open to an uprising as well."

I frowned, but Hale brushed my hand with his.

"Give them a chance," he urged.

I sighed, but briefly linked my pinky finger through his. "Fine. But make them stop asking me to repay my debt so I can finally sleep soundly at night."

Hale chuckled. "I'll see what I can do."

"This is all fine and good," Syrena interrupted, perching on the armrest of the emerald couch. "But how the hell are we supposed to get all these creatures out of here after we kill Aedan? Surely all the other Nethers will be in an uproar when they find out their king or god or whatever they think he is has been murdered."

"Can we do it while he's sleeping?" Xavier suggested.

Hale shook his head and crossed his arms. "There's too many. There's no way we could get them all out in one night."

Xavier nodded as he considered. "We also haven't established where everyone can go. The Fae won't respond well to a sudden surge of Nethers in their lands."

Ilora gave Tallys's shoulders another squeeze. "The Merrows are welcome in the lake at the palace of Merimaya.

When we get back, I'll sign a decree that no one is to touch them. Anyone found poaching or harming them in any way will be imprisoned without trial."

Syrena nodded in agreement. "Lerian will second the decree. The Merrows will be welcome on our shores, and the selling of their hides in the markets will be banned."

Tallys's eyes welled with tears, but not ones of sadness or fear like before. These were tears of gratitude.

"Are you sure your brother will agree to that?" I asked.

"I don't care if he does or not." Syrena set her jaw. "That's the way it's going to be."

"Alright, that settles the Merrows." Hale rubbed his chin thoughtfully. "What about the Piksis?"

I chewed the inside of my cheek, lost in thought, before glancing at Xavier. "They could live in the forests of Astoria, couldn't they? It's dense and heavily wooded, so they'd have their pick of trees to nest in." When Xavier nodded in agreement, I faced Hale. "Plus you said yourself they're often mistaken for fireflies. So maybe no one would even notice their arrival. Their only issue would be the owls."

"They're welcome in Merimaya too," Ilora cut in. Her hand had started rubbing comforting circles on Tallys's back. "The hills surrounding our lake have thick forests as well, and we have very few species of native owls."

"Well, that settles that." I leaned back against the wall and raised an eyebrow at Hale. "What about the Sluagh? Where do they go?"

Hale shrugged. "They're mysterious creatures. No one really knows where they home or hunt, they're only ever seen wandering. I'm sure if they received an invitation, they'd adapt and find a place. Or maybe they'll find a home in the lands beyond the sea."

I pouted and wrinkled my nose, pulling Hale's attention to its tip.

"I won't let anything happen to you," he assured me, leaning in and tenderly kissing my cheek.

Syrena sighed and crossed one leg over the other. "So now on to the most important part. Aedan. How do we kill him?"

"Hale can do it." Xavier gestured flippantly with his hand. "He can do his head-explodey thingy."

"Aedan can see through my head-explodey thingy, remember? What if I'm not fast enough and he sees it coming?"

"Good point."

"Maybe I could drown him," Ilora tried. "I'll practice harder and work with larger bodies of water. If I'm strong enough, and we get him by one of the pools, I could end it."

Tallys shook her head. "He could turn into something that can breathe underwater. I've seen him do it before."

One of Ilora's fingers absentmindedly found a strand of Tallys's hair and twirled it. "Shit. Good point."

"It looks like Lina is our only chance." Syrena's gaze landed on me, as did everyone else's in the room. "Can you manifest anything yet?"

Suddenly insecure, I tucked my hands behind my back. "Not really. Nothing but a spark."

Hale stepped forward, the power of his presence simultaneously exhilarating and calming. "How did you conjure it the first time?"

"I don't know. I just remember everything hurting." I squinted as I searched my memory. "That's all. The Fear Gorta inflicting pain, then something black and silver, then power."

"Have you tried reliving the moment?"

"Yes." I hung my head. "Nothing but the spark. I know it's in there, I just can't get it out."

"It'll come eventually," Xavier stated. "You're human. Magic still feels like a foreign concept to you. Once you get the grasp of it, you'll be unstoppable."

I offered him a smile in thanks, which he returned along with an encouraging wink.

"I agree." Hale's fingers brushed mine again. "Keep working at it."

"So what do we do until then?" Xavier asked. "We just keep puttering around and pretending we're actually considering negotiating with that homicidal maniac?"

Syrena's gaze hardened. "Do you have any better ideas?"

"We run."

This time, all eyes in the room turned to Tallys.

"Not everyone at once," she added, her dark eyes distant as she worked through the logistics in her mind. "Slowly. Over time. My sisters can sneak out the others little by little using the pool systems. If we move quietly, then by the time my master realizes what's happened, Lina will be able to take care of him."

My heart simultaneously swelled and faltered at Tallys's blind faith. Now there was more pressure than ever to grasp the magic inside and pull it to the surface.

"It could work," Ilora mused, nibbling her bottom lip. "When they leave the caves, the Merrows can lead the way into the ocean and take the others to the veil we entered through. Then they can hide along the Lerian coastline until we get back and make the decree so it's safe for them to reveal themselves."

"There are other ways to get to the Fae realm too," Tallys added.

We all turned to look at her at once. We'd considered the theory already, but hearing it declared as fact was still a shock.

"I don't know where all of them are," Tallys went on, "but I know they exist. Only Aedan knows the exact locations. He and the upper beasts he's sent through to carry out his will. The lower beasts who've escaped to your realm only found them by chance."

"Of course," Xavier muttered, blinking at the ground as he shook his head. "*That's* why Nethers kept popping up out of nowhere. No matter what Soren and I did, we couldn't rid Astoria of them all."

Tallys let out a horrified squeak, and Xavier quickly realized his mistake and grimaced in apology.

"How many ways in are there?" Syrena asked.

Tallys wilted and wrung her hands in her lap. "I don't know, I'm sorry."

"Does Erith know where they all are too?"

"I don't know that either. But I would assume so. My master shares everything with her."

Syrena groaned and rubbed her temples. "So let me see if I have this straight. Even *if* we get everyone out, and even *if* we kill Aedan, the Nethers can still enter the Fae realm to enact vengeance."

"We've fought different Nethers for centuries," Xavier countered. "We've always come out on top. The issue isn't the Nethers themselves, it's Aedan uniting them into one force. With him out of the way, they'll be without a leader once again and will go back to smaller, more manageable groups."

"You don't think avenging your murdered king would be good inspiration to stick together and continue his work?"

"We're also forgetting one thing," I cut in. "We have Erith to factor in."

"I'll deal with her," Ilora declared, her normally kind eyes icing over.

Xavier sighed as he rubbed the back of his head, mussing his dark curls. "So we just have to save everyone and kill Aedan and Erith. Simple. What could go wrong?"

When he lowered his hand, one rogue curl was left standing straight up, immediately bringing to mind my little brother. The thought of Wynn's cloudy spellbound eyes filled me with new motivation. I squared my shoulders and set my jaw.

"We can do this. I know we can. We bide our time, continue with the lie we've established, and when the Merrows have everyone out safely, we'll strike."

Syrena nodded and stood, holding her head high. "I think we should hit Aedan and Erith at the same time. That way the mess is contained, and there's no chance of one finding out about the other's death before we can get to them too."

Hale nodded. "Good thinking."

Xavier peeked at Syrena, the twinkle in his eyes betraying a sliver of admiration. "Looks like Lerian doesn't even need Commander Pax. Its queen has plenty of military prowess."

Syrena blinked at him, color rising to her cheeks. "Did you just give me a compliment?"

Xavier quickly looked away and shrugged.

"Not that I care," Syrena added, recovering from the moment with a haughty toss of her hair.

Xavier scoffed. "And the bitch is back."

Ilora rolled her eyes and helped Tallys to her feet. "I swear, if you two start up again, I'll be taking more lives than just Erith's."

Tallys let out a small giggle.

Ilora led her to the door, then gently placed her hands on Tallys's narrow shoulders. "Thank you for doing this. I know it's frightening. You're being extremely brave."

Tallys twisted her interlaced fingers, nervously shifting from one foot to the other. "We... we've never allowed ourselves something remotely close to hope. But now..." She looked up at the rest of us, a hesitant smile sneaking onto her lips. "Now for the first time, I think I might feel it. So thank *you*. Thank you for finally seeing us."

As Ilora guided Tallys out the door and into the hall, one glance around the room proved I wasn't the only one fighting back tears at her words.

When they had gone, Syrena let out a quivering exhale and returned to the couch, where she pulled her knees to her chest.

"Everything's going to change," she muttered, mainly to herself.

Xavier hesitantly lowered onto the seat beside her.

"What if no one else is open to it?" Syrena went on. "Ilora and I are only two people. Our territories will likely hate us for this."

"Then too bad," Xavier said. "You're the queen. You make the rules."

Syrena chuckled grimly. "Famous last words of every overthrown monarch."

Xavier dared to inch a little closer. "I'm going to go back and tell Soren everything I saw here. I know you don't believe it, but he's a good man now. I'll get him on your and Ilora's side too. That way, it'll be three of you against the world, not two."

Syrena snorted and rolled her eyes at his dry attempt at humor, but mumbled a thank you nonetheless.

Silence fell, and I was about to nudge Hale to direct him outside so we could give the two space when the queen spoke again.

"You know, when you're not being an insufferable ass you're sort of nice."

Xavier sat up a little straighter, and I could have sworn a pale pink hue tinged the apples of his cheeks. "Did you just give me a compliment?"

Not meeting his gaze, Syrena shrugged.

I *definitely* wanted to give the two space now. I touched a finger to Hale's, but he subtly shook his head, keeping his eyes glued to the two on the couch as a smile formed on his lips.

Xavier cleared his throat, suddenly transfixed by his knuckles. "Well, since I'm so nice, I guess I need to come clean about something."

Syrena looked over at him, eyes shining with curiosity and a cautious flicker of hope. "Yes?"

Xavier licked his lips, still staring at his hands. "I... I lied to you. The night we came to the Netherworld."

Syrena frowned, but remained quiet.

"I didn't sleep with Roric." Xavier shifted his gaze to the ceiling and sighed heavily. "A friend of mine likes him, and I wouldn't do that to her. All he and I were doing was trying to find a bottle of rum for a nightcap. I was planning on lacing it with a sedative so you ladies could slip out of the palace unnoticed."

Syrena stared at him for a few beats before her brows dipped low over her eyes. "Why did you tell me you slept with him, then?"

Xavier sighed again. "Because I'm an insufferable ass."

Syrena grunted in agreement, but didn't add to the insult.

"And..." Xavier fidgeted in his seat. "I guess I thought you being annoyed and angry with me is better than you not talking to me at all."

When he looked up at her, a melancholy smile colored his expression. Syrena's lashes fluttered as she noted it, but she quickly looked away.

"Well, if you're coming clean, then I guess I should tell you something." She swallowed and fiddled with her bracelets. "I was never going to do anything with him. I don't feel that way about him, and I'm not going to do anything with someone I don't want to just to prove a point."

"Why did you agree to the bet, then?"

Syrena hesitated before murmuring, "Same reason as you."

A corner of Xavier's mouth twitched from a contained smile.

"And maybe..." Syrena sighed. "Maybe I wanted a distraction."

"I'm good at distracting."

At that, a giggle slipped from Syrena's lips. "Yes, you are."

When they went quiet once more, I considered urging Hale outside again, but one glance at his face told me he was enjoying the scene too much to leave now. His lips were pressed together to keep his smile at bay, and his dark eyes sent silent encouragement in Xavier's direction.

Xavier cleared his throat again and cooly shook the hair from his face. "Do you think... maybe... we should call a truce? Just because we need to stay focused down here."

Syrena nodded eagerly. "That would make sense. And then once we're out of the Netherworld and find ourselves in need of distraction, our war continues."

"Right." Xavier met her gaze, his famous grin finally breaking out across his face.

Syrena smiled too, then slowly extended her hand for him to shake. "It's a deal."

Xavier slipped his fingers into her palm, his thumb skating back and forth along her knuckles. "It's been a pleasure doing business with you, Your Highness."

Syrena's face immediately fell into a scowl. She ripped her hand from his grasp before hauling herself off the couch, stomping into her bedroom, and slamming the door shut behind her.

Beside me, Hale sighed. "So close."

~

TALLYS INFORMED us she'd be spreading our plan among the Merrows, and if she could convince them of our good intentions and the queens' promise to protect them, then they'd begin the first wave of evacuations this evening. The young and the wounded were slated to be removed first, and after sharing the location of the veil we'd entered through, Tallys estimated it would take the weaker Nethers two days to swim there. Meanwhile, it would only take hours for the healthy. After talking to her sisters, they estimated we needed a week for the Merrows to evacuate before Aedan or those loyal to him began to suspect.

One week.

A week of pretending we respected Aedan and Erith enough to try and work things out. A week of pretending like I wasn't spending the majority of my time trying to conjure a devastating darkness from where it had rooted itself inside me. A week of pretending Hale and I weren't using our remaining moments sneaking fervent glances at each other, disappearing into darkened doorways to explore the other's body and mouth before someone passed by, and quietly slipping into each other's bedrooms when the world was meant to be sleeping. Hale was a drug I couldn't get out of my system, calling to me anytime we were apart and blinding me with a haze of lust whenever he was near. I craved his touch, his scent, his heavy stare and his smile, which had previously made so few appearances but now brightened the room more and more each day. It was almost enough to make me forget about Soren.

Almost.

But he was still there at the back of my mind when I'd see the glittering silver vines on my arm, or feel his dagger on my thigh, or occasionally when I lay awake at night with Hale's arms wrapped around me. How the embraces of two men I loved, who were equally passionate and intoxicating, could feel so different was beyond me. Hale's embrace, in a way, was more desperate. He held me tightly, as if I could be ripped away from him at any moment, while Soren's arms used to drape over me like he was daring everyone to try.

It was a strange mix of emotions the next few days. Anxiety and anticipation and frustration coupled with love and lust and longing. When a week had passed, I was mentally exhausted and time was an illusion. To all of us it simultaneously felt like we'd been here an eternity and no time at all.

But when we received a knock on the common room door one night, reality set in as our time ran out.

Nails tapping impatiently against her folded arms, Erith glared at me from the other side of the threshold. "Enough stalling. Let's negotiate."

I balked and glanced back at Ilora and Syrena on the couch. Their eyes were wide with panic. We didn't say it, but we were all thinking the same thing.

We needed a little longer.

Last we'd heard from Tallys, the Merrows had only moved part of their population and half of the Piksis. They'd had more difficulty remaining undetected than they originally antici-pated, and that made the going slow. We'd thought we could buy them more time by dodging Aedan's requests to meet with us, claiming we were too busy observing the Nethers' culture or caught up in meetings of our own, but apparently he'd grown impatient with our procrastination.

I turned back to Erith, racking my brain for a believable excuse. "Xavier's asleep. Can we meet with you after he wakes up? He gets cranky if he doesn't get enough rest."

"No, you'll wake him up now." Erith popped a hip, rooting herself to the spot. "Dinner's on the table. Don't want it to get cold."

"We already ate," Ilora chimed in.

Erith laughed. A cold, clipped chuckle devoid of even a semblance of amusement. "It seems you're misinterpreting our hospitality for stupidity. Get yourselves together and come to dinner."

She turned on her heel, but peered back over her shoulder. "The attire is formal. You have ten minutes."

"We need Tallys," I called after her. "We need her to show us the way there."

"You know the way," Erith stated, the click of her heels echoing down the tunnel after her. "You have ten minutes."

When she'd gone, I clicked the door shut and faced Syrena and Ilora, anxiety already eating its way through my chest. "What do we do?"

Ilora frowned. "We make these the longest negotiations in history."

# Chapter 44

When we'd changed into our clothes from the spring equinox, we made our way to the large tourmaline doors, which now seemed considerably more menacing than before. We knocked, and I blinked in surprise when we were again met by Erith. Dressed in a revealing black satin gown, she opened the door without a smile or greeting and beckoned for us to enter.

There was no one in the large quartz room except Aedan in Meer's form at the head of the table and Hale to his left. Hale was once again an alluring dark prince in his robe, ring, and obsidian circlet, while the Netherworld king was the embodiment of gaudiness in flowing gold robes, jewelry, and a matching crown.

"Thank you for finally gracing us with your presence." The king gestured to the empty chairs around an equally vacant dining table. "Please. Sit."

I slid into the open seat beside Hale, discreetly nudging his foot with mine under the table. He glanced up at me and smiled before returning his attention to Aedan.

"I was beginning to think you didn't like me anymore." Aedan pouted like a child being sent to bed early. "My feelings were starting to get hurt."

"Oh, come now, Aedan," I countered. "We all know you don't have feelings."

Syrena, who sat across from me, kicked my shin underneath the table.

Aedan sniffed. "See, I'd love to pretend that's just our usual playful banter, Lina, but I feel like we've known each other long enough now that we can start being honest." He leaned forward, propping his elbows on the table as his gray eyes narrowed. "So if I'm being honest, I think this pregnancy's made you a truly detestable cunt."

All my friends tensed at the word except Hale. I expected him to say something, or at the very least bristle the way I was, but he remained still, shamefully keeping his eyes fixed on the table in front of him.

It was Xavier who broke the stunned silence.

"Surely name-calling isn't the best way to start these sorts of things." He leaned forward, mirroring Aedan's position. "Which brings me to our first negotiation of the evening: I propose Lina keeps her big mouth shut, you, sir, attempt to rein in your obsessive need to toy with people's emotions, and we all keep words like *cunt* out of our mouths unless uttering it during deliciously filthy bouts of dirty talk in the bedroom. Agreed?"

Aedan stared at Xavier for a few tense beats before grinning ear to ear and turning to Erith. "He's just wonderful, isn't he? Can I take his form one night with you, my love?"

Erith took her time scanning Xavier's body. "You could take his form every night and I wouldn't mind."

Syrena irritably sucked her teeth. "I thought we came here for dinner. Why am I staring at an empty table?"

"Dinner will come after." Aedan leaned back in his chair,

his gaze roving over each of us individually. "As soon as we get this whole thing sorted out. And in regards to Xavier's proposition, I agree to the terms. No games. No name-calling. Nothing but the truth from now on."

"We will do the same." Ilora dipped her head respectfully.

"Wonderful!" Aedan clapped his hands, a blinding smile lighting up his face. "Then I can finally tell you I have no intention of negotiating with you."

The world ground to a halt, and all the air squeezed out of the room.

Aedan reached over and lovingly patted Erith's knee. "You see, negotiating is just another word for settling. And why settle when you can have everything? Isn't that what you always say, my love?"

His queen beamed back at him. "It is."

I frantically peeked at Hale, whose eyes were still glued to the tabletop, then glanced at Syrena, whose face had gone pale.

"I've been alive longer than you can even fathom," Aedan continued. "I'm an ancient being, and although I may not be a god…" He winked at me as if to say, *Good catch, Lina.* "I might as well be because I've seen it all. There is no trick in the book that can surprise me anymore. Which is why I know you have no intention of negotiating with me either."

My breath was escaping my body in shallow pants. Too panicked to be subtle, I dropped my hands from the table to my lap and grasped the hilts of my daggers to calm myself.

"Then why go through all this?" Ilora asked tightly. She sat as motionless as a statue, every muscle and tendon in her body taut. "Why let us stay here? Why offer us food and clothing and force us to attend parties as your guests?"

Aedan shrugged and picked at a piece of lint on his sleeve. "Boredom mostly. When you've lived as long as I have, things get dull. You have to find ways to entertain yourself. Like a child putting roadblocks in front of ants building their little mounds. After Lina figured out my hold on her dear, sweet brother, I was curious what else you might do."

Beneath the table, I nudged Hale's foot again. This time he didn't look at me, and for some reason that caused my anxiety to spike. Maybe he was hatching some grand plan like he had the last time. Maybe he'd shroud the room in darkness like he had then, and we could fight our way out again.

Or maybe he was just as frozen with fear as me.

"How did you know?" Syrena asked Aedan, but her gaze was locked with Xavier's. The two of them were having a silent conversation, searching the other's eyes for solutions.

Aedan cackled. "Oh, I'm so glad you asked." He swiveled in his chair and faced the door, snapping his fingers. "Bring her in, gentlemen!"

The door groaned open, and two massive Weirs entered, dragging a pitifully weeping Tallys with them.

My stomach wrenched at the sight of her.

She was nearly naked, wearing only a thin slip that was nothing but tattered rags on her emaciated form. Both eyes were severely blackened and swollen, one of her legs was twisted into an unnatural position, and aside from the countless bruises and bloody gashes across her gray flesh, sections of her skin were somehow crumbling apart like chalk and sloughing off her body.

"Poor, sweet Tallys." Aedan clicked his tongue as the Weirs tossed her at his feet. She screamed in agony as her bad leg caught wrong beneath her.

I looked to Hale again and gave his foot another fervent nudge, hoping he too would realize it was time to employ a different strategy. If Hale acted fast, maybe he could use his power to dispose of Aedan the same way he had the Fear Gorta.

Even if it wasn't enough to subdue Aedan entirely, it would at least give the rest of us time to strike.

But continuing his role of the dutiful prince, Hale refused to glance up from the surface of the table.

Aedan stood from his chair and crouched beside Tallys, tenderly brushing her sweat-drenched hair away from her face. The strands were tangled and matted with blood.

"I was so happy to see you all growing attached to her like I'd anticipated. It's hard not to feel for her, isn't it? So sad. So pathetic. And so very easy to break for information."

His gaze flicked pointedly to Ilora. She remained seated, but her hands had balled into fists, her nostrils flared, and her eyes shone with such fury that they left Aedan briefly stunned, forcing him into a few seconds of hesitation before he continued speaking.

"Although I have to say, little Tallys held out considerably longer than I expected her to. She must have truly believed in you all."

He laughed as his hand threaded through Tallys's hair, and with one firm tug, he ripped her off the floor and lifted her high. She cried out again, her eyes squeezing shut as her body went rigid from the pain.

Ilora said nothing, but her fists furiously slammed against the tabletop.

Erith sat back in her seat, nibbling at the end of a long fingernail and giggling at the scene.

Helplessness threatened to turn my limbs to lead. I needed something to cling to, a sturdy rock to ground me, so I turned to Hale. I expected to be inspired by a vengeful glint in his eye or his tensed back to signal his preparation for action.

But he sat as calm and stoic as before.

"Hale, we have to do something!" I whispered.

His frown only deepened, and he continued to look away as

Aedan went on.

"I've learned much throughout the years, one of the most useful being that everyone cracks eventually. You just have to know the right place to hit."

And with that, Aedan's eyes darkened to pitch black.

A bright white light flashed in the palm of his free hand, giving way to a dark fog that crackled and sparked like coals in a hearth. He smacked the darkness to the skin on Tallys's upper arm, which instantly caused her flesh to ignite, burn, and crumble into ash. Tallys's mouth opened in a tortured wail, her mutilated leg twitching in a helpless attempt to escape her captor, but Aedan kept a firm hold and grinned as he watched her flesh fall away. When a gaping hole was all that was left of the area, he moved his hand to another spot on Tallys's arm and repeated the torture.

"For fuck's sake, stop it!" Syrena screeched, slapping her hands flat on the table as she stood.

At her movement, the Weirs jumped forward and snarled, baring their fangs and defensively falling in beside their king.

Xavier darted to Syrena's side. He sized the Weirs up, taking note of their weapons and hulking size to weigh his odds of surviving a clash with them.

Tallys's screams continued to echo through the room, the high-pitched shrieks ringing in my ears.

I couldn't breathe. I couldn't think. I could barely move. With one last feeble plea, I reached out to my magic. I begged it for a flame, a flicker, *anything* to combat the dark lord's vicious attack, but it gave me nothing. I wasn't strong enough to beat him. The only person who was sat beside me, the perfect picture of a well-behaved prince.

Finally managing to break through my paralyzing terror, I grabbed Hale's forearm and gave it an urgent shake. "Damn it, Hale, just kill him!"

But his magic remained locked away, and his jaw stubbornly clenched shut as he ripped his arm from my grasp. Betrayal stung my heart and coated my tongue in dread.

Erith laughed harder.

Her amusement immediately died when the ground started to shiver and something rumbled far in the distance. Aedan removed his hand from Tallys's skin, bringing a stop to her agonized wails. We all scanned the room, trying to pinpoint the cause.

Aedan glared at the Weirs. "What is that sound?"

The world around us vibrated even more, the rumbling transforming into a dull roar.

I peeked at Syrena and Xavier, who were just as perplexed at what was happening as I was. A glance in Erith's direction found her equally confused as she gripped the side of the table to steady herself.

Then my gaze landed on Ilora.

Her eyes were enraged slits, sweat was splayed across her forehead, and her fists had unfurled, her fingernails now digging deep grooves into the surface of the table. Her stare was locked on Aedan, and her body shook as violently as the floor under our feet. She looked seconds away from bursting, and when the Weirs padded towards the door to investigate, we learned why.

A wall of water tore through the doorway, smashing into the men and hurling them head-first to the floor, snapping their necks on contact. The wave spiraled and headed for Aedan, flying at him with the ferocity of a hurricane. Hope swelled in my chest as the two neared, but just before their collision, Erith leapt to her feet and threw her hands in front of her. A shimmer of magic pumped from her palms, and the water instantly transformed into a solid sheet of ice.

Ilora collapsed forward on the table, gasping for breath at

the toll her power had taken on her. When Aedan cackled, she slowly looked up to meet his gaze.

"So *that's* why you lot were so overconfident!" Aedan tutted. "Naughty girl. It seems you've been playing with some very dangerous magic."

Ilora pushed herself upright and swiped the back of her hand over her brow. She sucked in a breath and let out a guttural shout, her battle cry paving the way for another torrent to crash in from the hall. Again Erith threw up her hands and transformed the water into ice in midair. The frozen wave cracked and shattered, crumbling into thousands of icy shards that scattered across the floor as Aedan cackled again.

"Like I said before. I know every trick in the book. Even the ones that give Fae like yourselves power down here. You didn't think I would force my beautiful queen to live here without her magic, did you?"

"You too, huh?" Xavier asked Erith.

The queen shrugged and kicked a shard of ice from beneath her shoe. "I'm no stranger to pain. It seemed a small price to pay. And thankfully, I was already fond of the mark it chose to give me." With a wry smile, she motioned to the circlet on her head and the dangling raw crystal at its center. "It feels strange if you sleep on it wrong, but damn do I look good in it."

Tallys attempted to wriggle out of Aedan's grasp, but he gave her another rough jerk, dragging a pained squeak from her lips.

Panting from exhaustion but refusing to surrender, the sound inspired Ilora to stand tall again. Protruding veins cut trails across her forehead, arms, and neck as she mustered all her strength to conjure a third tidal wave from wherever she'd found a water source nearby. The floor shook as the flood rumbled in the distance, and I latched on to the table in preparation for the watery rampage.

Aedan raised an eyebrow and smirked as Ilora struggled. "Admirable, Your Majesty, it really is. But if you think this little power of yours will be enough to finish me off, then I'm afraid you're going to have a rude awakening."

It was then that Aedan turned to Hale, who finally peeled his stare from the table.

"Son?" Aedan purred. "Will you do the honors?"

Hale gave a single curt nod before his gaze flicked to Ilora. Darkness burst from his palm, the stream of black mist slithering across the table and shooting into Ilora's mouth and nose. The room stopped shaking as Ilora went rigid.

My stomach dropped in horror.

"Hale, what are you doing?" I shrieked, grabbing at his arm. "Stop!"

But Hale tossed me off like I weighed nothing and stayed focused on Ilora. She twitched and gurgled, her eyes rolling back in her head as tears of blood bloomed in their inner corners and trickled down her cheeks.

A strangled sob escaped my lips, panic and confusion choking me as I tore at Hale's sleeve. "Hale, stop it!"

But he threw me to the side once more, knocking me to the ground and sending me tumbling. I groaned in pain as I skidded to a halt, my mind even more scrambled than before.

*This isn't happening. This can't be happening.*

The words continued to repeat, my mind unable to comprehend the sight of the lover turned callous executioner, the mouth that had explored every inch of my body now set firm, and the eyes that had stared into my soul now cold and glazed over. Hale and I had been at odds over Aedan at the start, but he'd changed, hadn't he? *We'd* changed. I'd accepted Nethers as friends, and he'd realized his king was a cruel trickster.

But he'd been the trickster all along.

My heart hurting just as much as my body, I weakly pushed myself to my hands and knees.

"Hale, this isn't you," I whimpered. "Don't do this! *Please!*"

But my cries fell on deaf ears.

Maybe some people really were too far gone to save.

The centers of my palms started to tingle as something deep inside unwound from my bones. A timid but terrifying force rushed to the surface, manifesting as black sparks at my fingertips.

My magic had awakened.

Only just, but it was a sliver of hope nonetheless.

Despite all my desperate attempts to reach it the past few days, I grit my teeth, mustered every ounce of control I had, and shoved the power back down. If I let go, if I did the same thing I'd done with the Fear Gorta in the caves, I would destroy everyone, including Hale.

And I couldn't do that.

No, I *wouldn't* do that. Not unless there was no other way.

Suddenly, an invisible barrier interrupted the mist, and Ilora fell to the ground in a heap. Hale's head angled to the side in confusion, and he sent his power forward twofold. Again it hit an unseen wall, making it impossible to continue its devastation.

"What do we have here?" Aedan flung Tallys to the floor and crossed his arms. "Not one, but *two* of you played the dangerous game for a little magic?"

His gaze shifted to Syrena and Xavier, holding on the latter's outstretched hands. After a few seconds, Xavier's arms dropped, and he collapsed to his knees, panting at the effort holding it for so long had taken. Aedan sighed and shook his head like a disappointed parent.

"I had such high hopes for our friendship." He shrugged and spun on his heel, latching on to Tallys's hair again and dragging her behind him as Erith joined them. Together they headed for the door. "Hale? Kill them all except for the human. I want to play with her first. And son?" Aedan looked over his shoulder and smiled. "Make them suffer."

Hale dipped his head, and without a moment of hesitation or a flicker of guilt, his darkness shot out of his back, splitting into three separate ribbons that snaked into Xavier, Syrena and Ilora as quick as lightning. My friends shuddered and seized, their eyes rolling back in their heads as the mist barreled inside them. The pressure in their skulls built, pushing droplets of blood out their noses, eyes, mouths and ears.

The deep-rooted power inside me stirred again, but my stubborn heart reined it in.

*I can save him. This time, I can save him.*

My magic chomped at the bit, but I resisted.

Instead of unleashing destruction of my own, I stood, took a running start, and hurled the whole of my weight into Hale's side like a battering ram, knocking him out of his seat onto the floor. The abrupt movement distracted him enough that his power ceased, releasing his dark hold on Xavier, Syrena, and Ilora. They crumpled to the floor, groaning and clasping their heads in agony. Across the room, Aedan and Erith stopped walking and looked my way, irritation written across their faces.

Hale and I rolled to a stop, my head hitting the quartz floor and clacking my teeth together. My vision reeling, I blinked furiously to get my bearings. Before I could, Hale was on top of me, straddling my hips and catching my wrists to pin them at the sides of my head. His darkness bloomed, lashing out behind him and returning to its mission of eradicating our friends. The mist tore into them again, their screams soon dying out as their blood flowed faster than before.

"Hale," I grunted, struggling against his hold. "Please, this isn't you!"

His eyes were devoid of any compassion as they glared down at me. In fact, they were devoid of anything at all. There was no pain, no anger, just a vast expanse of emptiness staring down at me like he had no idea who I was.

... Almost as if it *wasn't* him.

Almost as if he was spellbound.

The thought renewed my fighting spirit, hope surging adrenaline through my limbs and propelling me into action. My head the only part of my body I could move freely, I jerked it upwards to smash the top of my skull into Hale's nose. I heard a bone crack, and Hale loosened his grip ever so slightly as he flinched. His darkness ceased again, allowing Ilora, Syrena, and Xavier a reprieve from their suffering. I took the opportunity to twist to the side, crane my neck, and sink my teeth into Hale's arm. I then set my jaw and viciously yanked away. His flesh tore, and something warm and metallic dripped into my mouth as Hale finally released his hold on my wrist and sat upright.

Seeing my opening, I spat Hale's skin from my mouth and reached towards my thigh, stretching my fingers out in search of my dagger, but just as their tips brushed steel, Hale recovered and slammed his bloodied arm down again, this time catching my throat in his hand. He squeezed tight, cutting off my air supply, which sent my legs frantically kicking out behind him.

At the door, Erith sighed and stomped over to where my friends huddled in a mangled heap.

"Do I have to do everything myself?" she griped, swiping a knife from the table and setting her sights on Syrena. She squared her shoulders and tightened her hold on the weapon in preparation of the impending kill.

Despite my struggling, Hale's grip on my neck held firm, increasing in force until I saw stars and it became harder and harder to keep my eyes from fluttering shut. My free hand flailed beside me, still feeling for my blade but finding nothing except the ice-covered floor.

In the distance, Xavier grunted as he mustered his power at the same time Erith went in for a kill strike. She hit his wall, but undeterred, she went in again, then again, each blow that careened off the barrier taking heftier tolls on Xavier.

Darkness closed in on the outskirts of my vision, beckoning me to unconsciousness.

*Let go,* it whispered. *Let go, let go, let go.*

I fought against the voice, refusing to give up. Not on my friends, not on Hale, and not on myself.

Once more I reached for my blade but grasped nothing. My windpipe bent under Hale's grip, my body screaming in pain the way I would have if I were capable of speaking.

*Let go, let go, let go.*

I scratched at Hale's hand, raking my nails across his skin and leaving bloody trails through his brand.

Across the room, Xavier's power faltered, and Erith burst through his barrier, slicing furiously at Syrena, who barely rolled out of the way in time.

*Let go, let go, let go.*

I grit my teeth and grappled at Hale's fingers in a useless attempt to pry them away.

Darkness consumed my vision, the sounds of my friends' struggle growing faint in the distance. Eternal sleep was beckoning, and I could no longer ignore its call. I let my eyes shut, and finally embraced the weariness, the exhaustion, and the unthinkable pain.

But then... a glimmer in the dark.

The words echoed again.

*Let go.*

Realization lit up the expanse like a lightning bolt.

*This* was the source of the voice. This tiny sprout, silver and glittering, urgently whispering the words over and over.

It wasn't eternal sleep calling to me.

The words were in my voice.

It was me.

It was a firestorm of emotion.

It was fiery shadow grown into my spirit and entwined around my bones like a vine, begging its master to set it free.

It was my power pleading with me, begging, *Let us go. Lose control. Be free.*

So I obeyed.

I loosened the reins on the magnificent monstrosity, but kept a firm hold.

*Not too much. Just enough.*

Begrudgingly, it obeyed too.

Even half-unconscious, I felt my palms tingle as a black spark appeared. Followed by another. Then another. Then, like a flame igniting a brush pile, my entire hand went up in burning black, and the fingers around my throat eased.

When I heaved in a breath and my vision returned, the darkness cleared to reveal Hale on his knees, his hand in front of his face, watching as the brand on the back of it smoldered and sloughed away like cinders in the hearth.

"It can't be." Aedan's stunned voice reached my ears.

He stood in the doorway, limply holding Tallys's hair in his fist as he stared, slack-jawed, in my direction. He chuckled slightly and shook his head.

"Lina Calder, you never cease to surprise me. Unfortunately, that—"

Tallys twisted in his grip and kicked his knees out from under him, knocking them both to the ground.

When they landed, Tallys shakily hauled herself to sitting.

"The black stone, Lina!" she screeched. "He bewitched the—"

Aedan hissed a curse, flipped around, and shoved his hand to her face to silence her, sending a savage pulse of his power across Tallys's skin. She wailed as her nose, lips, and cheeks smoked and melted away.

Ilora screamed, immediately abandoning her, Syrena, and Xavier's fight with Erith to scramble across the floor towards Tallys and Aedan.

But I paid them no mind.

Setting my sights on Hale's black crystal circlet, I sat upright. With a final push of strength, I grabbed hold of the crown, tore it from his head, and smashed it to the ground where it shattered into a thousand shiny pieces.

Hale blinked.

Then blinked again.

An inhuman snarl ripped from his throat, and he tackled me back to the ground, his hand returning to my throat and squeezing mercilessly. I crashed back towards unconsciousness.

"Hale, please," I croaked. "I... I love you."

There was no recognition in his face, no shred of mercy in his eyes. In fact, his response to my words was simply to smack his crumbling hand across my mouth and stifle any more that might follow.

But the movement brought something else into focus.

A gold band around his middle finger, with a glossy black stone at its center.

An identical signet ring to the Netherworld king.

Thinking fast, I slapped my hand to his. His brand had completely sloughed off thanks to my previous attack, exposing rows of muscle and tendon that twitched beneath my palm, but I didn't care. I wrapped my fingers around the ring above the wound and reached out to my magic. Still crackling at my fingertips, it responded faster this time, sparking bright silver light before my palm went up in swirling darkness. The ring ignited, glowing like iron on a forge.

Hale shrieked with fury, his voice distorted and other-worldly. His own power unfurled with a vengeance and tore into my nose and mouth. The most excruciating pain I'd ever endured followed as the mist expanded, pushing at the walls of my skull in an attempt to crack it.

I wanted to stop.

I wanted to die.

I wanted to do anything to put an end to the misery.

But I'd made Hale a promise.

*Through good or bad, thick or thin, in this realm or any, I'm never letting you go.*

So I didn't.

I tightened my hold on his hand, my black magic unwavering even as Hale's free fist joined in on the violence. He beat at my face, bruising my eyes and splitting my lip, his screeches growing increasingly panicked and high-pitched. The pain in my head and body was unfathomable, unbearable, and the only thing keeping me conscious was the exhilarating rush brought on by the burning shadow barreling out of me. More of Hale's skin dripped away and fell to the floor as the ring glowed brighter and brighter until it shone like the sun.

Suddenly a mighty crack rang out, shaking the room, and the glowing gold burst into an explosion of gilded dust. Hale hurtled backwards and landed on his back with a thud and a grunt. I heaved in a lungful of air as his power dissolved and the pain ceased, the magic in my palm fizzling out like a doused flame.

When he hauled himself upright again, Hale groaned and rubbed his eyes, then blinked repeatedly as he took in the room with the same bewildered expression my brother had whenever a witch woke him from his own enchantment.

"What..." Hale glanced down at his hand, which was nothing more than singed bone and dangling scraps of flesh. "What happened?"

I crawled onto all fours and opened my mouth to answer, but another beat me to it.

"What happened..." Aedan growled, rising to his feet. "... Is this human whore has gotten in my way for the last time."

He sent a rough kick into Ilora's face as she neared Tallys writhing on the floor, then stretched his arms out wide. The crackling black appeared in his hands, and he swirled his arms in front of him, spiraling it into a whirlwind. Aedan's gray eyes landed on me and narrowed, and before I had a chance to process what he was doing, he hurled the darkness in my direction. It shot through the air so fast I didn't have time to leap out of its path.

But I didn't need to.

Hale lunged forward and shoved me out of the way, putting himself in my place. Aedan's power tore through him instead, instantly enveloping him in a vicious wave of destruction.

When the smoke cleared, there was nothing left of Hale except charred black robes smoldering in a heap on the floor.

I stared at the pile, the gravity of what had happened not clicking into place right away. Then it hit me all at once, cutting deeper than any wound, physical or emotional, ever had before.

Hale was gone.

He was actually gone.

*Let go.*

The reins I'd been holding on to slipped from my grasp, and a black haze swept across my vision.

# CHAPTER 45



"SHIT!" XAVIER EXCLAIMED.

He threw his arms out in front of him, summoning the remnants of his strength and stretching out his power as my head jerked backwards and my mouth opened wide in a blood-curdling scream.

It felt beautiful and ugly.

Holy and evil.

Full of pain and pleasure, and entirely uncontrollable.

Magic poured through my veins like molten silver, exploding from every pore on my body with a fiery vengeance and manifesting as a thick black shroud that flooded the room. Xavier's barrier wavered but miraculously held, protecting everyone in its vicinity, including Erith and Aedan, from instant annihilation.

Even when the dark wave ebbed, the smoky haze over my vision remained, my fingertips still sparked, and my body quivered as my power pawed at the ground, eager for more.

My gaze locked on Aedan. One look at the fury on my face

and the magic crackling on my skin and he took a cautious step backwards.

"Lina, you're out of control."

He sounded calm, but fear flickered in his eyes.

And *gods*, did I like that fear.

I stepped forward too. "Am I?"

"Yes. But it's alright." He changed tactics, his voice growing light and silky as he continued to back away. "I can help you. I can show you how to tame it."

"Why would I want to tame this?"

I followed his steps, filled with purpose. There was no heartache. There was no anger. All I needed was blood. *His* blood.

"Let's get something very clear, Aedan," I said, my voice as sickly sweet as his. "I am not something in need of taming."

Aedan gulped and took another step back.

"I am not a *pet*."

Another step.

"I am not a *whore*."

Another.

"I am a *king slayer*." I raised my hand, fiery death pooling in my palm. "And it's time for your reign to end."

Aedan's own power flared at the threat, his eyes darkening to pitch black as his own hands filled with orbs of burning dark.

It was almost enough to distract me from another black mist.

I almost didn't see it, too caught up visualizing Aedan's death to look down at our feet. But then the darkness thickened, sliding up Aedan's heels and inconspicuously weaving through his legs until it was a cloud blooming behind his back.

I lowered my hand, so perplexed by the mist that for a brief moment, I forgot my thirst for revenge. Aedan clocked my shift in attention, his brow furrowing in confusion, and slowly, he peeked over his shoulder.

It was then that the darkness formed a solid mass, and like fog wafting away from the ocean under the first rays of morning sun, it parted to reveal a man.

Standing behind him, naked but very much alive, was Hale.

My knees threatened to buckle at the realization, but there wasn't time.

When Aedan's eyes landed on him, Hale caught him by the shoulder. With one hand holding him steady, he plunged the other deep into the shapeshifter's back. Aedan went rigid as Hale's fist broke through skin, muscle, and bone. When Hale captured what he was searching for, he ripped his arm back out, letting Aedan sink to the ground as he held it high.

Dripping crimson in his palm was the Netherworld king's still beating heart.

Without a second glance, Hale stepped over Aedan's twitching form on the ground and strode over to me, presenting the bit of flesh like it was served on a silver platter.

"The honor is yours, King Slayer."

His terrifying smile was oddly contagious, and when I'd adopted one of my own, I took the heart from his hand. The organ was warm, slippery, and pulsing, its owner nothing but a feeble, wheezing creature on the floor in front of us. It was strange seeing the main character of my nightmares reduced to something so fragile. I held the source of so much pain and torment in the palm of my hands, and I controlled its fate. Aedan wasn't a god, but in this moment, I was his.

And while there might be some gods who are merciful, unfortunately for him, I'm not one of them.

Brutal power flowed from my fingertips, and Aedan's corrupt heart turned to embers in my hand.

His body shrieked and convulsed until it had shriveled into

a withered crust, while the heart puffed into ash beneath my breath and floated away. Only then did my eyesight return to normal and my magic retreated inside to coil around my bones until the next time I called upon it. Within seconds I felt normal again, and with that came the frantic pounding of my own heart, the trembling, and, as usual, the tears.

Hale raced to my side and caught me before I could collapse to my knees from the shock.

"I'm sorry," he breathed, gently taking my face in his hands and kissing my cheeks over and over. "I'm so sorry. I had no control. Did I hurt you?"

"I'll live," I managed, pushing him away so I could run my hands over his arms and chest in disbelief. "How did you... how are you..."

Hale laughed breathlessly. "Another trait I inherited from the Night Sylph, I guess. They can dissipate into darkness. Turns out I can too."

"You didn't know?"

"I never thought to try it. I wouldn't have even wanted to for fear of what people would think of me. But when Aedan went after you, my only fear was losing you. I must have done it just in time, right before Aedan's magic hit me."

Still stunned, I huffed a tiny laugh and brushed a strand of hair from Hale's eyes.

Eyes that were fully awake and held every emotion.

Even love.

"Are you sure I didn't hurt you?" Hale asked, brushing his thumb over the bruises forming on my neck.

"You hurt *us* a little," a strained voice piped up.

We turned to catch Syrena helping Xavier to his feet, the streams of blood down their faces already starting to dry.

"I'm going to have a headache for days," Xavier continued, groaning as he wiped his nose with the back of his hand.

Hale frowned and hung his head. "I'm sorry. I had no idea what I was doing. I was—"

"Spellbound," I finished for him. "Aedan has a habit of doing that."

"Had," Syrena corrected. She teetered on her feet, but beamed at me proudly. "I knew you could do it, Lina."

I peeked at Hale and grinned. "*We* did it."

Hale reached down to take my hand in his but sucked in a breath as he did. He glanced down, catching sight of his mangled arm.

I winced. "Sorry about that."

"Don't be," Hale replied, smiling to himself. "When it heals, the brand will be gone."

I started to laugh, but a weak cough met our ears.

Ilora crouched over Tallys, her healing blue light radiating over the damaged flesh on Tallys's face. All of us jogged over to join the women and knelt in a circle around them, anxiously watching as Ilora worked.

"Is she going to be alright?" Syrena asked.

In reply, Ilora's light dimmed, allowing us full view of Aedan's former slave. The gray skin on her face had darkened in the places he'd grabbed her, but Ilora had patched her up so her lips and nose were intact again. Most importantly, she was still breathing.

With Ilora's help, Tallys sat up, then looked around the room with a dazed expression.

"He's gone?" she croaked. "He's really gone?"

Ilora smiled and smoothed Tallys's rumpled hair. "Yes. You're safe now."

"Almost." Syrena's lips pressed into a tight line. "Erith escaped."

In all the commotion, I'd forgotten about the other half of Aedan's regime. A quick scan of the room proved her nowhere to be seen. She must have darted out while the rest of us were preoccupied.

At the mention of the icy queen, Ilora tensed, her eyes glinting with fury.

"Shit!" she hissed. "I'm going after her."

She moved to stand, but Tallys caught her arm and pulled her back.

"You can't!" Tallys cried. "She'll be raising the alarm as we speak. We need to find my sisters at the lake and leave as soon as possible!"

"I swore an oath." Ilora's lashes fluttered against furious tears. "I have to avenge my family."

"And you *will*," Syrena cut in. "Once you have a weapon on you and we're not grossly outnumbered."

"But if I leave Erith now, it gives her a chance to regroup and attack the Fae realm anyway."

"And if you go after her, you'll likely die anyway." Syrena took Ilora's shoulders in her hands and gave her a firm shake. "Think rationally, Ilora. You're too weak right now. We all are. Even the most feared generals have to retreat on occasion to preserve their troops and reevaluate their strategy. We have to do the same. It's not running away, it's stepping back from the battle so you can win the war."

Ilora chewed her lip, glancing at the door.

"You've done more than enough today," Syrena continued, her voice softening. "You've saved lives. Let that be enough for now."

Ilora's gaze finally rested on Tallys's pleading eyes, and her hardened expression eased. She sighed heavily, to which Tallys responded by gently squeezing her hand in support.

"Alright," Ilora conceded, melting at the innocent touch. "Vengeance can wait."

"Then everyone arm yourselves with whatever you can,"

Xavier ordered, already rummaging around in the pockets of the slain Weirs. "And Hale, put on some pants before I insist on stealing you from Lina."

He was still breathing heavily from the skirmish, and there were deep bags under his eyes, but it was good to see my friend still had his sense of humor.

Hale joined Xavier beside the bodies, quickly sliding off the smaller Weir's clothing and pulling it on before clapping Xavier on the back with his good hand. The two had a brief unspoken moment, with Hale nodding to him in thanks and Xavier bowing his head.

"Ilora?" I asked. "Hale's hand is in bad shape. Can you—"

"Of course." Even though pain and exhaustion shone on her face, she shuffled over and slipped Hale's fingers into her own. With a grunt, her blue light reappeared, and within seconds Hale's flesh regenerated and fused back together. Eventually it looked the same as it had before, only just as Hale had predicted, the Night Sylph brand was gone. A white burn scar in the shape of my hand was left in its place, but it wasn't nearly as noticeable as the crude symbol that had been there before.

Hale raised his hand to the light to examine Ilora's work, eyes glittering with emotion as he witnessed his skin without the presence of a slur. The symbol that remained on his neck bobbed as he swallowed hard.

"Thank you," he murmured.

Ilora nodded and dipped her head, offering him a sheepish smile before wandering back to Tallys.

Hale cleared his throat and straightened his shoulders, all signs of vulnerability washing away. "Everyone ready? We're probably going to have to fight our way out of here."

Xavier responded by smashing one of the nearby chairs to the floor, breaking it into pieces. He then handed two of the splintered legs to Syrena to use as clubs while he took up the others. I, on the other hand, proceeded to pull the obsidian-black blade from the scabbard strapped to my left thigh and returned it to its rightful owner.

"Ready," I told him, drawing Soren's blade for myself.

Hale nodded, and when Ilora had helped Tallys to her feet and wrapped a protective arm around her waist, he jerked his chin in the direction of the door.

"Let's go."

I followed close on Hale's heels, terrified of him slipping even an arm's width away. Twice now I'd been convinced I'd lost him, and I refused to allow a third. I was so close to him that when he exited the doorway, I ran face-first into his back as he came to a sudden halt.

"What is it?" I asked, peeking around his shoulder.

My blood ran cold.

Packed wall-to-wall as far as the eye could see was row after row of Sluagh. They stared back at us, sunken eyes round and unreadable, but their crudely fashioned weapons held ready to strike.

Darkness manifested at Hale's back, staying hidden as he surveyed the Nethers in front of us, carefully analyzing the situation to construct a plan of attack. His fingers twitched, his eyes narrowed, and I could practically feel the adrenaline heating his veins as he primed himself for carnage.

But instead of calling upon my own power to join in on the violence, I rested a hand on Hale's shoulder. Keeping his eyes on the threat ahead, he subtly raised one eyebrow in a silent question. I gave him a squeeze to communicate I knew what I was doing, then as slowly and unthreateningly as I could, I moved in front of him.

At the sight of me, the Sluagh hissed in unison.

But I'd grown accustomed to standing front and center in rooms of people who hated me.

Unswayed, I rose up tall and let my voice ring out loud and clear.

"A life for a life. That's what you said to me on that first Samhain." I stepped from the doorway and motioned inside, gesturing to the carcass on the floor with a gaping hole where his heart once lived. "There. There's your life."

When I turned back to the Sluagh, their eyes went even rounder as realization sank in.

"Aedan won't be hurting any of you ever again," I added softly. "You're free."

A peek at Tallys found tears of gratitude welling in her eyes. The Sluagh noticed them too, a dull murmur swelling among the crowd as they shifted in place.

"Not quite what we intended," a Sluagh at the front of the group stated. She looked me up and down, then glanced back over her shoulder at the sea of identical faces staring back at her. When she faced forward again, she lowered her weapon, the furious wrinkles on her brow relaxing.

"Regardless." The woman watched me a few seconds longer before a smile stretched across her thin lips. "Your debt is paid, Lina Calder. We have no quarrel with you anymore."

Relief fluttered through my chest, and I let out the breath I'd been keeping hostage in my throat.

The Sluagh dipped her head to me. "Be well, and give our love to the Changeling child."

I respectfully copied her movement. "I will."

She gave me another smile, then two fingers rose, snapped, and the mob vanished into thin air, leaving the hallway as eerie and silent as a burial ground.

"I'm never going to get used to them doing that," Xavier grumbled.

Hale grabbed my hand and gave it a proud squeeze before motioning for us to continue.

We rushed through the twisting maze of corridors as quickly and quietly as possible, but the going was slow with Tallys still limping and Xavier, Syrena, and Ilora weakened from Hale's vicious demonstration of power. In spite of that, we traveled through the tunnels relatively unnoticed, only needing to dispose of the occasional handful of Nethers we came across, which Hale or I efficiently managed with our blades.

When the shore of the underground lake came into view, we all breathed a sigh of relief. Our anxiety was lessened even further when shimmering, blue-tinged heads breached the surface.

"What happened?!" one of the Merrows demanded, before diving back down and emerging in the shallows, where she stood on two legs and splashed towards us. When she reached Tallys, her sapphire-hued hands flew out and took hold of her face, examining the discoloration left over from Aedan's fury.

"I'm alright," Tallys assured her. "But Aedan uncovered the plan. He's gone now, but Erith will be right behind us. We need to move fast."

The Merrow blinked in surprise. "He's... gone?"

Again, Tallys's eyes brimmed with tears. "He's finally gone."

The Merrow let out a single stunned laugh. Then she laughed again, this time louder. Then she threw her head back and cackled merrily, spinning to face her sisters' bobbing heads on the water.

"He's dead!" she shouted, punching a fist in the air.

The Merrows tilted their heads back and erupted in harmonious cries of joy, every high-pitched wail somehow melding together to create a haunting melody that echoed through the whole of the cavern. A few stray Piksis who had been hiding in the rocks nearby joined in the celebration, flitting over the water and sprinkling their gold dust in every direction, the glowing flecks raining on the Merrows as they laughed and splashed and somersaulted out of the water with glee.

The joyous display was over as soon as it began thanks to the Merrow on the shore urgently clapping her hands to wrangle her sisters' attention.

"Neith, Nixie," she barked. "You're the fastest. Find the rest of our sisters and tell them what's happening. Make sure they leave all their belongings and flee now. Meet us on the beach outside the mountains."

Two heads on the surface of the water nodded obediently and dipped out of sight.

"Ilayda, search the Piksis' forest for anyone remaining. If there are any, give them a ride through the pools and take them to the same meeting point."

Another blue head dipped in acknowledgement and disappeared beneath the waves.

"The rest of you grab hold of a Fae. Get them to the beach as fast as you can. Remember, they can't hold their breath like us, so make sure to come up for air."

A mumbled chorus of *Oh, that's right* and *I forgot about that* did nothing to calm my nerves.

The Merrows popped up in the shallows and started pairing off with each of us. Xavier went with the same periwinkle-lashed woman he'd been intimate with on the spring equinox, Syrena joined an adolescent Merrow with gorgeous cerulean eyes, Hale took the offered arm of a young lady with short midnight-blue hair, and Tallys stayed partnered with Ilora, her webbing and spiky dorsal fin appearing the second she set foot in the waves lapping against the shore.

The Merrow who'd delegated the tasks to her sisters stepped towards me, extending webbed fingers of her own.

"You're with me, King Slayer."

I swallowed my fear and grabbed hold of her. To my surprise, she wasn't cold and slimy like she looked. Instead, her skin was soft and warm.

"Can you swim?" she asked as she led me into bone-chilling knee-deep water.

"I'm not the best, but I can manage."

"Just kick your legs to help me out as best you can, and you'll be fine."

I nodded, sucking in a breath as the water swished at my hips and waist.

"What's your name?" I asked through chattering teeth.

"Aysu."

"Thank you for doing this, Aysu. We're very grateful."

The Merrow halted, seemingly immune to the frigid water that sloshed against our chests. When she looked at me, her eyes twinkled with emotion.

"No. Thank *you*. My people will sing songs about you for centuries to come. It is we who are grateful."

I barely had enough time to take a deep breath, let alone swallow the tightness in my throat, before Aysu leapt into the deep, dragging me down with her.

Underwater, time slowed even though the world around me rushed past, my surroundings nothing but a dark blur in every direction. As soon as my lungs were screaming for relief, Aysu somehow sensed it and would break the surface of a pool somewhere, staying just long enough for me to take in another lungful of air before she dipped back into the depths. The pattern continued five times, then ten, then twenty, until I lost track of how often we'd emerged in a random dark cave to breathe before continuing with our swim towards safety.

Just when I'd started to wonder if we'd been tricked and this was the Merrows' sadistic idea of fun before they took our lives, a light appeared in the distance: dim, gray, and dreary, but a beacon of hope nonetheless.

Aysu hurtled towards it, and when our faces burst into fresh air, we both furiously gulped the salty breeze like it was the elixir of life.

I looked out over the waves, relief flooding over me at the sight of water as far as the eye could see.

Not heavy, suffocating dark.

Not glowing algae or pale moonstone.

Not any form of crystalline cavern where morning, afternoon, and night didn't exist.

It was daytime, the air was open, and we were free.

# Chapter 46

Aysu swam towards the fog-heavy shore while I paddled behind. My friends were already there, sodden and weary, but just as relieved to be out in the open as I was.

Hale's hands caught me the second I arrived in waist-deep water, effortlessly hauling me from the waves onto the black sand shore before I could insist I was perfectly capable of getting there by myself. When my feet hit solid ground, Hale wrapped me in his arms and smashed his lips to mine, silencing every complaint and objection about to pass over my tongue. When he finally pulled away, he swept my cheeks into the curves of his palms, angling my face to look up at him as he beamed down at me.

"We did it," he whispered.

His body was shaking, so I tightened my arms around his waist to anchor him. "We did."

Hale's grin widened, and he lowered his lips to my nose, pressing a tender kiss to its tip.

"You two are so cute I'm going to vomit." Syrena stomped over, wringing water from the hem of her dress. Her words carried their usual bite, but her face held fond amusement as she watched us.

Hale grew serious. "Are you alright? I didn't hurt you too badly when I was spellbound, did I?"

Syrena shrugged. "We'll call it payback for how I treated you all those years."

Hale's frown deepened. "You treated me fine."

"No, I didn't." Suddenly finding it hard to look him in the eye, Syrena looked everywhere but. "I let my people believe things about you that were untrue. I barely did anything to defend you, and more often than not, I only treated you like my friend when it benefited me. And for that, I'm sorry."

She finally forced herself to meet Hale's stare. Her bright eyes were earnest, her shoulders slumped with regret.

"Why are you saying all this?" Hale asked warily.

Syrena shrugged and rubbed her arms against the chill. "No reason, really. Near-death experiences tend to put things in perspective, is all."

Her attention flicked to the freckle-faced man chatting with the Merrows farther down the beach.

"Anyway." Syrena shook her head, prying her eyes away from Xavier, and refocused on Hale. "I just wanted to tell you that. And I want you to know you still have a place in Lerian if you so choose. And this time, I promise to be a *real* friend to you, not just one of convenience. I won't allow you to be treated the way you once were. You have my word."

Hale blinked in surprise. With an expression brimming with uncertainty, he peeked at me. I responded by slipping my hand into his, soothing his worries with a warm smile and a loving squeeze.

"Wherever you go, we go together."

Hale's eyelids flickered, and his throat bobbed as he swallowed. "Lina, there's... there's something I should tell you."

His sudden seriousness set my heart racing. "Yes?"

He opened his mouth, but no words came out. Instead, he swept a pained gaze over my features, searching for inspiration in the lines of my face.

"Hale, what is it?" I pressed.

He remained silent for a few seconds more before sighing. "I don't care where I go, as long as you're with me."

I chuckled a little, my heart swelling with relief, and tightened my grip as I wove my fingers through his. "Agreed."

A faint smile appeared on Hale's lips, but it ended up looking more like a wince.

"Are you sure that's all you wanted to say?" I asked, analyzing his furrowed brow and the melancholy look in his eye.

Hale smiled again, a genuine one this time, and nodded.

The crunch of sand pulled our attention to Xavier trudging towards us. He fell in beside Syrena and slicked his soggy curls away from his face.

"The Merrows say they need a rest to renew their strength, then they should be able to get us back to the veil without stopping. Think we can give them a little time?"

Hale nodded thoughtfully. "I think we should be fine. No longer than a few minutes, though."

Xavier dipped his head and started back towards the group of women gathered near the water, the hue of their skin already starting to fade as they dried under the light of the silver sun.

"You're pretty good at this whole ambassador thing, you know," Syrena called after him.

Xavier looked over his shoulder, an eyebrow quirking upwards. "A compliment? What did I do to deserve such an honor, Your Highness?"

Syrena sighed and rolled her eyes, but a reluctant grin

sneaked onto her lips. When she faced us again, Hale's brows arched.

"What?" Syrena snapped.

He smirked and shook his head. "Nothing."

"Xavier was very brave back there," I mused, talking to Hale but glancing at Syrena out the corner of my eye.

"He was," Hale concurred, eyeing her the same way. "He saved lives."

Syrena clicked her tongue, spun away from us, and started for Ilora and Tallys further up on the sand. "Sorry to disappoint, but if you two are attempting to start a career in matchmaking, I will *not* be your first victim."

When she'd walked away, Hale turned to me and slid his hands around my waist, pulling me close. "A career in matchmaking. Maybe that's my calling when we get back."

I giggled and swiped another pesky strand of hair from his face, leaving my hand to rest on his cheek. "Maybe so. Your slogan can be, 'If a demon can find love, so can you.'"

Hale threw back his head and laughed, the rare sound glorious music to my ears. When he looked at me again he continued to smile, but there was that far-off look in his eyes again.

"Love, huh?" he murmured.

I'd lost him too many times now to be coy. Time was fleeting, and life was precious, and somewhere amid the chaos I'd decided that being subtle just wasn't worth it.

"Yes," I stated, draping my arms around his neck. "I love you, Hale. So deeply it abandons all logic and reason."

Hale gulped again, his fingers pressing further into the flesh at my waist.

"It's alright," I assured him. "You don't have to say anything back. I know you care for me. I don't need you to feel as strongly as I do. I love you, and that's fact. And nothing, not even your feelings, or lack of them, will do anything to change that."

"I *do* feel strongly, Lina."

My heart fluttered at those timid words.

"In fact..." Hale licked his lips and inhaled a shaking breath. "I... I think... I think I—"

A resonating howl pierced the air, cutting him off.

The Merrows instantly leapt up from where they lounged, erupting in a chorus of defensive hisses.

Both Hale and I snapped to attention, our hands flying to our weapons.

"What is it?" I asked, frantically searching the surrounding fog.

"Aedan's hunters," Aysu shouted, her stern voice a harsh contrast to her trembling hands. "They found us quicker than I thought they would."

A murmur of fear rose among the Merrows, their dorsal fins flaring as they backed towards the ocean's edge.

Another howl rang out, this time closer.

"We need to get back in the water," Aysu barked, the trembling finding its way into her words. "*Now!*"

At her command, we whirled and sprinted for the sanctuary of the sea. The Merrows were slated to get there first, then Xavier, me, and Hale, with Syrena, Ilora, and Tallys not far behind.

Aysu dove into the water, shooting out into the waves as far as she could, followed by the Merrows who had helped Hale and Xavier. The last woman, the smallest and youngest who'd aided Syrena, readied herself to leap into the surf, but the moment her webbed feet lifted off the sand, something hurtled out of the fog, snatched her out of midair, and tackled her back down to the ground. She screamed in surprise and terror, but a massive, hulking thing that was a garish combination of both man and wolf clamped its jaws around her neck, silencing her forever.

We skidded to a halt in alarm, the anguished shrieks from the Merrows over their fallen sister drowning out the pounding footfalls drawing near. Xavier glanced over his shoulder just in time, his eyes growing wide as he caught a glimpse of something behind me and Hale.

"Shit!" he exclaimed, throwing out his hands and sending a pulse of his magic forward.

A yelp rang out behind me, and I turned as another Weir, not a foot from my back, ricocheted off Xavier's barrier of protection and rolled across the beach in a flurry of sand and fur.

"Everyone get close to me!" Xavier ordered.

The statement was less for Hale and me and more for Ilora, Syrena, and Tallys, who were still a few paces behind.

Another Weir flew out of the fog, but this one Hale took care of by releasing a whip of darkness towards it. His power ripped through the creature with a vengeance, bursting its skull like a ripe berry and painting the shore red with its blood.

A second Weir leapt from the opposite side, aiming for Ilora, but again Hale sent his magic tearing into it. Then Tallys tripped and fell, and a third Weir pounced from the mist, its razor-sharp jaws open and ready for the kill, but Hale hurled his knife through the air. It whizzed into the creature's throat before Tallys ever realized she was in danger.

"Hurry!" Xavier shouted, hands still outstretched. His readiness paid off when a Weir leapt from the fog again, headed right for Hale, but one push from Xavier had it bouncing off his power and tumbling across the beach.

Another beast leapt at Syrena, but Hale disposed of that one with another ribbon of black.

Ilora's gaze was fixed on us, but her eyes went round in

surprise the way Xavier's had. I instinctively ducked, a pair of claws narrowly missing my head, but they collided with Hale instead and knocked him to the ground with a grunt.

"Hale!" I shouted, rushing after them as they struggled.

I stabbed my dagger down into the mound of fur and muscle that had pinned Hale, its point burying deep in a dense lump of flesh. The Weir lifted on its knees and roared in pain, then spun and swiped a claw in my direction. I jumped backwards, narrowly dodging it, and lost my footing. I clumsily landed in a heap on the sand, and the Weir returned its attention to Hale, who caught its snapping jaws as they went for his face. Grunting at the effort, his power tried to bloom from his back to defend him, but it fizzled as he focused on keeping the beast's teeth pried open as they attempted to devour him whole.

I scrambled upright and went after the Weir again, yanking my knife from where it had lodged in the creature's back and jamming it down again. The monster bellowed but kicked out a hind leg this time, catching me in the stomach and sending me flying as air whooshed from my lungs.

In the distance, more Weirs barreled towards us, howling and yipping eagerly at the thrill of the hunt. A river of water lifted from the ocean and battered the group, taking out a handful in its path, but it soon weakened and became nothing but a trickle. I sneaked a peek at Ilora, curious as to why her power had faded so fast, but found it was because she was already sending a separate stream in the opposite direction to keep another group of Weirs at bay.

We were surrounded on both sides.

I hauled myself upright and started for the Weir battling Hale. The creature's gnashing fangs were inches from Hale's face, dribbling drool and foam into his eyes and mouth. I stumbled towards them, catching hold of my dagger's hilt once more and tearing it from the Weir's skin, then raising it high to strike a third time.

A shrill screech sliced through the air, resembling that of a hawk but ten times as loud. The noise was enough to make the Weirs stop in their tracks and look up. I followed their gazes, catching only a whirl of black feathers before something plummeted from the sky above and a pair of talons struck the creature atop Hale, carving deep grooves into the back of its head. The Weir crumpled, and with a groan Hale shoved the body off him and scrambled upright. I ran to his side and gripped his arm.

"Are you alright?" I asked breathlessly.

"I'm fine," he panted, wiping the slobber from his face with the back of his sleeve. "What the hell was that?"

Ilora, Tallys, and Syrena finally arrived beside us, gasping for air from their mad dash. It was Syrena who answered the question, breathing heavy but beaming up at the sky.

"It's Veshti!"

As if on cue, the clouds parted and the winged woman plunged towards land, cleaving the throat of a Weir as it leapt at us, before landing solidly in the sand with her feathers splayed out on either side of her.

"Veshti!" I cried, laughing out loud with relief. "We thought you were dead!"

She shook her head, the gold in her hair and on her wrists tinkling with the movement. "No. Veshti alive. But not if stay here."

A Weir charged from the fog, headed straight for us, but Hale immobilized it with a fatal tendril of his darkness. Veshti watched the body fall, her wings rustling in surprise, then examined it before surveying Hale.

"Veshti like him," she stated, nodding appreciatively. "Very useful."

"Veshti!" Syrena ran up to her, offering one of her remaining bracelets. "Help us get back to the veil, and you can have as many golden snakes as you want. You can join our flock, and you never need to go hungry or fight to survive again."

Veshti eyed the gold piece, hesitating briefly before nudging the bangle back towards Syrena with her knuckle.

"Syrena keep," she demanded. "But Veshti still help."

With one powerful flap of her wings, she was in the air again and zooming towards a Weir lunging at Tallys. Her talons sank into its side, tearing the life from its body before it ever hit the ground.

"Everyone stay close!" Syrena yelled. "Head to the water. Xavier, protect our backs."

"Yes, Commander," Xavier quipped.

But he hadn't meant it as a joke, and Syrena didn't take it as one. Instead his words made her head lift high, her shoulders square, and she continued to dish out orders with the confidence of a born leader.

"Hale, Ilora, Veshti: defend the front."

In answer, Veshti dove at a Weir trying to sneak up behind us, and Hale sent a wave of black hurtling through three coming in from the right.

"Move as a unit!" Syrena instructed. "On three. One... two... *three.*"

Together we moved as one, our feet falling in tandem as we headed towards the waves lapping against the shore while the Merrows anxiously watched. Leaving the magic-wielding to those in better control of their powers, I paired up with Tallys, wrapping my arm around her shoulder and keeping her close as we both crouched low to the ground and followed the others across the beach. Beads of sweat dripped down Xavier's forehead as he kept his shield strong. Weirs constantly glanced off his barrier like pebbles of ice in a hailstorm, while the path ahead of us was nothing but a raging flood of water and black mist thanks to Ilora and Hale. Veshti also aided in clearing the way by swooping in and picking off any stragglers.

When we made it to the water's edge, Syrena sloshed into the waves and ushered Tallys and me forward.

"You two first," she commanded, flagging Aysu and the other Merrows down.

They obeyed the order, swimming into the shallows and extending their webbed hands to us. Once they'd drawn Tallys and me into the swells and away from danger, Syrena turned back to our friends.

"Boys, can you hold them off?"

"Yes," Hale stated, eyes narrowing as his darkness viciously swept through another four Weirs.

"Yep," Xavier grunted. He was clearly struggling, but his power held.

"Then Ilora's next." Syrena nodded to the queen of Merimaya, gesturing to the ocean at their backs. "When you see an opening, make a dash for it."

Ilora nodded, gritting her teeth as she focused on sending a furious tube of water crashing down on a pair of Weirs sneaking up on Xavier's left. When she was certain the creatures were drowned beneath it, she whirled and jogged into the surf, headed for Tallys, who was floating there waiting for her.

"Hale next," Syrena said.

Hale shook his head, keeping his eyes glued to the Nethers who had completely encircled them and were slowly pushing in. "You go. Let your sword and shield leave the battlefield last."

Syrena pursed her lips. "A good queen doesn't abandon her troops, she makes sure they're safe before she retreats."

"Listen to me, Syrena," Hale growled out the side of his mouth. "For *once*, just listen."

"Enough," Xavier snapped. His cheeks were ruddy from

straining, and as the Weirs attacked his barrier with more speed and aggression, the shaking of his hands worsened.

"Now's not really the best time to argue," he ground out. "I say on the count of three, we all turn and run. Deal?"

"Deal," Hale replied.

Syrena sighed. "Deal."

"Great." Xavier's jaw clenched, and he placed a foot behind him, readying himself. "One... two... three!"

Hale and Xavier dropped their power, and together the three spun and splashed into the shallows.

Hale got to the deeper water first, throwing his hands over his head and diving into the waves to surface alongside Ilora and Tallys in a swell further out. Xavier followed, throwing himself into a crest just before it smashed into him. But Syrena, who had been right on his heels, missed her window into the wave and was knocked backwards as it rolled into her. She tumbled underwater for a few seconds before her head popped up and she gasped in a breath, swiping saltwater from her eyes. Shakily, she found her footing and stood, lunging towards the deeper water once again.

But before she'd made it far enough, a Weir flew into the water after her, sank its teeth into her thigh, and yanked her back towards the shore before anyone saw it coming.

"Syrena!" I screamed out.

I started swimming for the beach to help her, but Aysu caught the collar of my dress and hauled me back again.

"You'll never make it to her in time!"

I attempted to shrug the Merrow off, but she was right. I changed tactics and looked up at the sky.

"Veshti!" I cried, throwing my arms over my head and thrashing in the water to get her attention. "Veshti, Syrena's in trouble!"

The movement caught Veshti's keen eye, and her gaze darted to the shore.

In the water not far from me, Xavier and Hale bobbed, focusing on the beach and attempting to stretch their power there. Xavier had no luck, but Hale managed to reach the Weir holding our friend. He made quick work of the creature, but as soon as he finished one off, another took its place. Even combined with Veshti's sharp talons swiping at the pack, they never seemed to get Syrena free long enough for her to make a run for the water. Her cries reached my ears, and even from where I floated I could see her blood staining the teeth and claws of the Nethers around her.

I swallowed my panic and shut my eyes, digging deep for that dark thing that lived inside me. It moved slightly, hesitant to leave its twisted vine around my bones. My body started to vibrate, and the water around me rippled.

... Except it wasn't from my power.

My eyes snapped open, and I looked down at the sea in surprise. The water had grown choppy, like a storm was roiling its surface, but there was no wind. Something else was disturbing the ocean.

Something from below.

I glanced at the Merrows, who seemed equally perplexed at first but soon erupted in terrified hisses. Before they had the chance to swim away, scales appeared in the water beneath our kicking legs, and I was struck by the horrified realization of their source at the same moment a giant serpentine head broke the waves.

The sea serpent we'd encountered before rocketed from the depths, its mouth opened wide in a deadly smile, but instead of swallowing us or the Merrows whole like I'd thought it would, it surged towards the shore. The Weirs barely had time to see it coming before it tore into them, smashing them beneath its colossal writhing body or slicing them in two with its knifelike teeth. The only one spared from its wrath was Syrena, whose battered body lay at the center of the snake's coil.

As the sea serpent struck at a row of Weirs attacking its tail, Veshti saw her opportunity. With a few flaps of her wings, she swooped down and scooped Syrena into her arms, cradling her like a babe, and leapt into the sky again.

"Veshti meet you there," she called down to us, already angling in the direction of the veil. "Hurry!"

Needing no further bidding, Aysu latched on to my hand and dragged me beneath the surface, hurtling through the murky deep even faster than before.

Again came the pattern of struggling for air, coming up for a breath, and diving again, until I'd lost track of time and location. Eventually a familiar rocky point came into view, and when we'd all gathered among its coral crags, everyone looked to me. Feeling the weight of the moment, I hesitated and peeked at Hale. He offered me a reassuring nod, which gave me the courage to take a deep breath, dive to the cave below, and lead the way to the new normal waiting on the other side.

Whatever that entailed.

# CHAPTER 47

THE ORANGE GLARE OF THE SUNSET HIT MY EYES AS I BREACHED the surface and gasped in life-giving air. One look at the precarious rocks and the palace nestled on the cliff overhead proved we'd made it back.

I treaded water, staring at the depths below, until there was a frenzy of air bubbles and one by one my friends and the Merrows emerged from the deep. Xavier was one of the last to appear, hauling a barely conscious Syrena with him. He was followed by Tallys aiding Veshti, who instantly thrashed and squawked and clung to a nearby rock to shake out her soaked feathers.

"Come on," Ilora called, beckoning the rest of us to follow her as she paddled towards the shore.

While Veshti remained out on the rocks to dry her wings, the tide helped push us in, allowing us to ride the swells towards the sand and making it a far easier journey than it had been swimming out. The Merrows helped us avoid the strong currents pulling us into the coral, and they aided Xavier in pulling Syrena's body onto the shore. Once she was safe on dry land, we all gathered around her.

There had been too much happening to take stock of how bad her wounds were, but seeing her now had my stomach twisted in knots. Her skin was riddled with savage bite marks and deep gouges from the Weirs' claws, and even though the ocean had washed away a significant amount of the blood, more was pooling around her.

"Out of the way," Ilora demanded, pushing into the circle and kneeling at Syrena's side.

Xavier stayed rooted beside her, dabbing at a gash on Syrena's brow with his sleeve and watching intently as Ilora summoned her blue light and sent the pulsing glow over the limp figure in front of us. Even the Merrows held their breath as they watched, wringing their webbed hands and murmuring among themselves. It felt like hours had passed, but it was probably only seconds before Syrena's wounds slowly closed. To our relief, she took a deep inhale, and her eyes fluttered open.

"Oh, thank the gods," I breathed, clapping a hand to my heart.

With me and Xavier's help, Syrena sat up, whimpering softly as her skin fused. Typically with wounds this size, a scar would be left behind after a healer's touch. But there wasn't so much as a mark marring Syrena's body when Ilora had finished with her.

"Well, that was a fun trip," Syrena groaned. "Let's never do it again."

All of us laughed, but none harder than Xavier.

"Excuse us." Aysu stepped forward and bowed her head. "Many of our sisters are still waiting. We need to return through the veil so we can show them the way through."

Ilora nodded. "We'll be here to welcome you when you get

back, and Syrena and I will get to work on a formal decree of your protection once she's feeling up to it."

Aysu dipped her head again, gratitude shining in her eyes. "Thank you, Your Majesties."

The rest of the Merrows also muttered their thanks before retreating. Tallys watched them go, then stood.

"I'm going with them."

At that, Ilora bolted upright, her brow creasing. "Are you sure you're feeling up to it?"

"Yes." Tallys hesitated for a moment, but soon rested a hand on Ilora's shoulder. "I'll be careful. I promise."

Ilora looked ready to argue, but after a tender squeeze from Tallys, she sighed. "Alright. But I'm not leaving this beach until you're back, so you'd better hurry."

A tiny bubble of laughter escaped the former slave. "I will."

They stared at each other a few seconds longer before Tallys forced herself to turn away and limp to the water's edge. She dove in, immediately disappearing from view, and true to her word, Ilora sat back in the sand and made herself comfortable, prepared to stay there for as long as it took.

The thump of footfalls pulled our attention up the beach. Out of habit I reached for my dagger, but stopped when a pack of Lerian guards crested the sandy hills. A familiar face marched among them.

"Dammit, you lot!" Roric Pax barked, fury etched into his face as he stormed towards us. "You're lucky I don't tan your hides!"

With Xavier's help, Syrena shakily stood. When her captain of the guard caught sight of her tattered dress and the blood drying on the sand, his hardened expression dissipated and his eyes went round with concern. He rushed to her side, gripped her shoulders in his hands and angled her body every which way in search of wounds.

"What happened? Are you hurt? Do you need a healer?"

Ignoring his questions, Syrena shimmied out of his grasp. "How did you find us so quickly?"

"I've had guards posted on the point day and night since you left." Realizing she was unharmed, Roric exhaled a sigh of relief, shaking his head as his authoritative tone returned. "A little birdie told me about a letter she received explaining where the four of you were headed the evening you bashed me over the head."

The commander glared pointedly at Xavier, who blew him a kiss in response. Roric rolled his eyes at the gesture and turned back to Syrena.

"What the hell were you thinking?"

Syrena stood a little taller, her voice calm and confident. "I was thinking I would accompany a friend on her valiant quest to save our world."

"You could have died!"

"Yes. For the good of my people I risked my life, and I'd do it again in a heartbeat. You can reprimand me all you want, but you'll accomplish nothing but wasting your breath."

Roric opened his mouth to speak but promptly shut it, exhaling loudly through his nose as he ruefully rubbed the back of his neck. "Gods, when did you start sounding like a queen?"

When he looked at her again, a fond smile had found its way to his face. Then his eyes flicked to the side, and he glimpsed Hale for the first time. Roric's jaw went slack.

"It can't be." Warily, he stepped forward. "Hale?"

"In the flesh."

Roric shook his head in disbelief. "How? They said you were dead."

Hale shrugged and casually kicked at a shell on the sand. "Apparently, I'm difficult to kill."

"Well, for that I'm glad." Roric closed the distance between them and clapped a hand on Hale's back. "Welcome home."

The warm gesture took Hale by surprise, but he kept his composure and politely dipped his head in the stoic manner he was known for.

I wanted to shrink into nothing when Roric's gaze shifted to me next, his eyes narrowing into olive green slits.

"*You*." He tapped his foot and shook his head. "You've created quite a stir, Lina Calder. Stealing away two queens, bringing Merrows to our shores, *and* leading an army onto our doorstep?"

At those last words, all of us tensed.

"Army?" Ilora scrambled up from her spot on the sand and jogged over. "Have the Nethers retaliated already?"

"It's not the Nethers. The army is from Astoria."

My stomach sank, the sensation only increasing when everyone turned to look at me like I knew something about it.

"Soren sent his forces here?" My voice became a pathetic croak as it tasted the forbidden name.

"Yes. They're camped on the outskirts of the city."

"How have we countered?" Syrena cut in.

"We haven't." Roric barred a pair of thick arms over his chest. "They didn't come to attack. They were coming after you."

My knees suddenly went weak as my mind spun in circles.

"What?" was all I managed to get out.

"When Willow found your letter, she came straight to me. We went back and forth on what to do, but eventually decided I would accompany her and your brother as they returned to Astoria to tell the king what you'd gotten yourself into this time. He had no idea you were even here."

Xavier stepped forward. "Yes, he did. I left him a note telling him where we'd gone, and I sent him letters every week I was here."

"I don't know about any note." Roric's frown deepened as he glanced purposefully at Syrena. "But apparently the king tried sending letters here, and *someone* has been making it very difficult for things to get in and out of the palace."

Realization washed over Syrena's face even before Xavier spoke his next words.

"Kaspar kept my letters from getting to Soren," he muttered, hands curling into fists.

"And he never responded to the king of Astoria's letters asking if you were here."

"There are people in Astoria who've likely done the same." Xavier chewed the inside of his cheek as he considered. "I know Magnus Tynan goes through Soren's personal documents, and he was in the castle the day we left. It wouldn't surprise me if he found my original note and kept it from getting to Soren too."

Roric nodded in confirmation. "Soren had no idea if you or Lina were even alive. He'd been going out of his mind with worry. After Willow and I met with him, he instantly made preparations to come to your aid. He and his troops have been here for days, scouting the coastline for the cave to the Netherworld that Lina mentioned in her letter."

As Roric's statement settled, it brought to mind a different set of words, ones I'd said to Syrena when my brother and I came to Lerian. I'd told her all I wanted was for Soren to fight for me. To go to the edge of the world for us if he had to.

And here he was, doing just that.

I inhaled a shaky breath, trying to ignore the massive piece of my heart that still ached for my past love, an ache that had never entirely gone away. Hale's eyes weighed on me, and I slowly met his gaze. He stared at me with that look of distant pain, which only increased the hurt in my chest. I never wanted to be the source of Hale's pain. I wanted to ease it, soothe it, pull it out of him like a healer draws out poison.

So I pushed aside the lasting remnants of love I still had for Soren and smiled at Hale to remind him *he* was the one I'd chosen, and would continue to choose, over and over, until the bitter end. To drive my point home, I reached out and slid my hand into his.

Hale collapsed to the ground as soon as our skin made contact, a tortured scream ripping from his throat.

I jumped back in alarm and watched in horror as his body seized, the pathways of his veins lighting up like lightning beneath his skin.

"What's happening?" I shrieked, reining in my emotions enough to fling myself to my knees beside him.

Roric hurriedly knelt in the sand beside me. "It looks like a broken bargain."

"What... what does that mean?" Fear and panic clutched my chest, making it difficult to breathe. My hands hovered above Hale's writhing form, shaking violently, while the rest of me froze. I was at a complete loss for what to do, too stunned and terrified to form a rational thought.

"When you make a bargain with a Fae," Roric explained, catching hold of Hale's shoulders to pin him in place, "it creates an invisible bond. If broken, the one responsible will suffer the worst pain imaginable until the end of their days, which never seems to be much longer after the breaking. The pain it causes is too great, and the body gives out under the strain."

"No, no, no..." I caught Hale's hand in mine, but he only screamed louder. "There has to be something we can do!"

"There isn't." Syrena knelt beside us. She swallowed hard, unable to look straight on at the agony twisting Hale's features. "There's no way to undo it."

"There has to be! You're Fae, you have all sorts of magic! What about a healer or a witch? Maybe they can—"

"We said there's no way to undo it, Lina," Syrena snapped. "There never has been."

I choked on a sob and looked back at Hale. Tears squeezed out the sides of his eyes, and each of his limbs was locked at a strange angle as his muscles spasmed.

Frantically, I turned to Ilora.

"You have to try and help him! You have to try to heal him! You're powerful, maybe you could save him!"

"Healers have tried to help bargain breaks for centuries," Syrena retaliated. Her expression was furious, but her voice broke on the last word. She smacked a hand over her mouth to compose herself, and ducked her head so we wouldn't see her eyes glistening.

"No." Ilora set her jaw, a look of stubborn determination washing over her. She shouldered her way into the circle. "Lina's right. The Hag added to my power. If anyone could do this, it's me. Everyone back up."

We obeyed, scooting further away from Hale as Ilora raised her hands over his body. The blue light came forward again. Ilora inhaled deeply and shut her eyes.

"Come on, Ilora, *focus*," she whispered to herself.

The glow in her palms started to pulse, slowly spreading over Hale's body, head to toe. His screams continued to drown out all other noise on the beach, the light doing nothing to ease the sounds of his torment or the way he jerked in place.

"Focus," Ilora muttered again, taking another deep breath in and out.

Shoulders shaking with silent sobs, I crawled over to Syrena. She slipped an arm around my shoulders and pulled me close.

"Come *on*," Ilora repeated, more firm this time. Her eyelids flickered but remained shut. "I know you're in there. I can feel you. You're strong," Ilora went on, her head tilting like she was arguing with someone standing in front of her. "You *know* you're strong. You're so strong it's terrifying, so you've stayed holed up in there. But people need you now. It's alright to be something unexpected, to be different. Being different is what makes you special, so stop fearing it. Come out. Come out and be exactly what you were created to be."

The light in Ilora's hands stopped pulsing. Instead, its glow stayed constant.

"Come out," she whispered again. "Come out, come out, *come out.*"

The light's color changed. The cool blue faded to white, then warmed to a golden hue reminiscent of the sun at the edge of the horizon. Ilora's eyes snapped open, her pupils matching the glowing gold, and her mouth parted as she gasped in a breath. The look of ecstasy on her face was one I knew well.

She'd grasped the full extent of her power.

Instantly, Hale's voice died down and he stopped seizing. His body went limp, but when I leaned in to see if he was nothing but a corpse, his chest rose and fell. Then a pair of dark eyes fluttered open, and I nearly collapsed with relief.

"Hale!" I cried, rushing forward and catching his face in my hands to plant a kiss on his cracked lips.

But then the lightning in his veins flared once more, followed by more of his violent thrashing and ear-piercing screams.

"No!" I wailed, looking back and forth between him and my friends. "He was fixed! You saw it, he was fixed! What happened?"

It was then that Xavier jumped into the huddle and pulled me off the man I loved.

"It's you, Lina!" he grunted, dragging me backwards. "The bargain has to do with you!"

I attempted to maneuver out of his grip, but he had too strong a hold on me. "I never made a bargain with anyone!"

"No, but they made the bargain about you."

I stopped fighting as the words sank in. Dumbly, I watched Ilora swoop in and send her new beams of healing gold through Hale's body once more, calming the spasms and easing his pain in a matter of seconds. When he'd returned to normal, his eyes met mine. Written over his face was the unmistakable mask of guilt and shame.

Still panting from the anguish, Hale miserably shook his head. "I'm so sorry, Lina. I should have told you."

A dull roar started in my ears at the same time a fire swept through my veins. It wasn't my magic roiling my blood, though.

This was nothing but rage.

"Who did you make the bargain with?" I asked, adopting the deadly calm Hale spoke in whenever he stood poised to tear the world apart.

Recognizing the tone, he gulped nervously.

My eyes narrowed.

"Hale," I said, my voice dripping sweet venom as I enunciated each syllable. "Who... did you make... the bargain with?"

Hale dropped his gaze to the sand. After a moment of silence, he sighed and mumbled, "Who do you think?"

*Someone who would fight for me, and go to the edge of the world for us if he had to.*

"Get up," I demanded. "Get up and follow me. *Now.*"

# CHAPTER 48

———

Soren and Hale sat beside each other looking like two children receiving a scolding.

Exuding the energy of a dog with its tail between its legs, Hale had trailed behind me as I'd stormed through the Astorian war camp. I'd barreled past every soldier or guard who tried to stop us until I blew right into the king's tent. Ignoring his look of surprise, I'd thrust a finger in his face and spat, "Both of you sit down," before he could even manage a hello.

"How *dare* you?" I snarled. "How *fucking* dare you? Who gave you the right to dictate my life for me?"

Hale opened his mouth to argue, but Soren nudged him with his elbow and shook his head gravely, pressing a finger to his lips to signal Hale should remain silent.

I paced in front of them, flailing my arms around me as the words tumbled out. "It's not so much the bargain, which is fucking idiotic by the way, but the fact that neither of you mentioned it. Not even once. You really think so little of me that you not only decided my fate, but you kept me in the dark for your own selfish gain?"

Again Hale made to argue, but Soren gave him another nudge to warn against it.

"Best to just let her get it all out," he whispered out the side of his mouth.

Foolishly choosing to ignore the advice, Hale spoke up.

"I just wanted—"

"I'm not fucking finished!" I screeched.

Hale clamped his mouth shut and wilted into his chair.

"You had more than enough opportunities to sit down and discuss this with me, but instead you wanted to preserve my opinion of you. You were avoiding a confrontation like *this*." I gestured between us. "In other words, you two were being *fucking cowards*."

I let out a furious huff and stomped over to the long mahogany table draped in maps and scrolls, leaning my backside against its edge as I crossed my arms and stared expectantly at the men.

"Well? What do you have to say for yourselves?"

Wary to attempt speaking again, Hale peeked at the king. Soren leaned forward and clasped his hands in front of him.

"You're right. We fucked up."

"Yes, you did."

I waited for him to argue his case, but he just stared at me, sitting with the mistake, taking all the rage I was throwing at him, and quietly accepting responsibility for his actions.

For some reason, that pissed me off even more.

"And you!" I flung another furious finger in Soren's direction. "What the hell were you thinking dragging your entire army to Lerian? What were you going to do, make them swim into the Netherworld one by one?"

"Yes."

I blinked. "That's *insane.*"

"You're right. I didn't think it through."

"See, that's your problem! You never think anything through!"

"You're right."

"Stop saying I'm right!"

"But you are."

I blinked again, staring at Soren for a few seconds to pick apart the expression on his face. As far as I could tell, he was being earnest.

"What are you doing?" I snapped. "Why aren't you arguing with me?"

"Because that's what a coward does when he's trying to avoid talking about what really matters. And I'm finished being a coward, Lina."

I scoffed and rolled my eyes, but it was mainly to hide the way his words made my heart melt and my skin tingle with the desperate desire to be close to him. "Well, that's new."

"It is." Soren averted his gaze to the overlapping rugs and furs on the floor of the tent. "Before I was afraid to speak candidly because I didn't want to lose you."

"And now?"

Soren looked up again, the sadness in his eyes instantly making my walls threaten to come down. "I've already lost you."

I swallowed hard, hating myself for the way I was beginning to tremble under his gaze.

"So all this." I gestured to the tent around us and the bustle of soldiers outside. "This isn't to try and get me back?"

"No." Soren shook his head, his attention briefly shifting to Hale. "You made your choice. I have to respect that. But it doesn't change the fact I would do anything for you." He looked at me again, adopting the measured tone of a military leader.

"And that includes providing my forces to aid you in your valiant effort to keep my homeland safe."

I peeked at Hale. He was watching Soren with that unflinching, analytical stare of his, jaw firm and lips pressed in a downturned line. He was studying him the same way I was, and I suspected he could find no lie in Soren's words either.

Refocusing on the king, I skeptically looked him up and down. "So you're done being a coward?"

"Yes."

"We'll see about that." I took a deep breath to calm my racing heart and lifted my chin. "Tell me why you don't want to marry me."

Soren tensed, his gaze flicking to Hale. "Now?"

"Right here, right now." I pursed my lips and readjusted my position against the table.

With Hale's stare boring into him, Soren was forced to look away.

"Fine." His intertwined fingers tightened, his throat bobbing with a nervous swallow before he spoke. "Again, it wasn't that I didn't want to marry you. I *did*. But... but I wasn't going to, for *your* sake."

"What's that supposed to mean? You didn't think I could handle being queen?"

"You've proven time and time again that you can handle anything life throws at you, Lina. What I mean is I wasn't going to subject you to a lifetime of disappointment with *me*."

I tried to keep my face neutral, but my brows nudged together in confusion.

Soren anxiously spun his signet ring in circles around his finger. "I've never told anyone this, not even Xavier. If it got out, it wouldn't be well received." He cleared his throat and forced himself to meet my gaze even though it looked like it pained him to do so. "The truth is, Lina... I won't give you children."

My mouth went dry, and I had to throw out a hand and grip the edge of the table to stay standing.

"I practically raised my brother on my own. I raised Xavier. In my mind, I've already been a father. And I'm content with that, and I wouldn't change it for anything. But... I don't feel the need to do it for real. I decided a long time ago that my line will end with me, so much so that a few years back, I went to a witch. The same one I sent you to in Astoria. She gave me an elixir that confirmed my decision, and made it impossible for me to sire children."

"What..." I rubbed my eyes. "What's Astoria supposed to do if you died, then? Who would become the king if you have no heirs?"

"I always assumed the responsibility would fall to Xavier."

A huff of disbelief passed my lips. "That's why you made him a courtier."

"I gave Xavier the life he has because I liked having him around." Soren shrugged. "But yes, in a way. As the years went on, I saw his kindness and loyalty and intelligence. All qualities of a good ruler. So I may have pushed him into the political side more than he would've liked. I'm sure he would've been content to do nothing but fight and fuck all day long."

We both couldn't help but laugh at the truth of the statement. When silence fell again, our eyes locked.

"I've never once felt guilt about my decision, Lina." Soren swallowed. "Until you."

A painful lump lodged in my throat, making it impossible to breathe.

"The second you came into my life I started to imagine a future with you, but then I saw the fierce love you have for Wynn. I started to think if *that's* so strong, I can't even fathom the love you'll have for a child of your own. The world needs more love like that. Children need more love like that from their parents. And if I married you, I would be keeping you from giving the gift of that love to a child. I won't ask you to do that for me."

I hadn't realized that as he'd been talking, tears had trickled out my eyes and down my cheeks. When Soren caught sight of them, his fingers twitched as he fought the urge to wipe them away like he had so many times before.

"The truth, Lina," he continued, his face remaining stoic but his voice cracking from the emotion coursing through him. "The truth is I am selfish. And I am arrogant. And I *am* a coward, because I wanted to hold on to you for as long as I possibly could. I wanted to keep you until you got tired of waiting for me and found someone else who could give you what you wanted."

Again his gaze shifted to Hale, whose eyes had dropped to the floor to stare blankly at a sheepskin rug.

"That's just it, Soren." I sniffled miserably. "You never asked me what I wanted."

Soren opened his mouth to protest, but thought better of it and sighed, choosing instead to nod. "You're right, I didn't. I assumed you feel the way most women do."

I sat with his words.

If he was being honest, then it was time for me to finally stop running and do the same.

Fiddling with the skirt of my dress to keep myself from falling apart, I sighed. "And *I* never asked you what you wanted, either, because I assumed you felt the way most kings do and would want as many heirs as possible. I was afraid to tell you the truth, because I too am selfish. And a coward. And wanted to hold on to you for as long as possible."

This time, it was Soren's turn to look confused. "The truth?"

A bitter laugh escaped my lips. "I don't want children. I never have."

Soren froze, his gaze locking with mine. Eventually he let out a shaky exhale. "So all the hurt and deceit—"

"Was pointless."

Hale's chair creaked as he leaned back and raised his eyes to the roof to stare blankly up at the tent's spire.

The king buried his head in his hands and groaned. "Gods. I'm a fucking idiot."

I chuckled miserably. "I am too."

Silence settled on the tent, the only sound my occasional wet sniffling and Soren's fingertips scraping against his stubble as he rubbed his jaw, lost in thought.

"Well." Soren's voice finally cut the tension, sounding light but still dripping with heartache. "We live and we learn, I suppose. Now we know what not to do in our future relationships."

He tried smiling, but it came out as a grimace.

I swallowed hard. "That's a good way of looking at it."

We both tried to laugh, but there was no joy in the sound.

I tried to ignore it, but there it was again. That magnetic, consuming pull to him, the one that seemed to connect our hearts and tug them closer. The feeling that had always been, until this very moment, near impossible to resist. But I did resist, and chose instead to look to another I'd never managed to stay away from no matter how hard I tried. His dark eyes were already fixed on me, the sadness inside them palpable.

I offered Hale a reassuring smile, but he didn't match it. Instead he sighed and shook his head.

"What?" I asked. "What's wrong?"

Hale looked away and examined the spot on the back of his hand where his brand once lived, now taken over by my handprint. His thumb traced the lines of my fingers, and when he spoke next, his voice was so quiet that at first I wasn't sure I'd heard him correctly.

"You two should be with each other."

Even Soren's head jerked up in surprise.

"What are you talking about?" I demanded. "I told you in the Netherworld, I'm *yours*. Through good or bad, thick or thin, in this realm or any."

Hale didn't respond. He continued to stare at his hands, his empty expression revealing nothing about what was going on inside his head.

"And you said you're mine too. Until the dark calls you home. Do you remember that?"

Hale nodded, a far-off look in his eyes. "I remember."

"So just like I said then, I'm not going anywhere—"

"I can't fucking touch you, Lina."

The harsh bark of his statement would have knocked me to my knees had I not been braced against the table.

When Hale's gaze found mine, it had hardened in an attempt to keep his emotions trapped inside, and his words became armed with a cutting edge.

"I can't kiss you. I can't hold your hand when the world feels like too much. I can't wipe away your tears when you're hurting. You can't tell me you could live a life without those things and truly be happy. I won't condemn you to a lifetime of misery."

"Loving you isn't condemnation—"

"You love him too, don't you?"

My mouth snapped shut. I couldn't bring myself to look at Soren, but I sensed his gaze searing into the side of my face. My mind was whirling, my heart in equal turmoil. I felt everything too much, and it was making it impossible to think straight or do anything besides stare back at Hale.

"No dodging the truth, Lina," he pressed. "Not anymore. Be honest with yourself. Do you still love him?"

I finally managed a glance at Soren. A sliver of hope flickered in his eyes. The look sent another miserable pang of heartache through my chest. I dragged my gaze away from him and refocused on Hale.

"Yes," I admitted, my soul splitting in half. "I do. But I already told you, I'm *yours*—"

"And you." Hale cut me off as he turned to Soren. "Do you still love her?"

"Yes," Soren said without hesitation.

Hale nodded like it was the response he'd anticipated. With a cool shrug, he said, "Then it's a clear choice."

"It's not!" I wailed.

"It is to me." Hale set his jaw and stood, looking less like the man I loved and more like the callous prince he'd become when Aedan enchanted him. He dipped his head formally, like we were nothing to each other, and in a monotone voice, he mumbled, "Goodbye, Lina."

A miserable sob wrenched out of me as Hale turned to go, but before he did, he glanced down at Soren still seated in his chair.

"Take care of her. Or I swear to every known god I'll bring you so much pain you'll be begging for death before I give it."

He spun on his heel and made for the flap of the tent.

In a flash, Soren stood and caught Hale's arm, jerking him to a halt. Hale angrily ground his teeth but faced him. My breath caught in my throat as the two glared at each other, and for a moment I forgot my heartbreak as fear came rushing to the forefront. A threat to a king was no small offense. In many cases it was even punishable by death. I prayed Soren wasn't the type to dole out something so extreme, but seeing the way the two of them were looking at each other now, I wasn't so sure.

A few tense beats passed before Soren spoke again, his voice calm but commanding respect.

"Before we made the bargain, I offered you a chance with

Lina. I said if there was any way you could give her your heart, then I would leave you to explore that. You said no then, but I assume if I asked you now, your answer would be—"

"Yes." Hale's hardened expression softened briefly as he glanced my way. "Yes, I think I could."

A flutter in my stomach added another level to the chaos churning inside.

Soren slowly nodded, his eyes narrow as he scrutinized Hale's features. "She cares for you, and you clearly care for her. Don't run just yet. Maybe there's a way to work this out so everyone can be happy."

Hale scoffed. "How?"

Soren released Hale's arm. "You like to watch, don't you?"

My stomach dropped, and Hale went as still as a statue.

"That's what Aedan said in the Netherworld," Soren pushed. "He said you watched me and Syrena all those years ago, and you watched Lina when she touched herself in bed."

The men weren't looking my way, but just to be safe, I ducked my face into my shoulder so they wouldn't see the rosy flush creeping into my cheeks at the memory.

Hale cleared his throat and uncomfortably shifted his weight. "It... it has become a bit of a habit, yes."

Soren faced me. It was hard to look at him at first, but when I finally did, his hooded gaze wasn't searching mine in spite. He seemed genuinely curious.

"And you like feeling his eyes on you, isn't that right?"

I started to tremble. Not from my anguish anymore, but because it seemed like both men were staring right through me. I was on display for them, my heart and soul carved open with nowhere to hide. It wasn't a negative sensation, though. In fact it was the opposite, and the flush from my cheeks had started spreading down my neck and chest, sweeping lower and lower the longer they looked at me.

"Remember what we said about secrets, Lina," Soren reminded me.

I licked my lips, glancing from one intense nearly black stare to the soulful deep blue of another.

"Yes," I whispered. "I do."

Soren nodded again, processing the information.

"And what about you?" Hale asked cautiously. "Would you be happy with that scenario?"

A charming grin crept onto Soren's face, suddenly making it very clear where Xavier had learned it.

"If Lina's happy, then so am I."

Hale watched Soren a little longer, thoroughly studying his expression to root out his true intentions. What he found eventually eased the tension in his shoulders.

"Part of me can still touch her, you know," he muttered. "I've done it before."

Soren's head angled quizzically to the side, and before he could ask what he meant, a puff of black appeared in Hale's palm. The muscles in Soren's back twitched as he fought the urge to step backwards in surprise.

"Can't Aedan see through that?" Soren asked hurriedly.

"Aedan's dead," Hale replied. "Lina killed him."

Two sets of eyes landed on me.

"Of course she did," Soren chuckled, shaking his head fondly.

"Of course she did." Hale gave me a proud smile.

My blush deepened.

Soren returned his attention to Hale, considering the darkness. "Show me."

Needing no further bidding, the mist morphed into a long black ribbon that sank down from Hale's hand like heavy fog and started in my direction. It slunk across the floor, maneuvering around the tufts of fur and through the tassels on the ends of the rugs until it arrived at my feet. It wafted upwards, gliding up my body until the tip settled against my shoulder. Timidly, the mist reached out a single silky tendril and grazed my cheek. My eyes unintentionally fluttered shut at the tender caress, every hair on my skin standing on end as the mist's cool, tingling breath licked all the way from my cheek to my collarbone.

As quickly as it had appeared, the darkness was gone, whipping back to Hale's palm and disappearing inside him. The mist remained a phantom on my skin, and I shivered before opening my eyes to find Soren and Hale each watching the other tensely.

Finally, Soren sniffed and looked Hale up and down one last time.

"Pull up a seat."

# Chapter 49



THERE WAS A LONG PAUSE.

Then, without breaking Soren's stare, Hale slowly wrapped his fingers around the wooden back of a nearby chair and dragged it beside him.

"Sorry, I'm a little confused," I said. "What's happening?"

Soren turned.

My heart thumped faster as I glanced back and forth between him and Hale as he strode across the tent towards me. When he stopped directly in front of me, the carnal hunger in his eyes made the heat in my body spread all the way down to my legs.

"We're giving him something to watch."

Without waiting for my response, he slipped a hand to the side of my face and pulled me into a kiss. The move took me by surprise, and I froze. I'd ached for his touch and taste for count-less nights, and here he was; warm and familiar, his scent wafting around me in a cloud that eased my worries, soothed my aching soul, and twisted my core with desire. It took a few seconds before I'd fully processed what had happened, but when I did, I hurriedly pushed Soren away. It felt unnatural, but I'd made a promise in the Netherworld, and I'd meant it.

My eyes darted to Hale across the tent, but to my surprise, he didn't look jealous, angry, or hurt. He simply lowered into the chair, his eyes never leaving my face.

"Something wrong?" he asked cooly.

Stunned, I opened my mouth to say something, *anything*, but no words came out. My busy mind was suddenly silent, too dumbstruck to overthink for once. I would have stayed that way had Hale not casually leaned back in his seat, jerked his chin to Soren, and said, "Go on."

Soren leaned in again, his kiss more passionate this time, but even after we collided, my gaze stayed locked with Hale's. It was a silent question, asking him if it was wrong to do this, if it was wrong to *want* this, but most importantly, if he wanted this too. The lust in Hale's eyes and the whisper of a smile on his lips made his answer clear.

I let my walls come down then. I melted into Soren, relishing the sensation of his lips as they toured the column of my throat, all the while holding Hale's stare and losing myself in the haze of his desire. When the king's fingers found the neckline of my dress and slipped one sleeve off my shoulder, though, I gasped and caught his hand.

Soren lifted his head to look me in the eye. Panting from the rising heat, he searched my gaze.

"Do you want me to stop?" he asked earnestly. "I will."

I hesitated, glancing back and forth between him and Hale. The ache between my legs informed me of the answer before my mouth could fashion the words.

"No," I breathed. "I don't want you to stop."

The hungry gleam made a reappearance in Soren's eyes. He circled behind me, returning his face to the crook of my neck and trailing his lips along the skin while his hand slipped the rest of my dress down. It fell to my waist, revealing my bare breasts. My skin prickled at the kiss of the air, but also from a rush of excitement. Across from us, Hale's expression didn't change, but he leaned farther back in his chair, his legs spreading in front of him and his head tilting to get a better view.

"Hale?" Soren's voice was muffled against my skin, barely audible over my increasingly ragged breaths. One of his hands stayed caressing my chest while the other slid towards my thighs.

"Yes?" Hale answered.

"Do *you* want me to stop?"

Soren's fingers slipped between my legs, jolting pleasure through my core and dragging a moan from my lips.

Hale's gaze ignited with lust. "Fuck no."

I leaned my head back on Soren's shoulder, rolling into his hips as his chuckle rippled warm vibrations through my body.

"Good. I don't want to stop either."

Soren released his hold on me and dropped to his knees. Reaching up to grip my hips, he spun me to face him and shoved my legs apart. I smacked a hand to the table to keep myself standing, a task made more difficult when Soren bunched up my skirt and buried his face between my thighs, his tongue finding my most sensitive spot and effortlessly drawing out a full-body shudder.

Groaning in pleasure, I instinctively ground my hips into Soren's face in time with his lapping mouth. When I looked up to see Hale watching me, his lips parted slightly as he admired the scene, my knees buckled entirely. Soren caught me before I fell, and without missing a beat, he pushed me back to standing with one hand while the other joined his mouth between my legs.

I threw my head back and moaned, resting another hand on

the table behind me to brace myself. The pressure inside was building at record speed, and it was only amplified the more I held Hale's persistent stare. His chest had started rising and falling faster, and his eyes constantly flicked from my face to my rolling hips and back again. When the pleasure coiled inside me, my own breath caught and my body went rigid. Hale bit down on his bottom lip and nodded, silently urging me on. The pleasure exploded at his command, and I didn't care who heard me as I cried out in ecstasy. Soren clutched me tight, holding me steady as I rode out every last blissful wave of my climax. Eventually I collapsed forward onto him, still squirming with lasting jolts of pleasure.

"Good."

Both Soren and I looked up at Hale's voice. Lounging in his chair, he was every inch a dark prince on his throne.

His gaze shifted to Soren. "Now let her taste herself."

There was a pause, and for a split second I worried Soren would take issue with being ordered around so brashly.

But the king rose to his feet with a devilish grin.

We both kept Hale's stare as Soren's fingers slipped inside my mouth, and I uttered an appreciative moan at the musky taste. The noise had Hale biting his lip again and an equally seductive noise rumbling up from Soren's chest.

"Good girl," Soren murmured.

"Very good girl." A full smile broke out across Hale's face. He looked to Soren once more. "Now make her come again."

My insides constricted at the order, but before I had a chance to respond, Soren stated, "With pleasure."

He shoved aside the scattered maps and papers cluttering the table and hauled me onto its surface before diving back between my legs.

Still sensitive from before, I was shaking instantly and had to bury my fingers in Soren's hair to anchor myself. The smile stayed plastered on Hale's face as he watched me, his hand slowly straying towards the object swelling against his trousers. Our eyes stayed locked as I inched closer to another explosion of pleasure, at the same time he began running his palm up and down the raised outline of his cock. Our breath synced, and after a few more precise sweeps from Soren's tongue, I was unraveling all over again.

When I'd finished, I could barely hold myself upright and flopped back onto the table. There I gulped mouthfuls of air and groggily swiped the strands of hair from my face that had dampened with perspiration.

Movement across the tent caught my eye, and I angled my head to see Hale standing from his seat. He took hold of a second chair and dragged it over to Soren.

"Care to keep the show going?"

Soren chuckled and unfastened the laces on his pants. "Gladly."

Hale grinned and returned to his own chair.

Before I fully processed what was happening, Soren dragged me off the table so I was sitting on his lap. His lips met mine, and after a long luxurious kiss, he pulled away just enough to nudge my nose with his.

"How about you?" he asked. "Do you want more?"

In answer, I eagerly ground against his cock, which was now pressing firmly into me. Soren inhaled sharply before an animalistic sound grated out of him. He spun me around so I was facing Hale, ripped aside the skirt of my dress, grabbed one knee, and yanked my legs apart so I was spread open. He pulled my back flush to his chest, but I did the rest, sliding my hand inside his pants, slipping him out, and maneuvering his tip to my center. Soren caught my face and forced my gaze to hold with his as he slid into me, both of us gasping the same breath at the intensity. I'd ached for him too many nights, dreamed about this stretch of him too many times, but even my wildest fantasies paled in comparison. He was jaw-droppingly, knee-weakeningly, overwhelmingly perfect, and everything seemed to disappear as he thrust into me. One of Soren's hands wove into my hair while the other rested on my hip, guiding me up and down but still letting me control the pace as he pumped in and out.

When I looked forward again, I discovered Hale lazily unhooking the buttons on his pants one by one. The image jolted a twinge of desire through me, making me desperate for any piece of him I could get. As if reading my mind, Hale arched an eyebrow and allowed a sliver of dark fog to bloom from his back. It inched forward, sidling up to the chair and snaking up my leg. When it flowed onto my bare chest, it brought with it a cool prickling sensation that had me moaning and shutting my eyes to savor it. When I opened them again, Hale was moving his hand up and down his length in languid strokes.

"Does that feel good?" he asked.

At his words, Soren escalated the speed at which he was thrusting, so all I could manage was a breathless nod.

Hale's mist thickened and slipped further down my abdomen. When it came to rest on top of my clit, it changed, swirling in tiny circular motions until it morphed into a breathy whirlwind. Unable to keep myself propped upright anymore, I sank back into Soren. He held me safe and close, but continued his punishing momentum.

"And how about that?" Hale asked, a smile in his voice. "Does that feel good too?"

With a moan, I nodded again.

Hale leaned forward, still working himself with one hand. "Let me hear you say it."

"Yes," I managed to gasp out, reaching behind me to latch a hand on to Soren for support.

Content with the confession, Hale leaned back in his chair, his chest rising and falling even faster. "What else would make you feel good?"

Soren increased his depth and speed, forcing me to tighten my grip and sink my nails into the back of his neck. He groaned in appreciation.

"Tell me what you want, Lina," Hale demanded. "Tell me what you want him to do to you."

"I want... I want..."

I couldn't form a sentence. There were no words in my vocabulary except stuttering moans, nothing in the world except pleasure.

"Come on, you can do it. Tell us what you want."

I licked my lips, my gaze holding on Hale's parted, panting smile.

"I want him to fuck me like he missed me."

Soren huffed a breathless laugh at the words I'd spoken all those months ago in Lerian. And just like he had then, he lifted me upright, hauled me over to the table, and flung me down on top. This time, though, he flipped me onto my stomach before dragging my hips towards him and plunging himself back in.

I gripped the sides of the table to hold myself in place as Soren hammered into me, and buried my face in its smooth surface to stifle my screams.

Another order came from across the room.

"Look at me."

With Soren pounding into me, I struggled to lift my head and meet Hale's eyes. But Soren entangled his fingers in my hair just hard enough for it to feel good, and with a gentle tug, he lifted my head for me.

Hale was stroking himself faster now, breaths escaping his mouth at the same rapid rate as mine and Soren's.

"Does that feel good?" he asked again. "Do you like when he fucks you like that?"

"I love it," I whimpered, the pressure inside me building with every grunt and thrust behind me.

"Then I'm going to watch you come just like this."

Everything inside me was tight, throbbing with overwhelming pleasure. Soren must have sensed I was getting close because he dug deep within himself and managed to pound even faster.

"That's it," Hale instructed, increasing his own speed to match ours. "Fuck her just like that. Give her everything."

The pressure built more and more, my legs shaking uncontrollably. Everything felt ready to snap, but the pleasure held in that stagnant, breathless place just before release.

"Let go, Lina," Hale barked. "*Now.*"

Soren drove into me one last time, and combined with Hale's words, the tension finally snapped and I hurtled over the edge. I screamed out, the pleasure so strong it almost hurt in the most glorious way, and I collapsed onto the table. Soren followed my lead and raced to a finish of his own, with Hale not far behind.

When our chorus of pants had diminished, Soren carefully slid out of me. I tried to stand but instantly collapsed, my body too deliciously spent to keep me upright, but Soren caught me.

"Easy," he chuckled, scooping me into his arms. "You should rest."

I pressed an exhausted kiss to his neck in agreement and let him carry me over to the pile of pillows, furs, and throws in the corner of the tent. He gently laid me down, watching in amusement as I nestled into them like a burrowing animal. When he caught a glimpse of something silver glinting on the skin of my right forearm, his face fell.

"What's this?" he asked, taking my arm in his hands and angling it to the flickering flame of a nearby lantern.

"It's a long story," I murmured, my eyelids heavy with exhaustion. "I'll tell you in the morning. Are you joining me or not?"

Soren sighed in exasperation, but still pulled off his rumpled clothes.

"Hale?" I called out.

Across the tent, Hale looked up from where he was buttoning his trousers.

"Will you stay too?"

He frowned and glanced at Soren, who shrugged as he settled into the pillows on my left. "I think there's enough space for you to sleep without touching her."

Hale's gaze darted towards the flap of the door. "I'm not so sure—"

"Please?" I pressed. "I want you with me."

Hale stared at me a few beats longer before taking a deep breath and giving a small nod. "Alright. I'll stay."

Another rush of heat spread through me, but this one was from joy.

Hale wandered over and lowered himself, rather uncomfortably, onto the pillows to my right, keeping a good arm's distance away. Soren pulled a blanket over the two of us, then tossed a separate one to Hale, who hesitated before grabbing it and politely dipping his head in thanks.

I shut my eyes and nuzzled into Soren's chest as his arms wrapped around me and pulled me in close. Just before sleep took over, I mumbled into the pillow, "I love you."

And I wasn't entirely sure which man I was talking to.

# Chapter 50



Soren didn't sleep.

Neither did Hale across from him, so the two spent the next hour listening to Lina's soft, drawn-out breaths and trying not to make eye contact with each other.

The flames in the lanterns were highlighting the auburn streaks in Lina's hair, which Soren was gently running his fingers through when Hale finally chose to break the silence.

"How are you alright with this?"

Soren looked up at him. "With what?"

"This." Hale gestured to the three of them reclined in the pillows. "If you love her, how can you be comfortable with her having feelings for someone else? Or being physical with someone else?"

Soren sighed and propped his fist under his head as he lifted his eyes to the roof of the tent in search of phrasing that made sense to him.

"I trust her. Lina rarely says anything she doesn't mean, so when she says she loves me, I believe it. And I trust our love is strong enough to endure whatever, and whoever, comes our way."

Hale considered Soren's words. "You're not worried she loves you any less because of it?"

Soren bent his head to press a tender kiss to Lina's cheek. "No. Her being with someone else doesn't make our moments together any less special. And her heart is so big, I think it's plenty capable of holding two separate loves for two separate people. Mine isn't, I don't think, but hers is. It's just another thing that makes her amazing. She has the capacity to feel so much."

Hale sniffed, his eyes flicking to the tip of Lina's nose as it wrinkled in her sleep. "Yes, she does."

The two of them watched her again, the silence stretching on for several minutes.

Soren usually hated silence. It left him alone with his constantly racing thoughts. To-do lists, mental notes to write to this lady, meet with that lord, check on those troops, ease dissent in these territories. Too much swirled in his mind at all times, and it only ever eased when he was with Lina. She could hold him or kiss him or look his way for just a second, and the world would stand still. Now she was asleep beside him, but to his surprise, the dark thoughts didn't sweep back in. Not even with Hale here. The man's wary, angry wall was practically tangible, but Soren wasn't swayed by it. In fact, his internal chatter remained dormant. Still, he should attempt to make the man comfortable. Because judging by the vicious frown cutting across his face, he most certainly wasn't.

"She doesn't usually do this," Soren mused, gently swiping a strand of hair from Lina's forehead.

"Do what?"

"Sleep this well. She tosses and turns all night. She can

never relax, not even when she's asleep. She has terrible nightmares."

"I know. I've slept with her."

Soren instinctively bristled at the edge in Hale's voice, but forced himself to rein in his emotions. He understood the hostility. Hell, he'd felt it himself once. But he knew better now. It had taken him a long time to figure out the two of them weren't enemies, and it still required the occasional reminder, so he couldn't hold Hale's response against him.

"Thank you for taking care of her down there," Soren said earnestly.

"She's plenty capable of taking care of herself."

"I know that. But she could always use an extra pair of eyes looking after her. The woman has a habit of finding trouble wherever she goes."

Hale failed in hiding his fond but somewhat exasperated expression as he stared down at Lina. "That she does."

Easy silence settled in again, but the dark thoughts still didn't come calling.

It was odd, but refreshing.

Eventually, Hale cleared his throat. "Lina and the queens of the western territories have invited a legion of Nethers to your lands."

Soren's whole body jerked in surprise at the statement. He searched Hale's face for a lie, but found none.

"Merrows, Sluagh, and Piksis," Hale expanded, eyeing Soren for some sort of reaction. "They were mistreated by Aedan, so the women offered them sanctuary. Xavier also agreed, and insisted you'd be onboard."

The dark thoughts finally returned, and with a vengeance. They swirled in Soren's mind, tensed his muscles, and churned his stomach with anxiety. Were his people in danger? What if they were overrun with Nethers? Would Astoria think he was unfit to lead? Would they go after him, or Lina, or Xavier as payback?

Rage rose in his body, heating his bloodstream, but Soren shoved it back down. That emotion was always his first impulse, but not always the truth. It was only an instinctual response to the conflict and confusion raging inside.

After a few deep breaths, Soren sorted through his jumble of emotions to find the right words. "I'm going to be honest with you... That terrifies me." He met Hale's eyes again. "I'm doing my best to listen and learn and grow, but it's not easy. I'm sure you know as well as anyone how difficult it is to unlearn things people made you grow up believing."

Hale's eyelids flickered as the statement hit him somewhere the truth hurt.

"But," Soren went on, "despite our sordid history with the Nethers... you're half Nether, and you're a good man."

At that, Hale went as still as a statue.

"Our people misunderstood and mistreated you, so..." Soren took another shaky breath. "Maybe you're not alone in that. Maybe other Nethers are in similar positions. And like I said, I trust Lina. Xavier, Syrena, and Ilora are wise as well. If they believe these Nethers are to be trusted, then... I'll do my best to welcome them with grace and understanding."

Hale blinked once.

Twice.

Three times.

"What the fuck happened to you?" he blurted.

Soren frowned. "What?"

"You're not the Soren of Astoria who pinned me to a wall and made me swear not to lay a hand on the woman he loved." Hale's eyes iced over. "That Soren would have rushed out and picked off the intruders one by one, then stuck their heads on stakes as a warning to the others."

"I only did that *once*," Soren snapped.

"To a horde of Night Sylphs," Hale bit back.

Lina flipped onto her side and nestled her face into Soren's bare chest. Both men stopped breathing in the hopes of not waking her. Lina mumbled a few lines of dialogue in her sleep, then picked up her quiet snoring once again.

"Do you blame me?" Soren whisper-shouted to Hale. "The Night Sylphs were wreaking havoc on every small village on the outskirts of Astoria and Lerian, preying on both woman and child. People were afraid to leave their homes after dusk."

"I remember," Hale spat. "The Lerian guards I was training with made sure to beat the shit out of me every night. 'So I didn't get any ideas from my relatives,' they said."

Soren's stomach dropped. Memories of his father's violent fists filled his mind, images of a shattered mirror cutting into his skin rising to the forefront. Suddenly it was Hale's face in that mirror instead of his own, crying and screaming for mercy, and it was just as nauseating.

"I'm sorry," Soren admitted, guilt hollowing his chest. "I'm sorry our people treated you like that. That *I* treated you like that. You didn't deserve it."

Again Hale's eyelids twitched as he fought to control the impact Soren's words had on him.

"Why the sudden change?" Hale asked. "What happened between last year and now to make you like this?"

"You happened."

Hale froze again.

"Listen. I'm..." Soren sighed. "I'm not especially good at talking about feelings." He gestured to Lina. "Clearly. But I'm going to try."

Lina moaned softly in her sleep and wriggled further into him. Soren couldn't help but smile, and took it as her subconscious encouragement.

"Hale, you upended everything I've ever known. I thought one thing about you, a belief the majority of our people also held, but that didn't stop you from sacrificing everything when the worst came. A Nether bastard had more honor in one day than I've had in all my long years, and the guilt of his death haunted me for months." Soren's fingers found their way to Lina's back and gently traced the line of her spine. "And if I'm being honest, this woman has caused me some pain too. But I'm grateful for it." He lifted his gaze to match Hale's stare. "If we don't let it destroy us, sometimes pain can be useful. It can transform us into a better version of ourselves if we let it. It forces us to learn difficult lessons, but necessary ones. It's because of you and Lina that I'm no longer the man who forced you into that bargain, and I apologize you ever had the misfortune of crossing paths with him."

Hale considered, a muscle in his jaw ticking before he looked away to toy with a loose thread on the blanket draped over his hips.

"I'm not sorry," he mumbled.

This time it was Soren's turn to freeze.

"I'm not good at feelings either," Hale added quickly. "But... that man was vengeful and powerful and strong. He would have killed for the woman he loved. I respected that. Hated him for it, but also respected him. That's exactly the type of man I want looking after the woman I care about."

"I'd still kill for that woman."

"Good. Because you're right. She has a habit of finding trouble. She needs all the help she can get."

The two of them chuckled at that.

Another wave of silence rolled in, and both men relaxed into the melody of Lina's slumber. Her breaths were soft, her heartbeat even, and her face completely serene. Soren was enraptured by her, and one peek at Hale found him watching her in the same way. When he sensed Soren's eyes on him, he looked up and frowned.

"Your younger brother died in that clash with the Night Sylphs, didn't he?"

Even after all these years, the mention of Silvain and that final fateful battle caused a twinge in Soren's chest. "Yes, he did."

"I remember the king and queen of Lerian talking about it in the days after. I'm sorry for your loss."

Soren dipped his head and returned his attention to Lina. "Thank you. It's not all bad, though. Like I said before, pain can transform you into a better person. That day was a turning point for me. Plus I gained another brother that day." A fond smile sneaked onto his lips at the thought of Xavier.

Hale nodded thoughtfully, then eased back in the pillows on his side of the pile. His shoulders sagged, releasing tension for the first time in hours.

"So what happens now?" he asked softly.

"With the three of us?"

"With everything."

Soren let out a breath that carried the weight of the world. "I truly have no idea."

Suddenly Lina sat upright, her bright eyes snapping open as she gasped in a breath.

Soren caught hold of her flailing arms, pinning them to her sides and pulling her to his chest like he had countless times before.

"Shhh," he soothed. "It was just a nightmare, you're alright. Breathe. Inhale through your nose, exhale through your mouth. We're safe."

"It was so real," Lina panted, her panicked words coming in hot bursts against his skin. "It was *too* real."

Soren glanced at Hale. He was watching Lina with a

worried frown, his fists tightening over and over as he fought against the instinct to provide her the same comfort Soren was.

"Do you want to talk about it?"

Lina clutched Soren tighter, her eyes glazing with a far-off look. "It happened right here. Right in this tent. Someone came in, and you stood up to talk to him, and he... he..."

Lina burst into tears and buried her face in Soren's chest.

Soren kissed the top of her head and rubbed small circles on her back. "It's alright, it was just a dream."

Again, Soren peeked at Hale. His expression was wistful as he stared at the two of them. Soren had no doubt he would do anything to change places with him, to be the one taking on Lina's pain instead. The thought had Soren's stomach wrenching with guilt all over again.

After a few minutes, Lina's trembling subsided and her breathing slowly returned to normal. She eventually unpeeled herself from Soren's chest and wiped her tear-streaked face.

"I'm sorry," she whispered. "I've never had a dream that vivid before."

"It's alright." Soren tucked a strand of hair behind her ear. "It's over now."

Gratitude shone in Lina's eyes as she nodded. "I'm glad you were here." She faced Hale and offered him a smile. "I'm glad both of you were here."

Hale opened his mouth to respond, but a voice from outside the tent interrupted him.

"Your Majesty? May I enter?"

In the blink of an eye, Hale evaporated into a puff of black mist, his clothes deflating and falling flat on the pillows beneath them.

The sight nearly made Soren scream out loud, and he had to clamp a hand over his mouth to keep it in as he scrambled backwards in alarm.

Lina caught hold of his arm and gave it a comforting pat. "It's alright. I forgot to tell you he can do that now."

Soren was about to shriek a few choice words about that being something worth knowing, but the voice outside called again.

"Your Majesty? I'm afraid this is urgent."

Soren glared at Lina to silently communicate they *would* be discussing this later, then took several calming breaths before clearing his throat. "Enter."

The flap of the tent rustled, and in stepped Lord Tristan Rourke.

Soren hadn't seen the young lord since that morning after Imbolc when Lina disrupted the nobles' breakfast. Beside him, Lina tensed when she saw the Astorian nobleman. Soren chalked it up to the fact there was nothing but a scrap of velvet protecting her modesty, so he handed her a second blanket to ease her mind.

"Lord Tristan," Soren greeted him, tying a silk throw around his own waist and standing. "What a pleasant surprise."

Tristan clocked Soren's state of undress and averted his gaze. "My apologies, Your Majesty. I didn't realize you were indisposed."

Lina tugged frantically on Soren's blanket, nearly making it slip off his hips. He quickly caught the hem and stepped out of her reach.

"Well, you said it was urgent."

Lina grunted.

Soren looked back at her and arched a quizzical brow.

Her eyes were round, and she was frantically shaking her head.

Soren raised his index finger to communicate he needed one minute before she could have his attention.

"What seems to be the problem, my lord?" Soren asked, facing the lord again.

Tristan glanced at Lina behind Soren's back and stuffed his hands into his pockets. "I think it's best we discuss it alone."

"Very well. Give me a few minutes to get dressed, and I'll meet you outside."

Tristan shuffled one foot and then the other. "Actually, I'd like to discuss it with you here. In private." He looked pointedly at Lina.

"The lady is resting, Lord Tristan," Soren said as kindly as he could. For some reason, the hair on the back of his neck prickled, and it worsened every time the lord fidgeted in front of him. "I'm not going to kick her out into the cold."

"Come now, Your Majesty, this is Lerlan. It's never cold here. It's a perfectly beautiful night."

Soren was finding it harder and harder to keep the smile on his face. "I said I'm not going to remove her, my lord. You and I can meet outside in a few minutes, once I'm decent."

Tristan glanced over his shoulder.

And fidgeted.

And shuffled one foot, then the other.

"I'd really like to speak with you here, Your Majesty."

There was another tug on the blanket around his waist, and Soren looked down. Lina had crawled over and was kneeling at his side, staring up at him with terror in her eyes as she shook her head. The hair on Soren's arms began to stand on end.

"What's wrong?" Soren asked.

"The dream," Lina whispered, her gaze darting back and forth between him and Tristan. "That's the man from my dream."

"Lina, it was just a dream."

Ignoring his brush-off, Lina leapt to her feet.

"He has a knife!" she shrieked, flinging a damning finger in

Tristan's direction. The velvet slipped from her body, but she didn't seem to care. "He has a knife hidden in his sleeve! He's going to kill you!"

Tristan scoffed.

Soren bent to grab the velvet at Lina's feet and quickly draped it over her naked body. Just because he'd come to terms with Hale seeing her intimately didn't mean he needed *every* man seeing her that way.

"It was just a dream," Soren repeated.

"No!" She grasped his hands in hers. "No, it's happening exactly like I saw it! He's wearing the same clothes, he's saying the exact same things, he's armed, and he's going to kill you!"

"Lina, I've known Tristan my whole life. He isn't going to kill me."

"He is! You have to believe me! *Please!*"

Soren peeked at Lord Tristan. "My apologies, my lord, the lady has terrible nightmares and—"

"It wasn't a nightmare!" Lina snapped. "I think it was a vision! Witches have visions sometimes and see glimpses of the future, and since I'm a witch, I think—"

Soren clapped a hand over Lina's mouth, daring a worried peek over his shoulder at Tristan. The man had stopped fidgeting and was staring at Lina intently. The unnerving look in his eye made Soren's stomach twist and roil uncontrollably even though he still wasn't entirely sure why.

Without warning, Lina's teeth sank into the flesh of Soren's palm, prompting him to hiss a curse and whip his hand away from her, shaking it gingerly.

"Hale!" Lina cried out, spinning in a circle as she scanned the tent. "Hale, I'm right about this! I know I am! Please, you have to trust me!"

"Who's she talking to?" Tristan asked. His cold gaze hadn't

left Lina's face once, and he stood as still as a predator poised for the kill.

All the warning bells going off in Soren's body finally broke through the stubborn blocks in his mind. He guided Lina behind him and turned back to the lord. "You're about to meet who she's talking to. Hale? Check him."

A wisp of black rushed in from the shadows behind the lord, growing tall and dense until it thickened into the shape of a man, and suddenly Hale was there: naked, vengeful, with his hands on either side of the nobleman's head, ready to snap his neck at a moment's notice.

"Show me your arm," Hale breathed in Tristan's ear.

The lord shivered at the unspoken threat behind those words, and reluctantly obeyed.

Hale reached down and flipped up Tristan's extended sleeve, and sure enough, a slender dagger glinted there. Hale expertly disarmed him, then lifted the knife to the lord's throat, holding it flush against the skin.

Soren stepped forward and pushed his face in close. "So this is what the South thinks of me? You think I need to be disposed of?"

"You or that cunt who's bewitched you," Tristan spat.

Hale tightened the knife on the lord's neck, pricking the skin enough to draw a thin line of blood.

"Please let me kill this son of a bitch," he growled.

"Not yet." Soren took another step forward, moving in so close he could smell Tristan's aftershave mixing with the acrid stench of fear. "You don't have nearly enough balls to have come up with this yourself, Tristan. Whose idea was this? Who sent you?"

The lord's mouth stubbornly pinched shut.

"Tell me who sent you, and my Night Sylph friend here swears he'll spare your life."

Hale shot him an indignant glare, but Soren only arched his eyebrows back to say, *I make the rules.*

Hale grumbled under his breath. "I swear."

Tristan gulped.

"Be smart about this, my lord," Soren urged. "Do what's in your best interest."

Tristan's shifty eyes moved around the tent in search of a way to wriggle out of the trap he'd gotten caught in, but when he found none, he conceded. Through gritted teeth he hissed a name, one Soren knew far too well.

"Lord Magnus Tynan."

The world melted away, and everything went silent. Rage didn't tear through Soren's blood. Betrayal didn't sit bitter on his tongue. He was completely numb, which let him think clearly about what he did next.

He patted the lord's cheek, and with an earnest smile, he whispered, "Thank you."

Then he pulled the dagger from Hale's hand and plunged it deep into Lord Tristan's chest.

The man gasped and gurgled, blood spurting from his mouth and dribbling down his chin. Soren dragged the lord in close, snarling in his ear so his words would haunt Tristan on his way to the Underworld.

"I said my friend would spare your life. I never said I would."

Then he loosened his grip and let Tristan fall to the ground in a bloody heap.

# CHAPTER 51

THE LIGHT DIMMED IN LORD TRISTAN'S EYES, AND EVEN THOUGH I'd grown accustomed to death, both by witnessing it and doling it out, watching someone's life leaving their body always spread an eerie chill through my blood. I shook off the sensation and refocused on Soren and Hale.

"Are you two alright?"

Soren nodded, the weight of the world seeming to rest on his shoulders as he and Hale dragged Tristan's limp body onto one of the rugs. "Comes with the territory, I'm afraid. Although it's never gotten this close before, and I never thought it would come from someone in my own circle."

"What do you mean, it comes with the territory?"

Hale grunted as he and Soren started rolling Tristan's body up in the rug and a few spare furs. "That was half the reason I was even employed in Lerian. My job was to protect the royal family and stay aware of any threats to it. In other words, I made sure no one attempted to assassinate them."

I guess I had known that, and I'd been aware of the rumors of insurrection around Astoria, but the gravity of it all had never truly sunk in before now. As far as I'd seen, royal life had just been a lot of meetings, paperwork, and extravagant parties, not looking over your shoulder every second, fearful someone was going to jump out and murder you.

"When your job is to lead," Soren went on, "you're bound to make some people angry, and because of that your life is in constant danger..." He trailed off, his eyes growing wide as he was hit by some unknown revelation.

"What?" I asked. "What's wrong?"

"I think I figured it out," Soren muttered.

"Figured what out?"

Ignoring me, Soren turned to Hale beside him. "What did you agree to when you accepted the bargain?"

Hale sat back on his heels and stared at the ground as he searched his memory. "I said I wouldn't lay a hand on Lina unless her life was in danger."

"And when is your life always in danger?"

The realization hit Hale too, because his eyes went round as well.

"If you're a member of the royal family," he mumbled.

Both men looked up at me at the same time.

Clutching the blanket to my chest, my gaze darted between the two as I tried to piece together whatever puzzle they'd put together without me. I didn't have to think long though, because Soren stood and finished it for me.

"What do you say, Lina?" he asked. "Will you marry me?"

# Acknowledgements

First and foremost, I want to thank *you*, reader. The life of an author is filled with self-doubt and imposter syndrome, and unfortunately I slip into darkness more often than I'd care to admit. But everyone who reads this series, sends me a kind message, or writes a glowing review battles that darkness. It is truly an honor to tell you a story that grips you, and I hope to do it forever.

Thank you Kari, my forever alpha reader, my sounding board, my unofficial story editor, my biggest fan, and my best friend. Thank you for your passion, your honesty, your patience, and your encouragement, all of which I wouldn't have gotten very far without. You're the Sam to my Frodo, and you'd understand the full gravity of that if you finally watched the Lord of the Rings trilogy like I've been asking you to. Still love you, though.

A big thank you to my talented and hardworking editor, who never ceases to amaze me with how she takes my gibberish and turns it into something readable. You're a superhero, Nia!

Thank you Dad, for loving me, supporting me, and always encouraging my art. I am your legacy personified.

And last but not least, I want to say a massive thank you to my incredible ARC team. Your love for this story and characters has exceeded my expectations. Sometimes I have to pinch myself because it still doesn't feel real that people love this series so much. You all brighten my dark days and keep me going when things start to look bleak. The work you do talking about this book on social media or sharing it with your friends is more beneficial than you know. You're a crucial part of this series, and I'm forever grateful. From the bottom of my heart, thank you.

I can't wait to give you all the next part of Lina, Soren, and Hale's story. What do *you* think will come first? A wedding, or a war?

Stay tuned to find out.

# Resources For Surviors

- National Sexual Assault Hotline 1-800-656-4673
- ChildHelp National Child Abuse Hotline 1-800-422-4453 (you can call or text, or use the live chat on the website), childhelphotline.org
- NCMEC - National Center for Missing & Exploited Children 1-800-843-5678, www.missingkids.com
- Child Welfare, www.childwelfare.gov
- RAINN - Rape, Abuse, & Incest National Network (they have a text chat option as well as a telephone hotline), rainn.org
- Joyful Heart Foundation (they have resources for survivors of sexual assault, domestic violence, and child abuse), www.joyfulheartfoundation.org
- NSVRC - National Sexual Violence Resource Center, nsvrc.org
- RALIANCE - Directory of rape crisis centers, raliance.org
- NSPCC - National Society for the Prevention of Cruelty to Children, 0808-800-5000 (UK)
- RCNE - Rape Crisis Network Europe, rcne.com
- Child Protection Helpline (Australia) (NSW) 13 21 11, (if calling from an international number) +61 2 9765 5117
- NASASV - National Association of Services Against Sexual Violence (Australia), nasasv.org.au

- For those wanting to provide support to loved ones who have experienced violence, remember to listen without judgment, offer supportive reassurance, acknowledge their pain, remind them it wasn't their fault, be present, and accept their decisions on healing. For more details, visit rainn.org/TALK